I0760833

REDEN BOOKS COLLECTOR'S EDITION VOLUME 1

THE TETHERED SOUL SERIES

LAURA C. REDEN

Reden Books Collector's Edition Vol. 1:

The Tethered Soul Series

Hardback: ISBN 978-1-954587-19-9

Laura's Book Count 4-7

Edited by:

Maxwell Anderson

Paige Lawson

Cover designed by Laura C. Reden

Cover Images:

© Adobe Stock / TT3 Design

© Adobe Stock / Extezy

© Adobe Stock / Deleon 8211

© Adobe Stock / Wings

'Till we meet again . . .

CONTENTS

THE TETHERED SOUL OF EASTON GREEN

Chapter 1 5
Chapter 2 11
Chapter 3 16
Chapter 4 22
Chapter 5 28
Chapter 6 33
Chapter 7 38
Chapter 8 44
Chapter 9 50
Chapter 10 56
Chapter 11 61
Chapter 12 63
Chapter 13 68
Chapter 14 74
Chapter 15 78
Chapter 16 83
Chapter 17 89
Chapter 18 93
Chapter 19 99
Chapter 20 104
Chapter 21 109
Chapter 22 114
Chapter 23 119
Chapter 24 124
Chapter 25 127
Chapter 26 132
Chapter 27 137

THE SECOND LIFE OF EVERLY BECK

1. Chapter 1 151
2. Chapter 2 156
3. Chapter 3 162
4. Chapter 4 166

5. Chapter 5 171
6. Chapter 6 176
7. Chapter 7 182
8. Chapter 8 187
9. Chapter 9 192
10. Chapter 10 197
11. Chapter 11 205
12. Chapter 12 210
13. Chapter 13 216
14. Chapter 14 222
15. Chapter 15 228
16. Chapter 16 233
17. Chapter 17 238
18. Chapter 18 243
19. Chapter 19 250
20. Chapter 20 256
21. Chapter 21 261
22. Chapter 22 268
23. Chapter 23 275
24. Chapter 24 281
25. Chapter 25 285

THE KINDRED SOUL OF NORA FAYE

1. Chapter 1 297
2. Chapter 2 304
3. Chapter 3 309
4. Chapter 4 314
5. Chapter 5 319
6. Chapter 6 324
7. Chapter 7 329
8. Chapter 8 336
9. Chapter 9 341
10. Chapter 10 346
11. Chapter 11 353
12. Chapter 12 359
13. Chapter 13 364
14. Chapter 14 369
15. Chapter 15 374
16. Chapter 16 379
17. Chapter 17 386
18. Chapter 18 392

19. Chapter 19 398
20. Chapter 20 404
21. Chapter 21 409
22. Chapter 22 414
23. Chapter 23 419
24. Chapter 24 424
25. Chapter 25 429

WHEN I WAS BECCA GREEN

1. Chapter 1 439
2. Chapter 2 442
3. Chapter 3 447
4. Chapter 4 453
5. Chapter 5 458
6. Chapter 6 463
7. Chapter 7 468
8. Chapter 8 474
9. Chapter 9 480
10. Chapter 10 485
11. Chapter 11 491
12. Chapter 12 497
13. Chapter 13 503
14. Chapter 14 509
15. Chapter 15 514
16. Chapter 16 520
17. Chapter 17 525
18. Chapter 18 529
19. Chapter 19 533
20. Chapter 20 538
21. Chapter 21 544
22. Chapter 22 549
23. Chapter 23 555
24. Chapter 24 560
25. Chapter 25 565
26. Chapter 26 569
27. Chapter 27 574
28. Chapter 28 579
29. Chapter 29 584

THE TETHERED SOUL OF EASTON GREEN

The Tethered Soul of Easton Green

CHAPTER 1

The first time I died was the hardest. I was a mess, not yet callused to say goodbye and overwhelmed by the fear of uncertainty. Still, it was one of my favorites . . . because that's the one in which I met Easton Green.

White knuckles gripped my steering wheel. My hands clenched tight as the tension turned to numbness. Mascara dripped from my cheeks. I lost my stomach, again. I was too young. There was so much I'd yet to see and experience. I'd never been in love.

The windshield wipers screeched louder than the stereo, and even though the heat was cranked up as high as it could go, I was still chilled to the bone. It must have been shock. Bad things happen to good people. That's what I told myself while forcing my concentration back to the road. The forest was barely visible through the condensation of my windows and the tears in my eyes. Few cars passed me on the winding two-lane road, momentarily blinding me as the wind threatened to push my truck outside of the lane. I shouldn't have been driving in my condition. Especially not with the storm. The angels must have been crying for me this dreary afternoon.

I wiped the snot from my nose on the sleeve of my forearm. I must have looked as terrible as I felt. I was a hideous wreck. Why me? What did I do to deserve this? It was the question that kept on giving. The more I thought about it, the more questions I had. Mom and Dad flashed into my mind, and my stomach dropped once more. This time, the thought came with pain—as sharp as a knife and as quick as deceit. How would I tell my parents? My brother? They would be even more devastated than I was. Certainly, it would be the worst part. I couldn't do it. I refused. Call it fear, call it denial, but I wasn't going to deal with any of it.

As I crossed the wooden arch of the New River Bridge, the silhouette of a man appeared, standing high on top the guardrails. *What was that!?* I lurched out of my trance as I slammed on the brakes. The dark phantom resided in the forefront of my mind. The truck hydroplaned, sliding recklessly until it skidded to a stop with one wheel on top of the curb.

My heart pounded. *Was I trying to kill myself!?* My hand wrapped around the rearview mirror, and I could see that he was still there, though I could barely make him out through the thick haze of the storm. I had to do something. Anything. But was this safe? I was confident the man was unwell, possibly planning to take his own life. I hesitated before unbuckling, but time was of the essence. I was going to die anyway. I would rather die a hero than whatever misery I had waiting for me in the seasons to come.

I pushed my door open and stepped out into the rain. "Stop!" I screamed, but my voice was lost in the howling wind. Rain pelted my face. "Stop!" My voice splintered. Either he didn't hear me, or he didn't care. I ran straight for him. The decision was made by my legs alone. Completely involuntary. As I parted from my truck, rain saturated my hair, and water seeped through my sneakers. The engine running, and the door gaped open. Never in a million years could I have imagined a scenario where I would run straight for a deranged stranger, but my body deceived me in more ways than one. My heartstrings pulled like those of a marionette. It was at this moment that I lost all control. Fate was simply unraveling at my feet.

"Don't do it!" I cried out to him.

Finally hearing my cries, the man turned his attention to me. He was no older than I was. His toes hung over the edge of the rail. It was a nine-hundred-foot plunge down to the river. And since this was the first rain of the year, it was sure to be particularly rocky. He would never make it. I stopped a good distance away, showing him my palms. I meant no harm. I only wanted to help.

"What?" he yelled back to me through the bellowing wind, one hand holding onto a cable for balance.

"You don't have to do this!" It sounded cliché as soon as it left my mouth, but it was true, and he needed to hear it. Unlike me, he still had choices.

He turned his focus back to the river rocks below. Taking advantage of his lack of attention, I inched my way closer. Slow and easy. "My name is Everly Beck, but everyone calls me Beck," I shouted through the rain.

I had once seen a special on tactics used to escape being held at gunpoint, and one of the tips was to let your attacker know personal details about you. Supposedly, the killer would be a little less murderous if they knew you shared common ground as dog lovers or tequila sunrise fans. Of course, this situation was different. The guy wasn't holding me at gunpoint. He wasn't trying to hurt me at all—only himself. And I hadn't seen a special on tactics to stop a suicide. I wished I had.

Still, I tried with what little information I had. "I know you're having a shitty day. I am too! We have a lot in common!" I took another gradual step forward. He looked at me, then turned to the depths below. *Shit! Too soon!*

"What makes you think I'm having a bad day?" he yelled into the distance between us.

Wasn't it obvious? "I see you're about to do something really . . ." I stopped. I didn't want to offend him in his fragile state. Who knows how much more he could take.

"What? Say it! I'm about to do something really, what?" he snapped as he let go of the cable.

"Oh, No! No! No! Don't do that!" I crouched, ready to pounce on him. But I was still too far away. After a moment of frozen fear on both sides of the exchange, I inched closer. In that moment, I was nothing more than a hunter. My focus sharp and narrow. My heart racing like a Maserati. I was more alive now than ever before, and I'd be lying if I said there wasn't a piece of me that was relieved to be worried about someone else for a change. My body began to tremble as my wet clothes clung to me, making the wind unbearable.

"Really . . . Permanent! Please, just come down from there!" The negotiation reduced to begging as I wrapped my arms tightly around my body. They offered me no warmth.

He began to laugh. I was taken aback by his outlandish sense of humor. He was anything but sane. He threw himself forward, and his feet slipped on the rail.

"No!" I screamed like never before, my voice shattered like glass on concrete. My stomach dropped as I lunged, closing the gap between us to grab him. My frozen fingers barely grasped the back of his shirt as he fell to the sidewalk. He landed on his side with a thud. My momentum continued forward, and I tripped over his body, laying me out on the ground beside him.

Our eyes met as I laid toppled over the stranger. I sucked in a quick breath as I released his shirt and retracted my hand. How did I find myself in such a compromised position with this man? The truck was far away now, but the door was still open and the stereo's faint sound drifted to us from the distance. The pounding in my chest told me I should get out of there; I should run. But I was frozen. Like the stranger before me, I was in shock. His dark hair was plastered to the side of his face, and rain collected at his chin, forming one steady stream to his chest. Like me, he was panting. Quick and shallow breaths laced with anxiety. I trembled as a strong gust of wind blew and sheets of rain pelted down on me.

Transfixed, I lingered a moment longer than I should have. He was unusual, alright; the whole situation was. I felt something I couldn't quite put my finger on. Something I would have liked to explore longer . . . had I not felt threatened by the uncertainty of the situation.

An earsplitting clap of thunder jolted me from my trance, and I jumped to my feet. The guy continued to lay on the curb, drowning in the rain. He wasn't a threat to me or anyone but himself. He was a broken soul. He closed his eyes and let the storm wash his resignation away. I glanced back at my truck before taking pity on him.

"Can I drive you somewhere?" I asked him. The closest residence wasn't for another five miles. He couldn't walk in this weather. We were both shuddering, most likely from the cold but maybe an adrenaline overload too.

He rolled onto his back and smiled up at me. "I'd like that," he said and held out his hand. I reached down to help him to his feet. His hand was freezing, yet he still had a firm grip. He stood about a foot taller than my average height. *Was this a bad idea?* My heart was galloping, my mind racing. The whole day had been a series of unfortunate events. I hoped I would live through the night, but I wasn't sure what my fate might hold.

I started to ramble nervously. *The more he knows . . .*

"I'm a full-time student. I'm studying to become a graphic designer." I stopped abruptly, wincing when I realized that dream would never come true. "Um . . . I work at a coffee shop, mainly because they help pay for my tuition, but I really love getting free coffee too."

I unlocked my passenger's door and sat in my now drenched truck. I shut my door, but the inside was just as wet and cold as the storm outside. The heater helped to calm my nerves—ever so slightly. I pushed my dripping, ash-blond hair out of my eyes before buckling up. He hadn't said much at all, and the silence got to me.

"I didn't catch your name," I prompted him.

"Easton Green," he replied as he held his hands up to the heater.

"Nice to meet you, Easton," I said. *Nice to meet you?* Was it, though? Nice? Or was it more like I had just met him in his darkest moment?

Why did I even bother trying to be polite at this point? I frowned, racked with self-doubt. "Where am I taking you?" I asked, hating everything that came out of my mouth.

He wasn't as scary as I thought a stranger about to jump off the New River Bridge would be. He was surprisingly normal. And I was predictably awkward.

"Um, it's just up here." He vaguely pointed into the distance.

I put my truck in reverse and backed off the curb. The ride was silent, except for the windshield wipers and the random claps of thunder that made me jump in my seat. I snuck little peeks at the wet stranger to my side as I drove. What was this guy thinking? He had presumably *walked* to the bridge in the middle of a storm in a T-shirt. I hadn't seen his car or any car for that matter, and now he was getting a ride home in my beat-up red truck. How weird was this thing we called life?

I came upon the small town of Clover. Easton was looking out his rain-drizzled window; nearly all of it was covered in fog. I drove slowly, allowing him the opportunity to talk, but he didn't say anything—not even the directions to his home.

Eventually, I had to ask. "Where do you live?"

"You can just drop me off here or wherever's convenient for you." He waved his hand about.

Drop him off wherever? Was he homeless? His clothes appeared new and stylish, even in their soaked state. I couldn't drop him off at a gas station in this storm. What was I going to do? I searched the road for answers. He probably hadn't eaten for a while. Maybe he didn't have the money to buy dinner. It was a terrible situation to be in. Here I was having the worst day of my life, but I still had a roof over my head and a full belly. I still had a loving family and friends. Fleeting or not. I wasn't broken. Not yet, anyway.

I drove to a diner. "Come on, let's get some dinner. Then you can be on your way," I said, feeling somewhat responsible for the guy I found on the side of the road.

I pulled into a parking spot. It looked like we were the only ones out in this weather. Unquestionably, I was the only one with a suicidal hitchhiker for a date.

"Red Brick Diner" flickered above the entry, the *B* temporarily failing to light. Bells jingled as I opened the door, and the smell of coffee and pie wafted through the air. Red checkered accents covered the diner and screamed, *stay—but not long*. A short, curvy lady with large breasts and a name tag, on which "Sue" had been scribbled, greeted us at the door.

"Just you two?" she asked as she grabbed a couple of menus, somehow managing to never make eye contact. I get it; life can be challenging, but if you're going to work as a hostess, a fake smile would be nice.

"Yes, please," I said, but she was already walking away. We followed her to a booth in an isolated corner. "Can we start with a couple of coffees, please?" I asked Sue as we took our seats. The light blue vinyl was stained brown, and I presumed it was where kids had wiped their greasy hands instead of using a napkin.

Sue said nothing in return, but I knew she'd heard me. *Rude.*

"I don't have my wallet on me," Easton said, apologetically. He was planning on taking his life thirty minutes ago; I didn't expect him to bring cash.

"It's on me. Get whatever you want," I said and slid the menu across the table, still shaking in my wet clothes.

Sue returned with two black coffees. I was eager to feel the heat from the inside out. She slammed the mugs down on the table, and coffee spilled over the edges. Was that necessary? I frowned at the puddle around my mug.

Easton reached for his coffee, brushing up against Sue's hand. "*You* . . . have the most beautiful eyes," he said, looking up at Sue.

What? What was happening?

She melted. A high-pitched sound came from her throat. Her cheeks flushed, and a grin larger than life stretched across her face.

"Aren't you a devil!" she snickered. "Let me know when you are ready to order; I'll just be over there. Take your time. Oh, and the clam chowder soup is delicious tonight. It might warm you up some." Sue walked away with pep in her step.

Who *was* this guy? I hid my smirk behind my coffee cup. Secondhand embarrassment was real. I knew my cheeks were as red as Sue's. And with my pale, washed-out complexion, the red in my cheeks was a noticeable pop of color. Even so, my emotions would not go unnoticed.

Easton looked at his menu as if nothing out of the ordinary had happened. Just another day for this young man. I stared at him in wonder. Something was weird about him. And I was nothing less than intrigued.

I wanted to know what was going on in his head. Staring at him certainly wasn't going to give me the answers I desired. If anything, it was going to make *me* look like the crazy one. The thunder clapped, and I jumped in my seat, spilling a few drops of coffee on my already soaked jeans.

"This storm is wild, huh?" It was the best I had. Making small talk with a stranger was hard work.

"The storm?" Easton looked out the diner window for a brief moment before continuing. "It's quite the rager . . . Why do you think people like to talk about the weather?" Easton asked before placing his menu to the side of the table.

What? Why was he challenging me? Why couldn't he just say something generic about the rain? It's crazy or I can't believe it . . . anything.

"I don't know. Because it's interesting?" I couldn't help myself from sounding sarcastic. But I *did* think the weather was interesting. Why else would people stare out their windows and watch the lightning dance across the sky?

"They talk about the weather because it's usually the only obvious parallel topic between them. It's happening all around them; therefore, they know they have something in common to talk to one another about," he said, staring at me, his eyes full of intent. And for the first time, I realized how remarkable they were. Light blue like the glaciers in the Antarctic, but surprisingly warm.

I suppose what he said was true. I had never thought of it like that.

"But you and I have something else in common, don't we?" he asked.

CHAPTER 2

Something in common? Did we? Was he dying too? Being so entranced in thought, I was startled when Sue asked for our order.

"I'll try the soup as you recommended. Thank you." Easton smiled at Sue as he handed her the menu off the table. Sue's cheeks turned red all over again. She had a crush. Easton was probably the first guy to show her attention in a long time. Had he not been so much younger than her, I'm sure she would've made a move. Probably with me sitting right across from him.

"Same. Thank you," I said, forcing a smile.

Sue didn't like me, and she showed it when she snatched the menu out of my hand and turned sharp on her heels. I was used to it by now. Most women didn't like me. I'd heard several times from friends that I was different than what they had expected of me. It must be my face. The way I carry myself. An invisible pheromone I put out. Something . . .

Easton's glacial eyes were burning a hole through me. Waiting for my answer.

"We do? What is it?" I asked, both intrigued and worried in equal parts. Did I want to know what I had in common with a suicidal homeless man?

"You're having a shitty day. You said so yourself, back at the bridge," Easton said, relaxed here at the diner as if he wasn't wearing wet clothes or sitting with me, a stranger. Why was he so comfortable? This conversation alone was freaking me out. I shuddered as water from my hair dripped onto my chest.

"You're right. I did say that." I didn't want to talk about it. I wasn't ready. "You clearly are having a shittier day than I am. Do *you* want to talk about it?" I asked him. I had to take the focus off of me. I wasn't the one ready to end everything, after all. I still had some fight left in me. As brief as it may be.

"I'm not having a bad day. Thank you, Sue." I jumped again. Easton helped guide his soup down to the table. *Where did she come from!?*

Sue placed my soup down in front of me. Her thumb dug deep into my clam chowder. I sighed, not able to thank her. Chills ran down my spine after hearing her thumb pop out of her mouth like a kiss. She was probably attempting to flirt with Easton. It was nothing but gross. And now my soup was tainted.

"But if you want to talk about what *you're* going through, I'd listen," Easton said before digging into his soup.

Me? Like I was the crazy one here? Huh . . . I guess it was a possibility.

"I don't want to talk about it." But as soon as I said it, the silence was deafening. My leg bounced uncontrollably under the table. All the tension I had been carrying around with me grew heavy. I didn't want to talk about it. But I needed to.

"You're not the only one dying, you know. We all are. Just at different speeds," Easton said casually.

I gasped. How did he know that? Was he a mind reader? A clairvoyant? I felt incredibly vulnerable, like he could see right through me. I tightened my wet jacket around me.

"How," I started.

"You told me back at the bridge. Remember? You were disgusted with me and how I could be throwing away my life when you didn't have the choice to keep yours." Easton paused, taking me in.

I didn't remember saying any of it to him. But it was exactly how I felt. My thumb-dipped soup stared back at me. I pushed the bowl away; I wasn't hungry anyhow. My memory must have lapsed at the peak of the adrenaline rush. I furrowed my eyebrows at the distaste of feeling exposed. He was the first person to know. I didn't feel as bad as I thought I might, though. Perhaps it was because he was a stranger. A stranger who had his own baggage and misfortunes. Like me, he couldn't possibly judge; he had no grounds for it. I felt his gaze on me, and I shrugged, unable to look back at him.

"What is it? Cancer?" he asked as if he were checking the flavor of a chocolate candy before popping it in his mouth. He returned his gaze to the meal before him.

I reached up to my neck and traced the lump with my fingertips. A small sound escaped my throat as if an admission of guilt.

Easton nodded before settling his crystal eyes on me. For a brief moment, I felt understood. I must be at a really low point in my life to feel like the only one who understands me is a soaking wet stranger sitting across from me in a stained vinyl booth.

"I've had it for some time." I looked everywhere but directly at him. The words fell out of my mouth. "I ignored all of the symptoms. I thought I was too young for something like this. It's my fault, really. I had a biopsy years ago, but it was inconclusive. They wanted me to come back for a repeat, but I thought there was no way in hell I was having a needle jabbed into my throat again." I winced at the memory of the pressure on my throat and the pain in my ears.

"I thought they just wanted my money, so I ignored it." My eyes drifted off to a faraway land. I felt empty inside. "And now, it's too late. There's nothing they can do." I found it odd that my eyes had begun to water since I felt nothing inside. In one moment, the truth was too much to bear, and then in the next, it was so far removed from reality that it couldn't possibly be my life. My fingertips traced my coffee mug handle.

Easton was the best kind of listener. The one who actually paid attention. No judgment. He understood, and he didn't try to fix anything or interrogate me with questions. He just gave me a warm body to talk to so I wasn't alone and the time to reflect on what lay deep inside. Had I been telling this to my parents, they would have jumped down my throat, grilled me on specific details, and made me feel guilty for not taking better care of myself. Guilty for taking their little girl away from them. Or perhaps, I would make myself think that all on my own.

Easton was gazing down into his coffee mug. He appeared sad. I knew that I was a downer, but somehow, I felt a little lighter after telling someone my secret.

"I'm sorry," I said. "I just—"

"Don't be sorry. It's life. You can't apologize for that," Easton said, his forehead creasing in defeat.

He was wise beyond his years—an old soul. I wondered what happened in his life to make him break. His hair was drying to an unruly dark mess that swept into his eyebrows. The reddish-brown bags under his blue eyes made me think that he hadn't slept in weeks. His skin was pale like mine. But unlike mine, which was genetic; his skin appeared white due to a lack of sunlight. I wondered if he was too far gone for the mood-enhancing benefits of vitamin D.

Sue came to our table with a check and a slice of blackberry pie "on the house." I dug out my wallet while she talked to Easton about the storm. I tried to hide my amusement. He didn't challenge her in the way he did me. Maybe he didn't care to. Sue took the card from my hand as she thanked Easton. I might as well have been invisible to her. It was so ridiculous; had it been a different day, I might have laughed out loud.

I caught myself wondering what Easton would look like with a smile. Though he wasn't my type: tall, slender . . . emotional. Challenging and intelligent. I was always attracted to the meatheads. The ones with more testosterone than they knew what to do with. The ones that had basic needs and basic brains. And subsequently, remarkable bodies. I never needed more than eye candy. I had fun with my friends, and I could always talk to my mom if needed. Still, I questioned what a smile would do for him.

"Are you going to be OK?" Easton asked me.

I found it odd that I was thinking the same about him. Somehow, he made me forget about my situation. If only for a few short moments.

"Yeah. I mean, until I'm not." How was I supposed to answer a question like that? I assumed it would be something I would learn over the next couple of weeks through trial and error.

"Are you?" I asked.

Sue crept into my peripheral vision. She wasn't going to spook me this time.

"Here you go. Just sign there." Sue handed me a pen with the receipt. I was tempted not to leave her a tip, but I played nice. "Don't be a stranger now, you hear?" Sue giggled, eyes set on Easton as her cheeks turned red once more. She retreated to the kitchen.

"I think she likes you."

Easton shot me a smile that did something to my insides. A weird flutter stirred inside.

I guess this was it. I'd lingered long enough. It was time I said goodbye. I grabbed my bag and slid out of the booth. Easton stayed put.

"Are you sure you're going to be OK?" I asked, feeling guilty about leaving him.

"I'll be just fine. It was nice to meet you, Everly," Easton said with a warm expression. How come it didn't sound out of place when he said it? I glanced around the diner. It's not like I had another choice. I wasn't going to bring him home like a stray dog. It was weird I even considered it. He pulled the pie in a little closer and picked up the fork.

"OK. You too," I managed to say. It felt off, but I didn't know why.

I turned around and walked out of the diner. The draft sent a shudder through my body as I opened the door. The rain pelted down on me, soaking me once more. I tried to shield my head as I ran to my truck. I cranked the heater up before stealing one last glance at the peculiar stranger I had met on the bridge. The waitress was making her way back to him. Huh . . . probably going to talk to him about the weather some more. I pulled away and continued homeward. But this time, I thought about Easton instead of my diagnosis.

I pulled into my driveway. It was my parents' house. They'd bought it as a rental. When I was old enough to move out, the place was vacant. It was only fitting that I moved in. The dead potted plants were finally getting some water with the rain. Mom would be happy about that. I knew they would get a drink at some point in time. Maybe they would grow back, and she would never know I neglected them in the first place. I ran to the door and fumbled with my keys. My hands were wet and slippery. Yeti impatiently barked inside.

When I finally opened the door, she jumped and barked rambunctiously, her bear-like body intermittently bumping into me. I peeled off my jacket and kicked off my wet shoes. They joined a shoe graveyard where five or six pairs lay scattered by the front door. I placed my bag on a small entry table before greeting Yeti. But her excitement only made me sad. What would she do after I was gone? Maybe my brother would take her. I would have to start bringing her over to his house to break her in slowly. Get her used to the idea. I padded barefoot to the heater. Even the carpet was cold under my feet. I tried not to think about it, but everywhere I looked was one more thing I had to deal with now, or my parents would have to later. I would have to start scaling back my already empty house.

Late that night, I found myself nose-deep in a hot bath. As the chill in my bones lifted, the heat helped to calm my aching heart, though tears continued to flow down my face. I didn't know how I would make it through the next few months of my life. The *last* few months of my life. I didn't know much about the emotional stages I would be going through, but I knew acceptance was one of them, and I couldn't wait to get there. If I could just get there.

My doctor's voice, low and callused, played through my head. "Terminal." Like a punch to the gut. By the time he said, "metastasized," I was barely listening to anything but the ringing in my ears. I winced. The punch was fake, but the pain was real.

With my eyes closed tight, I saw something different altogether, and I welcomed the change in thought. I saw Easton's rain-soaked shoes hanging over the rail of the New River Bridge. This, too, pained me. But in a different way. Without knowing Easton, I recognized that he was special. And the world needed special people; they were the glue that held the rest of us together.

It wasn't fair that he would have considered jumping. Regret boiled up inside of me. My eyes opened and focused on my red toenail polish—chipped fire hydrant red, nearly two weeks old. I should have stayed at the diner. I should have done more to help him. I played my regrets over and over in my head until the bathwater turned cold, and I became chilled once more.

CHAPTER 3

When my alarm sounded the next morning, I picked up my phone and threw it against my wall as hard as I could. As luck would have it, the alarm didn't stop. I tossed my heavy blue corduroy comforter off me and lay motionless while Yeti bumped her nose into me and bashed her tail into my nightstand. Why do I need to go to work anyway? Why do I need to do anything? I could just lie here and wither away.

As tempting as it was, the beeping of my alarm was maddening, and the dog needed to go out. I suppose I could be a contributing member of society for one day longer.

I pet Yeti on the head as I retrieved my phone from a pile of dirty laundry I'd been planning on doing for days. The screen had broken on impact. I sighed. Usually, I would tell myself, 'It only gets better from here,' but today was different, and I knew that was no longer true.

I took out a pair of crisp jeans from my closet; they were the only ones left that were clean. I pulled them on, jumping several times to get them over my butt. They would loosen up as the day went on, but straight out of the wash, they were much too tight. It was typical for cheap jeans to make a girl feel out of shape and start her day off with more self-esteem issues than any one person should have in a twenty-four-hour period.

I slipped my embroidered Fresh Grounds T-shirt over my head and brushed my teeth. The only thing I enjoyed about working was unlimited caffeine. And today, I needed it more than ever. I owned a coffee pot, but I usually got my coffee from work, even on my days off. The little shop was on my way to school, making it convenient for me to drop in on my way out of town. I sighed, looking into the mirror before deciding to embrace my pale, bare face, but I drew the line with naked eyes; I coated my lashes in black mascara. I knew my cheeks would pinken throughout the day, so I skipped blush and finished with a lip gloss that would darken my naturally rosy lips, ever so slightly. Without it, my face would look like a ghost. *How ironic.* After parting my hair to the side, I pulled back my light blond strands into a messy bun at the nape of my neck. It would be covered by my Fresh Grounds trucker hat anyway.

I said goodbye to Yeti and threw my apron over my shoulder before heading out the door. I surprised myself with how typical my morning was. When would it all change? It was difficult to imagine that one day I would be too feeble to serve coffee.

The storm had subsided, but the dampness and chill remained. A cool breeze blew, causing me to pinch my jacket closed around my neck. I started my truck and waited impatiently for it to warm up. The steering wheel was like ice under my hands, and my breath was visible. I switched the station on my stereo about every fifteen seconds. Every song made me feel *something*, and every emotion reminded me of my limited time. It was in my best interest not to tap into my feelings before work. If I did, I might never find my way out. I was about to pull into the parking lot before I turned off the stereo all together. I figured that music and I would have to part ways.

The warm air welcomed me from the post-thunderstorm breeze outside. But nothing was better than the smell of fresh-ground coffee. I inhaled deeply, trying to get even a morsel of caffeine in my system. Used books lined the shelves behind two old leather recliners. Fresh Grounds coffee mugs and T-shirts sat on the shelves for sale. Even though the place was packed, I recognized Greg's camel-colored jacket. He was about fourth in line. There was always a line here at Fresh Grounds, and Greg always seemed to be standing in it. He was one of our regular customers. We had tons of regulars, but he was one of the few I enjoyed serving.

I swung the bar door open and whispered my order to Lindsay as I passed by. She was in the middle of crafting marvelous latte art. Nobody could turn milk into art the way Lindsay could—not even the owner. Lindsay and I were longtime friends. We applied for the job together when the coffee shop opened up. Luckily, we both got a job and often worked together. My days were better when she was on schedule with me. I stashed my bag in the backroom and slipped my apron over my head.

"Hi, I can help you over here." I tied my apron behind my back as I stepped up to the open cash register.

A mom and two beautiful twin teenagers stepped up to my register. They must have been passing through Clover. A road trip, perhaps? I'd never seen them before.

"Good morning, I'll take two coffees with room for cream. To go please," the mother said.

As I entered the info into my register, one of the twins took a step forward.

Her long blond hair was stunning. A pang of jealousy rippled through my body, and I hated myself for it. She had it all, though: beauty, family, and from the looks of it, money. She was young—maybe sixteen. I bet she was the "it" girl at her high school.

"I'll have a grande caramel frappe, make that half caff, and extra whipped cream. Make sure you drizzle the caramel on the inside of the cup before pouring in the frappe. Oh! And a cheese danish—hot," the girl said as she raised an eyebrow. Huh, it figures she was entitled, too. One medium caramel frap . . . got it.

The second twin, a spitting image of her sister, stepped forward. "Um, I'll have the same." She looked away quickly, not making eye contact. It was clear that she wasn't the dominant twin. I looked between her and her sister before feeling bad for the girl. She lacked the confidence a girl needed to survive high school. It was as if her sister had absorbed it all in the womb and left her with nothing.

"Oh, and can you make it full caffeine? Sorry!" She shouldn't need to apologize for changing her order. I wish I could tell her to stand tall, take up space, and order her caffeine with confidence!

"Not a problem, and what's the name?"

"Hadley—" she said.

"Holly!" The sister barked from behind her.

I paused and looked at both of them before writing Hadley on all four cups. Lindsay slipped my coffee next to me, and I gave her a quick pat on the shoulder. The bitter americano soothed my parched throat. I would have a sugar-riddled frappe on break, but breakfast was always black and bitter. Much like prying myself out of bed in the morning.

"Good morning, Greg. How are you doing today?" I asked as he approached.

He had his camel jacket on as he did every single day of the year. I wasn't sure that I would recognize him without it. The doorbells jingled, and the line grew longer. My day had just started, and I already needed a break.

"I'm good, Beck. How are you today?" he asked as he opened his wallet.

It stung. How was I? I was terrible. Frightened. I was barely holding it together. And as of an hour ago, I was doing so with a shattered cell phone.

"Oh, same old, same old," I said. My life wasn't anything special before yesterday. What I would give to have my mediocre life back now.

"I'll have the regular. Oh, and Carol wants a slice of banana bread this morning," he said while flipping through the cash in his hands.

He was in his seventies, and he'd been coming here nearly every day since we opened. He was a good man with a kind heart.

"Here, keep the change." He placed a ten-dollar bill on the counter.

"Thank you, Greg. Have a nice day today. And tell Carol we said hello," I replied.

I survived the morning rush and was beyond thankful for my break. We weren't supposed to take breaks at the same time as other employees, but we only had a couple of customers, so Lindsay took the seat next to me. Her natural blond hair was dyed black. It made her blue eyes look electric. Her face was round and youthful, and her whinnied laugh was contagious. But today, I was immune to her infectious spunk. I had hardly been listening when she updated me on the potty training she had been doing with Capone, her new puppy.

"Hey, what's wrong?" Lindsay reached out and pushed on my knee.

Shit! My throat began to burn, and my eyes prepared for waterworks. *Hold it together!*

"Nothing!" I rubbed my eyes. "Allergies. They're driving me nuts," I said.

Lindsay bought it. I was pretty sure that I could pass off many of my symptoms on allergies. That's what I had told myself for the better part of the year, and I believed it, myself.

"That sucks. But hey, it could be worse." Lindsay shrugged while scooping whipped cream out of her drink with her straw. "I mean, people are out there dying with cancer and shit."

The blood drained from my face. I almost felt like I could throw up. I jolted to my feet.

"I gotta use the restroom before my break is over!" I blurted out and stammered to the bathroom.

"But your break just started!" Lindsay called out behind me.

I had been looking forward to my break all morning, but now that I had it, I wished I was working my shift. I couldn't talk to Lindsay about her squishy faced puppy. I lacked the appropriate excitement. And I sure as hell couldn't talk to her about . . . I don't know, allergies? Because that went south really quick!

I washed my hands under the warm water for far too long, trapped in the restroom because beyond those doors was a reality that I didn't have the tools to face. Again, I hadn't seen that tv special. I couldn't face my friend; she would know something was terribly wrong. But I couldn't hide in the bathroom all day either.

I dried my hands and left the comfort I'd found in the privacy of the restroom. A few more customers had wandered in, and Lindsay was working the cash register. I was thankful she hadn't been waiting for me to return to our conversation.

I was headed to clean up the mess I left on break when Easton's voice penetrated my mind.

"Easton," he said.

"Thank you. That will be right out," Lindsay said while writing on a cup.

Easton turned to walk away. I saw the side of his face and automatically looked away. What was he doing here? Would he blow my cover? What was I going to say to him?

"Everly?" Easton called out. I froze midway to the frappe I had barely touched on my break. Easton snuck up behind me. I grabbed my drink and stood to my full height before turning around.

"Hey! You found me!" I said, immediately regretting it when I saw his reaction.

His blue eyes filled with . . . what was that? Pity? I didn't need sympathy. Especially not from him. I took him in from head to toe. His hair remained unruly, even in its dried state, and he was wearing a wool grey trench coat and blue jeans. This time, he didn't look homeless—not in the least. Did I make that part up? Judging by the sunglasses hanging from the neck of his shirt, I would even go as far as to say he was well-off.

"That I did! How are you doing today?" Easton asked. His eyes scanning me up and down, a hint of interest in the corner of his eyes.

I felt overexposed. He knew my deepest, darkest secret. And now he was standing in front of me at my coffee shop, in front of Lindsay. It made my secret real. Tangible almost. I couldn't hide from it in the bathroom as long as he was there with me. I nervously glanced around, hoping nobody could hear us.

"I'm good!" I squeaked. I sighed and rolled my eyes. Sometimes I was the most exhausting person. We both knew I was lying.

Easton shook his head, understanding I wasn't ready to make my cancer a reality. He sat down on the old leather recliner in front of me and crossed his ankle over his knee. There was something about him that made me want to open up. I looked back to Lindsay again. She had the line of customers under control. I sat down on the edge of the other recliner and leaned into Easton.

"It's just that nobody knows. I can't tell them. But, I can't live a lie either." It came tumbling out of me. "I'm barely holding it together! And I don't know how long I can pretend I have allergies!" My eyes begged the stranger I met on the bridge for answers. I don't know why I thought he would have them. But I did.

Easton uncrossed his leg and leaned forward to meet me. He rested his elbows on his knees and clasped his hands together.

"You should tell your friends and family. You should tell everyone. I think it would help you cope with it in the long run. But start with your family," he said.

I thought about telling my mom, but she would fall apart immediately. How could that be good for anyone? Deep down, I knew he was right, though. I shouldn't keep it a secret.

"I'm sorry. I didn't even ask you how you were. How are you today?" I took a sip of my frappe, and my nerves started to calm as our conversation pivoted.

Lindsay walked over and placed Easton's latte on the table. It wasn't our typical practice to bring customers their coffee. Instead, we would call out their names and place their order on the bar for pickup. I hoped Easton didn't see her wink at me before she walked away. It's not what she thought; this was the furthest thing possible from a date. I would have some explaining to do.

"Today's a great day, now that I found you." Easton smiled as he buried his face in his mug. Was he flirting with me?

I laughed out loud. It was the first genuine laugh I had since my diagnosis, and as soon as I realized it, my smile faded. It was bittersweet.

"Don't do that," Easton said.

"Don't do what?" I asked him, shocked that he would tell me what to do, and a little fearful that he was in my head.

He leaned in again. "Don't cheat yourself out of happiness. You still have plenty of time to laugh. And you deserve it too." His forehead creased with his serious tone. It was true. *Everything* this guy said was true! I found myself nodding over and over again like a bobblehead as his words sank in. It was something I would need to remember.

I snapped myself out of his piercing gaze and looked down at my watch. My break had ended some time ago.

"I've got to go back to work," I said as I stood up and collected my trash. "Will I see you again?" I asked, keeping my eyes on the table. I didn't know what to make of him. He was confusing to me on many levels. But the one thing I did know was that he was the only person that understood me at the moment. And that brought me an immeasurable amount of comfort.

"I think I could make that happen." Easton smiled up at me, and I felt my cheeks flush. The door jingled as my mom walked through the door.

"Mom!" I blurted.

"Mom?" Easton said with curiosity as he looked over his shoulder.

CHAPTER 4

My mom wore a large cozy wrap that was more of a blanket than a cardigan. She had pale blond hair highlighted with silver strands. Her light green eyes were identical to mine.

I stepped away from Easton and gave my mom an awkward hug. "Hey, what are you doing here?" I asked.

"What? Am I not allowed to visit my daughter at her work? Come on! You haven't been returning my calls; what do you expect?" She held out her hands to signify the lack of options. Another customer came in behind her. Like building blocks, my apprehension was stacking higher, and higher.

"Sorry, Mom, I've had . . . a headache." I quickly glanced at Easton, who was raising his eyebrows in judgment but pretending not to eavesdrop.

"A headache! You can't call your mother because you have a headache? Geez, Beck, I was worried about you!" Mom said as she reached in for another hug.

"Sorry! I'll try harder to return your calls," I mumbled before glancing back at Lindsay. "Hey, I need to get to work. Can we talk later?" I asked, glancing around the room so that my eyes could land on Easton for a split moment.

Just do it. Be brave. "I, um, have something I want to talk to you about." My voice quivered.

"You do? Why don't you come over tonight for dinner? 5:00," Mom said—more of a statement than a question.

I grimaced. It was too soon.

"Tonight?" I tried to buy myself some time to think of an excuse.

"Yes, tonight! Your brother is coming tonight, and he is bringing his girlfriend. You can tell us your big news then. 5:00!" she said before lowering her voice. "Now, can you get me a cappuccino with a foamy heart on top?"

I sighed. I couldn't tell my family the news while my brother's girlfriend was present. I nodded, deflated and discouraged.

"Yeah. Just one sec, Mom," I said.

Mom always whispered when she asked for free coffee, even though I told her it was OK with the owner. I would have to ask Lindsay to do the heart for me, though, as I always screwed them up. I turned on my heels and headed back to work. I was utterly embarrassed that Easton had heard the whole exchange. Worse yet, my stomach dropped when I peered out from the espresso machine and caught Easton chatting with my mom. She looked amused, which wasn't saying much. Everything excited my mom. The world could be raining acid, and she would stare at it and marvel over mother nature.

He wouldn't tell her my secret, would he? The milk screamed as I started the frother. I watched my mom chuckle as I tapped the metal frothing cup with my palm to check for the perfect temperature. I guess she wouldn't be laughing if he told her. That was the only indication I had that my secret was safe.

"Hey, Lindsay, can you make a heart on top of this cappuccino?" I asked. She made me watch her for the hundredth time. But no matter how many times I watched *or practiced* with soapy dyed water, my latte art never got better. Lindsay executed a perfect heart, then took it a step further and made a swan, too.

"Show-off."

I slipped a coffee sleeve over the cup and grabbed a lid, eager to interrupt Easton and my mother from their chat.

"Mom!" I called from much too far away. "Mom, I've got your cappuccino, and Lindsay even made you a swan," I said, reaching the coffee out before I even approached her.

It worked. She took a couple of steps away from Easton and met me halfway.

"See? Isn't it pretty?" I said before slipping the lid on for her.

"Oh, I just *love* that . . . see what I did there? *Love,* and it has a heart . . ." Mom elbowed me in the ribs. It was so stupid it almost made me laugh, which reminded me of Easton's comment about cheating myself from happiness. I had a long road ahead of me . . . or, actually, maybe not.

"OK, Mom. 5:00 it is. I'll see you tonight," I said as I hugged my mom goodbye and tried to usher her out of my coffee shop before any further embarrassment could happen.

Mom resisted as she turned to Easton. "Goodbye, dear. Nice talking to you!" She waved her hand frantically at him. What on earth did he say to her? I frowned. I didn't have time for riddles, and that man puzzled me like no other.

"I'll be heading out too," Easton said, standing and joining my mother. "I'll walk you out." He turned to me and smiled. I didn't know what was behind his dimples, but I would have given just about anything to figure it out. I gave him an icy glare, but it only encouraged him more.

"Oh! That would be lovely!" Mom turned to me and winked as if she could still rope in the men. I shook my head and watched the two of them walk away.

"You have a lovely daughter," Easton said to my mom just loud enough for me to hear him. What was happening? I was about ninety percent sure he wouldn't tell her. I bit my lip, staring at the door as it closed behind them. Whatever this was, it was outside of my control.

"Beck! A little help here?" Lindsay called out. I grimaced when I saw the line had grown, and the customers were becoming upset. I must have been so wrapped up in thought that I didn't notice them come in. I hurried back to work. The hectic flow of customers didn't allow time for Lindsay to grill me on my odd behavior or the guy that I spent the rest of my break with. I found myself coming up with answers to her hypothetical questions while I worked. *He's just a guy I met the other day . . . No, I don't like him . . . I don't know why he was talking to my mother.* But she never asked. Not today, at least.

It was a long day at work, but this was just the beginning. The real work was ahead of me yet. I sat in the comfort of my truck in my parent's driveway, not yet ready to go inside. I was tired and emotional. Maybe I should just say I don't feel well and go home? The stomach flu *was* going around. My eyebrows raised as I considered the possibility of the lie.

Carter knocked on my window, and I jumped a mile high. If I had not used the restroom before leaving work, I might have peed my pants—just a little.

Instead of getting out of the truck, I stayed put and rolled my window down.

"Hey, dork," my brother said. He was holding his girlfriend's hand. I looked her over. Her dress was too frilly. Too short. I didn't like her.

"Oh my God. You must be Beck!" the girl said in a high-pitched tone.

"Actually, it's Everly." I corrected her. My brother frowned at my response.

"What are you even doing out here?" he asked. It was a valid question. One I didn't have an answer to.

I looked around my truck. "I'm just . . . I just got off work! So, I'm fixing my makeup."

He frowned, but his girlfriend understood. "Go on. I'll be inside in a minute."

He turned to walk away, and his girlfriend's high heels clacked on the driveway after him. It was too late to fake the stomach flu now. I pulled the bun out of my hair and shook the strands loose. A fresh aroma of coffee escaped my locks. At least I didn't work in a pho restaurant. Everyone loved the smell of coffee, right?

I walked to the front door, admiring the Japanese Boxwood bushes my parents had recently planted. The moment I placed my hand on the doorknob, my heart sank. I was weak, and I wanted to run away. I'd hide under the covers of my bed and waste away to nothing. One step in front of the other, I entered my childhood home, carrying my burden, heavy on my shoulders. The house was dark; no windows in the entryway. I passed the piano I'd taken lessons on as a child and failed to play since. Now it did nothing but collect dust—another manifestation of my failure. It took everything I had to enter the lively kitchen. Mom was blabbing about how pretty Carter's girlfriend was, and I could hear my dad talking to my brother about some hockey game. I wasn't sure where I fit in, but at least I showed up. Sometimes, that was the hardest part.

"Hey, Mom. I'm here." I held my arms out for a hug.

As if it wasn't hard enough to step foot into the kitchen, she burst into laughter.

"Oh, honey! Long day? You forgot to take your apron off!" Mom pointed at me as she chuckled. I looked down, disappointed, and ripped the thing off of my head.

"Hey, babe. Look, she forgot to take her apron off! I think she needs a drink!" Mom continued.

"OK, Mom. We get it. Yes, it's been a long day. Hey, Pop!" I called out to my dad as I threw my apron on the countertop.

The girlfriend stood awkwardly off to the side as I hugged my mom. I felt bad for her, even though I thought my brother could do better.

"Hi. I'm sorry I didn't catch your name," I said as I held my hand out to greet her.

She held her hands out wide, "I'm a hugger!" she said as she wrapped her arms around me for a fake hug. "I'm Chloe!" she said as she rubbed my back with her fingers only.

"I like your dress, Chloe." This time, it was a white lie, and those were OK by me. In all honesty, I did like her frilly white dress. The pink flowers were a cute pop of girly color. But it wasn't summer, and it looked like it had shrunk in the wash. Chloe smiled wide, showing red lipstick smudged on her freakishly white teeth. *Should I tell her?* I glanced at Carter, and our eyes met; he'd taken the time to put gel in his dirty blond hair. It always looked darker when he did that. His smile was genuine. I brought my attention back to Chloe before me. *Nah, I won't tell her.*

"So, Beck," she started.

"Everly." I corrected her. This girl would probably never earn the right to call me Beck.

"Sorry, Everly. I know it's weird, but even your brother calls you Beck. Well, when he's not calling you dork-face, or whatever. So, I'm just used to it. Maybe people will even call me Beck one day!" Chloe laughed, but I found her comment more disturbing than funny. Beck was a family name. Several of our friends had grown up calling us Beck. Sometimes it was confusing, but it was always an honor. I excused myself for that drink my mom had mentioned.

I walked over to the small counter space where we used to store the computer when I was a child. Now, it was filled with booze. I didn't want anything too strong. I knew I would need to drive myself home tonight. The sooner I could get out of here, the better. But I still needed something to take the edge off. I glanced over my shoulder at my mom. She held up a spatula covered in spaghetti sauce while she spoke to Chloe, a glass of red wine by her side. Red wine it was. I poured myself a half glass. I would have to see how the next fifteen minutes played out before helping myself to the other half.

My dad came up behind me and placed his strong hands on my shoulders, giving them a tight squeeze. The man didn't know his own strength.

"Easy, Pops, you're going to break me!" I spun around and swatted at his chest before hugging him.

"You're looking thin. You don't have weight to lose, my dear. You better eat up tonight," he said, just as he always did.

"I will. Don't worry." I said as I looked away. I knew he would pick up on my uncertainty if our eyes met. I swallowed the lump in my throat and turned the attention to the new girl.

"So, Pops, what do you make of her?" I gestured towards Chloe with my wine glass. She was laughing with my mom. A fake laugh, no doubt, but Mom didn't notice. Either that or she didn't care. She just loved attention any which way it came from.

Dad turned to watch the show. "She seems nice, you know? We've just gotta get to know her." He gave her the benefit of the doubt. He always saw the glass as half full. My mom did too. I'm not sure how I fell so far from the tree.

"Don't you think her dress is a little much?" I raised my eyebrows and took a swig of my wine. Not typically one for stirring the pot, I sure did have something against the girl. Maybe it was that her dress was too short. Her lipstick too loud. Her breasts too perky. Or perhaps, it was the fact that I was dying, and she was not. I shrugged my shoulders to brush off the thought. *It was definitely her chest.*

Dad laughed. "Oh, honey. You're never going to think a girl is good enough for your brother!" he squeezed my shoulder once more.

"Ah!" I shimmied out of his grip. That wasn't true, though. There was one girl that I thought was good enough for him. I took my last sip of wine. *That was quick.* We hadn't even started dinner. I poured myself the other half. I would take it easy.

After some more small talk and fake laughter, we all took a seat at the dinner table. I was blessed with the guest seat, the one I liked to call "the short chair." I sat about six full inches lower than the rest of my family, and I had to straddle the table legs. At this point, the stomach flu was looking pretty good. I would rather be wallowing in the bathtub alone than sitting in the short chair, watching Chloe win over my family with her lipstick teeth.

Carter tapped his fork along the side of his water glass. "I have an announcement to make. Chloe and I are getting married!"

"What!" I blurted out.

Chloe stopped clapping her hands when she took in my expression. Everyone stopped and stared at me.

"I mean . . . when?" I felt the heat cross my face and run down my back. I took another swig of wine which emptied my glass. I equally needed more and needed to drive my sorry self home. Now would be preferable.

"Well, we were thinking of April or May. Chloe wants to do it at the Bonnie Ranch inside the red barn," Carter said, and Chloe squealed, followed by more clapping.

April was a matter of weeks away. It was too soon. He didn't even know the girl. Why was I the only one to see this? I stabbed my fork into a meatball while my mind tried to comprehend this unfortunate turn of events. I caught my dad's empathic eye from across the table. He knew I didn't like the idea. And from the look on his face, he didn't either. But my mom was another story. She was thrilled to have wedding bells in her future. She wanted grandchildren.

They were going on about what flowers Chloe liked and who she might be able to snag for a photographer around here when I couldn't take it any longer.

I abruptly stood up. The short chair fell behind me. Making a scene was the last thing I wanted to do. Everyone was staring at me, again. This whole day had been one cluster of ill-fated events. In that moment, I thought for one second. I should just say it. I should say I have cancer. My hands balled up into fists.

"Oh, honey! I'm so sorry! You had news to share with everyone too!" Mom was trying to help, but that made it so much worse.

A cold sweat broke out across my neck and chest. *Say it! Just say it!* Carter rocked back in his full-sized chair and locked his hands behind his head.

"I . . . I have . . ." Mom had picked up Chloe's repulsive mannerisms in the blink of an eye. She silently clapped, encouraging me to say it. She looked so happy. Carter and Chloe, while making the biggest mistake of their lives, were happy too. I couldn't bring myself to do it. These people were *cheerful* people, made of light and positivity. I couldn't sweep them up in my tornado of illness. So, I did what I had been doing a lot lately: I lied—a *white* lie.

"I have . . . a boyfriend!" I faked a big smile and clapped silently.

I'd never *hated* myself more.

CHAPTER 5

"A boyfriend! I knew it! I'm going to be a grandma!" Mom waved her hands in the air like she had just won the lottery. Not one potential for grandbabies but two.

"A grandma? No, Mom, just a boyfriend!" I cleared the air, and relief washed over Dad's face.

"Oh, I know that, but first comes love, then comes marriage . . . then comes the baby in the baby carriage!" Mom was having the best night.

I rolled my eyes. Carter and I shared an exasperated look. Mom could be a bit much at times. The alcohol didn't help.

"She's not pregnant, dear! She's just got a boyfriend!" Dad looked up at me. "He's just a boyfriend, *right?*"

"Right! God, you guys. *Just* a boyfriend!"

Good Lord, these people! If this was how they reacted to my first real (and by *real,* I mean *fake*) boyfriend, then I didn't want to see what would happen when I told them I was dying!

"Oh, babe, you have to see him! He is *so* cute! And he's a charmer that one!" Mom said.

"Wait. What?" I asked, still standing.

"Easton, he's the most wonderful young man! I met him today at Fresh Grounds," Mom said.

My stomach dropped. Easton? My boyfriend? I scowled. I tried to see what my mom had seen at the coffee shop. Easton and I talking during my break. It must have looked like we were dating. What did he say to her when he walked her out? My eyes searched the table. It was all too much to take in. Or was it?

Maybe it could work? Maybe, I wouldn't have to tell them at all? They could be ignorantly blissful. Everyone could focus on the wedding instead of my health. Hell, I could even pretend that I didn't know I was sick in the first place! We would never have to talk about our feelings, and we could avoid the sad sympathy looks all together. My mind raced as I mindlessly rubbed my neck. It was a plan born out of fear, yet I saw no other way.

"Are you just going to stand there dreaming about your dork boyfriend, or are we having dinner?" Carter said, prodding me.

I snapped out of it and picked up the chair that had fallen behind me. "I'm sorry. I've got to run. I'm late, for, um, my date!"

I gave Mom and Dad a quick hug goodbye while rejecting Mom's several offers for a doggy bag.

"Congratulations," I said, quietly to my brother as I hugged him tight. I didn't have to agree with him to show him loving support. But it wasn't beneath me to tell him what I really thought when the time was right. But, tonight was not the night for honesty. I said my goodbyes, and I left with my burden. Only this time, it was heavier than when I came in.

I slammed my truck door closed. My eyes unfocused on the dashboard. That was a disaster! I failed my first real attempt at telling my family. And to be honest, it was most likely my last too.

I started the truck and made my way home, but not before swinging by the Red Brick Diner. Or as my brother called it, Red Ricks. I drove through the parking lot slowly as I tried to get a glimpse through the windows. There were about half a dozen customers, and I had no idea if any of them were Easton.

I sighed. I didn't know what I was thinking. I decided to go home because walking into the diner and ordering pie to go was too embarrassing. As soon as I made the call, though, loneliness crept in like a cold draft. I tried to push it out of my head by turning on the music, but then I remembered why it was off in the first place. The love song made me think about how I'd never given myself the chance to fall in love. And now, I would never know what it felt like. I didn't know how to help myself, but I wasn't ready to give up just yet. Yeti was waiting for me at home, and she would brighten my day with her big black doe eyes and wagging nub of a tail. She always did.

As I fumbled for my keys, Yeti scraped on the other side of the door. She was excited to shower me with love. Take my pain away. I was ready for it too. I opened the door, and she came bashing into me. I dropped my bag and kneeled, giving her face a vigorous rub.

Small bits of tan tattered cloth caught the corner of my vision. I lifted my head above Yeti to find countless pieces of chewed leopard leather all over the floor. The tiny ounce of pleasure my dog gave me quickly vanished. I stood up slowly and walked over to the first rogue leopard spot. It was still wet.

They were the first pair of brand-name high heels I'd ever bought, not even a week ago. I turned around to scold Yeti. Unleash all of my anger and frustrations about the impossible unfairness of this life! But she was cowering by the front door. If she had a longer tail, it would've tucked between her legs. I looked back at the mess on the floor. My fingernails were deep in my palms. There was no one to be angry with but myself. I guess I didn't have a purpose for shoes that would last me years anyway.

My bed was as cold and lonely as my heart, and slipping my legs under the blanket was just as miserable as hearing myself think. If there were a way I could shut it off, I would.

The walls of my bedroom seemed to enclose on me. I felt my heartrate pick up, and I knew I was on the verge of a panic attack. I was barely holding myself together. I scrunched my eyes closed as I thought about Easton's shoes hanging over the bridge. I didn't know his story, but I was beginning to empathize with him. Was it possible that he needed a friend too? My breathing began to steady. I shook the homeless man from my thoughts. It was weird I had even let him occupy this much of my mind in the first place. But when I realized that thinking of him made me feel less alone, I had no choice but to allow my mind to wander.

I reached over and turned off the light on my nightstand, and patted my bed. Yeti jumped up and made her way to the empty spot next to me. It was the space that should've been taken by a lover but wasn't—some day.

I tapped my pencil ferociously against my binder. My *closed* binder. My eyes uncrossed when I heard my name called aloud.

"Miss. Beck? Do you have anything to add?" Mr. Pillson asked.

Several students looked back at me, causing my stomach to drop. My hands stopped fidgeting as I straightened my back. I shook my head and opened my binder. I wrote Multimedia and Animation across the top of my page. I'd just finished dating the paper when I felt his eyes lingering on me.

Dawson was my kind of guy. The type of guy whose abs showed through his T-shirt. The type of guy who probably washed his car in his driveway on the weekends—shirtless. He did in my dreams, anyway. It was no surprise that this class held my lowest academic grade. I'd spent most of my time flirting with Dawson. I often tried to talk to him. Every day was *the* day I was going to be brave. But, just like all the other days before, I would psych myself out at the last minute, and bolt for the door leaving Dawson hanging back in the classroom.

I was a chicken that way. Never having a real boyfriend put certain pressures on a girl. I didn't flirt today, but I did hurry out of class. I couldn't strike up a conversation *now*.

I weaved in and out of the student body, up the stairs, and out of the classroom. It was my lunch break. I got a Diet Coke and a bag of Skittles from the vending machine. It wasn't the healthiest lunch available, but I no longer worried about my health. I had for nearly two decades now, and look where it got me. I took my loot to the tree I liked to sit under. Only this time, I passed it and walked to the parking lot. The ground was too saturated, and unless I wanted to look like I wet myself, I had to eat lunch in my truck.

I untwisted the Coke cap and took a swig. The carbonation danced in my mouth, and my eyes watered. It was one of my favorite feelings. *Sad* really. If you asked anyone else what their favorite feeling was, they would probably have a much different answer.

I watched a girl pass my truck wearing a skirt so short that she didn't have to bend over for me to see her underwear. I wrinkled my nose. Skittles exploded everywhere in the cab of my truck as I fumbled and the bag ripped open. My lap covered in the rainbow.

I skipped my next class, Principles of Design and Color, to eat Skittles off my floor mat. There was no point in me getting good grades anymore. I didn't even know why I came to school today in the first place. I mixed orange and red in my mouth as I took out a piece of paper and wrote.

Dear Easton . . .

I wrote several versions of my letter until the Skittles were replaced with crumpled up rejection letters. I stared at my name and number on an otherwise blank piece of paper. At least it was to the point. He would have to appreciate that, given my lack of time left. I shrugged to nobody but myself and finished my Coke.

The thought of attending my last class was less than appealing. Giving in to my new irresponsible mindset, I started the engine. My focus was now set on three places. The New River Bridge. Red Brick Diner. And lastly, Fresh Grounds. If Easton was the least bit interested in seeing me again, there was a small chance he would be hanging out at one of the spots we had previously seen each other.

I passed the New River Bridge, but only let off the gas a little. There was no need to slow down to see that Easton wasn't there. No parked cars and no homeless man standing on the rails. I trudged forward. The crisp air seemed to buzz with electricity. Maybe it was my destiny, maybe it was static, but I had a good feeling about this.

I turned into the empty parking lot of the diner. This time, I decided to park and head inside. The doorbells jingled as I crossed the threshold, the letter in my hand. I walked up to the bar, scanning the booths for a slender build and pale face with messy hair, and the eyes that made me forget I was sick. My stomach dropped, and for the life of me, I didn't know why.

A waitress rounded the corner, wiping her hands on a dishtowel. I recognized those boobs. Sue. I caught myself mid-eye-roll and forced myself to be polite. Maybe she was in a better mood today.

"Hi! Um, Sue?" I waved my hand, and even though she saw me, she kept walking. I scurried after her. "Sue?" My voice squeaked with the effort.

"I'll be right with you," Sue said and had the audacity to hold her finger up as if I were too dense to understand English. This time, I let my eyes do their thing. Sue busied herself behind the bar as I waited.

"Hi there! I knew you would be back!" Sue perked up so much that she looked like a different person altogether. Her whole face glowed. I scowled at her obvious distaste for me. I looked over my shoulder to see who the lucky customer was to have won the affections of Sue and her big bust, but I whipped my head back when I saw Easton closing in on me. My eyes bugged, and suddenly, I second-guessed the whole plan.

Easton placed his hands on the bar next to me. I slowly moved the letter in my hand to the inside of my jacket. I could feel him staring at me, but unlike Dawson from school, I needed something from Easton. I swallowed, refusing to look at him.

"Hello, Sue. How are you doing today?" Easton said, only quickly taking his eyes off of me. I peeked at him. His hair was the same mop of a mess, and he was wearing his wool coat—still not homeless. Why did I keep thinking this man was homeless?

"I'm doing better now that you're here, darling! What can I get you?" Sue whipped the dish towel over her shoulder.

"Ladies first," Easton gestured to me. My eyes met Sue's and her one raised eyebrow.

I swallowed again. "I'll have the pie. To go." It was even more embarrassing than I'd imagined last night. "Please," I said just under my breath. I knew it didn't mean anything to her. Still, I had to say it for me.

When Sue turned away, I looked up at Easton. "You found me," I said, unsure of myself. My cheeks warm, and my forehead creased. Easton smiled and pulled out a blue vinyl barstool and sat. I followed his lead.

Sue slid a box across the counter and handed me a check. "And what can I get for you, sir?" She shimmied her shoulders, too excited to stand still. I sat in front of the to-go container awkwardly.

"I'll have the same. It looks delicious. Did you make it yourself?" Easton asked.

"I did! How did you know that?" Sue placed her hand on her hip.

"Oh, just a hunch!" Easton leaned over the bar. "Between you and me, I don't think Bill is much of a baker!" Easton said, in a hushed voice, and Sue squealed. She looked back into the kitchen at who I presumed was Bill and giggled as she swatted the air.

I couldn't believe Easton put the time and effort into making her so happy. It probably wasn't much work on his side, but it sure did make her day. I wanted to be like him. I wanted to make someone's day, too. Not Sue's, though.

CHAPTER 6

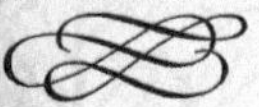

Sue placed a warm slice of blackberry pie in front of Easton, complete with a napkin and fork. I looked down at my cold pie inside of its to-go box.

"Can I have a fork, please?" I asked Sue. I forced a smile, but she never looked to see it. I suppose it was too late to ask for a plate.

"Funny how we keep running into each other," I said, knowing very well I came to the Red Brick Diner looking for him. I wondered if he was here doing the same. Sue placed a fork in front of me, and I smiled, but I didn't look to confirm my rejection. There was only so much a girl could take.

"Maybe it's fate," Easton said.

At first, I worried he might like me, and I was giving him the wrong impression, but then I remembered that he was the only one that knew my existence was temporary. Why would anyone want to get involved with that baggage? And if he were crazy enough to actually want me in my broken state, it was kind of like having a get out of jail free card. There were too many excuses to pick from.

"Maybe," I said, still contemplating my stance.

"Do you come here often?" Easton asked and took a bite of pie.

I ripped my box so the edges would lay flat like a plate. "I . . . don't, really. I just wanted something sweet." I shrugged.

I was still reeling from the soda and Skittles I ate off my floorboards. I frowned at the thought of my dishonesty. Was I ever going to tell the truth again? I slumped as I continued to disappoint myself.

"Actually, I came here looking for you." I took a bite of the pie and I tried to build the courage to keep going.

"You came here looking for me?" Easton asked, his eyebrows lifting. I feared his surprise came from me telling the truth and not that I was looking for him.

I pushed away the pie that I never wanted in the first place and turned my full attention to Easton. It was time to be honest. I owed that to myself.

"I tried to tell my parents, but it didn't go so well. They were so happy that I couldn't bring myself to tell them the truth. I don't think I'm ready to tell them, and I'm not sure I ever will be. Do you think that makes me a bad person?" I looked down at my feet, afraid of what his eyes might say.

Easton took a moment to think. I could hear it in his deep sigh. "No," he said in a tone too high to convince me that he was telling the truth. I peeked up at him. "I mean, it's your life. You get to live the way you want to, and that's the beauty of it, right? It doesn't make you bad or good to live the way you desire to," Easton said as he dug himself out of his hole. It worked, though. The profound guilt about my decision not to tell my family began to lift. The corners of my lips lifted as I nodded my head, accepting his point of view.

"Thank you for that. You've somehow managed to put my mind at ease. That's not an easy task. Especially not these days," I said.

"You don't have to thank me. I'm happy to help." Easton took his last bite and pushed his plate away. "Now, you said you were looking for me?"

Was my update not enough of a reason? I raked my mind for other lies. I couldn't tell him I needed him to be my fake boyfriend. It was absurd and embarrassing, and that was just the beginning. I pulled out the note from inside my jacket. It was just my name and number, thank God.

"I wanted to give this to you." I slid him the note on top of the bar.

His face bent with curiosity, and he opened the folded paper.

"You know, just in case you needed anything." I tried to make it sound like it was for him and not me. I don't know why that was my first instinct, but it was. I hated the way I felt like I couldn't simply ask for help. Sue gathered Easton's plate and handed him the check.

"OK, thanks for this." Easton smiled and put the note in his back pocket before turning his attention towards his check.

I'm not sure if he was calling my bluff or not, but I felt the panic creep in. Was that it? That couldn't be it!

"Um, well like, maybe you want to hang out or something? You know if that was the case, you could call me too." I waved my hand in the air as if it were nothing. But in all honesty, he was the only one keeping me sane, and I needed him for my mental health. I also needed him not to blow my whole boyfriend story.

Easton slammed the pen down on his check and turned to me. "You don't have time for games," he said matter-of-factly. His tone was sharp, his words cutting.

I looked away from his glacier blue eyes. It hurt to hear. I felt like Yeti cowering in the admission of guilt. He was right. He was *always* right.

"If you tell me that the number is for me to call if *I* need *you*, I'm not calling. Like I told you before, I'm fine. Would you mind telling me why you really came here looking for me? And what this number is really about?" Easton lowered his head to try to make eye contact with me. Reluctantly, I let him.

"You're right. I'm sorry. I don't know why I said that. The number isn't for you. It's for me. I need a friend right now"—my eyes began to well up—"and you're the only one who understands me . . . as odd as that is, given the fact that you're a total stranger to me. I just feel *really* alone." A single tear dripped down my cheek, and I wiped it away as quickly as it came. I tilted my head back and blinked several times, urging the tears to stop their madness.

"I would really appreciate it if I could just call you sometime or if we could hang out. That's all." I lowered my head to find Easton with an apologetic look on his face. My confession was all he wanted. Not the part that brought me to tears.

"There, was that so hard?" Easton asked and handed me his napkin.

I rolled my eyes. Damn boy. I blotted the corner of my eyes, and Easton chuckled at my theatrics.

"Look, I value honesty. If you want to be my friend, you have to be honest." Easton held out his hand.

I looked up into his eyes. They were full of sincerity. I reached out and grabbed his hand. It was warm and strong. My dad always told me that a firm handshake was important in a man. He would like Easton.

"Deal," I said, ignoring my omission of truth. Eventually, I would tell him when he wasn't a stranger, and I was ready to laugh about the lie I told my family.

We both stood and tucked in our barstools. Easton said goodbye to Sue, and I waited while he made her smile one last time. We made our way out of the diner and through the parking lot. Easton walked me to my truck. I opened my door but stopped before getting inside. The cold air wrapped around my neck, and I zipped my jacket as high as it would go.

"So, when are we going to hang out, friend?" Easton asked me, and a genuine smile spread across my face. It felt good to have a friend.

A black sedan pulled into the parking lot and caught my eye. I peered over Easton's shoulder. Heat washed over my cheeks as I realized that it was my mom. Again. My eyes grew wide, causing Easton to look behind him. *No. No. No . . .*

The clacking of my mom's shoes became louder. Easton was thrilled and took full enjoyment in my discomfort. He was probably the only person that would enjoy my embarrassment in my condition. And perhaps, it was the very reason I liked him. *Liked him?*

"Mrs. Beck! How wonderful to see you again. How has your day been?"

I prayed that she wouldn't say anything incriminating. But I knew my mother, and I knew that wasn't going to be the case.

"Easton! Hello again!" Mom laughed as she grabbed at his arm. "Dear, I just saw your truck as I was driving to the market and I thought . . . don't you have school today?" Mom looked down at her watch.

Clover was a small town. If my red truck was in a parking lot, every local in this town knew I was inside; and if Mom was driving to the supermarket and I was playing hooky, I was sure to be discovered. I thought this was frustrating when I was in high school, but it was even worse now that I was an adult.

"My teacher let us out early," I said, my eyes shifting between the two of them.

"Ohhh. OK. So, how was dinner last night?" Mom looked at Easton, then me.

Shit!

"Oh, yeah, we had fun. It was a good night." I nodded my head. Easton didn't have to know who "we" was, right? It could have been a girl's night out for all he knew.

"Well, I won't keep you two. Easton, I do hope you will come over for dinner soon?" Mom grabbed at Easton's arm again, and I sucked in a sharp breath.

"It's a date!" Easton said, smiling first at my mom and then me. Her face lit up.

All three of us stood in a silent web of lies until Easton broke the ice. "Well, I'll see you tonight then?" He raised his eyebrows at me and cocked his head to the side.

Tonight?

"Yes!" I said in absolute confusion.

Easton placed his hand over mine as I held onto my door and leaned down nearly two inches from my face. My stomach dropped as he closed his eyes and puckered his lips. My eyes grew wide with alarm. *What was he doing!?*

My mom lit up like a Christmas tree. I felt the pressure of her watching us and him waiting on me, and the seconds ticking by in slow motion. How long was he going to wait like a fool? I instantaneously decided to put him out of his misery. I rose up on my toes to close the inches between us and our lips met. I closed my eyes briefly before pulling away—as my stomach did somersaults.

Upon opening my eyes, Easton's smirk said it all. He got me. He got me good. Mom clapped. I was several shades of mortified.

The two of them turned to walk away. "I told you, you're her first boyfriend ever! So, she might come across a little timid . . ." Her voice faded into the distance.

I stood at my truck with my jaw dropped as I put the pieces together. "How wonderful to see you *again*." I assumed *again* was the first time they met, but clearly, it was not. I immediately regretted promising Easton a friendship built on trust. He had already known I was lying. He made me pay for my sins with a kiss. I brought my fingertips to my lips. I guess it could have been worse.

My mom walked into the diner, and Easton started his engine. I didn't know much about cars, but I knew that he definitely wasn't living rough. He pulled up next to me in his silver BMW and rolled down the tinted window.

"Hunters. 6:00 PM. Tonight," he said, pulling away before I could protest. My face contorted as I struggled to make out my emotions. I was irritated, deceived, angry . . . impressed, captivated, and excited.

CHAPTER 7

Red lace was too sexy. It wasn't a *real* date. Easton knew enough to know it was all for show. The dinner was more of a business transaction than anything else. What would I have to pay for a fake boyfriend? What did non-homeless Easton Green want?

My attention snapped back to the red lace. *No. I'll never wear that again.* I grabbed a sheer button-down blouse instead. The black top would have looked killer with my leopard heels. I bit my lip, thinking about the chewed-up shoes I never had the chance to wear. Alternatively, I slipped black boots over my jeans. They were weather appropriate at least. I threw on a necklace and grabbed my jacket before heading out the door. I was going to be early, but that's the way I liked it.

"Hello, I'm meeting somebody here at six," I informed the hostess. She checked her clipboard. I don't know how she could read it in this lighting. The ambiance was dark and romantic. Much too dark to read handwriting.

"You must be Everly?" the hostess said. I guess that her eyes had adjusted.

I smiled and nodded.

"Right this way." She turned and walked away.

I followed her through the small and intimate steakhouse. It was the only one in Clover. Every date happened here, and everyone knew who was seeing who. I spotted my dentist and his wife in the corner and pretended I didn't see them. My stomach dropped when we rounded the corner, and Easton came into my view. I don't know why I felt nervous. It was stupid, really.

Easton stood when I approached the table. He cleaned up nice. He was wearing a black-collared shirt and a smile. His hair styled with gel.

I received the menu from the hostess and took my seat. I thought about our kiss in the parking lot, and butterflies stirred in my stomach. I wouldn't say I liked Easton, but maybe I liked the way I felt around him.

"You look nice," I said before hiding behind my menu. The dim, romantic lighting was forgiving in the way he could no longer see my blushing cheeks and flushed chest.

"As do you," Easton said.

I glanced over the menu without reading. I had my order memorized since I was a kid. I never got anything but the chicken breast, mashed potatoes, and veggies. Mostly I filled up on the hot squaw bread and butter that came out as an appetizer. I slowly lowered my menu to take a peek at the boy across from me. I needed to get a read on the situation. His hair, slowly . . . his forehead . . . *dammit!* He was staring right at me! His hands folded on top of his menu. Confidence would be an understatement.

"OK, look! I told my family I had a boyfriend . . . it was my *mom* who told everyone else it was the 'cute boy from the coffee shop'" I curled my fingers into air quotes.

Easton's eyebrows lifted. "Cute boy?" he asked, clinging to the adjective.

Dear God! I'm either lying through my teeth or shooting myself in the foot. I stared at Easton blankly. I couldn't tell him that he wasn't my type! That his lack of abs left me with little to fantasize about! That would be . . . *evil.* I swallowed hard, and he just smirked back at me. Maybe I would go to hell.

"I'm sorry. This was a bad idea!" I said, starting to fidget for my purse.

"No! Don't go!" Easton pleaded, and my body stilled. "We don't have to be anything you don't want. I'm happy being your friend if that's what you need." He reached his hand out and placed it on mine.

I looked down at his hand. Warm on top of mine. I didn't know what to say. I didn't know what I wanted. I only knew that my pathetic life was better with him in it. I nodded and set my purse down. When Easton pulled his hand back, I wished that he hadn't.

"And I'm sorry I kissed you. I know I put you on the spot. It was only a joke," Easton said. I knew it was to get back at me, but calling it a joke hurt a little. I felt the ebb and flow between us, like an invisible string attaching us together. He pulls back, and I lean in.

"No, I know. That's OK. I know you were just getting back at me. I'm sorry I hid the fake relationship thing from you. I . . . never thought you would find out," I confessed. The honesty, as blunt as it was, felt good.

Easton laughed. "So, you're only sorry because you got caught?" he asked.

Now it was my turn to laugh. I thought about it. He was right as usual. "Yes!" I laughed again. It felt nice to laugh. Refreshing.

"My name is Kyle, and I'll be your waiter today. Can I get you started with a drink?" The waiter asked with his hands tucked behind his back.

"I'll have the red blend, please," I said.

"Make that two."

Now was my chance. I was going to make someone's day the way Easton had. I scanned the waiter for something to compliment him on. He looked . . . entirely average! *Just pick anything . . .*

"I like your shirt!" I blurted out.

The waiter frowned briefly before running his hand over a missing button. He faked a smile before dashing away.

"Oh, no!" My mouth gaped as I stared at Easton in disbelief. "I was just trying to say something nice, and he thinks I was sarcastic!" My eyes bulged with worry. I lowered my head to my palm.

"Oh, that's what you were doing?" Easton looked behind him, checking for the waiter. "Nooo, I don't think he was offended." It was his turn to fib.

"You're lying to me! We can't be friends unless we're honest with each other! You made a deal!" I accused him, finger-pointing and all.

"*I* made a deal that *you* couldn't lie!" Easton corrected me.

Was that how it went? I struggled to remember anything but the kiss.

"OK, from now on, nobody lies. Ever!" I said, and I meant it. I thrust my hand across the table for another handshake deal.

Easton hesitated. He swallowed and stared at my hand without making an advance. "What's wrong?" I asked him.

"Nothing," he said in an unconvincing tone before shaking my hand. It didn't go without notice that his once firm handshake had wilted. No longer the firm and confident dealmaker from the diner. I scowled. He's hiding something already. But I wasn't angry with him. I knew what it was like to have secrets. To be buried in shame and embarrassment.

Kyle placed two red wine blends down on our table, and I couldn't help but look at the missing button from his shirt. He took our order while nervously pulling at his clothes. There was a special place in hell for me.

Easton raised his glass. "To a friendship built on your honesty," he said.

I laughed. "Wait, you didn't think that would actually work, did you?" I asked through my amusement.

"To a friendship built on honesty," Easton corrected himself.

We tapped our glasses together and took a sip of wine. It was good—the perfect blend of sweet and cherry tart. I placed my glass down on the table with a sense of renewed life. I no longer felt alone. I effortlessly connected with Easton as long as I took off my armor of lies. I could do it for him . . . for me. Whatever it was, I liked it.

"How are you doing? Where's your mind at?" Easton asked.

"My mind?" It was pretty good until he asked. "Um, I'm . . . well, this helps." I gestured to him across the table. "You're a decent distraction. When I'm with you, I find myself forgetting that my life's imploding." I sucked in a shaky breath. It was unlike me to be so honest about my feelings. But I was trying.

"I *can* help distract you," Easton agreed.

My eyebrows furrowed. It's what I wanted to hear, so why was I upset? I played with my wine glass.

"Why are you doing this?" I asked, not wanting to know the truth.

Easton appeared to be caught off guard. He nodded, taking in my frustration along with a leisurely sip of wine. My irritation grew.

"Don't get caught up in your self-pity. You're going to get that from everyone else in your life, but you won't get it from me." He looked around the restaurant before leaning in. He spoke low and rushed. "I'm not your friend because you're dying. I'm your friend because I happen to like you. You're different. You're in an odd situation. And I enjoy being around you and your thoughts, emotions, and actions. Don't get me wrong. I'm just as selfish as anyone else out there, but I'm not doing this for a good conscience. I'm doing it out of my own damn self-interest. Don't you forget it!" Easton leaned back in his seat as Kyle brought us our food.

Frozen in shock, I needed a moment to take it all in. Buttered garlic swirled under my nose, and despite my distaste for the lecture, my mouth began to water.

I *didn't* want pity, and his brutal honesty is what I had just asked for, so I couldn't fault him for it.

"Are you mad at me?" I asked, trying to understand my ever-changing emotions.

"Mad? I'm not mad at you. You just need to hear the truth. Sometimes it hurts a little, but I've just vowed to be honest with you, so my relationship with you will be very different from my relationship with Sue at the diner. Does that make sense?" Easton asked as he tore apart his steak.

"You mean you don't think Sue has the prettiest eyes?" A small smile crept across my face as I began to forgive my new friend for snapping at me. Yes, the truth hurt, but the thought of not having him at all hurt more. Easton's eyes grew large, and his smile said what he did not.

"Look. This thing between you and I . . . it's different, right?" Easton motioned between us with his fork.

"Yes," I admitted.

"You don't have time for games, right?" he continued.

"No," I said, totally drawn in. I think I liked where this was going.

"So, let's just lay it all out on the table? Yes?" He nodded, willing me to do the same.

"Yes!" I said enthusiastically.

"You need a fake boyfriend to keep your parents in the dark because you're a coward and can't tell them the truth about your diagnosis," he said as I nodded greedily. It was all out in the raw open air, and I felt liberated.

"You're too afraid of pity, so you haven't told any of your friends. You're lonely beyond belief, and you need company." A smile spread across his face. "*My* company," he said.

I continued to agree.

"So, let's just do the damn thing! Let's be as real and as greedy as we need to be. And let's get you through the next several months." The candle's flame danced in Easton's eyes.

"Yes! Can we do that, please?" I asked. It was more than I ever knew I wanted. Who knew the truth could be so freeing?

Easton slammed his palm down on the table and our silverware clamored. "Yes!" he said—seemingly louder than he'd anticipated. He hunched and looked around nervously.

I felt electric. More alive than I had in a long time.

"OK, we've got to get to work! Hold on." Easton got up from the table and walked away. Where was he going? I waited impatiently, still too excited to eat.

Easton returned with a take-out menu and a pen. "OK, tell me all the things you've wanted to do in your life but haven't yet." Easton held the pen to the paper.

"Like a bucket list?" I asked.

"Yeah, yeah, like a bucket list. Do you have one?" he asked, staring into my eyes.

"No. I mean, not yet!" I said.

"That's what I like to hear!" Easton shook his pen at me, and I smiled, wanting nothing more in that moment than to be under his praise.

"Um . . . I've never seen the northern lights!" I said, rushed, and Easton scribbled it down.

"I've never bungee jumped! I've never gone camping! Or gotten a tattoo." It was all just spilling out.

Easton stopped writing and peeked up at me. "Wait, these are things that you *want* to do, not just stuff you've never done," he clarified, his forehead creased as he looked up at me with those eyes.

"I know!" I said, just as confused as he was.

"Nobody *wants* to go camping," he said.

I laughed aloud. "I do! I want to sleep under the stars and roast marshmallows!" I nodded my head as he shook his in disagreement.

"That's not—"

"Just write it down!" I said.

"OK," he muttered and began to write again. Our food was starting to get cold, but neither one of us paid it any mind.

"I want to ride a horse on the beach. I want to skinny dip . . . or go streaking! I want to crash a wedding!"

The word wedding stung as soon as it left my mouth. The fun had been replaced by an ache in my chest. My eyes settled on the dancing flame of the scentless candle on our table.

"I'll never get married, or dance at my wedding. I'll never fall in love . . ." The realization that my bucket list was impossible to fill was devastating. I sank in my seat. My throat burned as I held back my tears.

Easton continued to write, and I drowned myself in wine, proceeding to flag our waiter over to ask for a refill.

"Hey, weddings are overrated anyway." Easton shrugged, careful not to mention that falling in love was . . . totally worth it. But I could read between the lines, and I wondered what epic love story he had already experienced or would in his long life.

"Yeah, totally overrated." I shook away my tears. "Hey! We have to make your bucket list too," I said, trying to sound optimistic. I reached my hand across the table for my turn with the menu and pen.

Easton froze. He didn't like the idea as much as I did. "We don't have to do that. Let's just focus on you," he said and looked back to the menu.

"No! Come on. Don't be like that!" I protested and flapped my hand, begging for the menu.

"I've done a lot of stuff already; there's not much more for me to do," Easton said and batted my hand away.

I wouldn't accept his nonsense. "You're my age. What, like twenty-two, twenty-five? How have you done everything you want to do already?" I shook my head, not believing my "honest" friend.

Easton rolled his eyes before caving. He slid me the pen and menu. I silently cheered and took them from him. I flipped the menu over and wrote his name at the top.

"Ready!" I said.

"I've never crashed a wedding with you . . . I've never gone camping with you," Easton started in a slow and soothing voice.

My heart sank. "I've never danced at your wedding," he said, and my tears threatened to spill over again.

I didn't write anything on the menu. I just nodded and gazed into his eyes. We shared a moment of understanding. Neither one of us needed to say what we felt to know that it was kind, compassionate, and completely mutual. I didn't know his reasons for needing our friendship, but I knew the desire was shared.

CHAPTER 8

"I'll take it to go, please," I said to our waiter. Having only eaten a couple of bites, there was a possibility of me getting hungry later tonight. Easton read me his number as I entered the digits in my phone.

"You have to promise to call me if you need anything," he said with raised eyebrows.

"I promise. You too." I said.

"Any time of day or night, OK?"

I nodded my head. "I promise I'll call you," I said and smiled. "You too! This goes both ways." I pointed my finger at him in a flirtatious manner. He enjoyed it.

The waiter brought us our check, and I considered a way to right my wrong about the missing button on his shirt but ultimately decided I had dug a hole I couldn't climb out of. Easton paid, and I thanked him. I took the last sip of my wine before standing up and grabbing my purse. Where were all of the people? The restaurant was nearly empty. I checked my watch, it was almost 10:00 p.m.

"We've been here for four hours!?" I asked Easton, bewildered.

He checked the time on his phone and seemed to be surprised too. "Really?" he looked at me like someone was playing a trick on us, and I laughed. He placed his hand between my shoulder blades as we walked out of the restaurant. It was a friendly gesture, but it still made me blush, just a little.

I paused momentarily when I recognized someone I knew at the bar. Hope. I lifted onto my tippytoes, trying to get a look at the guy she was with. I was just like everyone else in Clover. Nosey.

"Someone you know?" Easton asked, looking at the couple at the bar.

"Yeah, that's Hope." I looked back at Easton as he took her in.

She was the girl next door. Not literally, but physically. She was beautiful, but most men looked it over, including my brother. He was too blind to see that she had feelings for him. Hope was his perfect match, and by the looks of it, she had started dating again. I frowned and kept walking.

"She's the girl I wanted my brother to marry, but he's too dense to see that she's the total package. Now, he's marrying some bimbo." I filled Easton in as our walk slowed to a crawl. He opened the door for me, and the cold air nipped at my nose.

"A bimbo! Is that right?" Easton laughed. "I haven't heard that one in a while."

I rolled my eyes at him. Chloe didn't appear to have brains—just a pretty exterior. I scowled when I realized that I had always gone for the same type. Perhaps it ran in the family.

"She's the dating type, not the marrying type if you get my drift," I said as I dug for my keys in my purse.

"Got it. So what's the deal with Hope then?" Easton asked, his hands tucked deep into his pockets.

"Well, our families used to be good friends when we were younger. They lived in the neighborhood. She always had a crush on my brother. He thought she had cooties. When they were fresh out of high school, they worked together at the supermarket. They spent all their breaks together and became fast friends. It was clear that she never lost feelings for him, but my brother never took the bait. I don't know why." I shrugged, looking back into Hunters' windows, but they were too dark to see inside.

"Maybe, it wasn't meant to be." Easton said.

I shrugged, not yet convinced. "I had a great night. Thank you." It was the most comfortable truth of the night.

Easton smiled back at me. "Thank you for not blowing me off. I thought there was a chance after my stunt in the parking lot today!" He laughed and looked down at his feet.

My stomach lurched at the mention of our kiss. I shoved him playfully.

"I'll get you for that. Someday," I promised him. I got into my truck and started the engine. Easton stayed by my door side. I rolled my window down a notch.

"Don't forget to call if you need me!" he reminded me.

I lifted my phone and gave it a shake. Then, I pulled out of the parking spot and made my way home with an empty belly and a full heart.

Easton's friendship was enough to keep the terrors away that night. My house was empty, but my mind was occupied. The bed was cold but not unbearable. And I was dying . . . but not tonight.

My alarm blared, waking me again. It was the fourth time I'd hit snooze, and each time I'd fallen fast asleep. I finally turned the alarm off altogether and rolled over. Not today. Work was the least of my concerns. Yeti rolled onto her back, wiggling and scratching, causing the bed to shake and my eyes to open. The more conscious I became, the more guilty I felt. Lindsay would be expecting me. I couldn't let her down. I groaned as I threw off the covers. I should just quit. Both school and work. I contemplated the idea as I got dressed and brushed my teeth. Maybe I wasn't ready to have full days of loneliness, but at some point, I wouldn't have another choice.

The silent drive to work got me thinking of my date last night. I'd be lying if I said I'd thought of anything else. A simple drive through Clover, and the diner lifted my spirits. Passing Hunters was equally uplifting. And Fresh Grounds made me flush with embarrassment when I thought of Easton warming up to my mom. A small pang of guilt seeped into my mind as I put my truck into park. Was I using Easton?

When I walked into Fresh Grounds, I was pleased to see Greg's camel jacket in line. The smell of coffee and all things pastry told me I'd made the right decision coming in to work. I whispered my order to Lindsay before checking into my cash register.

"Greg, I can help you over here." I waved him over. "How are you doing today?" I asked as I started putting in his order.

"I'm good. I'm good. I'll have the regular," he said, pulling out his wallet.

"And how is Carol?" I asked.

"She's good. She's all wrapped up in this book where a boy freezes himself. He wakes up twenty years later and falls in love. She says it's captivating but won't tell me the ending. Says I have to read it myself. She knows I don't read that stuff." Greg batted his hand across the air.

I laughed and took his money. "Maybe you would like it?"

"Me? No . . . I don't want to read about love. That's for you girls!" Greg shook his head as if I were crazy.

I giggled. "Your order will be right out."

"Thanks, Beck."

The line was small today. I grabbed my latte from Lindsay, and we chatted as I practiced making a heart out of foam.

"Why didn't you tell me you had a boyfriend!?" Lindsay hissed like the milk steamer.

My cheeks flushed, and for a moment, I contemplated which side of the truth she would fall on.

"He's *not* my boyfriend!" *Shit.* Wrong side.

"He's not? Because your mom came in here yesterday," Lindsay started.

"I just said that to her so I could get her off my back! Carter's engaged now, and my mom has been riding me about never having a boyfriend. She brings it up all the time." This part was true. She did bring it up whenever she could. "He's just a friend," I said, turning my latte heart into a cloud. I was surprised by how the last part was the part that made me feel guilty. He was a friend, but in a lot of ways, he was more than that, too.

"Oh shit! It was so bad that you had to make up a boyfriend?" Lindsay laughed hard enough to fold in half and slap her hand on the bar several times.

I grabbed Greg's coffees and set them on the ledge. "Greg, your order is ready!" I called out to him.

"So wait, wait . . . does that guy know? Because your mom sat down with him for a *while*! Lord knows what she told him!" Lindsay blotted her left eye with the back of her hand.

"I mean, yeah, I had to tell him." I couldn't help but smirk. Her laugh was so over the top, it finally got to me.

"Actually, I had dinner with him last night. I had to tell him the whole thing. It was utterly embarrassing!" Among other things . . .

"Thanks, Greg! Tell Carol to enjoy that book!" I waved goodbye.

"I will!" Greg held up his coffees.

Lindsay threw her hand on her hip. "No!" Her mouth opened into an elongated O.

I nodded.

"How did you even meet this guy?" Lindsay prodded.

I pictured the torrential downpour of the storm and Easton's wet hair plastered to the side of his face, his body shivering. He was a different person at that moment. I hadn't seen that guy since the bridge.

"School," I said, but it came out sounding more like a question than a statement. I was relieved when I heard customers walk in. I thought it would end there, but it didn't. Lindsay poked and prodded about Easton all day. I grew tired of dodging her questions, and I knew I wouldn't be able to keep my lies in order.

It was almost time for me to get off work when I got a text from Easton. I pulled my phone out of my back pocket and smiled instantly when I saw his name.

Easton: What are you doing?

I typed as fast as I could.

Me: Working.

I waited for his reply, careful not to let Lindsay see.

Easton: I'll be there in ten.

My eyes widened, and a wave of heat blanketed my back as I felt my cheeks pinken. I tucked my phone in my pocket and raked my fingers through my hair, trying to comb out a day's work.

"You OK?" Lindsay asked. She was oddly perceptive.

"Yeah!" I furrowed my brows . . . because why *wouldn't* I be OK?

How would she react when Easton came in? I hoped she wouldn't say anything.

Every time the door opened, I jumped, and Lindsay observed my sudden shift in mood.

When Easton finally walked through the doors, my stomach dropped. I was nervous all over again. Every time was like the *first* time.

"Oh! Oh!" Lindsay started, slapping my hip beneath the countertop.

"Shhh!" I hissed back at her. Easton saw the shuffled exchange between us, and it caused a stifled grin to appear on his face.

"You must be the infamous Easton?" Lindsay asked.

Shit! Here we go!

"Hi!" I said, taking off my apron and walking out from behind the bar to convey that this was not a three-way conversation.

"I have a proposition for you," Easton said into my ear as we walked into the corner of the coffee shop that resembled a used book store.

"A proposition?" I asked. I didn't know what it was, but he didn't need to say any more. I was in.

"Do you have plans tonight?" Easton's face lit up while he waited for my answer.

"Tonight? Um, no . . ." I was already planning what to wear in my head.

"OK, I'll pick you up at eight?" he asked, just as excited as I was.

I nodded. "Sure, I'll text you my address," I said, still unsure of what I was getting myself into.

Easton's grin widened as he started to step back towards the door.

"Wait, what do I wear?" I perked up.

"A dress." Easton gave me one last smirk before turning around.

Oh, no! Not a dress! I stood in the corner of the coffee shop, scowling. I knew I didn't have a dress. I hadn't worn one since prom, and I was pretty sure that when he said *dress*, he didn't mean a fuchsia floor-length gown. I was so distraught I didn't hear Lindsay when she came up behind me.

"Did you just break up with your fake boyfriend? Cause you look knocked sideways," she said," trying to read my face.

I closed my mouth and looked at her square in the eyes.

"Do you have a dress I could borrow?" I searched her eyes for the *yes* I so desperately needed.

"Um, yeah. I have a few dresses?" she started.

"Thank you! Oh my God, thank you!" I gave her a quick hug.

"What's going on?" Lindsay asked as we made our way back behind the counter.

"I have a date!" I shrugged and slipped my apron back on for the last ten minutes I had on my shift.

"Like, a *real* one?" Lindsay's face was lined with confusion.

I cracked. My shoulders dropped, and my back slouched. "I don't know!!! I don't know!" my voice came out whiny and annoying. I was no better than a toddler throwing a fit for candy at the supermarket. There were so many feelings and lies; I couldn't possibly keep track of them all. I didn't know if it was a fake date or a real one—if we were friends or something more. And if it hadn't been for the stupid kiss that I continued to lose my stomach over, I might just have a grasp on this thing. But as for right now, all I knew was that I looked hideous in dresses.

"It's OK!" Lindsay patted my arm. "Look, come over after work, and we'll try on some dresses, OK?" Lindsay looked at her watch. "The next shift should be here any second." And as soon as she said it, Amy walked in the door. "See?" Lindsay nodded, and I felt my panic begin to dissipate.

I sat on Lindsay's unmade bed while she rummaged through her closet. Clothes littered her floor, presumably dirty. Her cat took a liking to me today, but when it jumped onto my lap, all I could think about was its paws digging through its litter box. By the smell of it, the thing was nearby.

"So, I have this one that might be a little too big for you in the boobs, but you can try it on." She held out a teal satin dress that looked like the boobs were already inside. I nodded. This was going to be a disaster.

"There's this one that I wore to my sister-in-law's baby shower. It's more forgiving in the chest because you can tighten the straps." Lindsay threw a lacy floral dress on her bed. I nodded again, praying there was more.

"Oh! And there's this one, but it's kind of boring." She held a grey turtleneck T-shirt dress by her side. "And you have *no* idea what you're going to be doing tonight?" she asked for the third time.

"No! I have no freaking clue! It's seriously stressing me out!" I placed my palm against my forehead. I jiggled my legs so the cat would jump off me. I couldn't take the feces feet any longer.

"Well, don't do that, um . . ." Lindsay bit her lip, a habit she'd gotten from me. "I could . . . take a peek in my sister's closet?"

I sat straight up. "Really?" I asked with rising hope.

"Yeah, I mean, she usually comes home on the weekends, but I don't think she would notice. Here, I'll see what I can find. Be right back!" Lindsay scurried out of her room, and I gave a sigh of relief. I studied her Blake Shelton posters on her wall while I waited.

Lindsay was overly excited when she returned with what she thought was the perfect match. "Look what I found!" Lindsay shimmied her shoulders as she held out a baby blue slip dress. Simple, like me.

"Yes! Oh my God, thank you!" I jumped up and took the dress from her.

"Yeah, just bring it back soon, so I can pop it back in her closet, OK?" she asked.

"Absolutely! Thank you!" I hugged her briefly before getting on my way.

CHAPTER 9

I jumped when Easton knocked on my door. Even Yeti was surprised. She leaped from her bed, bounded across the small living room, and raced to the front door, barking all the way. She was ferocious when she needed to be. I held her by the collar as I opened the door. Easton was handsome in his navy suit, his top two buttons undone. I caught his eye for a split second before Yeti's strength overpowered mine; she pushed the door open and escaped from my grasp.

Lucky for Easton, Yeti was full. But what surprised me more than her lack of aggression was the fact that she wagged her nub tail in excitement. Small whimpers escaped her as if seeing an old friend. I'd never seen her act like that.

I watched Easton win the heart of Yeti in an instant, and I wondered if he'd done the same to me when I lost my stomach. I pushed away my nerves and called Yeti into the house.

"Sorry!" I said, noting the smudge of slobber on Easton's pants.

"Don't be. I love dogs. What's his name?" Easton asked.

"*Her* name is Yeti," I said with my back to Easton as I locked my door.

His proximity did weird things to my insides as I took in the smell of his woody, sensual cologne. I sucked in a quick and shallow breath of air when I spun around to find Easton much closer than I expected. I smiled nervously and tucked my hair behind my ear, trapped between him and my locked door.

"You look beautiful tonight," Easton said slow and calm.

My heart pounded in my chest. A part of me couldn't take the closeness and all of the emotions that came with it. Another, albeit a small part, wanted to see what would happen if we lingered like this a little while longer.

Only after sensing my nervousness did he take a step back and say, "Welp, we better get a move on it! Can't be late!" He walked to his car and opened the passenger's door for me. It was when he pulled back that I saw what I truly wanted.

So gentlemanly of him to open my door. This *was* a date then. It felt like a date. My eyes darted around the car, searching for the answers to my indecisiveness. I felt like a hamster on a wheel, running as fast as my legs could take me . . . in no particular direction and with no end in sight.

"Where are we going?" I asked, my forehead still creased with my unsettled feelings.

"I can't tell you that. It would ruin the surprise!" Easton flashed a dimpled grin at me before setting the car in motion.

A wave of excitement washed over me. I didn't let it last long before I protested. Ruining my life's positivity was a bad habit—and one I wouldn't have time to kick.

"I don't know why you're doing this!" I shook my head, angry at the things I couldn't control. Like this feeling like a date, even though it wasn't, and my emotions being all over the place. Why didn't I know what I wanted or how I felt? I pulled my dress down to my exposed knee. I feared he pitied me, even though he made it very clear the night before that he had not.

Easton took a deep breath. "You can't blame a guy for wanting to hang out with a pretty girl, can you?" He tried to diffuse my uprising frustration.

I rolled my eyes. People had told me all my life that I was pretty, but I'd never believed it.

Easton shook my shoulder. "Come on. We're going to have fun tonight. I need some fun," he said.

It was easier for me to think that he needed a distraction, so I went with it, allowing myself to try and believe it. When the image of him standing on the bridge crossed my mind again, I thought it might just be true. We were honest friends, after all.

"So, what do you do for fun normally? You know, when you used to be happy," I asked him and watched as his expression turned dark for a fraction of a second before changing to curiosity.

"Used to be?" Easton's eyes flickered from the road to me.

I looked out the window to the plethora of passing trees. The forest floor blanketed in pine needles and fallen branches. The car wound around the mountainside in tranquility. He didn't want to talk about it; that much was clear. I would have to find another way.

"I mean, your hobbies. Like, I'm in school for graphic design because I love it. I like to take a picture and change it around until it feels balanced and your eye can't help but move across the image in exploration. I've always loved art, ever since I was a kid . . . what's the thing you do, *or did,* that makes you most happy?" I asked, wishing I was comfortable with the silence and didn't feel the need to fill the air with the sound of my voice.

"Well, it isn't so much *what* makes me happy as *who* makes me happy." Easton's eyes flicked back to mine. "And right now, you're making me happy," he said.

Warmth spread across my face, and I lifted my hand to my forehead, subconsciously to cool my blush.

"You're a sweet-talker, Easton Green!" I stifled a laugh, and he did too.

"What!? It's true!" he claimed.

I shook my head, not believing a word he said. "We're *just* friends, and don't you forget it!" I reminded him.

Easton's mouth opened wide in protest, then closed again before saying anything. He scrunched his face, "Well, friends make each other happy, right?"

"Uh, huh." I shook my head as a grin spread across my face.

Our playful banter silenced when we crossed the New River Bridge. I looked out my window at the dusk lit bridge and decided not to bring up the night we met.

"What do you do for a living?" I asked, surprised that I hadn't thought to do before.

"I'm . . . in construction," Easton said as if he were uncertain how to explain it to me.

I nodded and looked around his car. High-gloss wooden finish and camel colored leather, it still smelled new. It seemed too nice to come from a mountain construction salary. Far too expensive to be driving into a construction zone every day. My eyes lingered on his hands, and though they didn't appear soft, they in no way resembled a man who worked with his hands. I looked from the absent calluses on his hands back to his eyes, where I detected his hesitation.

"I'm in the sales department. I connect the job's manager with the suppliers. It's more social work than anything else," Easton said as he furrowed his eyebrows.

Though it made a lot more sense, something in the back of my head was telling me to be cautious. I rationalized with myself. It explained the scuff-free hands, and he *was* good with people. It made sense for him to be a salesman, and with what I saw at the diner, he could probably make enough extra money in commissions to afford the car.

Though suspicious, I wasn't worried. Easton was more of a puzzle than anything else. I almost preferred the chase. It gave me something to think about other than my illness. The whos and whys of Easton Green dwelled rent-free in my mind. Every omitted truth he told, I stole away to unwrap in thought, late into the night when I was home and alone. It would help keep the terrors away at a bare minimum.

Easton was like my personal mystery novel. I read deep into the night, and I worked tirelessly, trying to find the missing pieces.

I filled the silence by telling Easton the latest about my brother and his engagement. I told him about my parents and how my mom had two sisters that

I adored when I was young, but I never saw them now. I told him about how we moved in the fourth grade and how making friends in a new school was easier than I imagined it would be. My mouth didn't stop until we pulled into a packed parking lot forty-five minutes out of Clover. Our headlights illuminated a man and woman walking through the parking lot holding hands. I was relieved to find I wasn't overdressed.

"Where are we?" I asked.

Easton checked his watch and smiled. "Right on time, come on!" He jumped out of his car, ran around to my side, and opened the door for me.

The brisk air rushed in, and a chill ran down my back, causing me to shiver involuntarily. I tucked my clutch under my arm. Easton reached out and rubbed my goosebumps to generate some heat, but his touch caused me to tremble more than before.

"Here." Easton stopped and took off his jacket.

"No! No! You keep it," I crossed my hands back and forth. He threw it over my shoulders anyway. His warmth that lingered inside the jacket now encapsulated me. I smiled at him. "Thank you." I'd seen it happen in the movies, but at twenty-two years old, I had never had a boy offer me his jacket. It made me both happy and sad.

Easton's expression creased with uncertainty when he caught the eye of a man ushering his family through the parking lot. I looked between the two of them.

"Do you know him?" I asked.

Easton guffawed, "Nope!"

The man seemed nice enough. He, too, was dressed in a suit, but unlike Easton, he wore a tie. He wrapped his hand around his little girl's tiny wrist. Easton swallowed hard, keeping his eyes away from the man's. We were all walking in the same direction, into the warmth of the . . . church? My eyes scanned for clues. The stained glass was a big one.

"That's the problem." Easton's gait began to slow. "I don't know him."

The man held the door open for his family and then us. Easton thanked him before taking the load of the door himself. For a moment, I didn't care where we were, as long as I could stay long enough to warm my limbs. But when the wedding march began to play, my heart skipped a beat. I froze. Easton grabbed my hand and pulled me through the double doors right as a bride rounded the corner.

"Easton! No! Wait!" I hissed in protest. He continued to pull me until we were sitting in the last pew—several eyes on us as we made our awkward entrance.

My heart pounded in my chest, and my mouth gaped open. Everyone rose at once. A bride, beaming from head to flawless toe, smiled at us as she walked past on the arm of her father. I threw my hand over my chest to capture my thumping heart and peered over my shoulder at Easton. His expression was that of excitement laced with anxiety.

He leaned in, close to my ear. "Act natural," he whispered, his warm breath tantalizing my ear.

"What!? You don't know these people?" I asked, looking around the room in fear.

I was an imposter. And I felt it too. Surely, we would get caught. We took our seat with the rest of the audience as the ceremony started. My eyes were the size of softballs. Easton held in his laughter, though his body quaked. He raised a fist to his mouth to pretend he was holding in a cough. I smacked him with the back of my hand.

"Are you being serious right now?" I bit my lip and tried not to catch the attention of those around us.

"Shhh. You don't want to get caught!" Easton said.

I seethed. How dare I trust this guy I didn't know! I didn't actually want to crash a wedding! The last thing I wanted was to be put in such an uncomfortable situation. Dew began to form on the back of my neck. I gathered my hair to one shoulder and began to fan myself.

Easton cleared his throat after a small outburst escaped his lips. A little girl with ebony skin and tight black curls turned around in her seat and watched us. If a five-year-old could tell we crashed the wedding, so would everyone else. I shrugged out of Easton's jacket and wiped my clammy palms on my dress, the sweat staining the satin.

As soon as the ceremony was over, I'd be darting to the parking lot.

I shot Easton a look that could kill, but he was too busy crossing off "crash a wedding" on the Hunter's to-go menu across his knee to see it. The realization that he was doing this *for* me and not *to* me dropped like a ton of bricks. He didn't want to be here any more than I did, but here we were because I said I'd never crashed a wedding.

When the groom recited his vows, my anxiety began to melt away. In the presence of love, I no longer had thoughts of fleeing to the car or wanting to kill Easton for bringing me here.

"I promise to cherish you through thick and thin," the groom said.

I listened to his shaky voice and watched as their love was professed in front of their closest friends, family, and the two strangers who snuck into the back pews at the last minute.

"I vow to be your guiding light when the night grows dark and your shoulder to lean on when life is too hard to handle on your own." The groom glanced down at the small piece of paper in his hand.

Easton placed his hand over mine. For reasons unbeknownst to me, I let it linger. His presence reminded me that I wasn't alone. And as much as he needed to have fun tonight, I needed his hand on mine, to tell me it was going to be OK.

When the ceremony ended, Easton pulled his hand back to his lap. The crowd broke out into small social gatherings. Many of the guests retreated straight to their cars. And a small line built in the hall next to the ladies' restroom. I cradled Easton's coat in my arms.

"Thank you for bringing me. I thought you were crazy at first"—I let out a laugh—"but then I realized this was exactly what I needed."

Easton laughed, "I think I was more nervous than you! But I'm glad we stayed." He smiled down at me. "Think we can survive the reception?"

"What!? No!" I said quickly.

There was no way I was sitting with the bride and groom's aunts and uncles and making up lies about how I knew them.

"I couldn't! Honestly! Don't make me!" I shook my head in all seriousness.

Crashing a wedding sounded fun, but I hadn't considered how nervous I would feel over getting caught. And from the relief in Easton's eyes, I could tell he felt the same way.

Easton chuckled and took the jacket from my arms, proceeding to place it over my shoulders as we walked into the cold with the rest of the crowd. "Are you sure you don't want to? We could stop and get dinner, then sneak back when everyone is toasted. You could even show me your dance moves. What do you say?" Easton asked, wagging his eyebrows.

"Oh, uh-huh, thanks for the offer, but I'm going to have to pass on this one. Plus, we already crossed it off the list." I shrugged apologetically. What was done, was done.

"Oh, thank God!" Easton threw his head back and sighed. "That was giving me indigestion!" Easton laughed at himself with one hand on his stomach. He was cute, trying to be brave for me. I bit the inside of my cheek and tried to cloak my smile. I didn't want to give him the wrong idea.

"Are you hungry? I know of a great place about fifteen minutes from here. It's on the way home too," Easton said as he opened my door.

"A bite to eat never hurt anybody." I tried to sound nonchalant as I crawled into the car. But the truth was, I was taken aback by the selfless gesture he made by taking me to crash a wedding forty-five minutes out of town. And I wanted more of his time.

CHAPTER 10

The dive bar Easton took me to wasn't what I was expecting when he asked me to dinner. We were overdressed, and frankly, I was out of my element. The bar and the wedding alike.

A bum lay outside of the bar. His clothes were tarnished with filth and so was his face. I subconsciously walked to Easton's other side, positioning myself as far away from the man as possible. But it wouldn't be this easy.

"Sam?" The bum struggled to sit up and get a closer look at us. A few beer cans crumpled under his weight, and to my surprise, a small dog appeared, nestled behind him. "Sam? Is that you?" he asked.

I glanced at Easton, hoping he would turn me around and usher me back to the safety of his car, but he did the opposite.

Easton's face softened as he reached for his wallet. He took out all the cash he had and bent down to give it to the deranged man.

"You can do better than this, Simon," Easton said in a quiet voice and handed him the cash. The bum grabbed at the money and started to count. I looked at Easton for an explanation, but he pretended not to notice.

Cigarette smoke marinated in the air, and a lively, probably drunken poker game carried on in the back corner. A pool table sat in the middle of the room where a man in a red plaid shirt and tattoos was trying to get lucky with a girl. By the looks of her attire, he would be successful.

"I know it's not much, but I used to come here to play poker all the time. The people are very nice; you have nothing to be worried about." Easton eyed my clenched hand pulling his jacket closed tight across my chest. I imagined that my face gave even more clues about my uncomfortableness.

Easton slapped the bar, catching the bartender's attention.

"Joey! Hey man, how are you?" Easton shook the bartender's hand.

The man with a long, thick black beard and brut body appeared incredibly happy to see Easton. I peeked around at the crowd; it wasn't what I thought when I pictured Easton's peers. Not that I had been thinking of him that intently.

"Who's the lady?" Joey asked.

"This is Everly. Everly, this is Joey, an old friend." Easton gestured to the bartender.

"Hello." I gave Joey a small wave and polite smile, still clenching the jacket closed.

"Hey, have you seen Clyde much lately?" Easton asked as he leaned over the bar and peered at the back poker game.

"No, man. I haven't seen Clyde for a while. He stopped coming in as much about three months ago." Joey picked up a wet glass and began to wipe it with a bar towel.

"Damn." Easton's forehead lined with worry. "If you see him, will you tell him I stopped in looking for him?"

"Yeah, no problem, man! Can I get you anything while you're here? You guys want a drink?" Joey's face lifted, hoping Easton would stay. Mine did the opposite.

"Um, yeah! That sounds great! I'll take a beer." Easton pointed at me.

I sighed. "Can I see a menu please?" I crawled up on the barstool.

"No menu. I got wine—white or red—beer, and hard alcohol. We also got nachos, peanuts, and . . . that's it!" Joey looked around the bar in case something else had slipped his mind.

I glanced down at the small picked-over bowls of peanuts. I thought about how many men didn't wash their hands after using the restroom had dug into the nuts. I assumed the nachos would be equally disgusting.

"I'll have a glass of red wine, please," I said. Joey smiled and turned around to fetch us our drinks.

"Old friend, huh?" I prompted Easton.

I placed my clutch on the bar but didn't take my hand off of it until I made one last glance around the room. He smiled and looked back at Joey before leaning into me.

"He's had a really tough life. I've spent countless hours on this side of the bar, walking him through life lessons that he hadn't yet learned. I think he's doing better now," Easton said, in a hushed voice.

Joey placed our drinks on the bar, and Easton straightened his back. I felt bad for Joey. I didn't know the details of his life, but I could easily picture how Easton's ability to connect with people had turned him into a counselor of the night.

"And Clyde?" I asked.

Easton's eyes darted away, and I assumed Clyde was a much longer story than Joey's.

"Clyde's my grandpa." Easton shrugged and took a sip of his beer.

His grandpa? I looked back at the couple, which were now making out against the pool table, and I wondered what kind of man Easton's grandpa was. I had my presumptions.

"Yeah, he . . . he's not that close to the family. Never was. When I found out he played poker here, I started coming to build a relationship with him. I've been coming here every couple of weeks to check in on him, but Joey says he hasn't been showing up." Easton looked down at his feet. No doubt to hide the worry in his eyes.

"Do you think he's sick or something?" I asked with growing concern for his grandfather.

"I don't know. Maybe? I don't have his number or address or anything. Joey says he only pays with cash, so I just give him his space when he goes off the grid for a while. Normally, he would reappear. I think it's more of an intermittent sobriety thing than anything else. I think it ebbs and flows with his depression." Easton peaked up at me, his eyes glassed over and filled with emotion.

I wondered about Easton's disconnected family life. I was positive that this was only the tip of the iceberg. I took a sip of wine, my eyes set on his.

"Did you succeed at building a relationship with your grandpa by playing poker here?"

"I did." Easton's smile reached his eyes. "And I learned a lot about poker too. It's quite fun. My favorite part is trying to read everyone's faces. Some are better than others at hiding their hand, but I can tell most of the time—if not *all* the time—when someone is bluffing." Easton chuckled at a distant memory.

"Hey! That's it! That's the thing you do for fun!" I perked up, excited about my discovery. "I just never took you as a gambler. You never cease to amaze me," I said, feeling the wine work its magic and alter my mood.

"Ha, yeah. Well, sometimes you've got to roll with the punches. I've found myself doing a lot of things that I never thought I would. All for a good reason, though." Easton held up a finger to Joey, who promptly brought me another wine.

"Oh! Thank you. You're not having another with me?" I asked.

"I would like to get you home safe." Easton smiled, every bit the responsible gentleman he was.

My first glass of wine did go down relatively fast, and despite being the only option for red wine, it wasn't half bad. Joey took away my empty glass. I took a long sip, and my eyes fixed on the base of my glass.

"Rolling with the punches . . . Is that what I'm doing now? Rolling with the punches?" I asked, wanting desperately to connect with him on a deeper level.

"Yes. It's what everyone does. You have to deal with it. There aren't many other options, you know?" He cocked his head to the side.

"You had a different option, though, didn't you?" I was too cowardly to look him in the eyes.

He sighed, and a stretch of silence spanned between us. "Excuse me, I need to use the restroom. Will you be OK here?" he asked.

I nodded, never looking at him. I regretted it the moment I said it. I always said the wrong thing, digging too deep too fast. I always pried. It was none of my business what was going through his head the moment I met him. And if I kept asking him, I was sure to lose him as a friend. I couldn't afford it.

I finished my wine and found myself eating out of the nut bowl by the time Easton resurfaced. I watched him on the far side of the room, saying hello to the poker players. Everyone seemed to know and love him. They must have all been fifty years and up, and I wondered why Easton would spend his time with a crowd much older and less fortunate than him.

The girl that was previously making out at the pool table slid her hand across Easton's back as she whispered something into his ear. I stiffened, and my stomach churned. I was frozen as I watched her caress him, and I seriously thought about going over there to break it up. But it was over before it started. Still, it was too long.

Did he like her? Did he know her? Did she not see me sitting over here in this sexy dress on *my date*!? It wasn't *really* a date, but *she* didn't know that!

After Easton paid Joey for the drinks, he made his way back to me.

"Are you ready?" his eyes flickered from mine to the peanut bowl my hand was scraping in. Easton looked back towards Joey, "Hey, can I get some nachos to-go?" I felt my cheeks flush.

"Sorry. I don't think I've had much more than a coffee today," I said as I wiped the salt off my hands.

"Don't be. I can get you something more substantial on the way home, but at least this will get you a little something in your stomach."

Easton turned to pay Joey for the second time, and I turned my daggers to the only other lady in the bar. Easton said goodbye and carried my nachos out to the car for me. I once again clenched his jacket tight as the chilly air collided with my warm body. It felt both cold and reviving at the same time—discomfort with a refreshing silver lining.

I stole a few glances at the bum, who was now asleep on the curb. His dog wandered a few feet away, looking for food.

"Hey, Easton? Why did you call that guy Simon? Do you know him?" I asked as I fastened my seatbelt.

"Who?"

"That guy." I pointed to the homeless man. "The one you gave all your money to," I said, confused. He knew very damn well who.

"Oh, no. I don't know him."

"Then why did you call him, Simon?" I asked.

"Um, it was on his sign. You must have missed it," Easton said as we pulled out of the parking lot and onto the main highway.

I thought back to the sign lying next to the pup; I very clearly remembered what it read: "Money Helps."

Easton didn't talk much on the way home. He said a few things here and there, mostly revolving around making me comfortable. I was quieter this time around. Far too interested in my melted cheese and undoubtedly subdued by the wine. I tried not to make a mess in Easton's prestigious car while I ate and stared out the window into the forest, which was black as the night that surrounded it.

Though I was with Easton—who was the only person that presently understood me—I felt the disconnect between us. I knew the answers lied in his mystery, but he didn't let me in. He didn't trust me as I did him. This realization made me feel alone all over again.

I looked at Easton's profile and let my eyes linger. His hair was becoming more unruly as the night progressed. His shirt was now wrinkled and slightly untucked. I wanted him to notice me. To see me. My nachos slumped down into my lap as my interest in them drifted to Easton.

I wondered what it would be like to kiss his lips. Not that measly kiss he tricked me into giving him at the Red Brick Diner, but a real and passionate kiss. My stomach dropped as Easton caught my gaze, and I looked away, blinking several times. I shook away the random thought and popped another chip into my mouth, rolling the salt between my fingers and trying to keep my mind off of what I really wanted.

"I had fun tonight," Easton offered into the silence.

I smiled. "Me too," I said.

I remembered him holding my hand when the groom recited his wedding vows and how my stomach felt weird and anxious. Maybe it was the cheese, perhaps it was the wine, but if I knew one thing to be true, there was a very strong possibility that it might be because I liked Easton Green. Not in the way I had been telling myself for the last week—the part about us being friends—but in the way that my life was ending, and all I wanted to do was spend my last days with him.

CHAPTER 11

The realization that I had feelings for Easton made the last fifteen minutes of the drive nearly unbearable. I fought through a small panic attack, and to my knowledge, I hid it well enough that it went unnoticed. I tried my damn hardest to push every single thought that came into my head, *out!* I didn't want to know about them, and I told myself that maybe it was just the wine talking. It wasn't, though. I knew that much.

We pulled into my driveway. My palms were sweating and my mind racing. Was he going to kiss me? We stepped out of the car, and he escorted me to my front door, his hand on the small of my back. I trembled as I dug for my key and Yeti serenaded us through the wood door.

"I just wanted to say, that—"

"Thanks! See ya!" I opened my door and slammed it in his face. Shutting the door of opportunity and heartache all the same. Yeti pushed her nose against my thigh as my eyes bulged out of my head, surprised by my own actions. I stood still and listened for Easton's movement, but as far as I could tell, he was just as stunned by my behavior as I was. My heart pounded against my chest. As quietly as I could, I took a step forward and lifted onto my tippy toes to look out my peephole. He was there, rubbing his chin in reflection. There we were, so close and yet worlds apart. But the thickness of the door wasn't the only thing that stood between us.

Two times he turned to knock on the door but ultimately gave up entirely and walked to his car. My heart continued to race. I lowered down, my heels pressing into the floor, and rested my forehead on the door.

This world was cruel. Like a black hole that swallows you slowly, torturing you along the way. I turned and threw my clutch at the wall and screamed at the top of my lungs, thankful that Easton was long gone and unable to hear my cries. The wrecking quakes hurtled through my body as tears washed down my cheeks. My nails dug into the back of my arms when I tried to comfort myself with a hug. Gripping tight like I might just lose myself all together if I didn't hold on for dear life. Only after noticing a feeling that should have been recognized as pain, did I realize I was squeezing too tightly. I didn't stop. The tiny sting from each fingernail was a blessed distraction from the terror that lived in my head.

My knees began to weaken, and my back slid down the door till my butt was resting on the carpet, and the loud, ugly sobs filled my empty home.

I fought it the best I could. The love I felt for him. I fought it, because It didn't make any sense to have when I knew it was fleeting.

Still, it grew.

I paid it no attention until it was too late; it'd taken hold of me. Like a vice around my chest and a weight around my ankle. And now what was I supposed to do? Add heartbreak to my bucket list? Or heart*breaker*? Assuming he may have feelings for me too.

It didn't matter if he did or didn't. All of it was equally tragic because I was a girl who was dying. And he was a boy who was not.

CHAPTER 12

The following day passed in a blur. It mostly consisted of me lying in bed, somewhere between sleep and consciousness, but I can't be sure. The curtains were drawn to black out the light, and a pillow covered my head for most of the day. At one point in time, Yeti made sure I couldn't ignore her, so I let her outside. It was then, when I was on two feet, that I picked up my clutch and checked my phone. It was shattered. Dead. If Fresh Grounds was calling me, I wouldn't have known.

I didn't let myself think of Easton. It was probably better to say goodbye now. As I did the night before with a slammed door between us. It would be easier this way.

At some point in the night, I woke. Only slightly to ponder if this was it. Was I dying now? *Could* I die now? I watched my favorite movie in my head. Nicholas Sparks' *The Notebook*. The two were so deeply connected to one another, their love carried them away. I willed it to happen to me. But each subsequent breath told me it was impossible. There was no love train out of this misery. And there was no easy way out. I was stuck, riddled with cancer and a broken heart, determined to stay in my bed until the day I was blessed to leave it all behind. Like a sweet release from the dark thoughts that plagued me.

Miraculously, at some point, I began to dream again. The swans from *The Notebook* surrounded me, and I, too, became a bird in flight.

The never-ending weekend finally came to an end. I had school today. And though I didn't care about learning anything new in the field of graphic design, I figured I could at least get out of the house. Sit in my truck with a piece of paper and pen. If I was fortunate enough, I'd manage some freshly combed hair and a full belly too. I was depressed and run down—miserable at best—but I didn't have to spend my last months bedridden.

By the time I got to school—teeth and hair successfully brushed—I was too late to make my first class. I didn't bother bringing my phone, as I never had the energy to plug the thing into the wall to recharge it. Still, it sat dead and shattered in my entryway. The less distraction, the better, I figured. I looked at my notebook, which sat beside me in the passenger's seat. I was going to need caffeine to get through writing these letters.

I was too much of a coward to stop at the coffee shop before school, so I walked to the vending machine for a Diet Coke.

The gentle rumbling of my engine soothed my nerves. I placed my notebook on my lap and the pen in my hand. I didn't know how to start, but I figured "Dear Mom," was as good of a place as any. I wrote nothing but the truth. Easton would be proud. I told her how I was sorry for not telling her of my illness sooner. I told her I was sorry for not letting her in. And I told her that I would change it if I could. If I was brave enough. The letter went on and on—nine pages of regrets and goodbyes. A few short, memorable stories that I held dear to my heart. I was only vaguely aware that the change of class had come and gone with the students around my truck.

I didn't cry. If anything, I felt the baggage I had been carrying lift. College was back in session, so I took out a clean piece of paper and continued to write. "Dear Pop," This letter wasn't as long and sappy. I didn't worry about crushing his soul like I did my mom's. He was a strong and capable man, and he would be the rock that held the family together.

When I got to my brother's letter, I found myself without words. All that I wanted to write was *Don't marry Chloe*, but it wasn't what I wanted him to remember me for. If he married that girl and his life turned out to suck the way I imagined it would, well then, I would be there to sit by his side in misery. It would be hell for both of us, I suppose. I sighed, finished my Coke, and wrote a nice letter, filled with my best memories of us as kids. I only mentioned once that if he ever happened to fall, I would be there to help him pick himself up again.

It was lunch break when I had three complete letters resting in my notebook. I stepped out of the truck to use the restroom and hit up the vending machine one more time. The wet grass beneath my shoes, the chilly spring air, and the buzzing studentry were invigorating enough to make me want to attend my last class. And that I did.

It would be one of the last times, though. I couldn't concentrate in the least. I found myself looking at the students one by one and wondering what their lives were really like.

Was her skirt so short because she didn't have a loving father? Did she show off her body because it was the only way she knew how to get attention from men? Or did she simply like the way it looked on her?

My eyes floated to a guy who was unquestionably the high school outcast. He most likely played in the band and had never been to third base. His acne would have prevented him from getting close to anyone. I wondered when he would peak. He would be rich in his forties, own a large advertising firm, and do it all with ease. He'd have a clear complexion, too. I wished I could tell him to wait just a little longer—that his time would come.

I looked down at my keyboard and smiled when I seriously considered telling the outcast my premonition. Trying very much to be like Easton at the diner, my intentions would be golden, but it would come out all wrong. I would end up telling him that one day he would no longer be a virgin, and his zit face would clear up. All he would take away from the conversation was that he was a loser, and I'd end up doing more harm than good. My smile faded as I concluded that I didn't have Easton's touch. And some things are better left alone.

When I pulled into my driveway, I was shocked to see my mom's car waiting for me. *Damn.* I was going to hear it from my mom. This and that. Me not answering my phone . . .

"Mom?" I called out to her.

"Everly? Where have you been!? I've been worried sick over you. The least you could do is answer your mother's phone calls!" She shook her head in aggravation and continued. "You don't answer your phone for two days! You weren't at work! Lindsay said you never came in or called out si—"

"Mom! Please, stop."

My eyes rolled into the back of my head. Ugh. Now I have to deal with this too? I noted the clutch on the ground, right where it had landed. My shattered phone on the entry table. Had she seen it?

"Why don't you go to the living room, let me get changed, and I'll make you some tea." I coaxed her away from the phone, and when she was out of sight, I hid it under a school binder.

"You can't do that again. Do you understand me? Just because you live in this house and not under our roof doesn't give you the right not to call me back. I'm your mother! And I always will—"

"Mom! I get it. Please. I won't do it again!" I shrugged. There was nothing else I could say. The next time would surely be the last.

"OK, OK!" My mom held her palms up to show her compliance. "We're having dinner tomorrow night, and your father and I want you to bring that boy you're seeing. I think you owe us that after this little stunt you pulled." Mom gestured to the space between us.

Just when I was about to swear Easton off altogether, I needed him to appease my parents. Funny how that works. I imagined his face through the peephole, and I cringed. If I wanted him to come to my parents for dinner and pretend to be my boyfriend, I was going to have to explain to him what happened the night I slammed the door in his face. I would rather die.

"Sure, Mom. Tomorrow. I'll see if he's available. There's a chance he'll be busy, but I'll ask anyway."

I took off my jacket and made my mom a black tea. She followed me into the kitchen, telling me the latest news regarding the wedding. I kept my mouth shut when Mom said that Chloe wanted daisies on every table. There was nothing romantic about daisies.

"What is that?" Mom came up behind me and grabbed at my arm.

My stomach dropped as I yanked my arm back to my side. I took a quick peek. It was nasty—all five fingernails. The scabs like crescent moons.

"Is that boy hurting you!?".

"No!" I stood with my mouth open, ready to explain anything that would clear Easton's name, but nothing came. It made him look all the more guilty.

"Oh, honey!" Mom said, her voice about to crack with emotion and her eyes glassing over.

"No, seriously, Mom. It's not—"

My mom collided with me, wrapping her arms around my back and squeezing tight. God, what did I get myself into?

"You're not listening to me!" I pushed away from her embrace. Her eyes were red, her heart breaking for me. And she didn't even know the truth. She couldn't handle the truth. It was a good reminder.

"I did it," I said—shame pouring out of me for losing control and for being too cowardly to admit why.

"You? Why would you do that? No, that's a man's hand! I can tell!" Mom grabbed my hand, now angry that I was covering for my boyfriend.

I wrapped my arms around myself and placed each finger in its hole, aligning the nails with the scabs. Mom stared in revelation. I think it hurt her more to know the person she loved was also the one she needed to protect me from. It would have been easier for her to wrap her head around a guy mishandling me. At least then, she could be angry. Now, she didn't know what to feel.

"It was an accident. I had a . . . panic attack, and it kind of just took over. I was trying to comfort myself with the security of a hug, but I was just too aggressive, I guess. I didn't even know I was doing it. I'm not trying to hurt myself, I promise." I said.

"A panic attack?"

"Yeah, I'm starting to get them. They've been coming on over the last couple of months. All the stress, I guess."

"What stress?" she asked, catching me in my lies.

I had no right to stress. I was twenty-two, worked in a coffee shop, and went to school for the arts.

"Self-inflicted stress?" I asked, unsure if that was even a thing.

"Maybe you should talk to someone? You know Maggie down the street has this counselor she's been—"

"Mom, no, I don't need to see anyone. Um, actually, Easton's been helping me get through it!"

"He is?" she asked.

"Yeah, you know, he talks to me in the middle of the night if I can't sleep. We text all the time. He makes me laugh. He's really good for me." I threw it all at her . . . anything I could to put her worried mind to rest.

Mom nodded and ran her hands down my arms. "OK, then. You just let me know if you need that number," she began.

"I will let you know, but as of right now, I'm just fine."

"OK, dear," Mom said, her voice laced with worry.

"What time tomorrow?" I asked. I had quite the show to put on now.

CHAPTER 13

"Beck! Where have you been!" Lindsay hissed at me when I walked behind the bar at Fresh Grounds.

"A caramel frappe. Toffee and whipped cream on top," I whispered back.

Lindsay's eyes grew dark. "I was worried," she said.

I sighed, not wanting to deal with her emotions. Mine were already too much to bear. "I'm sorry. I'll call next time."

"Kim, can you take over the register?" Lindsay asked the girl that was busying herself with the espresso beans. She was new and not yet comfortable with the register. Or the lattes. Or common sense. I gave her an encouraging smile as Lindsay pulled me into the back room.

"What the hell has been going on with you? You didn't show up for work, and both your mom and Easton came by looking for you. You didn't ca—"

"Easton came by?" I asked.

Lindsay frowned at my selective hearing.

After a long sigh, the hand on her hip fell to her side, and she said, "Yes. He came by yesterday. He said you weren't answering your phone . . . are you OK?"

"Yeah," I looked to my feet. My stomach sank, as I knew my acting skills were subpar.

"Beck?" Lindsay prompted.

I looked into her eyes. My throat burned as the weight on my chest threatened to crush me.

"I don't want to talk about it."

Lindsay's shoulders dropped. She thought about it for a moment before allowing me my privacy. She was a good friend. The best.

"You know Jacob isn't too happy with you, either. I lied and told him that you called in sick, but I wasn't on the schedule that day, so my story kind of fell to shit. You should pick up some extra hours or something to get back in his good graces."

"I'm not worried about Jacob," I said.

Jacob was my manager. It always bothered me that he was our age and carried no more managing skills than Lindsay or me. I was convinced that he had gotten the position because he was the only man that applied to work at the coffee shop when it opened. If he had a problem with me not coming into work, he could fire my ass.

"I'll make your drink," Lindsay said.

I took my schedule from Jacob's desk and frowned when I saw that I was supposed to work the night shift tomorrow. It would take a little effort on my part, but I was pretty sure Kim would fold and cover my shift.

"Hey, Kim? Can you cover for me tomorrow night? I have dinner plans." I called to her while she busied herself with unnecessary cleaning.

"Sorry! I've got plans." Kim's squinty eyes tried to look apologetic. I wasn't expecting Kim to be anything but meek. As disappointed as I was, I was also a tad impressed that she turned me down.

I sighed and spun around to find Lindsay with my drink in hand.

"I'll cover you," she said and handed me my drink. Whipped cream exploded out of the top, and toffee pressed against the clear lid.

"Oh my God, thank you! Have I ever mentioned how much I love you?"

We both chuckled, but I think that deep down, she knew it was true. We had been friends since we were kids, and while other friends came and went, she was my one constant.

"Oh! I almost forgot! I have your sister's dress in my truck!"

I retrieved the dress. The sun was warm on my shoulders, and the caffeine had lifted my spirits already. My eyes wandered the street, searching for Easton, hoping he would come around today as well. He was nowhere in sight, though.

After patching up my misstep with Lindsay, I went home knowing that my phone should now be fully charged. I had to call Easton, but I feared he would not be so forgiving.

I waited until evening to call. Pacing around my house, holding my shattered phone in my hands. I was too much of a chicken to listen to the message he had left me. I'm sure it said something about how I ended our date, and I didn't want to relive the embarrassment. I knew I was an idiot. If it were up to me, I would end my relationship with Easton now. Pretend I didn't have fun at the wedding and that my feelings for him were nonexistent. But it wasn't up to me. Not if I had my mom to appease. No, I needed Easton for my charade. How did my life get so complicated right when it was supposed to wind down?

The phone rang in my hands. Easton Green. I stiffened but answered. "Hello?"

"Everly?" Easton asked.

"Yeah, hi." I started to pace again, making small circles around my living room.

"I haven't heard from you. Are you OK?" he asked. The worry in his voice reduced me to guilt.

"Yeah!" I said, my voice high and fake.

Easton waited for the truth. He somehow knew me better than most, and yet not at all.

"Um, I just had a momentary lapse of self-pity. If that's what you would call it." I stopped my fidgeting around the room and leaned against a window. A bird scratched through the dirt, looking for food.

"Yeah. That's a pity party, alright." Easton said in a voice no different than if he were confirming the name of a rare insect. I smiled at his understanding.

"Why wasn't I invited?" he asked.

My smile grew, and the worry slipped away. "I didn't know that was your kind of party?"

"I'm so down to party! I would have brought the sorrow strobe light . . ." I laughed out loud as he continued. "The pity piata . . . the blue balloons—"

"OK! OK! Next time, you're invited!"

"That's what I wanted to hear." Easton paused for a moment. "Everly?" he asked.

"Beck . . . Call me, Beck." My heart melted. I hadn't planned on letting anyone else in. But there he was, making his way into my heart—one word at a time.

"Beck, I mean it. We can put on sad movies, and you can cry on my shoulder and pretend it's about the movie. I'll bring ice cream or just lie next to you when you want to shut out the world. Just don't shut me out too, OK?"

I took a seat on my sofa and mused over his offer. It was an inviting thought. I didn't want to do it alone.

"OK. But only because your pity parties sound so much better than mine." I laughed off the heaviness of the conversation.

"They are. I can guarantee it!"

"Oh, hey Easton. I have to ask a favor of you." I jumped up and began to pace again. This was the worst part.

"Yeah?"

"My parents want to meet my *boyfriend* . . . tomorrow." I cringed, saying the word *boyfriend*. My eyes shut tight, awaiting his response.

"Oh, wait. Is that me?" Easton said.

"Yes! Please?" Biting my lip couldn't help his answer come any faster, but I still tried.

"OK, I suppose I could make you kiss me—just one more time, though." Easton let out an exasperated sarcastic sigh.

I laughed out loud and was grateful he couldn't see the warmth in my cheeks.

"What! That's not part of the deal, buddy." I played hard to get while my heart fluttered with anticipation for the promise of a kiss.

I didn't have to wait for dinner the next night; it came quicker than a blink of an eye. I wore a plushy pink lipstick and tucked away my nerves. I filled Easton in on who he would meet on the short ride over to my parents' house.

"My dad is super easy to get along with; as long as you show him attention, he'll love you. My brother will probably be more difficult to get to know. His name is Carter, and he will have his fiancée, Chloe, with him. Don't mind her; she's . . . well, you'll see. And you know my mom, so—"

"Don't worry about it. I've got this. You know I went to The Acting Academy of Thomas Kelter?"

"You did!?" I asked, shocked.

"No," he said.

I slapped his shoulder with the back of my hand.

"But you believed me, didn't you?" Easton's expression lightened up, and his dimples drew deep.

I wanted to reach out and touch him again. This time, by the handful. I was in an impossible position. I was falling for this guy. But he didn't know it, and I had to keep it that way. On the contrary, my family had to believe the exact opposite.

"Oh no! All this time I was worried about you, but you're a natural! I didn't even consider me! I can't act! I'm the worst! Everyone sees through my lies! Besides, you and I barely know each other!" My eyes bulged, and I fanned my face.

"Beck, don't even worry. Just act natural. We're friends, right?"

I nodded.

"You like me, right?"

I nodded but a bit slower this time.

"Just act like you're hanging out with your friend. Which you are."

I continued to bob my head as Easton pulled into my parents' driveway. Carter was already here. Easton was right. No acting was required of me. My admiration for Easton was clear to see, and my parents wouldn't need to look further.

We began to walk to the front door, Easton grabbed my hand effortlessly, and through the ease of it all, I forgot it was an act.

He leaned down and whispered in my ear. "But this time, when I kiss you, try not to look so surprised."

Words of wisdom laced with promise. My eyes grew as my mom opened the door before us.

"Honey!" Mom reached her arms out for a grand hug, holding on much longer than usual.

"Hi, Mom. You remember Easton." I gestured to the calm and collected man beside me.

Not a hint of nervousness resided in his face. I marveled at him while my mom embraced him tightly and whispered, "Thank you for taking care of my baby," in his ear. I tried to ignore it, and Easton did a good job of pretending he knew what she was talking about.

"Always," he simply said. And I knew that wasn't part of the act. Mom felt it too.

The smell of spaghetti collided with boisterous introductions. Pop took to Easton immediately, as I had imagined he would. Carter shook Easton's hand with a sideways glare.

I hugged Chloe hello and found myself pleased that her lipstick and outfit were more subdued tonight. But even though her lips were mauve, her energy was still fire hydrant red. She wasn't the one for my brother, and I prayed he would see it before he walked down the aisle.

"Hey, there's my girl!" Before turning back to Easton, my dad squeezed me tightly. "Do you like hockey?" he asked.

It was my cue to leave the men to their sports and grab a glass of wine. I smiled at Easton as he accepted a beer from my dad, and his expression reassured me that he was more than equipped to handle himself alone.

I got a glass of wine and joined my mom in the kitchen. "It smells great, Mom. Thanks for having us," I said.

"Oh, I'm so glad you brought Easton! Your dad has wanted to meet him. Just look at them! They're hitting it off, don't you think?" she asked.

Chloe and I turned to follow my mom's gaze. Easton had the floor. He was telling some elaborate story, his arms reached out wide, and my dad laughed. Carter stood an extra couple feet away, and he chuckled, but it didn't reach his eyes. My brother glanced over at me, and I tried to give him a look that asked he at least try to get to know Easton. I could see him roll his eyes from across the room, but then he took one step closer.

"Oh, he is a cutie! I love that . . . thing he's got going on." Chloe waved her hand above her head.

"Yeah, he's got this hair that—actually it just works—whether it's been styled, or not. It even looks good when it's soaking wet." My eyes unfocused into a distant memory.

"Soaking wet! Ooh, that sounds like a story to me!" Chloe lifted her shoulders to her ears and brought her hands together in prayer. Her fingers tapping ever so slightly into the world's smallest clap. It took everything I had not to express my true thoughts. She wasn't evil; I knew that. It's not like I wished ill will on the girl; I just wished she would find a better match for herself. Someone more . . . I don't know. Shallow.

"There's no story. He's just a really nice guy, that's all." I tried to squash the curiosity burning in Chloe's eyes.

"He *is* a nice guy," Mom said. "He's been there to help Beck with her anxiety."

Mom threw salt into the boiling water. She never thought about keeping her mouth shut. I was used to it by now. She wore her heart on her sleeve and her mind in her mouth.

"Ohhh," Chloe cooed and her doe eyes widened. I could see the emptiness that resided within. Did she *know* what anxiety meant?

"What can I help you with, Mom?" I asked, eager to move the conversation along.

Carter came up behind Chloe and wrapped his arm around her waist. He stole a kiss on her neck, and I looked away.

Mom brushed my offer aside. "Nothing, dear. I've got it all done, anyway."

"So, you really like that guy?" Carter asked, not bothering to hide his feelings the way I did with his fiancée.

I glanced over to Easton; my dad had him fully engaged in the hockey game as he pointed to the screen.

"Yeah, I *really* like that guy," I said as natural as it came. The conversation moved onto the wedding, but my eyes continued to rest on Easton. I couldn't quite grasp how he managed to look so relaxed. As if he were home amongst his own family.

CHAPTER 14

I don't know if it were the warmth of the crackling fire or my apprehension about the topic at the dinner table, but I was sweating bullets. My dad asked Easton how we met, and I was very aware that the truth wasn't a story that could be told. Easton and I shared a quick glance before he chose to rescue me from my atrocious acting skills.

"We met on the New River Bridge," Easton began.

The heat poured over me, and even though I had been keeping my jacket on to hide the self-inflicted pain I displayed on the back of my arms, I could no longer survive being trapped inside the furnace. I shrugged off my jacket and pulled my hair into a ponytail.

"The New River Bridge! Is that right?" My dad engaged.

"Yes, sir. I was driving home from work when I saw Beck standing on the side of the road. She was looking at her flat tire like it was a UFO."

Dad laughed and slapped the table. Even Carter chuckled.

"Ain't that right!" Dad held his beer up towards me. I raised my glass of wine as I rolled my eyes. Easton was so good at this, I couldn't help but wonder why.

"Now, I was in no position to pass a pretty lady in distress. So, I pulled over. After fixing her tire, I asked her out on a date. To this day, I'm not sure if she wanted to or if she did it as a favor, but I like to think I won her over that night." Easton locked eyes with mine and slid his hand onto my knee. "The rest is history," he said.

I barely noticed how happy my mom was. I was too busy basking in the freefall. I don't know how he did it; every word out of his mouth was something to remember and reflect on. He had so much heart, I wondered how he could contain it. I reached down to his hand and squeezed it. We were acting like a couple, true, but we both knew nobody could see our interlocking hands under the table. That one was for us.

When everyone had their fill of dinner, I shrugged my jacket back on so that nobody would see. I helped my mom clean the dishes, and Easton attempted to win over my brother. It was no easy task, but I applauded him for trying. Mom scraped the leftover meatballs into a container, and Chloe collected placemats as she rambled on about the recipe she followed for the chocolate mousse pie she brought. As unsettled as the nerves had made my stomach, I was pretty sure there was a separate compartment made of steel that only always accepted dessert.

When the kitchen had been put back together, I rescued Easton from my brother. If he was as relieved as I imagined he should be, he didn't show it. He followed me to my parent's back patio. Small and quaint. A rose garden with a fountain and a view of the night's starry sky. I took a deep breath of the refreshing cold air and walked to the back fence line. The furthest away from the house, with the most privacy.

"How are you holding up?" I asked Easton.

"Don't worry about me. I'm solid. How are you?"

"I'm good. I can't thank you enough for coming tonight. You've made my mom very happy." Easton wrapped his arm around my shoulders, and though the cool air felt nice, I huddled close to him.

"I'm glad she's happy. You have an amazing family. You should consider yourself lucky," Easton said.

"Lucky?" I asked.

"Well, you know what I mean." He shrugged.

"Yeah, I do." I looked up into the stars, and after a stretch of silence, I said, "I *am* lucky."

Of course, I only saw that when I was with him.

Easton took advantage of my extended neck and lowered down to my lips. I didn't fight it. I couldn't. I lifted to my toes and closed the distance. He wrapped one arm around my waist and slid the other to my cheek. I kissed him long and deep, my passion and fear both exploding into fireworks. In that moment, I felt more alive than ever before. And by the time my heels returned to the floor, I knew I was falling in love.

"Um," I said, "you're quite the actor."

Easton shook his head. "You *know*."

It was all he had to say. I nodded and buried my head into his chest. "I know," I said.

We remained tight in the embrace for some time until Chloe yelled, "Time for dessert!"

I smiled. "I don't want to leave. And I *love* dessert. What are you doing to me?" I asked.

I looked up to see his expression. It seemed that I wasn't the only one fighting my feelings, and worry creased in my forehead.

"Is something wrong?" I asked, knowing damn well that my whole world was burning down.

Easton shook his head and smiled down at me. While I couldn't detect a difference in his smile, I could feel it in my heart. Something was wrong. I felt it like a bird with clipped wings. Our love had a ceiling.

"Let's get some of that pie before it's gone." Easton patted my back, and we made our way inside.

The dessert would have tasted better if I wasn't swallowing my emotions. One bite at a time. It did nothing to help.

As the night came to an end, we said our goodbyes and left hand in hand. And when the door closed behind us, I was unsure whether to let go or not.

Easton drove me home, neither one of us speaking. I stared out the window at the passing headlights and allowed myself to be swallowed by my fear. Only this time, it wasn't the cancer. This time, it was losing Easton.

When Easton pulled up to my house, neither one of us got out of the car. He set the car in park, and faint barks from Yeti sounded from the house.

I unbuckled.

"You have to tell them," Easton said.

"Tell them what? That we're not together?" I asked.

"No, never mind that. You have to tell them about your condition."

"Why!"

"Because!" He ran his hand through his hair in distress. "You'll regret it if you don't!"

"Huh, no . . . actually, I'll be dead, and the last time I checked, dead people don't muse over their past mistakes. And if there is such a thing as heaven, do you really think they'll allow regret through those pearly gates?!" The roller coaster continued.

Easton fumed. Quick breaths expelled from his nostrils like a fire breathing dragon. We were feeding off each other as the frustration of an impossible situation grew larger. But the truth was, he didn't know any better than I did about what happens after we die. He had no right telling me how I would feel. And judgment was the last thing I needed on a very long list of unmet needs. My heart pounded, and the tears burned my eyes. I should have waited for him to answer, but I continued to tear into him instead.

"You know, Easton, whatever we've got going between us, maybe it's better if it just ends now," I said. I got out of the car and slammed my door.

Easton jumped out after me but came to a stop at his taillights.

"End? Beck, come on." Easton's voice softened.

"No! Seriously. What the *fuck* is the point in all this? In you and me? We get close, and then it just makes everything that much harder? Why are we doing this to ourselves? It's a slow burn of torture, and while I might not live with the *regret*, you will! Is that what you want?" My tone sharp and forthcoming.

Easton took a step towards me. I took a step back.

"Beck. Don't do this," he said, holding out a hand.

My eyes dropped to the extended invitation to spend my last days in his arms. The cost? Shattering his heart in the wake of my departure.

"It's what I want," I said, sure of myself.

Our eyes lingered on each other for what seemed to be an eternity of pain and suffering. It was my hell on earth. Giving up the only man I'd ever loved. Setting him free in hopes that it would be in his best interest. I would have no way of knowing.

Easton closed the distance between us and brought his lips to my forehead. A warm soft kiss planted on my soul. And then he was gone. I didn't watch him leave.

I was mistaken when I thought it couldn't get any worse than the night that I scarred my arms. I crawled into bed, still half-dressed, and closed my eyes for the sweet escape of slumber. As it turns out, not feeling anything at all was worse than any pain I'd ever encountered. The roller coaster had stopped, and the numbness carried me away into a deep and loveless sleep.

CHAPTER 15

The numbness followed me like a shadow; only, it was there regardless of the light. I went to work and school but only to keep my mind off Easton.

When Dawson finally approached me in class, I was relieved to think about someone other than Easton. I couldn't believe that Dawson was my typical type. I used to drool over his abs—any abs really. Now I found myself attracted to Easton's body. The thick muscles of Dawson made me wonder if he would sink in a body of water, and I wondered where the days had gone when he danced around my head shirtless. There were no more dreams of soap suds and dripping sponges.

Easton ruined it all for me. I would never look at another male specimen the same. I only wanted Easton and his beautiful soul.

I skipped a few of my classes to sit in my truck and write one more goodbye letter. This time it was to Easton. Everything poured out with ease—all of my thoughts but none of the emotion. And I had a lot of thoughts. It all made sense to me. Easton was better off without me. My mind told me so. I detailed it in my letter. It was a simple note, only a one-pager. In the last paragraph, I professed that I loved him and that my only regret was not telling him in person. I signed the letter with a heart and prayed to God that heaven didn't allow regrets.

It'd been six days since I broke it off with Easton, and he called only once. I cleared his call when he did, and he never left a message. I would be lying if I said I never thought about calling him back. I did . . . all the time. But it was my love for him that kept me away. And it was my numbness that allowed me to survive the heartache.

On the seventh day, I decided to take a drive and wound up sitting in the parking lot of the dive bar Easton had taken me to. The bum was gone, and so was his dog, but the trash he left behind still remained. I parked and watched as a trickle of customers walked inside and never came out. It was only 3:30 p.m., but I assumed that addiction knew no time. Somehow, being here at the bar made me feel a little closer to Easton, and I wanted to savor it. My next stop would be the bridge, and I imagined that I would feel his presence even stronger there.

When I decided to continue on with my pathetic road trip, an older gentleman walked out of the bar on his cell phone. I cracked my window to listen to his conversation. Because I was a small-town girl from Clover, and that's what we do best.

"What? I can't hear you! Wait . . . that's better! Go on," the man said. He was slender—all but his belly, and I was pretty sure that he might be pregnant.

"No! No! Bring it by the bar. I'll be here 'til closing," he said.

Watching a drug deal wasn't going to bring me any closer to Easton, so I started my ignition.

It was through the rumble of my old truck that I heard him say, "Don't you Clyde me, you chicken shit!"

Clyde?

I stepped on my brake. My eyes shot around, suddenly aware of my surroundings. Clyde was Easton's grandfather! My heart picked up speed. What was I to do?

Clyde hung up the phone and grumbled a string of profanities. I feared he would walk into the bar and be lost forever.

I pulled out wide and stopped next to Clyde as he lit a cigarette. My window dropped slowly, causing him to step off the curb and approach my car.

I panicked.

"Do you know how to get to Clover from here?" My forehead drenched with worry.

"Oh, yeah." Clyde rested his forearm on my window seal and waved about his cigarette with the other hand. "Go south on Falcon—"

"Are you Clyde?" I blurted out.

The man looked at me with trepidation.

"Who's askin'?"

"Um, I'm a friend of Easton Green's, and—"

"Ohhh! Well, why didn't you say so!? How's that fella doin'?" he asked with a bright face.

"Good, yeah, he's good. Um, he misses you. He brought me here a little over a week ago looking for you," I said.

"Is that right!?" Clyde looked a little confused.

"Yeah, he said he hadn't seen you in a while and was worried."

"Oh, yeah. Well, I'm back now. Tell him to come by so I can whoop his ass in poker, would ya?" Clyde chuckled.

I knew I would no longer be talking to Easton to pass on the message.

"Yeah, I can do that. Um, maybe you should call him or something to let him know you're doing OK?" I interjected myself in a place I knew I had no business being. But I felt terrible for Easton. All he wanted was a relationship with his grandpa, and he had to gamble to get it.

"Call him? Well, shit!" Clyde took a long drag off of his cigarette and blew the smoke just outside my window. "I don't have that kid's number or nothin'," he said.

I frowned. "You don't have your grandson's phone number?" I asked him and immediately regretted my judgment.

"Grandson!?" Clyde scowled. An uncomfortable moment passed as my mind raced to fix what I had done.

"Is that kid in some kind of trouble?" Clyde asked. His face creased with the deep grooves of age.

"No! No, sorry, I think I was mistaken. Have a nice day." I placed my truck in drive, and Clyde took a step back, perplexed.

I pulled away quicker than I wanted to, and my tires made a small screeching noise that made me look even more suspect.

What the heck was that!? Easton lied to me? About his family, nonetheless. I traced back through my memory. There was no mention of his family at all except for what he told me about his grandpa. Why was he hiding from me? He was so comfortable on my sofa in the presence of my dad that it made it hard to believe he wasn't brought up in a loving home himself. I couldn't think of another reason for lying, though—other than being ashamed about where he came from.

I replayed every conversation we ever had. Most of it was about me, my life, and my predicament. Never once did he tell me what he was afraid of. He never added to the bucket list. His job was broad and somewhat unfitting. I didn't know what he liked to do, other than poker, and even that was soiled now. I didn't know Easton Green at all. And yet I loved him all the same.

I parked my truck on the side of the road by the New River Bridge. I got out and walked to the very spot his feet had stood on the railing, and I rested my forearms there. The river below was fuller now due to the major storm we had that night. It was the angel's tears that filled up the stream. I thought they were crying for me and my ill-willed fate. But as I looked out into the vast forest where the water met the sky, I realized something. They were crying for him.

Tears leaked from the corners of my eyes. My body was quiet, too damaged to feel the pain. I must have stood there for an hour. Maybe two. Not contemplating the end of my life but consumed with the mystery of his.

I didn't know much about him, but I knew his soul. It left its prints all over mine. Even though I put up a good fight, I knew we were meant to find each other. Like magnets, our destiny intended to collide. What I couldn't grasp was why. What lesson was I supposed to learn from falling for someone I couldn't have? And just like that, I realized it.

It wasn't about me, it never was. He needed me, probably more than I needed him. My life was next to over, but his wasn't. I didn't know my part yet, but I was sure I was meant to help move him along in some way or another.

I checked my watch. My shift at Fresh Grounds started in thirty minutes. I didn't want to leave Lindsay hanging, and since Jacob was working our shift, I thought I better show my face.

I was pleased when I walked into the shop, and the place was empty. Both Jacob and Lindsay sat chatting instead of working. Sometimes the night shifts were the best. Others, we would be bombarded with book clubs and first dates.

"Hey guys," I said, slipping my apron over my head.

"Hey!" Lindsay replied with large strained eyes.

She had something to tell me, but clearly, it would have to wait. Jacob nodded his head towards me and continued with his story about a feud with his cable company. *Good luck with that.* I ducked into the back room and took my time clocking in. I hated nothing more than terrible customer service, and even listening to someone else's story about it would make my anxiety start to rise.

I peeked around the corner to see if they were done—they weren't—but a third person caught my eye on the recliner in the corner. I watched intently as it became clear to me that it was Easton. His eyes were sunken and framed with dark circles. He looked unsettled, and I wanted to take it all away. Whatever it was.

I stepped out from the back room and watched as Easton caught my line of sight. Lindsay pointed in Easton's direction and grabbed my arm, pulling me close.

"He's been here since my shift started, over two hours ago," Lindsay whispered. Then, she gave Jacob an exasperated look to continue with his dreadful story. At least she was getting paid to listen to it.

I walked out to Easton. He stood, his eyes bluer than I'd ever seen.

"You found me . . ." I said.

Easton nodded, "I found you," he mirrored. His face was long, and I could see the pain he had tucked inside.

"Look"—he glanced over at Lindsay and Jacob to make sure we had our privacy—"I know you made your decision, but I can't help but be drawn to you. I can't move on from this," he said.

My body slumped. All of the numbness beginning to wear on me.

"I can, because I know it was in your best interest," I said.

"It's not!"

I smiled. "How do we know we're making the right decision?" I asked.

"I know." Easton placed his hand over his heart. "With the knowledge of three hundred years, I know."

The numbness shattered like glass, falling to the ground. I was in. Whatever it meant, wherever it went, I was in. I slammed into his chest, wrapping my arms around him tightly.

Easton pulled me back to look at my face. "Hey, want to get out of here?" he asked.

I looked between him and my manager. Jacob took his apron off; he must have been planning on leaving early due to the slow night.

"Yes!" I said to Easton.

I looked to Jacob, as he secured his baseball hat on his head and walked out from behind the bar.

"Jacob, I'm taking the night off!" I called out to him. He froze. Lindsay's eyes darted back and forth between the two of us.

"You can't. I'm leaving, and Lindsay can't close the place by herself," he said.

My eyes shot to Lindsay just as she gave me an approving nod of her head. My heart pounded with excitement.

"Then . . . I quit!" I said, wishing it came out more boss than it did. Easton sucked in a breath, and Lindsay's jaw dropped.

I took off my apron and placed it on the bar, giving Lindsay a wink.

"You can't," Jacob started.

"I just did!" I called on my way out.

"Call me!" Lindsay yelled as the door swung closed.

As soon as Easton and I were in the open air of freedom, we began to laugh. I'd never seen him laugh like this; it was beautiful and enormously contagious. We laughed so hard we cried, and I was forced to cross my legs so that I remained a lady. I didn't know where we were going, but we couldn't stay, so we crawled into Easton's car and took off. The laughter faded, and like aftershocks of an earthquake, it would come back now and then.

"Ohhh my God! That was . . . one of the best moments of my life! I feel so . . . free?" I looked to Easton for validation.

He nodded his head. "Free!" he confirmed.

"How should we celebrate my retirement?" I chuckled.

"I know a place." A coy expression spread across Easton's face.

"Come on, no secrets this time. Where are we going?"

"We have another bucket list item to cross off. The truck is packed, just in case I was lucky enough to win you over," Easton grabbed my hand in his and brought it to his lips. He kissed it. "We're sleeping under the stars."

"We're going camping?"

"Yup. I have sleeping bags, a tent. Marshmallows . . . And now you."

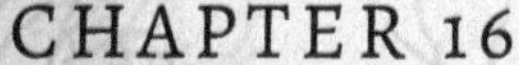

CHAPTER 16

I worried for the vanity of Easton's BMW as he rolled over thick tree roots and rocks, only wincing when I'd hear the bushes scrape the length of the car. If he cared, he didn't show it. It was dark out when we reached the clearing. He seemed to know the place by heart and took no wrong turns.

"How prepared are you, exactly?" My eyes tried to stretch the distance but couldn't see past the glare of the window.

"I know what I'm doing!"

"But it's going to be cold, and there are probably bears, right?" I asked in a tone of worry as my excitement melted into apprehension.

"Oh my God, Beck! I told you, you wouldn't like it, but you wanted to sleep under the stars! You romanticized this in your head, and I've vowed to give it to you!" Easton reached over and jabbed a few fingers into my ribs, causing me to giggle. "Now get your butt out of the car, bears and all, because we have work to do."

I opened my door and stepped onto the gravel, afraid of what I couldn't see. Easton and I met at his trunk, where he pulled a beanie over my head. He had thought of everything.

"Grab the tent and place it in the clearing. You can get to work unrolling it. I'm going to try to get a fire started," Easton said.

I grabbed the tent and walked out to the beams of the headlights. I unrolled the tent and pulled the corners as far as I could to make a square. Several sticks cracked under my feet, startling me each and every time. I never thought I would die in the woods at the hands of a bear, but the reality was slowly sinking in. Even though I was frightened of the vast wilderness at night, I couldn't think of a place I would rather be than here with Easton underneath the Milky Way.

A small sense of pride lingered after I completed my first task. I took it one step further and turned the poles into two long straight sticks. Easton had been successful with the fire, and flames jumped, hungry for more dried leaves and deadwood. With his help, the tent went up easy, and I was eager to get the bedding inside and zip up the door, closing out all of the nocturnal eyes.

Once the tent's inside was complete, Easton took four large rocks and placed them by the fire. He pulled bottled waters out of his truck and emptied them into an old beat-up canister that he placed on top of the fire. I smiled at the amount of effort he had put into tonight.

"What if I had said no?" I asked.

"Said no to what?"

"Tonight. Would you still have gone camping?" I huddled in the door of the tent.

Easton laughed. "Do you really think I would torture myself for no good reason?"

"Hey!" I laughed. "It's not that bad, is it?"

Easton plopped down next to me, resting his forearms on his knees. "Nothing is *that* bad when I'm with you," he said.

"But a little bad? You can admit it!" I poked his side.

He wrestled my hand. "Yeah, you're a total pain in my ass. It's bad! It's bad, alright!" he pulled on my hand, drawing me in and kissed me. "I've got it . . . *bad* . . ." My heart sang, my head swam, and my body propelled towards Easton. He barely caught me, and our bodies hit the floor of the tent with force. I struggled to kiss him and rip my jacket off at the same time. He rolled me over, and the weight of his body compressed mine. His woodsy cologne intoxicated me with a desire I'd never felt so sure of. I pulled him in close with the free hand I had, running my hand up into his hair. I tightened my grip on its silky texture —my other hand pinned inside the arm of my jacket. I moaned, lifting my hips into his.

Easton pulled back, both of us out of breath. He stared at me for a moment before whispering sweet warmth into my ear. "We have all night."

His words did nothing to break the urgency I felt. I needed him *now*. "Isn't this what you want?" I lifted my head and planted slow seductive wet kisses down his neck.

"Beck," he said, his voice laced with pain. I pulled away to see his eyes. "You have no idea!" he shook his head.

I was more than surprised when he rolled off of me. He brought both hands up to his head and grabbed hold.

I perched up onto an elbow, "Wha—"

Easton ran his palms down his face and covered his eyes.

"What is it then? I mean, don't stop on my account. I want to do it! I do!" I begged him to hear my words. I leaned in to kiss him again. This time, he shied away.

"I know, I know. I just, I don't want to take advantage of you," he said.

My old friend, anger, began to rumble in my blood. I struggled to keep my voice calm. "Are you telling me . . . that this is a cancer thing? Now?"

Easton pulled his hands away and gave me the full weight of his heavy heart through his eyes.

"This has nothing to do with that and everything to do with me."

"What, it's not you, it's me? That's the line you're trying to feed me right now?" I accused him.

"No! That's not it at all!" Easton studied my face. He couldn't possibly understand my anger.

"The truth is that I care for you." Easton shook his head, and the gloss in his eyes sparkled by the light of the fire. "More than you'll ever know. It's like I've waited my *whole* life for you. Now, I don't want you to feel rejected . . ."

I rolled my eyes and looked away. He totally understood, apparently more so than I did, but I was embarrassed that it was as simple as that. Rejection.

"But Beck, I can't move this relationship any further than where it is. You don't *know* me . . . and if you did, I don't think you'd feel the same way."

I furrowed my eyebrows. What was he talking about? I didn't need to know where the guy grew up to know I loved him.

"I can't do that to you. I can't have you fall for a guy you can't know. And, I know how you feel. I see it when you look at me. I feel it too," he said.

I watched the flames flicker in his eyes, as he watched our water boil and spit out of the canister. Neither one of us cared to remove it from the fire.

My anger fell to the wayside, and I placed my hand on his back, the moment of lust and fury now behind me.

"Tell me?" I asked. I was ready for it. Whatever skeletons he had in his closet, I was ready to meet them face to face.

"I can't." Easton shrugged.

"Yes, you can. And I won't go anywhere."

He continued to shake his head, his eyes fixated on the boiling water.

"Easton?" I asked, and when he refused to look at me, I wrapped my hand around his chin and pulled his face to meet mine. I placed a soft kiss on his lips and whispered, "I'm falling in love with you. And there's nothing that you can say that will turn me away. I'm in this for the long run." I scuffed. "Or *my* run, however long that may be."

Easton pressed his forehead to mine and my heart ballooned out of my chest.

"I've been falling since the day I met you on the bridge. I've never hit the ground so hard, and I'm afraid of what it will do to me when you're no longer here," Easton confessed. I nodded. It was what I was worried about for him.

"There are only two options. We do it wholeheartedly, or we don't," I said. But there was a third choice that I left out on purpose. The one where we stay together without ever scratching his surface.

"I've made my decision. That's why I'm here tonight. Risking my life with paper thin shelter, and a real chance of being frozen alive," Easton joked.

"I'm here too. I know it's the right decision for me, and I really hope that somehow it's the right decision for you too," I said.

"It is. You don't worry about me. OK?"

"OK," I said.

"Promise?" he asked.

"Promise." This thing was going to be hard for both of us. But somehow, we couldn't escape it. We were bound together by a weird and mystical force, unseen by the human eye.

"At some point, Easton, you're going to need to open up to me."

It took some time for an answer, but finally, he said it. "I know."

I rested my head on Easton's shoulder till my heart began to slow, and the tension lifted away. My eyes grew heavy, and the fire died down to ash and embers. I crawled into my sleeping bag and Easton placed the heated rocks from the fire near our feet. I snuggled up to him, lying my head on his arm as we watched the stars twinkle from the top of our tent. We saw three shooting stars that night. And all of my wishes were for Easton's walls to drop.

I didn't try to kiss him again. There was a kind of honor between us. He didn't want to feel like he was tricking me into loving him, but he also wasn't ready to talk. I had no other choice but to wait. Ironically, time was the only thing I couldn't give to Easton.

I was no princess, but I sure did feel all the peas lying on the forest floor that night. Worse yet, I heard all of the sounds of the living. And at one point in the night, I sat up and armed myself with a flashlight.

I woke at first light. The bags under my eyes were probably a close match to Easton's, but I was happy. Waking next to him was a gift, and I felt blessed to cross another item off my bucket list.

"Coffee?" Easton asked as he lit a new fire.

"Please." My voice cracked, and I coughed the morning phlegm away.

I stood up and stretched, my body ached. I wouldn't be surprised if I had multiple bruises on my hips and shoulders.

"How did you sleep?" I asked Easton.

His hair was unrulier than I had ever seen it, and that was saying a lot.

"Um . . ." His voice was high enough to tell me it was no walk in the park for him either.

I chuckled. "One and done. Me too."

Easton laughed. I joined him on a small blanket next to the fire and examined my surroundings. Everything looked different in the light. The birds chirped near and far, and the lush green branches lifted and lowered with the gentle breeze.

"We didn't do marshmallows last night," I said.

"Let's have them with our coffee," Easton said before getting them out of the trunk of his car.

"Do you have skewers? Or should I find some sticks?" I called out to him.

"I've got skewers!"

Easton handed me everything I needed to make roasted marshmallows and then proceeded to pour our coffees. It was quiet until the caffeine brought me back to life.

"If you have time, I would like to show you a great spot. It's about a forty-minute hike," Easton said.

"Yeah, that sounds great. It's not like I have a job to get to or anything," I smiled.

We finished our coffee and marshmallows before taking down the tent. We packed the belongings into the back of Easton's trunk, and we set out on our hike. Being amongst nature with his kind soul was grounding. I soaked in everything: his gate, his laughter, and the way the sunlight lit his eyes into a trillion shards of crystal. I took in the green dragonfly that followed Easton like a lost puppy. I wanted to take every morsel of the memory with me so that when I took my last breath, I could come back here, and my heart could smile one last time.

We came upon a large clearing in the forest. One larger than life dead tree overlooked the Truly River before it bled into the New River. It was breathtaking. Easton held my hand and led me to the tree. We picked a spot nestled in its roots, which was large enough to make for excellent seating.

"It's beautiful. How did you find this place?" I asked.

Easton shrugged, "I've been here before," he said.

He was good at being vague. I wondered if he had come here with an ex-girlfriend, but if he had, I guess I wouldn't want to know. Or would I?

"Have you been in love before?" I asked, still unsure if I wanted to hear his answer.

Easton shot me a look of concern for my well-being. Huh. *Guess I shouldn't have asked.*

"I've loved before," he said, choosing his words carefully.

The dragonfly had returned and taken a particular interest in Easton. It must have been attracted to his scent. I couldn't blame it; I was too. Easton smiled like a child and watched as the insect fluttered around his face. The green exterior glimmered in the sunlight like a magical creature. I think I liked watching his wonder more than the oddity of the flying bug itself.

"Silly thing, isn't it?" I said.

"It's quite something," he replied.

I looked out to the river and watched as a flock of birds swooped down to the water and back up again.

"I wonder what it's like to fly. Do you think I'll get my wings when I die?" The flock soared over our heads.

"I don't know what I think. It's complicated, I guess. Maybe there are different options?" Easton said.

"Like what?"

"Oh, I don't know." Easton picked up a small stick and began to draw in the dirt.

Sometimes it was like pulling teeth to get him to talk. I only wanted to know what he thought.

"You know, there's no right or wrong answer. Sometimes I wonder if blackness is the best option. As much as I fear it, I think I fear the regrets more. You taught me that!" I flicked a pebble at him.

"Hey! That wasn't my intention. I don't want you to worry; I just want to help you make the right decisions." Easton picked the pebble off of his jacket and tossed it aside.

"Easton?" I asked in sincerity.

"Yeah?"

"I love you," I said, not wanting any more regrets. His face softened, and his eyes lit from within.

"I love you too, Beck." Easton placed a hand over his heart before leaning over and showing me with a soft and long kiss. He pulled away with a smile so content that I could stay in the moment forever.

"I don't want you to hide anything from me. I know you said I don't know you. But I do! I know the impact that you have made on my heart. And there's nothing you can say that will change that." I took a deep breath, "Do you believe me?"

"Come on Beck, that's not fair," Easton said.

"What's not?"

He sighed in exasperation. No words followed.

"You're afraid that I won't love you after you tell me. Do you know what I'm afraid of?" I asked.

Easton looked at me, afraid of what I might say. I saw in his eyes that my fear was the chink in his armor.

"I'm afraid that the one I love won't let me in. I'm afraid our relationship will be stunted, and there's not a damn thing I can do about it," I said, not realizing how I felt until I said it.

I understood all my anger from before. Blanketed under this simple statement. It was lack of control that I feared most. I couldn't control my health, how Easton felt, or if he wanted to open up to me.

Easton considered my words. His eyes squinted in the sun and his laugh lines deepened in the absence of humor.

"Are you afraid of dying?" Easton asked before he looked over the river.

"Of course, I am. Who wouldn't be?" I said.

"I was too. The first time I died."

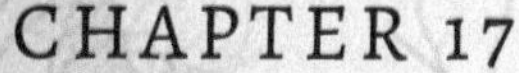

CHAPTER 17

I whipped my head to Easton and observed him carefully as he built the courage to continue. My mind raced from medical conditions to accidents, but nothing prepared me for what he said next.

"I would like to say that practice makes perfect, but that's not the case when it comes to death. Sure, it gets easier with time, as many things do, but perfect is an unachievable goal for the human race."

His words flowed like the melody of a sweet song, but he was singing in a different language—one I didn't understand.

I watched his face contort with the pain that only life on earth could offer. He momentarily took the break he needed before continuing down a slow path to honesty. I knew it was my time to listen, and I tried my damn hardest not to judge him for what he believed to be his truth.

"I'm what's called a Tethered Soul, Beck." Easton's gaze dropped down to the dirt before him. He looked as broken as the day I met him. "No matter how many times I die, my soul returns."

I sucked in a quick breath when he finally looked at me. His irises, electric blue, were flanked by bolts of red.

"I've lived a dozen lives over the years. It never ends for me. I'm like a prisoner." Easton broke our contact and looked back over the river. A single tear fell from his eye.

I knew Easton had been hiding something, but I didn't expect it to be this. I didn't know how to react. I felt stupid for believing him, but I did. He was my proof, sitting right there in front of me. He was no normal man. He was an old soul, and now I knew why he remained so comfortable in his own skin.

Easton continued. "In all my lives, I've never loved someone like you. You're it for me. And when you pass on to another dimension in time . . . I'll remain. A new place, a new family, but I will *always* . . . have the same broken heart, and the same damn tethered soul."

Easton ran his hands through his hair, and the tears flowed effortlessly. I mindlessly rubbed the knot in my throat as I struggled to put the pieces together. He would have to feed me more because right now, I only saw the tip of the iceberg. And there was a lot yet to uncover.

"Say something! Anything!" Easton pled.

I didn't know what to say. I was stunned, unable to form complete thoughts, let alone a comprehensible sentence.

"I love you."

It was the one thing I knew to be true. My whole life was upside down. I didn't know right from wrong or up from down, but I knew that I loved Easton Green. No matter how many lives he lived. Or believed he had.

I moved over to Easton and sat as close as I could, resting my head on his shoulder. I wasn't quite sure what was happening, but I was there for him either way.

"So, I'm sorry. I'm just trying to get it all straight. You've lived . . . *multiple* lives?" It felt as dumb to say aloud as it did to hear it.

Easton responded as if it were an everyday conversation about the weather. Only, this time, he was personally affected by the storm.

"Twelve or thirteen, probably. I lost count."

"Thirteen!" I said, sitting up to look at his face. He looked away as if he were ashamed.

I scrambled to my feet.

"Don't go!" Easton cried out.

I took a deep breath, "I'm not! I'm um, I'm just trying to come to grips with what you're telling me. That's all." I shook out my hands and began to pace.

Easton stood and dusted the dirt off his pants.

"Let's walk," he said.

"Yeah." I agreed. I needed something to do with my arms and legs. I needed moving parts and the passing scenery. I needed to understand.

"I know, it's a lot to take in."

I laughed out loud. I tried to stop for fear it was coming off as rude, but my nerves wouldn't allow for it.

"It's not that I don't believe you. I do! I just . . . I'm having a hard time understanding," I said as I interlocked my hands in weird and uncomfortable formations.

"OK! I can help with that!" Easton was excited about the development of my reaction. It was something he could work with, and as I told him before, I wasn't going anywhere.

"You have memories of when you were a kid, right?" he asked.

I nodded.

"Like two years old, three years old?"

"Sure . . ."

"OK, I do too! But I have them with different families, all around the world."

"What!?" I stopped walking.

He was explaining it well, but my heart was still picking up speed.

"It's true. I'm always me. My soul, my memory, my personality. Always. But my situation is different. My adopted parents, siblings, the country, the lifestyle: that changes every time. I've grown to adapt. I've learned to read people—understand them. I know what makes this world turn and understand motive more than anyone you will ever meet. I've learned it all from experience." Easton ran his hand through his hair and gave me a hopeful expression.

"So . . . I'm sorry! I don't know what to ask! I'm so confused! Who are you now? Who were you then? Are you even a construction sales rep—"

"I am Easton Green. And I love you, more than any soul I've ever met! If you let me love you, I will show you the greatest love of a lifetime. Everly, please don't give up on me!" Easton stilled and squeezed my hand tightly.

My heart melted, and my body slacked.

"I don't fully understand Easton, but I wasn't lying when I said there was nothing you could say to change my mind. And if this is your reality, I want to know about it. Count me in. Always."

I hugged him, pressing my ear up to his beating heart. *Lub-dub, lub-dub, lub-dub.* I held on until I felt I was beginning to digest the gravity of what Easton had told me.

"So, you are or aren't a construction sales rep?" I joked.

Easton smiled but wasn't ready to laugh.

"You got me! I'm not a sales rep."

"I knew it! I knew it!" I shouted and pulled away to push his chest playfully.

This time he laughed at my excitement. "How did you know?"

"Your hands are too soft!"

Easton examined his hands, "What? Are you saying I have girly hands?"

I laughed off the tension, and we continued to poke fun of each other. Our walk back to the car consisted of me trying to pick out which morsels of information he fed me were fact and which were fiction.

So far, it'd been my favorite game yet. It was better than any game I obsessed over as a child. I learned that he didn't have a job; he never needed one with his investment knowledge and maturity to invest young. Though that never stopped him from getting a job he wanted. I learned that he did have a family, albeit adopted. He cared for them but said that only a few select people left an impression on him and that sometimes it was easier not to get attached. I learned that his last life was stationed in sunny California, where he spent his days surfing and being a beach bum. It was a real shame that he couldn't bring his tan with him.

When we got back into his car, I was pleased to see Easton take out the Hunter's to-go menu from his glovebox. He crossed off camping before folding it back up into a neat square again.

CHAPTER 18

Pearl buttons lined the sheer opening of Chloe's back. It was a lot of skin to show, but she was comfortable with that, and I would rather see her back than her chest. Unfortunately, I saw that too. Her cleavage popped out of the sweetheart line dress as she continued to pull on it. The gown trailed to the floor and pooled beyond her feet. It was a beautiful dress. I nodded in agreement with my mom and Chloe's mother and grandmother.

It was sweet that she invited me, and I felt myself opening up to the possibility that she might not be as bad as I originally thought. We all had deep dark secrets, after all; what if hers was that she was secretly awesome? Far-fetched, but possible.

Chloe clapped, and both our mothers mimicked her enthusiasm with the same applause. Her grandmother smiled a toothless grin from her wheelchair.

"OK, but I still think it's a toss-up between this one and number two!" Chloe announced.

"Pumpkin, *this* is the one!" her mother said.

"Really?" Chloe said in a tone that could call a wolf pack home.

Chloe's mom nodded her head, and the tears began to fall. It was an emotional moment for them. Chloe trotted to her mom in her heels that were too high and too big, and they embraced, both crying and speaking in dolphin.

It was hard for me to be excited for her when I knew I would never have a wedding of my own. I wasn't even sure I would make it to their wedding. I felt my secret growing larger by the day. It was like a black cloud that followed me everywhere I went. Only I knew the severity of the storm ahead.

"That's going to be you one day," Mom whispered in my ear. I frowned—nothing like rubbing salt in the wounds.

"OK, enough of that! Everly, try on your bridesmaid dress?" Chloe asked.

"Huh?"

I was horrified. The last thing I wanted to do was put on a purple satin gown and show off how ridiculous I looked to a group of people. But apparently, Chloe didn't have close friends—it was a major red flag—so, when she asked me to be her maid of honor, I had to comply. It was probably my best acting yet.

A saleswoman with beady eyes ushered me to a dressing room where the purple dress hung waiting for me. I couldn't tell if it was her tiny eyes or that she was judging me for my lack of excitement and loyalty to the bride. I closed the door and sighed, giving myself a small moment of pity before making a fool of myself.

After dressing, I checked myself out from every angle I could. The tri-fold mirrors made it easy, and every angle I saw I hated. I never found myself to be girly. Dresses looked awkward on me at best. My knees were too knobby, my hips too straight. I looked like a thirteen-year-old boy in a nightgown. And what's worse? I had to stand on a miniature stage and have four women judge me on it. I gave the mirror one last distraught look before I met my fate.

"It's a pretty dress, but I don't know if I can do it justice. My hips just—"

"I love it!" Chloe squealed, sealing the deal.

"I do, too!" I lied.

I was pretty sure only the grandma caught on. Well, her and Miss Judgmental Eyes. My cheeks turned red under the scrutiny, and my shoulders slumped in defeat while the tailor pulled, pinched, and pinned my dress.

"Honey, you look like you're losing weight!" my mom said.

"No, I don't think so."

"What's your secret?" Chloe asked, and the room lightened up. "I've been mowing down celery like it's going out of style! But I'm only two pounds away from my wedding shred weight! I think I can do it!" Chloe checked herself out in the mirror.

I was relieved when I was dressed in my clothes again. Jeans and a hooded sweatshirt: nothing was more comfortable than that combination. I prayed I wouldn't have to wear the purple dress for an entire evening. The thought of standing in front of all the guests wearing nothing but a thin satin draping freaked me out—enough to wonder if I could call out sick and leave Chloe at the altar with no backup. I wouldn't do it, of course, but that didn't mean it wasn't tempting.

The five of us went to lunch after the fitting. It was a cute café, wrought iron tables lined the sidewalk, and I was able to people watch instead of engaging in conversation. Each person that passed, I wondered if they were a Tethered Soul like Easton, and I imagined what kinds of lives they had lived in the past.

"How are things going with your boyfriend, Everly?" Chloe asked.

I jumped when I heard my name, snapping back to reality. *Boyfriend?* I suppose it was true. Easton was my boyfriend now. I liked the way it sounded.

"It's good!"

"Ohhh, look at that! She's getting embarrassed!" my mom cooed.

Drawing attention to it only made it worse. If I was pink before, I was red now.

"Mom!" I tried, but my attempt failed.

"I've never seen her this smitten by a boy before! Not even Evan Styles! The boy she pined after for two years and they went to homecoming together! I thought she had it bad then, but now? Wooo . . ." Mom fanned her face, and I rolled my eyes.

"Evan was just a fling, Mom." I looked to the other women. "It was nothing. Don't listen to her."

"Do you love him?"

It was a bold question coming from Chloe. I couldn't believe that she would pry like that in front of our mothers and her grandma. But before I could think of something clever to answer, all the women, including the grandma, made all sorts of high pitch squeals. I cursed my God-given face for deceiving me in the way that it did.

"Ohhh, I remember my first love . . ." Chloe's grandmother said.

"Yeah, Grams married my grandpa super young. They were high school sweethearts!" Chloe announced.

"Aw, that's so sweet!" My mom placed a hand over her heart.

"Just because that geezer was my last love doesn't mean he was my first!" Chloe's grandma spit through her missing teeth.

It was the best thing I'd heard all day. I loved a senior with an attitude. I sat up straight in my chair, eager to listen to her story. After the waiter took our menus, she began.

"Two boys were fighting over me my first year in high school. Frank and Harold."

"Frank is my grandpa," Chloe added.

I loved it already.

"Frank was handsome, but nobody held a candle to Harold. He was a bad boy, he lived on the wrong side of the tracks, and I loved him more than anything. We used to sneak around so my parents wouldn't find out."

"Grandma!" Chloe said.

"My parents were friends with Frank's parents. They were a good family. Hard-working. I liked Frank well enough, but he was no Harold. When my parents found out I was fooling around with that boy, they forbade me to see him."

"What did you do?" I muttered.

"Oh, I had to listen to them. They'd whip my butt with a belt if I didn't. Lash my tush until it bled! You can't do that these days. They'd think you're a bad parent. Abusive, they'd say."

I chuckled and found myself wondering how old Easton's views dated back. I briefly pondered if he valued waiting until marriage before having sex. I winced, remembering when he turned me down in the tent. I was thankful when Chloe's grandma continued with her lisp-ridden story of forbidden love.

"After a while of Frank trying to get to know me, I caved. There's only so much will power a young girl has, and I was bored. I started to go out with him to help me get over Harold. And eventually, I did."

"But Grams, you love Grandpa, don't you?" Chloe asked.

"Oh yeah, I love the crusty geezer. It took years for it to grow through. Some love is meant to be. Some love . . . well, you can make it work."

Chloe and her mother were visibly disturbed by her confession. Although from Chloe's mother's expression, I imagined she'd heard the story before. I was sure I was the only one who thoroughly enjoyed the grandmother's confession. It struck true for me too. And I took pleasure in the idea that I had chosen my Harold.

The five of us continued our lunch. My panini was delicious, but my appetite only allowed for a small portion. I took the leftovers home with me in a box. It would make for a good dinner. All and all, the day wasn't too bad. I began to look at Chloe as a Frank. Maybe it was a love that wasn't instant or true, but it had the potential to work regardless. I hoped for my brother's sake that their love was a hidden Harold.

I would have met Easton at Fresh Grounds, but I was too embarrassed to show my face. I told him to meet me in the parking lot across the street instead.

I called Lindsay and told her all about the romantic night camping Easton had put together for me. I left out the part where he may or may not be a mad man. The jury was out, but I loved him nonetheless. It sure did make for some interesting conversation, and I was thankful to have a new focus. I promised Lindsay I would still come into the coffee shop, but she had to tell me who would be on the schedule first. I didn't need the wrath of Jacob.

When Easton jumped in my truck, he gave me a quick peck on the cheek.

"What's the secret mission?" he asked.

I had something that I needed to do. Due diligence, if you will. But I was slightly ashamed of myself for it. That's why I needed backup.

"Do you remember that girl we saw at Hunters?" I asked.

"No. I don't remember a girl. However, I do remember you making a young man feel as small as a boy when you pointed out that his shirt was missing buttons. Was the girl before that, or after that?"

I shot Easton a look. He held up his palms, "Joking! I was joking!" he said, before mumbling under his breath, "True story though . . ."

"Hope, the girl on the date. She was the one I wanted my brother to marry," I said.

"Oh, yeah, I remember. What about her?"

"I went to Chloe's dress fitting today, and I'm having a hard time accepting that she's the right one for my brother. I just want to talk to Hope. Do a little sleuthing," I said like a true Clover girl.

Easton was apprehensive. I could tell he disapproved of me meddling in their relationship.

"I don't know how to say this, Beck—"

"Just say it!"

"I think you should trust your brother and respect his decisions. You don't know his heart."

Easton made a good point.

"I know his mind! And I know he's attracted to shiny new things! And I know that when the newness of their relationship fades, he's going to wish he'd picked someone with more depth. But it'll be too late then! He'll have a baby! I know my brother, and he's making the wrong decision! Hope is the manager at the supermarket; I'm just going to talk—"

"I have an idea!" Easton interrupted. "Before you talk to Hope, why don't you talk to your brother?"

I frowned.

"Have you ever talked to him about this?"

"No," I admitted.

"Out of respect, I think he should be your first stop. Then, maybe even Chloe. And a far, distant third, Hope. And maybe not even then . . ."

I threw myself back in my seat under protest. He was right, as usual.

"So, no Hope?"

"No Hope."

"Come with me to talk to my brother?" I asked Easton. He was pleased with the new direction, and we were on our way.

It was a Wednesday, and I knew my brother would be working. We went to K & C's Concrete, and it didn't take long for me to find him.

"Hey, Dork! What brings you here?" Carter said, eyeing Easton and me.

"Hey, do you have a second to chat?" I asked.

"Now? Is everything OK?" he asked. It made my stomach turn.

"I just wanted to talk to you about the wedding. That's all."

"Oh, OK. I'm due for a break. I'll meet you at the benches by the deli in five," Carter said before heading back inside.

I squeezed Easton's hand, thankful he was by my side. My brother and I didn't have conversations beyond name-calling, but it didn't mean I didn't care.

I sat with my back toward the fading sun. A little warmth hit my back, but it wasn't enough. A shudder ripped through me. I couldn't tell if I was cold or incredibly apprehensive. Was I doing the right thing? I wanted to pull out, but it was too late. Carter sat down opposite me.

"So, what brings you here? You never come to my work!" Carter said with a less than welcoming tone.

"I . . ." I looked at Easton, my eyes begging for help. He placed his hand on my knee and squeezed. But that's all he offered. He was going to make me do this all on my own. I deserved as much.

"I wanted to give you my blessing!" I couldn't believe it when the words came out of my mouth, and by the looks of my brother, he didn't either. I was too scared to say what I actually thought.

Carter took off his sunglasses and squinted into the sunlight.

"Look Beck, I know you don't like her, but you don't see who she is when we're alone," he said.

"No! I know!" It was something I'd just realized in that moment.

"She's kind, and she cares a lot about other people. She's a good person. And she doesn't show it all the time, but she's deeper than you'd know."

"Totally!" I nodded, never doubting him for a moment.

"She's incredibly insecure. You wouldn't know it by looking at her, cause she's hot as hell, but it comes out all weird. Lots of makeup, showy clothes, an over-the-top personality. But when she's with me and we're home on the couch, and she's got no makeup, and my old baggy t-shirt on; that's the woman I chose to marry. Just give her a chance, Beck. You'll like her." Carter glared at me, part pleading, part warning.

"No! Yeah! I get it! I'm here for you, and I can't wait to get to know her better. She's going to make a great addition to our family," I said, feeling no better than scum.

Thank God, I never went to Hope!

Carter put his sunglasses back on and stood up. I guess we were done talking.

"Wait!" I blurted out. No regrets. "It wasn't Chloe; she was never the problem. It's me. Nobody will ever be good enough for you, in my eyes. I'm sorry I ever doubted your decision."

For the first time, I watched my brother look at Easton with a softening of his eyes. Approving almost. He knew Easton was right for me, too. Besides, it was likely that my feelings about Chloe were similar to his own for Easton and the confession resonated all the more for that reason. Carter nodded and slapped Easton on the back before heading back to work. And when he was out of sight, I refused to look at Easton's "I told you so" face.

CHAPTER 19

"I know you want to say it," I said.

Easton held up both his hands, saying nothing. *Smart boy.*

"If you're not going to say it, I will. You were right. I had no business meddling in my brother's relationship. How could I have been so blind?" I asked, mostly thinking aloud, but more than interested in knowing if Easton had an answer.

"When you're emotionally invested, it's easy to have your judgment clouded," Easton said. He was too kind.

"Yeah, but your judgment's never off. You always know best. You knew today when I wanted to talk to Hope." I prepared to go on and on, but Easton cut me off.

"And that took a very, very long time to figure out, though. It can be difficult still, and I'm sure I'll continue to make mistakes. I'm not perfect." Easton shrugged. "We're human," he said.

"You are?"

"I am what?"

"Human?" I asked.

Easton's face fell. "Seriously?"

"What!? I've never met a . . . a . . ." I waved my hands about in the air. I didn't know where I was going with this, but it sounded worse the longer it continued. "I don't know, OK? I don't know what you are." I sank in my seat.

"I'm a human, as are you," Easton said.

I rolled my eyes. "Well, last time I checked, we don't come back from the dead, so—"

"What, do you think I'm a zombie?" Easton was beginning to find it humorous. I was too exhausted.

"Look, I'm sorry. I've had a long day. They made me try on this awful purple dress, and then I got spit on by this toothless grandma . . ."

"What? Really?"

"Yeah, actually, she was amazing. The spitting, not so much."

"Why don't you come over for some dinner? We can watch a movie?" Easton offered.

"I would love that, but I have to get back to Yeti. I don't have it in me to stay out late." Too bad, because I was dying to see his place. No pun intended.

"I'll come to yours then."

"Really? I'd love that, as long as you don't mind me being so tired?" I wanted to spend all my hours with him, but I was still exhausted from camping. It had been a couple of days ago, but I was dragging, nonetheless.

"You go home, get on pajamas, and I'll pick up dinner and bring it over," Easton said. It was nice not to have to plan anything.

"That sounds great," I said.

When I got home, I spent my time picking up the breakfast plate that I left on the kitchen counter and the random socks that Yeti had stolen and dispersed throughout the house. I had just enough time to brush my teeth before the doorbell rang.

"Hi, come on in. Um, sorry about the . . ." I motioned towards the pile of shoes by the front door. There would be other things that I would be embarrassed about too, but I had to let it go if I wanted to enjoy my time with Easton.

"I hope you like Mexican food?" Easton held up a bag from the only Mexican restaurant in Clover.

"It's my favorite!" I said.

I felt a little awkward with Easton in my house. It was a funny thing that happened to the mind. My insecurities about the cleanliness, lack of décor, and absent furnishings—no matter how insignificant—still overpowered everything else that had happened in our relationship. All the while, he'd recently told me his deepest darkest secret, and it was beyond any fear of a messy kitchen. I felt the insecurities all the same. I was eager to look past it all and get to a place where we were entirely comfortable with each other.

"I want to see your place; I'm curious where you live," I said as I pulled out paper plates and real silverware.

"I'd like that too. But, don't have high expectations. It's nothing fancy."

I pointed around my kitchen. The original cabinetry from the eighties, the stained grout between the white tiles, and the one attempt I'd made at a decoration: a chicken statue. Easton smiled and cocked his head to the side.

"Are there others like you?" I asked, suddenly curious if there could be another him out there.

I watched his face contort as I mindlessly unwrapped the food. Easton took a seat at the kitchen island.

"There are. Not many, I suppose. I've only met a few dozen or so."

"Really? A few dozen?"

"Yeah, um, remember the homeless man outside of the bar?" Easton's face softened with what I assumed was empathy, maybe sadness.

"Nooo!" I said, drawing out the word.

Easton chuckled, "Yeah, that's Simon. He's all but given up. It's a hard life, and I understand why many choose to drown themselves in drugs and alcohol. They're just trying to escape." Easton plated a chicken burrito and doused it in salsa.

It was sad to me too. I never looked past Simon's dirty face. It was becoming a theme in my life—one I'd like to nip. I had so much to learn but so little time.

"He called you something; it was like he knew you . . ."

"Sam?"

"Yeah!"

"The first time we met, my name was Sam. That's what he'll always remember me as," Easton said.

"You get a different name each time?" I asked before taking a bite of my dinner.

"I'm always adopted under the same name. Half of my parents honor my given name—It's Easton Green, by the way—and half of them change it, sometimes using a variation similar to the original and sometimes changing it altogether. I used to care and legally change my name back the second I turned of age. I don't care so much anymore."

"Wow." I took a moment to let it sink in: multiple lives, multiple names.

"But how did Simon know that you were like him?" I asked, intrigued. I could probably ask questions all night and still not finish.

Easton worked to clear the food in his mouth, holding a napkin over his lips while he chewed.

"Sorry, there's just so much to understand." I apologized for the interrogation; it wasn't very hospitable of me.

"No, don't be sorry. I like it. I've never been able to talk to someone about this before—"

"You've never told anyone!?" I blurted out.

"I have—a couple of times. Um, I've told one of my best friends before. It didn't end well. And I've told a few parents, all in my early lives. Every time, I regretted it. The worst was when I was put under psychiatric care," Easton said with a shrug.

My jaw dropped. "But you took a chance telling me," I stated.

"I did." Easton put his food down for a moment of reflection.

"Why?"

"God, I knew it was going to go one of two ways. I was so scared, and every life experience I had was telling me not to." Easton shook his head and stared off into the distance.

"What changed your mind?"

Easton's focus came back to me. "I couldn't stunt your chance at love. If you chose to leave me, that would be a valid decision, but I didn't have the right to make that decision for you."

"Thank you for giving me a choice." I smiled at him, realizing that he'd given me a choice, and I wasn't as stripped of control as I previously thought.

We finished our dinner. The conversation flowed effortlessly, even in my exhausted state. Easton picked a movie about a man able to travel through time. It was no wonder why he proclaimed it as one of his favorites. He lay on the sofa, and I crawled in front of him, careful not to block his view. No matter how mind-bending or heartbreaking the movie may have been, I was never going to last. I fell asleep in Easton's arms. My guess would have been in the first five minutes.

I felt more at home in Easton's arms than I ever had in my house alone. And while his arms kept the terror away, I still dreamed of death. At the very least, I was unconscious when the dream played out like a movie; it was much better than being awake and gouging out the backs of my arms and threatening the life of my cell phone. But, even though I was asleep during this particular dream, it still took up residency in my mind the same as a memory would. And I was disappointed when I awoke with a memory of drowning to death. The nightmares hardly seemed fair. I had enough horror to deal with in my real life, and I didn't need it in my sleep too.

The despair drained from my memory when my eyes focused on Easton. He sat in the recliner, reading a book and sipping coffee from Fresh Grounds. The sunlight brushing the side of his face. I was pleased to see that he had stayed the night.

"Good morning," Easton said, taking me in.

"Good morning."

"I brought you a coffee. Thankfully, Lindsay was working, and she knew your order. I think she left you a little note on your coffee sleeve." Easton held out my coffee.

The note read, "Call me!" I read her message aloud and chuckled. I'd been neglecting her and my family. I knew it wasn't right, but it was the easiest path for me at the moment. I missed her.

"I see you found the blankets." I lifted the blanket he had draped over me. I had a small stack of throw blankets in a cupboard tucked away in the hall.

"I didn't snoop, I—"

"No, it's fine. Thank you. And thank you for the coffee." I rarely had coffee upon waking. It was nice.

"Did you sleep OK? I thought about moving you to your bed, but I didn't want to wake you. You seemed . . . restless," Easton said.

"Oh, I slept fine. It was just a dream, but . . . um, actually, I slept better than I have in a while. I think it's because you were here."

Easton smiled, and I blushed. I hid behind my coffee cup.

"You know, the house gets lonely. And the quieter it gets, the louder my thoughts become."

Easton nodded without saying anything. Sometimes it was nice just to know somebody understood.

"Well, I've got to head out. I have some errands to run. Are you going to be OK today?" Easton closed his book and placed it under his arm.

"Oh! Yeah," I shook my head. Why wouldn't I be OK? I had stuff to do too. Like sleep.

"You should call Lindsay. I know it's hard, but I think it would be good for both of you to spend a little time catching up. It seemed like she missed you." Easton smiled before turning to leave.

"Yeah, maybe I will," I muttered. He had always been right in the past; I'm sure this was no exception.

Dear Lindsay, I wrote.

I didn't call her. Nor did I visit. But I did take a nap, and I was productively writing my goodbye to Lindsay. It was hard work. Draining work. By the end of the letter, I'd need a hot shower to wash away the emotion.

I told her why she was my best friend, and I shared my most hilarious and treasured memories with her. And I told her why I was too much of a coward to talk to her in person. I asked for forgiveness, and I begged her not to feel sad. I wrote my wish that she would only remember me with a smile.

The day had come and gone when I caught wind that Chloe was having a bachelorette party the following weekend. For an introvert such as myself, a bachelorette party was a dreaded event. The thought of pretending to have something in common with a bunch of ladies on a party bus sounded horrendous. Nonetheless, I committed myself to give it my best shot. I owed it to Carter for doubting him. And to be honest, I was a little intrigued to get to know the real Chloe—the one that Carter knew and loved.

CHAPTER 20

So, what did you say you were going to school for?" I asked the girl next to me.

I'd already forgotten her name. She had a short pixie cut and cute freckles. I wanted to call her Alice, but I knew that wasn't right. I wouldn't chance it.

"Um—" she started.

"Suck it!" The crazy one yelled to the one with long blond hair and a penis straw.

The limo bounced, and I tried to hold on to the leather seats. It was uber hot, and the six of us ladies had packed in tight like sardines. The smell of alcohol permeated the air, and I was thankful you couldn't get drunk off the smell alone. I was taking it easy. I had a weak stomach, I said. It wasn't entirely untrue.

"Um, I'm just taking general ed classes. I don't know what I want to do yet," not Alice, said.

I nodded. It was so awkward when the conversation died. Now I had to do all sorts of work to come up with other questions. I picked up my cell phone as if I had a notification ping that only I could hear. I scrolled through several apps, buying myself time before having to talk to someone again. Chloe was the only one I knew—and not well either. I was hoping we would have some time to get to know each other, but by the looks of the half-empty tequila bottle, and the still setting sun, tonight was going to be a long one and not for talking.

At some point, maybe I could sneak out early. I wouldn't be missed. That was for sure. The five girls all knew each other from high school, and one of them, as early as elementary. They had all sorts of inside jokes and a plethora of things to talk about. I was the only newcomer. And I was not open to making new friends.

Quite the opposite, actually. I was in the market for downgrading. Saying goodbye and closing the door. I shouldn't have come.

I texted Easton. I prayed he would tell me to hold tight and that he would bail me out. He didn't. He was overly optimistic that I would find some fun by the end of the night. I threw my head back and braced myself for another bump; then, I spent all of my energy on joining the party. I started with a shot.

By the time we got to the karaoke bar, I was feeling sick to my stomach. I didn't know if it was my condition or not, but I hadn't been able to consume alcohol the way I used to. Each and every time, my tolerance would shrink. I knew I shouldn't have had any, but I wanted desperately to rid myself of my social awkwardness that came with being an introvert and the burden I carried of keeping a secret with the magnitude of cancer.

We stammered out of the limo. All of us had penis headbands, except for Chloe. She had a crown, a sash, and a ball and chain around her ankle. It was degrading at best. Everyone stopped and stared. I wished I was intoxicated enough not to notice, but I wasn't. I was on the cusp of being chattier but also starting to yawn at an accelerated rate. I was ready for bed, and it couldn't be later than seven.

The girls tumbled into the bar. I lagged behind. Something was off; it was either motion sickness or déjà vu. I stopped altogether on the curb as the others disappeared into the karaoke bar. I saw something I recognized. But what? I looked around the busy streets. A car honked as a guy hung out the back window with his phone. Was I a celebrity? No, I had a penis on my head. I snatched the hideous headband off of my head and hid it under my jacket. My stomach churned in humility. I was safer with the pack.

It was then, when I made my decision to head inside, that I saw him.

There, across the street, tucked behind the trash cans, was Simon. Like a hidden gem. I knew I recognized something, and it was his dog that came out to greet us when we unloaded from the limo—looking for scraps, no doubt. I crossed the street, thankful I no longer was getting the attention from onlookers, and came upon Simon sleeping on top of newspapers. His sign was different this time: "Need Help to Feed Family." Poor guy. It was his only hope; he probably changed it out all the time, testing it like an advertisement. Seeing what sticks can be hard work. I knew that from my design classes at the college.

"Simon?" I said.

He was out cold. His clothes were so dirty that they were nearly black, and the deep wrinkles in his face showed pale against the dirt on his skin. His hair was so greasy, I wondered when the last time he had a proper shower. I stood above him—his dog whimpering—and I wondered what I could do to help this Tethered Soul.

"Simon!?"

I forced out a louder call, but my voice cracked. It'd been doing that a lot lately. I rubbed at my neck. The little dog begged at my feet, and I just stood there helplessly. The least I could do was give him a proper meal. Maybe the smell of hot food would wake him.

There was a taco shop two blocks down, if I recalled correctly. I made my way there and ordered five rolled tacos with guacamole and sour cream. I was back in no time, and Simon had woken up naturally. He sat, back hunched against the wall of a steakhouse. It was probably prime picking when they brought out the leftovers. I'm sure his dog loved it as well.

"Simon?" I said again.

Simon's eyes widened at the sight of me and then dropped to the container of food. His dog stood on two legs and danced.

"I know you probably don't remember me, but I'm Beck. I'm East—Sam's friend." I corrected myself.

Simon nodded. It was a brief encounter, and it was dark, I didn't blame him for not remembering me in his drunken state.

"I brought you some food. Are you hungry?" I asked as I sat down beside him.

"Yeah!"

Simon took the food, his eyes large in wonder. He tore into a rolled taco. But no matter how hungry that man was, he still had the loyalty to share with his dog. Simon gave him one full taco. It was a generous gift. As if that wasn't enough to melt my heart, he offered me one next.

"Oh!" I waved my hands about, "No, thank you, I've got to get back to a thing."

Simon looked at me with questioning eyes.

"Yeah, my brother's getting married, so I'm here with his fiancée, celebrating." I pulled the penis headband out from my jacket and gave it a little shake.

Simon began to laugh; a toothless smile spread across his face, and I laughed with him.

"There! Over there!" Chloe yelled to the crazy one. Her long arm pointed at me from across the street.

Shit.

"Looks like the penis sisters found me!" I said to Simon, and we laughed some more.

The girls crossed the street, "What are you doing out here, Everly? We've been looking all over for you!" Chloe said.

"Yeah! We looked in the bathroom. Twice!" the crazy one said.

I rolled my eyes. Not on purpose. It was natural.

"OK, yeah, I'll be right there," I said, not wanting to leave the wisdom tucked within this homeless man. He was like a unicorn that only I could see.

The girls exchanged shifty glances.

"Like, let's go then. Now." Chloe had *hero* written all over her face. She would later tell the story as if she saved me from the dangerous homeless man.

I sighed and looked over to Simon. "Do you like to sing?" I asked.

The girls began to whisper. At least, they thought they were whispering. Simon chuckled and pointed to his chest.

"Yeah! Come with us! More food and drinks too!" I said.

Simon was quick to his feet. The girls were apprehensive—that was until the crazy one screamed.

"Wooooooo! Partaaayyyy!" She thrust her arms in the air as if she'd just won a boxing match and ran across the street. More cars honked, and Chloe ran after her, her legs pinned at the knees. I knew that run. The girl had to pee. I crossed the street slower than the girls before me, remaining at Simon's side. He was a stiff man, and I assumed sleeping on the concrete would do that to the young and old alike.

The karaoke bar was loud for being at half capacity. The night was early, and I was thankful we got in when we did. Our party was by far the most obnoxious. Even worse than the woman singing "My Heart Will Go On." I was embarrassed for her. She was most likely in her early forties, and she was not here to party. No, this woman was serious; she probably came here after work to fill the void of never becoming a professional singer. When she stretched out her voice, it was clear why this had never taken off for her. She felt it deep within her and looked like she might cry at the sound of her own vocals. Others might cry for a different reason. It was hard to watch.

The waitress got an extra seat for Simon. Most of the girls were taken aback by his presence, but the girl not named Alice gave me an approving smile.

"Hi, I'm Audrey."

Audrey! I knew it wasn't Alice!

"Hi."

Simon gave her a toothless grin. He was so happy, and I felt grateful that I was able to brighten his day. It was fate that our paths crossed, and I was glad I came. Easton was right *again.* I did find a patch of happiness on this bachelorette night.

Simon ordered the kitchen sink and two shots of bourbon. When his food came, I ended up taking one of his shots with him. You only live once! Well, not Simon. He lived a lot.

"To Simon, and the amazing life he's had the opportunity to live."

I held out my shot glass, and the five other girls did the same. Bourbon, vodka, two Sex on the Beaches, and one dirty martini joined forces for a brief moment in the middle of the table to celebrate Simon's life. It was nothing short of a miracle.

The night was a blast. I admittedly spent some of it throwing up in the bathroom, but that was only because my tolerance was zilch. Chloe showed us that she had somewhat of a decent singing voice, and at one point in the night, the crazy one showed us that she was wearing a neon pink bra. Simon got on stage to sing after some coaxing from the other five girls and me, and we all sang "Livin' on a Prayer." I only knew the chorus; Simon didn't know any of it. But that didn't stop us from singing our hearts out. It was a night I needed. And I was grateful.

When the time had come to say goodbye, I left Simon with all the cash I had in my purse, as Easton had. It wasn't much—sixty dollars perhaps—but he was touched. I said goodbye to Simon's dog and finished up with a tight squeeze around Simon's neck.

"Take care," I whispered.

The five girls said goodbye to Simon, giving him high fives, and pats on the back, thanking him for singing with us on stage. Simon beamed like a new man. I wondered if I'd ever see him again.

I felt good on the ride home. Tired beyond belief, but happy. I never got my time with Chloe, but Simon was an unexpected surprise that made my night worth the exertion. Something about being in the presence of an old soul made me feel grounded like I was one with nature. And Mother Nature was a beautiful thing.

CHAPTER 21

I was already half asleep by the time the limo dropped me off. I threw my shoes into the shoe graveyard and padded barefoot to the kitchen. I forced myself to drink a full glass of water before bed. My full belly made me feel even more nauseous, and I ended up throwing it up no more than five minutes later. I must have been really down on myself because Easton answered a text I didn't remember writing and came over to help. I knew enough to know I was embarrassed and that texting him was probably a mistake.

Easton was nothing less than a saint, though. He tied my hair into a ponytail and fetched me water. When I settled into bed after a hot shower, I begged him to stay. He didn't hesitate. He crawled into bed with me, and I was thankful for the warmth of his body. I nestled my face into his neck.

"What did you do tonight?" I mumbled into the darkness. His hair smelled of cherry cigars.

"I played poker tonight."

"Did I ever tell you I ran into your grandpa?" I fumbled on my words as I remembered the odd exchange I had with Clyde.

"You saw Clyde?" Easton asked.

"Yeah," I said, partially aware that I was incriminating myself.

"Where?" Easton's tone was confused. Possibly suspicious.

"Oh. Um." My eyes searched the black void of my room, worried about how he might take my stalkery, "At that bar, the one you took me to."

"You went to the bar? When?"

I took a deep breath. "I went when we weren't talking. I think I was trying to run into you. I missed you," I said. After what seemed like an eternity, I blurted out, "I was stalking you, OK?" I felt much better now that it was out. It didn't feel like stalking at the time, but looking back now, the truth of the matter was clear. I was a crazy girlfriend, and I was ashamed.

"Hey, it's OK; I was just worried for you. That's probably not the safest place for you to be alone."

Easton was understanding and forgiving.

"I just wanted to find you. I—"

"Shhh, it's fine." Easton ran his hand through my hair. "Did he say anything to you?" he asked.

"It was an . . . odd, exchange. He kind of acted like you were just a bar buddy and not his grandson. Now looking back . . ." I glanced up at Easton, and though I saw nothing, I stared, waiting for his answer.

"He knows me as a poker buddy. I know him as a little brother."

I sat straight up, "What!?" I wanted to search his eyes, but it was so dark that all I could see was a moonlit silhouette.

"Two lives ago, he was my little brother. When I moved out for college, he was seven. It was a bad home. An abusive one. It's always weighed on my heart. I shouldn't have left him there alone. But, it's not the first time I've seen it. Lived it. And it won't be the last. I spent my last life looking for him to no avail. I ended that one short. I was twenty years old when I gave up on that one."

Easton played with my locks, reflecting on his past life.

"I found Clyde at that bar, completely by chance. He didn't remember me, but I knew it was him. I made it my mission to get to know him and hopefully find a way to enrich his life. So far, I've only made him laugh. He's a tough nut to crack, and I think his substance abuse makes him damn near impenetrable. Still, I try."

"It makes so much sense now."

I laid my head back on Easton's shoulder and pondered the awkward conversation we had outside of the bar.

I began to chuckle. "I probably looked like such an idiot to him!"

Easton found amusement in this. "I'm sorry. Grandpa just seemed like the closest thing I could think of at the time to convey how much he meant to me."

I traced hearts over Easton's chest. The pad of my finger barely pressing into his T-shirt. I felt terrible for him. It made me think of ways to make him feel better.

"That reminds me. Guess who I ran into tonight?" I said.

"Who?" Easton's heart was beginning to pulse under my hand.

"Simon."

"You ran into Simon? Tonight?"

"Yeah," I began to chuckle again. I rolled over to grab my phone.

"I brought him to the karaoke bar with us, and we all sang on stage together! It was a riot!"

I pulled up the multiple selfies I took of Simon and me, Simon and the crazy one, Simon and the girl who was . . . still not Alice. I paged through the photos in the dark, and Easton squinted, as the light was bright in his eyes.

"I don't remember that girl's name, but she was nice. And that's when Simon and I took shots!"

Easton shot me a look I could only see by the light of my phone.

"What? I didn't drink that much; It was only like three or four drinks."

Easton continued to stare in disbelief.

I laughed, "I'm serious! I don't think my body can process liquor like it used to. I felt sick after just one drink! But, then I drank more to squash the social awkwardness. It's a real struggle sometimes."

Easton's disbelief turned humorous. His face cracked into laughter.

I laughed too, but I didn't know what we were laughing at, just that his mood was contagious. The more I laughed, the harder he did.

"Beck?" Easton managed to squeak as he wiped a tear from his eye.

I sat on the edge of the bed. My phone was still lighting up his glorious smile.

"Huh?" I giggled, half dazed, half confused.

"That's . . . *not* Simon!"

"What!"

I grabbed my phone from him and examined the photos. Easton was laughing so hard now he was rolled over to his side, his arm hanging off the bed. I shot to my feet and flipped on the overhead lights. I studied the selfies as if they would conjure an explanation.

They didn't.

I wanted to say something, but my jaw just hung open as I watched Easton roll around in hysteria. My face flushed; I wanted to get him. But all I could think of was the pillow. I grabbed a throw pillow from the floor and chucked it at his face. In a million years, I would never make that shot, but tonight, I did.

The pillow knocked the laughter right out of his mouth. Now he was as shocked as I was.

We stared at each other for a split second with pure animalistic instincts. Without a strategy, I picked up the second throw pillow, but I was too slow. The first of the ammunition was fired back and already hurtling toward my head. I turned as it slammed into my shoulder.

I screamed.

Easton flew out of bed, ready to attack; I screamed louder and tried to run away. He was impossibly quick. He grabbed me around the waist, and I laughed so hard that no sound escaped my throat.

Easton grunted, pinning me to the bed. I fought with as much strength as I had. It wasn't nearly enough to make a difference.

Both of us struggled to catch our breath. Our heart's throbbing against each other.

I broke out into laughter once again, but something in Easton's eyes melted my hysteria into depths of desire. The air shifted. For a moment, I took it in, the look in his eyes, the pounding of his chest. It was a moment I never wanted to forget.

"Do you," Easton began, breathless.

I rolled my bottom lip in between my teeth, trying to freeze time. I wished I could live in that instant forever, basking in the light of Easton's most cherished love.

I lifted my head, searching his eyes just long enough for my lips to find his. Time slipped away as we succumbed to our passion. It was the moment of a lifetime—the moment when I learned the difference between having sex and making love. I had never done the latter. It was the night I was able to convey just how much Easton meant to me. And I did so with every slide of my hand. Every plush kiss of my lips. The driving thrust of my hips. It was a slow, sultry dance to a melody only he and I could hear. The emotional bond we had, collided in a storm of lust and desire.

The sunlight penetrated my eyelids, and I scrunched my eyes while spreading my arms wide, stretching, and reaching. When I felt nothing but the cold sheets to my side, my eyes flung open, and I sat up.

I looked around my room for signs of Easton, but everything was unnervingly still. The dust sparkled in the air as it sank to the floor. In the distance, a car door slammed. My love, not lost. Not yet. I bolted to my bathroom and took a swig of mouthwash. My head pounding all the way. I perked up when I heard fumbling in my entryway. I spat and hurdled back into my bed, finding my warm spot. My anticipation grew with each footstep on the stairs.

"Hey, how are you feeling?" Easton asked, holding a tray of coffee and a bag of what I presumed to be pastries. I could get used to this. A flush of my cheeks was enough to answer his question—and more. A dimple kissed his cheek.

"I feel surprisingly light today." My eyes wandered the bedding. Easton laughed.

My heart began to pound. Maybe it was embarrassment, for the heat of passion last night was now out in the open daylight. Perhaps it was so surreal that I wanted to see if it would happen again.

My mouth watered as the nutty warmth of coffee wafted through the air. Easton closed the distance. He placed the coffee and the bag of treats down on my nightstand. Without a thought in my head, I reached out. Wrapping my finger into his belt loop, and I pulled him toward me.

Sometimes, it's luck. Sometimes the stars align so perfectly, the unthinkable happens. Then, there are times where dreams meet reality. It boils down to fate.

It didn't matter where my stars fell from here on out. I'd found Easton, and I wasn't going to let go—today, physically speaking. We'd spend the day fooling around in bed until the daylight gave way to the darkness. Beyond that, I don't know what it meant. But I'd have to imagine that when I passed on, my heart would be staying with him. Because I was no longer its owner.

CHAPTER 22

Chloe's mom placed a delicate crystal tiara in her daughter's hair. It was the finishing touch to the most beautiful bride I'd ever seen. Even though she wasn't the bride I would have handpicked for my brother, she was the one that was meant to be. And that made her beautiful. Sometimes there are right choices and wrong choices. Sometimes it's right for *right now*. I had high hopes she would be my brother's *Harold*. And if I, for some reason, turned into a ghost after all of this was over, I would follow them and do what I could to keep them on track. Likewise, I might haunt her if she ever did him wrong.

It was probably my ignorance talking. Perhaps my love for my brother. But it was hard to imagine anyone having a bond like the one that I shared with Easton. I knew it was special. But I would even go as far as to say it was one-of-a-kind love. And if that was the case, where did that leave Carter and Chloe? Where did that leave all the other couples in the world? Was love on a spectrum?

"She looks stunning, doesn't she?" Mom whispered in my ear. She had tears in her eyes.

"Mom, you're going to ruin your makeup before the wedding even starts!" I shook my head. What was she doing? "Control yourself," I scolded with a half-smile, both appalled by and poking fun of her weakness.

She slapped my shoulder and dabbed the corners of her eyes with a tissue. "Stop that!" she hissed.

It was in those tears that I realized how difficult this evening would be for me. Because for every tear my mom would shed, I would have none. I couldn't find it in my heart to forget my unfortunate fate. Though, that's what I needed to do for the happiness to peek through. It's not the dying part that upset me, but all the things I'd never be able to do. All of the moments I'd miss out on. And on such a momentous night, I realized I was afraid to watch what I could never have.

My mom handed me a full glass of champagne. My stomach churned. I looked around the room at the women brought together as a mark of Chloe's past and future.

I was neither. Chloe's mother held her glass up, "To my little girl, my starlight, my Coco . . ."

I sighed. On accident.

"I'm so happy you've found your soulmate. To a life filled with happiness and babies! Lots and lots of babies!" Her mom held her champagne in the air and gave Chloe an air kiss on both cheeks. Her grandmother grumbled something inaudible as she lifted her glass before downing it in two gulps.

I didn't pretend. I just placed my champagne flute, as full as it was given to me, on a table near my side. My mom set her empty glass on the table before picking up mine and swallowing it. She gave me a look, out of the corner of her eye, as she gulped it down. A look I didn't recognize and couldn't decipher.

I walked down the aisle on the arm of Carter's best friend Nick. His best man. Fresh daisies and red ribbon lined the church's pews and covered an arch above the minister's head. Guests filled the seats, and I could feel the stares. I was suddenly less focused on the irony of my childhood dream—walking down the aisle with my older brother's best friend—and more focused on not tripping. My heels were a good four inches, and that was about four inches more than I knew how to walk in. I never had the chance to practice, though I had planned to. Nick smiled and nodded at the strangers on each side of the aisle. He was a natural, and had my life taken another path, this could have been my reality. I looked down, not to see a white wedding gown but a thin satin shift dress. Purple.

I took my place on stage and stole a peek at Easton. He sat in the second row, wearing a black suit and a warm, encouraging smile. His hair was gelled so that it still looked disheveled, but in a way that would not come undone. I imagined him standing in the mirror, trying to get it just right. It was working to calm my nerves.

When the "Wedding March" began, and all invasive eyes turned to the back of the room, I took a deep sigh of relief. I looked down at my heels and took several therapeutic breaths. I didn't want to see the bride in all her glory. I was afraid of what I might feel. Jealousy was the green-eyed bitch, and I didn't need that weighing on my conscience. I looked to Easton instead. Our eyes met. A stolen moment in a room full of people. He gave me the courage to face my inner struggle. To face the bride as she walked down the aisle—a vision that is every little girl's dream.

It was as painful as I imagined. Chloe beamed with love from head to toe. Her normal tackiness subdued. And if I didn't know her, I might even say she looked elegant. Her hands were buried deep in daisies and a large red ribbon bow. Her tiara sparkled as much as her eyes as she set her sights on my brother. Carter's gaze met hers, and it wasn't until that moment, when I saw the joy emitting from my brother, that I realized I had room in my heart to be both happy for them and sad for me, all at the same time.

I threw my head back, willing the tears to suck back in their ducts, but it was no use. I was my mother's daughter. I gave up, lowered my head, and they ran freely down my cheeks. I glanced at Easton, who was now sympathetic. They must have been some tears if he could see them from the second row. I only hoped that waterproof mascara wasn't a gimmick.

If I thought I was losing it then, I was mistaken. My tears were just warming up. A mere appetizer to a five-course meal. The night was young, and the handwritten vows had yet to begin.

"Chloe, when you came into my life, I wasn't thinking of settling down and getting married. But when I got to know you, and I saw what you were doing to me, I knew that I would be stupid to let you go. You make me want to be a better person. And I promise you, from here on out, I will strive to be the best husband there ever was. And with you by my side, I think I can be that for you. I love you." Carter's vow was shaky and full of promise.

It's the second time in my life I'd seen my brother speak with such depth and emotion. The first being when Easton and I cornered him at his work to talk about his bride.

I didn't have a good view of Chloe's face, so I peered down into her bouquet of daisies in my hand when she spoke her vows.

"Carter, it's with—" Chloe cleared her throat and stiffened her notes in front of her, and began again.

"Carter, it is with you, that I have finally found myself. I know, when I look into your eyes, not only who I am, but who I want to be. Thank you for being the kind, loving, and accepting man that you are. And thank you for taking me on as your co-captain. It won't be easy; I can promise you that. But it will be a life to remember, full of love and laughter. I can't wait to see what our future holds with my hand in yours. I love you." Chloe choked. I lifted my eyes to see her folding up her notes into a tiny square.

My mind drifted to a faraway place; a place where it was me who was slipping into a wedding gown, and Easton waiting for me at the end of a long and lush rose covered aisle. The beautiful imagery in my head was shattered when the minister spoke.

"In sickness, and in health . . ."

My stomach cramped like a small dagger had been thrust into it. The rush of bitter acid in my throat. It was enough to make me cough. Tears welled up again, but this time for a different reason. My mouth was now sour, and I was relieved that soon, I would be able to get off the stage and out of the limelight. *Soon*, I promised myself.

"You may kiss the bride," the minister said.

My brother kissed his new bride, at first sweetly, then bending her over backward. Her leg kicked up in the air, and everyone cheered. My heart was so happy for him, but the smile never came. I hated myself for it. I felt like a burden. And if I could change anything about this whole process, I would change my control over how I acted. I wanted my genuine emotions to show. But it never came out that way. My happiness was shadowed by jealousy, and my fear was hidden in anger. My lack of control was clouded by sadness.

"You did great!" Easton reached for my arm. The masses were on their way out of the church. Some lingered behind to talk to friends or family.

"I cried," I informed him.

Easton smiled, "I know." I shot him a look of concern before he added, "but you can't tell!" in a rush of words, aimed to make me feel less self-conscious.

"I'm glad that's over. I felt like I might pass out, and there was this one point where I threw up in my mouth! Just a little." I pressed my hand to my forehead. All of the emotion was taking a physical toll on me.

"The hard part is over. Now let's have some fun." Easton grabbed me tight around the waist and pulled me into him. "Wow, this dress is thin!" His eyes widened and his grasp tightened.

"I know! I feel so naked!" I admitted.

Easton's hands wandered, stopping ever so slightly over my sacrum. "Are you . . ." His eyes glistened as his palm searched for a panty line.

I shook my head, trying to contain my embarrassment, though reveling in the fact that I could excite him so easily. "You dirty dog, is that all you think about?" I joked.

"Well, it's hard not to notice these little details about you." Easton squeezed my waist, and I squealed in response.

The room was nearly empty, and I was aware that we should be heading to the reception hall. It was only a ten-minute drive from the church, and I couldn't be late.

"I'd love to hide here with you, but I need to get to the reception," I said.

"I'll drive."

It was a beautiful day for a wedding. The sky was painted in orange and pink as the sun set for the night, tired after a day's hard work. Easton and I walked hand in hand to his car, and I stabled my wobbly balance with his strength.

The reception hall was grand and I was impressed that it felt intimate, given its size. The dim overhead lights gave way to the romantic fairy lights sprinkled throughout the tables and buffet. Candles glowed on every white tablecloth, and daisies were tucked in every nook and cranny. It was a lot of hard work that came together in the end in one beautiful display. My eyes wandered over the tables, and the guests finding their seats. I was sitting between Easton and Nick. If I had it my way, I wouldn't spend the night sandwiched between an old ember and a current flame. But, as I stated before, I was not in control of this beautiful disaster that was my life.

I took my seat, thankful for the reprieve. It had only been a handful of weeks since I was diagnosed, but I felt the toll beginning to take hold. The air had shifted ever so slightly, and I was starting to notice things. Little things. Like, I always felt like I was fighting off a cold. I had to take a three-hour nap mid-morning just to have the strength to socialize tonight. I imagined it must be how the elderly felt. Napping. Being exhausted from doing nothing more than watching their soap operas. It sounded quite nice, actually. Tranquil almost.

I noticed my voice cracking more often too. Now and then, it would feel like something was lodged in my throat. A pill capsized halfway down. My breathing had been reduced to sucking air through a straw. The moment I noticed that the symptoms were too apparent to ignore, I began to hide them. Much like I did with my doctor's missed telephone calls, I tried to sweep my destiny under the rug. Out of sight, out of mind. But I knew it didn't work this way, and I knew at some point—hopefully, later than sooner—they would not go unnoticed. It was then, and only then when I would succumb to telling my parents.

CHAPTER 23

Nick took his seat next to me but not before he held a chair out for his date. She was a pretty, blond-haired girl, and if I wasn't mistaken, I thought she looked a lot like me. But unlike me, she wore a dress that was both sexy and obscure.

"Hey, Beckette, you did great out there!"

Nick called me by an old familiar nickname. He called my brother Beck, and even though my friends called me the same, he had to have a way to differentiate between the two of us. Hence, Beckette.

"That was nerve-wracking, huh? All of those eyes!" I turned my attention to his girlfriend. "Hi, I'm Carter's sister, Everly."

I reached over Nick and shook her hand. Ugh . . . it was a limp one. Before I could introduce Easton, Nick had done it himself, leaning into me as he shook Easton's hand. The whole exchange more like a game of Twister than anything else.

I felt the subtlety of his lean into my chest. Not noticeable to either of our dates, but a closeness deemed unnecessary. It seems that I may not have been the only one with revived memories of our youth dredging up old feelings by walking down the aisle together.

I reached my hand over the back of Easton and rubbed his shoulder. A public display of affection. Nick responded with a mirrored image as he claimed his date. The small talk began. Nick sized up Easton, asking what he did for a living and yada, yada, yada. I once valued this information myself. Not because of how fat his wallet was with potential but because of the insight of interests and drive. Now I only cared what Easton's soul looked like. Not his face or body. I didn't care what he did for work or fun. One hundred percent of my love for him was based on something intangible and something you could never uncover with a question from across the dinner table.

Our last couple joined us at the table, completing our setting for six. It was Alice and her date. A cute nerdy boy with box-rimmed glasses and suspenders.

"Hi everyone. Hi Everly!" Alice waived to me.

I smiled, thankful to have someone I liked at our table.

"I'm Audrey, and this is Benjamin."

Audrey!

My heart skipped a beat at the thought that I almost introduced her to our table under the wrong name . . .

"Oh! I've heard so much about you and all the fun you had with . . ."—Easton looked at me, eyes filled with mischief—"Simon!"

I thrust my jaw to the side and gave his shoulder a squeeze that was more like a pinch. *He wouldn't!*

Audrey threw her freckled face back and cackled like a witch. "Oh, your girl Everly's a riot!"

"Ohhh, you have no idea!" Easton's eyes beamed.

I stiffened at his side. My face flushed red with the embarrassment of spending an entire evening with a man I thought was someone else. The only thing more embarrassing than that would be if Easton told the story right here, right now. The butterflies swirled in my chest at the very thought.

I was lucky enough to be reminded why I loved him so much; he kept my secret a joke between the two of us, right where it belonged. But the embarrassment of that night wasn't all under lock and key. Audrey had memories of her own to spill, and that she did. The table laughed along with her as she retold her version of the night. I laughed at the fact that the truth was far more outrageous. And she would never know.

Everyone stood with applause when the bride and groom were announced. Waiters and waitresses swarmed the room, spreading salad plates and pouring either red or white wine. I chose red, even though I wouldn't take more than a taste. My hot plate of chicken breast, asparagus, and garlic roasted potatoes looked as divine as it smelled, but it wasn't enough to bring back my appetite. I spent a long time moving the food around on my plate so that I would look at least half engaged, but the truth was, my stomach had turned sour during the ceremony, and it had yet to recover.

"How do you all know the bride and groom?" Benjamin gestured to the rest of the table guests with his fork.

I took a deep breath, preparing myself for an answer, but Nick beat me to it.

"I've grown up with the Becks. Carter and I go way back! Everly too." Nick put his elbow in my side.

"Yeah, it was Nick, my brother, and Hope. A couple other kids that I didn't know very well too, but we all lived in the same neighborhood and grew up together. There was always a plethora of neighborhood kids at one house or another at any given time," I added.

Nick knew that I never hung out with them. Nobody wants to hang out with their little sister, anyway. His angle made me nervous, and I wondered if he was trying to intimidate Easton. The joke was on him, though; that would never work.

"How did you two meet?" Nick's girlfriend asked Audrey.

"Oh, we met in middle school, but we didn't start dating until after high school graduation." Audrey shook her head as if there was no story there. "What about you guys, Everly? How did you meet?" Audrey threw the ball in my court.

A panic set over me. I wasn't as rehearsed as Easton was. "Oh!" I scrambled to remember the story he told my parents about the bridge. He'd altered it so that I had a flat tire.

"We met at a college party!" Easton said as he stretched tall and placed his arm around my shoulders. "Craziest night of my *life!*"

This ought to be good . . . I couldn't keep my smile in. I was embarrassed about the lie yet excited to hear the make-believe memory. It was a new identity. And if I could be someone else just for that moment, I was going to do it.

"I saw her there." Easton placed a hand out like he was remembering me, and I snickered, covering my mouth with my hands. "She was like an angel. I fell for her without ever knowing her name. She looked at me from across the room, and we just knew." Easton's voice trailed off as he shook his head back and forth for dramatic flair.

I was sucked into the story as was the rest of the table. Only Nick stirred with disinterest.

"The cops rushed in, and everybody fled each and every way. But my eyes were set on Everly. I made sure that where she ran, I followed. We darted out of the house and down the streets. The crowd dwindled to half a dozen of us. It was someone's bright idea to take refuge in his friend's house that was only a couple of blocks away. But his friend wasn't home! What were we to do now?"

I bit my bottom lip and watched Easton capture the attention of the table.

"He started to check the windows! He said that his friend always left one open. And there it was, a window in the back of the house, unlocked. We took turns crawling through the window. We turn on the lights, start making quesadillas. Not long after that, the cops burst into that house as well! One went out the window, one got caught, two fled through the slider door, and Everly and I . . . we hid in the pantry!"

I burst into laughter. The others were on the edge of their seat. I watched Easton wrap up an epic story.

"Nine hours! Nine hours, was how long we had to hide until the homeowners left the house, and we could sneak out. It was the best damn nine hours of my life! And we've been together ever since."

The girls swooned, myself included. Even Benjamin thought it was an impressive love story.

"I thought it was his friend's house!" Audrey choked out.

Easton shook his head, "In his drunken state, he miscalculated by two doors down! Turns out it was an old retired English professor's house. Mr. Rottermen."

Audrey wailed, and I gave Easton a kiss on the cheek. And for a split second, I forgot that it was merely make-believe.

The bride and groom were called to the dance floor, and we watched as they shared their first dance. Carter was uncomfortable, no doubt, but he hid it well. The moment Chloe's father stepped in to have the father-daughter dance is the moment I felt my throat close. My eyes no longer able to watch; I dismissed myself to use the restroom. All the while, I thought about how I would never have the chance to dance with my pops at my wedding.

I stood in the bathroom much longer than necessary. If I were hiding from my emotions, it was a poor hiding place. I ran my hands under the cold water until they felt like ice. Then I placed them on my cheeks and the back of my neck. I was tired already, but I had a little while longer to last.

By the time I resurfaced, the heartfelt scene had dissipated, and the party had started. Drinks were flowing, and the dance floor was on fire. I was thankful that it would be all downhill from here. There was still the cake to cut, but I didn't see how that could make me sad. Maybe I would be sad if my appetite hadn't yet returned, but that was one thing that I was confident I could handle.

I took my seat next to Easton. Our chairs were now turned to watch the dance floor. I loved to watch people dance. Some didn't care, some were gifted, others nervous and awkward. My favorite was when there was a combination of the ones who didn't care and the ones who were incredibly inept. They made for the best entertainment. I'd once seen a guy run and dive onto the varnished dance flooring, sliding like a penguin on his belly. He took out three people ending in a small dog pile in the middle of the crowd.

I was so content I didn't notice Nick when he approached us.

"Dance with me!" He held his hand out in front of me, vodka permeated the air.

"Oh, no, I couldn't." I shook my head and looked at Easton. Not for permission, but for rescuing. He smiled, not an ounce of jealousy in his eyes. If anything, maybe there was some sympathy. Not for me but Nick. Easton knew he would never have a chance.

I rolled my eyes, now feeling sorry for the sucker myself. I placed my hand in Nick's as I glared at Easton. He laughed and waved me farewell. The dance Nick and I shared was that of me taking a step back and him following. Him wrapping his hand around my waist, and me twisting out of it. It didn't take long for Easton to see that it was no longer fun and games. He stood to attention and made his way over after reading my several glaring attempts to call for help.

Nick was harmless, but I didn't want someone's paws all over me. Especially not in this dress. Just before Easton approached us, the song turned to a slow romantic number. Nick caressed my back one last time before Easton tapped him on the shoulder.

"Mind if I cut in? This is our song," Easton lied.

He didn't wait for Nick's sloppy rebuttal. In one swift motion, I was secured in Easton's arms where I belonged.

I laid my head on his chest and sighed in relief. "Thank you."

"How are you holding up?" he asked.

I closed my eyes for a moment and then let it all fall out.

"Honestly? It's been a ride. I keep thinking about how I'll never have these memories of my own. It's hard to watch my parents." I looked up at Easton. "There's just so much I want to do, and there's not enough time." I searched the depth of his blue eyes, but it was dark, and I couldn't find my way into them.

Easton stopped our slow momentum.

"Marry me," he said.

My heart skipped a beat. Did I hear him correctly? I scanned his eyes more frantically now.

"Marry me!" he said again.

CHAPTER 24

"Marry you?" I repeated.

It took me a long while to process his request. I'd all but forgotten we were in the middle of a dancefloor. Time stood still.

"Why would you want to do that to yourself? I mean, it's one thing to have love and loss, but it's another to be a widower your whole life. Surely you don't want that title. And for what? I'll love you just the same . . ."

"I want to marry you! I'm not going to be a widower . . ."

Easton grabbed my elbow and led me to a more private place to continue our conversation without others overhearing. There, out in the hall, he said it. The thing I never considered. The thing that made me hate and love all the same.

"I'm not going to let you die alone!" Easton's forehead lined with pain.

His words like a dagger to my chest. I wouldn't have the man I love die on my behalf. Even if he would resurrect sometime later or believe that he would.

"No! Are you crazy!? You can't do that!" I hissed. Eyes darting down the length of the hall. Still, no one within earshot.

"Everly, I don't think you understand! I've died a handful of times over, and I'll be damned if I let you do it alone!"

My skin began to heat. It's all I remember until I woke in Easton's lap with a small crowd hovering over me. Regrettably, one of them was a paramedic.

"What's happening?" I asked Easton in a storm of confusion and faintness.

"Shhh. Everything's OK. You've just been out for a little while," Easton said.

I looked at the paramedic; it must have been longer than a little while. The questions began to fire, but I couldn't answer any of them truthfully. None could be said in front of my mother, who was standing behind Easton.

"We should take her in, run some tests," the paramedic said to my mom.

My protest went unheard. Neither Easton nor I had a say in the matter, and before I knew it, I was placed on a gurney and rolled out of the reception hall. I convinced my mom that Carter would never forgive her if she left his wedding early and that Easton was more than capable of going with me to the hospital.

My mom watched me from the curb as they closed the ambulance doors. I was utterly mortified by my grand exit. And I'd thought the purple dress was bad.

"Is it Tim?" I asked the paramedic as I tried to focus my eyes on his name tag.

"Yes, it is."

"My boyfriend asked me to marry him, so I passed out," I mumbled.

Maybe it was the needle in my arm, or maybe it was Tim's kind face, but truth poured out of me now that my mom was out of sight.

Tim chuckled. "Is that the boy who's following us in that beamer?"

"Yes."

"You did all that to get out of saying, no?" Tim asked.

"No! I wanted to say yes . . . but here's the kicker: I have cancer." I rubbed my throat as I said it. "Have you heard of anaplastic thyroid cancer?" I asked.

Tim's face contorted with sympathy. He'd heard of it. Less than one percent of thyroid cancer mutates into such a demon.

"It's spread, and I don't have long."

"Why didn't you tell me this back at the wedding, dear?" Tim asked.

"I haven't told my parents," I admitted. It would be the most expensive therapy session I'd ever receive.

Tim sighed and ran his eyes through the cab before returning to me. "And what about the boy?"

"He's the only one that knows. I told him the night we met."

I thought back to it, surprised by my behavior. It was then when I realized I never actually told him. I wouldn't have. Not even in a fury of panic.

"Are you afraid to marry the boy because of what it will do to him when you're gone?" Tim asked as he checked my vitals.

"Something like that," I mused.

"Well, dear, I don't have an answer for you. But if the boy asked, and he knows, I'm guessing he's already made his decision." Tim had no idea how profound his simple comment was.

He was right. Easton had already made his decision. He was going when I was. Regardless if we'd end up in the same place or not. It wouldn't stop him from trying. I couldn't control Easton's life any more than I could control mine.

I ran through the gauntlet of tests, and Easton waited patiently. And when the doctor came in to tell me my latest updates, he was there by my side. The cancer was in my thyroid, trachea, lymph nodes, and now my liver. It would soon spread to my lungs and bones. It wasn't news to me, but hearing it out loud was a different kind of pain. The kind that made your face wince and your body squirm. The hours ticked by, and the sky had begun to lighten by the time I was discharged. I would later tell my mom it was dehydration.

That was, until I found the right moment for the truth that would shatter her heart. Was there ever a fitting moment for such a thing? The burden was now too heavy to carry on my own. I needed to admit it to myself and everyone I loved that I needed help. I could see now from this event that it was unfair of me to place such a heavy burden on Easton alone.

"Easton?" I asked, looking out his car window.

"Huh?"

"I don't believe I ever told you I had cancer." I turned my attention to his face. "How did you know?" I studied him. He glanced up into his rearview mirror, then to me.

"I *know* things. I can't explain it."

"Try." I was short.

"The same way I can tell if another is a Tethered Soul, I feel it. Their spirit's age, fine like wine. Perfected as much as a flawed being can be. I feel their pain—too grand for one life alone."

Easton glanced over to see how I was taking the news, then he studied the road ahead of him. "It's the same as when I met you. I knew when you pulled me off of the bridge . . . the very instant when I looked into your eyes on the sidewalk. Your heart was meant for me. A perfect soulmate in an imperfect world. But I felt your time was limited, like a battery draining low. I would live forever, and you would perish shortly thereafter meeting you. The only thing worse was the thought of never knowing you at all."

Easton spoke quietly, his words laced with the heartache only he could ever know.

"Yes," I whispered. The word spilled out onto my breath.

Easton's brows furrowed as his eyes shifted between me and the road.

"Yes," I said. My voice raspy, but I meant it with all that I was.

"I want to marry you! I want to spend the rest of my life loving you. I don't have much to give, but—"

"Beck, don't. Let me be the judge of that." Easton reached over and squeezed my hand. His eyes were wet with love.

CHAPTER 25

"It was just dehydration! . . . Yeah, they gave me an IV, and I went home."

I paced around my living room, watching my feet as they continued their shuffle. It was the moment I lifted my gaze and caught Easton's expression that I knew I was doing more harm than good. I listened to my mom on the other line. Then, with a heavy heart, I asked.

"Mom? Can I come by today?"

The minutes began to tick as soon as I got off the phone. Ninety short minutes was all I had to prepare myself to tell my parents that they would be alive to bury their daughter. I grabbed at my stomach when it churned with nausea and sat down on the sofa. Still exhausted from the night spent in the hospital, the climb I had ahead of me seemed damn near impossible.

Easton rubbed my shoulders and kissed the top of my head. I looked up at him, suddenly upset that I had made this decision, here and now.

"Don't make me do this alone!"

"Never. I'll be right by your side," he said.

"Hi, honey! Come on in!" My mom kissed my cheek and pulled me inside. "Thanks for taking care of her, Easton!" Mom kissed his cheek, too.

We stepped into the shadows of the house. My eyes took longer than usual to adjust. Dad was watching a game on TV and said hello with a wave from the couch. My first concern was getting him to turn the TV off. Sure, it was as simple as asking, but I'd never asked my parents to stop what they were doing and give me their full attention. I didn't want to worry them. And yet, that's what I had come here to do. I dispelled the thought with a shake of the head. It had to be said. I believed that now.

"Can I get you two an iced tea? You have to stay hydrated!" Mom said. I wished it was that simple.

"Yeah, that sounds great, Mom."

I moved to the sofa and joined my dad. He gave me a pat on the knee. The secret that I'd been holding in since early March was growing heavier. It came out by way of clammy palms and ringing ears. My legs began to tremble.

"Well, you didn't miss much last night. After you left, everything kind of just wound down. We threw rice at your brother and his wife. Oh! I get to say that now! His *wife*!" Mom said.

Two ice teas were set in front of Easton and me. He took a polite sip, but I was too nervous to move.

"I'm so glad you two are paying us some attention! I know you're so busy with work and school—it's like I never get to see you anymore!" Mom said. More bricks added to my already too heavy load.

"I quit my job!" I blurted out. It was the first of many to come. Dad flinched but continued watching the game.

"Oh, well . . . if you need help with the bills, I'm sure we could—"

"I stopped going to school, too. So . . . maybe you should stop paying for my tuition."

That got my dad's attention. He reached for the remote and turned the TV off. Nobody said anything. The tension boiled inside me like a pressure cooker. I rubbed my wet hands onto my jeans. I wanted to say it in a way that wouldn't hurt, but I feared it would tumble out just like my other confessions and catch fire.

My mom cleared her throat, unable to say anything nice. She held it in and waited for my dad to speak.

"You kids these days think that a college education isn't worth squat, but—"

"There's more, Dad. Dad?" He continued to talk over me. Ramblings of the value I couldn't see.

"Dad!" I yelled.

The mood shifted. What once was disappointment was now shock. Soon, it would be devastation. I should have rehearsed it. Came up with the perfect way to tell them. But I didn't, and they were going to have to live with my mistake.

"I . . . didn't pass out because I was dehydrated. I passed out because I'm fighting . . . um, an illness. And my immune system is working really hard, but it can't do it all," I said.

I refused to look at them, but I could feel the disarray pass through the thick air.

"What? Like cancer?" Dad asked.

"No! Don't say that!" hissed my mom.

"Yes," I replied.

Mom sucked in a sharp breath. I kept my eyes glued to the floor. A shower of shame rained down upon me. As if it were my doing, my choice.

"Well, we're going to fight it! I'm going to call Doctor Allen. He'll know what to do!"

Mom jumped to her feet. She walked herself in a couple of circles before making it to the phone. Fight or flight was a common reaction. Like my mom, the fight was my first response too. Until the doctor showed me the images. My chance to fight was fleeting.

Arguing erupted overhead as Pops tried to change her course of action. Shots fired back and forth, fueled by fear. I sat silenced. My knuckles, white. When Easton reached his limit, he stood and began to speak of the facts. And just as he did, my parents shifted their focus to learning what they could instead of changing what they'd yet to understand.

"Everly had papillary thyroid cancer. The symptoms were easy to overlook, and she was young. She had a biopsy done via fine-needle aspiration. That's when a tiny needle goes into the nodule and collects cells. Unfortunately, the specific cells collected in this fine needle tip were not the cells that were mutated, but the surrounding cells from her thyroid. Her results were inconclusive. It's a usual reading. More times than not, it means there's no cancer."

Easton commanded the room much like he did when he told the make-believe story of how we met at my brother's wedding. I assumed that he had gathered all of this information after he read my medical files in the hospital. Perhaps he'd spoken to my doctor. The air was so thick that I was sure I would suffocate right then and there, never making it my full term. My parents were frozen. It was the most I'd ever seen them focus on anything in my entire life. They absorbed every morsel of detail that Easton spilled, while I sat on the couch dripping with guilt, sweat, and tears.

"On rare occasions—less than one percent—thyroid cancer will morph. The cells will mutate into a highly abnormal and aggressive form of cancer called anaplastic. The prognosis is poor. And in Everly's case, it has already spread. I regret to inform you that she is not a candidate for chemotherapy and radiation. Her cancer is resistant to treatment." Easton spoke with poise. His performance was captivating.

Darkness blanketed the sky as it did the hearts of my parents. It took a long time to convince them this was their new reality. What felt like an eternity, was probably closer to a couple of hours. But they were some of the most challenging hours of my twenty-two years. There had been breakdowns, and several stages of acceptance. Shock, anger, denial, and bargaining. I knew that they would continue to play on repeat for quite some time, but I held on to the hope that eventually, they would cycle out of these stages and move through depression and finally, one day, acceptance. Possibly, they could find happiness there.

Mom was stuck in denial. She was racking her brain over all the possibilities. As if I hadn't already considered all of it.

"Mom, stop! I'm exhausted! I've already accepted that I'm on the fast track. I'm not saying you must also, but you need to respect my decision during this time. I'm not a kid anymore! I'm the mature woman that you raised me to be, and this is my life. And I've chosen not to spend the rest of it in the hospital or hovering over the toilet, sick. I don't want an experimental treatment! I don't! There's nothing they can do anyway. And I'm OK with it. I'm focusing on my quality of life now. And Easton's been helping with that. We've been experiencing things I've always dreamed of. It's been some of the best weeks of my life, and I mean that!"

Mom's face melted into her hands, and she began to weep again. Pop helped to hold her as her knees buckled. It was hard to witness and even worse to know I was the cause of it.

"I'm sorry I didn't tell you sooner. I wish I'd been stronger. I wasn't. I was afraid of hurting you guys."

Despite how much I cared for them, I just wanted it to be over. I willed them to see it from my perspective—to give me the green light that I needed to live my life as I saw fit. I pushed off the couch and walked to the fireplace. Had there been a fire going, my arm wouldn't have been so cold pushed against the red brick. Easton was getting antsy too. He'd moved to the kitchen to get some water.

"Look, I don't know what's going to happen when I die, but if for some reason I'm still here on earth, following you two around, I'm going to be really pissed if you guys are sad all the time. I just want you to be happy when you think of me. I want to be celebrated. I want to feel the love, not the sorrow!" I ran my fingers through my hair as I felt the last remaining fight drain out of me. "Would it be too much to ask for that while I'm alive too?" I searched the eyes of my mom, then my dad. Both sets were red and swollen.

After a long moment of unspoken despair, my dad pulled me into his embrace. Everyone was out of things to say and had all but given up. I pressed my ear against his heart and took comfort in its beat and the smell of vanilla tobacco.

"There's one more thing," I said.

Pops groaned. He couldn't bear any more news. I looked to Easton, and for the first time that day, I felt a shift in my mood. I buried my face into my dad's chest and squinted my burning eyes tight for a moment before pulling away.

"We're getting married . . ."

Easton's face lit with pride as he thrust to his feet and re-entered the room, ready for hugs. My parents were a little slower to react.

My eyes flickered between the three pairs of eyes. Two uncertain, and one losing hope. Did I need to explain myself? Wasn't it obvious? Had we not gone through this for the last two or three hours? "Pop! I love him! And I'm going to spend the rest of my life with him! Now, I would appreciate it if you celebrate our love and give me this last memory!" I said with a hand on my hip.

Like clockwork, my mom raised her arms to Easton, pulling him into an embrace and welcoming him to the family. It took a little coaxing, but it's what I wanted to see. A genuine smile spread across my face and into my eyes. My dad cried.

Regardless of the pain, heartbreak, and sheer exhaustion, I walked out of that dark house feeling lighter than I had in a long time. I felt the gravitational pull that tethered me to earth, to my body . . . disconnect. My spirit was beginning to free. I was halfway packed for my departure, and I wondered if this was a mandatory step in me letting go. As Easton opened my car door for me and I caught his eye, I realized something else.

The second half to cutting my tether was saying goodbye to Easton.

CHAPTER 26

It was well after dinner by the time that Easton took me home. He stayed to feed Yeti and made a small batch of pasta for the dinner that we'd missed. I didn't eat.

"Thank you. I couldn't have done it without you," I said. A plaid throw blanket wrapped around my shoulders.

Easton ate his dinner, leaning against the refrigerator. "I was happy to be there for you. It's never an easy conversation to have."

"You act like you've had it before. And how did you know all that stuff? I didn't even know all of it!" I said.

"I used to be a doctor. I glanced at your chart when you were resting at the hospital."

A doctor?

Why did this surprise me? I pictured Easton back in my parent's living room, breaking the news to them. It seemed as if he'd done it a hundred times before. And if I stretched my imagination just a little further and pictured him with a white coat, holding a clipboard, it almost made sense. My eyes began to blur as visions of my blue-eyed boyfriend became a doctor, and I knew it was time for me to go to bed. My mind was cooked, my heart hurt, and my eyes were playing tricks on me.

Easton stayed with me as he had been doing more often. I slept better with him here. Sometimes in the middle of the night, I would slide my foot over until I found his warmth. It was enough to soothe my anxiety and put me back to sleep. Other times, I would go overboard and wake up smothering him. But tonight, I did neither. Tonight, I slept like I was already six feet deep.

When the morning came, so did my mom. Easton let her in while I was still dead to the world. I woke up to the chatter downstairs. I slipped on a robe and headed down the stairs to see her, only stopping halfway when I heard her soft-spoken voice.

"Then you can text me when you're on your way. It's going to be her brother and his wife, her friends, Lindsay, Lisa, Shannon—"

The stairs creaked under my weight. I made myself known.

"Mom? What are you doing here?"

"I, um, well I wanted to see you. I know that last night was difficult. I brought you coffee and flowers."

Mom stood grasping a coffee from Fresh Grounds. The bags under her eyes were as dark as her eyebrows, and she was still dressed in the same clothes from yesterday.

I took the coffee from her and wrapped my arms around her. Only then did I see Easton was sitting at the kitchen island in his boxers. He took the moment of my embrace and scurried upstairs. Presumably to get dressed, but maybe to give us privacy as well.

"Mom, I'm worried about you."

"No, you listen to me," Mom said. She sat me down at the island where Easton and she had shared a secret conversation just moments before. "I know I look like *trash*, but that's only because I stayed up all night . . ."

I raised my hand and slapped it down on my leg.

"I had a lot to think about. Now, I'm not saying I'm OK with this, but your dad and I talked, and we've come to the conclusion that you have enough on your plate. And the last thing you need is to be worried about us. We want your days filled with love and laughter. And, honey"—her eyes began to water, and her voice rose—"I promise you that I'm going to try my hardest to stay that way after too. And I hope that it can put your mind to ease."

Her chin wobbled as large tears ran down her cheeks. She crumbled into my chest. I wrapped my arms around my mom and held her as she wept. Tears streamed down my face as I stared out my window with blurry vision. Yeti's instincts took over and she nestled my mom, helping to break her episode.

"I know it's hard, Mom, but that's what I want. Thank you."

We shared our coffee talking about the wedding. I told her how I envisioned it. No minister, no music, no audience, just Easton and I professing our love for one another and committing to the short time I had left. I was tired as it was, and I didn't want to have to entertain guests. In addition to that, I didn't want to say goodbye to all of them. It was hard enough to tell my parents. Extending that conversation to aunts and uncles, friends and co-workers . . . *no thank you.*

A wedding was about devoting your love to someone, and that's all I wanted from it. And maybe a ring. Nothing fancy. It could be made of twine or the stem of a daisy—just something to slip onto my finger.

It wasn't easy to convince my mom that a wedding could be anything other than traditional, but after a squeeze of her hand and a flash of pleading in my eyes, she stopped to listen.

My mom visited every day after that. Mostly, she would come mid-day as not to barge in before Easton had a chance to get dressed. Sometimes, my dad would accompany her. I would gush to her about Easton, and she would cry every time. But she was sleeping and changing her clothes, so things were looking up. Both of my parents were run down, but they tried their hardest to stay positive for me. Even though I could see through their charades, I appreciated the effort.

I was thankful that my parents did the heavy lifting when it came to Carter. They told him in private so that I wouldn't have to do it myself. When he had time to collect himself, he came over to see me. Chloe stayed back, but she baked homemade cookies and sent them with Carter. I knew she wanted to give us privacy to talk, and I respected that. But Carter and I didn't talk much. It wasn't his language. It wasn't that he didn't care—just that he didn't express himself with words. I still felt all of his emotion as we sat together in my living room. And I felt his body trembling when he hugged me goodbye. We all express ourselves in different ways, and a part of me took to the way Carter did it.

In the following days, I showed my mom where my letters were. We both cried over that one. And I told her all of the things Yeti liked and didn't like. I told her I wanted to be cremated.

There were few possessions I held dear to my heart, but I made a list of things that I felt were essential and I wanted my parents to disperse to loved ones. The rest, I wanted them to donate. And soon too. I saw no purpose for them to store boxes of my things in their garage for years to come. It wouldn't lessen the pain, and it wouldn't bring me back. My "keep list" contained only three things.

The first thing I cherished most in this world was a pair of diamond earrings my grandmother had given me when I graduated high school. She'd gotten them as a Mother's Day gift from her late son. The uncle I'd never met. Because she cherished them, I was nothing short of honored to have received them. I treated them as such too. I pulled them out of the top drawer of my dresser, where they'd been resting in a felt bag.

"Grandma gave me these."

My mom knew very well what they were. Her mother wore them every day for two decades. That was, until she gifted them to me.

My mom sat quietly on my bed, reminiscing over the earrings and the very situation we found ourselves in.

"Actually, I'm going to wear these for the ceremony," I said.

It was funny how I saved them for a special occasion only. I never thought there would be a shortage of time or special occasions for me to wear them. If I had, I would have worn them every day as my grandmother did. It was a foolish way of thinking. And If I had it to do all over again, I would enjoy the things I loved most. I would wear them out until they were unusable, and then I would love them some more.

Instead of placing the earrings back in the drawer, I slipped them into my ears. My mom jumped up to help me with the backings. When she pulled away, tears had formed in her eyes. It wasn't often that I saw her without them.

The second tangible item I loved too much to see thrown out was my first stuffed animal. It was a tattered old frog that my mom got me when I was in utero. She thought I was a boy. It was a dream she had of two boys playing outside by a pond—fishing for crawdads. It could have been a premonition, in fairness to her, because my brother and I did go on to do that. And I could have passed as a boy with a baseball cap and a mud-painted face. Either way, I loved the frog. And I always imagined that I would give it to my firstborn.

"Can you give this to Carter's baby? When he has one." I shrugged. "Maybe you could tell him it's from his Aunt Everly."

Carter's kids would be cuties. They would have his light complexion and Chloe's great bone structure. They would be loud and outspoken until it came time to express their emotions. They would have my green eyes.

My mom took the frog and cradled it in her lap. She forced a smile and waited patiently for me to continue.

"And, last but not least, these." I resurfaced from my closet, holding three diaries—one purple suede, one zebra print, and one, a more mature faux leather. Each resembled the maturity at which I started the journal.

I sat down on the bed next to my mom, and a picture fell out of the first book I opened. One of Lindsay and I in the sixth grade. Fake blood ran down our mouths and covered our hands. I remembered that day like yesterday.

"That was Halloween. She had the capsules of fake blood that you pop in your mouth," I said. I could still remember the way they tasted—like cough syrup.

I flipped through the zebra print diary. Pictures were glued to the pages, and a colorful display of rainbow ink bled across the pages. I ran my fingers over the imprinted pen marks. The more emotion poured onto the page, the more the words felt like reversed brail.

"What's that?" Mom pointed to a receipt I had taped into the journal.

"Huh. That was a receipt for a movie."

I glanced over the entry and read a quick blurb about how the love of my life sat behind me and threw popcorn at me during the movie. I was sure that he was the one. But I was eleven, and he was nothing more than a cute stranger.

I closed the journal, embarrassed by what was inside.

"On second thought, maybe we burn them?"

Mom laughed. She took the journals from my lap and added them to her collection of strange things that I deemed essential.

"I would never do that! I can't wait to read them. I'm allowed to read them, right?" she asked.

Should I let her read them? All I knew was that I cherished them. My memories and personal thoughts captured in three books. I wasn't sure that they should be *read*. What if it hurt her feelings? The last thing I wanted was to leave her with lasting anger from when I hit puberty!

My face contorted in regret. "No, seriously . . . let's burn them!"

"What! No! We can't do that!"

"Mom, I can't have you read all the times I was mad at you and took it out on my diary! That's cruel and unusual punishment!"

Mom's face twisted with the realization that there were in fact, negative things hidden deep within the pages.

"I won't read them, then. I'll wrap a bow around them and place them on my nightstand. I'll keep them close, but I won't read them."

I searched my mom's eyes. She was unwilling to let them go up in flames and smoke. Something so important to me couldn't be lost in such a way. I gave in.

"Tie it *tight*," I said.

CHAPTER 27

Music filled the air, and my mom twirled with a glass of wine in her hand. It was mid-day, and I happen to know she skipped breakfast. I only cared that she was happy, and it appeared that she was. She set her glass down, humming to the music, and separated a lock of my hair to be curled.

I watched myself in the mirror. I wasn't sure if my bathroom lights were washing my already pale complexion out, or if I was losing what little color I had, but my face was lackluster and sallow. It wasn't the familiar face of a glowing bride.

"Now, do you want it up, or maybe like this? Oh! This is romantic . . ." She held a single strand from the front and pinned it back behind my ear.

"Yeah, I like that."

"It's going to be cold, you know. A storm is coming in. You're going to need to wear a jacket. Even if it doesn't match your dress!" Mom said.

"I know."

I couldn't help but wonder what the girl in the mirror would look like a couple of years older and healthier. Mom finished my hair, placing a crystal pin in my trestle. She was right; it was romantic.

I stepped into my dress, holding on to my mom's arm for balance. While the dress was white, it was anything but traditional. More of a sundress than anything else. Woven eyelet flowers and lace. The straps were thin and crossed in the back. The length hit just above the knee but it had a generous and even sexy slit up one leg. It wouldn't show unless I took a step. Or perhaps twirled.

"You look gorgeous!" Mom clapped her hands to her mouth.

"Mom, stop! I look like I'm going to a backyard barbecue!" I tried to downplay the moment. But the truth was, I felt pretty special, and I was fighting back the tears myself.

"Can you put a little makeup on me?" I asked.

Though I never wore very much makeup myself, it wasn't because I didn't like it. I just preferred the natural look. Today, though, the natural look was unsettling. It had been growing worse as time slipped by. My mom dusted a muted mauve over my cheeks, bringing them back to life. A light highlight almost made me look lit from within. If I didn't know any better, I would say I looked almost thriving in a youthful, healthy way.

"Thank you, Mom," I said.

"Oh, honey. Thank you for letting me be a part of your special day. I wish I was there to see you."

"There's nothing to see. We're just spending time together. It's . . . I don't know . . . personal. It's only fitting to keep it private."

Our wedding was going to be as unique as our situation. One dying girl, and one undying boy. A love that would last forever. It wasn't for prying eyes. Only for the two of us to share with one another.

"Hello?" Easton called out from downstairs.

"Looks like it's that time!" I said to my mom. "Are you sure you can drive home?"

"Oh yeah. I've only had one glass!" Mom walked beside me as I went down the stairs, supporting my elbow even though I was barefoot and arguably more stable than she was.

Easton clasped his heart at first sight of me in my sundress.

"I'm honored. What did I do to deserve you?" Easton muttered as his eyes took in the length of me.

"Oh, I have to take a picture!" Mom waved her hands wildly and pranced over to her purse to retrieve her phone. I rolled my eyes. Though I completely understood and wanted a picture myself, I still hated to stand for the barrage of photos. It took away from the magic of the moment.

Easton wrapped his warm arms around my waist, and my mom snapped several photos as he kissed my temple and beamed with pride. I ignored my mom for a moment and reached up to his face and pulled him in for a kiss. All time stopped, and the camera faded away.

That was, until she said, "Wait, I didn't get that. One more time?"

I threw my head back and groaned.

"One more time!" Easton agreed.

I laughed, and he devoured my face, making ridiculous animalistic sounds, and the camera snapped over and over again.

"OK, Mom, we've got to go before it starts raining!"

We said goodbye to my mom and promised to see her that night for dinner. Only I knew it was something more than that. I'd overheard her and Easton talking about it. She was planning some sort of reception for us. I had to make the internal decision not to fight it. I would have to act surprised too. That was something I wasn't good at, but I hoped I could pull it off.

I slipped on some flats—I wasn't going to walk through the field in heels—and my mom handed me a jacket. I scowled when I realized it would clash, but I took it anyway. Easton and I both sighed in relief as the car doors shut and we were finally to ourselves.

"You look absolutely stunning, and if we didn't have to beat this storm, I would have taken you upstairs to ravish you," Easton said.

I giggled. "*After* my mom left."

"Yes! *After*!" Easton's eyes widened with his smile.

Though it was now the seventh of May, the wet weather of April had lingered. Perhaps it was the last storm of the season. The sky that was once on the cusp of turning warm earlier in the week was now grey and chilly. The condensation lingered in the air like a low-hanging cloud. We drove over the New River Bridge, my gaze glued to the very spot we met. I turned my focus to Easton.

"Why were you going to jump that day?" I was confident now that after everything I knew, he would finally tell me the truth.

Easton grabbed my hand and brought it to his lips for a warm kiss.

"When you've lived as much as I have, it's easy to become picky. I no longer live past my twenties. I choose not to. Being old is hard work. Your mind starts to slip, which can be difficult for someone, such as me. I have a lot of memories; it can be messy when reality turns into a spectrum. Plus, your vision starts to go, your body begins to ache. Things that used to be fun, just aren't anymore. That's why I prefer to live my lives basking in the glow of youth. Then, I choose to start over. Go back."

"That's so sad!"

"Yeah, it is. But I can't continue into my thirties. That's when families start. It's just not my place."

"You've never had a family?"

"No. Not until now." Easton looked over at me with a warm smile.

We pulled into the same spot we did the time we were almost eaten by bears. Our campsite was now unrecognizable with new growth. We got out of the car, and I slid my arms into my jacket. A part of me wondered why I even bothered with a dress in the first place. I was chilled from head to toe.

Hand in hand, Easton and I waded through the tall wet grass. And all the while, his winged dragonfly remained by his side.

"Oh my God! I think that's the same one as last time!"

"It is," Easton said.

I could tell there was more to the story, judging by his calm demeanor.

"And? Are you going to tell me? Or leave me guessing?"

Easton laughed. "It's a loved one. From time to time, they visit after they've passed on. Sometimes it's a dragonfly; sometimes it's a sunset painted just for me; And sometimes it's as simple as a draft in stale air."

"You're telling me your ex-girlfriend is coming to our wedding?"

Easton laughed louder. "No! It's not my ex-girlfriend."

I giggled, stepping over a fallen tree. My dress soaking up the dew and becoming wet against my legs.

"Have you ever gotten chills? Goosebumps out of nowhere, and you knew it was something. Or someone?"

I nodded. "I've felt it. It's like that thing you can't explain?"

"Yeah! That's it! That's the bond you've shared with someone that still exists when they don't."

I thought about all the times I felt the presence of someone that wasn't there. The times I was so captivated by a bird in flight or the beauty of a sunset. I wondered how I would show myself to Easton in the years to come.

We approached the clearing where Easton confessed his life's secret to me. The dead tree was lit with twinkling lights that glowed through the thick grey fog like fireflies. White roses covered a stand-alone trellis, and music played softly into the air. Not a soul in sight. My heart skipped as I cupped my hands around my open mouth.

"What's this?" Tears pricked the corners of my eyes.

"Beck, you have a lot of people that love you."

Easton tucked my hair behind my shoulder and leaned down for a kiss full of magic and wonder. I'd never felt so loved in my entire life. The chills from my wet dress melted away with the beauty of our spot. It was majestic and spellbinding, like a fairy tale made for me. The dead tree was brought back to life with the love of my family and friends.

I picked up a rose from the arched trellis and breathed it in as I looked out to the Truly River. It was invisible due to the cloud cover, but that didn't make it any less beautiful. I was nearly convinced I could step off the cliffside, and the low hanging clouds would carry my weight. I wondered what it would be like to nestle into the plushness of a cool cloud and fall asleep. I turned to Easton as he was setting up a tripod and a video camera.

"What are you doing?" I asked as I ran the thornless rose through my hands.

"It was at the request of your parents. The only way they were willing to accept our privacy for today was to capture it on film. They wanted to have a movie made of it," Easton said.

"So, I have to wait to consumate our marriage. Is that what you're telling me?"

Easton laughed. "Well, I'm sure there's an *off* button around here somewhere!" he said with a blush.

He pushed record and joined me under the trellis. His hair, weighted down by the moisture, fell to the sides of his eyes, making them look more vivid in contrast. I wrapped my arms around his waist and rested my head on his chest. I closed my eyes and listened to the soft playing music. "Surrender" by Natalie Taylor. The words—"My love will find you"—floated around us. Easton began to rock us into a slow dance. Our feet never left the ground.

"Easton, you found me. And for that, I'm so thankful. But for the life of me, I can't figure out, why now?" I dug my chin into his chest and gazed up into his eyes.

"I've been looking for you, for a very, very long time." His fingers twisted in the back of my hair as he spoke. "I can't tell you why now. All I know is, we were meant for each other. And I wouldn't have it any other way, no matter how short our time."

"Same."

"Visit me? If you can," Easton asked.

"You mean like a dragonfly?"

"In your own way. Whatever you choose. I'll know it's you," he said.

"I promise." My voice came out horse, the tone splintered.

Easton squeezed me tightly, and his chin began to quiver. I buried my face against him wanting to crawl inside and live there forever. Maybe I would. Live inside his heart. Perhaps that would be the only place I existed after this.

With a heavy heart, Easton pulled me away and lowered onto one knee. I took a step back as he opened a small box between us. A single oval diamond sparkled against the blue felt of the box. The light danced inside the diamond as Easton's hands trembled.

"I can't tell you I know what the future holds. I don't know. But if I know one thing, it's that I will never stop loving you. If you let me, I'll carry a piece of you with me, wherever I go."

I dabbed the tears in the corners of my eyes with shaky hands.

"Yes! Absolutely! Take as much of me as you can fit. Take it all! I want to stay with you forever," I said to Easton, and anyone else who was listening that may grant such a wish.

Easton took the ring and threw the box over his shoulder. We both chuckled as he slid the diamond ring onto my ring finger. It was a perfect fit.

"I love you," I said.

"I love you, Beck." Easton wiped away a tear with the sleeve of his jacket. Then, with one quick sweep, he lifted me into his arms and swung me around, dipping me backward towards the camera.

"She's mine! All mine! Mrs. Green!" Easton shouted to the video recorder. I giggled like a schoolgirl. Of course, we weren't legally married, nor was I legally changing my name. It was so much more than that. Something documentation could never touch.

Easton spun me around until I couldn't take anymore, and I begged him to stop. By the time my feet touched the ground, my head had continued to swim. My vision was just becoming sharp when I saw Easton shaking a bottle of champagne.

"No!"

He popped the cork, and champagne exploded into the air and rained down upon us. I screamed and took off, running behind the old dead tree. Easton chased me, spraying every last drop he could. The taste of almond champagne dripped from my hair and down onto my lips.

We ran around the tree like kids in love. The bottom half of my dress tinged with the color of earth and bark embedded into the lace. By the time Easton caught me, I was begging to be captured. I made myself clumsy just enough to fall to the ground in a bed of tall grass. Of course, he would never let me fall alone. I laid my curled hair onto the ground and searched his eyes as he realized that the fall was merely a ploy. I bit my bottom lip and his head whipped around to examine the camera's position.

"Are we out of sight?" I asked.

"Uh-huh." Easton said, breathing harder now than when he was chasing me.

Excitement sparked in his eyes as his lips crashed into mine, our love manifesting in its own celebration. One that would leave me too much of a mess for my surprise reception. Perhaps, I should have thought of that before I enticed Easton to make love to me on the forest floor underneath a tower of roses and fairy lights. Although, I assured myself it wouldn't have changed anything.

I lay, basking in the afterglow, on his outreached arm. My legs were itchy from the grass, and I watched the misty grey clouds dance through the sky. We talked about life until the first drops of rain crashed down on us.

"We should go," Easton said, looking at me.

I sighed and turned to look back at him. Our noses were nearly touching and grass was peaking up all around us.

"I guess it's time," I said. I didn't want to leave.

Easton helped me up, and I made it to my feet. My balance off for a minute or two. He collected the small speaker and camera and turned them off.

"They'll never know," Easton said as he placed the camera in his jacket pocket.

"Do we leave all this here?" I asked. The raindrops coming more frequently.

"Yeah! They'll come to clean it up tomorrow. Come on, let's go. We still have to hike out!"

By the time we reached the car, it didn't matter that my dress was soaked in champagne and I had grass stains riding up the back. We were drenching wet. Same as the night I met Easton.

"Déjà vu!" I said after slamming the car door closed.

Easton laughed, "Who would have thought on that stormy evening that we would be married by May."

"Me," I said.

"Oh! Come on! You didn't know what you thought of me!" Easton laughed.

I echoed his laughter.

"That's not true! I thought you were deranged! And most likely homeless . . ."

I giggled, knowing that Easton was appalled by my honesty. I bet he never saw that one coming. I pulled down the sun visor and checked myself in the mirror. I looked like a drowned rat.

"Good Lord! I can't go to my parent's house like this!"

Easton tried to be supportive. He tried to hold in his amusement, but my white dress was green with lover's passion. He burst into laughter.

"We'll make a pit stop. Two, actually. I should change too! I'll just text your mom that we're going to run a little late."

"OK, good call. Hopefully we're not too late though. I would feel bad."

I turned the heat on and kicked off my wet shoes. Huddling into a ball for warmth near the vent.

"Think you will move some of your stuff in?" I asked.

"I've been sneaking some things over slowly. It feels weird to be at my place now. It doesn't even feel like home!"

"And my place does?"

"*You* feel like home. And your place is covered in your things. It's comforting," Easton said.

Thunder cracked, and the sky lit up in a brilliant blue seconds later. I watched the electricity dance outside my window like a show made only for my eyes. Nature had never been so beautiful to me as it was in the last couple of weeks. The colors of the earth had never been so brilliant.

We continued our drive talking about what he would move over and what he would do with his place now that it would be vacant. I tried to coax him into telling me what my mom had planned for the surprise reception, but he was a stubborn one and wouldn't budge.

"Next week, if you're up for it, let's take a trip."

"Where to?" I asked.

"The beach. I want to get you on that horse, and we can gallop through the water! Do you still want to do that?" he asked.

"I forgot about that!" I looked into the sky, waiting for the next light show. "Hey, do you still have that menu?" I asked.

"Yeah, it should be in the glove box." Easton motioned to the compartment before me.

I opened it, and the to-go menu of Hunters fell to the floor. I marveled at the markings: only my bucket list items, none of his. Now I knew why. He'd done everything that he ever wanted to do, and then some. Getting married was probably one of the first "firsts" he'd had in a long time.

"Oh! The northern lights sound pretty good too!" I said, even more interested than the day I mentioned it. I picked up a pen and scratched off "get married."

"Which one did you mark off?" Easton asked.

"Get married. Oh! And dance at my wedding. You wrote that?" I asked as I drove a line through it.

"I barely remember saying it," I confessed.

I coughed, struggling to clear my throat. It wasn't until I pulled my hand away that I saw the bright red blood and tasted the copper in my mouth. I froze, not quite understanding why my hand was painted red. Easton's eyes flickered over to me and I hid my hand in my lap, ashamed. Streaks of blood now on my white dress. I felt Easton's concern, but I didn't look. Not until I heard it.

A horn sounded, long and loud, until the screeching of the tires became deafening. I lifted my head just in time to see the semi plow into the front passenger's side of our car. The headlights blinding the rain-soaked windows. The impact jarring as it sent us through the guard rails of the New River Bridge.

And just for a moment, time seemed to still. The free fall in slow motion as Easton's car plummeted to the river below. All I remained concerned with was hiding my blood-stained hand. The realization that my life was ending there and now had not yet registered.

The force of the crash knocked me half unconscious. I was barely aware that Easton was trying everything he could to free me from my seat belt. But the doors were totaled and fused shut. My seatbelt was jammed. And the same blood on my hand that I'd been desperately trying to hide, now spilled from my head as well.

Ice cold water was rushing in as Easton panicked around me. My consciousness slipping. My fate had found me. It wasn't until the water trickled up to my nose, did I regain full awareness—my adrenaline making one last lap. I struggled to free myself, but couldn't. I tried to hold my breath as the water swallowed me whole.

And there he was. Easton, by my side. His seatbelt free, and his window kicked through. He stayed. I didn't want that for him. And watching his life end was far worse than leaving my body behind. But in these last fleeting moments, I admittedly was comforted by his presence.

As I stared into Easton's eyes through the cold river water on my last breath, hundreds of images flooded my mind. My brother, giving me his last hug. My parents, handing me flowers after my dance recital when I was seven. Easton's shoes hanging off the guardrail of the New River Bridge. The smell of puppy breath and the taste of almond champagne kisses. All as real as if they were happening in the present moment.

I saw the reception at my parent's house. I watched as my mom fell to the floor when the cops told her the news. My reception turning into an impromptu funeral. I wondered if the camera would ever be found, and what picture they would choose to blow up at my service. I hoped it would be the one of Easton kissing me while I laughed wholeheartedly. I bet that was a good one.

My body protested the lack of oxygen. I gasped for air, and ice water rushed into my lungs. I watched the little bubbles escape Easton's nose until I could no longer feel the cold in my extremities. Easton faded away into a sea of darkness, and my mind was finally at rest. I used to think dying was the worst thing that could happen to a person. As it turns out, it's not . . .

Passing away is actually quite natural. I knew how to do it without ever practicing.

Two months ago, I thought the angels were crying for me. One month ago, I knew they were crying for Easton. What I would later come to realize was, they were never crying at all. They were merely washing away the mistakes—the broken and defective. Cleaning the slate for something new. Something better. I would come to understand that this wasn't the end of my life . . . but only the very beginning.

THE SECOND LIFE OF EVERLY BECK

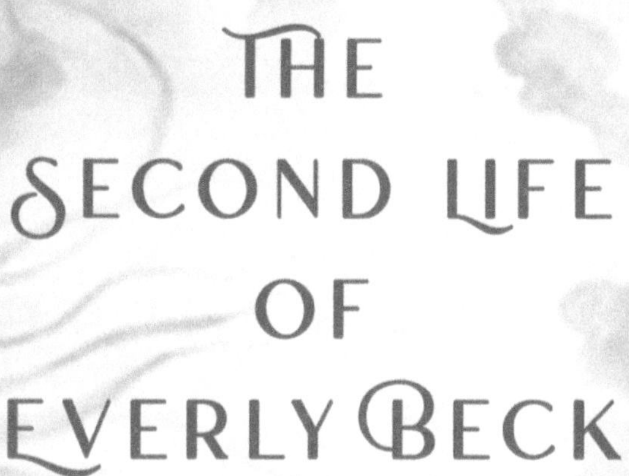
The
Second Life
of
Everly Beck

CHAPTER 1

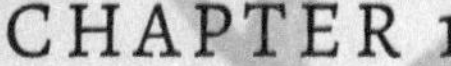

It was the fourteenth time I died, yet the first I wanted to live. Love will do that to you. The fear of losing Beck was far greater than anything I had ever experienced before. It was too soon. I was promised months longer—possibly a year. The wreckage stole everything from me. I didn't know it was an option for her to follow me. I'd never turned a mortal soul into a tethered one before. But that's how much I loved her. Enough to not let go, in sickness and in death. I meant it when I said, *forever.*

As a kid, my memory was clouded, leaving me with major gaps in my timeline. To put it simply, it was the best part. The ignorance. It truly was bliss. Though, for every gift that youth offered, there were drawbacks. Mine was that I had a secret to keep. In all honesty, it was a curse. An isolating burden that would cause me to squander my talents. To be seen but not noticed. If I had opened my mouth freely, I would no longer be "gifted," I'd be a "prodigy," and that was the line I drew between being normal and being something else entirely. A Tethered Soul was a tortured soul.

As a young boy that'd been around the block a dozen times or more, I mostly lived in the present. Being young was the best part of it all. No responsibilities. No backache, stiff knees, or dilapidated vision. I was damn near invincible. Or at least, that's what it seemed like. But unlike every other childhood I'd lived before, this one showed great promise when a little towheaded girl moved in across the street.

This is the story of my second life with Everly Beck.

Beck had survived death. I'd never been more sure of anything in my life. That's why I found myself in an underground gambling ring making dirty money; I had someone to provide for. Somewhere over the horizon, I had a wife, and I wanted to give her the world. There were, however, a few tasks that needed completion first, and I'd been working through them tirelessly. First, I had a standing appointment to see Clouse Charles, assuming he was still alive. Either way, at 3:00 PM, in the basement of a back-alley bar in the most dangerous part of Stills, I'd be handing over a large sum of cash for something much more valuable to me. It wasn't the first time I'd rubbed elbows with men such as these. Feral, savage beasts. Each with an outstanding criminal record. Because when you've been around as long as I have, it's hard to keep finances above board.

I was winning amongst the testosterone and cigar smoke when a leggy redhead placed my drink on the table with a wink. I'd seen that face before—the one that begged for a reason to run away and start anew. I smiled at her, taking in the invitation. She was a pure heart, much better than this place called for. I briefly imagined how I could turn her life around. How her troubled blue eyes could shift in the light of day. I could save her from this life. I wanted to. But I couldn't save them all, and my heart had already been given away. She wasn't Beck, and no matter how I pretended, none of them were. I took a sip of my drink, focusing on the game again, and when it was my turn to lay cards down, I did carefully. I collected my chips at the protest of the beast at the round table.

The men shouted, throwing their hands in the air. One went as far as repositioning his gun on the table to point in my direction. I won the pot when it mattered most, but lost often enough to make it believable. This wasn't the kind of place where you wanted to be taken for an outsider. All of these men had short lives ahead of them, and none were bright. Their energy didn't lift into the air; it sank like a heavy poisonous gas that cloaked the ground in darkness.

I'd been inhaling cigar smoke for four hours in anticipation of my meeting, but I couldn't keep this up much longer. My welcome had worn. When my 3:00 showed up, I withdrew from the game and cashed out with the bartender. I patted Clouse on the back and pretended not to notice as he marveled at my stature the way he had twenty-some years ago. "Still drinking scotch?" I asked. He smiled, and his silver-flecked beard split in two as he laughed out loud. "Two," I said to the bartender, tipping him a chip from my winnings.

"Easton Green, you never change, son. I wouldn't believe it if I hadn't seen it with my own eyes." His voice trailed off.

"You're looking well yourself. Do you have the key?" I asked, sliding him his drink.

"Do you have my cut?"

I didn't mess around. I trusted Clouse. He'd been part of a long line of men that dealt with Tethered Souls and other powerful, dangerous beings. Keeping their safe deposit box keys for gaps of time that made little sense to anyone, printing fake IDs and passports when needed. They never asked questions, and they always delivered. All secrets were safe for a cost. I was happy to pay. I slid him a briefcase, and he handed me a single gold key.

"Will you be back, Mr. Green?" Clouse said, peeking into the briefcase, satisfied.

"Always. Keep my account open," I said, throwing back my shot and patting him on the back. It would be the last time he saw me, given his age, but there would always be someone on the other line ready to answer the call of a Tethered Soul—assuming the price was right. I left without turning back, and my stomach twisted when I heard shuffling in my wake. My hair stood on end when a gunshot echoed up the stairwell. The blood drained from my face as I took two stairs at a time. I had seen so much crime that sometimes I could convince myself to turn a blind eye. It was easy to do when the men had black mist pooled at their feet, but as I walked down the alley, I struggled to dismiss the leggy redhead who deserved better. It wasn't my world, however, and I had no choice but to keep on walking.

I proceeded to the bank and withdrew more than enough to get me started with a new life. Over the years, I'd dump my overflow into the account before making my exit into the next life. It was the only nest egg I had, and sometimes, I didn't even have that. I'm not sure what Clouse's men thought Tethered Souls were, but by the service they provided, I had to imagine they thought we were vampires or werewolves. Something that could not only siphon their blood and tear their flesh, but would do so at the drop of a hat. If they had only known we were like them, lonely and broken, caged birds unable to fly . . . well, I don't think they would work for us at all. And my guess was, that's the precise reason Tethered Souls said nothing about who or what they really were to anyone.

I moved swiftly down the streets. The cold air nipping at my nose, and my breath visible. I threw the tail of my scarf over my shoulder and hailed a taxi. The second task at hand was finding an engagement ring. What I dreamed of giving Beck was her original ring, but I knew it was either six feet deep in the Clover Cemetery or her parents had it locked away in a keepsake box amongst her belongings. I considered this when I thought about how meaningful it would be to give her the same ring, but I wasn't about to break into her parents' house looking for it. As tempting as that may be, I needed a replacement.

Doorbells jingled above my head as I walked into a jewelry store. The air was warm and stale. A security guard stood at the door with his arms folded across his chest and a gaze that could deter even the stealthiest of thieves. "Can I help you?" a man asked. His hair was slick and jet black.

"I'm looking for an engagement ring. Simple yet elegant."

The sales agent led me to a row of glamorous bands that gleamed under the encased lighting. My eyes wandered over all the possibilities that could represent my eternal love. As I lost myself in the beauty of my bright future, I heard my eight-year-old adopted brother call out in a memory that was anything but distant . . .

"Trampoline?" Tanner said, halfway out the door.

Becca and I knew there was no time like the present. We took off at a full sprint through her kitchen and out the back door. Her backyard was marvelous. They had a pool and a trampoline. I could almost feel the heat beaming down on me that sunny day. The towheaded girl crawled onto the trampoline and turned around to give me a hand. We were friends the second our hands met.

That day, the three of us jumped high enough to reach the sky. My heart pounded with excitement, and I laughed at the little girl's hair as it stood on end every time she fell. We didn't have to say anything to know we shared an undeniable bond. That was one advantage of being a Tethered Soul. I didn't like it so much when I was old, but then, I could live like that forever and be happy. That day, the day I met my neighbor, the three of us were as free as birds, and my soul soared with no limits.

We played every day that magical, sweltering summer. But it all ended when school started and my family moved across the country. Back then, I couldn't figure out why it felt like déjà vu the very moment I said goodbye to Becca. It hurt me in a way I could only understand when I was older. Even though my memory hadn't yet bloomed, I knew I was losing a very special piece of myself that day.

The older I grew, the more I was convinced of two things. The first, was that Beck was alive, going on her second life. I didn't know how, but I could only imagine that my love was strong enough to pull her soul to mine, and somehow, she stayed behind with me instead of moving on. The second, was that for a brief moment in time, she used to be my neighbor. I felt the gravitational pull towards her when I was young, but now with the clarity of my memory in full force, I could see the synchronicities. The bright blond hair, the green eyes, her name. Becca Reed. It was so close to Beck, it was possible that her new parents named her after her real last name. I never asked.

"This one," I said. I chose a single diamond that sparkled with resounding hope. It looked just like the original had, and I couldn't wait to find Beck and slide it onto her finger. This time, we'd have a proper wedding. And this time, it really would be forever. The only obstacle standing in my way was the third and final task at hand; I had to find her. I'd searched for loved ones before. Scoured the earth for little brothers, past parents, favorite mentors, and one time, a dog. But I'd never searched for her—I'd never looked for another Tethered Soul. When I started with records of her adopted parents' names and a past partial address, nothing had turned up. As was the case with most adopted kids, her records were all marked confidential.

It was hard to remember, but if I recalled correctly, my first few lives had been messy. Of course, nothing had been worse than the original, though. I was nearly six when I died, and until that day, I was nothing more than my father's whipping post. I tried to block it out, but lucky for me, my subconscious did that all on its own—something for which I was thankful for. But the lives that followed were dark and lonely until the rules of the game finally made sense to me. I needed to be there for Beck during this confusing time, because remembering the impossible can be an uphill battle. Especially if the ones you trust to confide in don't accept you for who you really are. And they don't. They never do. Everly was the only person I'd ever told that loved me just the same when all was said and done.

In an ever-changing world, I had always stayed the same, and I knew Beck would too. If I had to guess, she was somewhere out there, trying to get an education in graphic design. It was the one and only clue that I hadn't yet investigated. I hoped she would fall into my lap much like she did on the New River Bridge. Appear out of thin air. Her soul not tethered to earth, but to me. Our love like magnets, fate willing us together.

It didn't happen. Not yet, anyway.

I'd spent two years checking out the golden coast and watching every equestrian that galloped through the crashing waves. It was one of her bucket list items she'd yet to check off, and I somehow envisioned her there with a golden tan and a wild mustang beneath her. Eventually, I rented a home up north, hoping to run into her during a breath-taking display of the northern lights. It was there, underneath the sky's green glow, that I'd find her wrapped in a blanket in need of my warmth. When that, too, never came to fruition, I spent nearly a year crashing weddings while traveling across the country. But I wasn't about to give up. No, I was just getting started.

It hadn't occurred to me earlier that Beck might return home, and I expect that this is because my first life wasn't one I'd ever return to myself. When I tried to empathize with how Beck might feel, I knew I had to go to Clover. There was something about home that could draw a warm soul in, and I had hoped that would be the case with Beck and the small town in which she had grown up. When the plane touched down, I ordered a cab to take me straight to the bridge. The New River Bridge.

CHAPTER 2

I stared out the window of the taxi as memories slowly took hold. While most of the commercial space had developed over the years, the lush pines of the forest remained the same. My heart picked up pace as the New River Bridge approached, and I rubbed my clammy palms onto the knees of my jeans. "You can drop me off here, sir," I said.

"Here?" The cab driver asked.

"Yes, thank you." I handed the driver a twenty and hopped out of the cab with nothing but a backpack slung across one shoulder. I stepped onto the curb and marveled at the bridge and the rushing water below. The air was electric, and my skin buzzed with memory. Now, all I had to do was find her. Again and again and again. My never-ending story was finally taking shape. The only problem? Where was she?

My fingertips grasped the platinum band in my pocket, twirling it from side to side as I stood at the very place we met, *and died*. She wasn't here either. Not today anyway. I breathed in the electricity in the air and I could feel that I was closer here than I had ever come before. Her energy seemed to waft in the air and wrestle in the trees. My eyes grew large as I took in the genuine beauty of the river and the optimism that it stood for. It was beautiful here, despite the pain.

I ran my fingers over the engraved plaque that read, "In loving memory of Easton Green and Everly Beck." It was a lifetime ago, but it hurt like yesterday. I shook the image of Beck's searching eyes submerged in the icy water of New River—an image that plagued me. Nothing was worse than helplessness, and I felt its full wrath in the wreckage that stormy afternoon.

I shook the memory from my mind, replacing it with a happier one:

"Easton! Come on down!" Mom yelled from downstairs. She was an impatient woman.

I rolled my eyes and let out a sigh. "I'm coming!" I yelled. She wouldn't hear me if I didn't yell, and I laughed at the ridiculousness of it.

Tanner threw his pencil, standing in compliance, and I followed him downstairs. He and I were the same age and adopted the same month. Mom and Dad had gotten two of us to keep each other company—like dogs I'd always thought. I liked dogs, though, and I enjoyed having a brother. As far as having a sibling went, Tanner was a good one.

"The new neighbors moved in. We're going to greet them and bring some cookies. Go wash your face, Tanner. You have marker all over!" Mom hissed.

I didn't want to meet the neighbors. I'd been watching them out my window for a week. They had a girl, seemingly my age. She wore too much pink. Tanner reappeared, the marker faded by ten percent, no more. Mom let out a sigh and ushered us out the door while she grumbled something unkind to our dad. Tanner and I snickered behind them.

The day was dreadfully hot, and the sun beat down on my back, making meeting the girl next door even more dreadful than it had to be. My brother and I took turns seeing who could shove each other harder before my dad interjected, swatting us from behind. Tanner gave one last groan before Mom rang the doorbell, holding her perfect plate of cookies. We appeared to be the perfect family, except none of us shared DNA, and nobody ever talked about it. I wasn't the only one with a secret.

A woman opened the door, still drying her hands on a dishtowel. The women exchanged pleasantries, and once the warm cookies were handed over, the lady invited us inside. As much as I had protested before, I was more than willing to step into the air conditioning. My family and I sat on the sofa, Tanner and I like perfect gentlemen when it mattered most. The neighbor called her daughter down to meet us.

"Becca, come meet the neighbors!" she called. I still remember my cheeks getting hot in anticipation. But everything changed when I saw her. It was like I had finally found something I didn't remember losing. I smiled, gripping the bridge's railing as I grounded myself in the present moment.

The low hum of a motor whizzed by, and I looked over my shoulder, though I shouldn't have. It was tricky being back in town just one life over. I had a good chance of running into someone I once knew, and since I looked identical, only a little younger, it was something that I had to be aware of. It had happened to me before, coming face to face with past loved ones—it frightens them. It's painful to see someone they once loved but had to close the door on so that they could move on with their life. I didn't want anyone from Beck's past to see me. I pulled the baseball cap down to shield my eyes.

I stood there for hours, willing her to find me. I watched the river run wild. Listened to the blackbirds crowing above as they searched for prey. I counted the cars that passed by: eight. All the while, I slouched with an empty heart and a fear that I couldn't see. If I had only known she was safe and happy, I could take the time needed to find her. But I knew nothing for certain, and it was draining.

People like to say it's a small world, but you only hear that when a coincidence occurs. In reality, far more people are missing their chances than getting them. And more opportunities are lost than found. I wouldn't allow Beck to be a lost opportunity, though. I was going to find her if it was the last thing I did. Luckily, I had a lot of time on my hands, making the probability of keeping my promise strong. I lingered on the bridge until sunset, unable to pull myself away from the feeling of being closer to Beck than I had been in years. When the sun dipped behind the mountains and the air dropped several degrees, I decided today wasn't the day. I'd begin again tomorrow with fresh eyes and enthusiasm.

I hitched a ride to a nearby hotel, only stopping when I saw the Red Brick Diner along the way. I asked the taxi to pull over and keep the meter running while I grabbed some dinner to go. It wasn't the Red Brick Diner anymore, though, as all things change over time. Now, "The Taste of Italy" glowed above the doors, and unlike the Red Brick's signboard, this place had all of its letters in fully working order. It had a fresh look too. After a moment of debate, I decided I would take the chance of being seen, though I hid under the bill of my hat the best I could.

I tugged at my collar, trying to hide the lines of my jaw as I walked into the pizza joint. You never know what will spark a memory in the minds of the mourning, and sometimes it's something so little that it can't be described at all.

The smell of freshly made bread comforted me, and my focus turned to the grumbling in my stomach and the watering in my mouth.

"Can I help you, sir?" It was a perfectly round lady with a chip on her shoulder. Sue.

Did she remember me? I took a step back and looked down at the ground.

"Well? Can I help you or not?" she said.

"I'd like to make a to-go order," I said, looking everywhere but into her eyes. A pinball machine rattled and chimed as two kids thrashed about, their entire world spinning because of two quarters and a red button. A boy riddled with acne on what appeared to be his first date. And a couple sitting across the room from him with shifty eyes. His parents?

"Well, what'd ya want? I'm no mind reader!" Sue barked.

I looked her in the eyes. She needed this more than I worried about getting recognized. "I'm sorry, you just have the most beautiful eyes! You probably hear it all the time." I shook my head and looked away, hoping that she was as easy to win over as she was years ago. The Hawaiian pizza looked phenomenal.

"Oh! You devil, you! Stop that!" Sue giggled like a schoolgirl. My heart sank for her. So grumpy. So unhappy. She just wanted to feel special. But she was so scared of rejection, she made everyone hate her before they ever got the chance to see her.

"I'm serious! You go home tonight and tell your man, he's a lucky one!" I said.

"Ohhh, well, believe it or not, there hasn't been one of them in a long while. But I have to say, if you weren't so young, I might've gone after you, you handsome devil!" Sue trailed her hand ever so slightly across one of her large breasts, even though she was well into her seventies and I was twenty. Her efforts made me chuckle, and a slight warmth spread across my face. Sue bounced with amusement.

"Well, I guess in another lifetime, huh?" I said.

"Guess so. What can I get for ya, dear? The pesto is really good tonight." Sue pointed to a picture on the wall.

"Pesto? OK, that sounds great, I'll take one to go, please." It wasn't my favorite. But the girl needed a win, and I'd already committed to being in her corner.

I paid Sue with a nice tip and sat in a booth while I waited for my pizza. I watched the people go about their lives, and I wondered who they were and where'd they go. I wondered what kept their minds satiated when the daily grind wasn't enough. I had my guesses about all of them, but I looked for clues that would stand for evidence. It was when I was mid-evaluation of a businessman ordering dinner, that I saw a girl with blonde hair escape into the ladies' room. My stomach dropped at the cool ash tone of her locks. I jumped to my feet as adrenaline coursed through my veins.

Was this it? Had she come home, looking for me? For her parents? I scanned the room before moving booths to one a little closer to the women's restroom, where she could not escape without me seeing her face in full. As the seconds ticked by, my palms started to sweat and the beating of my heart echoed in my ears. What would I say to her? How would she react when she saw me? Would she still love me?

The ladies' room door swung open, and my breath caught in my lungs. But when she emerged, my breath let out freely in despair. She was just another face —just another almost. Her skin tone was light, and her lips a contrasted pink; she looked a lot like Beck, but no doubt it was a different soul.

"Green! Pizza for Green!" Sue called out, her voice booming over the chatter and arcade games. I got up, disappointed, and retrieved my pizza but not before I put on a cheerful face for the server that had worked well past her prime.

"Don't be a stranger!" Sue called.

I turned around and waved to her. The blond haired girl caught my eye as her boyfriend reeled to get her attention as she stared mindlessly at her phone. "Everly! Look at this!"

I stopped dead in my tracks, my feet unable to keep momentum. Could it be her? Was it possible I'd forgotten the face of my soulmate? I shook my head, dispelling the thought. I could never forget. Then I realized as I peered over to her table, the girl must be Beck's niece. I squinted my eyes shut, taking a split second to absorb the pain, and then I forced myself forward. Tightness closed around my chest as I came so close but not close at all.

By the time I arrived at the hotel and got situated in my room, my pizza was cold. I tossed the box on the table and grabbed a slice, sinking my teeth into the cheesy pesto. It wasn't half bad, though Hawaiian would have been much better. I threw myself on the stiff bed and landed with a thud. Nothing like a rock-hard mattress to pair with my cold dinner and lonely heart.

I pulled up directions to Beck's old college on my phone and wrote them down on a hotel notepad. It would be the first place I checked tomorrow morning. Once I exhausted my efforts in research, I turned on the TV. Four slices of pizza and two hundred channels later, I fell asleep with the lights on and my shoes still tied tight. Sometime in the middle of the night, I'd kick them off and climb under the covers, but it didn't matter; I would never have a good night's sleep on that mattress anyhow.

I woke with a jolt; the room lit with the sunrise. It was the same dream I'd been having for the past month. The one with the woolly mammoth sized twin boulders. I dodged one successfully, but the other was about to shake loose and there was nowhere for me to run. I hopped to my feet and shook off the dream. Already dressed for the day, I collected my things and checked out of my room. I would have grabbed a coffee in the breakfast bar, but I had an itch for Fresh Ground's coffee, and I hoped they were still open some twenty years later.

I threw my backpack into the taxi and clasped the driving directions tightly. I didn't need directions for Fresh Grounds, though. That was still locked into my memory. Staring out the window, I reminisced about all the local spots Beck and I had once frequented. Hunters still stood strong, though it had received a facelift at some point over the years.

When we pulled into the parking lot of Fresh Grounds, I was disappointed to find that the place had closed, but at least what had opened in its place was yet another coffee shop. The cab driver parked, and I walked into what was now Stanford's Coffee. The little coffee shop had the same library vibe as before. Perhaps even more vintage now than it used to be. A few people waited in line, and I busied myself examining the changes. The faces of the employees were different, though the average age remained the same; they all were young adults. The seating configuration was a little different too, as they had replaced the leather chairs with old, green suede sofas that were decorated with ornamental wooden feet. The books on the shelves were so old they were falling apart.

"Sir, can I help you?" a young lady called to me.

I took several strides forward, unaware of my surroundings and lost in memories.

"May I have a latte to go, please," I asked as I pulled my hat down around my eyes.

"Sure, that will be $3.99," the pixie cut barista said.

I frowned, took out my wallet, and handed her a five-dollar bill.

"Thank you. That will be right up," she said.

I placed my change in the tip jar and busied myself looking at the old book spines. The smell of a good book only intensified with age. I imagined what treasures they hid within. What wise, artful words were left behind though the authors themselves were no longer here to share their stories.

"Latte, to go!" the barista called out.

I picked up my coffee and headed straight for the cab. "Step on it, my friend," I said to the driver. As we got closer, the gentle tugging at my soul became increasingly urgent. I knew I was on the right path.

CHAPTER 3

Norton University was breathtaking as I stared out my window. The institution was made of stately red brick and covered in old ivy. The lush green lawn stretched for what seemed like miles. Students everywhere. My eyes scanned the crowd, trying to find Beck, but there were too many to vet them all. I didn't know if I was in the right proximity or not. Still, I had to try.

I stepped out of the car, and the gravel crunched under my shoes. The spring air was crisp and full of promise. My eyes bounced from every ash blond head as I made my way through the courtyard. Small groups of students with books in hand gathered at the benches and leaned against various trees. I listened to the conversations as I passed—in one ear and out the other.

"Brian's a prick. Don't listen to him!"

"Did you see the latest episode of . . ."

"Sorry, I have to work tonight. But maybe I can . . ."

I took the stairs two at a time, eager to get inside. It didn't disappoint. High vaulted ceilings. Ornamental wooden staircase. The college was stunning. I could see why Beck had chosen it in the first place and why she might return. I walked the halls checking countless class names until most of the students had disappeared and the chatter quieted. When a tall slender woman wearing a name badge passed by, I thought I better ask for help.

"Excuse me? Can you point me toward graphic design?"

The lady slowed her rushed pace just long enough to answer my question. "Yes, you're going to want to head over to the west wing." She pointed vaguely as she spun back around and continued on her mission. As my luck would have it, I'd been wandering in the wrong direction.

Making my way across campus once more, my memory drifted back to the day Beck and I had pretended to wed as children. All I had to remember her by was the one photograph. We had been eight years old the day we got married. She made me wear her dad's dress coat and tie. She wore her mom's dress and sunglasses. Beck held her pet bunny—our witness—who was also dressed for the occasion. Her mom thought it was adorable and snapped a photograph. Printed two copies for us to keep. It had hung on my bulletin board back home. Every now and again, I'd take it down and wonder where she was and how I would find her. If it was truly her—and I knew it was—we'd have an eternity to find one another. But if I was lucky, I wouldn't have to wait that long.

I scanned the classroom plaques, which told me I had made it to the arts wing. I passed several classes where Beck may have been, had she chosen the same career path as she did in her last life. I picked an introductory graphic design class to kick off my investigation. Slipping in the back of the class with little disruption, I took an open seat next to an older gentleman. My spirit lifted at the sight of people learning in all stages of their lives. Whoever said you can't teach an old dog new tricks was simply inept. The man smiled at me as I took my seat.

I placed my backpack on the ground. Unlike all the other students here, my backpack was filled with clothing, not books. My stomach wrenched with excitement at the thought that Beck could be sitting just a few rows over. Would she make a scene when she saw me? Scream? Drop her books and bound into my empty arms? Would I propose to her right then and there? *Should I?* Right here in front of everybody? I saw it then, myself on one knee, presenting her with the ring. She'd be cupping her mouth, stifling her squeals, and the students would be spellbound. The story would turn into gossip, changing along the grapevine until it was a different version altogether. It was kind of romantic in its own way.

I lost myself in the daydream. It wasn't until the gentleman next to me packed his stuff that I snapped back to reality. Faces were passing now, and I searched them one by one.

I spent my day on repeat until the school day was done and I'd marked off three classes and one lunch hour. Unless I wanted to come back every day of the week and sit through as many classes as I could, I would have to find a better way. I pondered the idea of hacking into the school's database and searching the attending student list and schedules. Unfortunately, in all my years, hacking was one of the few things I never studied.

I swung my backpack over my shoulders and started the long walk to the parking lot. My eyes searched the various faces as I questioned if my childhood neighbor had been Beck at all. I was young and impressionable. Had I made it all up to comfort me in a time of grief? Was I in love with my childhood neighbor, *and* the girl from my last life? I frowned at my fresh worry with distaste, and I rubbed my hand across a furrowed brow to erase my angst, though I still felt it in my chest. Surely, there wasn't two loves in my life. As I walked through the sea of bodies, I was transported back to the ridge of my dream, where the monstrous boulder had begun to rumble.

I sighed. I thought living a few hundred years with no purpose was hard, but nothing could be worse than finding your purpose and losing it. Now that I'd felt Beck's love, I couldn't go back to a life of solitude. My very existence clung to the hope that she was alive and waiting to be found. *"You found me."* Her voice still floated through my mind, clear as the day she had said it.

I located my ride and opened the trunk. As I threw my backpack inside, I caught only a split-second glance of the back of a head. Ash blond. Ducking into the passenger's side of a white truck. Frozen, I watched as the truck drove away. Before I knew any better, she was gone. What made that blond head any different from all the others? I hadn't even seen a face, yet somehow my sights were set on this girl and this girl alone. Could I rely on my wrenching stomach? Or my eyes that saw only the back of a girl? I couldn't. But something inside me was telling me I *should* listen to the pulling on my chest. Like an anchor set in my heart.

Even though I knew Beck would most likely not come to school every day of the week, I did. After leasing a new black BMW, I finally had a place to gather my belongings. It was my first step out of the transient life and into one with roots. Never being one for commitment, I yearned to have it all with Beck.

I brought a laptop, sat under a large oak tree with a vast view of the open courtyard, and busied myself in the stock market, buying and selling stocks until I was sick of making money. The sun made its way across the sky, and I remained still beneath it as I waited for her. I knew now that I didn't need to see the faces passing by, I only needed the tugging in my chest to become so strong I'd be forced to follow it. Two days is how long it took for that familiar feeling to resurface, but it might as well had been an eternity beneath the oak tree.

Nearly forty-eight hours after my first potential sighting of Beck, it happened again. My heart pounded, and my palms moistened. The smell of grass became overwhelming and the sun almost too bright to see. Tiny goosebumps stood to attention on my arms as if receiving the signal. Every sense I had was now sharper, as I knew my chance had arrived, and I couldn't miss it.

I searched for what I could not see but knew was close. A group of three blond girls walked by. In the far distance, I could see a figure similar to Beck's. A small frame positioned on the stairs. A face buried in a hoodie, reading a book. None of them were Beck. It was only when I started to doubt myself that I saw the white truck pull into the parking lot.

My posture straightened, and tree bark scraped into my back. Regardless of the distance between us and the small blurry figure that stepped out of the passenger's seat, I knew it was her. Like knowing wholeheartedly, I loved Everly Beck despite never having the time to confirm it. Like trusting yourself, even though time and again it had been proven that you shouldn't. I didn't have to see her face to know it was her, because I felt my heart stop in my chest. I sighed in relief, for I had finally found her. And then when my heart started to beat again, this time it was . . . stronger.

I swallowed the bile caused by unruly nerves and scrambled to my feet at once. My laptop fell to the tree roots below. My hand found its way into my pocket, and I slid the cool platinum ring onto the tip of my finger. I watched as Beck situated her backpack and adjusted her hair before a large brute of a man rounded the truck and slid his arm around her shoulders. My stomach tanked. Together, they walked onto campus, talking amongst themselves. Beck glowed a little differently than before.

My nervous fidgeting stopped, and my jaw slackened. The ring felt foreign and misplaced in my hand. A dull ache spread across my abdomen—as if I'd been hollowed from the inside out. I thought finding Beck was the only obstacle that stood between our happily ever after, but I was wrong. Ignorant. Like a young boy in love for the first time, I hadn't realized that there would be unforeseen obstructions. Boulders on a steep ridge.

I watched them walk through the courtyard in slow motion as they made their way to the grand staircase. Beck playfully shoved the guy, and he grabbed her back into his possession. The sun suddenly became too hot, even as the shade cast down upon me. I stared as Beck and her boyfriend disappeared into the college. There I remained, frozen in her wake. Unbelieving.

CHAPTER 4

It took longer than I'd like to admit before I was collected enough to sit down again. But when I did, I got to work, mentally putting the pieces of what I had known to be true back together again. I wrapped my head around the idea that I might have to watch Beck be torn between her current romance and her past one. I knew she would come back to me. It was fate—like simple math. But what I didn't know was the grey matter that blended the black and white together. I didn't know how long it would take for her to become mine again or how steep the road ahead might be. Either way, I was in it for the long run. Not because I was noble, but because I had no other choice.

Beck was the first thing in my many lives that made any sense. Her becoming tethered to live out her second, third, fourth chance with me by her side . . . that was nothing other than destiny knocking at our door. I had to see it through. And she did, too.

I remained under the shadows of the tree, waiting, thinking. I wasn't entirely sure what had to be done, but I knew I had to see her again. I hoped that when she caught sight of me, it wouldn't matter that she had a boyfriend. Nothing would matter. Time would stop, and we would reunite. Start a new life unbound by time. I tried to convince myself that this was the only possibility. Because how could her boyfriend's love ever live up to what we had? It *couldn't.*

Before lunch rolled around, my eyes fell on Beck once more. I felt like a coward for not rushing up to her, but I couldn't move. The fear of being unloved froze me. An eternity of knowing love was right outside my grasp. Surely it would put the fear into anyone. Beck's boyfriend threw such a wrench into my ultimate plan that I didn't know how to proceed. It certainly wasn't with the ring in my pocket.

I watched Beck as a friend of hers approached. They talked for a bit before Beck set her bag on the ground and threw her hair up in a ponytail. She was even more beautiful than I remembered. And I could see that she had a long life ahead of her this time. The energy that surrounded her was strong and youthful. Somehow, her eyes found mine as she reached to pick up her bag. And for a moment, I felt it. We were back together. She and I like Bonnie and Clyde. My heart stitched back to a complete piece. A smile spread from my lips to my eyes.

But just as quickly as it happened, it unraveled at my feet, the stitches in my heart pulling apart all over again. She'd looked directly at me and then away. *Nothing* happened at all. Was it possible she didn't see me? I pried my eyes off of her blond locks and looked all around me. I was the only one in the general vicinity. Maybe her vision was blurry like mine? Maybe the thought of seeing me again was so far-fetched that she just dismissed it?

But when it happened again, I no longer knew what to think. My heart beat against my chest. She saw me alright. She'd even stolen a second glance before going back to class. Perhaps the life she had made for herself was preferable to the one she had shared with me. The one where she had died. I could see how I might remind her of terrible times. My face was the last thing she saw before drowning, and her eyes burrowed into mine with her last breath. All I could hope for now was that she didn't associate me with the grim end of her brief life and turn me into baggage. I was so much more. I *could* be so much more.

I stayed put all day except for one trip to the restroom that I could no longer ignore needing. I hurried back, sure I hadn't missed another sighting. A small sense of relief washed over me when Beck emerged from the exit doors and into the courtyard where I had squandered my days away. I clenched my jaw as her boyfriend found her hand and walked steadily by her side. I hid behind my sunglasses like a true yellow-belly. When Beck cocked her head behind her shoulder with the direct intention of finding my figure under the oak tree, I found the courage to lift my sunglasses and meet her gaze, eye to eye.

She was close enough this time I could see the grimace on her face. Her hair caught wind in slow motion and danced under the sunlight, trailing behind her. My heart ached, and I grabbed at my chest to feel the pounding under my palm. Ever so slowly, she turned her focus ahead, and before I knew it, she was driving away. Just as quickly as she had come, she had disappeared, taking my hope for our future with her.

I sat for a long while under the tree, unpacking my predicament. I was pretty sure she knew it was me, but she wasn't yet sure she wanted another lifetime by my side. It was worse than any circumstance I had come up with in my head. By the time I was nearly suffocated with self-doubt and pity, I took my remains back to the hotel for another sleepless night.

It was a long, lonely evening. Even more so than the nights before. I could imagine the rejection when she was finally forced to say it aloud. "I don't want a second chance with you." It hurt enough in my mind, and I wasn't sure what I'd do if those words ever spilled from her mouth. I'd die right then and there of a broken heart. But that's not even the sad part. The sad part would be when I was born again on the same day to grow up and feel the pain all over again.

I'd all but given up for the day. I'd had enough of myself and wanted nothing more than to quiet my mind. It was too cruel—in only the way that honesty could be. I undressed and noticed something that made my night even darker and more disheartening. The ring in my pocket was missing. I checked furiously through my four pockets several times over. I scoured the hotel floor, retracing my steps through the tiny room. It must have fallen out with my hope while I sat under the oak tree for hours upon hours.

Was it fate? Was life telling me that Beck was no longer mine? I imagined the diamond sparkling in the grass, and I wondered who would be the lucky person to find it. For a split second, I thought about driving back to the college with a flashlight. But enough was enough, and I had to know when to quit. It was late, and my soul was in a million pieces sprinkled throughout Clover. It was quitting time. At least for today.

I woke in a panic. Sweat-soaked sheets and a heaving chest. *The ring!*

I scrambled out of bed and grabbed my belongings. I raced to the college as quickly as I could. I didn't know which fear was greater, someone else finding the ring or it being consumed by a riding lawnmower. Either way, I had to find it . . . fast.

It was Friday, and from what I gathered, Beck only attended school on Tuesdays and Thursdays. I wouldn't see her for five more days. I was neither saddened nor discouraged; I was hopeful. I hoped that she would have clarity by the next time I saw her. I hoped that I would have had enough time to pick up the pieces of my heart before standing before her. Nobody wanted to be broken. And first impressions were everything. Well, second first impressions . . . but they were basically the same thing.

I had a hard time finding a parking spot, but when I did, I picked up speed across the lawn. The anxiety reached new levels when I saw two girls had taken up residency under the oak tree. No doubt they had found the ring. They probably had a long discussion this morning about whether they should turn it in or keep it. How in the world would I convince them it was mine?

The girls fell silent when I approached them, both staring at me questioningly. I did a quick assessment. They were of the intellectual type. Cute in their own right, but clearly not girls that were used to the attention of the opposite sex. I didn't want to come off too strong. My focus landed on the books between them. Bookworms. Some of my favorite people were the ones who loved to lose themselves in the pages of a good book. I'd done enough reading in my days to fit into most book club meetings without a misstep. I wiped my palms on my pants as their foreheads creased with confusion over my intentions.

Honesty. It wasn't the only way in, but it was the best. These girls could probably spot a fraud a mile away, and I was tired of acting.

"Hi." It started off rocky.

"Um, hi?" One girl looked to the other. She went for the prim and proper yet vintage vibe and had an apparent love for mustard yellow and other muted colors. Her friend pushed her glasses up the bridge of her nose and stared at me, waiting.

"Any chance you've seen an engagement ring in the grass? It dropped out of my pocket yesterday, right about here, where you're sitting."

The girls immediately began searching the grass. They'd not come upon it yet. I crouched down to examine the grass with them.

"Sorry, I haven't seen it."

I crawled around on my hands and knees until the girls were so uncomfortable, they abandoned their post. At first, I was excited to see if it had been beneath them, but there was no such luck. With the girls gone, it was clear I wasn't finding the ring. Someone else already had.

After nearly an hour of searching, I retreated to my car. Water-soaked knees and two empty pockets. I suppose I didn't need the ring, anyway. I had gone to bed last night hoping for a better day, but this morning was off to a terrible start, and the boulder had begun to roll down the mountain. I needed a coffee.

Stanford's Coffee was buzzing this morning. I stood in the back of a long line of caffeine-hungry consumers. My mind had finally fallen quiet, and I gazed off into the distance, thankful for the reprieve. Every few moments, I would awaken to take another step forward. But when the doorbells chimed, and the air shifted with familiarity, my mind perked alive once more. I relished the moment of wonder. I loved the feeling of familiarity. It was like nostalgia, and it never got old. A red box with a bow. Who was it? What was it? I didn't want to find out. I only wanted the feeling of hope to spread until my mind was bright and clear again. I took another step closer to the register.

The sound of a woman talking to her friend several customers back pinged. She was the source of the familiar feeling alright, but I couldn't place the voice. Clearly, it had changed with time, and it would take concentration to find the subtleties.

"I don't know. I need to talk to John. See what he thinks," the woman said.

I took my last step forward and greeted the barista at the cash register. I ordered a large coffee, black, and an egg sandwich. I gave her my cash and my name before turning around to meet the mystery voice. And when I did, I was pleasantly surprised.

Beck's old friend Lindsay was standing in line. Age had been kind to her, and she was a beautiful middle-aged woman. Her hair was a natural dirty blond and her blue eyes glistened with sadness. She and her friend wore pink nursing scrubs, but I didn't bother checking her ID card. I knew it was her without a shadow of a doubt.

It was a standing room only, so I found a place near Lindsay where I could wait for my coffee. I listened with my back to her.

"How long do you think you will be out of work?" asked the friend.

"I don't know, I'll try to get back as soon as I can," Lindsay said.

"Don't push it. We have more than enough staff to cover you, and you'll need rest to recover."

"I know, I know. That's what they say." Lindsay was clearly upset with her situation, and it disappointed me that she didn't have Beck to help ease her through whatever she was going through. "But four to six weeks is a really long time."

"I've heard the laparoscopic hysterectomy recovery is shorter, though. Jess had one, and she was moving around after a couple of weeks. Her major complaint was being tired—um, hi! I'll take a cappuccino to go, please. What do you want, hun?" the friend asked.

I didn't know what was going on with Lindsay, but I figured that with her job, whatever it was, at least she knew the right people to get the best help available. I only wished her blue eyes weren't so sad.

"Easton! Order for Easton!"

Startled, I took my order from the table. As I made my way out, I caught the eye of Lindsay, but this time they were anything but sad. It was worse. Her forehead lined with disbelief, and her mouth slightly parted. Fear struck my chest, and I cursed myself for not having worn my baseball hat. I pried my eyes from hers and headed out of the shop in a rushed gait. It hurt me to know that Lindsay was standing inside that coffee shop with a flood of emotions and memories, and it was all my fault. I should have been more careful.

CHAPTER 5

Tuesday had come, and I was up early to see Beck. I had convinced myself that I wouldn't let her get away as easily this time. I would approach her, no matter what fears ran wild in my head. I would complete this one simple task: talk to the girl. I breathed in the deep crisp air of the campus lawn and cloudless sky. Today was the day I'd find out where I stood. After five days of living with the questionable voice in my head, I was ready to meet my reality. It couldn't be worse than the irrevocable damage I had already done by drilling into my head.

I perched under the oak tree, hoping that Beck would look for me there. While I waited, I couldn't help myself from running my hand through the wet grass. No diamond in the rough today. I sipped my coffee and waited patiently, searching every student that crossed the campus. When the brisk morning air became warm and sultry, I knew Beck had arrived. I looked to the parking lot to see the white truck in search of parking. Of course, her boyfriend would be with her.

Beck's eyes met mine even before she made her way out of the parking lot. She was looking for me alright, but this time, her friends were too. There was something in the subtlety of her movement that held me still in my place. I wanted nothing more than to run up to her, but her eyes told me I shouldn't. I swallowed the lump in my throat and leaned against the tree again. Maybe lunch would be a better time to make good on my promise.

It was close to noon when Beck resurfaced. Her arms locked with a tall girl; her hair as dark as chocolate. They made their way to the vending machine. I closed my laptop and tucked it under my arm and made my way over. It was now or never, and I convinced myself that nothing could be worse than waiting another two days for my chance to talk to her. My heart thumped in my chest as I approached the vending machine.

"You have to come! Payton is coming!" Beck said to her friend.

I took a deep breath and stood behind them.

"Oh, go ahead. We're finished," Beck said and grabbed her friend's arm, squeezing it tight. Our eyes met briefly before she hid behind her friend.

"Thanks," I mumbled, fumbling with the dollar in my hand and the laptop under my arm. This wasn't how I envisioned our reunion going. Disappointment washed over me and I tried to act as naturally as possible, but I was no stranger. Her eyes returned to mine, flicking back and forth between me and her friend. I tried to carry on with my selection in the vending machine, but I feared I was much more awkward than that. Beck's stare was more prominent now, and her jaw hung slightly. She could no longer hide behind her friend—not with that expression hanging in the balance. I was right there in front of her, and she had to say something. Anything.

I wanted to kiss her. I wanted to take her in my arms and never let go. But I just stood there, trying to smooth out my dollar bill, afraid of everything that could rain down on me. I'd never been so afraid in all of my lives, because the truth was, this was the first time I had something to lose.

"Nolan is bringing James. You're not going to want to miss this one," Beck said before her attention fell back to me. "I'm sorry, do you need help?" she asked.

"OK." And just like that, I was back on the New River Bridge. Rain-soaked lashes and her beauty still crystal clear. It was like meeting her for the first time all over again. Innocent. Hopeful. Full of possibility.

Beck took the bill from my hand as if in slow motion, her hand nearly brushing mine, close enough for me to feel the warmth. Her sweet scent—coconut—almost bringing me to my knees. I was so hypnotized, I barely noticed the vacancy in her eyes; she didn't share the same nostalgia that I was swooning over. She couldn't feel the palpable bond pushing us together. She couldn't feel it.

"I know you," she said, her eyes still searching for the answer. The impossible answer that wouldn't make sense to anyone in their second life. And that was it. That's what had happened. She wasn't stuck trying to figure out if she wanted a second life with me. She was simply trying to figure out who I was.

I could say so much, but in that moment, all that came out was a simple, "Yes," and I don't even think it was fully audible. I hoped she could read between the lines. My eyes filled with so much depth that surely, she could read me like a book . . . if she would just look deep enough. Long enough.

She couldn't.

The silence stretched between us until I saw the slightest shift in her expression. Her mouth opened to speak, but no words came out. She slowly let her hand fall—a tree in the forest—until she was pointing directly at my chest. "Oh . . . my . . . god," Beck began.

My heart felt like it had been hit by a semi-truck. The impact of her remembering me was so poetic, so magical, so memorable. It was better than in my dreams. I couldn't pry my eyes off of her. *Go on, Beck. Say it. Say you've missed me. Say you love me.* "I," I started.

Like clockwork, as summoned by the Devil himself, along came her boyfriend and wrapped a possessive arm around her shoulder.

"Can I have some?" he asked as he grabbed the bag of skittles from her hand. Beck's eyes remained on me, and her boyfriend took notice of our undeniable connection. "What's up? You know this guy?" he asked, frowning at the intensity of the moment. Our bond was so strong, it was tangible.

Beck's eyes reluctantly pulled away to look at her boyfriend. "Yeah! You wouldn't believe it! But this used to be my neighbor when I was a kid!" Beck said, and they looked back at me for confirmation.

Neighbor? Just a neighbor? It was like a dagger to the back. I never saw it coming. I wanted to take her by the shoulders and remind her of the life we shared—the memories of champagne and grass stains, but everyone was staring, and now was not the time. I resisted the urge and nodded slowly, confirming that, yes, it was true–we used to be neighbors. I had the picture to prove it, and it was right there in my wallet.

"Holy shit! Easton?" Beck shook her head in disbelief. "I *knew* I recognized you! What are you doing here?" Beck's voice was loud and boisterous, and I could tell that this was no act.

"I'm a student . . . here," I said and immediately wished I hadn't. I committed to the lie either way.

"Oh my god! It's a small world," she said, her eyes bursting with wonder.

It wasn't small though. It was an immense and infinite world capable of the unthinkable. All kinds of inconceivable things she couldn't remember.

"It really is," I lied, taking in the distrust of her boyfriend. The moment settled, and I knew my time was closing in. I had to do something so that this wasn't the end. I needed a way into their inner circle. *Her* inner circle. "Actually, I just moved here. I don't know anyone, and it's really something to run into an old friend." The word friend caught in my throat as if it were laced with acid, and I coughed to help clear the distaste. "Maybe you could show me around sometime?"

Beck smiled and her eyes lit up like a clear night's sky, full of stars and promise. "Absolutely! Sorry, how rude of me. This is Brooklyn," Beck motioned to her friend who was patient and welcoming. "And this is Nolan," Beck raised her hand to her boyfriend, and he glared at me in return. His expression screamed territorial but there wasn't an ounce of insecurity. If I looked like him, like I belonged on the cover of a men's fitness magazine, I probably wouldn't feel threatened by me either. But little did he know that I already had Beck's heart.

"Hey, I'm Easton. Nice to meet you."

Beck and her friends turned away, but Beck nodded with her head for me to join them. I crammed the unspent dollar back into my jeans and joined Beck by her side as I clung to the idea that she had not introduced Nolan as her boyfriend. He felt it too, and I wondered if it was a misstep or an intentional withholding.

"So where are you living now, Easton?" Brooklyn asked. I liked her immediately, she was a kind, gentle soul.

"Clover." I watched Beck when I said it, looking for any sign that it meant something to her. If it did, she had one hell of a poker face.

"Oh, that's not too far!" Brooklyn nodded approvingly.

"You guys, Easton and I were *best friends* when we were kids! Do you remember my trampoline?" Beck leaned in with a wide smile.

Everyone took a seat at a nearby bench and spread their belongings across the table, taking up real estate. Beck set down a half-eaten bag of Skittles and a Diet Coke.

"I remember your trampoline and the countless days of summer we spent in your backyard." *I remember marrying you. Not once but twice.*

Beck threw her head back and laughed. "Do you remember when my rabbit scratched your brother, and he flung her at you, and you fell into the pool?" She managed to choke this out between fits of laughter. Not a care in the world. Beck was no longer dying but thriving. It was a Beck I'd never known before—but wanted to.

"Yes, I remember drowning in your pool. You refused to save me!" I teased her. I knew how to swim, of course, but I pretended to sink to the bottom hoping she would jump in and rescue me. It scared her, though, and I regretted my decision when it was all said and done. The look in her eyes was one I wasn't expecting. I was sent home after that. The parents had a long talk with us about pool safety that night.

"I was . . . *terrified* of the water!" Beck admitted. And I knew why.

"You still are!" Nolan said.

"Hey! It's . . . unnatural. We're not meant to be underwater, OK?"

Brooklyn frowned. "You really need to get over that fear. It's super weird! What kid doesn't love the pool?"

Beck lifted her shoulders. Her eyes darted frantically. "I don't know! Me, I guess?"

I watched her intently and wondered if she had any memory at all of drowning. My heart broke for her. I imagined there were a lot of unanswered questions and inadequacies buried deep within her. I did the only thing I could think of at the moment, and I changed the subject.

"I remember we got married that summer."

The conversation quieted, and Beck bit her lip and smiled up at me. "I remember that too." Her voice was endearing. Brooklyn's eyebrow raised, and Nolan snatched the Skittles out of Beck's hand, eager to interrupt the memory.

"Yeah, well, maybe we'll get married in Sin City next weekend! My birthday gift to you," Nolan said before emptying the remaining candy into his mouth.

Beck elbowed him playfully, and Brooklyn made cooing sounds in the background.

I'd been so busy trying to locate Beck that I didn't realize my birthday was coming up. Since she and I died in the same accident, on the same day, we shared the same birthday as well. But birthdays were like any other day of the week to me. They stopped being special when you'd had so many of them.

"Hey," said Beck, patting my arm—"That means it's your twenty-first birthday too!" The group was taken aback by this anomaly, and Brooklyn raised her brows in question.

"Twenty-one!" I said as any first-timer would; with excitement.

"Hey, Becca, our class is starting in five. We should go," Brooklyn said. I loved Everly Beck with all my heart, but who was Becca Reed? And how would I get her to remember me? The girls gathered their belongings.

Lost in thought, I watched my heart walk away on the arm of her friend. What was life throwing at me now? When I thought losing my soulmate was the worst thing that could happen, then this? I find her, and she doesn't remember me? Was this a cruel joke? Was it even repairable?

"Dude!" Nolan snapped from the other side of the table. I'd forgotten he was still with me. I glanced at him. He held his hands out like I was supposed to know that Beck was taken and I wasn't allowed to stare.

I stole one last glimpse of her before complying. "Sorry, man. What class do you have next?"

The first thing I did when I got back to the hotel was start a hot shower to rinse away the stench of defeat. When I finally relaxed, I lingered, unable to pull myself away from the scalding water and steam that enveloped me. My eyes cut through the mist, and Beck's drowning eyes haunted me. The fear of losing her all over again built until my eyes burned with tears and my breath quickened. I wondered if it would have been easier if I hadn't known Beck's love at all—easier than looking into her eyes and seeing an empty, forgotten bond. Was Becca Reed only the shell of a girl I used to know? Used to love? I placed my palms against the cool shower tiles until the tears ran dry.

It was when I closed my eyes that night that I returned to the nightmare that had been plaguing me. The boulder rolled down the mountainside, picking up speed, and I had nowhere to run. When I tripped and fell flat onto my stomach, the boulder began to crush me.

CHAPTER 6

I didn't make it to campus until a little before Beck would be out for lunch on Thursday. Not because I hadn't tried. I did. I sat in my car at 7:00 AM. The motor running, my hands tight on the wheel. I just never made it past park. I like to think of myself as a strong, multi-faceted, capable guy. But no matter how much experience I'd had throughout time, I wasn't prepared for being in love with someone who looked at me like a stranger. Being forgotten was one of the most painful events I'd experienced. And that was saying a lot.

I had to win Beck's heart all over again. Honestly, I wasn't sure I could. Today, my highest hope was that she would take me on a tour around the campus. It was so insignificant, and yet, I wasn't even confident I could achieve it. A part of me didn't want to try.

My stomach was so sick by the time I finally saw Beck that it was difficult to look her in the eye. She seemed well, though—possibly happier than I'd ever seen her. I questioned if I would hold her back in this life. My specialty was being a beacon of light in the lives of the dark and fallen. Now that Beck was thriving, I wasn't sure that I had anything to offer her. I couldn't shake the thought of letting her live out her life and finding her in the next one.

"Are you alright? You seem kind of down," Beck said.

"Oh, no. I just didn't get much sleep. That's all."

"Oh, I'm sorry." She didn't buy it. The telltale sign was the ruffle of her brows.

"Hey, do you think you could give me a tour?" I asked with nothing left to lose. I was surprised when she said yes. It was enough to elevate my mood a notch or two. When I pushed off the bench and we put some distance between us and her friends, I felt even better. Beck and I alone, walking side by side. It was the small things. I had to believe that one of them might spark and later, catch fire.

Despite the cool spring air, Beck wore a white sundress. It looked amazing on her. It would have looked even better if her boyfriend's jacket hadn't been draped over her shoulders.

"Have you not walked around campus yet?" Beck asked.

"Um, no!"

"You must be busy. Do you have a full schedule?"

I'd not thought this far. "Oh, wait, no I've seen this wing. Let's check out the library? I've been dying to see it."

"Oh, yeah, OK." Beck nodded, and we changed course. "I still can't believe we ran into each other. And here, of all places. I mean, it's not like we grew up here or anything. It's *so* weird," Beck rambled.

"Like, it was predestined?" I asked with a smirk.

Beck looked at me and smiled. Her cheeks flushed pink. It was the first time I felt like I was talking to her. The old her.

"Yeah, you could say that," she said.

"Well, it couldn't have come at a better time, because, like I said, I just moved here, and I could really use a friend. I'm happy to have found you." I opened the door for Beck and briefly placed my hand on her back as she passed through.

"I'm glad to have my friend back too. Um, is there something else going on I should know about?"

I lowered my gaze to the lobby floor. We were inside the college now, and I needed to keep my voice down. "It's nothing. I just found out I was adopted, so . . . ":

Beck gasped.

It was kind of a dishonorable move, but I was working from the ground up. Not only were the odds stacked against me, but her picturesque boyfriend was too. I knew she would empathize with the shock of finding out I was adopted, and maybe I'd be in the club again. The Beck and Easton Club of Tethered Souls. It had a nice ring to it.

"I'm so sorry. Your parents just told you?" Beck asked.

"Yeah, just recently. Right before I moved here."

"And your brother? Is he adopted too?" Beck opened the doors to the library. It was a beautiful sight. Massive and historic. I took a deep breath; I loved the smell of books.

"Um, yeah. Tanner was adopted too." I waited for her to confess her adoption.

"Shit. That must have really thrown you for a loop, huh? Are you going to find your real parents? I mean . . . biological? Sorry!" Beck scrunched her shoulders up to her ears with a pained look on her face. *Real parents.*

She really didn't remember me, or she would have remembered that I didn't have parents. She never would have faltered, calling parents "real," just because they shared your DNA. And apparently, she didn't know she was adopted either. How had she not known this about herself? Why hadn't her parents told her the truth yet? It would be hard for her when she came to realize the truth. I only wished she had found out about her family sooner. It probably would have made it easier to accept what she now was. Not to mention the fact that it would have made my job a little easier too.

"No, it's alright. Um, I don't think I'm going to look for them," I said while I ran my hands down the spines on the bookshelf. They weren't people I'd want to find, even if I had the opportunity.

"If you don't mind me asking, why wouldn't you?" Beck leaned against a wall of books.

It was a hard question to answer, even if it was a lie. "I don't think they were fit to be parents. They didn't want to be found, and I can respect that. I'm just happy they gave me a better chance than what they had to offer." Only the first part was true—that they weren't fit parents.

Beck nodded, her eyes falling on a student walking in our direction. Our private conversation became less intimate, and our connection faltered. She turned around and pulled a book off the shelf and paged through it while she waited for our privacy to return. My eyes burrowed into the back of her head, and I yearned for our connection to return.

"That's a good one. You would like it," I said, coming up behind her.

Beck's eyebrows raised. "You've read this one?"

"Yeah."

She smiled. "That's random."

"I've probably read most of these books," I said honestly.

"Oh wow. You're a big reader!"

It was my turn to smile back at her. "I've got a lot of time on my hands," I said. I wish she understood. But she just looked at me in question. After a moment, she grabbed a book from behind her without ever looking at it. "This one?"

I glanced at the cover. "Yes."

Beck stacked the book on top of the other and took off down the aisle. She paused near the end of the fiction aisle and grabbed a small green novella. "This one?"

I chuckled. "Yes. Though I don't think you'd like it as much as the other two in your hands," I said.

Beck's eyes slanted, "And what makes you think that? You don't even know me."

"Do you want to read about the Siege of Kazan?" I challenged her.

Beck's eyes quickly scanned the back of the book before she bit into her lip and looked back at me with large doe eyes. "No," she admitted.

I closed the distance between us. "Beck, you seem to forget that I was your *best* friend. And at one point in time, I was even your husband."

Beck snorted. "Oh my god, Easton! That was like, a lifetime ago!"

"Precisely," I said. It took everything I had not to lean in and kiss her. I wondered how it would be received if I did. Right here in the library where fiction ended. "One lifetime ago is not enough to change who you are. I'm sure you've changed, Beck. I mean, I know you have, but I still know you to be the little girl you were at eight years old. And I still see my best friend when I look at you." I stopped myself from bleeding out right there amongst the books. The truth was, I saw so much more than that. But she wasn't ready to hear it. Not today, she wasn't.

Beck smiled, and her eyes glistened. She placed a hand on my shoulder and pulled me in for a hug. "God, I've missed you," she said. My heart dropped. I wanted to hear it over and over again.

God, I've missed you. It echoed in my head.

"And if you ever need to talk about your parents or anything, you can call me. OK?"

"OK. Like anything?"

Beck pulled away too soon and checked her watch. "Oh, shit! I'm *so* late!"

I pretended I too had somewhere to be. "Oh man, where'd the time go?" I looked around, shoving my hands in my pockets.

Beck shoved the books back into a random spot on the shelf, and I tried not to cringe at the disorder.

"Hey, a group of us are going to Sin City next weekend to celebrate my birthday. And actually, it's your birthday too, so you should come!" Beck said as an afterthought.

Sin City? "Yeah! I'd love to!" It wasn't my scene, but I'd do anything to be by Beck's side.

"This is going to be so much fun! Let me get your number real quick, and I'll keep you updated," Beck said as she glanced behind her as if time itself was coming after her. We exchanged numbers in a hurry.

"I'll call you," Beck called out as she charged off to make the remaining bit of her class.

I smiled and nodded. "I'm looking forward to it!" I called back much too loudly for a library and reaped the consequence when someone shushed me.

I had woken up with the highest hope of getting a school tour out of Beck. A tiny fraction of time alone with her. What did I get? A lot more than that! A whole weekend with her . . . and her boyfriend. I pushed my back up against the bookshelf. Her boyfriend. What had I gotten myself into now?

When my questions went unanswered there in the library, I resolved to head out. I'd already fulfilled my purpose of coming to the college today, and since I wasn't actually a student at Norton University, it was time to be on my way. But not before putting those three books back in their rightful places. I wouldn't allow Beck to sin by accident.

It's funny how an instant can change a perspective. One moment in the library. One look of curiosity. It was enough to set the hook, and I'd be there for Beck whether she wanted me as a friend or something more. At this point, I'm not sure she could get rid of me if she tried.

I'd need a house if I was staying long-term, and from the looks of Beck's schooling and friend base, I would be here awhile. There were a few options, but nothing exciting. Nothing in Clover was. The options I had available to me when I moved to Clover previously—to develop a relationship with Clyde—were slim to none. I chose the best house, but it still needed work, and while I had the time, I found myself living with the dysfunction instead of fixing it. I knew that would be the case for my next house as well, and I'd have to choose wisely if I ever thought Beck would move in with me.

I settled into the hotel for the night, anxiously awaiting Beck's promised call. Time moved beyond slowly, and I busied myself looking for real estate nearby. When the hunt bore no fruit, I watched a movie. And then, another. By the time 9:00 came, I couldn't wait any longer. The phone-checking had become impulsive, and I questioned why I hadn't called her myself. She was probably waiting for me to call, like I was waiting on her. Without any more thought, I picked up my phone for the umpteenth time and dialed her number. Was it too late? Would she answer? I pushed it all aside the moment I heard her voice.

"Easton Green. You know, I still can't believe that our paths have crossed for a second time."

My stomach wrenched at the sound of her voice. "I'm glad they have," I said.

"Um, about Sin City . . . now that you've had time to think about it, did you still want to go?" Beck sounded off, regretful perhaps, and I knew why. Though I didn't want to admit it to myself.

"Yeah! I can't wait. I'm . . . I'm looking forward to meeting some new *friends*." My eyes dropped to my lap and moved across the bedsheets in defeat.

"Great! I'll send you our flight information, and the hotel reservation, and you can book your stay. It's going to be so much fun!"

"Cool!" I cringed.

"OK. I'll, um . . . , I'll see you next weekend then," Beck said in a much lighter and more confident tone.

"OK. Bye."

"Bye!"

I wished I hadn't called. The realization pulled me down like a cinder block tied to my ankle. Beck didn't like me. It was as simple as that. The subtle drop in her tone when I made an advance was obvious. The pickup when I used the keyword *friends*. She was afraid of leading me on. I was just an old friend that she now had the pleasure of pitying because of my adoption sob story. Had she not been dying in her last life, she never would have given me a chance. Beck was out of my league.

I ran my hands across my face and scrubbed my eyes. Would Sin City be my personal nightmare? Would I be "friend-zoned"? Had I really said *cool*?

CHAPTER 7

On the heels of my embarrassment, I had preparations to make before my trip with Beck and her friends. I needed to secure my position at the college as an attending student. I needed a home in Clover. And lastly, but possibly most important, I needed to go shopping. Sure, I should pick up a couple of shirts and swim trunks, but what I really needed was a birthday gift for Beck. An engagement ring would not suffice for a girl who couldn't remember.

I drank down the bitter, black hotel coffee as I swiped through job openings at the college. My laptop sprawled across my lap, and a pad of paper to my side that read "Student? Job?" The list was slim. I figured if I couldn't get in as a student, as the enrollment period had already closed, I could at least shoot for a job at Norton. Anything that gave me a purpose to be on campus, because the stalker look wasn't what I was going for.

The college was in search of a janitor and a math professor. Although I didn't enjoy math, I was good at it. Good enough to be a college professor. And I suppose if push came to shove, I could try for that position. Still, the chances were bleak without teaching credentials, and I didn't have time to ask Clouse to fabricate the necessary materials. I wasn't sure if he'd made it out of the bar that day anyway. If for some reason the university hired me for a position, I could twist my way out of telling Beck I was a student. Picking up the pad of paper to my side, I jotted down the details of the open position.

I flipped the page and wrote "home?" and revisited the houses I was looking at previously. Of course, they were both still for sale. Nothing moved quick in Clover, but if I wanted my story to be plausible, I had to. I made a couple of phone calls and scheduled the viewings later that evening with the real estate agent, Tina McFay. She sounded as if it would be her first viewing in a week or longer but didn't want to appear too open. She pushed me off until the evening. It worked out well, as I had errands to run anyway.

I got dressed in a new variation of the same clothing I had shoved in my backpack and set off. I felt the need to get to the college as soon as possible, but the simple fact that I didn't have clothing for an interview prompted me to go shopping first. The closest strip mall was nearly forty-five minutes away, and I spent the entire drive mulling over the perfect gift for Beck. I couldn't give her what I wanted most, and the more I thought about it, the more I realized my options were limited. Unless I wanted to be an ex-neighbor with a restraining order, I needed to settle on something simple. Flowers were always a pleasant choice, but they'd die, and it's not like she wanted to tote flowers around with her on the plane. A bracelet was too romantic for a supposed friend. Chocolate was an excellent choice, if it wouldn't melt. I must have run through two dozen terribly unfitting gift ideas by the time I arrived at the mall.

As I began weaving in and out of the shops, I noticed the demographics were eighty percent women. The men were either in tow with a girlfriend or hidden in groups of friends, and I wondered what all these people were doing off on a Friday afternoon. They couldn't possibly be shopping for fun, could they? A way to pass the time and empty their pockets in doing so? I browsed the store names above every door and passed on most. But when I walked by a store filled with things that sparkled, I stopped dead in my tracks. If I knew one thing, it was that girls liked things that sparkled. Like a moth drawn to light, girls had been pining after shiny objects since as far back as I could remember. And that was saying a lot.

I pulled the door open and entered the tiny shop filled with crystal objects. The air was still and stale. With little traffic to compete with, I immediately stole the attention of the store clerk, an elderly lady who was past the age of retirement but wouldn't have it any other way. Despite how high she had climbed on the ladder of life, she had more time than most. Her cheeks fought gravity and lifted into small painted red cheeks on her weathered face.

"Can I help you?" The woman asked, clasping her bony hands together. Right away, I could tell that this interaction may be the highlight of her week, and it was my duty as a Tethered Soul to make it count.

"I'd love some help. I need to get a special gift, but I'm not sure what I'm looking for." I walked up to a glass enclosure with tiered shelving and spinning trivets of glistening treasures.

"Well, you came to the right place! My name is Patsy, and I'll be helping you out today. Let's start with some questions. Who is the gift for? And what is the occasion?" Patsy asked. I could tell I'd be spending more time here than I would like, but the sooner I accepted it, the easier it would be. So, I shook off my impatience and gave Patsy the best customer interaction she'd have in a long while.

"Well, Patsy, it's an interesting story. Do you have time for a story?" My eyes glanced around the empty store, and I feared it appeared as mockery. Of course, she had the time. But Patsy's age-worn eyes didn't pick up on the subtlety.

"Oh, do tell me! I just love a good story."

"OK then. It begins with a girl . . ."

Patsy's eyes lit up. She was hungry for a real-life love story.

"We used to be neighbors when we were kids. I loved her then, when I was eight." I pulled out the picture of Beck and me on our second wedding from my wallet. This photo had a special place in my wallet, hidden behind a tri-folded blank check. The picture was worn and had a mark through the middle where it had been folded so many times before. The photograph was of our pretend backyard wedding. Beck held her rabbit, and I wore a suit that extended well beyond my limbs.

Patsy gasped, bringing one hand to her stolen heart, and one shaky hand to the old photograph. It was among the few belongings I kept from my current childhood.

"Does she love you, too?"

"Well, see, that's the problem. My family moved that summer. We lost touch for so many years. I only recently ran into her by chance at a college we both attend."

"Oh!" Patsy made a high-pitched sound somewhere between a statement and a question. Her eyes glistened with the tears of hope.

"Yeah. I think it's fate . . . I really do," I said. And I wasn't lying. Beck and I were fated mates. Even if she didn't know it yet in this lifetime. We both knew in our last one. And I'd like to think we knew it as kids, too—when our subconscious ran wild and we weren't yet caged by plausibility.

"So, you want to give her a gift? I know just the one!" Patsy hobbled to a desk nearby and unlocked the glass lid. She lifted out a large crystal heart that came to a sharp point, and I couldn't help but to see the resemblance to my own beating heart with its sharp, possibly dangerous edge.

I smiled at the mere thought of handing Beck a large weighted heart for her birthday. I steepled my fingertips under my chin and pretended to consider Patsy's perfect pick.

"See, the thing is . . . I don't want to come off too strong," I said.

Patsy's eyes lowered to the heart in her hands. "I see . . ."

"It's her birthday, and actually, I think she has a boyfriend. So timing is important, and I don't know that this is the time to tell her I love her. Not just yet."

"Oh! Yes, that's good thinking." She brought her hand to her cheek and let her old eyes wander the shop in thought. I took a deep breath and let it out slowly. I wanted to look around the shop myself, but I knew letting her help me was more important. It was when Patsy had a second perfect pick that I realized

I would have to buy something just to make her happy, and I would have to shop for Beck's birthday gift elsewhere, and I was OK with that.

"It's the perfect birthday gift for a girl in love," Patsy said.

"You know, I think you're right! It's perfect!" I stared down at the crystal bear holding a bouquet of pink balloons. I couldn't possibly give it to Beck.

"Isn't he the cutest bear? I'll wrap him up for you. She's going to love it." Patsy hobbled behind the register and wrapped the bear in white tissue paper. I lowered my forearms to the glass table between us and stretched my back. I let my eyes wander over the land of glimmer below until wandering was the last thing they wanted to do. My sights glued to a small crystal dragonfly no larger than a quarter. It had a green, beaded body and peridot wings. *That* was the perfect gift.

"Patsy? Can you throw in that little dragonfly too?" I pointed to the corner of the display where the dragonfly rest.

"Of course, dear!"

I wondered if it would mean anything to Beck. If she would look at it and know it was something more special than eye candy.

Patsy wrapped up my gifts with the speed of a tortoise and then checked me out in the same fashion. I glanced at my watch. I'd spent an hour in the store. I had to pick up the pace if I wanted to get to the college and make it in time for the house tours that evening.

"Thank you, Patsy. I couldn't have found the perfect gift for my girl without you." I said.

"Oh, dear. You go get her, you hear?" Patsy said.

I winked at her before exiting and sliding my sunglasses back over my eyes.

I dashed into the first shop that displayed men's clothing in the window and picked up three collared shirts, two T-shirts, and an extra pair of jeans. A black blazer also found its way into my hands to help with my first impression, if I was fortunate enough to snag an interview. My sizes never changed, and it made shopping effortless. I left the store carrying a large paper bag and one tiny, pink, plastic one. I knew I should take the time to get a proper pair of dress shoes, but I was feeling the pressure to move on with my day.

I had picked up my pace, but soon found myself in the wrong place at the wrong time. Right as I was about to step off the curb into the parking lot, a nearby pretzel stand caused my stomach to rumble and my mouth to water. I checked my watch again. I barely had time to grab a quick pretzel and soda before my drive to the college. As soon as I made the decision to wait in the line, my sense of urgency dissipated. It had happened to me many times over my past lives. Tugging, pulling, urges to be somewhere or do something. They never made sense . . . until they did. Till I discovered the true meaning. More often than not, I wondered if I was merely a pawn in someone else's scheme.

It was my turn to order, and I took a step forward to meet the young teen working the register. A tall striped hat was part of her uniform—the worst part.

"I'll have a pretzel and soda to go, please," I said.

"Name?"

"Easton."

"That will be seven-fifty."

I gave her a ten, and when I received the change back, I dumped it in her tip jar. She thanked me with a smile. I waited for my order to be complete, and in doing so I unwrapped the crystal bear. I hadn't planned to give it to Beck, and I certainly didn't want to tote it around with me in my backpack. I examined the bear in my hand and concluded that Patsy was right; it was the perfect gift. Just not for Beck. I looked around at all the people passing by the pretzel stand and placed the bear on top of an open table in plain sight. The tightness in my stomach finally put me to ease as I left the gift where it needed to be. I turned my back on it and waited for my order, realizing I wasn't hungry at all.

It wasn't long before I heard the gasp of a girl behind me. No doubt, it was at the sight of the bear on top of the deserted table. A gentle tug at the corner of my lips pulled upward, and pride replaced the tension I had felt in my chest. It was in these unique moments, few and far between, that I stopped wondering why I was a Tethered Soul, and simply was.

"Oh my god! Hanna, look!"

"Whose is that?"

"I don't know. It was just sitting here?"

"OK, that's . . . weird!"

"Do you think . . ."

"We should turn it in. It's clearly somebody's . . ."

"I think it's . . . yours?"

There was a moment of silence before I could hear the muffled bout of emotion threatening to boil over. I wondered what the bear meant to her. Had her mother given her a teddy bear with pink balloons? Had she bought a crystal bear for her best friend or a sister before they passed? Could it be the same make and model? I didn't need to know what it meant to the girl to know that it was special to her. The stifled cry was contagious, causing my throat to burn. I knew exactly how she felt as I held back the pain I shared with a person I'd never met but knew had loved and lost.

"Easton! Order for Easton!"

My attention snapped back to the food, and I gathered my bags and my pretzel to go. When I turned to leave, the girls passed me on the way to the counter and asked, "Do you know if this belongs to anyone? It was sitting at that table over there." They both pointed to the table in unison. Only one girl had blood-shot eyes, and equal parts pain and hope streaming down her cheeks.

The teen working the checkout replied, "No. Nobody has sat at that table all day. If you want it, it's yours."

I'd passed just before hearing them gasp once more, and I walked away with a smile on my face that was deep enough to touch my heart.

CHAPTER 8

Now that I had Beck's birthday gift squared away, it was time to secure myself a reason for showing up at the college. Then, if I was lucky enough, a home as well. But when I found myself sitting in front of the dean, my hope all but slipped away.

"I'm so sorry. You will have to wait for open enrollment. We're not currently accepting students. And the math professor's position was filled this morning, Mr. Green." The dean, a woman late into her fifties with ebony skin and a brilliant blue scarf tied around her neck, examined my resume. It was the best prefabrication I could make with such brief notice.

"I understand. Perhaps the professor will need a teacher's aide? I could be of help," I countered, pulling at my blazer collar, hoping I looked sharp.

"We have all the aides we need at the moment. But check back with us. You never know what the future holds." She clasped her hands together and rested them on her desk. A sure sign that she was ready for me to leave her office. I clenched my jaw. Not yet ready to give up.

"Are there any job openings at the college? Anything?" I asked, sounding more desperate than I intended.

"Well, there is one . . ." I raised my eyebrows and leaned forward in my chair. "We *are* in need of a janitor."

". . . Anything . . . *else*?"

"No, Mr. Green. That's all."

I sighed. I needed a reason to be here. I needed time. Time to grow with her. Time to uncover the truth with her. Time to make her love me again. And I couldn't do that if I didn't attend the college.

I cleared my throat, trying one last option. "I spoke with the counselor earlier who said you may have room for another student and that you might consider an exception?" It was a blatant lie, of course. The counselor told me just the opposite, in fact.

The dean furrowed her eyebrows and I could tell her trust towards me was fading.

"For a donation of course." It was a Hail Mary. I had to try. I watched her expression change from one of annoyance to slight interest. I had to strike while the iron was hot. "Perhaps—"

"Mr. Green, with all due respect, I don't think you're capable of a bribe bountiful enough to bend the rules. Now, if you don't mind, I have quite a bit of work to do, and I'd prefer to get back to it. Thank you for coming in." With that, she picked up her pen and began to work while I was still seated in her office.

My mind raced in circles. Should I take the janitorial position? Would that get me closer to Beck? Should I donate the money I took from Clouse and forgo buying a home in Clover? Somehow all of my options were terrible. None managed to inch out above the others. I ran my hands through my hair and stood to make my exit. I walked slowly, giving myself the time to change my mind within the seconds I had left in the dean's office. When I heard her voice again, I knew it was fate giving me a fighting chance.

"Mr. Green?" The dean asked.

A smile spread across my face and I spun on my heels to face her. "Yes, Dean?"

"The tag is sticking out of your blazer collar." The dean smiled as she watched my face heat. By the time the door had closed behind me, my mouth was parched, I had no security at Norton, and I was utterly humiliated. I reached behind my collar and ripped the tag off throwing it in the trash on my way past the counselor.

By the time I reached the parking lot, I'd come up with a Plan B. I wasn't proud of Plan B, but when push came to shove, I had no other choice. I'd show up on the days Beck went to class, and I'd pretend I had class too. I'd lie. *Simply lie*, until one day—and hopefully, that day was sooner than later—she would remember me. Our life. Our love. And I could be in her life beyond school. But until then, it looked like I had some acting to do. Luckily for me, I had practice.

I must have played the exact moment the dean smiled at my embarrassment a hundred times before I arrived at the Clover Real Estate's office of Tina McFay. Since I hadn't just donated my savings to weasel my way into college, I would have enough for a down payment on a home. I wrapped my hand around the cold metal doorknob, and just as I pulled the door open, Tina just about fell out. She stumbled on her heels before standing tall and adjusting her clothing.

"You must be Easton! So nice to meet you. Thank you for coming in today!"

I shook her hand, which was petite and warm. She was attractive enough to be on a magazine cover. And if I had to choose which type of magazine, I'd have to say swim. Her pencil skirt hugged her curves, which resembled an hourglass figure. Her teeth were perfectly straight and perfectly white, and her hair was long and lustrous.

"We have two houses to look at this afternoon. Let me just grab my notes and we can get a move on it." Tina turned to grab her notes, and my eyes dropped slightly. I wondered how much her looks played into her job. Did she sell more houses because she was easy on the eyes?

I took a deep breath and examined my surroundings. Her office could have been a spread in a magazine, but not from a swim edition—more like home decor. I gave my head a shake, dispelling my thoughts as I moved to the entryway table, on which sat a stunning bouquet of tulips and a bowl of etched wooden balls. Everything matched and flowed effortlessly. It was probably a language Beck understood, being in graphic design, but all I could do was appreciate it.

"Do you stage the houses you sell?" I asked.

"I do! Most of them need it!" Tina said as she shoved a notebook into her bag.

"I like what you've done here." I vaguely pointed to the shelves that were lined with photographs in heavy farmhouse framing.

"Thank you! It's a fun pastime. Are you ready?"

"Yeah!" I clapped my hands and then followed Tina to her car. When I stepped inside her car, I was thankful that it was clean and odor-free. It was a simple task, but one that was unattainable by most.

"So the first house we're going to is the smaller one. It's about twelve hundred square feet, but it has a nice location. It's at the end of a cul-de-sac, which personally, I enjoy. And if you plan on having children, I just think it's a safer option, as well."

I thought about it. Children. I'd never once seriously considered it. The first time I died, I was just a child myself. After I found out what I was, or more rather, *who* I was, I didn't think it would be fair to have children. Now, after all of these years, I was positive I was incapable of having kids. The chances of a mishap would have happened by now, and no such thing had. I was sterile alright.

"I'd love a family one day," I said.

Tina smiled a warm and endearing smile. "I would too."

My stomach dropped with unease. "I already have the engagement ring, so as soon as the time is right, I'm going to ask my girlfriend to marry me. I doubt she will want to wait long to have kids." I made my stance clear as day. Tina's eyes lost their sparkle. But the uneasiness in my stomach went away.

We pulled up to the first house. Option A. It was indeed tiny—old too. Red brick peeked out from behind the overgrown weeds and covered the bottom portion of the house. An abandoned scooter rest against a tree. The driveway was long and skinny, and the windows needed replacement.

"I know it's not much on the outside, but if you can imagine a facelift, and some yard work, I think this would be a beautiful fixer-upper." Tina framed the house with her hands. I nodded, unsure if I could see her vision.

We stepped inside, and the stale smell of mildew escaped into the open air. I looked at Tina with a doubtful expression, but she charged forward with confidence.

"This is the living room!" she said. I stared at the brown shag carpet, and my eyes flicked to various stains, which reminded me of the spots on a cow's hide.

It couldn't have been more than ten steps into the home before Tina said, "And this is the kitchen," in the same cheerful tone. Small was an understatement; we didn't need to walk any further than the front door to see the kitchen, living room, and dining room. In fact, I could see the backyard from where I stood as well. Though larger than an apartment, this house felt smaller than a cardboard box. I followed Tina into each room, the tour lasting a full two minutes. When she finally stopped to examine my face, she agreed we should look at Option B.

Once outside in the fresh evening air, I took a deep breath. Expanding my lungs as full as they could stretch. The smell of overgrown grass never smelled so clean. A part of me wanted to stop Tina right then and there and tell her that whatever the second house looked like, I'd take it, because it couldn't be worse than this one. But in true Easton fashion . . . I was wrong.

Option B was *worse*. The house was larger, which was nice, and the smell was at least tolerable. But it was . . . sinister. And if I had to guess, I'd say the house was haunted. As if the subtle constriction of my throat and the icy pockets of stale air weren't enough to convince me, Tina had to disclose the multiple deaths that had taken place over the last few years in the house, and it was more than any one home should endure. I wondered what mysteries lay inside. No, I had enough on my mind; I didn't need to lie awake at night and feel encapsulated by the darkness and evil that lived there. I'd rather spend my free time ripping out brown carpet and breathing in mold.

To say I was disappointed with how my day turned out was an understatement. Although I found the perfect gift for Beck's birthday, I had no job, no tie to her schedule at the college, and now, the only two homes in Clover were nothing short of atrocious. But if I didn't attend Norton as I said and I didn't have a home where I said, then what *did* I have? I was desperate to make my story plausible. Desperate to give myself a shot.

Just when I thought I had no chance in hell of ever laying down roots in Clover, I had to remind myself of the ending to my recurring nightmare. The boulder had crushed my leg, or so I thought. Despite the momentum it had from barreling down the hill, however, something had stopped it dead in its tracks—just above my ankle. When the fear subsided, I could see that there was a perfect tunnel etched into the perfectly round boulder. My foot was free, and I could slide out unscathed. I crawled out from underneath the boulder and I stood inches from it, marveling at the hazard that had never touched me but almost killed me.

I had to remind myself that losing the ring wasn't the end, Beck forgetting me wasn't the end, and this wouldn't be how my story ended either. It was then that I pictured Beck wearing a hard hat and a tool belt. It's when I saw her laughing in the kitchen with a spatula. And it was when I saw her running through the tiny house wearing nothing but a bedsheet that I put an offer in on the house.

I came in low, even lower than what the house was worth, but Tina said that the home had been on the market for a year, and had no offers to date. We were sure my offer would be accepted. And at the end of the day, Tina would have some cash in her pocket, and I would have one less lie to carry on my shoulders.

CHAPTER 9

I counted down the days until the trip in both anticipation and dread alike. I couldn't wait to spend more time with Beck. There was a burning in my belly that told me I would inch my way closer to her heart if I had the time to do so. I couldn't think of a better way than to celebrate our birthdays together on a weekend away. But a nagging sensation gnawed at my thoughts, never letting me forget that Nolan wouldn't be far away. Behind every smile, every shared moment, and every glitter of hope, Nolan's eyes would burrow into me like those of a blood-sucking tick.

The funny part was, I couldn't blame the guy. He had impeccable taste. It only bothered me that he didn't feel the way I did for Beck. How could he? Our bond was something no college fling could come close to matching. Still, somewhere deep inside me, and unrelated to my conscious thoughts, I feared our untouchable bond wouldn't be enough. Or possibly never discovered. And it was foolish if I thought a crystal dragonfly would be the gift that kept on giving. No, it had to be something more. A kiss, perhaps?

I stumbled over my own two feet at the very thought of kissing Beck again, and I looked around to see if anyone had caught my blunder. If they had, they didn't care to make a mockery of me. It was about time for Beck's lunch, and I sat waiting on the bench she frequented. When her friend Brooklyn spotted me, she came to keep me company.

"Hey there. How are you today?" Brooklyn asked. Her long dark hair was parted down the middle and brushed slightly in front of her eye.

"Just another day in paradise," I said.

Brooklyn laughed, shaking off my sarcasm as she sat down. "I heard you're going to Sin City with us next weekend. Are you excited?"

"Yeah, I can't wait. It'll be nice to get out of this town and see the city." I had lied so many times. Pretended I was naive or inexperienced. It flowed out of me like the air expelled from my lungs, and half of the time, I never even realized it. It was a means of survival and nothing more . . . but it could prove the barrier that kept me from getting close to others.

"Me too! I've never been there. So excited!" Brooklyn said in a high-pitched tone. I looked up to catch her eyes, which were so warm and golden, they reminded me of spun honey, but that wasn't even the most interesting part. It was the boredom reflected in her eyes as she claimed to be excited that interested me the most.

"Hey," Nolan said as he took a seat.

"Hey," Brooklyn responded.

"So, what do you guys do in Sin City? Do you gamble?" I asked.

"I just drink, man. Maybe drink by the pool during the day?" Nolan said. I was slowly peeling back the multiple layers of Nolan, and the more I did, the more that hope crowded out my insecurities.

"I'm not twenty-one yet," said Brooklyn, "but I've got a fake ID, so I'm covered."

Beck kissed Nolan on the cheek, and he swatted her on the rear, making her yelp and drawing attention from those around us. I tried not to show a reaction of any kind. "Can I see it?" I asked Brooklyn.

"See what?" Beck asked, sitting down and pulling her bag onto her lap.

"My ID." Brooklyn handed me her ID from across the table. I looked at it closely for telltale signs of being a fake but couldn't find any. It was as real as any other I'd seen.

"Wow, that's legit. Where did you get it?" I asked.

"Oh, I have a guy." Brooklyn placed her hand under her chin and posed like a cherub. I laughed and wondered how far from the truth it really was.

"And your friend, James, does he have one too?"

"No, Brooklyn is the baby of the bunch. James is . . . what? Twenty-two? Twenty-three? I think he started at Norton late," Beck said.

"He didn't start late. He's just too dumb to pass his classes!" Nolan barked.

"Stop that!" Beck smacked him with the back of her hand. "James is actually very smart."

Nolan laughed out loud, "Are you serious? Have you met James? He can't sit still long enough to study! He's probably never read a book!"

I looked to Brooklyn during the quarrel, and she offered me an eye-roll. "Where is James? Does he go to school here?"

"Yes, but our classes don't align." I nodded, eager to make up my own theories about the man they called James.

A girl walked by on her cell phone, giving everyone a quick wave before meeting up with a guy. "Oh, that's Payton. She's coming to Sin City too," Beck pointed to the girl. Nolan seemed to take a particular interest, but I preferred to watch Beck lick the lid of her yogurt. I pretended to listen to Brooklyn talk about something that happened in her class today, but the truth was, I was too busy stealing glances at Beck. Only when Nolan stood up abruptly and crumpled up his lunch bag to throw in the trash can did I turn my head to peek at Payton. Her arms were wrapped around the guy's neck, and his hands rested dangerously low on her back. I watched Nolan slam his lunch into the trash. Beck's eyes flickered about. I didn't know how unstable her relationship was, but I gathered it may be rocky by the time this group was several drinks deep—in a place called Sin City, nonetheless.

I showed up on Thursday at Norton University, just long enough to catch Beck passing through the halls. I told her I had an errand to run at lunch, but that I'd see her at the airport. I didn't have errands to run, but I did fear wearing out my welcome. Figuring if I was going to be with Beck for a full weekend, I'd better give her a little space now. And if all went as planned, the statement "Absence makes the heart grow fonder," would ring true.

I spent the day at the old dive bar where I used to meet Clyde the second time around. I was reminded of the evenings I labored to make up for leaving him behind in an unfit home. He never did let me in, and ultimately, I realized we were more alike than I ever imagined us to be. Still, I wished I had a third chance to make it right. Simon had been nowhere in sight. I only hoped that he had moved on to a better life. And if I didn't find him in this one, perhaps I would see him in the next handful of lives to come. Joey no longer worked at the bar, which was to be expected at his age, and all the regulars had been replaced. Somehow, it felt more like home to me than the place I'd grown up. I knew that when I sat down in that dark grungy bar—whether or not I recognized the faces around me—that Clyde was with me.

After showering the stench of smoke and booze off my body, I packed a bag for the trip. It was nearly everything I had with me when I moved out of my home. Precisely enough to get by and not an ounce more. I sent an e-mail to Tina about the house and dabbled in stocks before I set my alarm for the morning flight. And when I closed my eyes that night, I hoped I would return to Clover a different man.

I filed onto the plane, careful not to bump the shoulders and elbows of the already seated passengers. The seating was open, and it was clear by the order in which the plane was being boarded that I wouldn't be sitting with Beck. She took a middle seat, her friend Payton by the window, and Nolan on the aisle. I squeezed past Nolan as he placed his carry-on overhead and found the second-closest seats available. Behind them and across the aisle sat James, Brooklyn, and I. Brooklyn would have been my second choice, and I could tell that the feeling was mutual.

James was a shorter, husky guy. His eyes were as dark as the mole on his left cheek. For what he lacked in height, though, he made up for in noise. I knew the key to his affection was none other than attention. It was the simplest personality to crack. I'd known my fair share of attention-seekers. Loud and boisterous, sometimes reckless and unforgiving. The need to be seen and heard trumped every other need . . . or so it would seem. But somewhere deep down was the need that always came up short—the one that was unmet and hidden away. I expected James to be no different, but what made him the most unique was not how bright his candle burned but how short the wick was. He wouldn't live a long life.

The flight attendant gave her spiel about safety, and though I had it memorized, I stared vaguely in her direction so I wouldn't appear rude. You didn't have to be an attention-seeker to want to be heard or respected; that was a shared personality trait amongst them all. Myself included.

Brooklyn fiddled with the air spout above us, and James opened his backpack, revealing a plethora of snacks. Had I not known better, I'd say he robbed the gift shop.

Brooklyn looked at me with a sympathetic eye. "It's a shame, huh?" she said, hurt filling her eyes.

I looked between her and James, and my skin turned warm. "What is?"

Brooklyn's gold eyes shifted, and she returned to being the carefree girl that I saw most of the time. "That he didn't get us any chocolate. Oh, can I have one of these?" She pointed to a roll of Sprees.

"Yeah, yeah! Take whatever you want," James said.

Brooklyn picked her candy, and James took his time digging through the salty and sweet for the perfect choice. I ran my hands through my hair, closing my eyes. It was all too clear that I was stressed. It was a slip-up, and I hadn't meant to show it.

Of course, Brooklyn would catch the one time I let my act fall for a brief breath in silence. "It's OK. I get scared too. I brought some shots. Let's take one now, so takeoff won't be so bad—because that's the worst part. Well, that and landing," Brooklyn said.

Even though fear of flying was not my issue, a shot may still be the fix.

"That sounds great. Thanks." A little something to take the edge off was exactly what I needed.

Brooklyn pulled out six shots. When the flight attendant turned her back, I passed three over to Nolan.

"Bottoms up!" James said and downed his shot. Brooklyn smiled an encouraging smile and wished me a happy birthday before she gulped half of the clear liquid, shaking her head a multitude of times before going at it again. I swallowed mine whole.

I wasn't much of a drinker. Not in this life, and not in most before. There was a time—a life—when I tried desperately to escape my cyclical, never-ending existence. But the drinking never fixed the loneliness, and to be honest, it just made me an asshole. That life went by in a blur. I was a burden on society, the worst part of many people's day. And then it ended. I died recklessly, just as I had lived. And then I started anew. When I looked back on that life, I always came up with the same question: what was the point? Since then, I'd rather feel the pain and be able to live with myself at the end of the day.

"Oh, God! It's *so* bad! How did you guys drink the whole thing like that?" Brooklyn stomped her feet against the floor like a child throwing a tantrum. Her twenty years of age were reflected in her acquired taste that was yet to be. It wasn't until a shiver ripped through her body that I laughed at her, lifting my mood. The warm liquid chased away the worry that I carried onto the plane with me, and I was so grateful that I asked for another.

James, Brooklyn, and I took another shot, this time not sharing with the other three. Brooklyn buried her face in the crook of her elbow and coughed as James and I laughed. No matter what happened on this trip, I was along for the ride; and for the first time since being invited, I was OK with that.

CHAPTER 10

The plane took off, throwing us back against our seats. Brooklyn grabbed hold of my wrist and then James's too. She scrunched her eyes closed tight, and I tried to comfort her the only way I knew how. I rattled off statistics.

"The chance of this plane crashing is only one in five-point-four million. You have a greater chance of being struck by lightning or mauled by a wombat. Just take a deep breath . . . and maybe another shot. Before you know it, we'll be in Vegas." While I may have included some of my own statistics, I was sure she wasn't listening to me either way.

Brooklyn took several deep breaths, and sometime after her third and fourth shot, she relaxed. Her body was heavy and her lips loose. She leaned in and divulged secrets about her friends. I soaked up every word like a sponge while James snored against the window.

"Payton's always had a thing for Nolan, even after they broke up in high school. She just can't seem to let him go. She won't admit it, of course, because Becca is her friend, so she pretends to be happy for them, but really, she's jealous as shit!" The smell of vodka lingered on her breath as the truth spilled out.

"So, is Beck serious with Nolan?" I asked.

Brooklyn sighed and looked up to the ceiling of the cabin. "Um, I mean, it's complicated. They're not like *exclusive,* if you will, but"—she took a moment to pop a Spree in her mouth and mull it over in her head—"I honestly think Beck likes him more than he likes her."

As much as I was happy that their bond was breakable, I still ached for Beck that she'd not been loved properly.

"I mean, look at him. He's gorgeous. Who wouldn't fall all over his feet?"

I looked in their direction, and a pang of jealousy drifted over me. "Do you like him, too?" I asked.

"Me?" Brooklyn pointed at the remainder of the Sprees, an extension of her finger, to her chest. "I wouldn't. He's not my type. He's . . . well, maybe? I mean, no! No, I don't like him. I like to look at him, but that's not the same thing. Huh, I'm saying too much aren't I?"

"No, you are saying just the right amount, actually."

We laughed, and I could tell she wasn't worried about me keeping her secrets.

"Can I tell you something?" I said. After much deliberation, I concluded Brooklyn put a lot of weight on trust. And though she was spilling everyone's secrets at the moment, I could tell it was more to do with the occupation of keeping her mind off the plane crashing than the alcohol erasing her inhibitions. Plus, the gossip was child's play compared to the secrets she really held dear. Her soul was buried at the depths of the ocean, and I wondered what had put it there. A trauma was my guess, but I wouldn't pry, as it was none of my business. The way to her heart was trust, and I knew how to be loyal. Brooklyn sensed as much, and I assumed some of that was why she'd chosen to open up to me.

"Anything!" Her eyebrows lifted in curiosity.

"Don't tell anyone, but"—her eyes focused on mine, the gold glimmer warm and inviting—"I always felt deep down in my gut that Beck was my soulmate. And one day, I plan to marry her," I said, all acting aside. As if two marriages weren't enough, I wanted a third. A traditional one.

Brooklyn sighed at the depth of my seriousness. "Oh my god! I got chills! I totally believe in that kind of stuff!" She lifted her arm between us, and it was covered in tiny goosebumps. "You know, I see it. It all makes sense. So much sense." She scratched her head, smiling off into the distance. "Now, can I tell you a secret?"

I leaned in, all ears. "What?"

"She's the missing piece to your puzzle." My brows pulled together, not understanding. Brooklyn pointed at Beck. "It's her. She's your missing piece," Brooklyn said in a whisper with a slight lisp, then gazed off in Beck's direction.

I followed her line of sight, and watching as Nolan lowered his head to Beck's. I was grateful that I could only see the back of her chair. Her soft giggle lifted into the air, and my stomach dipped, knowing that I'd not been the one to make her laugh. Still, through the pain, I enjoyed the sound.

Just as I was about to ask Brooklyn to elaborate, she turned to me, announcing she needed to use the restroom. I pressed my knees together and shifted to the side as Brooklyn straddled me ungracefully and crawled out of the row, making her way to the back of the plane.

I closed the hotel door behind me, thankful that Beck's room was adjacent to mine but more than a little disturbed that she was sharing it with Nolan. Brooklyn and Payton were placed in a room down the hall, and James was on the first floor, which suited his need to be amongst the bustling casino guests and flashing lights.

I unpacked, trying not to think about all the things Nolan was doing to Beck at the very moment, and I couldn't be more grateful that we didn't end up with adjoining rooms. Sharing a wall would be my new nightmare, making the boulder pale in comparison.

I tried to dispel the thoughts and unwelcome images with a shower. This couldn't really be my second life with Beck? I had amounted to nothing more than supporting best friend. Her birthday twin. Her old neighbor. Did she really not remember me? Our entire life before this?

I willed myself to remember my second life. It was a long time ago, and while I remembered that it was more difficult to understand the situation I had come upon then, I didn't have the clarity I needed to assess Beck's situation. I didn't know how to uncover the hidden memories because I had forgotten what it was like.

I dressed and spent a few extra moments messing with my hair. When it protested, I gave up. It didn't matter anyway. My eyes searched the mirror, looking for answers regarding how I ended up here and how I could find my way out. But the reflection only mocked me with unruly hair and dark shadows under my eyes. I was startled by the loud knock on my hotel door, and I left the man in the mirror for another time.

"Ooh! Don't you look handsome!" Brooklyn said as she stumbled into my room on the arm of Payton.

Payton was a cute girl with an athletic body; short and muscular. Her hair was long and mousy brown. It was thin and dry, and despite her toned body, I could tell that she didn't take care of herself.

"Where is Ev . . . Beck?" I asked the girls.

"She's probably in pound town right about now," Payton said, rolling her eyes.

Brooklyn backhanded her shoulder a little harder than I think she meant to, and I could see that my secret was already out by the way Payton responded with wide regretful eyes.

I turned away from the girls as they made themselves comfortable on my bed, and I stared out the window to the streets below. The people were like ants swarming the city. The girls talked about their plans for the night, and I only half-listened while the other half of me was with the people out my window. It was easier to think about them than "pound town." I ran my hand through my hair, disheveling it further.

Much more time passed than I would have liked before Beck and Nolan appeared. His hair was ruffled and his shirt wrinkled. The sight of him made my throat restrict, and I wondered how I would possibly make it through an entire weekend away with these lust birds. My prior resolve to settle in for the ride faded away with the buzz I had long ago, leaving me with a much more sober and somber tone.

"Let's get some drinks at the bar and do a little gambling while we wait for James. I've been dying to play the slots," Beck said as she swiped through her phone. My eyes trailed from her silver earrings swinging by her neck down to the curves of her thigh before darting away the moment her gaze lifted.

"Why don't we go to the buffet? Ribs, shrimp, pizza, all on one plate!" Nolan said holding his arms out as if there were no possible way anyone could refuse the thought of a heaping plate of mismatched food. I couldn't help it when the image of him hunching over a plate of meat scraps crossed my mind. How could she possibly be attracted to him? And now Payton and Brooklyn too? I watched him, my jaw slightly dropping as I scrambled to find the answers to his appeal, and finally resolved to the idea that his lure was not meant for me to see.

"OK, well, you do you . . . I'm going to get a margarita at the bar. We can meet up later." Payton threw her hands up in the air and walked out of the room. Brooklyn laughed and stumbled behind her, leaving Beck, Nolan, and I in an uncomfortable circle of awkward silence. Not soon enough, Nolan answered a phone call, taking several steps away. It wasn't much, but I felt the privacy between Beck and I return.

"How do you want to spend your twenty-first birthday?" I asked.

Beck slid her phone into her bag and took a seat on the edge of my bed. "I don't know. I just want to order a drink at a bar. At a pool. At a club. I'm going to be so mad if they don't card me! That's all I really want, to be carded. I want to flash my ID as much as possible this weekend." She leaned back onto her elbows, exposing an inch of flesh and the crevice of her belly button. My heart lurched, and I forced my gaze up to the ceiling.

"I'll make sure that they card you. Everyone in this forsaken city will think you're a minor, if that's what you want for your birthday," I said, avoiding the length of her body on top of my bed. Beck laughed, eyeing me suspiciously.

"What about you, birthday boy? How do you want to spend your twenty-first birthday?"

I wanted to spend it with her. Just as she was now. A smile on her face and a sparkle in her eyes. I wanted her to remember me. I wanted Nolan to be no more than history, and I wanted my future promised with a ring on her finger. "I . . . I want to try my hand at poker," I said as I felt the weight of my shallow lie. Though, it would be nice to pocket some cash for the weekend.

"Do you know how to play?"

"I used to play with my . . . grandpa." And for a moment I was back in the bar playing poker with Clyde and his drunken buddies. His foul mouth would always run, and his tough exterior never wavered, but the times that he laughed so hard he slapped the poker table and the chips would rumble were enough to keep me coming back time and time again. My lips twitched with a smile.

"Maybe you could teach me?" Beck's eyebrows raised, and the smile spread well beyond my face.

Nolan ended his call and informed Beck they were going to the buffet. Beck invited me, but I didn't need to look at Nolan to feel the radiating disapproval from him. I settled, promising to teach Beck how to gamble after their dinner.

We split after the elevator, and I made my way to the casino floor. The room was buzzing with cigarette smoke and high stakes. Most were drowning in the disappointment of lost wages, leaving few with chips in their pockets or optimism in their hearts. I spotted Brooklyn and Payton at the bar talking to a couple of men; I'd leave them to it.

After evaluating several tables, I found one to my liking and pulled up a seat. Three players, all men, and a dealer who was probably in her late sixties, early seventies. She wore a short skirt and a revealing top as part of her uniform. Her lips puckered with the wrinkles that only a long-time smoker earned in due time.

"Yes, pull up a seat, hon," she said in a splintered voice.

I joined the table, and the dealer counted me in. Two of the men eyed me, and the third didn't notice me at all. I was pretty good at poker because of my ability to read people, but I cursed myself for never taking the time to learn how to count cards. As the game began, I committed to learning in this lifetime, starting with this very game.

Time was lost as if in an alternate universe. It was a phenomenon that happened only to gamblers, and as I sat at that table, I was not immune to its powers. That's why I was surprised when Beck placed her hand on my shoulder some three hours later.

"There you are! I've been looking all over for you!"

"You have?" I looked around. I was nearly four thousand dollars up, and there was a new player at the table.

"Yeah, we finished dinner a while ago and we've all been at the bar."

I looked back as far as my eyes could stretch. There in the bar was a small group of people gathered around James as he told a lavish story with so much animation, he had an open ring around him further than his arms could reach. I returned my attention to the table and reaped my winnings, thanking the dealer with a tip.

"Wow, you're really good!"

"Oh, just beginner's luck," I said. Beck's brows knitted as I pocketed my chips. We started back to her friends, but before we got far, she asked if I knew how to play the slots.

"I don't play, but I'm sure we could figure it out together. Sit down, let's see," I said.

Beck took a seat at a nearby mermaid slot machine. It was her third serious consideration, and I poked fun of her every time she switched machines. She cracked every knuckle on both of her hands before shaking them out. The stress radiated off of her in sheets.

"Are you OK?"

"Yeah! I'm just getting ready," Beck said.

I laughed at her theatrics. "Alright then. If you're ready to lose some money, put the coin in, and pull the lever."

Beck looked at me like I was deceiving her. "Is that it?" she asked.

I shrugged, "Um, maybe push one of these buttons?"

"Oh my god! You don't even know how to use this thing!" Beck swatted at me, and I jumped backward when all I really wanted was to dive in close. Our playful banter was like a small sense of recognition. Her welcoming an old friend back into her life. The closer I got to her, the more I craved it. We messed around on the slots for a little while until Beck was sick of losing her money. Then, we took some of my winnings, and I taught her how to play roulette.

"Make sure you card this one. I don't think she's old enough to be here!" I said to the man in charge of the roulette.

He looked at me, unamused. "I'll need to see *both* of your IDs." Beck sucked in a quick breath and snickered into my shoulder. We handed our IDs to the man, who was twice my size. He gave them back with slight annoyance.

"Sir, I think your hair is on fleak!" Beck said. My eyes widened as I looked back to the man's head of thinning hair. Though I couldn't see the top, I was still sure that there would be a round balding patch. He frowned, causing Beck's cheeks to turn crimson.

"I thought it was a compliment. It was supposed to make him feel good. It doesn't work for me. It never has," Beck whispered, turning her face away from the man. Beck didn't know that she was still loud enough for him to hear, but he and I did.

I smiled an apologetic smile and handed him our bet. At least some things were still there hidden within Beck, and I briefly wondered if the alcohol would be the key that unlocked even more yet. After much deliberation, Beck chose black, and I think she enjoyed it more than pulling the lever on the slots. It was something in the way her eyes sparkled that made me want to reach out behind the nape of her neck and kiss her long and deep. But when I realized I couldn't, my smile began to fade as my eyes lingered on her lips.

Beck looked up at me after we lost, catching the desire in my eyes. She bit her lip, meeting my gaze before breaking. "Come on, let's get back to the others. I don't think you can afford to teach me any more games," Beck said as she grabbed my arm and led me away.

I followed her back to her friends, leaning into her arm, and when she stumbled, I was there to catch her. If I hadn't expected to see Nolan around the corner, I would have kept my hand wrapped around her tight; but that wasn't the case. The small group in the bar had downsized, and only James and a petite but equally outgoing girl remained. Several empty shot glasses fell over and rolled around on the table when James brought his fist down in a fit of laughter. My brows shot up as I counted.

"Where's everyone at?" Beck asked James.

James appeared surprised to see us, and it was clear that we were interrupting his conversation. "Oh, I don't know. They left a while ago." James vaguely waved to the exit sign. His eyes were red and glossy.

Beck took out her phone and stepped away to make a call. She must be reaching out to Nolan. I turned back to the table before me, and James and his new friend were carrying on as if I was no longer present.

I thrust my hands into my pockets and looked around the bar. One gentleman in particular caught my eye. He was a little older than the rest of the crowd. Forties perhaps. He sat alone, red hair resting to the side of his face. I didn't have to see his eyes to know he was a Tethered Soul. I could feel it. The same way someone knows when they're being watched, even though, presumably, nobody's in the room with them. I simply knew that in this bar full of strangers, he and I were the same. He'd lived many lives before, and his energy was palpable. The tortured pain of loneliness so thick I could reach out and touch it. On the contrary, Beck's was weak. So weak that she didn't even believe it to be true, and had I not known her in our last life, I wouldn't have believed it either.

"I can't get a hold of anyone. I think I'm going to turn in for the night." I could see the disappointment etched in Beck's face.

"What!? You can't do that! It's your birthday! You've got to celebrate!" I grabbed her hands and raised them into the air, forcing her to cheer for herself. It worked, but not for long. Her smile was fleeting.

"Well, I don't know what to do. I mean, I don't know where everyone is."

"What does everyone have to do with anything?" I said, trying not to let her see my disappointment. I wasn't enough. Not yet.

"Well, what do *you* want to do? It's your birthday too!" she said.

"I would take it personally if you ditched me on my birthday. Let's go have some fun! If not for you, then do it for me!" I knew it would work. She couldn't let someone down.

"OK! Yeah, you're right. I'm in! What are we doing?" Beck pushed the pale hair out of her face and rubbed her hands together in anticipation. A second wind.

I used this opportunity to take a page out of my playbook. "You know, I've always wanted to go bungee jumping, and I think that can be done off one of the skyscrapers here." My stomach knotted while I said it. The last thing I wanted to do was jump off a building, but if I thought that Beck's life would be enriched by doing so—and I did—I would jump right alongside her.

"Really!? Oh my god! I've always wanted to do that!" Her eyes were large and filled with excitement.

"Yeah! Or, we could get tattoos!" It was also on her list, and if I had my choice of being stabbed by a needle one trillion times or jumping off of a skyscraper, I would choose the mutilation.

"No way!" Beck's mouth popped open, the light catching her lip gloss. I tried hard to keep my eyes on hers, but they kept dropping to her lips. Beck's expression shifted, and the window of opportunity for an epic night was closing fast. "Maybe we should wait until—"

"Let's order ourselves a cake and take it to the hot tub. We can give everyone a little while longer to resurface, and if they don't, then we'll jump off a building by ourselves. Deal?" As I continued, Beck's lips sealed tight in deliberation. "We can't celebrate our birthdays without a cake. We need to make a wish, right?"

"Deal! You had me at cake . . ."

It wasn't my favorite plan, but at least she wasn't going back to her room alone to wait for her boyfriend. We didn't need to say goodbye to James. He wouldn't remember it tomorrow anyway. My eyes jumped from James to the Tethered Soul at the bar before leaving. He hadn't turned around, and I hoped that I would run into him again before the weekend was over.

CHAPTER 11

Beck dropped her towel on a nearby chair and kicked off her flip-flops. She reached her hand up to her hair and gathered it in a small ponytail and my eyes ran down her side, remembering our first time together. My jaw hardened, and my heart beat out of rhythm. Just as she lifted her head to look at me, I whipped my gaze away. Afraid I had given myself away, I made it worse by stumbling over my flip-flops. I looked back at her and caught the tail end of her smile. Of course, she saw it. I shook my head, disappointed in my lack of agility. I placed my card key on a small patio table before covering it with my towel, and then I pulled my shirt off over my head. If I wanted Beck to notice anything, it was this, but her back was turned.

I tried not to stare as Beck tiptoed into the hot tub. Her body was enveloped by the heat as steam rose around her. It was like a dream coming true before my very eyes, and I never wanted to wake up. My eyes trailed from her shoulders to her hips, noting the subtle differences from one life to the next. She was stronger. Healthier. Her skin, however, remained unchanged. Just as pale, it glistened like alabaster, even in the night's shadows.

"I really do want to bungee jump," she said, turning around to take me in. I was just as sun-deprived as she, but my skin didn't glisten with the multitude of undertones like hers. She was simply stunning.

I stepped into the water and the smell of chlorine permeated the air and burned my nostrils. Pins and needles pricked my toes as I stepped deeper. My eyes set on Beck.

"I just think I would feel so free . . . like a bird in flight. Do you think it feels like that?"

I couldn't help but let out a short, blunt laugh as I felt jumping would be the polar opposite. "No! I'm pretty sure it feels like your life is ending."

Beck splashed me in protest, and I flinched as the scalding water slapped at my chest. But I didn't think. I knew. I'd never bungee jumped before, but I had gone skydiving. And I related the freefall to anything but a bird in flight. "Birds are peaceful up there in the air. I think you've confused flying with falling."

Beck raised a brow. "Then why did you want to do it!?" she asked. It was a valid question. One I couldn't answer truthfully.

"I think it's good to do the things that scare you. It's what life's about, you know?"

Beck smiled softly and looked down into the water.

"Speaking of, I thought you were afraid of the water?" I could see Beck blush even through the dim light and thick steam.

"Not when I can touch the bottom." Beck rolled her eyes. "It's so embarrassing. It's just this really weird irrational fear. I don't know what else to say about it."

"You don't have to say anything. Maybe you drowned in another lifetime or something?" I tested the waters and watched her intently for any show of recognition. And for a split second, I thought she seriously considered it. But then the air shifted, and I let the breath out that I hadn't known I was holding.

Beck laughed dismissively. "Oh, come on!" She rolled her eyes as if it were the stupidest thing she'd heard and picked up her cocktail and sucked down a substantial amount.

I wasn't ready to give up just yet. I waited, letting the thought simmer a while longer. Her eyebrows furrowed as she played with her straw. "How did we get here?" Beck asked as she swiped her hand across the rumbling bubbles of the water's surface, her eyes unfocused.

"What do you mean?" I asked.

"I mean, we're already twenty-one, and I don't know about you, but I have nothing figured out. Sometimes I feel like I don't even know who I am. I thought I would have a plan by now, you know? But I don't. Not even close. Do you ever just take a moment and reflect on your life, and wonder how the hell you got here? Do you ever wonder where you're going? Or what even matters in the first place?" Beck threw her head back and stared up at the stars. I watched as the steam rose and collected under her chin. Her exposed throat begged to be kissed.

"You have no idea," I said, taking her drink from her and placing it on the hot tub's edge.

Beck looked at me, her eyes filled with sympathy, a shared understanding. "Sometimes I feel like my entire life has been a lie. I wonder if there's more out there. There has to be more to it than this."

She searched my eyes, desperately seeking understanding. "I worry more than I would like to admit that I'm living the wrong life," she said.

"The *wrong* life?"

"I mean, what if I took the wrong path? What if I get lost? It would be the wrong life. The one that wasn't meant for me."

"I know this may not seem like much coming from me, but I think you're living an extraordinary life," I said. I inched a little closer, fighting my instincts to comfort her.

"You do? What makes you think that?"

"Your heart runs so deep that I think you can make the impossible happen, and whoever you choose to open your heart to will be the luckiest soul to ever walk this earth." It poured out of me. No regrets.

Beck lifted one dripping hand and ran it through her hair. Her mouth partially separated as she bit into her bottom lip. And if I wasn't mistaken, I thought I saw a flash of hunger in her eyes.

"I wonder if our paths crossing a second time is a coincidence or something more. I feel something when I'm around you. Something I can't explain." Beck lowered deep into the water, her chin partially submerged and her eyes burrowing into me.

"Try?" I said.

"I couldn't even begin to explain it. And I'd be afraid of coming off like a complete lunatic. It's . . . I mean, it's . . ." Beck closed down and turned away from me. She moved to the opposite side of the Jacuzzi, one arm resting on the cold pavement as she looked into the distance.

"How about I tell you how I feel instead? I'll be the lunatic for both of us." I closed the distance between us and looked out into the darkness as she did.

Beck laughed nervously. "OK then . . . Give it your best shot."

"I feel like the stars have aligned ever so perfectly for our lives to intertwine . . . *again*." Beck brought her wet hands to her eyes, pressing her palms deep into her sockets. When her back rose with her heavy breath, I feared I had said too much. Too soon.

"Easton Green, *who are you?*" She cocked her head to the side and raised her eyebrows in question. It was more of an accusatory look than a warm invitation. My chest constricted and I swallowed down a bullet of worry. She knew I was more than a neighbor. That much was obvious, but the truth was still cloaked, and I feared it may scare her once she figured it out.

I closed my eyes and tilted my head up to the night sky. I didn't know what to say. *Who was I?* She was asking me, point-blank, and I couldn't answer. It was an impossible situation. In love with a girl who simply didn't remember me, and if she did, her entire world would crumble to her feet. It was in that moment that I wondered if I was better off not knowing her at all. If this would be slow torture, a new cage . . . another tether.

What she did next was the last thing I'd expected. Her body pressed against mine, and she wrapped her hand around the nape of my neck, pulling me down to her. I lowered my head as she lifted onto her toes, planting a wet chlorine kiss softly on my lips. I opened my eyes to see a flicker of desire reflect in her expression, and she was no longer Becca but my Everly Beck. She'd come home. I hated myself for ever thinking the pain wouldn't be worth it because in that moment, I knew I could chase her for all of eternity.

And then, without notice, as if awakened abruptly from a dream, her affection drained from her face and regret washed over her. "Oh my god, I'm *so* sorry! I don't know why I did that!"

"No, no, no. Don't be sorry!" I reached my hand out to grab her, but she was already stepping out of the hot tub. "Don't go, Beck!" I pleaded.

"I'm so sorry. I need to find Nolan!" Beck grabbed her towel and took off in a half walk, half jog, wrapping her towel tightly around her chest. In an instant, I was left with nothing more than her forgotten flip-flops and wet footprints on the pavement floor.

Three employees holding a small cake with a lit candle passed Beck on her way out. I closed my eyes, wishing them away, but when I opened them, they stood at the hot tub's edge. Two girls and one boy sang one of the worst renditions of "Happy Birthday" I'd ever heard. And that was saying a lot. Maybe it was the collective lack of talent, or maybe it was the pain of my broken heart boiling with the fear of losing my soulmate. But either way, it was one of the most difficult fifteen seconds I'd ever faked. When the coyote call was finally over, they held the cake out for me to make my wish. The candle danced wildly as if even it were protesting. I was so humiliated, I blew the candle out almost instantly, never making a wish at all. Which was a shame, because I could really use one.

"Where should we—" The three of them looked around for a place to put the birthday cake.

"You can just put it with my towel over there. Thank you," I said.

I didn't wait for them to leave. I took a deep breath and submerged myself to the bottom of the hot tub. The heat burned my cheeks, offering me temporary relief from the actual pain I felt inside. I knew now that the spark between Beck and I was not a fluke. The tether between her and I was still as strong as ever. Present, though her memory was not. And if I could hold on, just a little while longer, maybe she would come around.

I racked my brain, thinking of the possible ways I could help bring her memory back. I wondered how I could get her on the New River Bridge. How I could take her to the open field overlooking the Truly River and sit her in the roots of the dead oak tree. It wouldn't be a simple task, but it was a goal I could work towards. It was a goal I could focus on. Maybe then she'd come back to me.

An elderly couple approached the hot tub. The woman was holding onto her husband's arm for support as she took her first steps into the water. They smiled politely at me.

"Do you need a hand?" I asked.

"Oh, aren't you a sweetheart." The lady reached out and placed her small, frail hand in mine. I helped guide her down the steps as she yipped and yipped over how hot the water was.

"Well, what did you expect? It's called a hot tub for a reason, Marge!" The old man bickered.

I couldn't help but laugh, and through all the pain and suffering my heart had been through tonight, I couldn't help but find the humor in this geriatric couple. It was the blind leading the blind. They most likely had fallen into a rut where they only spoke to each other through jabs of criticism or sarcasm. And if I had to guess, they wouldn't have it any other way. I never wanted to grow old, but in that moment, I wanted nothing more than to grow old with Beck.

"You think you're so tough, why don't you come in here!"

"I'm coming! I'm coming! Someone's got to put your robe on the table! The Lord knows you won't do it." The man shuffled in his trunks to the water's surface.

"What's that?"

"Nothing!" The man grumbled as he stepped into the water. "Damn that's hot!"

"I *told* you!" The woman looked at me and shook her head exhaustedly.

"Yeah, it's a little hot, but it will feel good once you get used to it," I said.

The man froze, staring at me and patting his bare boobs. "Where are my glasses?" He looked between me and his wife.

It was the reason I never wanted to grow old before. I had no reason to wither away in body and soul if I had no one to do it with.

"They're on your head, you dummy!" She looked in my direction, and for the life of me, I couldn't figure out why I was included in the conversation. "I swear, he'd lose his own butt if it weren't attached!"

I chuckled, and the old man groaned as he took another step into the water. He waved his hand dismissively as if he'd heard it all before. I wondered what growing old with Beck would be like. And though I was worried I'd never have the chance to find out, I let myself hope. If I had made that wish, I would have wished for one long life with Beck.

"You two have a nice night," I said as I stepped out of the hot tub and grabbed my towel. Alone and deep in thought, I strolled back to my hotel room. But when I came to my room, I was shocked to see Payton slip out of Nolan's suite and stumble away, adjusting her clothing. She barreled down the hall, walking anything but straight. If she noticed me at all, she didn't say anything. I looked over my shoulder and watched her round the corner, twisting her ankle in her heels and nearly falling to the floor.

"God damn it!" she cursed, sharp enough for me to clearly hear it down the hallway. Her cutting tone was not from the pain of a twisted ankle but, rather, regret.

CHAPTER 12

I pushed my door open and stepped inside my room, wondering where Beck had been, and if she had any knowledge of Payton's presence next door. I paced the depths of my hotel room in my towel until I couldn't take it any longer. After dressing in dry clothes, I headed to Brooklyn's room, hoping to find Beck. But when Brooklyn answered the door, I didn't see Beck wounded like I thought I might. Instead, I was surprised to see Payton there. If I had to guess, she was probably using Brooklyn as her alibi.

"Easton, come in. Have a drink."

"I'm just looking for Beck, have you seen her?"

"No. Payton, have you seen Beck?"

"Nope!" Payton said from inside.

"Come in!" Brooklyn echoed.

"Thanks, maybe later. See ya," I said, already making my getaway. Beck was nowhere in sight. And both girls appeared confused about where she might be. Only one of them was being honest, though.

I texted Beck, asking to talk, but she didn't reply. Tapping my phone across the palm of my hand, I stood beside the elevators, waiting for the reply that would never come. I took one last sweeping look for Beck down in the casino and bar before returning to my room for the night.

When the elevator door opened, a couple making out in the corner startled and separated. The man was wearing more of her lipstick than his partner. I joined them as they snickered behind my back. The elevator air was thick with anticipation—theirs and mine—but if we had to agree on one thing, it was that the elevator doors couldn't open soon enough. I closed my eyes and counted in my head until the electric buzz of people and machines crowded my senses.

Cigarette smoke clouded the floor, and the slots chimed obnoxiously. It was easy for one's senses to be overloaded. I tried to block it all out. Focus. I needed to hone in on my tether. But after walking a few laps around the casino and lobby, I found myself in the shadows of the hotel bar. Beck was nowhere to be found.

The redheaded soul sat hunched over the bar as if he hadn't moved an inch in the past decade. My shoulders dropped, letting go of the tension I'd been holding since Beck left me at the hot tub. Before opting to join the gentleman, I took one last peak—as far as my sight could travel. When Beck's ashen hair was nowhere to be found, I sat. The man's hair swept in front of his face, yet the hard lines of his jaw were still visibly tightened. He was like stone, petrified and historical.

"Two of whatever he's having, please," I said to the bartender.

I adjusted my barstool closer to the bar, and the gentleman ever so slowly turned to me. When he did, I could see the years of pain etched in his eyes. They were green with gold flecks. He was an Irishman. Middle-aged on the outside, but his soul reached well beyond the time I'd seen. He studied me, as I did him. I waited for him to speak first. Perhaps he didn't want to talk at all. Either way, I'd be here to let him know he wasn't alone. Even if it were for just a drink.

The bartender placed two whiskey and sevens in front of us, and I handed him my credit card and ID.

The bartender looked at my ID and smiled. "Happy Birthday, man!"

"Thank you."

The Irishmen slid his empty glass to the bartender, who took it with an exasperated glint in his eyes. He'd probably been here longer than this evening alone. Maybe days or a week.

"Huh," he grunted after sipping his refreshed whiskey. "I haven't come across one of you for a long time."

"Few and far between," I nodded, slugging back a gulp. The amber liquid lashed out, burning my chest and settling in my belly.

"They sure are." He held his glass up to cheers mine. The glasses clinked together, and I slapped his back before finishing my double shot.

"Do you have time for a story?" I asked. His need for camaraderie was nearly tangible, but he was slow to open up. He reminded me of Clyde in this way, which made me like him even more. I knew *my* story would breathe life back into him. He didn't speak, but instead, turned his focus to me. I told him all about Beck. Her cancer. Our crash. Finally, her forgotten love. I'd lost all sense of time. One drink after another, and I could have talked for hours. Probably did. I thought he almost didn't believe it, but by the time I finished speaking, I could see that he did. His jaw had slackened, and his eyes took on a softer tone. He not only believed me, but he was moved by my story.

"She's here?" he asked, peering around the bar.

"Yeah. Somewhere."

"Damn. I'd never heard such a story." He shook his head. An unheard story was hard to come by when you'd been around as long as we had.

"Me neither! I was hoping you'd have some advice for me!" I took a deep swig of my drink. It was most likely the one that put me over the edge.

He laughed, "Me? Oh, no, no, no. Just because I've seen a lot, doesn't give me the right to hand out advice. Lord knows I've made a muck of my own lives." He shook his head and took down the last of his drink, proceeding to watch his ice in the bottom of his glass as he swirled his tumbler around in small circles.

"I guess you need more practice." I laughed under my breath, and the stone man found the humor too. His hunched back bounced before his face fell flat once more.

"Yes, fella. That's surely what I need. But if I know one thing, it's not in the cards." He stood up and threw his jacket over his shoulder. He was a tall man, much taller than I expected. "Now, I don't do this regularly, and I have half the mind to tell you not to listen to me. But I'm going to leave you with a bit to chew on."

"Alright then." I swiveled in my barstool and clasped my hands in my lap awaiting the Irish advice from a man who hadn't yet figured out his own life. Despite the many tries.

"Tell her the truth," he said, blunt and harsh—true to fashion.

It hit harder than I'd imagined it would. The word *truth,* burning a hole in my stomach far worse than the whiskey. As if I'd been the one hiding it from her. I never wanted to hide anything from her.

The man placed his gigantic hand on my shoulder and squeezed. "Take care of yourself."

I nodded.

He was halfway out of the bar when I yelled after him, "Hey, I didn't catch your name!"

"William!" He waved over his head as he disappeared around the corner.

I woke abruptly that morning with a text from Brooklyn. The ping pounded in my head, nearly rupturing my temples.

Meet at the buffet for breakfast in ten.

I jumped to my feet, grasping at my temples. *Water.* I needed water. I opened up the mini-fridge and grabbed an overpriced water. Ripping the cap off, I guzzled it down. I brushed my teeth as I dressed one-handed. I barely had my shoes on by the time the hotel door slammed behind me. Beck's room was quiet, and despite checking my phone a million times over, she had not texted, and I wondered if she would be at breakfast.

I wasn't hungry until I caught the smell of bacon and syrup wafting in the air as I neared the breakfast buffet. I immediately spotted Brooklyn and Payton at a table near the entry. I sat down next to Brooklyn and across from Payton, who repelled my eye contact.

"Morning! How was your night last night? Did you ever find Becca?" Brooklyn asked.

"No, I didn't. She never stopped by your room?"

Brooklyn shook her head but then lifted her gaze and said, "Speak of the devil!"

I whipped around to see Beck, her face pale and puffy. She too avoided eye contact. Nolan was quick on her heels, and he had a distinct air to him. If there were a word for his aura. I'd say . . . *smug*.

Nolan took the seat furthest away from me, leaving only two options for Beck to choose from. She opted to sit between Nolan and Payton. *That's* how much distaste she had for me?

"Where's James?" I asked.

Payton laughed, "You'll be lucky if you see James before the plane ride home." When our eyes met, there wasn't an ounce of guilt behind them. I couldn't tell if it was because she wasn't sorry or she thought she hadn't gotten caught.

Nolan let out a muffled huff and added, "*If* he makes the plane."

Everyone seemed to agree it was a real possibility that James would be stuck here in Sin City. I gathered it was for no reason other than his lack of responsibility and short-sightedness. From what I saw last night in the bar, I was sure that he could be easily sidetracked by anyone who gave him their undivided attention.

Our server approached with a full pot of coffee, and my stomach turned sour at the sight alone. After our coffees were poured, our table was released to the madness of the buffet. Everyone split, and I took special notice that Beck started in the opposite direction of Nolan. Had she seen what I saw last night? Did she suspect Nolan was with Payton? Perhaps the most important question was, did it matter?

I took a clean plate into my hands and snuck behind her at the fruit and yogurt bar.

"You're avoiding me . . ." I saw no point in beating around the bush when I had so little time to talk to her. It wouldn't be long before we were in earshot of one of her friends. And in a matter of seconds, she could be at the omelet station, and I'd be standing in the middle of the bustling buffet . . . with Nolan.

"No!" Beck said in a sharp tone.

"Yes, you are. Strawberries?" I held a spoonful of strawberries between us and she paused, softening a little before moving her plate underneath the spoon. Ripe red strawberries rolled across her plate.

"OK! I am. It's awkward! And I'm sorry about last night. I feel like an ass. It's just, it shouldn't have happened," Beck admitted.

It was a blow but not an unexpected one. I'd already had the night to feed upon her regrets. I pushed them aside and trudged forward. "Beck, we're friends, right?" I'd used this a time or two on her before, and it worked well. There was no reason to think it wouldn't now.

"Um, yeah. Sure."

Unconvincing. I furrowed my brows. "Whipped cream?"

"Yes, please," she said. Interesting, how she was so sure she wanted whipped cream on her strawberries but not so sure that her neighbor from when she was eight—her two times over husband, her soulmate—was worthy of such a simple title as *friend*. I slopped the whipped cream on top of her fruit, and it was the glue that held the berries together.

"Don't think for one second that our *friendship* is so easily disposable. If you want to forget this kiss, it's as good as forgotten," I said, hushed.

Beck stopped and looked up to meet my eyes for the first time since our kiss in the hot tub. And in lieu of a response, she nodded.

Just because lying was so easy for me, it didn't make it acceptable. William's advice rang through my head. I knew that deceit was wrong. But it came with the territory. And if Beck was more comfortable thinking I'd forgotten last night's kiss, then so be it. The truth was, I was like an elephant. Every detail of all my lives was preciously preserved in my memory. Except for the first few lives, that is. They were . . . fuzzy. I presumed this is how Beck's memory would work as well. In a couple more lifetimes, she wouldn't remember I had lied to her. And my highest hopes were that she wouldn't remember a time when her love for me fell absent.

Our group ate breakfast while rehashing the night before. Trying to figure out how each puzzle piece fit together—the when's and how's of how everyone ended up separated. I caught a few stolen glances between Nolan and Payton while Beck moved her food around on her plate absentmindedly. James showed halfway through breakfast somewhere between our first and second helpings of unlimited food.

"James! You're alive! I was beginning to worry!" Payton called out.

"No, you weren't!" James said.

"You're right, I wasn't!" Payton laughed.

James approached our table, and his hungry eyes scanned the massacre of dishes and uneaten food on the table. He grabbed Nolan's shoulder and squeezed it tight, intending to inflict as much pain as possible, but Nolan was nearly twice his size. "Oh, man! You're eating Polish sausage? That's a *bold* move!"

Nolan pulled away from James's grip. "No! It's good! You should try it!"

My stomach turned at the very sight of his sausage link. Mixed splotches of brown and grey. Three down, one left to go.

"I'm all good! I think I'll pass on the water-rhea!" James took off in search of food as the table chuckled in his wake.

The chatter continued in James's absence, but when he returned with his breakfast, the conversation took on a whole new life. It was crude and brash, and I loved every moment. Shots flew in every direction. Some aimed at my hair, some fired toward James's sex-capades from the night before, but most . . . Most were aimed towards Nolan and his grumbling stomach.

He tried to play it cool, but when his knuckles turned white, and sweat beaded at his hairline, I about rolled out of my chair laughing. I wanted desperately to control the sound that exploded from our table, but I couldn't think about the other guests' dining experience with that ferocious rumbling coming from the depths of Nolan's intestines. No, all I could think about was air! I needed to breathe but couldn't! My head was nearly resting on the table, I was so doubled over, and tears streamed from my eyes. All of my worries had been chased away by laughter. Every time I thought I had a handle on it, Nolan's stomach would grumble again, and the group would erupt into a fit of laughter. Even Beck. *Especially* Beck.

Finally, when Nolan couldn't play tough anymore, he slammed his fist down on the table and said, "Screw this!" and stormed off. Through teary eyes, I could just make out Nolan trotting off, tail tucked as he ran straight to one of the nearest restrooms.

It was the best thing I'd seen in years, and I wished I hadn't eaten so much because my stomach was taking a beating from laughter. There was no doubt in my mind about having pulled at least one abdominal muscle. Brooklyn rubbed her eyes so viciously, mascara ran down her cheeks, making her look like a panda bear. Beck wiped away the tears from her swollen eyes. If she enjoyed it more than she should have—and I think she did—I knew why. She must have had her suspicions about Nolan's loyalty.

By the time breakfast was over, I had a new fondness for Beck's friends. James and his endless stream of dialogue were truly a brightly burning candle. One day, I imagined I'd miss having him around. And when the dust settled, Brooklyn put eye drops into her eyes, the excess streaming down her mascara-stained cheeks, before winking at me with a marked sense of pride.

CHAPTER 13

With breakfast over, the group retreated to their rooms. I lingered. It was an invitation for Beck to pick up where we'd left off, and it didn't go unnoticed. She turned, playing with the sleeves of her shirt. Only after she opened her mouth did she close it again and stare at her shoes. She didn't have to say anything to express herself. I could feel it in the surrounding air. Her worry collided with anticipation and burst into a plume of wonder. It was enough to make my heart swell. At the very least, she wasn't mad at me.

"What are you going to do today? It's your last day in Sin City, and your boyfriend has food poisoning," I said.

"He's *not* my boyfriend!" Beck's face filled with distaste.

Surprise washed over me. "Wait, he's not?"

Beck's eyes scanned the casino, looking for answers in the flashing lights, and when she found what she was looking for, she said, "Come on!" She grabbed my arm, pulling me to her side.

"Where are we going?"

"We have living to do!"

A snort escaped me. "And what does that mean, specifically?"

"We're going bungee jumping!"

I was thankful she didn't turn around to see my face when she said it. If she had, she would have witnessed an awful shade of green in my cheeks. My gait slowed naturally as I instinctively tried to postpone the leap. But she only tightened her grip and charged forward. Sometimes the girl knew just what she wanted. Who was I to get in the way? I swallowed the sour taste of fear and told myself to suck it up. I had to be brave for Beck, and that's precisely what I intended to do. I had the entire trip to the launch pad to get myself there.

I caught up to her, side by side, and scanned her expression. It was cold, her eyes vacant. She didn't want to live. She just had something to prove. My guess was that it had to do with Nolan. But if she wanted to prove to herself that she didn't need him to have a memorable twenty-first birthday. Who was I to judge? I loved her either way, and I'd be jumping off the tallest skyscraper in the state to prove it to her.

"You're sure you want to do this?" I asked, my long legs in stride to keep up with her pace.

"Absolutely!" She continued, her sights set on hailing a taxi.

Beck didn't glance in my direction until we were inside the cab, and even then, it was brief. She looked away the second I returned her attention. I knew she was hurting inside, and I wanted desperately to take that away for her, but it was hard to do when she refused to let me in. I pulled my gaze away from the back of her head and stared out my window.

It was a short distance to the destination, but the traffic caused the ride to be much longer than expected. When we arrived, I tipped the cab driver and helped Beck out of the car. She placed her hand in mine, and I gripped it tight, not wanting to let go. She pulled her hand back when she was upright, and I couldn't help the wash of disappointment that spread through my chest.

"Do you want to talk about—"

"About what?" Beck asked in a tone that was intended to be light and airy but only sounded disingenuous.

I nodded, taking the hint that now was not the time for her innermost confessions. Perhaps it would have to wait until after we lost our breakfast.

We signed up for the jump and were thrust into a twenty-minute educational course. They taught us what to expect, what to do, and what not to do. Beck's focus was intense, but I mainly paid attention to her. Dying would be a bitch, but it didn't hold as much weight for me as it did everyone else. I thought back to William, the Irishman, and imagined he would jump without even taking the safety course. Me, on the other hand, I'd just let the lesson float in one ear and out the other while I dreamed about my wife.

The time had come for our jump, despite my efforts to stop time altogether. The elevator filled with tension so thick that Beck was having trouble keeping her breathing under control. Her face flushed, and her hands were restless at her side. I couldn't help but smile.

"What? Don't give me that look!"

"You're really scared, aren't you?" I asked.

"No, I'm not!"

I stared at her in disbelief and called her out on her bluff. "Liar!"

A sharp *bing* signified we were at the top of the skyscraper, and Beck jumped a fitting mile high. I bit my cheek as Beck's body betrayed her. The elevator doors opened, and I tried my damnedest to hold it in, but I was busting at the seams. A loud boisterous laugh escaped me and I covered my mouth with not one but both hands. The angrier Beck got, the harder I laughed. I could hardly hear anything the guy said when he was binding my feet. Tears welled up in my eyes, and I clutched my stomach. It was breakfast all over again as my nerves transformed into hysteria.

"Stop that!" Beck hissed as her feet were being bound. The smallest curvature of her lips told me that in some small way, I was helping to distract her. It wasn't on purpose, though. I couldn't help the fact that she pretended to be so confident, but when the time had come, she was crumbling to pieces. It was *so* Beck.

The two men helped Beck and me to our feet, and gave us one last rundown of instructions before walking us out to the edge of the building. Beck and I stood on two red Xs in front of an endless panoramic view. The air was cool and the sky cloudless. The world bustled below, unaware of our pounding hearts above. I looked down at the congestion of traffic below, and I couldn't help feeling relieved being so far removed from it all. If I wasn't about to plunge eight hundred feet down, I might see how this would remind Beck of a bird in flight.

Triple checks were being made on our safety before we were told to walk to the edge. I smiled at Beck, but my face fell flat when I saw she was not having the same experience as I was. Her face was pale as a ghost, and her eyes the size of golf balls.

"Hey, Beck. Look at me!" Ever so slowly she turned her head, and our eyes locked. "You are an incredibly strong woman. You don't need Nolan or anyone else for that matter. You've got this!" Beck puckered her lips and blew out a breath she'd been holding tight. "We're going to do this together, OK? You wanted to live, and this was on your list. Right here, right now, you're going to check this off! You're going to be a bird, and it's going to be just like you're flying! You still want to fly right?"

Beck nodded slowly, tears forming in her eyes.

"OK, I'll be right there with you. I promise, Beck. I'll be right by your side! Do you trust me?"

Beck sucked in a breath and nodded once more. Her hands were balled into white fists at her sides.

"Alright, I'm going to count to three, and you're going to tip forward. On my count! One!"

A small squeal escaped Beck's throat.

". . . Two!"

"Fuck, fuck, fuck, fuck," Beck said under her breath. I curled my toes in my shoes and felt the ledge give way underneath them. Suddenly I was back on the New River Bridge on the cold, wet night that I met Beck.

"Three! Go!"

Shit! I closed my eyes and let my body fall forward. Gravity sucked me into its vortex as I plunged downward. Time sped and slowed to a crawl, all at the same moment. Beck let out a guttural scream that slipped into the distance between us. The freefall was one I'd felt before and similar to what I would have felt if I had jumped off the New River Bridge. I braced myself for the darkness. The darkness that only followed death. In the moment, bursting with adrenaline, I'd forgotten that I would open my eyes once the fall was over.

This jump was made for the thrill. Coming close to death but not yet touching it. It wasn't a thrill to me—to someone who had died a dozen times too many. And no matter how many times I might take a jump like this, my life would start over again. And again.

I was lost in the moment of falling. Wrapped up in the feeling of dying—without death—that I didn't realize something was wrong. Off. Beck's scream was not by my side. And when I heard it, the feral sound stretched until it was gaping between us.

I opened my eyes to see the world spinning and tumbling. I flailed around, trying to get an understanding of the world as I knew it. The tension on the bungee reached its max capacity and recoiled like a rubber band. Blood rushed to my head and my feet pulled before I was falling in reverse. This was an entirely new feeling and one I liked even less. But it was on my up that I could see that Beck's bungee had never left the platform.

My speed slowed until I was nearly floating in midair. Then the fall came again. And again. And again. When the torture was finally over, I hung upside down, suspended from the skyscraper, my eyes wanting to bulge from my head as the pressure built. My arms outstretched overhead, and I swung slightly as they pulled me up. All I could think was, *She didn't jump.* I couldn't believe she didn't jump! Beck didn't know it yet, but she was my partner. We didn't have one lifetime together but an infinite amount of time on this earth. Had she known that, I'm confident, she would have jumped. But because she didn't, I'd spend the rest of my life getting her back.

When I breached the platform, and my body was finally resting upright, my head spun. I could feel the blood funneling down to my extremities. Chasing away the pins and needles. When my vision finally cleared, I turned to look at Beck, who hadn't spoken a single word. Her eyes were huge, her hands cupping her mouth. A small squeak sounded but nothing comprehensible. We stared at each other while the men untied my legs.

"I thought we had living to do?" I cocked my head to the side.

"I'm so sorry!" Beck finally said.

"It's OK. It's my fault. When I said, I'd be by your side, I assumed, that went both ways. But I was mistaken," I said, shaking my head and pretending not to care. But the truth was, I was *so* going to get her back!

"I'm seriously so sorry! I couldn't do it!" Beck grabbed her stomach, still shaken.

I scrambled to my feet, a little unsteady, and held my arms out for a hug. She came bounding into my arms, and I wrapped them around her tight. The smell of coconut brought me back to a time when I was tangled up with her in bedsheets. I wanted to live in the memory but forced myself back to the present. Another nervous man was being strapped and lectured. He peered at me nervously.

"It's OK, really. But you owe me," I said with a smile.

Beck laughed a wildly nervous laugh. "Deal!" she said. Her breath was warm against my neck, and I didn't want to let her go.

She pulled away. "How was it? Tell me everything!" Beck asked as we walked to a nearby lookout point. The same magnificent view but with the safety of guardrails and plexiglass.

"It was amazing . . . really like spreading your wings and flying," I said.

Beck tipped her head back and laughed out loud. I joined her and shook my head. "Honestly, though, the worst part was opening my eyes and seeing that you weren't by my side."

Beck's laughter fizzled out and her eyes glistened. The air began to shift between us, and I could feel her coming back to me. Her face regained some color, and her cheeks turned pink.

"I'm sorry about last night," Beck said, looking at her feet.

"About leaving me in the hot tub? You know I had to listen to the world's worst rendition of Happy Birthday all by my lonesome, right? And then I gave our cake to an old grumpy couple. I didn't even get to make a wish."

"About the kiss." Beck corrected me.

"Oh?"

"I shouldn't have kissed you. I think I just drank too much. Got swept away." Beck waved her hand in the air dismissively.

And if I looked just deep enough, through the hurt of her cutting words, through the fear of losing her again, I could see it. She was saying what she thought she needed to say in order to protect herself. I remembered a time when she admitted to having a nasty habit of destroying her chances at happiness. She was her own worst enemy. The hand that held her down.

"Well, I sometimes do that to women."

Beck snorted, and unfortunately, we both knew I was being sarcastic.

"You know, it's like I feel this weird connection with you. I feel so . . . so *grounded*. Is that a thing? I don't know. I just don't want to jeopardize that with something as stupid as Nolan drama. You were my best friend. And I'd like it if we went back to that," Beck said.

I could see right through her. The shift in her eyes. Her posture. She was afraid of the feelings she had inside. Perhaps the memories too? So, she was building a wall. Brick by brick.

"Can I ask you something?"

Beck stared out at the cars below. "Anything." Her tone was warm and inviting.

"Did you want to jump?"

Beck looked at me, eyebrows knitted. At first, it appeared that she thought the question was simple. Stupid even. But then, when she really thought about it, her thoughts delved deeper and deeper. "I did. I wanted to," she said so in question.

"So, why didn't you?"

Beck wasn't surprised by this question. She knew it was the difficult part that followed her first answer. She wanted to, but something stopped her. *She* stopped her. But why? Why would anyone get in their own way?

"I was afraid."

"Afraid of what, though?" I asked.

"I don't know. Of dying!" Beck shifted uncomfortably. It was my cue not to lay off but to push further. Dig deeper.

"Did you really think you were going to die if you jumped?" I asked.

Beck's cheeks turned pink. Her hand raised, then fell aimlessly. "I don't know. What do you want me to say?" Her voice rose in frequency.

"I just want you to be honest with yourself. That's all. It would be nice if you were honest with me too." I mumbled the last part.

Beck thrust a hand on her hip and huffed out a sharp breath. I stood still, watching the world below. Then I took a step onto the bottom rail.

"What are you doing!" Beck hissed, looking over her shoulder.

I rested my forehead on the plexiglass and slowly lifted my hands away. The view was almost as clear as standing on the launch pad before jumping. "Join me."

It took a moment, but Beck did. I reached for her hand and pulled it away from the glass. She whimpered, but this time, I didn't let go. When her breathing gave way to slow and even breaths, I could see the thrill in her smile.

"Wow," she said, turning as much as she could to look at me as our foreheads pressed against the window and our hands locked tight at our sides.

"Hey! You can't be up there!" A security guard yelled.

Beck squeaked, and we both made a mad dash to jump off the rail. We awarded ourselves an escort down the one-hundred-and-three-story elevator. Snickering all the way down. And nothing in this world felt better than when I looked into her green eyes, and I knew the smile on her face was there because of me.

CHAPTER 14

The day warmed as the sun crawled high in the sky. Traffic moved all around us while Beck and I stood still. She was lost. She was away on a birthday weekend that had turned out to be nothing like what she planned. I wondered what her weekend would have looked like if I hadn't tagged along. Perhaps Nolan wouldn't have found himself alone with Payton. I couldn't help but feel responsible for the turn of events. I needed to make it up to Beck. Make sure she had an unforgettable trip.

"So, you've always wanted to bungee jump, but"—I shook my head and sighed—"what else have you always wanted to do? Maybe there's still time," I said, checking my watch.

Beck rolled her eyes. "You're never going to let me live that one down, are you?"

"Nope!"

Beck accepted her fate with a heavy sigh. Then a look I was beginning to recognize crept across her face. "I should get that tattoo. Yeah, I should totally get a tattoo!" Beck said, eyes widening in excitement.

"Then you should! Let's do it!" I said.

"You're going to get one too, right?" Beck asked.

Me? I'd had my share of tattoos. In one life, I was covered with them. Not just from arm to arm but everywhere. They'd become addictive. The art was beautiful when fresh. Until it wasn't. Until I wanted something different. When the time came, I wanted to express myself differently and couldn't. It's true that I enjoyed them, but I also never had one I didn't regret at one time or another. "This one's all you . . ."

"Oh, come on, you baby!" said Beck in a playful tone, shoving my arm.

"Oh! I'm the baby?" I stopped walking and slowly raised my finger to point at the now distant skyscraper that I'd leapt off, while she stayed permanently affixed to the surface in safety.

"OK! OK! I take it back! Please, let it go! You're not a baby."

I remained frozen, pointing, unsatisfied.

"You're . . . brave!" Beck pled.

As soon as she said it, I only hungered for more. "And?"

"And . . . adventurous!" Beck said.

"And?" I prodded. Beck tilted her head in protest, but I encouraged her to keep going with a wave of my hand.

"And . . . spirited, kind, um . . . attractive . . . kind of . . ."

My accusatory pointer finger fell from the skyscraper, and I closed the distance between us. She stood her ground when I lowered down to her. Slowly. Slowly enough to gauge if she would let me kiss her. If her eye contact told me anything, it was that she was open to the idea of another kiss. One that was sober and in the open daylight of clear cognitive thought and emotions. I brought my lips close to hers before brushing by them. Trailing my lips against her cheek, making my way to her ear. Then I whispered, "*Kind* of?"

Beck let out the breath she'd been holding in, and I couldn't contain the smile that pulled across my face. The tension, having peaked, came crashing down around us. Beck took her frustration out on me, wailing on me two palms at a time as I flinched away and laughed at her. This was going to be fun. I liked this Beck. The one that didn't have impending doom on the edge of her heart. The one who fought back.

"You! Little! Errrr!"

I hailed a taxi as Beck stole little glances at me from behind the curtain of her hair. I pretended not to notice, but it wasn't any good with the foolish grin I had plastered on my face. I couldn't for the life of me hide how I was feeling inside. We had that in common. But by the time we pulled up to the tattoo parlor, it was clear that Beck was feeling something else entirely.

"Are you sure about this?" I asked.

"Yeah!" Beck squeaked.

I'd heard that confidence not too long ago. "You know, because it's not too late to fail at this, too," I said and smiled.

"Stop! I'm going to do it!" Beck said, convincing herself more than me.

We walked into the parlor, and the buzz of a tattoo gun was the first thing that brought me back to the hours I'd spent in the chair. Drawings covered the walls and the man who greeted us alike.

"Can I help you?" the man asked. His thin frame covered in colorful ink and large studs adorned his ears.

"Hi, um, this one was thinking about getting a tattoo today. Do you have availability for a walk-in?" I asked, not staring at the man himself or his tattoos but my reflection on his shaved head.

The man looked at his watch. "I guess it depends on what you want. I have an appointment at 3:00, and I can squeeze you in if it's simple enough. Do you know what you want?" The man looked between Beck and me.

"I do. And yes, it's simple," Beck said.

I was surprised that she already knew what she wanted. She'd put some thought into this before. I wondered what she valued enough that she would display it on her body for years to come. I hoped whatever she chose wouldn't be a part of the lie she'd grown up believing. Because then, I'd feel obligated to speak up.

"Then let's do this. I'm Zack, and I'll get some paperwork for you. You can fill it out while I draw you up a sketch and get the quote ready. What is it you wanted to get?"

I looked down at Beck, curious. "I wanted to get an infinity symbol. Right here." Beck pointed to her side. My heart just about dropped into my stomach. The girl remembered more than she led on.

"Why?" I mumbled under my breath. Barely audible.

Beck peeped at me before accepting the paperwork from her soon-to-be tattoo artist and filled out her information.

"Why?" I asked again, slightly louder.

Beck stopped writing and looked up at me, "Why what?"

"Why that?"

Beck shrugged. I thought something profound would come next. A clue, perhaps. Or a memory that she made into a dream. But when she said, "I don't know. I like it!" I had to second guess if it was a sign at all. Maybe I was trying to will a memory that simply wasn't there. Did she like it in how girls liked to draw hearts? Or did she like it in the way that resonated with her on a deep and meaningful level?

I watched Beck make a small *x* on the human body drawing of her paperwork. She wanted her infinity symbol on the side of her ribs in a place that I imagined her bra would cover. Hidden, intimate. I waited on a bench while she approved the sketch and paid the cashier. When the artist was ready, I moved a chair to be by her side.

Beck removed her bra and blushed a bright crimson as she shoved her sexy undergarment in her purse. She lay down on the chair and lifted her shirt high, struggling to keep her chest hidden and get comfortable at the same time. My eyes trailed down her ribcage, and my heart quickened.

"I need you to rest your arm over your head like this." Zack held his arm against his ear, and Beck imitated him. She looked at me while he wiped down her skin. Tiny goosebumps pimpled her side, and worry pricked the corners of her eyes.

"Hold my hand?" Beck asked.

I rolled my chair closer to her, took her hand in mine, and held it tight, stroking her knuckles with my thumb. "You've got this. Why don't you tell me why you choose the infinity symbol? Other than just liking it. There's got to be more to it than that."

Zack tested his gun, and Beck flinched at the sound.

"It's OK, honey. I'm not starting yet. I'll let you know first," he said.

Beck nodded, embarrassed, before she turned her attention back to me. "Um, I think that sometimes . . ." She looked back down at the gun and struggled to focus. But I needed her to. I needed her to focus on what she was telling me. "I think that, there are things in this world that . . ." Her eyes dropped once again.

"OK, honey. We're going to start. Just a light pricking feeling. Try not to jump."

"In this world that, what Beck?" I asked.

"That never truly—"

The gun pierced her skin and Beck yelped, jumping two feet into the air. Zack pulled his gun back and yelled, "Fuck!"

"Nope!" Beck leaped off of the bed. "Nope. I can't! I can't do it!" Beck became unglued, her eyes fear-stricken and her body tremulous.

I didn't have to ask if she was sure. I knew. Everyone knew. I looked back to Zack, whose mouth still gaped open, the gun still lifted into the air. "We're going to take an intermission. But if she finds the courage to come back and finish—which she won't—we'll call and make an appointment first. I'll get your card on the way out," I said. Beck was already halfway out of the parlor, and the door was swinging closed behind her.

"Sorry, man. I told her not to move! She's going to have to come back to get that fixed!" Zack said.

"Oh, no. Don't worry. Yeah, I'll get her to come back. It might just take a little time is all!" I lied. I knew we were on a flight out first thing tomorrow morning. And I knew by the look on Beck's face that she wouldn't give this a second chance.

As I walked out of the parlor, I couldn't help but remember taking Beck to crash a wedding. She was absolutely horrified. And when I brought her camping, it was no different. I didn't bother taking the man's business card on the way out. I was too deep in thought. What made this girl so afraid of what she really wanted? I found Beck pacing the parking lot. I grabbed her tight, pulling her into my embrace. She trembled against my body and sobbed. "Shhh."

"I'm so embarrassed!" Beck said when she had settled enough.

"Shhh, it's OK." I stroked the back of her head and pondered over what was holding her back. But perhaps the most important question wasn't what was holding her back, but what propelled one forward. "I thought you wanted to get a tattoo. It was on your list!" I said.

"My list? Why do you keep saying that?" Beck pulled away. Her eyes red and laced with confusion.

Shit. "I mean, you said you'd always wanted to get one." I looked away and hoped the moment would pass.

"I did! I thought I did. I don't know what's wrong with me! I have this bad habit of self-destruction. It's like I get so close to the thing I want, and then I find a way to destroy it," Beck echoed. I remembered her saying it two decades ago. It would not be an easy fix, but we had the time to work on it. I wanted that for her.

"Well, let's take a look and see what you got," I said as I reached out for the hem of Beck's top. She helped guide her shirt up to her ribcage. My brows peeked, and I hid my mouth behind my hand.

"What? Is it bad?" Beck asked, unable to see.

I tried to tell her it wasn't. I tried! But it just came out as full-blown manic laughter that busted the seams of my cupped fingers. What I saw could only be described as a . . . comma. A comma that was made by a passenger in flight. One that hit turbulence.

"Oh my god, Easton! Is it that bad?" Beck tried to manipulate her body. Bend and fold in every which way to see it. She couldn't. I spun around to gather myself but ultimately folded in half, bracing my hands on my knees. I wanted to get Beck back for making me jump off the skyscraper alone, but the poor girl just couldn't help doing it to herself. And I couldn't help but laugh at her mishaps. I'd probably laughed more in the last two days than I had throughout the whole of this very life. I prayed Beck would never grow out of it. Because her lack of grace might have been my favorite thing about her.

"What the hell is that?!" Beck squawked as she held her cell phone out to her side.

"Congratulations! It's a twig!" I said. Beck lifted her head, but her jaw remained on the floor.

Beck and I finished the day at the drug store, getting her a salve and bandage for her skewed comma tattoo before heading back to the hotel. She didn't seem overly concerned about checking on Nolan, and I didn't blame her. I'd had the best day with her. It was epic, really. And I took pleasure in knowing that every time she would see the ink on her bare body, she'd think of me. Maybe not favorably, as I did laugh pretty hard at her in the parking lot, but all the same, she'd think of me.

That night I could hear her and Nolan fighting from across the hall. His tone was loud and accusatory. Hers high-pitched and sharp. And I couldn't imagine a situation in which I felt so helpless. I sat with my back against the front door of my room and listened to the rise and fall of their argument. I couldn't make out what they were yelling, but I guessed it either had to do with Payton or me. Perhaps both.

I wanted them to break up but not like this. Not with pain. I never wanted that for Beck. I ran my hands through my hair, wishing it all away. Dreaming of a time when Beck and I were together again and there were no more secrets. And no more Nolans.

Irishman William's advice rung vividly in my head. Neither qualified nor founded but still solid. I weighed the possibilities of telling Beck the truth. Her past life, who I really was, and what it really meant to be a Tethered Soul. And had I not had so much to lose, it might be worth it. But for now, when I still had the smallest chance to be with her, I had to hold off. Save it for a time when there was no going back, and I was all out of hope. There *would* be a time. *That* I was sure of, but the time was not now. I steepled my fingers under my chin, thinking about how afraid she was to jump. I couldn't imagine what learning of her immortality might do to her.

Having grown tired of listening to the muffled dispute between Beck and Nolan, I opened my door and slid the lock in between the door jamb. I hoped that Beck would see it as an invitation if she didn't want to stay the night with Nolan after their fight. I left the bathroom light on for her and crawled into bed. I closed my eyes, exhausted from the emotional distress of the weekend, and drifted off to sleep.

CHAPTER 15

It was some time into the night when I dreamed of Beck. Her warm body against mine. The scent of coconut-infused hair curling around me like a vice. So real I questioned if I was asleep at all. When my dream slipped away and Beck remained tangled in my arms, my mind raced to gather the fragmented pieces. My eyes fluttered as I looked around the darkness of the room, and I remembered I'd left the door open for Beck. The small light peeking out from the bathroom cast a warm glow on her cheekbone and illuminated her resting eyes.

I thought long and hard about what she needed in that moment, and as much as I wanted to close the distance between her lips and mine, I knew she was a lifetime behind me. Unlike me, who held my spouse in bed, she was lying with a friend. A neighbor.

A single teardrop fell upon my hand. I squeezed her a little tighter but said nothing. Sometimes, pain just needed to be felt. And it helped to have someone by your side. This wasn't the time for questions. I knew that much. I nestled my forehead into the back of her head and tried my damn hardest to go anywhere but the field of wet grass on the day we wed.

I woke before my alarm went off. It was hard not to with Beck on my arm. Like waking up to gifts early Christmas morning, I was too excited for sleep. I watched her eyes twitch in the early morning light before attempting to withdraw my arm. She rolled off of it, still sound asleep. Once free, I padded barefoot to the restroom. As quietly as I could, I began packing for the airport. I knew Beck would have to do the same, but I dreaded waking her up and sending her back to Nolan's room to pack her belongings. It hardly seemed fair.

My ears perked when I heard a faint vibration. I opened the bathroom door to hear the sound magnify and Beck stirring in bed. Her phone rested on top of her bag, and I nearly tripped over her suitcase in my pursuit of it. *Smart girl.* She must have packed last night. I grasped her phone to silence it but not before seeing the dozens of text messages left unread by Nolan. My eyes landed on words like *fault*, and *Easton*.

"Was that my phone? What time is it?" Beck murmured.

I spun around with her phone in my hand, trying not to look suspicious. "Sorry, I was just trying to silence it. Are you OK?" I asked.

Beck ran her hands through her tangled hair and squinted into the light. She said nothing. I brought her the phone and sat at the foot of the bed while she paged through her texts. A moment later, she tossed her phone onto the fluff of the hotel comforter, shaking her head.

"Nolan hooked up with Payton," Beck said.

"I'm sorry."

"He thinks I have a thing for you. He said it was my fault," Beck said, watching her fingers intertwine.

I swallowed. Afraid of what she might say next.

But when nothing else came, I had to ask. "Do you? Have a thing for me?" I regretted it the moment I said it. The timing was off. Her mood was off. I looked down to my lap, as I could see Beck shake her head in my peripheral vision. I wished I had been more patient. The silence stretched between us, and though she was near, I felt our distance grow.

"You are so . . . infuriating! You waltz into my life after all these years, and I don't see where you fit in. I don't know where you belong in my life because I already have a best friend, and I already have a boyfriend. *Had* a boyfriend. Yet there's just something about you. About us. And I don't understand it. So, if you have to know if I have a thing for you . . ." Beck paused. She was talking herself out of what she really wanted. Her fear of being loved was swallowing her whole, and it was so loud, I could almost hear the turmoil between her ears.

"Beck, you deserve a life with no regrets. If I had to guess, you have a few from this weekend. Don't make another one. Tell me. Tell me how you really feel," I pleaded.

I could tell I struck a chord with her when tears filled her eyes. "I'd be lying if I told you there wasn't a piece of me that was drawn to you."

My heart pounded, and my hands balled into fists filled with the bed's comforter. Through clenched teeth, I asked what I knew I shouldn't: "How big is the piece, Beck?"

Her face was devoid of color. Whatever it was, I'd hit it on the head.

"I don't know," Beck whispered as tears streamed down her cheeks.

My lungs expanded, and I knew not to push further. I threw my head back and closed my eyes, basking in the small confession she had made. She didn't know how much yet, but she knew that some part of us belonged to one another. There was only one problem. Why did she look so afraid? I released my white-knuckled grip of the bedding and raked my hands through my hair. "OK, well we don't have to have it all figured out now. We can figure this out together." Concern filled the empty spaces in my mind until I could hardly think straight.

"I can't—"

My cell phone alarm chimed, loud and intrusive. I jumped to turn it off, but by the time I returned, the window of honesty had closed. The emotion that filled Beck's eyes was now dulled. Her walls were back up, and her feelings were hidden deep inside. I was left with more questions than answers. I should have felt like I had just won the lottery, but I felt no such victory.

"We can't be late for our flight." Beck threw off the blanket and bolted to the restroom, promptly shutting the door behind her. I let her be while I drowned in my fears. I gathered what little clothing I had and threw it into my suitcase. Then I picked up my laptop. It was when I opened my backpack to place it inside that I saw Beck's birthday gift. I stilled, not knowing if I should give it to her or not. I was almost positive the moment had passed. Several of them over the span of the weekend would have been preferable to this one. I set my laptop down and took the small bag out of my backpack. Reaching inside, I pulled out the small box that held the crystal dragonfly.

As soon as I saw the green wings, I felt the need to give it to her in this imperfect moment. *A piece of me* rang through my ears, swirling inside me—a song of hope. I clenched the tiny box to my chest and spun around with the determination to give it to Beck and the need for her to remember. It wasn't the perfect time, but the perfect time may never come for us. It had to be now. I knocked on the bathroom door.

"Yeah?" Beck asked.

"I have something for you." I placed my palm on the door jamb and leaned into it. Beck opened the door slowly. Her eyes found the tiny box for a moment before lifting to meet mine. "Here. It's your birthday gift."

"You didn't have to get me a—"

"I know. But I saw it, and it reminded me of you."

Beck opened the box. Nerves crawled under my skin like an army of ants, and I wanted to squirm. I crossed my arms over my chest and watched her intently. The green-bodied dragonfly emerged from the box and sparkled in Beck's hands. Her eyes, as green as the emerald wings, were transfixed on the gift. I couldn't tell how she felt about it. The seconds ticked on, and I felt more restless by her silence as the time passed.

What seemed like an eternity later, Beck lifted her gaze to meet mine, and I could see the recognition behind her puffy eyes.

Both of us jumped when a thunderous knock rapped against the hotel door, breaking the moment I had waited twenty-one years for.

"Time to go!" James yelled.

"Do you think Becca is in there with him?" Payton asked.

"Well she's not with Nolan," Brooklyn said.

Beck pushed past me, hand clasped around the dragonfly. She grabbed her suitcase and her bag, and I nearly jumped to get out of her path. She swung the door open. "Hi! You guys all ready?" Beck asked in a tone that I could only describe as the opposite. The opposite of everything she'd just conveyed with her eyes. The opposite of everything she felt when she held the crystal in her hand. Was this her plan? Were we just going to pretend this didn't happen?

I shoved my laptop into my backpack, a little more recklessly than I intended, and followed Beck out of the room with my suitcase in tow. James wagged his eyebrows at me and elbowed me in the ribs as the girls whispered a few feet down the hall. Nolan appeared in his doorjamb adjacent to mine, and the air shifted once again. For an instant, I thought he was going to say something. But it never came. The bags under his eyes said he'd had a sleepless night. James was good at diffusing and sucked Nolan into a story about a girl he met at the bar almost immediately. I dragged behind the group, lost in thought.

Beck kept her distance from both Nolan and me. She even worked hard at avoiding eye contact. I wished I could say the same for Payton and Brooklyn; they wouldn't stop staring. I wondered how much Beck was telling them. How much more they knew than I did. Beck knew she had feelings for me—that much was clear—but she didn't yet feel comfortable opening up to me. And if she couldn't talk to me, then it was possible that I would become the thing that she wanted but wouldn't allow herself to have. I'd essentially be the freefall she was too afraid of. Or the tattooed twig. I couldn't let that happen. I wouldn't be another failure in her life.

While waiting to board the plane, Brooklyn texted me from where she sat only one row away.

Do you want to sit with Beck on the flight home? I could sit with the guys.

It was a small act of kindness, but it meant the world to me.

You're the best!

When it was time to board the flight, Brooklyn positioned herself just behind James and Nolan. I trailed far behind the group, pretending to be consumed with e-mails on my phone. It wasn't *all* a lie. The real estate agent, Tina, had messaged me saying I was in escrow and there was an opportunity to rent before the purchase was complete. I'd be going home to my very own brown shag carpet. Brooklyn sat in the row with the guys, and when it was my turn to take a seat, the only one open was next to Payton, who was currently trying to get Brooklyn to sit in the open seat.

Brooklyn winked at me when I passed by, and I tried to hide my smile. James was still entertaining Nolan with nonstop chatter.

"Brooklyn, sit here!" Payton said. Heat crept over my face as I looked to Brooklyn. She placed a set of earbuds in, pretending not to hear. I pushed my suitcase overhead and Payton moved her purse out of my seat. By the time I had my backpack tucked under the seat before me and my seatbelt fastened, the row had turned ice cold. Beck stared out the window, and I wanted to reach out and take her hand. I would have if Payton wasn't in the middle of us.

It wasn't long after takeoff that Payton stuffed earbuds in her ears and closed her eyes. I tore off a piece of my napkin and chucked it at Beck. It hit the side of her head that drew a curtain between us. She patted the side of her head before pulling the balled-up napkin from her strands. She unraveled it, flipped it over, set it down, and looked back to the window. I did it again. She unfolded the napkin, then refused to look at me.

I found a pen in my backpack and took what was left of my napkin under my drink. Realizing I never told her how I felt, I knew I had to convey it somehow. But how do you tell the woman you love the depth of your feelings? How would I squeeze it onto half a napkin? I bit at the back of the pen, running it over my teeth.

When the idea came to me, I set pen to paper. I drew a small circle and labeled it "My piece." Then I drew the same thing again but labeled it "Your piece." Then I connected the two circles to make an infinity symbol. The drawing wasn't great, but it was still better than her tattoo, and she'd paid for that. I wadded up the napkin and chucked it square at her forehead. This time she looked at me with a frown. Was it wrong that I enjoyed her aggravation nearly as much as her laughter? But when she opened up the napkin and studied the drawing, her eyes took on a fresh look. And this one I liked the most.

CHAPTER 16

In need of a bed, I went to the hotel that night. I was tired from Sin City, and I wasn't yet ready to face the smell of my new home. Plus, I hadn't gotten the keys from Tina yet. All I wanted was a hot shower. Scorching hot. Then, a night's sleep that stripped me of my fears and breathed new hope into me. I wanted to wake with the morning sunlight and stretch my arms wide, thinking *I've got this!*

I showered in the searing water, which was enough to melt away my negative thinking and send it straight down the drain. Then, I sent Tina a brief e-mail about picking up the keys the next morning. I held my phone in my hand, wanting very much to text Beck but not knowing what to say. If only she had accidentally told everyone I was her boyfriend, this would be so much easier. But the truth was, she didn't need me this time. No, this time . . . I needed her.

I stared at my phone for some time before building the courage to craft a text that wouldn't just be alluring but safe. More than friends, but friendly enough. It seemed near impossible until I deleted ninety-five percent of my text.

Meet me Monday in Clover. I have something I want to show you.

It wasn't a question, and I had given her no way out. I watched as the burbling bubbles told me she was already texting back, and my stomach knotted in anticipation. I wondered if she had been holding her phone in pursuit of texting me as well. I waited patiently at first, but when the bubbles disappeared and no text followed, I couldn't help but text her a time and address and hope for the best.

The address was that of my new house. Not that I wanted to put her off with the smell of mildew or the stains in the brown shag carpet, but more that I wanted her help. I wanted her input on what made a house a home. I wanted to take the focus off the tension between us, and fix something. Achieve *something.* It didn't have to be us right now, we had lives upon lives to figure us out. We just needed a small win, and maybe that came in the form of shopping for a rug or a sofa. Perhaps she would want to take on the challenge with me.

It was early Monday morning, and I packed my scant belongings from the hotel into my backpack. I grabbed a coffee in the hotel lobby—sure to put hair on a young boy's chest—before checking out. It was nice to finally close the door on the transient living that I'd done in my search for Beck. Now, it was time to put some roots down. I met with my realtor, Tina McFay, to sign the paperwork and pick up my keys. The escrow was just beginning, but I could rent for the first month, and the owner was kind enough to let me begin the renovations. Good thing too, because the house was inhabitable as it was.

I took the gold key in my hand and waved goodbye to Tina. It was a new beginning for me in a life that seemed to run on forever. Somehow, this house . . . this life . . . I could see with Beck. It was a new start for me. I cherished that. I stole another glance at my phone; it must have been the trillionth time. Beck still hadn't replied, and I had no idea if she would show today or not. I still had a couple of hours to kill before I would be stood up, and I had a long list of items I needed to purchase. The top of the list was a bed, but perhaps even above that was deodorizer and hand soap. The basics.

The smell of crisp pine trees rushed into my car as I opened my sunroof, and a concentrated ray of sunlight warmed my skin. It was a beautiful day for new beginnings. I hoped Beck would feel it too.

I may or may not have gone a little overboard at the hardware store. I hadn't realized it until I was faced with the problem of packing everything into the trunk of my car. Perhaps I should have waited on the bags of wood chips and the potted flowers. But the thought of live flowers in front of the house was one I was sure Beck would like. I couldn't pass on the gardening gloves covered in purple flowers, either. It was absolutely overboard. I was aware, but I did it anyway.

Amongst the entire gardening section that I had purchased and stuffed into my trunk, I also picked up a crowbar and sledgehammer. I was very much looking forward to using them both. There wasn't a particular wall or cabinet I was planning on removing right away, but I knew I wanted to hack something, and I thought I'd better be prepared.

By the end of the night, I would need to purchase a mattress and pillow so that I'd have a place to sleep. I didn't have time to do it now, in case Beck showed up, so I planned to make a run right before dinner time.

I pulled up to my new house just before noon. I would not call it a home for some time—not until it had earned the right. I turned my ignition off and stared at the old house hidden behind the growth of weeds and chipped brick. For a moment, I thought of the house as a metaphor for my life. Beaten down. Old beyond its days. And ready for new beginnings. A fire lit in my belly, and I wanted to transform the house immediately. Pour all of my tethered restraint and sorrows into it and make it something beautiful.

The car warmed in the absence of air conditioning, and I was forced to step out and meet my future, face to face. A lot of hard work lay before me, but I was grateful to have something to take my mind off of Beck. At least here, I could control the outcome.

I popped my trunk and sighed before starting my very long project. By the fourth bag of wood chips, I was ready to rip my shirt off and jump into the pool. There was no pool, of course. Not in this part of town. I pulled my shirt over my head and threw it into the trunk of my car before picking up the fifth and final bag of wood chips. Gravel crunched under the weight of tires behind me. I spun around with the bag on my shoulder to see a grey single cab truck pull into my driveway. I shielded the ray from my eyes and squinted into the light. I had hoped it was Beck, but I didn't recognize the truck. The windshield, lit up by a blaring glare of sunlight, hid the driver's identity.

"Is this your house?" Beck said as she stepped out of the truck. She came. A wash of relief fled through me.

"Is that your truck?" I answered with a question of my own.

Beck slid her phone into her back pocket and approached me at the trunk of my car. "It is." She played nervously with her keys. I watched her eyes drop, taking in my bare chest, and I felt somewhat exposed. I didn't bare the type of body she was accustomed to. I was no Nolan.

"Good! Because I'm going to need a truck!"

Beck nodded, knowing she was sucked in. "Is that why you called me here? Because you needed a truck?"

"No, I swear! I didn't even know you had one. But, uh . . . Now that I do, you absolutely have to help me. Like, a lot! I barely fit all of this into my car, and there's going to be more. A lot more," I said.

"Really?" Beck asked, peering into my car.

"Yeah. I don't even have a mattress to sleep on. I mean, what do you want me to do, sleep on the floor? Strap a mattress to the top of my car?" I twisted to the car behind me. Beck smiled. "It's the least you could do for a *friend*, right?"

"I suppose so." Beck rolled her eyes. "Do you need help bringing stuff in?"

"That would be great. Grab what you can. I'm going to toss this bag with the others," I said as I walked the bag I had slung over my shoulder to the pile I had made underneath the front window. I thought it would make a perfect place for a flower bed.

"Where do you want these?" Beck followed me with two pots of flowers in her arms.

"Here would be great!" I said. We continued to unpack my loot. The wood chips and flowers were finally unloaded, and what remained were bags that needed to be taken into the house. Beck made fun of me for the purple gardening gloves she spotted within the bag. I was too much of a coward to tell her I bought them for her. Instead, I claimed it was my favorite color. While it wasn't my favorite color, it was one that reminded me of a very revealing dress she once wore to her brother's wedding. And for that reason alone, it was a special color. We stacked as many bags as we could fit into our arms before heading inside, and I immediately regretted not attempting to air the house out before she came over.

"Remember how our parents were a part of that group when we were—oh my god! What is that smell!?" Beck hid her nose in the crook of her arm as the bags swung across her chest. It was worse than I'd remembered. The mildew.

"That's just mildew from the house being closed up for so long. It should air out after we open some windows." We placed our bags on the nearby kitchen counter.

"That's *mildew*?" Beck asked with her face buried in her arm. For the first time since she got here, I was worried she wouldn't stay.

"Yeah, that's just—ack!" My stomach wrenched, vomit nearly propelling out of my mouth.

"Easton! That's *not* mildew!" Beck opened the backdoor slider and ran outside. I had no choice but to follow her.

"Yeah, that's just the smell. You'd be surprised. There's probably a wall with mold growing rampantly underneath the drywall or something. But, um, don't worry. I bought a candle," I said looking back at the bags on the kitchen counter. They seemed so close yet so far away.

"A candle?" Beck looked at me with eyes of doubt.

"Yeah, I mean, it's a mosquito candle"—my voice rose—"but they put off a smell, and I figured it was better than nothing. I'm just going to open all the windows and doors and light that candle. We'll be inside in no time!" I really wished I had my shirt to hide my nose in, but I had to use my hand instead. I ran through the house, opening the windows and doors while breathing through my mouth. My tongue pressed firmly against my teeth. When I crossed the threshold of the kitchen into the hall, I realized the smell was originating somewhere around the stove. I ran to the backyard and gasped, more dramatically than intended. Beck laughed at me. I stood shirtless and sweaty in front of her, my hands on my hips.

"Have you had lunch yet?" I asked.

"I could eat. I could always eat."

I smiled, thinking back to a time when Beck was sick and her appetite fleeting. It was nice to hear she'd gotten it back.

"Change of plans. Let's let this whole thing breathe," I circled my hand toward the house, "while we get lunch. And a mattress." I looked down to the ground, hoping she wouldn't protest. I couldn't be more relieved when she agreed to spend the day with me.

"There's only one problem," Beck said.

"What's that?" I asked.

Beck pointed through the slider to the front door, "We've got to get to the other side."

I laughed, and a split second later I had her hand in mine as we ran through the house in one breath. Beck was laughing on the other side, and I was left wondering how such a rancid stench—which was definitely *not* mildew—could have possibly brought a smile to her face. I took my shirt from the trunk of my car and pulled it on as I jumped into the passenger's side of Beck's truck.

"Are you just going to leave your doors open like that?" Beck started her ignition.

"Are you kidding me? There's nothing to steal, and if there were, I don't think the burglar would survive in there!"

"Good point!" Beck said as she backed out of my driveway.

It was when Beck asked for directions to the store that I found my opportunity to cross the New River Bridge with her by my side. There were two ways out of town, and I led her to the one that crossed the bridge. The closer the bridge drew, the more I feared her reaction. It felt almost cruel. Like I had been hiding this secret of who she was and then forcing her to remember. I thought I had done the right thing by letting her memory come back to her slowly, but now I worried I should have spilled the truth long ago. Like any friend would. I immediately felt the weight of my decision as the bridge drew closer.

CHAPTER 17

My heart thumped in my chest as I wiped my clammy palms on my pant legs. The New River Bridge was right around the corner, and we would cross it soon. Beck messed with her phone as she tried to pay attention to the road and find the perfect song at the same time. I was worried that she would miss it altogether . . . but even more worried she wouldn't. It was possible that she had been on her phone when she crossed it the first time on her way to my house, had she taken the bridge.

"Did you come to my house this way or did you take the backside of the mountain?" I asked.

Beck set her phone in her lap and surveyed her surroundings. "Um?" She looked out her window, eyebrows scrunched.

The truck jolted when it lifted onto the steel bridge. My eyes rested heavily on Beck's. She placed her foot on the brake and the truck crawled to a stop. What was she doing? I looked out my window. A teen girl was stuck on the side of the bridge with a flat tire. We had just gotten onto the bridge, and I didn't want to stop here, but Beck found it in her heart to stop and ask the girl if she was alright. Beck rolled down my window and yelled, "Do you need help?"

The girl examined us before saying, "Not unless you know how to change a tire?"

Beck looked at me, and I nodded with a sigh. "Yeah, I'll just pull over!"

As I stood on the side of the bridge, jacking the car up, I realized it was the exact lie I fabricated when Beck's father asked how we met. Beck, however, was the girl with the flat tire in the version I had told. As I listened to the girls chat, I suddenly became worried that Beck's dad would pass us on the bridge and see his daughter standing on the side of the road with her deceased boyfriend. It wasn't a good look for either of us, and I had been foolish enough to forget my baseball hat in my car.

I lifted the replacement tire out of the girl's trunk and slid it onto the post. I listened for hesitation in Beck's voice, but I detected no signs of despondency. I worked as quickly as I could to move the girl off the bridge without Beck and I becoming discovered. Relief washed over me when the girl drove away in her lopsided car, which now had three regular tires and one miniature one. Only two cars had passed by in that time, and from what I could tell, they were no one of importance in Beck's past life.

"Thanks for doing that. I just remember what it was like being a new driver, and I'm glad that we could help her." Beck started back for her truck.

"Oh hey! Look at that, want to take a quick look?" I pointed down the bridge and hated myself for it. But the truth was, if Beck didn't figure it out soon, I might just blurt it out over lunch.

Beck hesitated, "Um, we should really get you that mattress."

"Come on. Just real quick. I bet it's . . . something to be remembered." I cringed. I was the worst.

With Beck's truck already pulled off to the side of the road, we walked a quarter of the way down the bridge. Beck was quiet—even more so than usual—and I could tell she was teetering on the cusp of uncomfortable and full-blown panic. I watched with large eyes.

"Do you feel alright?" I asked, stopping when I reached the spot in which we met.

Beck's face was devoid of color. "I'm OK. I'm just scared of heights."

"You seemed OK when we were on the skyscraper . . . apart from the jumping that is," I said.

"Yeah, that was different." Beck looked over the edge with a deeply creased forehead. I peered over the edge with her. It was a long way down, and the water was moving more freely than the night we had met. Beck pulled at the neck of her shirt. "Do. Do you ever get that feeling," she whispered, barely audible, "that you've been here before?"

My stomach dipped over and over. "What do you mean?" I asked.

"I feel like I've been here before. Like, physically, *right here*." Beck ran her hands along the top of the railing. Her eyes ticked back and forth, looking for answers. She paused before peeking at me, "I feel like I've been right here . . . with *you*."

I sucked in a deep breath, wishing I had a plan. A map. Any protocol to follow. But this was a new situation, and I didn't get many of them anymore. I'd figured all of this out on my own over the course of my first couple of lives. Nobody was there to hold my hand through it, and I didn't know if I was pushing her too fast. Or perhaps it was too slow?

"Oh my god, don't listen to me. I'm crazy. I'm a crazy person!" Beck nodded her head to herself as if she had repeated that mantra her whole life. I hurt for her.

"You're *not* crazy," I rebutted.

"Yes, I am. You have no idea. You think you know me, but you don't."

It pained me to see her struggle. I knew what she was going through, and I knew I had all but one of the answers she sought. All but why. I didn't know why it happened to me, to her, or to any other Tethered Soul.

"If you're crazy, Beck, then I'm crazy too."

She raised her eyebrows as if I was making light of the situation. Like I couldn't possibly understand what she was talking about.

"What, you're crazy *about* me, I take it?" Beck rolled her eyes dismissively, and I could sense her panic dissipating.

"I'm a lunatic for you! I just can't get enough of you! And I *do* know you. I understand how you feel, right now," I said. The corners of her lips lifted.

"I feel like I've known you my entire life. Is that weird?" she asked.

I pushed off the bridge and pulled her into my arms. She felt like home. "You have," I said, and I didn't mean since we were kids. There was nothing like holding Beck in my arms. It was like allowing two magnets to click together. The birds crowed above, and the warmth of the sun hit my back. "You're probably getting hungry. Do you want to go get that lunch now?" I asked.

"Yeah, let's do that," Beck said with a kind smile. I slid my hand down her arm and interlocked my hand in hers. But as I started for her truck, Beck's hand slipped from mine. She stopped clear in her tracks and her face fell flat and cold. It was the moment I feared most.

I did a double-take, my hand feeling more than a void in her absence. "Beck, what's—"

"What is that?"

I turned to follow Beck's trembling, accusatory finger. My throat dried and my insides melted. Beck pointed to our memorial plaque. I raked my hands through my hair as she slowly squatted, examining it. Her head tilted ever so slightly as I waited for destiny to rear its ugly head. And I knew *I* had brought this on myself. On her. Beck swiped her fingers over the plaque and abruptly stood, tears filling her eyes. "Never mind! Let's go."

"Beck, wait!" I called out to her, but she kept walking. Unfortunately for her, fate was not something she could run from. I picked up my pace and grabbed her by the shoulder. "Beck, I think we need to talk." I placed my emphasis on *think,* because again, I did not know what was best for her. It was a lose-lose situation, and at this point, my only real hope was that I wouldn't lose Beck all together.

"What! About what? What could you possibly know about what I'm going through? Unless you *do*. Unless you *have*. Unless you've *kept it* from *me*!" Beck stretched her arms out wide, baring her open heart as an easy target.

"What if I told you, that . . . when I walk out on this bridge, I get memories, too?"

Beck's arms slowly dropped to her side and her eyes slanted in pain. Her face was soaked with sympathy and stained with fury.

"What if I told you that . . . I know why you're afraid of the water?" A small sound came burbling from Beck's throat, and she cupped both her hands over her mouth. "What if I told you, that you are my . . . home? And that I've loved you since *before* you moved in next door." I shrugged.

I didn't know what else to tell her, but it sure as hell would not be that we were already married! Not yet anyway—not while she was a flight risk. *Home.* The word stuck in my head. It wasn't the perfect choice, yet it was the closest thing to it. And somehow, it held more meaning than love. The word used by every other person in this world with a crush or infatuation. But none of them had survived death for their loved one. We had something unique, and it didn't have a title.

Beck swiped a tear that fell from her eye, and she peered back at the bridge behind me. She pointed down at the large arch but couldn't choke out what she wanted to.

"You remember, don't you? Some of it, at least?" I asked. Beck's head shook up and down. Demanding. "I can fill in the blanks, Beck. If you let me," I pled. Closing the distance between us, I placed my hand on her shoulder, but she shrugged away. She'd turned to stone. Sharp as an arrow. And I was her target.

"I only have one question. Who. Are. *Those people?*" Beck's pointer finger shot out like a cannon and exploded into a plume of accusation and betrayal.

I looked down the bridge, fearful of who I might see, then grabbed my chest and sighed when nobody was there except the gentle spring breeze. "Which people?"

"*Those* people, Easton! The ones that had this entire bridge dedicated to them! Who are they!? Because one of them is *you* . . . and I don't know the other!" Beck yelled, her voice splintering into past and present lives.

I was so worried for Beck, I'd forgotten all about my name being on the plaque. I rubbed my eyes, shaking my head at the impossible situation that I'd found myself in. "OK, you want to know the truth?" My voice had risen to match hers. It wasn't the time to lose myself, but I was exploding with repressed emotions, and her tone was taunting me. "Those people, Beck! Those people who died on this bridge twenty-one years ago . . . *They're us*!" I threw my hand down, driving my point home. *Home.* I watched as Beck became unglued. Large tears streamed down her face, and her pale complexion was now red in the heat of the battle.

My heart pounded in my chest, and I could hear the blood pumping between my ears. I regretted yelling at her and needed to show her how sorry I was. That I'd be there for her. I reached out for her as she stepped back. Her body was trembling.

"No! Don't touch me!" Beck's eyes laced with the fear of the unknown. "*You*. You're the crazy one!" Beck took one more slow step back.

"Beck, don't do this," I pled.

"*You're crazy!*" Beck screeched, fleeing to her truck. She started her ignition as I tried to open the passenger's side door, but by the time the door was half open she'd hit the gas and sped off, nearly taking my arm with her. I stumbled, trying to catch my footing as I jogged into the middle of the bridge with my arms reached out wide.

"Beck! Come on! *Fuck!*" I spun on my heels as a car horn sounded too close for comfort. And this time . . . this time, it *was* Beck's dad.

I leaped out of the way, and for a split second, he and I locked eyes. "Damn it!" I said to myself, tilting my head up to the blue sky, my hands square on my hips.

I took to the edge of the New River Bridge, thinking of the day I almost jumped. My heart had filled with sorrow as the rain pelted down on me. I'd lost everyone I'd ever loved. And worse, I had stopped letting them in. I had locked my heart up so tight, I couldn't breathe. I'd been mourning for hundreds of years but somehow still found a way to hurt myself worse. I'd been suffocating, and as I stood on the bridge's rail, I knew that it could all be gone in a moment's time. My pain erased. And for a few short years, I would forget all the agony I'd brought onto myself. And in that moment, I had committed to starting over.

That was, until Beck had pulled over. Her green eyes had shone even in the storm's wrath, her life burning bright as the end neared. I took pity on her at first, but quickly felt my heart beating again. I hadn't felt that alive in centuries, and I had no idea what it was. Not until she tried to distance herself from me had I realized that my heart was opening to her. And as I'd taken her in, all the pain from lives lost simply fell into place. Like the ebb and flow of an ocean's current—lives lived, lives lost, lives journeyed onward. And somehow, Beck's love had showed me how to accept it all. She'd thought she needed me because she was dying. But really, I needed her, because I was living and I didn't know how.

CHAPTER 18

Stranded with nothing more than my toxic stream of conscious worry, I walked toward the new house. At some point, I'd call for a taxi, but for now, it was probably best for me to walk off some steam. It wasn't the first time Beck and I had fought, but it was the first time she'd found out her life was a lie. All of it. Every single thing she knew to be true, shattered in a moment's time. I didn't try to convince myself that I understood. Instead, I took out my phone and texted her to come back. I begged her to turn around and talk to me. Five text messages later, and she hadn't replied. Not even burbling dots, a sign of an attempt. Three phone calls later and she had turned off her phone altogether.

I walked a couple of miles before calling for a ride, but it still wasn't enough to clear my mind. And I imagined no amount of miles would cure what had manifested in my heart, soul, and gut. As if the day couldn't get any worse, the taxi dropped me off at the house that had been left to air out. I hadn't even gotten my mattress.

Later that night, I was fortunate enough to find a dead raccoon tucked behind my refrigerator. It was a monstrous pile of fur decomposing in the tight space. Tiny worms slurped through the open holes in its flesh. The sight was enough to make someone sick, and I had a long debate in my head over which was worse: the sight or smell. After the debate was settled—it was the smell—I used all of my trash bags as gloves. The better option was the purple gardening gloves, but I still wanted to keep those for Beck, in case she returned. *When* she returned. I scooped up the rotting raccoon and ran him to the nearest outside trashcan. As for the juices left behind, I'd have to wait until I bought bleach and rags from the store the following day.

I skipped dinner. I'd like to say it was because of a broken heart, but truthfully, it was a combination of the hollow feeling inside my heart *and* the worms that took my appetite away. I'd nearly thrown up three times when taking the body out. It wasn't a strength of mine. No matter how many awful things I'd seen in my time, my stomach never grew stronger. Nor did my gag reflex, which matched that of a teenage girl. The smell had improved greatly with the removal of the raccoon, and I left the windows open to vent the house that night. When the sky grew dark and the air chilly, I retreated to my car. It would be a miserable night without sleep, but I couldn't bring myself to crawl back to the hotel when I had just bought a house. Maybe it was the stubborn part of me, but I'd sleep in my car for a week if I had to. It wouldn't be the first time, and I was sure it wouldn't be the last.

Bundled in two jackets, I used a pair of rolled-up jeans as a pillow. At some point in the night, I fell asleep despite the cold and discomfort. I woke frequently to unknown noises and nightmares centered upon the New River Bridge. It was Beck and I drowning again in a trapped car and her eyes watching me painfully. It was my death in 1727 when I was trapped in a burning house. Smoke filled my lungs as the heat encapsulated me. It was World War I when a bullet pierced my chest. Blood drained slowly until my limbs ran cold and I no longer feared what lay ahead. It was my first life . . . when I died as a child at the hands of my father. Beck watched them all while I lived every death, back-to-back. I'd never felt so exposed—not in my unconscious or waking hours. I had a lot of history to unpack, and the look in her eyes reminded me that I was not normal. Nor would I ever come to be.

I tried to sleep after waking in a puddle of my own sweat, but after the nightmare, I lay across my back seat, forcing shut my eyelids and racing mind. Losing Beck would be worse than all my deaths put together. Would she still want me now that the truth had been exposed? I didn't know how much of it was within my control, but if she had become a Tethered Soul because of her bond to me, I'd have to believe that she wouldn't walk away. At least, not in *every* lifetime.

Since I couldn't fall back to sleep, I was up before sunrise. It was one of the most beautiful views our earth offered, yet so many rarely saw it because it was easier to stay nestled in the warmth of blankets. Today, not only did I want to see the sunrise, but I needed it. Watching the morning unfold, my existence was a fresh slate, which made the necessity to move forward with Beck all the clearer. And if I was being honest, my house could use a couple of extra hours airing out.

I started my car and cranked on the heat before making my way to a nearby gas station. It was there that I got not one but two coffees. The gas station clerk sympathized with me and the dark gaunt rings framing my eyes. She told me I should go back to bed, and whatever I had planned for the day could wait a few extra hours. I smiled warmly, but I knew that there was no hiding from my problems—the same way that Beck couldn't hide from hers. They'd be there, life after life, always waiting. And while the extra sleep would sure be nice to rid the fire from my eyes, it wouldn't make my day any easier.

I double-fisted my coffees to the car and started up the mountain. There were many spots with spectacular views and places large enough to park a couple of cars side by side. I pulled into the very first one I came upon as the sky lightened. I checked my phone again, but there were no messages from Beck.

I wondered if I should go to the college and continue my charades of being a student or if I should give her the space and truth that she deserved. Personally, I wanted to track her down, spew the truth out all over her and give her no other choice but to absorb it. If she was going to leave me, it better be that she knew the truth and still chose a different path. I wasn't OK, however, with her leaving me under any misconceptions of who I was or what had happened. Still, I knew what I *should* do. Respect her space. Give her time to compartmentalize. Allow her to come back to me all on her own.

The sun released its brightly burning rays from the horizon and I watched with a sorrow-filled heart. They say it's better to have loved and lost than never to have loved at all. And as I watched the full strength and beauty of the sun emerge that morning, I agreed. Heartbreak was worth it. Sure, my life would go on in endless despair for centuries to come, but I was better for knowing her.

I wasn't surprised to see an unknown vehicle sitting in my driveway when I pulled up to my house, even though I had invited no one. Before I could park my car, I saw Brooklyn, with her long, dark-chocolate locks, emerge from the vehicle. She slammed her door and crossed her arms at her chest. I didn't know what was coming, but I could make an educated guess.

"Good morning, Brooklyn. I see you found my house," I said.

"Easton, I don't know what the hell you have done to Becca, but you've really thrown a wrench in my plan," Brooklyn snapped.

"Your plan?"

"I basically had her feeding out of your hand! And this is how you repay me? Could you have . . . less game?"

I'd never seen this side of sweet Brooklyn, but I never doubted it existed. "What are you talking about?" I grabbed my bag of bleach and rags from my trunk and walked up to my house. Brooklyn was quick on my heels.

"You said she was your soulmate! I've been doing everything in my power to match you two up. And then you unravel it in one afternoon! She never wants to see you again, and what's worse than that? She went running to Nolan last night!" Brooklyn shut the door behind us and her nose wrinkled when the air hit her nostrils.

"Nolan!"

"Yes!"

"Well, why did you let that happen?" I said.

"Me?" Brooklyn's jaw dropped.

"I'm sorry. You're right, I know. I'm sorry," I said. Placing the bag on the counter, I mindlessly pulled out my cleaning supplies while I told myself I deserved this. A long stint of silence spanned between us. "I'm sorry, why are you here?" I asked, suddenly confused.

"You sure do have a lot to learn, you know that?" Brooklyn scowled.

I threw the rags down on top of the plastic grocery bag and gave her my full attention. Whatever she came here to say, she'd better say it before I shut the door on her. I was in no mood, and she didn't know what she was talking about.

"And I suppose you've got it all figured out?" I asked.

"Well, a lot more than you have. I mean, what have you been doing all of this time, anyway?"

I looked around the house and turned up my palms. "I bought a house. And I took a decomposing dinosaur to the trash last night with my bare hands. I bought a bed. What have you been doing?" My brows knitted together. My fondness for Brooklyn was fading.

"Oh my god." Brooklyn's face displayed a mixture of confusion and amusement, but mostly it was the amusement that twinkled in her warm honey eyes. "You don't know?" she asked, though it was more of a statement.

I looked her up and down, from head to toe and back again. What was she hiding from me? I let out a slow, measured breath and then asked. "Know what?" in a tone that was sharper than I intended.

Two car doors slammed shut, and I knew that my bed had arrived at the worst possible time. "Know what, Brooklyn?"

Her eyes flicked to the front door as a loud knock rapped against it. For a second, I stilled, giving her the opportunity to explain, but when she didn't speak up, I went to open the door.

"Hello. I have a setup today for Easton Green."

"Yes, that's me."

"Sign right here." I signed the paperwork against the door and handed it back to the man wearing blue coveralls. "If you show us where you would like it set up, we can get started."

"Absolutely. Right this way."

The men came in, carrying several large boxes. I shot a look to Brooklyn, begging her to wait, but when I returned, she was already gone.

It was nearly three days before Beck showed up at my front door. And when I realized she'd come back to me, I had the distinct feeling that Brooklyn was partially to thank. Beck stood with a bag of hot food and a can of deodorizer spray in hand. We stared at each other, sizing one another up in silence. So much tension passed between us, but I still wasn't sure where she stood. From what I could tell, she was here to say her goodbyes, and for that, I wasn't ready. "You're early. I wasn't expecting you for a week, or two."

Beck rolled her eyes. "You weren't at school . . ."

It was as good of a time as any to flush out my lies. "I don't attend Norton University, so there was no point in going to school if you didn't want to talk to me."

Beck's eyes lifted as she took it in. I could see her wheels turning. She was questioning other things I had told her. I ran my hand over my jaw and looked down at her shoes. Her feet twisted in trepidation.

"Look, I'm sorry I left you on the side of the road. It was kind of an asshole move."

"It was," I agreed.

"I feel like . . . I should run wildly in the opposite direction from you. But what can I say? You have this weird piece of me. You always have."

"We belong together, Beck. Don't run from me. *Stay*." I encouraged her.

"Well, I wouldn't have come with dinner for two if I was going to apologize and leave. Can I come in?" she asked.

"Oh, yeah, come in." I held the door open and resisted running my hand down her back as she passed by me.

"It's . . . surprisingly better." Beck shrugged. "But I think I should still spray this." She gave her can a little shake.

"Yeah, go ahead."

Beck walked around the house spraying an obscene amount of deodorizer into the air while I sorted out the bag of food she had brought over. I didn't have the heart to tell her I'd already eaten. "I can't believe mildew smells that bad!" Beck muttered.

"I think I've gotten used to it. I barely smell it anymore. But let's take the food outside," I said. There was a small stone bench in the backyard we could eat our dinner on. Beck nearly emptied the can in the kitchen air before joining me outside.

"I'm actually a little surprised you came back. I mean, I knew you would at some point, but I wasn't entirely sure how long you would make me wait," I said.

"I didn't want to come back here," Beck said.

My jaw tightened, and my stomach dipped, "You didn't?"

"As you could probably imagine, I have a lot of negative emotions associated with you. It's no cakewalk to look at your face and wonder if something was real or a nightmare." Beck's hair fell in front of her face, and she tucked it behind her ear.

I nodded, hating the way my very face brought her pain. "Then why are you here?"

"I have . . . so many questions. I have questions so loud I can see them when I close my eyes. I have so many questions that I'm physically sick. My stomach is knotted, and my is head pounding. And if I have to go through one more night like I had for the last few nights, I might as well drown myself all over again!" My gut wrenched. Beck swallowed hard and looked down at her lap as she placed one soft hand over her mouth. Then, timidly, she turned to me. "That is what happened, right? We drowned?"

I re-wrapped my taco and placed it back in the bag. There was no way I could eat my way through this conversation. "What exactly do you remember?" It was as good as any place to start.

Beck's knees bounced, and she looked up to the dusky sky. "Honestly, I remember nothing. I have these flashes, though. They're like, um . . . like snapshots of memory. I've always thought they were repetitive dreams, and I'd had them so many times that they burned into my mind like a genuine memory would. I have this . . . memory? I guess you would call it? Um, it's of us, and we're underwater. There's blood all around, and it's cold yet numb at the same time. And I can just close my eyes, and you're still there, still staring at me with those glacier blue eyes, until . . . until you're not anymore."

Beck's eyes shifted, and her voice fragmented. She lifted her hand and shrugged her shoulders in doubt. "I don't know? I don't know. This is all so stupid! I don't know what to believe!"

I pulled her in for a hug and this time she allowed me to comfort her. She buried her head into my chest, and I wrapped my arms around her back.

"And I feel things too! Like I have some sort of weird gravitational pull to you, and I knew there had to be an answer, but I just couldn't figure it out! I want to feed the homeless! Like, I think about it *all* the time!" Beck choked out in a half cry, half laugh into my shoulder.

My face contorted in amusement and torture. Neither of us was able to define the flood of emotions tied to something so unlikely. I wanted her pain to stop first and foremost, but then I wanted to tell her stories of our past life. I wanted to see her laughing again. And I dreamed of fast-forwarding to the part where we left off twenty-one years ago. "I know it's hard. I've gone through it too."

"You have?" Beck pulled away, suddenly optimistic.

"Yeah, a long, long time ago."

Her eyes narrowed as she tried to stifle her cry. "What does that mean?" She frowned with a subtle warning that I must answer her question but in a way that wouldn't add to her already overloaded consciousness.

"I have this . . . *gift*?" I questioned myself by her reaction, and when she didn't completely lose it, I continued attentively. "When my life ends, I simply get the opportunity to do it all over again." Beck's reservation was painted in the creases of her forehead. "And now, you have this gift too!" I couldn't look her in the eye when I said it. I had always viewed my gift as a curse. A cage binding me to this world. I would never meet my maker or see what was on the other side of the veil.

CHAPTER 19

"Wow, you're immortal? *I'm* immortal!?" She'd been sucked into my phony optimism. I'd sold it for more than it was worth.

"Well, no. Not technically."

"Oh . . ."

"Immortal people don't die. We're the opposite. We die . . . a lot." And when it passed my lips, I knew I could no longer sell this as a gift.

I watched carefully as Beck started to see the controversy, but I desperately wanted her to think that this was a legacy we were chosen for. And perhaps we were? "But we get to do it together! And after a couple of times, you will have a pretty good memory of it all. It's only the beginning when your subconscious blocks out these memories of past lives. It's a defense mechanism, really."

Beck fiddled with the taco wrapper between her fingers. "You remember all of your past lives?" Beck looked at me with pink puffy eyes and a hint of hope. She was taking this better than I'd thought.

"Yes, I remember all of my lives. My last one is where I met you. And we fell so deeply in love, somehow, you became Tethered as well."

"Tethered?" Beck asked.

"Yeah, there's a name for our condition. *Gift.* We're called Tethered Souls, or at least that seems to be the most common name I've heard amongst our kind. I guess it makes sense because our soul is bound to keep coming back. But since I met you, I've questioned that."

"What do you mean?"

"Um, I just mean that I've never known a Tethered Soul to love another, and I question its meaning." I shrugged, and Beck stared at me like I was an open book she could no longer process. All the answers were there before her, ready for her to pick up, but she couldn't.

"There are others?" Beck said in a worried tone.

I waved my hand. "Don't even worry about that. They're just people," I said. She fed off of my temperament, and I could sense that her anxiety had started to dissipate. Her flustered skin was finally regaining its usual pale tone, and her breathing had slowed to a steady ebb and flow. We sat in silence until our attention fell to our dinner. Beck took her food out of the bag, and we ate in my backyard in reflection.

"Thanks for dinner," I said, breaking the silence. Beck was so emotionally drained that she could barely respond. Her eyes glassed over as she chewed slowly and methodically. "Hey! I have the best idea!" Beck's dreary face turned ever so slightly in my direction, as if she'd just woken from a deep sleep. Her flaxen hair draped over the corners of her eyes. "Do you want to demolish something?"

Beck brushed her hair from her face and tucked it behind her ear. "Like what?"

"Literally, anything!" The edge of her lips curled upwards as the light returned to her eyes, one sparkle at a time. "I bought this sledgehammer, and we can just . . ." I shook my thumb back at the house with an impish smile.

"Really?" Beck asked.

"I've always wanted an open floor plan!" I said with a shrug.

Beck picked up the sledgehammer with a gleam in her eyes. She found her grip while she lifted it up and down, trying to get a feel for the heaviness. I pointed to the wall that separated the dining room from the living room, and she approached it with determination. She took a wide stance as if she were playing baseball and took one last approving look in my direction with brows raised.

"Wreck it!" I hollered through cupped hands. Beck took a deep breath and swung the sledgehammer into the wall, yelping as it struck the drywall. She flinched, and the hammer stuck in the middle of the wall. Beck shook her hands and wiped them on her jeans. From my particular angle, I could see the hammer poking out on the other side of the wall.

"I . . . I need to try again. That one was just practice!" Beck tried to pull the hammer out of the wall, but when it didn't budge, she stopped and looked toward me for help.

"You can do it!" I said.

Beck tried some more before turning her frustration onto me. "Seriously, the thing is stuck!" She slapped her palm on her side.

"Use your foot for leverage!" I said, busying myself as I tried to set up my

Bluetooth speaker. Just finding the settings app was difficult enough amongst the sea of unused apps on my phone. Pairing was going to take me a while.

"Eerrr" Beck growled, and I turned, amused, just in time to see the sledgehammer break free and Beck propel backward onto her butt. The sledgehammer went flying backward over her head, clamoring down to the floor.

"Beck! Are you OK?" I approached her with an open hand for help up, but she wasn't ready. Her chest was rising and falling in pure frustration. Her face was beet red, and loose strands of her hair lifted with each huff. As soon as I smiled, I knew it was the wrong reaction. Her brows furrowed, and her eyes squinted into a devilish glare. It was precisely the reason why my smile grew to an outburst of laughter. Beck liked that even less. She scrambled to her feet and grabbed the hammer that landed several feet behind her. "Wow, take it easy!" I said, baring my palms.

She didn't. Every bit of frustration, anger, and fear came barreling out on that wall, and this time when she struck it, she didn't recoil. The music kicked on, stoking Beck's internal fire, and she tore into the wall as if it were every lie ever fed to her, every misconception she ever had, and every mistrusted person in her life. She broke into that wall like it was her cancer, and she'd had enough.

I wasn't going to admire the view from afar, although it was quite satisfying. I wanted in on the action. To destroy that demon with her. Together. I picked up my crowbar and hooked it into a hole she had torn into the wall. Then ripped the side of the drywall off. It was too easy. I tossed the crowbar over my shoulder as Beck took another overhead hack into the wall. I kicked at the exposed beam and it cracked. The music blared, and the beat drove another kick. The beam snapped in half.

Beck's face was flushed, and pieces of her hair stuck to the sweat on her forehead. She took a moment to catch her breath before she tossed the sledgehammer onto the ground and tried her hand at kicking the beams with me. She wasn't quite strong enough to get it on her first or second try, but the house was old and the beams gave way after a handful of her tries.

"This is for living a lie!" She kicked the beam and then looked toward me, waiting.

"This is for . . . having to lie!" I broke another beam in half.

Beck scowled at me, not quite approving of my confession. Then she let it go and yelled over the music, "This is for Nolan, that cheating son of a bitch!" She slammed a right hook into the only clean patch of drywall.

"Ahhh!" Beck pulled her hand back and tucked it in between her thighs, doubled over, holding her breath. The music blared on in the absence of our demolition.

I placed my hand on her back and waited for her to stand upright again. When I was convinced that would never happen, I lowered to my knees and gently pulled her hand out from between her legs. Without the pressure against her hand, blood rose to the surface of her knuckles. "Wow, you really did it, didn't you?" I looked up to see Beck's teary eyes and full cheeks.

"He deserved it!" Beck said as she lifted her hand to examine the damage.

I huffed and pointed to her bloodied hand. "But did your hand deserve that?" I asked. Beck rolled her eyes and pushed her shoulder into mine, causing me to take a step back to catch my balance. I smiled at her, then looked back to the wall. If I hadn't known better, I'd say a bomb went through the center of it. "It's just what I wanted," I said as I framed the wall between my hands. Beck laughed, and I went to the kitchen to turn off the music and fetch her some ice from the freezer. Making do with what I had, I wrapped the ice in a small hand towel and took it to her. She held her hand out, trembling as I took it in mine and slowly lowered the ice down onto her knuckles. Beck winced, and I lifted the ice off for a moment before placing its full weight on top of her hand. "How's that?" I asked.

Beck nodded, still panting from the workout. Heat radiated off her body, and I found a subtle comfort in the way her chest rose and fell with every breath. Pressed against my own, her palm was moist and hot. The whole thing made my heart regain its momentum, though I had been still for some time. I examined the green flecks in Beck's eyes before my gaze dropped to her mouth as she bit down into her bottom lip. She was so close I could smell her cherry lip balm. But it wasn't enough. I needed to taste it, too.

I lowered my lips to hers, and my chest exploded when she lifted onto her toes to meet me in the middle. My eyes closed, allowing me to see more clearly than I had in months. It was the moment that I was sure I could live this life over and over, and every drop of insanity would all be worth it. Beck backed me up against a standing beam in the ruined wall. My back pressed into shards of broken drywall as I deepened my kiss. She responded with matched passion and urgency. The flutter in my chest swelled. The heat in my belly deepened lower yet.

I carefully took my hand off the ice and ran my hands up into Beck's hair. The ice pack slapped against the floor, and ice cubes kicked back at my legs. Beck wrapped one icy hand under my jaw while the hot one slid under my shirt and up my back. All the tension I'd carried with me came to a head in this heated moment, and I swept her up into my arms and carried her to my bedroom. She planted kisses down the side of my neck as I hurried down the hall. Grateful that I'd bought a bed just days earlier.

I took a deep breath, allowing my lungs to be filled to maximum capacity. Then, ever so slowly, I let all the strain I'd been living expel in one exhalation. The boulder had spared me, and I was unscathed.

Sometime after the passion had settled, when all was right in the world, and when Beck had finally found her way back into my arms, I closed my eyes and basked in the sublime. I could finally breathe again. We stayed there entangled as the sky grew black, and the house darkened. When Beck pulled away, I tucked my hands behind my head and watched her pull her shirt over her head and shimmy into her jeans. Her eyes trailed around the empty bedroom before settling on the bare mattress and sleeping bag tangled underneath me. "Is this all you have?" she asked.

"Yeah. For tonight."

Beck singled out a thick lock of hair and wrapped it around her mouth, hiding her smile. A chuckle escaped me, though I was unsure why. She'd just looked so cute. So happy.

"You need me," Beck said, sitting next to me.

I smiled and placed my hand on her knee. There was absolute truth to what she said. It was even an understatement. The moonlight cast shadows across the side of her face, and even then, her beauty was undeniable. "I love you, Beck," I said as sure as the day we wed.

A slight curvature spread across her lips before she turned her head away and ran a hand through her hair. I wasn't expecting to hear it back, nor did I need to. But I did have to tell her how I felt.

"I—" Beck started.

"You don't have to say it back. I understand," I said, sitting up to rub her back.

"No, I want to, it's just—" Beck's shoulders rose.

"Shhh." I hushed her, leaning forward to kiss her on the forehead.

"I struggle because I feel like I know you," Beck went on, pointing her good hand at her heart and tapping her chest. "But here . . ." She pushed a finger to the side of her temple. "I don't have the pieces."

Though I understood, it was difficult to be told that you were forgettable. Especially after the love we had just made.

"I just need a little more time."

I forced a smile, thankful that my face was hidden in the shadows. "Well, you're in luck, because there's an unlimited number of days for you and me. Take all the time you need, but no more, you hear?" I said.

"OK, deal," Beck said with a smile.

Beck and I spent another hour sitting on my bare mattress, discussing her past relationships. Nolan included. She had anticipated that he wouldn't be faithful, but it never kept her from trying with him. Her intentions were to have fun, but she wound up liking him more than she planned. Because of that, she was hurt when he did what she knew he would. She talked about how she had an unhealthy pattern of picking guys who either couldn't commit or couldn't keep her attention. Of course, she didn't need to tell me. I already knew from the conversations we shared before. Still, I enjoyed her new take on relationships, and I could spot the subtle changes in her growth even though she couldn't.

I kicked myself for not having a first aid kit after I ran Beck's blood dried hand under tempered water. I patted her knuckles dry with a clean paper towel and apologized for not having bandages. When Beck was ready to go, I didn't press her to stay. I knew she had a lot to sort through in her head, and I was confident that she'd be back fairly soon. I made it my goal to have full bedding in place by the time she did.

The work progressed nicely with my house in the following weeks. I had replaced all the carpet with a light grey hardwood. Nearly all the smell left with the dead raccoon, and what had lingered was gone with the carpet. I spent my time working on the ruptured wall, while Beck went to school. Most days, she would come by in the evenings and help me with whatever project was on the list for that day. It was just how I imagined. We painted the bathrooms, and Beck decorated them in soft neutral colors. On the weekends, we spent hours in the dirt, planting flowers and getting sunburns. We cooked in the kitchen together, and she wore my T-shirts like tunics around the house. Slowly but surely, Beck began to feel comfortable in her Tethered skin.

Nearly a month had gone by when I said something that had shocked Beck. It never crossed her mind, and it seemed to have rattled her to her core. I wanted nothing more than to continue our forward momentum, but it was a look in her eyes that told me to tread lightly.

CHAPTER 20

"I'm . . . adopted!" Beck barked.

I stared up at her, dumbfounded, my jaw unhinged. I thought she knew. How could she not know? I lowered my paintbrush into the paint pan and tried to look anywhere but directly at her. The paint bucket was as good a place as any to wait it out.

"Seriously!? My mom and dad aren't my mom and dad?" Beck's mouth hung open. I knew she wasn't looking for an answer, so I steadied my course while the seconds ticked by. "Well, then who the hell is?" she asked.

Unlike me, Beck had parents. In fact, I saw one of them on the bridge just moments after she'd left me high and dry. Had she stayed just a little longer, we would have caused her father a lot of pain. His healing would have torn open like a fresh split on a scabbed knee. If Beck wanted to know her parents, there were stories I could tell her. Though that wouldn't ease her shock now.

The very first life I lived was under the roof of an abusive family. I never had the chance to grow up. I never had the chance to see my fifth birthday. Once I got a couple of lives down the road, I learned that how I had grown up was anything but normal, and for the most part, parents weren't meant to be feared. I was a true lost soul. But Beck was different because even though she didn't remember her parents . . . I did. And they were everything a child could ask for and then some.

"I've got to call my mom! Or *whoever* she is!" Beck lowered off of the ladder and tossed her paintbrush in the pan, causing white paint to splatter my pants.

"Whoa, whoa, whoa! Are you sure you want to do that?" I asked.

"Why wouldn't I?"

"I don't know. It just seems like something you should think about first." I tried to save her from herself, but the woman was a damn tornado when she set her sights on something.

Beck beat her cellphone on the palm of her hand and paced the length of my living room. Fifteen minutes and one iced tea later, she slammed her glass down on the kitchen counter and declared a road trip.

"What?" I asked.

"I thought about it," she said.

"Well, that's—"

"I need to talk to my parents. And you're right, I should think about it first. I can do that in the car. It's nearly a six-hour road trip. That's plenty of time to figure out what to say or ask. God damn it, I should have seen the writing on the wall! Our parents were in that parenting group when we were young, and after you mentioned you were adopted, I realized that's what the group was for . . . I just never thought my parents were there for them. I imagined they were there to support your parents! God, I can be so dense sometimes!" Beck rambled on at the speed of light.

"No, don't say that. It's easy to overlook something when your heart steps in the way." Our minds played tricks on us all the time. Most people couldn't see anything clearly if they were emotionally wrapped up in it. And this was very emotional for a first-timer.

"I've got to go." Beck checked her watch. "I'll pick you up tomorrow morning?"

I smiled and nodded, not entirely convinced that come morning, she'd still want to confront her parents in person. I'd be by her side either way.

9:00 AM struck, and I was all but sure that Beck had given up on talking to her parents. Though that hadn't stopped me from packing a bag as soon as I woke, and it sat ready by the front door. I sipped my third cup of coffee, staring at my unfinished wall while I replayed her reaction over again in my head. I wondered if she would feel up to painting today after school; if she even made it, that was. If Becca was anything like Everly, she'd skip school and lay in bed wasting away. But what I was coming to believe was that Becca was a stronger version than the girl I had known before.

One hour and one fresh coat of paint later, a long honk blared in my driveway. The low rumbling sound of bass grew before a car door slammed shut. I opened my front door, paintbrush in hand, to see Beck bounding forward with bright eyes and beautifully short shorts. "Aren't you supposed to be in school?" I asked.

"What do you mean? I thought we were going to see my parents?"

"Oh, yeah, of course! I just thought that maybe you would have changed your mind once you . . . had time to think about it some more." I set the paintbrush in the paint tray, and Beck took a step inside.

"Then what's that?" She pointed to my bag by the door.

I shrugged. "Proper planning?"

"Come on, let's go."

I looked around the tiny house with longing, but there was nothing here that couldn't wait a few days. "Give me a minute to lock up."

"OK, I'll be outside!" Beck said.

I hammered the lid onto the paint can and changed out of my construction clothes. When I stepped outside, the first thing I noticed was that Beck wasn't driving her truck. A black jeep sat eagerly in my driveway. The second thing I noticed was that Beck wasn't driving. Brooklyn was. I turned my back on the jeep and locked my front door, then swung my bag over my shoulder as I approached the back passenger's side. Brooklyn waved excitedly, and it was clear that I wasn't the only one who'd had three cups of coffee this morning. She and I hadn't talked since the day she accused me of "not knowing," whatever that had meant. But I could see by the smile on her face that it was water under the bridge. And if I was going to spend six hours with her in a car, I was happy to dismiss it as well. Just not forever.

I threw my bag into the back, wincing when I saw how much luggage had fit into Brooklyn's trunk. Not as much as they had packed for Las Vegas but similar. "I'm sorry, I didn't catch how long this trip was, and by the looks of your truck, I may or may not have . . . grey hair by the time I return," I said as I crawled into the back seat. I'd never understood the obsession of needing so many options. That is what was behind me, taking up half of the Jeep. It was shoes. I knew it. "Good morning to you too, Easton!" Brooklyn said.

"Good morning, Brooklyn." I shook my head, giving her an eye full of unfinished business.

Beck reached behind her seat to hand me a hot coffee they'd picked up while filling the vehicle full of gas. She shot me a glance that could only be described as "*I'm sorry*," but I didn't mind. In fact, despite our last heated conversation, I thought Brooklyn was good for Beck.

"I'm not sure if you knew this, but Brooklyn and I went to high school together. So when we were looking at colleges, Brooklyn found Norton University and practically begged me to come with her." Beck rolled her eyes.

"I did not beg!" Brooklyn said.

"You did! She did." Beck nodded before turning back around, laughing.

"Wait, Brooklyn chose Norton?" I tried to read their faces, but the back seat did little in terms of view.

"It's where I'd always dreamed of going." Brooklyn glanced into her rear-view mirror, fixing her eyes on me. They burrowed deep into mine, and though I couldn't read minds, I could read hers now.

"So we moved out here together and got an apartment close to the college.

Anyway, long story short, she's going back to see her parents too. We've done this road trip a few times now and really have it down," Beck said.

I listened to the girls chat about a TV show. They were four seasons deep, and the drama ran as deep as the blue ocean. I stared out the window. When we crossed the New River Bridge, Beck busied herself by digging through her purse frantically. I leaned forward and gave her shoulder a squeeze, and she was so plagued with tension that it was contagious. I, too, became tense.

"Jesus Becca, what'd you forget?" Brooklyn said, trying both to keep her eyes on the bridge and look into Beck's bag for clues.

Beck threw her purse on the ground, and her eye caught on the window. I watched her reflection as she studied the bridge. I didn't know if it was the transparency of her eyes or true vacancy, but there was an emptiness in them. "Nothing," Beck said in a soft tone.

I sipped my coffee even though I was on the verge of being overstimulated and belted in place, no way to expel the energy coursing through my veins. I settled in for the long haul. Brooklyn filled the air with stories of high school Becca, and I wished I could reciprocate my favorite of the times we'd shared in the past. Then, when Beck couldn't withstand any more humiliation, Brooklyn switched gears to talk about her parents. They were both attorneys, and her brother was in law school. She called herself the black sheep of the family, and I wondered if that was the common thread between Beck and Brooklyn's friendship. Perhaps that was the reason I took so well to Brooklyn, too.

What should have only taken six hours would turn into an eight-hour road trip. Possibly longer. I learned more about Brooklyn in that time than I had ever aspired to, but I didn't mind. As much as the girls talked, and it was second to none, they never seemed to mention Beck's adoption. I gathered that Brooklyn wasn't yet privy to the information, and therefore, I kept my mouth shut. When the caffeine finally dissipated, my eyes drooped, and I fell into a dream like state of semi-consciousness.

The dream was nothing less than magnificent. The best part was, I was awake enough to control the outcome. Beck and I got to her parents' house, but they had taken off for a weekend getaway. We had the house to ourselves and treated it like a vacation, lounging around the pool and drinking her parents' liquor cabinets dry. I spent the days watching Beck under the sun and the nights admiring her new tan lines. One night, I convinced her to skinny dip with me. The water was chilly, but the hot tub was ready and waiting. I watched Beck undress as I stood naked by her side. Our toes breached the edge of the pool. I counted down from three with no intention of taking the polar bear plunge myself. Little did she know, I'd be getting her back for our bungee jump incident.

When I yelled three, Beck leapt into the pool, arms straight in the air and screaming until she hit the water with a splash. I stood at the pool edge bent in half laughing.

"Oh! Is he smiling?"

"What?"

"He is."

"Bet he's dreaming about you."

External whispers penetrated the boundaries of my dream, but nothing was more alluring than Beck's face when she came up for air to see me padding to the hot tub, dry as could be. I sank back into my subconscious, where Beck showed me just how angry she was with me in the sweltering hot tub. I awoke with a bump. My head slammed against the window.

"Ah!" I grabbed the side of my head and surveyed our surroundings. Brooklyn looked behind her seat and snickered. I pushed myself upright and wiped the drool that was seeping from my mouth while both girls laughed at me.

"Nice dream, Easton?" Brooklyn teased.

"Stop!" Beck sank into her seat.

"Very, very nice," I said. Both girls laughed with embarrassment, and heat rippled under my skin. Even with my eyes open, I could still see Beck enveloped in steam. I rubbed my eyes, trying to bring myself back to reality. Though it was the last thing I wanted to do.

"Well, we're about thirty minutes out."

"So, we'll be there in an hour?" I asked. Brooklyn's jaw dropped, but she had no comeback. I ran my hands through my hair and straightened my back, settling in for the last hour of the drive.

CHAPTER 21

It was dusk long before we met our destination and I had grown restless. I stretched my arms overhead, a groan escaping my throat. "Call me if you need anything. Love ya!" Brooklyn waved out the window as she drove away. I looked to Beck and then back at her parent's house. Not only was it massive, but it was dark, too. I was pretty sure that nobody was home.

"Did you tell them we were coming?" I asked.

Beck looked back at the house before pulling the handle out on her suitcase. "No, but I have a key."

"Well, are they going to be OK with you bringing a guy home?" I followed her to the large wrought iron doors.

"They don't care! They're going to be excited to see me . . . and they'll love you! You've got nothing to worry about." Beck pushed open the door and rolled her suitcase into the foyer, fumbling for the lights.

"Ahh . . ." A woman's muffled moan snapped us to attention. My pupils grew large, trying to cut through the darkness. My heart beat against my chest as I realized we had made a terrible mistake. Just as the lights flicked on, a naked woman rolled off the sofa and hit the floor with a thud. A man flailed his arms, spewing a long list of profanities as he covered his lap with a decorative throw pillow. The gold tassels swayed as the veins in his neck bulged. Beck cupped her mouth with both hands, dropping her bags to the floor. The suitcase handle slapped against the tile below, and the woman crawled on all fours behind the couch.

"What the fu—" Beck's dad hissed.

"Oh my god!" Beck squealed as she bolted out of the room, ultimately leaving me behind, staring at her naked father.

I had half the mind to reintroduce myself, but I wanted to make a good first impression. As slim as my chances were now—due to unforeseen circumstances—it didn't keep me from trying. I acknowledged him with a curt nod before making my slow exit. The panting and cursing faded as I ventured deeper into the house in my attempt to find Beck. I began to meander, though not aimlessly. I dragged my fingers across a full bookcase, catching a few titles I knew and loved. I admired some framed photographs of baby Beck in the hallway. Partially listening to the symphony of her parents' argument that played softly in the background. When I came upon the kitchen, it was obvious that we had come at a *really* bad time. Red roses unwound in a tall crystal vase, and the remembrances of mixed drinks lay on a wooden cutting board. Grains of salt and pools of lemon juice indicated a rushed mixing.

I briefly wondered if we'd be getting a hotel tonight when I heard a door slam and an echo in the distance. I still hadn't found Beck when her dad came upon me in the kitchen. His collar was popped and his pants were falling without the security of his belt. His face was nearly beet red. And if I hadn't known that Beck was adopted, I might say she'd gotten her complexion from him. I'd seen her flush like that more than a time or two.

"Who are you!?" he barked, still breathing heavily.

"Hello, sir. I'm Easton Green. Um, your old neighbor?" I reached my hand out, but he did nothing more than stare at it with cinched brows.

Beck's mom rounded the corner, wearing a white satin robe that hugged her body like a second skin. "Who are you? And where's Becca?" She tied her robe with a fierce double knot.

"Hi. I'm Easton Green, your old neighbor?" I extended my hand for the second time, and much like the first, she denied it too. She looked nothing like Beck with her dark features, and I was surprised that adoption had never occurred to Beck as a possibility before.

I pulled back my rejected hand and stuffed it into the pockets of my jeans, "I'm a—" I began, determined to make them like me.

"You know, maybe now is not the time. You should go," Beck's mom said. I had nowhere to go. My mouth fell open, but no words came out. The three of us waded through the awkwardness until Beck rounded the corner with a vengeance.

"What the fuck, Mom?" Beck said, holding her hand high in the air. "Who the hell is *that!?*" she gestured to the man fidgeting with his belt.

What? Oh, no! My eyes darted from Beck to her father, not father . . . to her mother.

"Uhh, I'm going to get going, Lil," said the man. He hesitated for a moment before striding out of the kitchen.

"Does Dad know about this?" Beck hissed.

"Your father is away on a business trip," she said before giving me a long and uncomfortable gaze.

"You know, I should go too . . . I'm just going to go . . ." When my declaration had gone unnoticed, let alone unprotested, I followed the fool who'd walked out moments earlier.

I followed the man I'd thought to be Beck's second father outside but not before he collected his shoes from under the sofa. I took one last look into the house before I closed the wrought iron door, leaving the argument behind. "So what's your name, man?" I asked.

He studied me, scanning the length of my body. "Charlie," he said reluctantly.

"Hi, Charlie. I'm Easton," I said. The air had grown cooler, and the stars began to shine through the twilight sky. I took a seat on the curb while Charlie approached his car. With one foot on the floorboards of his car, he paused and looked me over one last time.

"Do you need a ride somewhere, kid?" he asked. I would have accepted if I had somewhere to go, but I didn't know this town from Adam. My time was best spent waiting it out on the curb. I hoped Beck would fetch me shortly.

"No, I'm OK. I'll be fine here. Thanks, though." Charlie gave me a quick nod before leaving, and soon I was left to my lonesome. I tried to adjust my seat, but no matter how I sat, the curb was uncomfortable. I spent the next half-hour watching the glowing lights flicker on and off in the surrounding windows—families watching TV—and trying to stretch my hearing as far as it could take me. When I thought they were finally done and it was safe to return inside, it would start up again. The rise and fall of the mother-daughter dispute finally ran its cycle, and I received a text from Beck asking me where I had been hiding.

Beck found me on the curb. I stood, letting her fall into my open arms. "I'm so sorry you had to see that," I said.

"Yeah. I'm sorry you had to see it too. Apparently, he was her art instructor," Beck said, and I couldn't be more grateful her head rest on my chest and she was unable to meet my gaze. I cleared my throat, buying myself time to gather a reply. "You know, I shouldn't even care. They're just two random people having sex. It's not like she's my mom anyway, right?" Beck pulled away to read my face.

"Well, I wouldn't go that far. I mean she raised you, right?" I said, and Beck sighed, letting a strand of hair twist around her finger. "Parents are the people who raise you. Sometimes, people have biological parents, and other times, it's who they learned under. It's about who made them feel safe and loved. Who taught them right from wrong. And sometimes, that may look more like a village than two people alone. I don't know, Beck. It's a perspective, I guess. I think you will have to just see what feels right when the dust settles." I shrugged, and a shiver rippled through my back. "It's cold out here. Are you warm enough?"

"Oh, yeah. Sorry. Let's go inside."

"What about your mom?" I asked.

"We won't even see her. Her room is on the opposite side of the house," Beck said as she pulled on my hand.

"Maybe we should get a hotel tonight. And however long we're planning on staying. I'm not confident I'm welcome."

"It's been such a long day, I just want to forget all about it," Beck said. I doubted that could happen with her mom still home, and despite the feeling that we were both invading her mother's privacy, I followed Beck back to the house. I kept my eyes peeled for white satin robe while Beck rummaged through the refrigerator, pulling out an assortment of meats and cheeses. She placed an apple, paring knife, and cutting board in front of me before looking through the cabinetry in search of crackers. I chopped the apple and assembled the charcuterie board that looked surprisingly appetizing for the short time it took to throw together.

Beck grabbed a bottle of wine before meandering into the backyard. "Let's eat out here. There are space heaters." I nodded and before picking up the charcuterie board. I gave a quick look around the kitchen, and when I was satisfied that I wasn't being watched, I stole a red rose from the crystal vase and spread the petals over our appetizer. I hoped the romantic touch would bring a smile to Beck's face.

I placed the cheese board on a table underneath the heater. Beck worked to get the heat burning, and I uncorked the wine. The backyard was beautifully manicured, and I admired the landscape and work that had been poured into it. "Did you want me to get some glasses for the wine?" I asked Beck. When the hot tub snagged the corner of my eye, my skin heated as I remembered my dream. Though just as quickly as it came, the memory turned from embers to ice as I realized that this weekend was anything but the one that I had dreamed up in my head.

"Nah, I don't mind drinking out of the bottle," Beck said.

"Oh. It's going to be one of those nights?" Beck rolled her eyes at my sarcasm and we both made ourselves comfortable in the lounge chairs underneath the heater. I started on the cheese and crackers while Beck got to work on the wine. She passed me the bottle, and I took a sip, careful not to spill.

"I just can't believe it. These people . . . I thought they were my parents, and now it's like I don't even know who they are. What's worse . . . I don't know who I am." Beck's stare sank to the bottom of the pool.

"I know who you are."

Beck looked at me. "Do you?" I began to nod, but Beck was more serious this time. "Seriously, you say that, but do you?"

"Well, yeah." I looked up into the sky briefly, confirming my answer. I knew I loved her. And I knew she had a large heart, a kind eye, and a loving touch. I knew my heart belonged to her. And I knew she was her own worst enemy. But would these things help her find her identity? Probably not. "I know your first parents. And your brother," I said.

"I had a brother?" Beck straightened, shock passing through her eyes.

I took another sip of wine and tried remembering how long it took me to regain my memory. "You really don't remember your brother?" I asked, passing her the bottle.

Beck shook her head and held the wine in her lap, tapping her nails against the glass. "I mean, I guess I do. Now that you say it, I feel like it must be true."

After a moment of silence passed between us, I leaned forward. "You should try the cheese. I think it's smoked Gouda." The smoke on my tongue danced with the red wine, and I was happy to eat nothing more than cheese for dinner underneath the warmth of the heater.

Beck smiled at me before dropping her gaze to the rose petal charcuterie board and frowned. "Did you steal my mom's roses?"

I froze, mid-chew. "What is wrong with you?" Beck asked.

I sucked in a piece of cracker and let out a barking cough.

Beck huffed. "You know you deserve that. Stealing roses from my mother's mans-tress . . ." Beck rolled her eyes at the ridiculousness of the situation, and I coughed up a cracker.

"It adds a romantic flare though, don't you think?" I said, still hacking.

Beck smiled and begrudgingly agreed. She loosened up just enough to try the smoked Gouda, causing her eyebrows to rise with surprised delight. "You know, if I close my eyes, I think I can see them, and I wonder if it's really my family, or just some fraction of make-believe I've conjured up in my head." Beck licked her fingers before wiping them on her jeans.

"God, I really wish there was something I could do to help you remember them. I mean, not just them but everything. I wish you remembered it all! What was it like when we were on the bridge? You seemed to remember once you were back in that specific location. Maybe we could, I don't know, imitate that by bringing you around town?" I asked.

"Yeah! Maybe? Do you think it could work?

"It already has, hasn't it?" I asked.

Beck tucked her hair behind her ears and wrapped her arms around her knees. "Kind of. When we were at the bridge, I felt . . . unsettled. The feeling gnawed at my stomach until I could no longer ignore it. Then, I saw your name on the memorial plaque, and I just lost it. In that moment, I knew that my intuition was correct and that, while I had thought I was crazy my entire life for feeling things I couldn't explain, finally, there was an answer. There was a plaque. I knew you were the secret's keeper, and I both blamed you for keeping it from me and needed you expediently."

"Lives," I said.

"What?" Beck looked to me, resting her cheek on her knees.

"You get to say *lives* now. Plural."

"Oh. Yeah. I guess." Beck directed her gaze to the stars above us, and I lowered my lounge chair so I could see them too. "I want to see them, Easton," she said in only a whisper.

"Who? Your family?"

"Yes. You have to take me to them."

"Oh, no, no, no. That's a big one, Beck. We can't do that."

"Why not!?" her voice rose.

"Beck, imagine you had a child. Now imagine you outlived that child. After twenty-one years of grief, you still wouldn't be healed. What do you think it would do to them if you suddenly came back into their lives? At the same age, no less! It's *not* fair to them."

Beck sat quietly for a long while, digesting my comments. "But I need closure too."

My stomach dropped. In my hundreds of years, I'd never thought about my own needs in the grieving process, and perhaps that's why I never healed myself. I briefly wondered if I'd even given anyone other than Beck the chance to touch my heart at all. I'd been so afraid of losing everyone I loved, I never even allowed my heart to open up.

My chest was heavy with regret, and I vowed to myself that I would take down my walls. I watched a small shooting star dart across the sky before fizzling out, and I brought my hand to my chest. My slow, methodical heart beat under my palm. Sometimes, I couldn't believe I was alive in the first place. I didn't know how I'd come to be Tethered, but I knew that in that moment, I could do it better.

"I have a compromise for you to consider," I said after much thought.

"What's that?"

"We can stalk them."

Beck let out a stunted laugh. "What? Really? You want to *stalk* my parents?"

"It could be fun," I said, perching up on my elbow to look at her. "We can get binoculars and donuts, and we can sit in a stake-out car down the street from their house, waiting, for hours for them to check the mail. It will be nothing short of entertaining, and if we're lucky, it might help bring some of your memory back, too. Maybe you could get a little closure that way?" I reached over and took the bottle of wine from Beck's grasp.

"OK. Let's do it." Beck's tone was devoid of excitement, and I might have gone as far to say that it was a little annoyed.

"What is it? You don't think it will work?"

"Honestly?"

"Yeah, honestly."

"No. I don't think it will work."

"Why is that?" I asked.

Beck ran her hands through her hair in distress, causing my confusion to peak. "Because I don't remember you . . . and I've seen every inch of you."

I writhed in pain. The blow had been unexpected. I knew she was having trouble piecing everything together, but I hadn't known the extent of it. My jaw tensed as I watched the pool's surface ripple under the moonlight. This certainly wasn't the way I thought the weekend would go. "You don't remember me?" I asked in disbelief.

"Apart from your eyes, through the blood-stained water, and my lungs full of the icy river, I have no memory of you. Any of it, really." Beck's voice had run cold, and the vacancy behind her eyes had returned. No wonder she couldn't say she loved me back. The only part of me she remembered was the worst moment of her past life. My eyes were her grim reaper. I shut them tight, wishing she didn't feel pain every time she looked into them.

Our trip ended one day short. Beck's dad was coming home, and her mom didn't want us around when he did. Understandably, they had to talk. Beck never had her chance to sit down with her parents and ask them questions about the adoption. It was devastating for her to walk out the front door with no better sense of identity, but she clung to the hope that she would find herself through the lenses of binoculars on her old street. During our trip home, Beck told Brooklyn everything—aside from being cursed to walk the earth forevermore, of course. And after hours in the car, she had finally let go of some tension. Brooklyn even got her to laugh a bit, and for that, I was thankful.

I spent the rest of the road trip reflecting on my lives, dedicating myself to making Beck's life easier, happier, more enriched. That was the simple part. It was the poolside promise that I had made about loving without reservation that I'd need to work on. It was hard when everyone moved on and only I remained. It was hard to open up to the pain of saying goodbye. Especially when it wasn't a matter of *if* but a matter of *when*. But despite the inevitable hurt, I vouched to not only feel the broken hearts but the beating ones, too. I was going to love again.

CHAPTER 22

I stopped at the donut shop before we got started. It was in every cop movie that featured a stake-out. And even though I'd had a plethora of career experience in my past, I never once considered being a cop. It was a real shame too, with my talent for regeneration. But could I live with all the crime at the end of the night? Was I strong enough to witness the corruption and the fate of the less fortunate? Could I then knock on homes of the unknowing? Could I continue to fight, through the thick of it, without letting it destroy me from the inside out? I'd like to think so. I steepled my fingers under my chin as I wondered if I could pass the physical entry test.

"You want this one?" The lady behind the glass window pointed to a pink sprinkled donut.

"Um, sorry, yes I'll take one of those, and a powdered one, and two cronuts please." I dug in my pocket for cash as I pictured myself as a police officer. I couldn't quite put my finger on why it didn't look right in my head, and I shook the image away when the clerk asked if I wanted coffee.

"Two, please."

"That will be $8.89."

I handed the clerk a ten and placed a couple of bills in her tip jar. I picked up Beck from her apartment, leaving the donuts in the car but taking the coffees with me. The warmth from the cups were a welcome contrast to the brisk air against my knuckles. It felt nice to be near campus again, as I had avoided it in my attempts to finish the renovation of my house. After I climbed the stairs to Beck's apartment, I kicked the door lightly with my foot, trying not to spill the coffees in my hands.

Brooklyn opened the door in short shorts and a crop top. She crossed her arms attempting to hide her chest as she called for Beck. "Becca! Easton is here! Oh . . . Is that for me?" Brooklyn asked, lashes lifted.

"Uh, yeah!" I looked down at the coffees, trying to remember which one I had been drinking out of, but when I couldn't recall, I handed her the left one.

"You're so sweet! Thank you!" I gave her a quick nod, my gaze lingering while I searched for what she claimed to know better than me. "Where are you guys off to?" Brooklyn said, sipping my coffee.

"We're having a picnic," I said.

"A breakfast picnic?"

"Exactly." Brooklyn's eyes lowered to half-mast as she realized she wasn't the only one with secrets.

Beck was quick, and I'd have to wait for another time to finish my conversation with Brooklyn. She didn't appear as worried as I was. Beck grabbed her bag before giving me a quick peck on the cheek. She took the coffee from my hand and waved Brooklyn goodbye with her pinky finger. "I have donuts and binoculars," I said.

"I brought a trucker hat and oversized sunglasses!" I laughed, realizing that I typically had those things in my car, ready at all times. "I'm really nervous." Beck tried to smile through a clenched jaw.

I stalled and pulled Beck in for an embrace. "You have nothing to be nervous about. We probably won't even get a sighting. Not for a few days, anyway."

Beck pulled away, and her brows stitched together.

"I mean, we're totally going to see them. We're going to see them so hard!" I smiled and slapped the bill of Beck's hat, tipping it down to the bridge of her nose.

She smiled her pearly whites and lifted the hat to see again. "Now that's the spirit! Let's go stalk some old people!" Beck said.

We got in the car, and I made my way to Clover, trying everything I could to make Beck wait for the donuts until we were in position, but she didn't understand my vision and swallowed the pink one nearly whole. "They're such a treat! I never eat these!" she said through a mouthful of pink glaze.

"I can see that!"

"What are these brown ones? They look . . . incredibly boring." Beck stared into the box, hunting for her next kill.

"Uh, those are the best ones! They're a mix between a croissant and a donut. You have to at least try it. Not now, though. Just wait."

Beck did as I asked, and I laughed every time I saw her eyes flicker back to the box. It wasn't until I pulled into her old neighborhood that my excitement shifted and I became apprehensive of the whole plan. There were so many things that could go wrong . . . and so few that could go right. "Do you recognize any of this?" I tried to capture Beck's expression, but her head was turned away, looking out the window. If only the back of her head could talk.

"I don't know? I mean, it looks like every other neighborhood, doesn't it?"

"True. But if you had to say which house on this street was yours, which one would you choose?"

Beck looked to both sides of the street before leaning forward in her seat. Her hands gripped her seat and her knuckles were taught and white. I drove slowly, allowing her time to look at each one in thoughtful deliberation. My heart fluttered at the sight of her house, but I tried to remain unbiased. "Well, if I had to choose, I'd say that one with the little bushes that lead up to the front door."

I don't know why it shocked me that she was right, but it did. "What makes you think it's that one?" I asked.

Beck looked at her other options and then back to her old home. "I can't say for sure, it's not anything in particular. Just a feeling. A draw."

"A tether?" I asked.

Beck turned her head slowly and looked into my eyes, "That's *exactly* how it feels. Look!" She raised her arm between us, and it was covered in goose flesh. The tiny hairs on her arm were standing straight up.

I grabbed her hand and kissed the back of her knuckles, which were nearly healed from her demolition mishap. "You're right. That's it."

Beck nodded, taking it in. I parked on the opposite side of the street, making sure our view was the best it could be without being too obvious. I looked to Beck who was no longer consumed with the pastries, and I handed her the large sunglasses to hide behind. I pulled my old trusty cap on and we sat in silence, staring at the house. After ten minutes or so, I reached for the box of donuts. I bit into a cronut while I held the binoculars up to my eyes and tried to peer through every window of the house. If someone was home, I couldn't tell. "I think I might want to try being a cop," I said.

Beck let out a snort. "Yeah. You should do that."

I turned to her, but her face was no more than a blur. I lowered the binoculars slowly. "You laughed," I stated.

"No . . . there was something in my throat." Beck rubbed her throat, reminding me of the way she did when she had cancer.

"You literally snorted."

"No, I just think, you know . . . if you're going to be a cop that maybe you should start lifting weights or something. Maybe."

I stared at her, unable to see her eyes through large tinted sunglasses. Her thin pressed lips were all I needed to know that she was stifling a giggle.

"Are you saying I'm not masculine enough to be a cop?"

Beck slid her glasses down the bridge of her nose and peered up at me with her large green eyes. "Honey, that's precisely what I'm saying."

My jaw unhinged, and my eyes grew with wild delight. "You!" I ripped my seatbelt off, "Little!" I began to crawl over to the passenger's seat and Beck squealed. My head hit the ceiling, and my knees kicked into my chest. My foot caught the center console, and my hands grabbed fistfuls of Beck to steady myself. She screamed, much too loud for a stake-out. It was a rookie move. Fully on top of her, I reached down, fumbling to find the seat recline lever. "Say it. Say I can be a cop!" When her mouth glued shut, I ripped the lever, and we both fell flat against the reclined seat. Beck laughed so hard her face turned red and a vein bulged in her neck. She looked just like her mother's art instructor. I showed no mercy, jabbing my fingertips into her ribs and blowing puffs of air into her ear. She squealed like a boar and fought like one too.

In my attempts to seek revenge, I hadn't even noticed a woman approaching Beck's window. Two knobby hands pressed against my tinted window, making binoculars of their own. Eyes of papier mâché peered down at us. Who knew how long she had been watching? Beck hissed at me when I rolled my window down. "What are you doing?"

"Can I help you, ma'am?" I asked. The lady was appalled by either our display of affection or the fact that she had gotten caught—which one I couldn't tell. She muffled some inaudible words under her breath before walking away, her wiener dog trotting behind her. I opened Beck's door and nearly fell out of the car. I got up, dusting off my clothes, stood to my full height, and walked back to the driver's seat in stride. The lady shot me several dirty looks over her shoulder. And by the last look of utter distaste, I wondered what she truly thought was happening in the parked car.

"Do you think she's going to call the *real* cops? You know, the ones with muscles?" I asked Beck.

"Jesus, you can't let anything go, can you?" Beck was amused by my sarcasm, which only made me want to lay it on thicker.

"Too bad we don't have a dog to walk. If we did, we could get closer." I regretted it the moment I said it. Something in the way Beck's eyes sparkled screamed *mischief*, and I wasn't sure I was up for it.

"I've got a . . . compromise."

I didn't like the way she said it. "No."

"Wha—"

"No."

Two hours later, Beck and I stood at her parent's front door wearing navy blue jumpsuits and face coverings. Beck insisted on holding a clipboard, and I made her promise that under no circumstances would she speak. She rapped on the front door, and nerves coiled in my stomach. It was the very moment I tried to avoid, and here I was, against my better judgment, knocking on the door. I prepared my opening line about needing to test for termites. I'd use several of the neighbors as referenced clients. But when nobody answered the door, I was relieved. Though, relief was quickly chased away by a more powerful, gut-wrenching anxiety when I turned to Beck to see no sign of disappointment in her expression. The twinkling in her eyes told me I was in for much worse than a knock on the door.

"What are you trying to do to me?" I hissed as she tiptoed through the boxwood bushes toward the backyard.

"Quiet!" Beck hissed as she tried to open the first window she came upon. I knew right then and there I'd be spending the night hiding in the pantry with her.

"Beck, seriously, we can't get caught!" I followed her to the slider, and her eyes grew with excitement when the door rolled down the tracks, which officially meant breaking and entering. I let out a trapped breath, as I knew I'd do just about anything to make her happy. "OK . . . but get closure and then get out!" It was my only stipulation—that we do it quickly.

"Closure. Got it." Beck disappeared into the house and the drapes sucked outside, blowing into the mid-morning air. I pushed through them, following her blindly. My eyes searched the house frantically while they adjusted to the dim shadows. It looked similar to what I'd remembered. And at least I knew it was the right house and her parents hadn't moved. That would have been a different kind of disaster—one that I wasn't prepared for.

Beck moved quickly, making her way to a large hutch covered in framed photos. She stilled when she found a picture and pulled it close to examine. I wanted nothing more than to comfort her in that moment, but the thought of getting captured on videotape consumed my thoughts. I scanned the room for small red lights and anything that blinked. I couldn't imagine how her parents would feel watching their daughter's ghost rummage through their house, and I didn't want to be haunted by the thought.

It wasn't until I caught a tear rolling down Beck's cheek that I stopped looking for security cameras and came to be by her side. "We were married?" she whispered. Her hands gripped the picture frame tightly as if it might slip away at any moment. "Why didn't you tell me!" Her whisper turned to a hiss.

"I . . . I was going to—"

"You seriously just pretended to be my *neighbor* . . . when you were really my *husband*!?" This wasn't a whisper at all. She was furious. But this hardly seemed like the right time to discuss it, as we stood in the dark home we had broken into.

"It . . . it was a delicate situation!" She had to know that.

"You let me get screwed over by Nolan, knowing damn well that I loved you!? That I'd already found my match? You just stood by the wayside letting me make mistake after mistake?"

"How was I supposed to know you would choose me again? I honestly didn't think you could love me twice. I had no choice but to let you choose on your own terms!" I said in a hasty yet hushed voice, still aware of our surroundings even though she was not.

She swiped the tear from her cheek and tucked the picture of us on our wedding day under her arm. It was the one where I planted kisses all over her face and she tilted her head back in exquisite loving laughter. I remembered the moment like it was yesterday.

"Wait, what are you doing? You can't take that!"

"Why?"

"Beck! Seriously? Take a picture with your cellphone or something, but leave that here!" I begged.

Beck sighed, giving me a look that could set fire to rain-soaked logs. She placed the picture down on the hutch and pulled out her cellphone. Hastily, she snapped photos of every picture she could before following me to another room. "Which room was mine?" Beck asked.

"I don't know. You didn't live here when I met you." We opened every bedroom door, peaking in quickly. But before Beck could shut the master bedroom door, there was something that caught her eye, rendering her motionless. "What is it?" I asked. When she didn't answer, I began to worry. I pushed the bedroom door open, and Beck walked inside. "What did you find?" I whispered, searching for red blinking lights.

Beck didn't answer, and I was suddenly pulled in a different direction than she. I took one last look at her as she approached the dresser, and I turned my focus to the nightstand. There was something about being a Tethered Soul that allowed you to know without reason. The draw was so deeply embedded in my chest. It was like an anchor digging into the ocean floor. I stepped up to the nightstand, pulled the top drawer open, and lifted the small box from within. I didn't need to open it to know what was inside, but my eyes couldn't survive coming so close and not witnessing it one more time. I opened the box, and Beck's first wedding ring sparkled—even through the bedroom shadows.

A car door slammed. Then another. The sound was so close, it had to be in the driveway. We froze, twisting to see each other and hoping someone had an answer. But neither of us was prepared for this. My feet felt heavy like I was sinking into quicksand. My mind raced. We didn't spring into action until keys entered the front door, at which point full-blown panic ensued. On pure instinct, Beck grabbed my hand, leading me to the master bathroom. She closed the door behind us and worked to open the small window that led to the side yard. I realized I still had the ring in my hand and as much as I knew I should, I wasn't able to let it go. I thrust it into my pocket before boosting Beck up so she could climb out the tiny window. When it was my turn to squeeze through, I was thankful for my lean build. Had I been any stronger, I might not have fit at all.

I slid down the wall, the stucco scrapping my palms as I tried to find gripping. Hanging half way out the window, I was about as graceful as a fawn still learning its footing. I fell to the bushes below with a thud, leaving one shoe behind in the restroom. I scrambled to my feet and peered into the window at the lone shoe in the middle of the floor. There was no way I could retrieve it in time.

"Let's go!" Beck hissed.

"My shoe?" I tripped on my way out of the bush, falling onto my knees.

"Leave it! Let's go!" Beck took off, running to the car, her back half-hunched. I looked back at the window, knees and palms pressed into the wet lawn. I took off after her, limping with one shoe, and one wet sock. We slammed our doors shut. "Go! Go! Go!" Beck wailed, and I peeled out. My heart was beating against my chest like a butterfly trapped in a glass jar. I flew around the corner onto the main road and blew through a yellow light, speeding down the straightaway.

In reality, it would probably be hours before Beck's parents went to draw a bath and noticed the shoe, and even then—at their age—they might just place it back into the closet without a second thought.

By the time we were some way down the main road and my speed had slowed, Beck and I began to laugh. My anxiety lifted, and the high of the thrill took hold. "I can't believe my shoe came off!" I said, and Beck snorted. "And did you see me squeeze through that tiny window? How's that for being manly? If I had been twenty pounds heavier, I wouldn't have made it out alive!" I claimed.

Beck grinned. "Yeah, you're a real modern-day Cinderella . . ."

CHAPTER 23

We hid the getaway car inside my garage. After hunkering down, Beck and I ordered Chinese food for delivery. Still riding the wave of adrenaline, I was saddened that Beck didn't feel the same way. I wanted to celebrate a victory, but she was anything but victorious.

"Do you mind if I stay the night?" Beck asked.

"Stay the night? Beck, you can stay the night every night for the rest of your life! Quite frankly, I've been a little surprised that you haven't moved in with me already." She forced a smile. "What is it?"

"Move in with you?" Beck's eyes grew with shock.

"Well, you *are* my wife," I said cautiously.

"*Was* your wife."

I swallowed the lump in my throat and nodded in agreement. "I'm sorry I didn't tell you earlier. I want you to know, I thought about you every day. And after I finally found you, you seemed so happy that I questioned if I was right for you, this time. I wanted to tell you, but I was afraid," I said.

"Afraid of what?"

"That it would be too much, too soon. That having a past life would upset you. That you wouldn't love me like you promised."

"So you kept it to yourself?"

"No! I let you choose. I let you ask. It's different! I'm sure I could have done it better, but I tried my best to not interfere with your decisions and memories. And you chose me! Again! Without even knowing you had before. Don't you think that's invaluable for us to know?"

Beck closed her eyes, and when she opened them, they took on a warmth that was previously absent. She nodded. "I'm sorry for being upset. It's just a lot to take in. I don't want any more secrets between us, OK?"

"None?" My eyes darted to the corners of the room. I had a lot of secrets and a lot of lies. So much so, sometimes I wondered what was true and what was fiction.

"Easton!" Beck popped a hand on her hip.

"I love you," I said cowering.

Beck sighed, opening her mouth but ultimately closing it without repeating the words back. She hadn't said it yet, and I was starting to worry. "Come here," I said, holding my arms out. She wrapped her arms around me and pressed her ear against my chest.

"I can hear your heart beating," Beck said.

I rested my chin on the top of her head and sighed.

"It's just, I went looking for closure, but now, I think I'm too afraid to get it."

"What do you mean? Are you afraid to look at the pictures you took?" I asked.

Beck pulled away from my grip. "No. I'm afraid to read these." She lifted a stack of journals from her bag. They were tied tight with a large burlap bow. My stomach dipped, realizing I wasn't the only one who stole something from our last life.

"What are those?" I asked.

Beck's eyes began to water, and she looked anywhere but directly at me. "I recognized them. They're mine!" Beck said defensively.

"Beck you can't! You shouldn't have! I never should have let you—" I stopped myself there, knowing that I, too, was guilty of meddling in her parents' lives. I left a shoe on their bathroom floor, for God's sake. I scrubbed my eyes and exhaled long and deep. The doorbell rang.

"But they're mine . . ." Beck said.

"I know," I said, the ring burning a hole into my leg. With a frown, I turned to answer the door. Our Chinese had arrived. I thanked the delivery kid and brought the bag of food into the kitchen.

"I know . . . Maybe you should read them, and then we can put them back?" I nodded, devising my plan. I couldn't bear the thought of breaking back into the house, but it was the only answer I could come up with. "Do you think it will help you to remember?"

"I don't see why they wouldn't. I remembered that they were mine. I just knew without a shadow of a doubt. But, if I'm honest, a part of me doesn't want to remember. When I saw the picture of us, it made me feel sick inside. How could I marry a man and forget him? When I saw these journals, I knew they were the answers to all my questions. The only thing I don't know is . . . am I strong enough to read them?" Beck said as she tucked a strand of her hair behind her ear.

"I could read them to you?"

"No! I mean, no, I can do it by myself. I just need a little space and time," Beck said.

"Well, make yourself comfortable. I can build a fire, and you can settle in with a blanket and read your past memories."

After dinner, we did just that. I built a fire and Beck began to read. She started with her first journal, the one she wrote when she was a child. Judging from the amusement on her face, I imagined it was going well for her. I busied myself setting the new tile backsplash in the kitchen while Beck made random sounds from the living room. Every now and again, I'd steal glances at her, curious what she'd uncovered. I was eager for her to get to the part where she met me, and I wondered if she would let me read it.

An hour later, I was halfway through the mosaic and Beck was onto her second journal. Her amusement began to lessen, and by the time she was a few pages into the third book, tension had soiled the air. Her face was lit by the glow of the fire, and her tears were highlighted with the dancing flames. Nothing would have made me feel better than to rush to her side and promise that everything would be OK. Wash away the pain of old memories with my kisses. But she didn't need that. She needed space. And time. Two things that proved to be challenging for me.

I ended up taking a deck of cards to my bedroom and shutting the door to give her privacy. I knew she wouldn't have that back at her apartment with Brooklyn, so I tried my best to give her what she needed here. I practiced counting cards until the early hours of the morning as I listened to muffled sounds come from Beck in the living room. When some time had passed in silence, I went out to check on her. She lay on the sofa with the journal opened across her chest and pink swollen eye sockets. She must have cried herself to sleep. I pulled the blanket over her and threw another log on the fire before going to bed myself, though I wouldn't sleep soundly.

When morning came, Beck was gone and so were the journals. The blanket had been tossed to the floor. Worry spread through me as I checked the front yard and saw my car missing. But when I hurried into the kitchen, a note was taped onto the coffee pot dispelling my concerns. Beck was at school. And the fact that she was well enough to go to class told me that everything was going to be alright. Perhaps it would be even better than alright.

I grew excited for the possibility that Beck had finally found herself. Her identity uncloaked. I couldn't wait to look into her eyes and see my girl. The one I had fallen in love with on the bridge. Sure, she was the same person, and I had been looking into the same green eyes for months now, but I'd been searching those emerald flecks for recognition. And that was something I had missed deeply. I picked up Beck's ring and slid it into my pocket, unsure if the time would come for me to give it to her. But I'd rather be ready than not, and I was hopeful.

I called a taxi to drive me to Norton University. The sky was bright and cloudless, and I couldn't help but think it was the perfect day to welcome Beck back home. Being with Beck . . . her memory and all . . . That was my dream come true. And I never would have imagined it was so important until it wasn't there. A whole life erased. The secrets we shared. The things we said, and the things we didn't. The living we did while we were alive. The moments we shared before we weren't. It was a bigger part of who we were than I had realized. Beck knew she loved me, but without her memories, she didn't know *why*. And maybe that was why she hadn't admitted it. Maybe today was the day.

When I arrived at the college, I bought a coffee from a vendor on campus and waited for Beck under the oak tree. My tree.

I waited with all the patience in the world. The wait was almost euphoric with anticipation. I listened to the chatter within earshot about weekend plans and test grades. The birds chirped in the oak tree, and a gentle breeze blew by, rustling the leaves. I ran my hand through the damp grass and my back went rigid when I felt what I knew to be a diamond ring under my fingertips. Slowly, I plucked it from the blades of grass. It was in perfect condition, no gouges from a lawnmower sucking it up and spitting it out. The diamond still sparkled as it did in the jewelry shop months ago. I dug into my pocket and pulled out the original wedding band to compare them side by side. They were different, slightly, and the original was a little misshapen, having been pulled from the wreckage.

As I looked over the two rings, the past and the present, I grew unsure of which ring to give to Beck. "What have you got there?" Brooklyn asked, startling me. I nearly dropped both rings into the sea of grass, never to be found again. I shoved them in my shirt pocket, hopeful they would be safer there. Brooklyn eyed me with her golden eyes and one lifted brow.

"Hey, Brooklyn. Have you seen Beck today?"

"No, she didn't come to school today. In fact, she didn't come home last night. Is everything alright?"

I patted my pocket, causing both rings to jingle. "Oh, yeah, everything's fine. I just thought she was at school today, so I dropped by to have lunch with her. Have you heard from her at all today?" I asked.

Brooklyn took a seat next to me and then checked her phone. "No, I haven't, but uh . . . Did I see a ring in your hand?"

I looked to Brooklyn, caught red-handed, and I couldn't help but smile. "Maybe."

"You're really going to do it?" Brooklyn looked unsure of how she felt about it.

"Yeah, I really am." I pulled out one ring, it didn't matter which one my fingers found first, and I handed it to her. It was the new band.

"Wow, Easton, she's going to love it!"

"Think she'll say yes?" I joked.

"Well, yeah. How could she not?" Brooklyn handed the ring back. I eyed her suspiciously. Brooklyn shrugged, "What?"

"What do you mean, how can she not? She has a choice . . ." I had made sure of that.

"I know that. It's just, you guys are kind of fated, though, right? Do you really think you have a choice when it comes to fate?"

I looked into her eyes, trying to read between the lines. "Fated?"

"You know, you said she was your soulmate and your puzzle piece—all of that sappy stuff." Brooklyn rolled her eyes and began to gather her things.

"Wait, but you were the one who said—"

"I'm sorry, Easton. I've got to run. I don't want to be late for class. Good luck!" Brooklyn said.

"Brooklyn, wait!" I said, catching her by the wrist. "Wait!" She spun, her eyes meeting mine. "Talk to me," I begged.

Brooklyn sighed, letting the fight escape with her breath. "OK. I . . . I sometimes have these dreams."

She stopped there, as if it were enough to answer my rising suspiciousness about her. "And?" I let her arm go, and she rubbed her wrist mindlessly.

"And, they sometimes come true."

"Sometimes?" I asked.

"*All* the time."

"Do you get these dreams often?" I asked.

"I've always gotten them. But not many know, so you can't say anything to anyone. Not even Becca."

"I won't," I promised before knowing if I was able to keep it. Brooklyn frowned. "Did you have a dream about her?"

"I've had a dream about the two of you, and it didn't end well." Her eyes creased, and she looked to the ground.

"And by that you mean?" I pushed her to continue.

"I mean, you two didn't make it."

"Like, we split up?" I asked, dreading the worst.

Brooklyn let out a stunted laugh that was anything but funny. "No, like you guys died," she said, worry lining her forehead.

I almost burst into laughter but fought to contain myself. Here I thought that Beck wouldn't accept my proposal, but it was only death. That, we had done before, and we would continue to do it a thousand times over. Poor Brooklyn, she had been worried about a premonition, but little did she know, it was already in the past.

"Well, if you're so worried about us dying, then why have you been trying to pair us up?" I asked.

"I can't control my dreams. They just kind of will me down a particular path, and then once I'm there, they take on a new form. I knew that she was meant to be with you. Not that asshole Nolan. But it wasn't until more recently that I saw your death," Brooklyn said.

"Look, I appreciate you telling me this. But I don't want you to worry over nothing," I said, placing a hand on her shoulder.

"It's not nothing," Brooklyn said.

But I couldn't explain it to her. She was now the one who didn't understand. And while I thought her ability to dream of reality was neat, I had a wife to find. "Of course not. I'll be very careful. Thank you for looking out for us. You're a good friend." Brooklyn bit her lip, looking like she could go on for days about her dreams. "I've got to go find Beck, I'll catch you later," I said, and she nodded reluctantly before heading to class.

There, under the shade of the tree, I stood stranded and slightly sidetracked. I called Beck's phone again to no avail. Where would she go if she had remembered everything? What would she do? A thought sparked, and I was on the phone calling another taxi. I had to get to the ridge of the Truly River.

I waited for my ride in the parking lot, where I had spotted Nolan talking to a girl by his truck. She was neither Beck nor Payton, but a third prospect. Long black hair that touched her waist and highlighted her bare skin between jeans and crop top. Nolan's stance was wide, encapsulating her between his legs. He pulled out his phone as she did hers, and I presumed they exchanged phone numbers. I wondered where his relationship stood with Payton, but when my ride rolled through the parking lot looking for the rideless, my attention fell back to my missing girl.

I watched the perfect day pass by through the cab window and hoped my inclination was right about where Beck had run off to. When the cab pulled up to our old campsite and I saw my car parked at the mouth of the hiking trail, I finally got the relief I'd been waiting for.

I thanked the cab driver and walked up to my car, placing a hand on the front hood. The car was cold and therefore had been parked for some time. I set off, jogging down the trail, eager to meet my bride. The pines passing by and tall damp grass nipping at my calves. A slow burn spread across my chest as my heart worked to keep up with my pace. Once I reached the clearing, I could see Beck there at the cliff's edge. The wildflowers danced in the field between us, and Beck's hair looked alive, set to motion by a cool gust. Every step closer was a step closer to my fate, and I could feel that I had nearly grasped the brightly burning star that I'd once wished upon so long ago.

CHAPTER 24

I walked through the field, my hand over my shirt pocket. The rings clamored together, past and present clashing. Beck turned around and offered me a slight smile, though it didn't reach her eyes. I wrapped my arms around her waist and rested my chin on top of her head. I said nothing. The view from where we stood was astonishing and grounding all at once. If you came here to look down at the Truly River not knowing who you were, you would at least leave knowing who you *wanted* to be.

"You found me," Beck said softly. I squeezed her tight. That I had.

"You remember. Beck, I've waited so long for this moment. I love you. I've loved you through sickness and health. Through life and death and back again." I reached into my shirt pocket and lowered down onto one knee. The ring I grabbed was the original, and it shined brightly under the ray of the sun. Beck turned around, stunned to see my intention. "Will you make me the happiest man and be my wife . . . again? Now, and forever?"

Beck brought her hand to her mouth, leaving me to read her eyes alone. Her tears left me guessing for far too long, and my heart nearly exploded out of my chest in anticipation of her reply. "Beck, say something," I begged.

"It's coming back . . . slowly. You know how you can look at a picture of yourself as a kid, and you smile and say 'I remember that,' only you don't—you remember the picture? It's like that. I read my journals, and I remember, but it's like I only remember what I wrote. I understand how I felt, but somehow it doesn't translate. I don't feel that way now. It's not the same, Easton, I was a different person then. It was—"

"A lifetime ago?" I asked.

"Yes. That's exactly it." Beck's eyes were filled with sadness and marked with doubt. I found them to be contagious.

My gaze dropped to the ring in my outreached hand. Had she not felt the same way about me now? Beck lowered to her knees and sat back on her heels, taking the ring from me, but not placing it on her finger. I sat down, defeated. "Beck, do you still love me?" It was the only question that mattered now.

"That's the thing, Easton. I do love you . . . but is that because I remember I did? Is it because I'm supposed to?" Beck ran her finger down the dent in the ring, and I watched as the sparkle of the diamond dimmed as her face fell. "I almost feel like I'm stuck between two people. I don't know who I am anymore! But if I know one thing . . . I'm not her. I'm not Everly Beck." Beck handed the ring back to me abruptly as if the pain of having it was too much.

"But you *do* love me?"

"Yes." Beck grabbed my hand.

"Say it?" I asked. "I need to hear it. I've waited so long to hear it."

"Easton, I *love* you. I just—"

"Stop! That's all I need," I said. I couldn't take what was coming out of her mouth next. And I still needed the first part to sink in.

I took the other ring out of my pocket and stared down at it for a moment before handing Beck my heart of glass. I knew I was asking a lot, but I couldn't live with the regret if she left me now. "I want to be with you. Beck. Becca . . . The first life, the tenth . . . It's all the same to me. It's natural to be scared. But you don't have to do it alone anymore. I'll be here for you whether or not you put this ring on your finger. I just want you to know that."

"What's that?" Beck asked. I looked at her as she stared into my hand holding not one but two diamond rings. "Why are there two?"

I shook my head, nearly giving up. "I'm a lost soul, Beck. What more can I say? You know, before I met you, I thought I had it all figured out. I'd go about my life, trying to make other people happier. I thought I would brighten the world one Sue at a time, and it worked for a while . . . but then you came along, and everything changed. I found balance when I found you. Everything hurt more deeply, but the love you showed me was well worth the pain, and more. You took down my walls, and I never want to build them again. You're the center of my universe, Beck, but if you want to know who you are . . . you're so much more than that!" I watched Beck melt before me as my words struck a chord with her, and the green in her eyes softened to match the grass. "Let me ask you this, Beck: who do you *want* to be?"

Beck picked a wildflower and pinched off the purple petals one at a time, entranced in thought. "Well, I can tell you who I don't want to be," she said.

"OK then . . ."

"I don't want to be that girl I used to be. The one who thought life was . . . cruel. But I don't want to be the girl I am now either! The one who's too afraid to try!"

"Beck, you have all the time in the world to craft who you want to become. Learn the lessons you need. The hand you've been dealt is nothing more than chance. But it was you who chose to deal with it bravely, and that's been a choice. Nobody can take that from you. I know you won't believe me when I say this, but I've already seen incredible growth from you. I can't wait to see the person you blossom into . . . if you let me."

Beck plucked her last petal. "He loves me," she murmured. A smile spread across her face. "I'm just scared."

"I know." I reached over and lifted the hem of her shirt.

"What are you doing?" Beck squirmed.

"Let me see it?" I asked.

"See what?"

"The twig."

Beck's mouth fell open. "What? Why?"

"It's literally the epitome of your fear. Come on!" I laughed. Beck rolled her eyes and lifted her shirt, baring a cat scratch in black ink across her ribs. I covered my mouth, laughing into my hand. Beck's eyes sparkled, and I could see that the fear no longer held her back.

"Seriously, though, why do you have two rings?" A small amused laugh escaped her.

"I thought . . . that the second I found you, you would bound into my arms. I'd kiss you a thousand times and when you finally let go, I would lower onto one knee and propose. I thought we would pick up right where we left off," I shook my head at my stupidity.

"And we lived happily ever after," Beck smiled and flicked the flower stem away.

"Yeah. That's exactly what I thought."

"That's so sappy!"

I laughed at her bluntness, and the embarrassment caused my face to warm. I guess I was a hopeless romantic. I never gave it much thought. I glanced at her and she winked at me. My heart lurched in my chest. "Yeah. Pretty fucking stupid!" I said, and both Beck and I burst into laughter, letting all the tension fade between us. She shoved me and I flinched before grabbing her and pulling her into me. She fell against my side and inched lower to rest her head in my lap. Her giggles trailed off, and she looked up to the sky. I dug a palm into the grass behind me.

"This reminds me of grey skies and rainfall . . . a slow, tender dance. And if I close my eyes tight enough, I can almost taste the champagne on my lips." Beck smiled with her eyes sealed. The sun beamed down on her face, allowing her skin to shine almost ethereally.

Her memory was painted not only with her words but in the smile on her face. It was almost real—like I could taste it too if I just closed my eyes. "Beck? That memory wasn't written in your journals," I said. Beck's face compressed under the sun, and a stream of fresh tears ran into her hair. When she opened her eyes, she didn't need to confess her love for me or place a ring on her finger because I could see it not only in her but all around her. Like fireflies glowing and gleaming in the air, tucked between blades of grass and tangled in her pale blond hair.

"Easton, I don't know what I would do without you. I may have a lot of self-discovery left to do, but I'm my best self when I'm with you. I love you, and I want to spend the rest of my life with you. Not only our past life. Not only this one. But the future ones too. I'm all in. It's you and me, OK?" Beck let her tears run freely as she gazed up at me, her eyes full of love and promise.

My heart mended back together, stronger than it was before it had broken. Beck chose me. *Again.* And it wasn't because she was down and out or because she had no other choice. She chose me because I'd won her heart, and she'd have it no other way. "It's us against the world," I said.

Beck snickered as the tears fell. She nodded in agreement. "You and me." "Which ring do you want?" I asked.

Beck sat up, placing a finger to her lips. "I want the first one—the original. It's been through a lot, and I'm not done with that girl yet." Beck smiled widely and held out her left hand. I glided the ring onto her finger. Despite the dent, it still fit her perfectly. She held it out for both of us to admire. I took her hand in mine and kissed it.

"I have a safe deposit box I can send the other ring to for safekeeping."

"You mean, for another life?" Beck asked.

I wiped her tears away with my thumb. "Yeah, something like that. Hey, Beck? If we're ever separated, I think it's important to have a meeting place."

"Wait? Why would we ever be sep . . . Oh." Beck laid back down on my lap, looking at her ring.

"May seventh. Every single May seventh at the New River Bridge. If we find ourselves starting over, I want you to meet me there as soon as you can," I said, stressing the importance.

"May seventh, the New River Bridge," Beck repeated. Reassurance washed over me like a warm blanket, and Beck and I took a deep breath in unison. She looked back up to the sky and reached her hand out in front of her as I stroked her hair. At first, I thought she was admiring her ring, but then I saw her pinching at the open air. Her eyes green and wondrous, she looked in between her fingers, perplexed. "Hey, Easton?"

"Huh?"

"What are these?" She tried to catch another but came up short.

I chuckled and marveled at her as she saw what love looked like for the first time. "It's love, Beck."

"It's . . . magical," she whispered.

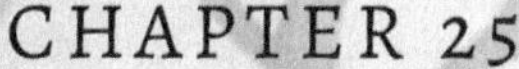

CHAPTER 25

Neither one of us was ready for reality. We remained in the clearing above the Truly River for hours. Beck asked questions about her cancer, and I helped fill in the missing gaps in her memory. She told me stories she'd read in her journals and picked flower petals until the sun made its voyage across the sky.

When it was time to head back to reality, Beck and I strolled hand in hand on the trail under the pines. Beck tossed me the keys from her bag and I unlocked the car before we got inside. I pulled my seatbelt across my chest and noticed that Beck sat still and silent. She paged through her phone, which was filled with missed calls and texts. Several were undoubtedly from me, and I became insecure when Beck twisted with unease.

"What? I was worried, you weren't answering."

"It's from Nolan. James was in an accident!" Beck said in shock. I looked away, feeling her hot gaze on me, but I was too cowardly to meet her stare. I swallowed, feeling the push and pull of bad news on a beautiful day, and I put my car into reverse and pulled out of the pines. "He's at the St. Peterson Mercy Hospital. Do you know how to get there?" Beck asked. I did, it was the same hospital that Beck had been taken to by ambulance after her brother's wedding. I nodded, and we were in for a shift in the tide.

Beck stayed on phone calls between Nolan, Payton, and Brooklyn, and by the time we pulled into the hospital, there was a small group of James's close friends huddled in the waiting room. The few I knew were from our trip to Sin City, but there were several faces I'd never seen before. Beck ran into Brooklyn's arms, and I wondered if she'd had a dream about James, too. I took a seat, resting my elbows on my knees and hanging my head, my hair flopping into my face. The dread spread throughout my chest as I waited for news that only I could know to spread to his friends.

It was a scene I'd seen a few times too many and one I had never wanted to see again. It's hard enough to watch someone leave this world of old age—a perfectly natural occurrence that happens every single second—but when a person is young, short-changed, and unready . . . it's even more unfathomable. I wanted to be anywhere but in that waiting room, but I had a job, a love, and a breaking heart to protect.

James's friends talked amongst themselves as we waited for answers, and I gathered the bits of information that I could and pasted them together. From what I understood, James was on a job painting high on top of scaffolding when he tripped and fell. He landed in a compromising position and there was damage to his spinal cord and head. He wasn't conscious when they brought him in, and I knew he was already gone, though monitors would most likely keep him alive for hours or even days longer. I watched his friends lean on each other, and when I saw no evidence of his parents, I asked Brooklyn where they were. "They're out of state on vacation. Nobody has got a hold of them yet," she said. I threw my head back and scratched my head, exasperated.

"I can't stay here. I need to walk. Tell Beck that I'll be right back, OK?" I asked.

"Absolutely. Oh, and Easton?" Brooklyn said. I looked over my shoulder as Brooklyn mouthed, "Congratulations," with an empathetic smile. I patted my heart and turned away. It was hard to be happy in the wake of a tragedy.

I fled the scene and made my way to the cafeteria for a coffee. Unbeknownst to me, Beck had followed. "Can I get a coffee please?" I asked.

"Just one?"

I looked behind me, startled to see Beck. "Two please," she said.

"Hey, I'm sorry, I just needed a breather," I apologized.

"I get it." Beck gripped my arm tight and rested her head on my shoulder, exhausted from an emotional couple of days. We took our coffees and headed to a nearby table littered with creamer and sugar packets. It was when Beck took her lid off, that I saw her mother enter the cafeteria. As quickly as I could, I spun Beck around, shielding the visibility of her face.

"Ah! What'd you do that for?" Beck held her arms up, covered in hot coffee. Beck's mom looked towards us to see what the commotion was about, and I ducked my head.

"Shhh, wait!" I hissed.

Beck slapped her hand down on her thigh, "Easton, I'm covered in coffee!"

"Beck, it's your mom. She's here!" I whispered into Beck's ear.

Beck turned around slowly and I grabbed her wrist, leading her out of the cafeteria. Both of our coffees remained behind. Once in the safety of a stairwell,

Beck looked into my eyes with an unwavering sense of knowing. "It's my dad, Easton. I just know it. I have to see him."

"Beck, we can't interfere. They won't understand," I pled.

"I'm not asking permission, Easton! I'm doing this with or without you, I'm only asking for your help!" Beck didn't wait for my answer and spun on her heels, ready to charge out of the stairwell.

"I can find him," I said, and Beck stopped. "This way," I said.

Together, we checked with a nurse. I told her I was Beck's brother, Carter, and she pointed us in her father's direction without a second thought. Beck squeezed my hand as we walked down the halls looking for her dad's room. When we found it, she took a moment to gather herself before entering.

Beck's dad lay resting while monitors captured his vitals. A clear breathing tube was threaded above his ears and under his nose, and his bedsheets were folded pristinely across his chest. The past twenty-one years had not been kind to him, and the broken heart of losing his daughter had shone in the crevices etched into his forehead.

"Pop?" Beck whispered.

"Shhh, we can't wake him," I said.

Beck pulled a seat near his bedside and sat down. Her face compressed with heavy emotion. I stood by the doorway keeping an eye out for her mother, and when I was convinced that we had some time alone, I picked up her dad's chart and read. Beck reached for her father's hand, causing my heart to skip a beat, but I couldn't tell her not to. Not just because she wouldn't listen but because the fear of her parents seeing her was far less than the fear of Beck not saying goodbye. In all honesty, had I been given the chance, I would risk it too.

She brought his hand to her lips and kissed his knuckles. Gentle tears rolled off her cheeks and dripped onto her lap. I watched as she finally had the chance to say goodbye to her dad, even if it was an entire lifetime late. I couldn't pry my eyes off of them, and I felt my own tears burning the corners of my eyes.

"I'm sorry I didn't get a chance to say goodbye, Pop. I thought I had more time. I thought it was going to be different," Beck murmured, lowering her head. Broken.

The corners of her dad's lips pulled up in a strained smile, and his eyes fluttered open. My stomach dropped and while I felt adrenaline course through my veins, Beck was the polar opposite. She remained calm and complacent. Confident that she was right where she ought to be.

"Everly? Everly, is that you?" he said through the drugs and heavy eyelids.

"It's me, Dad, I'm here. I'm here." Beck kissed his hand repeatedly, squeezing it tight.

"Oh, Beck! Oh, Beck. How I've missed you." He began to cry, his body brittle and quaking.

"Don't cry, Dad. I'm doing good. I'm happy, and I have Easton. He's taking care of me, so you don't need to worry about me anymore." Beck's dad looked at me, and his eyes grew wide. It hurt me to see his wounds reopening, and I wished it didn't have to be this way. I ran my hands through my hair and scanned the halls once more as my heart nearly lurched out of my chest in anticipation of what would come next.

"What's it like, Beck? What's it going to be like?"

Beck looked at me, taken aback by his question. My mouth fell open.

"Um . . ." Beck looked back to her father, her leg bouncing nervously. She exhaled long and methodically, collecting an answer that she would never know to be true. "It's like kicking your shoes off after a long day's work. It's like birds flying over a pond on a warm afternoon at sunset. It's um . . . it's football and a cold beer . . ." Beck's voice strained, barely audible anymore.

"Will you be there, Beck?" His eyes filled with tears.

"Yeah, Dad. I'll be there . . ." Beck pushed his white hair off of his forehead and ran the back of her hand down the side of his face.

"Listen, Dad. I can't stay. I have to go, but um . . . can you tell Mom something for me?"

Beck's dad covered his face, trying to stifle his sobs.

"Tell Mom that I borrowed my journals, but that I will give them back soon, OK? I don't want her to worry she failed me by losing them. It was me. I took them. And Dad, tell her I love her. Carter too." Beck stood to hug her dad goodbye.

When he pried his incredulous eyes off of her and placed them onto me, I walked over to him and leaned in close to his ear. "Sir, thank you for raising such an amazing daughter. You don't have to worry about her. I'll keep her safe. I promise," I said.

Beck buried her face into her sleeves, wiping away her tears. "Take care of my daughter," her dad said through a splintered voice, and I forced a smile and nodded.

"I will."

Beck looked to her dad when I joined her side and she whispered, "I love you, Pop."

He nodded, burying his eyes deep into his palms, sobbing even heavier yet. "I love you. I love you," he cried.

I looked to Beck, "We should go," I said. She nodded in agreement right as the footsteps approached the door. I panicked and pulled Beck behind the privacy curtain of the shared patient room. Beck's eyes were large with shock, but wider yet when we heard her mother's voice on the other side of the thin vale.

"Oh, honey, I'm here. What's wrong?"

"B . . . Beck . . . Beck" her dad murmured.

Beck cupped her mouth with both hands, trying to silence her cry. Her tears ran down her cheeks and onto her interlocking fingers. I rubbed her back, trying desperately to keep her calm. The damage we had done was sinking in, and it would only be made worse if we showed ourselves now. My own heartbeat became deafening, and for a moment, it was the only thing that I could hear. That was until code blue was called.

Panic ensued on the other side of the curtain, nurses yelling, instruments clamoring. Above all was the screaming from his beloved. Beck began to hyperventilate, and I sat her down on the empty hospital bed as I blocked out the trauma as best I could by placing my hands over her ears. I fought to get her attention, which was no effortless task. When I had her eyes locked onto mine, I worked even harder to keep them there. We took deep breaths together, and I held her hands tight. As tight as I could.

"Clear!" a nurse yelled, and a thump sounded shortly thereafter. Beck and I held our breath until a tiny beep sounded for the second time. "We have a heartbeat! Let's get him to surgery now!"

Beck jumped off of the bed, weak at the knees. I stabled her trembling body in my embrace, and we listened to the commotion leave the room and trail down the halls. The curtain steadied in the wake of the storm. Only the feeble weeping of Beck's mother was left on the other side. So close, yet . . . still a lifetime away.

Beck had called the hospital that night for an update on her father, and when she got the news that he didn't make it, she started checking the newspaper for funeral updates. James hadn't made it either, and Beck was having a difficult time processing it all. She said it was easier when it was herself that was dying and that she would take their place if she could. She didn't understand why she couldn't. Why she got a second chance when they only had one shot.

Beck stayed at my house every night, and every day we moved in more boxes of her things. The once fixer-upper was fast becoming our home . . . my favorite place to be. Brooklyn gushed over Beck's ring and was happy to help her pack in the short stints that Beck spent at their apartment. Brooklyn even spent some time over at our house, and she quickly became a friend of mine as well. She promised to help Beck plan the wedding, and I relinquished all rights to any opinions I might have.

The following week ended with not one but two funerals. James's service was packed with new and old friends, co-workers, fellow students, and family. Brooklyn held Beck's hand at the burial and she often spun her engagement ring mindlessly. When the crowd thinned, Brooklyn's empty stare turned to me as she asked if I could fetch her jacket from her car. I welcomed the chance to step away for a breath of fresh air, though the heavy heart would follow. I strolled down the dirt path a little slower than usual as I played with her keys in my hand. I rummaged through multiple garments in Brooklyn's car before settling on the only one fancy enough to go with her dress. Passing James's friends on my way back to the grave, Brooklyn had her arms wrapped around Beck as she stroked her hair. "Is she alright?" I asked, approaching.

"Just a little shaken up is all," Brooklyn said. I handed her the jacket from the car, and she let go of Beck to put it on. Beck's eyes flicked to me before turning back to Brooklyn. She gave her a quick nod before asking me if we could go home. Beck was silent, overcome with emotion, and by the next day at her father's funeral, she had said that she was numb. Hollow from the inside out.

The sun was high as we sat on a hilltop bench across the cemetery. Beck wore a large sunhat and matching black sunglasses. She could have passed for a celebrity in her mysterious way. There was a smaller gathering for her father, but that was to be expected at his age. Beck pointed out past relatives as she remembered them, and I pointed out her new niece that I had seen at The Taste of Italy. When the crowd dispersed after the burial, Beck's immediate family stayed behind, throwing flowers into the hole where her father's casket was lowered.

"Everly? Can you watch Wes? I don't want him to fall," Chloe said, pointing to the little boy. Beck's niece scooped up her little brother and bopped a white rose on his nose. We watched as he squealed trying to capture it. I squeezed Beck's hand, and a rogue tear tumbled down her cheek from behind her sunglasses, finding its way into the crevice of her lips.

"Is it always going to be like this?" Beck asked.

I thought about how many people I'd held at arm's length. How many people I'd distanced myself from so that I could protect myself from this very moment. I had been doing it wrong all along. "If we're lucky," I said.

Beck's face was shielded by the brim of her black hat, but I could see her red lips twitch with disapproval. "How could you ever associate this feeling with luck?" Beck asked, as she stared down the hill at her family as an outsider.

I took a deep breath. I had been thinking about it a lot lately. "Because it means you're doing it right. You couldn't possibly hurt like this if you haven't loved like that," I said.

Beck let out a small sound that caught in her throat, and she pulled her hand away to wipe her cheek. It was then that a beautiful amethyst dragonfly fluttered up to Beck, landing on the lilac peonies she held for her father. I smiled and looked to Beck to see her lips press together before she lifted her hand to cup her mouth.

"Wow, Beck. It's really something, huh?"

Beck pulled her sunglasses down the bridge of her nose and peered at the dragonfly. A tender smile breached her lips, and I knew in that moment the stars had aligned just perfectly for us. I didn't know how or why. But I knew I had finally found my forever within her gentle soul.

"You know what my dad always used to say?" Beck asked as the purple dragonfly took flight.

"What's that?" I asked, watching it flutter to meet her family below. My heart warmed when I saw Beck's nephew take notice, chasing it around the grave site. Not a care in the world.

"When one door closes, another one opens . . ."

THE KINDRED SOUL OF NORA FAYE

The Kindred Soul of Nora Faye

CHAPTER 1

I was going to live forever. It could have been a gift, or maybe a curse. I didn't know. But it was my second chance at life, and I intended to make the best of it. I never expected it would have turned out the way it did. This is the story of how my first life *should* have gone; and maybe then, I never would have been a Tethered Soul.

Every inch of my skin was sun kissed. My spirit sailed into the summer air as my body grew heavier in the poolside lounge chair. Without opening my eyes, I reached for the sweet Mai Tai, bringing the straw to my lips. The drink washed down my throat and settled like ice in the bottom of my empty stomach. I rolled the straw between my teeth before drawing another sip. A soft moan escaped me, and my lips curved upward ever so slightly. This was living alright. If I could do this every so often, I would surely die a happy girl.

"Why do we wait for someone to get married to celebrate like this?" Brooklyn asked from the lounge beside me.

"I don't know. We should do this all the time."

"Let's do that."

"Uh, huh."

"Promise? You're not going to get married and forget about me or turn old and grumpy . . ." Brooklyn asked.

"What? Who do you think I am?" I forced my eyes open to look at her. The sunlight ricocheted off her oil-slick skin, nearly blinding me. She was starting to burn.

"Well, you know. People who get married stop hanging out with their friends and stuff. They get boring when they slip into a rut."

I sat up and reached for the sunscreen. "I'm not going to be like that. We're going to do this all the time. That's a promise."

"Good," Brooklyn mumbled.

"Now, you should probably put more of this sunscreen on; you're turning pink." Brooklyn lifted her sunglasses and peeked at her torso, then shrugged, waving me off. I finished the rest of my Mai Tai, the straw slurping the fine drops of liquid between the ice.

"Another round." It wasn't a question. Neither she nor I wanted this feeling to fade. I couldn't imagine a better bachelorette party. I told Brooklyn I just wanted to relax, and she booked a weekend away at a winery. We had massages scheduled, manicures, pedicures, wine tasting, you name it. If it was under the umbrella of pampering, we were doing it. However, I would be hard-pressed to leave this lounge chair in my current state.

When the sun's rays became too hot against my skin, I rolled to my stomach, draping my arm over the lounge. My knuckles lay against the cool concrete in the shade of my chair. "Hey, Brooklyn?"

"... Huh?"

"Why didn't you ever tell Easton that you were tethered?"

A stint of silence stretched between us for so long I thought she might have fallen asleep. "Because I don't tell anyone."

"But, you told me?" I pressed.

"Well, that's different. I *had* to tell you. And you're my best friend, so there's that."

"Huh. True," I murmured. "Wait, why, though?"

"Why what? I need the server. Have you seen her?" Brooklyn asked, sitting up.

"No, I'm face down. I have seen nothing but my shadow. Why did you *have* to tell me?" I pressed.

There was a loud sigh, and I could tell I was killing her buzz. "Excuse me? Hi, can we get more of these?" Ice rattled as Brooklyn shook her drink back and forth. "And, do you want anything else?"

"Fries! Can we get some fries? Or, oh, chicken tenders! With ranch dressing!" I blurted my order out in fragments, the only way my brain was processing.

"Good call. Two of those, please," Brooklyn said.

I stood unsteadily and lifted the back of my lounge chair to a seated position. I fixed my towel, dancing as my feet burned on the cement, and sat back down as quickly as possible. My eyes adjusted to the sunlight once again and settled on a lady swimming laps in the long rectangular pool before us. "I don't want to die again." The scattered thoughts escaped my lips.

"Honey, we get to live forever. Just as long as you remember the plan, that is," Brooklyn said. I nodded, though I was sure her eyes were closed, and she couldn't see me.

"I remember," I said, thinking back to the day of James's funeral. Brooklyn had sent Easton away to tell me of a dream she had. I was accustomed to her dreams. I had heard about them all the time, and after the first few came true, I hadn't questioned them again. I never wanted to move to the small town of Clover, but when Brooklyn woke with a dream that my future would be found at Norton University, I couldn't refuse. You can't change fate, she always said. And that was true until she formed the plan. A plan to get around fate. "I know you didn't tell Easton that you were Tethered, but you told him about your dream?" I asked, my recollection fuzzy. It was nearly a year ago, and I had a lot going on at the time, with my memory coming back to me in fragments that would shatter my reality. I adjusted finally, but it took time.

"Yeah, I told him about the dream. He couldn't care less." Brooklyn waived her hand through the air dismissively.

"Really? He didn't care?" My brows stitched, and I pried my eyes off the woman doing laps to look at Brooklyn. She was surely burnt now. The pink in her skin turned to red honeycombs across her legs.

"Either he knows you're going to die and doesn't care, or he thinks I'm a quack," Brooklyn said. Eyes gazing down the bridge of her nose as she lowered her sunglasses.

"Huh?" My jaw fell open, the alcohol hindering its closure.

"Don't get me wrong . . . He loves you; he really does. I don't doubt that for a second. But, I don't think he knows the half of it."

"Really?" I asked.

"Yeah, I mean, he really hasn't lived that long."

"Oh. Yeah . . . I have a lot to learn, too, I guess," I said, the weight settling down on my shoulders. I was still new, only on my second life. I might as well have been an infant.

"Don't worry, I've got your back," Brooklyn said. And I knew it to be true; she'd never steered me wrong. She had been there for me through thick and thin, and her dreams had been a beacon of light for us both. It wasn't until I came to her crying after I had seen the plaque on the bridge–riddled with confusion and distrust–that she told me she too was a Tethered Soul, and that was the reason she'd been drawn to me in the first place. She said my energy was a little brighter than others, the depth somewhat twisted. Whatever that meant. I hadn't seen the things that she and Easton spoke of. Except for the fairy lights I had witnessed in the clearing the day he proposed. Apparently, it took time to open one's senses to the other intangibles and invisible fields of emotion and energy. It all seemed weird to me, but then again, so did having a former life.

Chicken tenders and greasy fries came from the heavens above, and I dug in as if I hadn't eaten in a week. It surely felt like it. I became famished the second the first fry graced my tongue. The Mai Tai in the pit of my stomach soaked into french fries and ranch dressing, making for the most joyous of gatherings. If I thought I was happy an hour ago, well, I'd be wrong because there was a new standard now, and it included fried food. "It doesn't get better than this," I said.

"Just wait, it will," Brooklyn said with a mischievous glow.

A broad smile spread across my face. "You're right! We have massages!" I shimmied my shoulders to the beat of my jaw chewing. Brooklyn giggled, and I looked over in time to see her tilt her head to the side and shrug. She was leading on to something else, something I didn't know about. I didn't pry. Surprises were best served shaken with a dash of shock.

We finished our lunch by the side of the pool, and by the time I finally stood, I nearly fell backward onto my lounge chair. Brooklyn laughed, and I grabbed onto her arm for support while we strolled back to our room. She could have been more supportive if she had stopped swaying herself. We stomped through the bushes every now and again as we veered off the path, and each time we would blame the other. When we finally approached the four villas at the end of the path, Brooklyn fumbled with the keycard, trying to unlock our door to no avail. "Hurry up. I have to pee," I whined.

"It won't open!" Brooklyn jiggled the door.

"It's upside down!" I took the card from her and slipped it in what I was sure to be the correct way, but it didn't open.

"Wait, what room are we?" Brooklyn asked while glancing at her watch.

"We're thirty-one." I looked up to the door, and the numbers flickered in and out of focus. "Does that say thirty-one? Or thirteen?" I asked.

Brooklyn laughed, checking a message on her watch before grabbing my arm and pulling me forward. "Come on, I think we're in the wrong section. Our villa is on the other side of the winery."

"No!"

"Yes!"

"I'm going to pee my pants!" I claimed.

"You should have done that in the pool, my friend. Now let's go. We can't be late!" We trudged on for what seemed like a small eternity through grape vines and red roses. When we approached, the villa marked thirty-one—for the second time—our door unlocked with ease. I ran straight for the bathroom.

"Surprise!" screamed from within the restroom. I jumped, startled by the group of girls packed like sardines behind the door.

"What! What are you guys doing here?" I said, my hips swaying from side to side as they took turns in giving me a hug. Audrey, Terra, Grace, and Kennedy had all flown in a week early to celebrate with me, and to say I was shocked was an understatement. And then there was Payton, who came even though she slept with my boyfriend on my birthday. It had been many apologies later, but despite the regret she expressed and the full year that had passed, I still didn't trust her. And that would never change. But somehow, through the death of James, and the friendship of Brooklyn, we all remained friends . . . of sorts.

I danced my way to the toilet while the girls filed out of the bathroom, closing the door behind them. "We wanted to surprise you!" They yelled.

"Did you know?"

"Yeah, were you surprised?"

I washed my hands under the cold water, the sunscreen turning the sink water milky. I looked at myself in the mirror, my eye liner pooling under my eyes. *Good god!* I had to pull myself together! Fast! I was happy my friends were here; it just wasn't the surprise I'd imagined. With this crowd, I would have to kiss my weekend of relaxation away. It was a shift in mindset that I wasn't prepared for and was struggling with as I stared at my reflection in the mirror. I wiped under my eyes, smearing the liner as I opened the door to several expecting eyes. "I had no idea! You guys totally got me!" I said.

The girls squealed in delight, and another round of hugs began. "We have twenty minutes until our massages, let's start heading that way," Brooklyn said, managing our time by her watch. Her eyes must be more in focus than mine, and I wondered if she had drunk as much as I did by the pool. Then, I suspected that she had taken me to the wrong villa on purpose. I narrowed my eyes at her, and she returned my gaze with a mischievous smile. Brooklyn was always full of surprises. Right when I thought I knew her, she always did something I found shocking.

"You guys have massages too?" I asked.

"Yeah! We're not missing out on any of the fun!"

"I'm getting a Swedish massage."

"I'm getting the hot stone one."

"I don't know what I'm getting; I just picked the one I couldn't pronounce," Grace said. We all laughed as we left the villa.

"That's our room," Kennedy said, pointing to the villa next door.

"Yeah, and that's Audrey's and mine," said Terra.

Brooklyn swung her arm around my shoulders. "Payton is rooming with us this weekend," she said. I forced a smile. Several conversations were happening simultaneously, and my focus bounced back and forth between them like a pinball machine, never landing long enough to grasp the entire topic at hand. After trying and failing, I defaulted to taking in the view of the gardens as we passed by. The chatter passing in one ear and out the other.

Audrey opened the door, and the girls filed in. The scent of lavender washed over my senses, and the sound of trickling water came from various corners of the spa. The air conditioning felt nice on my warm cheeks, and I knew then I'd be falling asleep the second I laid on that massage table.

"Oh, you got some sun!" Brooklyn said, pointing to me.

I turned to her, shocked to see how red she appeared under the artificial light. "Me? You should see you!" I said, laughing. Kennedy and Terra laughed, agreeing with Brooklyn that I was far more burnt than she. If it were true, I'd be in trouble. Brooklyn checked us all in while I perused around the spa boutique picking up tiny purple gems and opening jars of mud that smelled like green tea. And before we knew it, we were handed robes and sandals and shown to the changing rooms. I picked a locker with the number three on it for the best chance at me actually remembering where I had stashed my clothes. Fifty-three. It shouldn't be that hard.

"Oh my god, Becca! You are so burnt!" Terra said. I looked down to where my swimsuit had shifted lower on my hips, and a stark white band wrapped around my body like a belt. My eyes grew as I rushed to the full-length mirror.

"What the hell?" I gasped. "I'm fried!" I said in a squeaky tone. The girls nodded, laughing at me in agreement.

"You are going to blister! I hope you won't be peeling when you walk down the aisle. That would be a nightmare!" Terra finished tying her wavy brown hair into a messy bun and picked at my side strap, examining my burn. "What's? You have something . . ." she said.

"What?" I lifted my arm, trying to see what she had.

"You have . . . what is that? It looks like you have a pen mark on you." Terra licked her thumb and began rubbing the skin on my rib cage. I twisted in the mirror to see my unfinished tattoo. My face felt impossibly overheated, and I was thankful that she couldn't see my flush through the burn of my skin. "It's not coming off." Terra continued to press into my side.

"Stop," I whispered frantically. Quiet as to not alert the other girls.

"But you have . . ."

"Stop, it's a tattoo," I whispered.

"What?! You have a tattoo!" Terra blurted out, catching everyone's attention.

"Wait, *you* have a tattoo!"

"She has a tattoo?"

"What!?" It came from several directions in the locker room and seemed to echo off the walls. I brought my palm to my forehead as everyone except Brooklyn came to investigate.

"Where?" They asked as they all searched my body.

"What did you get?" They stared right past it.

I gave up. Lifting my arm to the ceiling in defeat, but their eyes continued to explore every part of my body. The anticipation churned my stomach as I waited for them to realize they were already looking at it.

"That's it. Right there," Terra pointed out. I sighed, cutting through the shock and ugly gasps.

"OK. I know. I didn't go to get a pen mark on my side. I went to get an infinity symbol. But the guy totally messed up!" I folded my arms across my chest.

"No!"

"He messed up?"

"What!"

"How?"

I searched their hungry eyes but ultimately couldn't give them what they wanted. The truth tumbled out. "Well, he messed up when I leaped out of his chair!" I couldn't help the embarrassed smile that split across my face. Terra laughed, and Kennedy covered her mouth with both hands to smother her hysterical giggle.

"Shut up!"

"You didn't!"

The hazing belted from all five girls. Brooklyn was the only one who had already known about my mishap in Sin City.

"Oh my god, Becca! Only you!" Payton slapped her knee, laughing at my shortcomings. I didn't blame her. I did it to myself. And one year later, it was quite funny.

"Yeah, it's a one-of-a-kind, alright," I agreed.

CHAPTER 2

The seven of us stepped into the spa waiting room. Grace and I filled up on cucumber water while the others talked about how hot they hoped their masseuse would be. One by one, we got picked off. And when an exceptionally attractive man called Terra's name, the rest of the girls moaned in jealous disappointment. I smirked behind my handful of complementary grapes; glad it wasn't me who'd been called. I was the second to last called by a petite woman with a soft voice, and what I would later come to find as firm hands. The massage was relentless, and despite what I had originally thought about falling asleep, the pain of it all kept me wide awake, sobering me muscle by muscle. By the end of my forty-five minutes, I felt beaten and battered. Just the way I liked it.

"Make sure you drink a lot of water to help flush the toxins out," my masseuse said, as I left her room.

"I will, thank you." I took the water and drank it down in a few large gulps. I made my way to the ladies' room and showered the oil out of my hair. I took my time opening the bottles in the shower and smelling each and every one. I may have gone overboard when I found a eucalyptus spray that turned the shower into an invigorating steam room. When I emerged, I felt like a brand new woman. Slightly tired from the sun and alcohol, but refreshed nonetheless. I ran into Grace by my locker. "How was it?" I asked.

"It was good," she asked, uncertain.

"You don't sound so sure of yourself," I said, pulling open my locker, surprised that I had found the right one.

"Well, like, they really get in there you know . . ."

I closed my locker door slowly, revealing Grace's brown bewildered eyes.

Her strawberry blond hair slick with massage oil; it almost looked as dark as her freckles. "Got in . . . where?" I asked.

Grace's eyes jumped to Terra, who strolled in. "Oh my god. That was just what I needed! He was so hot!" Terra let out a loud sigh and pulled her robe off.

"I mean, like, they all massage your butt, right? That's normal?" Grace's eyebrows pinched together, and she nodded her head, trying to convince herself that she was being ridiculous. I didn't know what to tell her. I'd never felt uncomfortable during a massage, and frankly, I'd never thought about what was standardized either.

"Well. . .what kind of massage did you get?" I asked.

Grace shrugged and shook her head. Brooklyn and Payton walked in chatting, and the volume picked up, echoing off the bathroom walls. "Like his hands were so firm!" Terra continued to gush over her masseuse.

"You sure it was his hand?" Payton teased Terra.

"Wow! Hey now!" I said, looking between the two. Terra laughed and wagged her brows, causing us all to giggle. Kennedy and Audrey strode in next, never missing a beat and jumped in immediately to tease Terra. If I had to pick a wild one out of the group, it would be Terra. She was a Spanish spitfire with unruly hair. Out of all my friends back home, Terra was the one who liked to kick it up a notch. I thought she might even give Payton a run for her money, but the night was young, and only time would tell.

We took our time in the spa's bathroom. Everyone showered and took advantage of the luxury creams and complimentary hair products as I did. I went on and on about the eucalyptus spray, making sure everybody tried it. By the time we left the spa, we were pampered to the upper limits and almost ready for our next adventure. Which, to my knowledge, was wine tasting and dinner reservations. The only thing we had to do in preparation was get dressed and maybe put on a little bit of makeup, and we'd be tasting in no time.

Nearly two hours later, we emerged from our rooms. Everyone appeared to be the best versions of themselves, and voices clamored in the air about clothes pairings and eye shadow. Audrey, in particular, loved my heels, and we somehow had a full conversation about them and them alone on the way to the wine tasting room.

"Well, have you tried the moleskin?" Audrey asked, her hand wrapped around the crook of my arm.

"Moleskin?" My upper lip curled as we walked into a large tasting room. Wine-soaked barrels permeated the frigid air, and I took a deep breath in before letting out a shudder.

"Just try it. You'll thank me later," Audrey said, patting my arm before letting go. I looked back at her and nodded. I'd have to remember the stuff and try it. But somehow, I knew that coming off the bachelorette weekend high, I would never remember a second skin made of a rodent. I shrugged to myself in contemplation as I stepped up to the bar. I took out my ID and slid it to the bartender; it never got old.

"Which one are you going to start with?" Audrey asked.

I scanned over the list of tasters. "I think I'm going to do the reds. Oh, look, the port comes with a chocolate!" I said.

"Sold. I want that one. Think I could start with that one?" Audrey asked.

I laughed. "I think you have to go in order, but you could ask?"

Grace slinked up beside me while I waited for my pour. "I don't know what I like. What should I get?" she asked.

"Um, I don't know. Why don't you start with a light white wine?" I said. Grace nodded and pointed to the first white wine on the tasting menu. In the dim lighting, her hair looked void of red and she could easily pass as brunette. I smiled up at her timidness and watched as her brows furrowed with thought.

"Are you sure you want to marry this guy?" As soon as it slipped out of her mouth, the fear set in, and she tried to cover her misstep. "No! I mean, I don't mean are you sure, I mean, you're sure? Like how do you know you're sure? . . . When did you know you were sure?" Grace took a breath and stared at me with beady eyes waiting to assess the damage.

I giggled and took a sip of my first taster. Tart. The back of my jaw came to life. "You're fine! I know what you mean. He's the one. I just know it." I said, my cheeks warming.

Grace stared, her eyes unblinking. "But *how* do you know? I don't even know what wine I want to commit to tasting. How could you possibly know what man you want to spend the rest of your life with?" she asked, making a valid point. I could see how one might be perplexed over this very question. And I was so young. How was I to know what I wanted? But the answer was simple; I just knew.

Kennedy's brows rose and nodded as she joined the interaction making it two to one. "Yeah, how do you know?" she asked.

I sighed, my cheeks surely beet red, and that was before the embarrassment. Audrey and Terra turned around to make four pairs of eyes, staring and waiting for me to say something profound. I wasn't the first man on the moon, but I was the first out of my friends to get married, and that was pretty close. "Because I can't imagine my life without him. And I wouldn't want to," I said, skirting around all of our history.

It would have been easier to say that I'd died once, and my heart refused to let him go. My love for him was so strong that he literally breathed new life into me. It would have been easier to say that I never had a choice. That my heart picked his, or vice versa–I'm not sure–but whatever had happened was outside of my control. That it was fate, and it was bigger than him or me. But because saying all of that was not an option as I stood, twirling my glass with one sip left, I said this: "When you know, you know!"

To their dissatisfaction, each and every one of the four girls groaned in protest. Greedy, wanting more direction. As if I had somehow found the key to success and refused to share it with them. I swallowed my last taste, and my next pour came without asking. Dry. Fruity. Better than the last. It reminded me of my second life.

"But you've only known him for a year, how do you know?"

"Yeah, I've dated Landon for three years, and never once was I like, 'This is the man I want to marry!'"

I laughed, touching my glass to my nose and trying to hide behind its transparency. "That's because you didn't know!" I exclaimed.

"Exactly!"

"Exactly!" I agreed. "If you knew, it would be a different conversation, right? It would be more like, 'I never want to be apart from him. I love him now, and I'll love him till the end of time! And I can't wait to share my life with him,'" I said, noting a raised eyebrow from Brooklyn one wine barrel away.

"That's so sweet, Becca. I'm so happy for you," Grace said.

I smiled at her, and she leaned in for a quick hug. Her hand lingered on my back, rubbing away her worry. "Grace, you don't have to worry about it. You will know. And if you don't know, maybe he's not the right one," I said. She finished her pour of white and bared her bottom teeth, wincing. "You don't like it?" I asked.

"Oh, I love it!" Grace said, eager to please, but it was anything but the truth.

"No offense to you . . ." Terra started. I braced myself for the undoubtedly offensive comment about to spill from her lips. "I just don't think I could ever be sure that I wouldn't want a different man in my life. Like, how could you pick one, and only one? I don't think I could settle for just one," Terra said, eyes crossing in a downward gaze. Grace's lips pulled down as she looked away. Audrey's eyes grew large and fixated on my expression. "But like, no offense," Terra snapped out of her trance and waved her hand, erasing rude parts of her comment.

"It's OK. Marriage isn't for everyone. And if you feel like you're settling, I would highly recommend you don't marry! But for me, I wouldn't settle if I had anything less than Easton," I said. And the truth was, I wasn't offended by what she'd said. I knew that she just hadn't met the right person yet, and one day if she did, she would have a different perspective altogether. If she didn't, well, at least she wouldn't "settle," and that was fine too.

Terra must have felt bad for her comment because she spent the rest of the wine tasting trying to make it up to me with over-the-top compliments and gestures. I must have told her three separate times her comment didn't bother me, but when she wouldn't let it go, I told her we could call it even if she gave me her port chocolate. She gladly gave it up, and I savored the dark, bitter-sweet chocolate between sips of the syrupy port. By the time we had strolled to dinner, my heels were in my hands, and I padded barefoot down the pathway.

Dinner was a perfect mixture of laughter and delicious bread rolls. The wine helped keep my body warm in the air-conditioned restaurant as I picked at my plate of chicken and potatoes au gratin. We talked about the wedding briefly, going over the final dress fittings and place settings. I filled in Payton about how Brooklyn and I knew the rest of the girls from back home. Grace and I met in the third grade when I had to take her to the nurse's office after she scraped her knee on the asphalt. She cried the entire way there, and I remember it feeling like life or death in the moments it took to walk to the main office. She was friends with Kennedy, and I slipped into their small friend group seamlessly after that day. I met Brooklyn, Audrey, and Terra in high school. But when the conversation pivoted, and the girls wanted to know how I'd met Payton, the air shifted, and I was no longer warm.

"And you met Payton at Norton University?" Audrey asked.

"Yes, she was friends with a couple of the guys there, Nolan and James. And Nolan and I shared a class, so we started hanging out," I explained.

"Isn't Nolan the guy who cheated on you?" Audrey asked. Though it was an innocent comment, my stomach churned. My face flushed. They had no idea that Payton was the one who he'd cheated with.

"Um, yeah. But we weren't exclusive or anything, so . . ." I said, trying to diffuse the conversation.

"Still, what a dirtbag!" Audrey said of Nolan.

"And didn't he sleep with your friend or something?" Terra pressed.

Acrobats flipped in my stomach. The whole circus had shown. I stuttered. "Uh, uh, he . . ." My eyes jumped to Payton, and I wish they hadn't. Her head held high in a dismissive fashion. It only made me angry.

"Oh, and wasn't James the one who died?" Terra continued, digging the entire table into a hole we could not escape from.

My face drained, and somehow, I wished we were still talking about Payton and Nolan. I found I preferred anger to helplessness and sorrow, and I would rather dwell on how Nolan cheated on me than how James was denied a long and beautiful life that he very much deserved. I could not answer the questions as they came.

"Yes, James is the one who had the accident," Brooklyn said, as a matter of fact.

"Oh, shit! I'm so sorry, you guys. It's been a tough year, huh?" Terra said, looking from Brooklyn, Payton, and me.

Brooklyn squeezed my hand under the table, and my eyes dropped to my half-eaten chicken.

Payton nodded. "The worst," she said.

CHAPTER 3

Payton drowned her regret with another glass of wine. At least, I assumed it was regret. Perhaps she was just uncomfortable with the topic, or the point of view at which it was shared. I knew she had her reasons for sleeping with Nolan, and none of it was shared at the dinner table that night. Thank god. But it caused for an uncomfortable walk back to our villas. Payton and I couldn't be further from each other as she led the way, and I trailed in the back. I didn't know what to expect when Brooklyn, Payton, and I were alone in our villa for the night, and I didn't want to find out.

But when Payton unlocked the door and an exceptionally well-built firefighter was sitting at the dinette set, I knew I wouldn't have to deal with Payton for quite some time yet. His blond hair was a mess, and his stubble had been growing just long enough to give the illusion that he was a little rough around the edges. A bad boy, helping good people. He stood to his full height, making me feel small, and when all the girls pointed directly at me, I melted. My insides disintegrated, leaving me with not a bone to stand on. This guy was unbelievably attractive, and I didn't want to take my eyes off him. But the last thing I wanted was for him to notice me at all.

He strode towards me. My stomach lurched as he swooped me off my feet and placed me on a chair in the middle of the villa. Brooklyn started playing music, and Payton started pouring shots. The girls were hollering, and the bass bumping. All of it was happening so fast my head began to swim. And then his jacket was coming off. The screaming began as my friends turned into feral beasts. He peeled his jacket off his arms, exposing his shirtless, very tan abs and red suspenders as he swung the jacket overhead. He placed it around Kennedy's shoulders, and she screamed, jumping up and down as if her teen crush pop star had reached downstage and grazed her fingertips.

I sat motionless in the wrought-iron seat in the middle of the room. Hiding in plain sight. Brooklyn passed by and placed a tiara on my head, and Audrey draped a sash over me that read, "bachelorette." As if I wasn't already a target, now I had a red bullseye painted across my chest. I didn't want any of it. The stripper turned his attention back to me, placing his boot between my legs, resting on the edge of my seat. I spread my legs, not wanting the sole of his boot to touch my jeans. My back straightened as it pushed against the chair. I noticed some of the girls laughing at my expression, and I tried to loosen up, but my face was frozen in shock.

The firefighter's hips rolled to the beat of the music as he slid one red suspender off his shoulder to hang waist side. And then another. Before I knew it, oil was being rubbed down his chest and onto his abs. My eyes were transfixed, and I was pretty sure I hadn't blinked since we arrived at the villa. Then, a collision of fear and excitement plowed through me. I swallowed hard, and when he turned to let the other girls help rub the oil in, I escaped from the hot seat.

The girls hooted and hollered, and I grabbed a shot on my way out of the villa. I threw it back before the door closed behind me. And I was thankful to hear that the commotion continued in my absence. I walked to a nearby row of grapevines and sat under a trellis near the parking lot. Taking a deep breath, I did what I knew was forbidden on a night like tonight. I called Easton.

"Hello?" Easton answered on the other line. My heart warmed at the sound of his voice.

"Hello," I said.

"Is everything OK?"

"Yeah," I said, small and meek.

"Beck, what's wrong?" Easton asked.

I sighed. "Nothing's wrong. I just wanted to hear your voice."

There was a pause on the line. "I miss you too. I'm just picking up my brother from the airport; he should be out any minute."

"Are you excited to see him?" I asked.

"Yeah, I think it will be nice. I haven't seen him since I moved to Clover. It's probably been over three years or so—"

"They got a stripper. . ." I blurted out, unable to hold it back any longer.

Easton laughed carelessly on the other end, and I didn't know if I should be relieved or offended. "I know. Brooklyn told me everything before you left. Is he as good-looking as she said he would be?" he asked, sounding genuine.

My face flushed as I walked my fingers around on the bench. "Seriously?" Sometimes I questioned if he had a jealous bone in his body. Not that I wanted that. I didn't. But I could have stood to hear a little worry in his tone.

"Well, I mean, I know he's not as ripped as I am, but she said he'd be good-looking." Easton laughed at himself, and I joined in. A commotion sounded on the other line, and then I heard a door slam shut. "Hey, man. Good to see you!"

"Hey, brother!"

"Beck, say hi to Tanner . . . She's on speaker," Easton said.

I smiled, though he couldn't see me. "Hi Tanner, I can't wait to see you," I said.

"Hey, neighbor!" Tanner said. It seemed like a lifetime ago, but I managed to hold on to a few memories of Tanner. From what I remembered, he wasn't half bad. Of course, Easton was my favorite.

"Well, listen, I don't want to keep you from all the fun–she has a stripper–"

"No way!"

I rolled my eyes, having the news spread like wildfire.

"Yeah. So go have a good time. Not too much fun, though, you hear?" Easton said. And there it was, the bit of worry I'd been waiting for.

I laughed. "Alright," I said with a big, goofy smile. Someone caught my eye in the dark of the night, and when I turned, startled, I was glad to see it was Brooklyn approaching me.

"Now's your chance, Bec. Once you're married to this fool, there will be no turning back!" Tanner yelled in the background.

"OK, I'll go have some fun. I look forward to seeing you again, Tanner. Make yourself at home."

"You know I will!" he replied.

"I love you," Easton said.

Brooklyn sat down on the bench beside me. I smiled up at her and held up a finger. "I love you too. Bye."

"Bye."

Brooklyn put her arm around my shoulders. "Everything OK? I've been looking everywhere for you."

"Oh yeah, I just wanted to call Easton." I shook my phone.

"You know that's strictly against the rules, right?"

I chuckled, and Brooklyn's face cracked into a sympathetic smile. "I'm sorry, I'm terrible at this."

"Yes. You are. What's the problem? Is he not hot enough for you? Because I told them to send the hottest one," Brooklyn asked, half-joking, half-seriously confused.

"No, god no. He's . . . great. Um, he just makes me a little uncomfortable." I smiled apologetically.

Brooklyn laughed and shook her head. "Well, honey, I don't get you, but that's OK. You can't be worse than Grace. She's back there cowering in the corner. I think she might have locked herself in the bathroom when I left." Brooklyn laughed.

I laughed and clutched my hand to my mouth. "Oh no! Poor Grace. We should go save her."

"Yes, you probably should. Come on; it won't be that bad. I promise." Brooklyn stood and pulled me to my feet. We began walking back to the villa, and this time, I was sure we were headed in the right direction. "Are you OK with the whole Nolan thing?" she asked.

"Oh my god! That was so awkward!" My eyes bulged as I grabbed hold of her arm and squeezed.

"They don't know it was Payton, huh?" she raised her eyebrows at me.

"Not a clue!" I said, exchanging a look of unease between us.

"What's Easton doing tonight?" she asked, changing the topic.

"He's picking up his brother, Tanner."

"Oh! Is he single?" Brooklyn wagged her eyebrows. I laughed and gave her a light shove. She giggled and took the crown off my head. "Don't worry. I've got this. Just have fun, OK?" Brooklyn flashed a mischievous smile.

We slipped into the room unnoticed. The stripper was down to a red thong, and his suspenders draped down the sides of his legs. His pelvis hadn't stopped thrusting and rolling since I'd left. And I was pretty sure the drinks hadn't stopped flowing, either. Brooklyn whooped and hollered, dancing up to Payton and placing the crown on her head. She didn't think a thing of it as she shimmied with her empty shot glass. Brooklyn said something into the stripper's ear, and he nodded. I had a feeling I was off the hook. I pulled the sash over my head and took a deep breath before joining the fun without a target on my back.

The party continued for another couple of hours or so. When I thought I couldn't possibly laugh any longer, I did. Terra fell off the bed at least three times, and Payton slow danced with the stripper. The other girls never stopped dancing as Grace and I cried with laughter. By the time the firefighter was dressed again and ready to go home, the party had clearly come to an end. The girls were beyond tired, and the music had died down to white noise. Shoulders were slumped, and mascara smudged as all the girls had outdone themselves. My cheeks hurt so bad; they would be sore tomorrow. I thanked the gentleman on his way out. I thanked each of my friends with hugs as they trickled out of the room and off to bed. And when the door finally closed, and all was quiet, I looked around to find Payton asleep at the foot of the bed. I looked to Brooklyn and shrugged.

"That wasn't too bad, right?" Brooklyn asked.

I shook my head. "I haven't laughed like that in a long time. I had a lot of fun. Thank you," I said, sincerely.

"Did you see him suck Terra's toes?" Brooklyn's eyes bulged.

"Oh! Oh my god! I just about died! It was the most disgusting thing I've ever seen!" I grabbed my stomach, still churning at the memory. We chuckled, recapping the night while we took off our makeup in the bathroom.

When we were done in the bathroom, Brooklyn curled up in the bed that Payton lay across while I got the other bed to myself. I closed my heavy eyes and drifted off to sleep. But it wasn't long before I woke to sounds of vomiting from behind the closed bathroom door. I squinted my eyes and assessed my surroundings. Payton was gone, and Brooklyn was fast asleep, mouth agape and snoring as she often did after a night of heavy drinking.

I tiptoed into the restroom, holding a bottle of water. Payton's cheek lay across the toilet seat lid. "Oh, Payton . . . are you OK?" I asked. Clearly, she'd had better days.

"Nooo. I'erd too mush," Payton mumbled.

My head ached, too, but I was in no position to complain. "Try to drink some water," I said, holding out the bottle for her. She took it, taking slow sips as if she had fallen back asleep between each one. Her body convulsed, and I grabbed the water from her. Awful sounds escaped her throat like the exorcist had been trying to escape. She retched, vomiting into the toilet. I gathered her hair, holding it back while she emptied the entire contents of her stomach. When her episode had calmed, I fetched her a wet wash cloth and ice. She wiped her mouth and nose while I tied her hair back.

I sat down against the bathroom cabinets and rested my head on my knees. We sat in silence. Both probably drifting in and out of consciousness, until her voice brought me back sometime later.

"I'm surry," she slurred.

I lifted my head and looked about the bathroom. "Sorry?" I asked.

"I'm surry fer what I did." Payton's eyes had parted, and she stared at me through tiny watery slits of her lids.

I took a deep breath, already having known that this apology would come after the dinner conversation had dug up the past. "We talked about this already. I know you're sorry. It's OK." The truth was, it was more complicated than that. I couldn't control the standards that she held herself to, and we weren't very close friends when it happened. And if it hadn't happened the way it did, would I still have run into Easton's arms? I wasn't sure. I'd like to think so, but who's to say. Did that make sleeping with Nolan OK? No. It didn't. But it was hard to say I'd been damaged after I had come out on top.

"Iz not OK. I'm surry," Payton repeated.

I watched her for a moment while I tried to gather my thoughts. The truth was, it all seemed so insignificant after James had died. Somehow, it seemed like it was a choice that she and Nolan had made about how they wanted to live their lives. And as long as I did nothing that I was ashamed of, I was honestly OK with what had happened. I didn't feel like a victim because I lost nothing but a few nights' sleep. And actually, it felt like I had nothing to do with it in the first place. I couldn't understand where she and Nolan were coming from when they did it, but I didn't need to.

I said the only thing I could think of. "I forgive you." Payton closed her eyes, and a small lone tear crossed the bridge of her nose. It was true. I had forgiven her, but I wasn't one to forget as easily.

CHAPTER 4

I opened the door, Brooklyn on my heels, holding my pillow. I tossed my bag in the entryway, where I typically kicked off my shoes. The subtle smell the house inhabited was like a warm hug telling me I was home and the party had come to an end.

Tanner walked out from the hallway, his eyes grew large, and his brows peeked. "Bec!" He held his arms out wide, and I bounded into his embrace.

"Tanner! Oh my god! Let me look at you!" I pulled away. My eyes traveling the length of his body. His golden sandy hair and dark chocolate eyes. His sun-kissed skin led me to assume he'd spent his days outside soaking up the rays, and I was jealous. "Man! You look great! I can't believe how tall you've gotten!" A broad smile crossed his face, flashing with pride.

Easton appeared, and though it had been over a year and two lives of being with him, my stomach still fluttered. "Hey! Wow! You're sunburnt!" He scanned my face and shoulders. "I mean, how was it?" Easton asked, grabbing me around the waist and planting a kiss on my cheek. I winced when his chin scrapped over my sensitive skin.

"It was so much fun. All of my friends came early so they could surprise me," I said, turning to Brooklyn. She stood in the doorway, hugging my pillow. "Oh, I'm sorry. Tanner, this is my friend Brooklyn," I said, motioning in her direction.

She smiled with a coyness that I'd never seen before, and my brows pinched in confusion. She slowly placed the pillow on top of my bag and took a step forward to meet Tanner. "Hello," Tanner said, shaking her hand. Her face flushed as she slid both hands into her back pockets. I turned to Easton, but he hadn't seen what I did. "God, Bec, I swear, if someone told me when I was eight years old that my brother would marry the girl next door, I sure as hell wouldn't have believed it!" Tanner chuckled. A smile appeared on Easton's face as he drew me in for another kiss. This time on the lips.

"You and me both, Tanner!" I said.

"Well, I should go. I know you have a lot to do." Brooklyn's voice was soft, and even though she was a sweet soul, her tone usually came off more confident.

"OK. I had a great time. Thank you!" I hugged her tight. She lingered for a moment before disappearing into the bright daylight in the front yard.

"So, how was the stripper?" Tanner asked., causing Easton to roll his eyes. "What?" he shrugged.

"He didn't hold a candle to you two handsome men . . . even in his thong," I said as the warmth spread across my cheeks.

"Ewww!" Tanner laughed, batting a hand in my direction.

Several wasted hours and one nap later, I made spaghetti for dinner. It was nice having Tanner around, as it reminded me of the old days. The days where all I cared about was how high I could jump on the trampoline. How famished I had become from running all day under the sweltering sun. And when I could see Easton next. The days where my biggest fear was what lay beneath my bed when the lights went out and the depth of the pool in the backyard. I longed for the time of my youth when I had not known of my cancer or the wreckage that stole my life. I wondered what would have happened if I never died and my cancer was cured. If Easton and I lived a long and happy life the first time around. I didn't know for sure, but I assumed I wouldn't have had the second chance at love that I was living now.

I watched Easton laughing with his brother over our small dining table for four, and I had never felt more at home. For all the things that had happened in my life, all the uncertainty and pain . . . it just made sense when I was with Easton. And seeing him with his brother made my heart feel whole again.

The boys looked at me expectantly, and the room grew quiet. My eyes pinged back and forth between them. ". . . I'm sorry, what?"

"The bachelorette party. How was it?" Tanner asked.

"Oh! Yeah." I nodded. "Well, I had thought that it was just going to be Brooklyn and me at the villa getting massages, but when we came back from the pool–"

"Now, is that where you got your third-degree burn? Or was that later on?" Tanner asked.

I said nothing but shot him a snarky look. He laughed like I imagined my brother would when he poked and prodded at me for the same reaction. Is this what it was going to be like? Was Tanner going to be like a brother to me? I guessed it made sense, after all, seeing as he was going to be my brother-in-law. "Like I was saying when we came back from the pool–"

"There was a naked guy in your room?" Tanner popped off again.

"Damn it, Tanner!" I snapped.

Easton and Tanner laughed, and I could tell that I had been outnumbered. I sighed before stabbing a meatball on my plate.

"OK. OK. I'm sorry. Continue, please," Tanner said.

"No."

"No. Come on. Come on. I'll be quiet."

"When we came back from the pool. . ." I said slowly, anticipating his next remark. When it didn't come, I continued, "Audrey, Grace, Kennedy, and Terra had driven down early to surprise me. And um, Payton was there too," I said. Easton was quiet, listening, waiting. Tanner bit his cheek. I continued cautiously, "We got massages, went wine tasting, had dinner . . . and then the stripper came–" I shook my head.

"Ahhh!" Tanner belted and laughed out loud. I shook my head, trying to dismiss it, but it lingered until the next topic was well under way.

"So, what are you doing these days, Tanner?" I desperately tried to maneuver away from the oil slick set of abs that had rolled mere inches away from my face. I knew we were all still thinking about it. But I prayed I was the only one envisioning it.

"Well, I'm an Interpretation Analyst. I do a lot of interpreting and a lot of analyzing, and–"

"You mean you sit on the couch all day playing video games?" It was my turn to fire off, and I intended to do so relentlessly.

Tanner's jaw dropped open, half insulted, half impressed at my quickness. "Uh, yeah. That's exactly what I meant when I said I was analyzing. . ."

"Oh my god!" I laughed. The banter extended well after dinner and flowed into the night. Tanner's affection for Easton was apparent, and if I hadn't of known any better, I'd have said that Easton was warming up to the idea of having him around for the week. It wasn't like Easton to get close to people, but he'd expressed to me that he wanted to change and that he was ready to open his heart, even if it meant hurting more in the end. He started taking Tanner's calls shortly after we got engaged. The boys talked on the phone about once a week until it had become second nature for Easton. I knew having Tanner stay with us was a big step for Easton, and I enjoyed watching him come around to the idea of family. I couldn't be more grateful that I was the girl who got to share her life with these two special guys. And I could feel that I was growing a chosen family around me. I knew Tanner was thankful for the opportunity to have his brother back in his life, too.

The seamstress pulled at the loose material around Grace's waist. Grace and Payton wore terracotta rust, Audrey and Brooklyn were in the cinnamon rose dresses, and Terra and Kennedy in the desert rose ones. All would hold mauve, cream, and mustard flowers, complementing the warm sultry tones in their dresses. They were stunning, each and every one of them.

Terra sat down on the sofa next to me in the fitting room. She handed me a mimosa, and we cheered our flutes together, causing a high pitch chime to echo in the air. "I know I give you a hard time about getting married at twenty-two, but I just want to say that I'm so happy for you. And I don't doubt your instincts for a second." Terra smiled at me, a tear forming in the corner of her eye.

"Aww, Terra. I know. Thank you," I said, squeezing her tightly.

Terra sniffed. "I can't wait to meet this mystery man. I mean, I know I'll love him, but still. I'm really looking forward to it."

"I can't wait!" I said, my jaw clenched tight with nervous energy. I'd been planning the wedding for a full year now. I knew it wouldn't be perfect—was such a thing even possible?—but I had been working tirelessly so that it would have the best chance possible. I loved Easton beyond this life, and I knew I wanted to marry him without a shadow of doubt. But would Grace's dress still pucker at the waist? Would my vintage bouquet appear dull and lack luster instead of muted? Because I specifically wanted it to look muted. And I knew it was going to be weird that Easton only had three people coming compared to my thirty-five . . . But *how* weird? Weird enough to ruin the ceremony?

"Becca?"

My eyes snapped to Maripat, the seamstress. I released my fingernails from the meat of my palms and stood to follow her into the dressing room for one last try on. The dress was stunning. It hugged my figure, showing off my curves. The back cut into a low v and flowed into a long lace train. I had Maripat add spaghetti straps to the mermaid fitted dress so I wouldn't have to worry about it slipping. The dress fit a little snugger than last time. Having fit like a second skin, I worried what would happen when we couldn't button it before the wedding.

"And you're still set on no veil? Correct?" Maripat asked. I nodded with a nervous smile. What if that was the wrong decision? "It looks beautiful," she said.

"Thank you. I love the straps. I would never have known the dress came without them." I traced the stitching with my fingertips.

"Thank you, dear. Now let's get you out of this dress, and you can join your friends."

The afternoon unfolded with paninis and tea at a favorite local eatery. The girls filled me in on the funny stories that had continued after the bachelorette party, spilling over to their stay at the nearest hotel. I struggled to stay engaged as the wedding was closing in. My mind raced, double-checking and triple-checking lists in my head. And when I had finally gone over every single worry in my head, I'd create new ones.

It wasn't me. I wasn't the type to turn into a monster as the wedding neared. But there was an undeniable shift that happened deep inside my mind as the prior forty-eight hours began counting down. My brain was dripping with worry, shorting out my circuits. Steam made of stress and anxiety expelled from my ears. I found it challenging to form complete thoughts as there was always a part of me stuck on the wedding. It wasn't until later that night that Easton called attention to it. Further expressing his perfect match for me, he helped ground me and wash away the worry. It was the stories of our past life that I loved hearing the most. I had some of my memory back, but I had never gained full clarity. The pieces I uncovered were still fuzzy and somewhat questionable.

"We married overlooking the Truly River. Well, we called it that, but there wasn't an officiant," Easton said. The fire casting a light show of shadow and highlight on the side of his face as we sat on the sofa.

"We didn't need anybody else," I said, recalling the need to marry before I was too sick.

"It wasn't for anybody else. It was just for us. And this wedding is no different," Easton said.

My gaze dropped to my fingers, entwined in the crocheted lap blanket. "I know."

"We're doing this for us, and as long as we're married at the end of the day, we will have succeeded," Easton said.

My brows lifted. He was right. He always was.

"Seriously! The building could burn down, the band could not show, and the cake could have a hair in it. Literally, everyone could get salmonella!" Easton's voice raised, "But if we walk out of there married. . .we've done it! Game over." Easton held his arms in the air, and I giggled. Letting a little stress roll off my back. "Right?" he asked.

"Yeah, no, you're right. But salmonella would be pretty bad—" I nodded.

"I know you, Beck. Don't you go adding food poisoning to your list of things to worry about. That's not what this conversation is about!" Easton warned.

He knew me so well. I mentally crossed it off the list. "I remember I ruined my dress. It was a white sundress. And by the time we left, it was trashed. I didn't care then. I don't know why I care now," I said, remembering the grass stains and rain-soaked sundress. It was one of the few memories I uncovered, and I held onto dearly.

"You had greater things to worry about back then. Hopefully, you can use that to put this wedding into perspective. We're getting married; that's all that matters. The rest is just a party. And you know what makes an epic party?" Easton asked.

"What?"

"Party fails," Easton shrugged.

I smiled. Eventually, it grew to show my teeth and beyond into rolling laughter. "What's a party without party fails?" I shook my head in disbelief. It was a point of view I'd never considered and was glad to have looked upon now. We finished the night with ice cream and an hour of streaming party fails on TV. By the time I went to bed, I almost wanted to trip over my wedding dress and fall flat on my face. Almost.

CHAPTER 5

The wedding dress hung by the window sill and draped down to the floor. The warm glow of the sunrise behind it. Somehow, the lacy number represented the beginning of something new and yet, the continuation of something old all at the same time. I stood in front of it, the steam from my coffee warming my chin as I marveled over every ornate detail. The stitching was seamless, and the eyelet lace, intricate and mesmerizing. A rooster crowed in the far distance, bringing my focus back to me.

"I'm here! I'm here! Sorry, I'm late!" Brooklyn whirled into the room like a storm. Her dress draped over her arm as she balanced two coffees, her purse and a gift bag.

"No, you're right on time. I'm just early. I couldn't sleep."

"That's understandable," Brooklyn said as she unloaded her things. "Wow, it's really beautiful, isn't it?" she said, looking at the gown.

I smiled. Somehow calm after the last two days of tension. I suppose it had finally run its course. Either that, or Easton's party fail pep talk did me right. "I want to remember this moment forever," I said as Brooklyn came to my side and locked her arm in mine.

"And you will," she said.

I shot her a sideways glance, and we both laughed. The thought of living forever was both exciting and daunting. I hadn't fully settled on which side of the fence I fell. Easton thought it was a curse, but my best friend found it to be a blessing. I wanted to be like her. I did. But every time I felt lucky to have a second chance, my stomach dipped with trepidation. Leaving me more confused than anything else. Sometimes I wondered if there was something that I failed to see or understand, and I feared it would swallow me whole when I realized it. When I finally saw the prison Easton had spoken of.

"It's your big day, Becca. You deserve this. Are you ready?" Brooklyn asked.

"Let's do it!" I said, beaming from head to pedicured toe. Whatever prison awaited me was neither now nor in my immediate future, so I pushed the worry down deep where it belonged. Because I had a wedding to celebrate.

A knock on the door startled me. Brooklyn checked her watch. "That's your beautician. Right on time. I already like her." Brooklyn crossed the room and opened the door. A man waltzed inside, carrying what I could only describe as a black toolbox. His black hair gelled like a hard helmet against his head.

"Oh my god! This ranch is stunning!" he said, his cheekbones high and mighty, carved out with contour and highlight.

"Hi! Um, I thought Remy was coming?" Brooklyn said while glancing into the hallway.

"Honey, I am Remy!"

"Of course, I'm sorry. . ."

"Happens all the time," Remy waved dismissively. "Is this the bride? Oh, she is so burnt!" he exclaimed, setting down his things.

"Hi, I'm Becca Reed." I reached out to shake his hand, a little embarrassed.

"Soon to be Mrs. Green," Brooklyn added with a wink.

I settled in for what was scheduled to take one hour. I wanted all the glamour, but I still wanted to look like myself. But Remy had a plan, and I trusted him and his cheekbones to get the job done. He had a way about him that made me want to gush about everything. Easton, the wedding, girlfriend gossip. And I did. I don't think I stopped until he spun the chair around, and I came face to face with my reflection.

My heart skipped a beat. I couldn't believe that I was the very creature that looked back from my reflection. She was beautiful. And the best part was that I still recognized myself. Brows lifted, cheekbones more defined. The bow of my lip was exaggerated. And my eyes! My eyes were framed with just the right amount of shimmer and lash. Not overpowering my emerald eyes but enhancing their natural color.

"Remy! You're a genius! I love it!" I stammered as he pulled locks of my blond hair down to frame my face.

"Oh, honey! I'm so happy!" he placed both hands on top of his heart. A woman snapped candid pictures of the moment. I was so wrapped up in my ramblings to Remy that I hadn't noticed the photographer's arrival.

A sniff echoed behind me. "Mom! When did you get here?" I asked.

My mom stood in the door jamb, a tissue pressed under her nose. "Just now. Oh, baby, you look so beautiful!" she said. She came in for a hug, and I could sense Remy tense with worry that his masterpiece would smudge. Several snaps of the camera clicked like rapid fire. I wasn't used to being the center of attention, and it made me slightly uncomfortable. But if there were ever a time to receive so much attention, it was now, when my hair and makeup were crafted in to a masterpiece. I almost felt like a princess.

"I have something for you," Mom said, rummaging around in the depths of her purse.

"Oh yeah? You didn't have to get me anything, Mom."

"Well, technically, I didn't." Mom pulled out a small butterfly clip adorned with crystal chips. My heart swelled. "This was given to me when I was a little girl. Of course, I was never allowed to wear it. But I remember cherishing it from afar. I always imagined I would give it to my little girl one day." Her voice broke as she brought a tissue to her nose again.

Her eyes fluttered about, and only I knew she was reminiscing about how she never had that little girl, so she adopted me instead. I never talked to her about it after my first failed attempt. One moment slipped away, giving way to another chance that was also not perfect. By the time my perfect chance had come around again, my emotions had settled back down, and I didn't feel the urgency to bring it up. But when I saw the emotion behind her eyes, I knew what had caused it to be there. And when I didn't think it was possible, I loved her even more because of it.

"So it's your something old." Mom handed me the butterfly and wrapped her arms around my neck.

"It's perfect. Thank you, Mom," I said, fighting back the tears that threatened Remy's masterpiece. I glanced at him quick enough to see his eyes narrow.

"And here is something blue," Brooklyn said, handing me a little gift bag.

I opened it slowly, too aware that my every move had been captured on camera. Inside the bag was something silky and blue, but when I pulled it out, my cheeks flushed at the sexy lace garter belt. "Brooklyn!" My eyes popped as I scrunched it up into a tiny ball.

"Woo, girl! Let me see that!" Remy snatched the sexy number out of my hand and held it up for everyone to admire. My cheeks lit on fire.

"And that's not all. There's more to that outfit, but you will have to open it in private," Brooklyn said with a broad smile.

I laughed. "I can't wait till you get married! Thank you! It's—"

"Sexy!" Remy said, twirling it around his finger. And that it was. I'd never owned something so sexy, and in just a handful of hours, Easton would pull it off in front of every single one of my wedding guests. I fanned my face, and Brooklyn laughed.

"Let's get that dress on. We still have some photos to take before the wedding starts, and it looks like we're a little behind." As tall as Brooklyn was, she still needed to lift onto her tippy toes to reach the dress's hanger. Remy stepped out of the room, giving us privacy while both Brooklyn and my mom helped me climb into the dress. When I was decent, the photographer started taking candid shots again.

The second my last button was secured, Mom started weeping again. "Oh, baby! You look so beautiful!" she said in a broken voice.

I smiled at her, fanning my face and blinking my long lashes. Doing all I could to not let the tears gather. Brooklyn let Remy back inside, and he had my crown of flowers with him. He secured it tight on top of my head and pinned the butterfly clip to a visible break in the flowers. It was the perfect touch. "I think you made the right choice to leave out the veil," Brooklyn said. Seeing it all together, the dress and the flowered crown, it was everything I had waited for. And I couldn't understand why I had been so stressed over such a beautiful occasion.

I said goodbye to Remy, just as the other girls filed in for their hair to be done. They were excited to see me in my dress, and I wanted to stay and talk but couldn't. I was ushered out to several ranch markers for photos. The red abandoned tractor, the windmill, the horse corral. The Bonnie Ranch was stunning, and I had no doubt the pictures would reflect that. Brooklyn and Payton joined me for photos, and Grace, Kennedy, Audrey, and Terra trickled out when their hair was complete. The more of my bridesmaids that arrived, the more fun the pictures became.

"You still have time to run," Terra whispered in my ear. I whipped my head to face her right as the camera snapped. Was she still pressing this runaway bride thing? "*If* you wanted to," Terra shrugged.

"Thanks, but I'm good." It was the only thing I could think to say. My forehead creased, but the moment I remembered Easton's comments about party fails, I relaxed again and started counting. A rude comment from one of my closest friends was the first of many failures. I was sure of it.

Before I knew it, guests started to arrive. I parted ways with the bridesmaids, and the photographer and I walked back to the room across from the red barn where we would marry. I watched nervously out the window as the last guest trickled in as I waited for my dad. I hadn't seen him much since I moved to college, and it had been even less since he and my mom split. I knew it was going to be difficult for them to be together today.

The door creaked open, and my dad peered inside. "Dad!" I jumped up and wrapped my arms around his neck.

"Oh, Becca, you look beautiful in that dress!" His eyes scanned over me, and I blushed with pride.

"Thanks, Dad," I said.

"Are you ready to do this? You sure you want to marry the guy?" he asked sincerely.

"Dad! Why does everyone keep asking me that?"

"Well, dear, probably because you're twenty-two. You're just a baby!"

I tilted my head to the side, "I'm more grown-up than you realize, Dad," I said.

"Oh, I don't doubt that." Dad held his arm out, and I wrapped my hand around the crook of his elbow. We walked out to the side of the barn. The warm air soothed any residual nerves I had from before, and the smell of hay burned into my memory as a cherished moment. I'd probably think of my dad every time I smelled it from here on out.

I stepped on the front of my lace gown, propelling myself forward. My hand tightened around Dad's arm, and he was quick to grab ahold of me. I never hit the ground, but I did tear the front of my dress.

"Oh my god!"

"That was a close call!" Dad said.

"My dress is ripped!" I looked up with disappointment. My dress was not only ripped before I even managed to make it down the aisle, but the hem was dirty too.

"It's OK. Nobody will even notice." Dad's forehead creased, mimicking my worry. I nodded, looking back at the damage.

"Party fail number two," I said.

"What?"

"Oh! Did I say that aloud?" I took a deep breath. The music started, queuing me to walk down the aisle. "It's nothing," I said, smiling. I meant it. A ripped wedding gown was nothing if I walked off this ranch married to Easton.

My eyes lingered on my dad's warm brown eyes. They were not of my blood, but they were family. He loved me all the same, and I felt every morsel of it. I wrapped my arms around his neck and squeezed him tight as the music continued. "Thank you for being my father. Every day. Even when you didn't have to. Even on the days when I was difficult. And even now, after you and Mom split. I know I haven't always been easy to love, but you always made it effortless for me to love you back," I said, tears dampening my eyes.

Dad hugged me tightly. And I could tell by the second wave of emotion that poured out of him that he was beginning to wonder if I knew of the adoption. He pulled away, his body shaking, and smiled warmly. "I won't let you fall, dear. Ever . . ." For a moment, I thought he was about to say my actual name, Everly. I wondered what it would feel like if he had. Dad cleared his throat and straightened his back. He faced forward like a soldier ready for battle, and I joined him as we began the walk down the aisle together. Kicking my dress before planting each step, I knew even if I stumbled that my father would catch me.

CHAPTER 6

We rounded the corner of the barn, and I was met with a sea of hungry, attentive eyes. Each set was straining to get a glimpse of me as I walked down the aisle. It was more attention than I thought I could withstand, and I felt somewhat faint until my dad squeezed my arm, reminding me he was there to catch me should I fall. I scanned the crowd, recognizing faces I hadn't seen in some time but still meant the world to me. Friends from back home, aunts and uncles. Their warm smiles made my cheeks flush and my back heat. I looked back to the rip in the hem of my dress and took a deep quivering breath. Dad squeezed my arm. "You're missing the best part," he said, nodding to the alter.

I followed his gaze, almost afraid of the emotion that would pour out of me. I was barely holding on by a thread as it was, and I had only seen my distant friends and family. I knew that standing on that alter were my best friends. My closest companions. My soon-to-be brother-in-law. And the very love of my lives. My soulmate. And on a day like today, when my emotions were high, I had to take it all in, but in small segments. Pieces at a time, so that my heart wouldn't explode.

Muted mauve and cream flowers lined the alter. A beautiful halo of color around the man in black. My soon-to-be husband. He stood tall and confident. His typical dark, unruly hair had been tamed. I lowered my gaze from his hair to his eyes, where our gazes locked. I sucked in a quick and deep breath as if seeing him standing there was like fresh oxygen to my hungry lungs. As if he were the reason I could breathe again, and in a way, he was. His face, as he stood at the altar, was something I'll never forget. Awe-stricken. His mouth partly open. Eyebrows lifted, and eyes glassy. I could practically see his heart fluttering, and I knew mine had synced with his the moment our eyes met.

My life was just better with Easton. I didn't expect my friends to understand the depths of our relationship. How could they? And the feelings I had were not ones I could put into words. But if I had to choose a word to sum it all up, *lucky* is the only one close enough. I don't know how I ended up finding Easton on the side of the New River Bridge that stormy night, and I don't know how my soul survived my death, but I knew I was one lucky girl to have captured the heart of Easton Green.

My dad kissed my cheek and whispered, "I love you," in my ear. I smiled at him with a full heart before I took my place by Easton. His eyes fixed on mine as I took the steps alone.

"Dearly beloved, we are gathered here today to unite Easton Green and Becca Reed . . ." The words faded into the background as I stared into Easton's glacier blue eyes. My entire world right before me. The love I had for him created meaning beyond my wildest dreams. It was my second chance at my first love. And I was fortunate enough to see how it would have rightfully played out had I not been previously robbed of life. Robbed of my happily ever after.

Though standing in front of Easton, in my white gown, and in my second life; it truly was my second chance, and I owed it all to him. Without him, I doubt I would have been tethered at all. I would have had to live with some regrets. Some unlearned lessons. And essentially, a heart that never knew just how much it could love. Easton sucked in a deep breath and I caught myself doing the same. Mirroring his every move.

My eyes never left his as Brooklyn took my bouquet and Easton took my hands. "Becca. Beck. I'd like to say that I've waited a long time for my heart to find yours. But the truth is, I never knew love like this could exist. You've breathed new life into me, Beck, and I promise you today, and every day thereafter, that I will do my best to do the same for you." Easton lowered his gaze, clearing his throat. My stomach swam with anticipation and admiration. I squeezed his hands, not once, but twice. "In a world where love is the greatest power, and time is the most valuable currency, I vow to give you a very rich life. And I can't wait to spend my forever, with you by my side," Easton said, his tone soft like we were the only two people in the barn.

Awe-stricken, I choked back my tears. My chest tight as my heart expanded. I took out the vows I'd written on a piece of paper. Hands trembling, I tried to steady the page. The words were a blur as tears filled my eyes. The only sound was that of the pounding of my heartbeat between my ears. I looked up from the fuzzy words into Easton's eyes and smiled. Tiny sparkles floated around him. Without looking, I knew it was his love bursting into the air like tiny fireworks.

I crumpled my vows into a ball and threw it over my shoulder, unable to speak. Leaping forward, I wrapped my arms around the nape of his neck and kissed him deeply. Easton grabbed me tight. My feet lifted off the ground as I deepened my kiss. I placed my hands on both sides of his cheeks as the distant sound of cheering erupted into my consciousness. I pulled back, laughing with embarrassment. A single tear rolled down Easton's cheek, and I swiped it away with my thumb. He lowered me onto the ground. And the officiant threw his notes behind his shoulder and tossed his arms up in the air. "I guess I pronounce you, husband and wife! And I'm sure you'll kiss the bride again," he said. And we did.

I turned to the crowd I'd forgotten were present, and Easton held up our intertwined hands. We laughed as they cheered, and Brooklyn gave me back my bouquet.

It was when we were taking photos that Easton caught my hand and slipped on the wedding band. Diamonds sparkled the full length of the band, making for quite the beautiful light show. "It's beautiful!"

"It's called an eternity band. I thought it was only fitting," Easton said.

"I love it!" I spun around, turning my back on Easton as I tried to fish his band out from my bust, but the slippery little thing kept slipping lower into my dress. "I can't . . . get it!" I spun back to face Easton. "I can't get it!" I laughed, rubbing the ring that was now pressed against my ribs. Thank God the dress was tight enough to hold it there. It shouldn't travel any lower.

Easton's eyes dropped to my neck line and then lower. His fingers traced mine over the ring. "I can't wait to get that ring tonight," he said in a hungry voice. My stomach dipped, and then even lower yet.

"OK, let's get another one by the tractor!" The photographer called out. Where did all these people keep coming from? My cheeks burned with embarrassment. I buried my face in Easton's chest, hoping to hide from the surrounding eyes. But when I heard the camera snap repetitively, I knew I was no longer safe. Easton's brother slapped his back, urging him toward the tracker.

"Come on, you two! You will have all week for that. I promise!" Tanner said.

"Can we leave now?" Easton asked.

"What! No! You guys can't leave now! The party hasn't even started!" Brooklyn said on my flank.

"Yeah!" Terra echoed.

I leaned into Easton and whispered quiet enough for only him to hear, "It will be worth the wait . . ." I said seductively.

"We heard that," Tanner said. I moaned, throwing my head back as the boys laughed. Easton squeezed my hand and winked. I knew I would be painted red in every single shot. Thankfully, I knew the photographer could fix that.

The pictures would have been awkward if they were with anyone else, but with this bunch, it was painless. Hysterical even. It was apparent that Tanner had been spending time with the bridesmaids because they all passed around a flask and shared an inside joke I was not privy to. I enjoyed seeing them together. I couldn't help but think Easton and I were making our own little family of tightly woven friends.

The MC introduced us as Mr. and Mrs. Green when we entered the larger barn set for dining and dancing. The sound of my new name sent a shiver of excitement down my spine. After being Everly Beck and Becca Reed, I'd held the name of Mrs. Green, and I loved it. It had been the easiest one to identify with that I could remember.

The wedding party took their seats. Easton and I in the middle, and some bridesmaids next to Tanner for balance. He didn't seem to mind, and neither did Grace and Kennedy by his side. However, I had to wonder about Brooklyn, who kept looking in his direction.

Even though I had been famished, I found it difficult to get down a quarter of my meal. A mixture of guests coming to our table to talk, the tightness of my dress, and nerves kept me from getting my fill. And when Brooklyn told me it was time to make my rounds, I abandoned my dinner altogether, for I knew it would grow cold.

I spoke to every table, and though I loved every moment, I couldn't help but be reminded of the wedding reception I never had in my past life. The one I somehow knew had happened and somehow saw my mom collapse under the news the cops had brought to my doorstep. Was this what it was supposed to be like? Would it have been this way, only with different faces? Or would they all have been too sad that I was terminal to be truly happy for me?

As I fought my past that never came to be, I was called to the dance floor for the father-daughter dance. A bolus formed in my throat, unable to swallow it down. And though I didn't cry, I knew my eyes were red from the burn. I almost scratched the father-daughter dance altogether. I knew it would hurt. I knew I'd have to be strong to get through it. But ultimately, I decided it was all a part of the healing process. Well, that and I couldn't take it away from my dad. He didn't deserve to be stripped from the father-daughter dance just because I missed my pop. I knew too that if I didn't do mine, then Easton wouldn't do his with his mother, and it would snowball into this thing that I was tired of overthinking. So, I told myself to suck it up. Be brave and fearless.

However, what I hadn't expected was the entire event had left me with very raw emotions. Memories that I hadn't even remembered until this night. And worse yet were the dreams. The ones that never came to be but haunted me in the mirrored moments of my parallel life. Riding side by side by a life that ended, I watched what could have happened unfold before my very eyes. And it was beautiful . . . But what I couldn't realize until this very moment was that the beauty hurt just the same as the sorrow.

"Just one step at a time, honey. Follow my lead," Dad said, taking me in his arms.

"Thank you, Dad," I said, forcing a smile.

He made small calculated steps, and I followed him, careful not to step on my dress again. I breathed in his cherry cigar smell that leached into his coat and was swept away in memories of him teaching me how to ride a bike. How to build a campfire. How to barbecue.

I was aware of all the eyes watching us but thankful for the dim lighting as my emotions were exposed for all to see. Front and center. I swallowed hard, actively pushing memories of my late pop out of my head. And then feeling guilty when I had succeeded. Feeling guilty when the happiness crept in. And when I felt the father's love of the man who danced in my pop's place.

I had kept it together. Locked it up tight. Buried it down deep . . . I had worked tirelessly to be strong, but when a song came on that my pop had sung to me as a kid—the only song he knew the lyrics to—I lost it. Completely and utterly lost it. Dad pulled me into his embrace as I wept. Wept for the dad who wasn't here to give me away. And then wept harder when I knew that, actually . . . he'd been here all along.

I opened my blurry eyes, lifting my head from my dad's shoulder, and looked around the room, expecting to see his face and those kind eyes that I'd missed so much. But when I couldn't see him, I closed my eyes once more, swaying back and forth to the slow song, basking in the feel of his presence, both far and near. His pride for me on this special day. And his deep unconditional, and undying love for me. I basked in the glow of knowing the song Pop played was his gift to me. A present for me to know he's OK. And it was OK for me to be happy. Because this slow, steady song that played not only in my heart but for everyone to hear tonight. . . was *not* on my wedding play list.

CHAPTER 7

I wiped the wet tears off my cheeks as Easton and his mother stepped onto the dance floor. He looked at me with concern, but I forced a smile to let him know I was OK. I was *OK* . . . I *would be OK*.

The moment I stepped out of the limelight, Brooklyn took my arm and ushered me to the restroom. Grace had been waiting in the ladies' room for us and held the door open as we approached. "Are you OK?" Brooklyn asked. My eyes shot to Grace, and judging from her expression, perhaps my breakdown was worse than I even knew. I sniffed, my nose still running as I approached the sink. Startling myself as I looked into the mirror. *Three.*

This fail was epic: It could have counted as three *and* four. I looked like a raccoon from the smudged eye liner. My cheeks were not only missing make-up where I had wiped away my tears, but they were also exposing my residual sunburn and flaking skin. The only way to remedy this situation was to finish the rest of the wedding in the dark.

"Shit, you guys! What am I going to do?" I stared back at the girl in the mirror, and I was shocked to see that she looked nothing like the last reflection I'd seen before walking down the aisle. "Is Remy still here?" I asked.

The girls' eyes filled with worry, and I knew his shift was over long ago. The three of us sat in a moment of silence. Black mascara crumbled in bits that littered my under eyes. And though it had been waterproof, I had rubbed nearly all of it off my lashes. Brooklyn wet a paper towel and began to blot at my face. I let her take care of me as my eyes fell unfocused on the sink faucet. "What happened, Becca?" Grace asked.

My eyes flickered to Brooklyn, who most likely understood why I had broken down. “Oh, she . . .” She began a cover-up story like any true friend would.

“I recently found out I was adopted,” I blurted out.

“Ohh!” Grace’s eyes grew wide. She was not expecting that.

“And . . . that my biological father had just passed,” I added. It felt good to get the truth off my chest. Even if there were parts that I still hid deep inside.

Grace threw a hand over her mouth. “I’m so sorry, Becca!”

“It’s OK,” I said. Though clearly it wasn’t. I didn’t know why it came out so dismissive as the proof was written all over my face that I was anything but OK. “The father-daughter dance was just . . . hard. That’s all.” I shrugged.

“Yeah, I can only imagine!” Grace said.

“But, I mean, nobody really noticed, right?” I asked, looking between Brooklyn and Grace. Their eyes met for a second before they agreed in unison.

“Yeah!”

“Right! Yeah.”

I sighed. Grace couldn’t lie to save her life, and I knew Brooklyn too well to know she was only trying to make me feel better. Brooklyn opened a small cosmetics bag and worked her magic. When I looked back in the mirror, I looked nothing like the girl I had when Remy made me up. But at least, I was presentable. Sort of. “Thank you,” I said, hugging them both.

“You know you can talk to us, anytime,” Grace said. I smiled at her. Wishing that I could. That my secrets weren’t so out of this world that I had to keep them locked inside. Maybe then I wouldn’t have melted down in front of all my wedding guests.

“I will. Thank you,” I said with no intention of ever telling her I was on my second life, and of all the pressures I carried on my shoulders to make it better than my first one.

By the time we had re-entered the barn, the party had kicked up a notch. I was glad to see that my breakdown was all but forgotten, and everyone was enjoying themselves. I found Easton standing awkwardly with both of our parents near the back wall. I straightened my back, sucked in a breath of confidence, and strode over to them. Easton reached out far before I was in arm's length, willing me to hurry by his side.

“There she is!” Easton’s dad reached out to hug me. Followed by a warm embrace from his mother. I knew they saw my episode on the dance floor, but I was more than OK pretending nothing happened.

“Hi, thank you for coming,” I said.

“Oh! We wouldn’t have missed this for the world!” Easton’s mother said.

“I see you’ve met my parents.” I smiled.

“Yes! We just met, Mr. and Mrs. Reed.”

My mom looked down at the ground, rubbing the back of her neck. My dad flinched, opening his mouth but ultimately closing it without correction. They were newly split after a long stint of trying to make their marriage work. In the end, my dad felt he could no longer trust my mom for cheating on him. And as I would internalize it, I seemed to think it was my fault for walking in on her. Though I knew it wasn't. It had nothing to do with me at all. Except, perhaps, that the only reason my mom confessed to sleeping with her art instructor was because I had found out. Either way, it was a big step for them to be here tonight, standing next to each other. Cordially. And I had faith that if I could survive the father-daughter dance, they could survive this awkward night together. If not for themselves, then for me.

"Hey, you doing OK? You seemed . . . It seemed rough out there?" Mom asked.

My eyes flickered to both sets of parents before landing on Easton's calming gaze. "Yeah. I'm going to be OK," I said before returning my gaze to her. "Just a moment of reflection, I guess," I said. The parents nodded understandingly. Or so they thought. I caught my dad's eyes as he was trying to evaluate my mother's expression, and I assumed he was wondering if she knew that I had knowledge of the adoption. Her face showed no telltales.

The MC came on to the speaker, announcing that a few guests had requested to make speeches and asked everyone to take their seats once again. My stomach churned as I said goodbye to both sets of parents and headed for my seat. Once there, Easton held my hand on his lap. "Are you OK?" he whispered, leaning in.

"Yeah, I'm OK." I nodded. But when the concern didn't leave his face, I followed up with, "Seriously, I'm OK."

Tanner took the stage, looking incredibly nervous. The microphone shrieked, and the audience recoiled, causing me to giggle into the back of my hand. He wiped his palms on his slacks. "I feel like you all have been hearing a lot of positive, loving things about Easton and Becca over the last couple of nights. So . . . buckle up," Tanner flipped his note card, and my face grew warm. The crowd laughed, eager to hear the roasting. My nerves flared.

"Oh, shit. . ." Easton muttered, amused.

"I just want to start by saying how beautiful Becca looks tonight. Doesn't she look beautiful?" The crowd clapped, looking back at me, and my stomach dropped. A smile spread across my face. I was going to kill him when I had the chance. "And so do all of Becca's friends and bridesmaids. They all look really, really beautiful! Really, stunning—did I say that I was single?" The crowd laughed, and Brooklyn reached over and grabbed my leg, squeezing it with a firm grip. Excitement passed through her eyes. Did she really like him? Brooklyn was never phased by guys.

"It may come as a surprise to you all that Easton and I are adopted." Easton went rigid by my side, but my eyes immediately flicked to my mother, who at that moment looked to me as well. My stomach somersaulted. Even from across the room, I could see in her face that she was calculating the reason I looked to her during that very statement. I would have to talk to her soon but now was not the time.

"That's the reason why I got the looks, and he . . . well, he looks like that." The crowd laughed, and even Easton broke. He leaned forward, placing his elbows on the table as he engaged in his brother's speech. "After bringing Easton home, my parents said, 'He's so wonderful. We want another,' which is how I came to be in the Randolf family. Randolf, you ask? Yes, Easton changed his name when he legally could at eighteen so that it would match his birth certificate."

Worried eyes began to look back at our table, and I slowly leaned into Easton and muttered, "Four . . ."

"Four what?" he asked, never taking his eyes off Tanner.

"Four wedding fails."

"Has there been four already?" Easton asked, raising his eyebrows.

"Yes, but this has potential to turn into multiples," I said, smiling back at everyone. Easton laughed and leaned over to kiss my cheek.

"Three moments stick out in my memory I'd like to share with you about Easton tonight. The first is when he tried to drown me in ice cream when we were young," Tanner said, flipping his note cards.

"Good god, he's still going," Easton muttered, shaking his head.

"You see, I had become too much of a treat. With my dashing looks and all," Tanner said, causing the bridesmaids, in particular, to giggle. Tanner was quite a looker, and perhaps that was what made it so uncomfortable. "But Easton never had to worry about being second best, because he was the true shining star of the Randolf household. But even though he had the brains, Easton saw it fit to eliminate his competition. Thankfully for me, he didn't have the muscle for it, and I survived the first attack." Tanner took a moment to let everyone quiet down before he continued. I peeked over at Brooklyn, who practically had stars in her eyes. The way she looked at Tanner on stage nearly made me blush.

"The second memory I have is when he would teach me math until my brain would explode. Seriously, it exploded all the time. And at that point, Easton would just do the work for me so that we could go play. Sorry, Mom!" I laughed, and Easton nodded, confirming the story to be true.

"But the third memory that sticks out in my mind, even more than when he tried to kill me in my lactose rich dessert, and still, more than when he pushed me to be a better man . . . And ultimately giving up on me . . . was when a little girl moved in next door." Tanner said, and my heart warmed. My friends and family started to look back at me once more, as this was not a story many of them had heard.

"You see, this was no regular little girl. She was fun! Even when she wore too much pink. She and Easton became best friends, and I often stayed home while they played to finish my homework. Funny how Easton stopped doing my homework when he saw how that played out for him, huh?" The crowd laughed. I pinched my cheeks, which were on fire.

"Yup, you'd never believe that Easton found his wife at eight years old. But he did." Friends and family looked around, shocked. My parents and closest friends nodded, confirming it was, in fact, a true story. I smiled, thinking they didn't know the half of it.

"Easton told me so after the very first day he met her; he said that he would marry her. I thought he had finally gone crazy, but it actually happened. Just three short weeks later! Yup, I have the picture to prove it! Officiated by a rabbit, but nonetheless, they married in her backyard that summer. And when we moved away—and Easton did my homework again, no surprise there—Easton's heart broke a little. You see, he never gave up looking for his bride!"

The crowd awed, and I leaned over to kiss Easton on the cheek. He moved swiftly, and our lips met. "No girl was good enough for Easton in high school. Or so he said. He matured late, and I see his muscles have yet to come in. But hey, your voice finally dropped, am I right, buddy?" Tanner gave Easton a thumbs up, causing Easton to sink into the seat a little. I lost it, laughing so hard I was sure my cheeks would cramp. Easton chuckled, shaking his head at his brother, then slowly and reluctantly returned his thumbs up. Tanner continued.

"So, I'll wrap this story up for those of you who don't know it. Easton changed his name and moved out of the Randolf household as soon as he was legally allowed to do so. Soon after that, he stopped taking our calls and basically vanished. Until one day, some three years later, he called to tell me he found his bride." I placed my hand over my heart as it melted in my chest. I'd never heard this side of the story.

"And slowly, from that day on, Easton started answering his phone when I would call. He came back into my life, and I don't think that would have happened if it weren't for his lady here. So, let's raise our glasses," Everyone raised a glass of champagne. "And cheers to the fact that Easton was too wimpy as a kid to drown me in a bowl of ice cream!" I nearly spit out my champagne. "Oh, and cheers to Becca too, because I think she's pretty great!" I clapped ferociously, standing up. Easton rose to his feet too and started a slow clap. I loved every second.

I stood when Tanner approached our table and kissed him on the cheek. The smell of Tequila strong on his breath. I wondered how much he had to drink to deliver his speech and how far he veered from his original one. Easton slapped his back while he gave him a quick embrace. He said something in Tanner's ear as I placed my chilly hands on my warm cheeks, trying to massage out the tension from laughter. "Oh, I can't wait until he gets married," Easton muttered. And I laughed all over again. Only stopping when I noticed my mom had taken the stage.

"Hello, everyone. What a wonderful speech, thank you. Um, I'm Becca's mom. Um, wow, this barn must have a great antenna because this is a great reception!" A bark lodged in my throat, making a weird sound as I grabbed

Easton's leg underneath the table. Few laughed, but mostly out of discomfort. I bit my lip, waiting for her attempt to recover.

"Um, well, I've been preparing this toast for a long time now, so I hope it's not burnt!" Mom said.

"Oh, no!" escaped me. Easton burst out in laughter as my mom looked frantically around the room. Second-hand embarrassment had never been so real.

"Becca is such a beautiful daughter. Loving and kind. She's the kind of girl you don't worry about introducing to your parents. That's why she didn't introduce us to Easton's parents until twenty minutes ago. . ."

I shot Easton a look, and we both said it. "Five!"

"Five, this is definitely number five!"

The speech went on in what was intended to be not only funny but loving. Very loving. It just never quite went anywhere at all. Not before my dad interrupted with a speech of his own. And he could only get a few words in before breaking down and crying into the microphone. And it didn't end there. No, speeches came from many of my bridesmaids, too. But the best one came from Brooklyn, which wasn't a speech at all, but a complete shutdown.

"Thank you for all the lovely speeches. Now, if I could get all the single ladies up here, Mrs. Green is going to throw the bouquet!" she took the microphone with her, which I could only secretly thank her for. I'd have to tell her how much I loved her for that when the time was right.

"Thank god that's over!" I laughed, shielding my face behind my hand. "My poor parents!" I said.

Easton laughed, "Please tell me someone got that on video!" Easton peered around the room, "Are we having this taped?" he asked.

"No, probably should have, though."

"Go throw your bouquet. Let's see if we can get number six," Easton said, nudging me out of my seat.

I chuckled, standing up. I grabbed my bouquet of muted mauves, off whites, and mustard yellow flowers. It was every bit the vintage look I was going for. I hated to throw such a beautiful bouquet, but I couldn't argue with tradition.

I stood with my back to the bridesmaids and a few other women, mostly young. I was happy to see my mom hadn't joined. "One, two, three!" I threw the flowers over head with as much might as I had. A loud thud sounded, followed by gasps from the crowd. I spun just in time to see flower petals floating down from the large industrial-sized fan. Mustard, mauve, and cream petals began to litter the dance floor. In the tragedy's wake, it was almost beautiful.

A moment of stillness passed before someone screamed, "It's mine!" and took off running to the back of the barn where the bulk of the bouquet had spat from the fan. My eyes met Easton's as a dozen single ladies ran to the back of the room. Two toppled over each other. Chairs were knocked over, and a table cloth pulled, sending several glass champagne flutes crashing to the ground. A few grunts ensued before Payton raised her arm high and mighty, thrusting the tattered bouquet into the air. About a third of the flowers were missing, leaving cut stems in their place, but surprisingly, the rest had held up pretty well. I clapped as Grace pulled Terra off the floor. I snickered and held six fingers up to Easton from across the room.

CHAPTER 8

Six wedding fails. That's how many it took to make the perfect wedding. By the time the sparklers were lit and our friends and family formed a tunnel for us to pass through, Easton and I were ready to take our love somewhere more private.

"Ready, Mrs. Green?" Easton asked, taking my hand.

"Ready!" I said, grabbing as much of my lace dress as possible and lifting it off the ground. We sprinted through the sparklers, a beautiful whirlwind of bouncing, flickering lights. And by the time we reached the end of the tunnel, Tanner and Brooklyn had shaken champagne bottles and popped them over head. Champaign rained down on us, taking me back to the clearing that overlooked the Truly River on the evening we first wed. I looked to Easton as we ran to the car, and I wondered if he had lived in the constant realm of déjà vu, in how I had today.

Easton opened my door, and I crawled into the back seat. Scooping my lace train off the ground before closing the door. Easton ran around the back of the car. With a slam of his door, we were one step closer to finally being alone. The driver pulled away, and I kissed Easton's champagne-soaked lips as the wedding cans clanked behind the car. We watched the glow of the sparklers disappear into the night as the wedding had finally come to an end. "Success!" I said.

"It really was," Easton said. "But the best is yet to come."

I raised my brows. "That's a big promise," I said.

"Well, as you may have heard . . . I eventually hit puberty so . . ." I giggled, causing Easton to wag his brows. We spent the rest of the ride to the airport caught between lusting over each other or laughing at something that had happened at the wedding. And in no time, we were waiting to board the plane.

Several people had come up to us saying "Congratulations," because I was the only one in the whole airport wearing a wedding gown as far as I could see. I itched to take it off, but I feared it might be cutting it too close. And missing our flight was one wedding fail that I didn't want to come to fruition.

"I don't know how we got here so late. I thought we were good on time," Easton said, checking his watch.

"I think our flight moved up to an earlier slot. We should have checked it this morning," I said, gripping my luggage handle and yanking it off the train of my gown.

"Should have. Guess I was too excited to see you in this dress to think about it," Easton said, his eyes trailing down my figure. I smiled.

"Congratulations! You look so pretty!" A woman said as she passed by.

"Thank you!" I said, blushing. "I need to get out of this dress," I hissed to Easton.

"Flight 3838, ready to board!"

Easton looked at me with large, round eyes. "Do you think you have time?"

I looked nervously to the passengers lining up for the flight and then back down the way we came in. Not only were the restrooms far away, but I doubted I could take the dress off by myself. "I don't think so! What am I going to do? I can't wear this thing for a nine-hour flight! I'm suffocating as it is!" I fanned my face, feeling the panic rise.

"It's OK. No worries. You can take it off on the plane." I shot him a look of doubt, causing him to follow up with, "I promise. I'll help you." I nodded. Unconvinced, but accepting that I had no other choice. We got in line, and it moved swiftly. My suitcase rolling over the lace train of my dress again. Easton bent over and picked it up, holding it while I walked. "See, I can help!" he said. I smiled, thankful for all he did.

We funneled onto the plane, taking our seats over the wing. Easton placed our luggage overhead, and I sat next to the window. "Do you want to take it off now?" he asked.

I looked around. People were still filing onto the plane. "I don't think we're supposed to use the bathroom until the plane gets in the air," I said. Easton took a seat next to me and patted my leg. "Thanks, but . . . I can't wait fifteen more minutes," I told him.

Ten minutes later, and I couldn't wait any longer. The plane hadn't even begun to move, and I was on the verge of hyperventilating. "I've got to take it off!" I said, standing. Not a single thought could process through my head if it didn't involve ripping this corset off and freeing my lungs. I made it to the back of the plane before getting turned around by the flight attendant.

"I'm sorry, there's nothing I can do. You have to wait until the plane is in the air and the seatbelt lights have turned off," the flight attendant said. I nodded, taking quick, shallow breaths on my way back to my seat. Of course, being afraid of flying wasn't helping my situation. I would have been nervous normally, but it was the dress that made me feel claustrophobic. I placed my hand on my stomach and tried to slow my breathing.

"What's wrong?" Easton asked by the time I got back to my seat, still wearing the dress.

"They won't let me in the bathroom!" I crawled over him and plopped down in my seat. He gathered the train of my dress and pulled it out of the walkway, pooling it at my feet.

Easton took out the brown paper bag in the seat pocket before us. "Here, breath into this." I protested with my bulging eyes, not wanting to look more ridiculous than I already did. "Just do it!" he said. I followed his orders and began breathing in the bag.

The flight attendant came by and slipped me two bottles of vodka. "Don't tell anyone. I'm not supposed to hand these out. But it should take the edge off."

"Thank you," Easton said, taking the bottles. I continued breathing into my brown paper bag, and Easton handed me an uncapped bottle. My eyes scanned his in question. "She's right. It'll help," he said.

I lowered the bag and sucked down the bottle. Barely able to swallow it all, I coughed as a shiver split down my spine. Easton smiled. "Stop it!" I snapped. My eyes darted to the second bottle. "That one too!" I reached over him, taking the drink from his hand. The clear liquid was even worse the second time, and my reaction was no better. Aftershocks ripped through me like jolts of electricity. Easton smiled, trying hard not to laugh. "Stop that!" I said, picking up the brown bag again and placing it over my mouth.

Eventually, the plane lifted off the runway. The force pressed me back in my seat, adding even more pressure to my anxiety-ridden chest. My nails dug into Easton's forearm as he rattled off the most ridiculous statistics I'd ever heard. "Did you know that you are seven times more likely to die of a paper cut than to crash in a plane? And nearly thirty times more likely to witness a real-life mermaid?" He said in all seriousness.

"What?" I crumpled my paper bag, finally able to breathe. My thoughts were consumed with mermaids as the claustrophobia fell to the wayside. How much had I drunk again? Because one of us was crazy, and I didn't want it to be me. By the time the seatbelt lights turned off, I was in a different mindset altogether. The fear had become amusing, and the tightness of my dress only a game.

"Hey, Easton?" I asked. He leaned in, looking up at me from underneath his lashes. "I don't think I can get this dress off by myself. You're going to need to help me." The looped buttons were far too complicated for me to manage behind my back. And in a moving cabin, it would be impossible.

"Sure, anything I can do to help." Easton peeked at the back of the plane before turning back to me. "You go first, and then I'll slip in behind you when no one's looking," he said.

I nodded. Every single pair of eyes lifted to me as I passed through the aisle. It was like walking down the aisle in the barn, only this time I didn't have my father's strength beside me, and the eyes that stared back were neither proud nor loving. They were strangers, and I had no idea what they were thinking. All I knew was that I needed to get out of this wedding dress as soon as possible. I tightened my grip on the change of clothes in my hand.

I opened the cabin door and stepped inside. But before closing the door, I saw the lace of my dress's hem peeking out from under the door. I bent down to pick it up, but the other restroom across the aisle caught my eye. What if Easton had walked into the wrong stall? I smiled, almost wanting to see it happen. But then I left the lace closed the door. This way, there would be no mistaking. I turned to look at myself in the mirror. My hair had not budged one bit from the ceremony, but my makeup had done several things. My lips were bare and lashes naked. I suddenly became more self-conscious for all the thoughts that passed through the passengers' heads as I walked by.

A light tap rapped on the door before opening. Easton pushed his way in as quick as a storm. His chest pressed up against mine in the tiny stall, and I felt my heart quicken. My eyes searched his, mere inches from his face. "Uh, it's a little tight in here," he said.

I tried to take a step back, but my heels hit the base of the toilet. The front of my dress yanked me forward. "You're standing on my dress," I said, trying to look down.

Easton picked up his foot but had nowhere to go. He grabbed handfuls of my gown and tried lifting it out from under his feet, nearly knocking me over in the process. I burst out into laughter, and Easton cupped his hand over my mouth. "Shhh. We have to be quiet," he whispered. His eyes locked on mine with conviction, but I was far more guilty than being too loud. A smile spread across my face that I could no longer hide.

"Hey, have you ever heard of the mile high club?" I asked in my most seductive tone. A tone that I was sure could only come out after taking shots on an empty stomach.

"No. Don't start that. We have to get you out of the dress and then get back to our seats. Can you turn around?" Easton asked.

"Would you like that?" I asked, dropping my shoulder.

"Beck . . ." Easton warned.

"Yes . . ." I bit my lower lip.

"Turn around!" Easton said, not having any of it.

"Ugh, fine!" I tried to spin, but Easton was still on my dress. I nearly toppled over. My hand slammed against the back wall and Easton's hands tightened around my waist, catching me. Bent over, I turned slowly, giving it one last try. I winked at him. As sexy as I could wink, I did. But when both my eyes closed, I had to try again . . . and again. Why couldn't I wink? I thought everybody could wink?

"Beck! Please!" Easton begged. I couldn't tell if he was annoyed or just taking pity on me, but maybe it was a bit of both.

"Jesus! Is there nothing I can do to turn you on?" I demanded.

"Beck, you don't have to try to turn me on. This just isn't the place or the time. Damn it, how do you take this thing off?" he hissed.

"But, mile high club . . ." I whined.

Easton stilled. The air shifted, growing thick with lust. I knew I had it in me to seduce him. When he couldn't hold himself back any longer, he slowly leaned forward, his breath hot against the nape of my neck. "Is that what you really want?" he whispered.

My breath quickened. I was in no position to make decisions. But something inside of me screamed for me to live my life, and I was pretty sure it was the alcohol. "Yes!" I gasped.

Easton planted a wet kiss on the back of my shoulder, sending shivers down my spine. I lifted my head, exposing my neck, and he trailed his mouth up to my ear. My hand tightened around the base of the sink, and my head began to swim.

"Take off the dress!" I said in a breathy, needy voice.

Easton undid the uppermost buttons from the corset, and I could expand my lungs for the first time since slipping on the dress. I sucked in a deep, much-needed breath of air. He lifted the gown from the floor, bumping into me. I laughed out loud as I nearly fell into the toilet. "Shhh," Easton said from behind as he stifled his own laughter. I gripped the top of my corset and yanked it down with as much force as I could, freeing myself from the tightness and suffocation.

A glisten of gold flickered from my bust, dropping into the toilet bowl below with a splash. I went rigid. "What was that?" Easton asked, bumping into my back and pushing me forward to get a look over my shoulder. His body pressed against mine, forcing me to take a step forward. Tripping, my hands hit the back wall once more. Only this time, one of my hands landed squarely on a button, pressing it until the toilet flushed fiercely. I watched Easton's wedding band vanish in a violent vortex below. My heart stopped.

"What? What was that?" Easton repeated, still arching over my shoulder. Turbulence struck, and the lights flickered on and off. I pushed my hands into either side of the cabin walls, trying to hold on. The lights went completely out, and my heart pounded in my chest. Then, in the blackness of the cabin, a knock rapped on the door.

"Ma'am, you're going to have to go back to your seat. The seatbelt light is back on. Ma'am?"

"Shit!" I said, tugging at my dress.

"Ma'am!"

CHAPTER 9

After a long sleepless night on the plane, we landed on the main island of Tallaway. The sun had recently risen, but already the air was warm and thick with humidity. We were ushered through security and placed in the back seat of a taxi, our belongings in the trunk. The island of Taiseen was a thirty-minute boat ride from the main island.

"Welcome to Tallaway!" Our driver said.

"Thank you, sir," Easton said before his eyes settled on me. "How are you holding up?" he asked.

A tired smile spread across my face. "I didn't sleep very well on the plane. But other than being sleepy and a little embarrassed, I'm good," I said, my wedding dress draped across my lap.

"You're still embarrassed? Why? Don't be . . . You're never going to see those people again," Easton promised.

"Yeah, you're right. I just wish I didn't have to walk back to my seat with a half unbuttoned wedding dress!" I let out a huffing laugh. "You should have seen the stares they gave me!" My eyes lost focus in the memory.

"Oh, I know. I got them too," Easton said. I giggled because it took a lot to embarrass him. He was usually so set on not making a fool of himself and denying his desires in that miniature bathroom. I think that walk of shame did him in though, and it was almost worth it to see the flush in his cheeks.

Easton paid the driver, and he helped us load our bags onto the boat. My cheeks painted red when I realized the small boat was occupied with not only us but two other couples from the plane. My eyes dropped the second I remembered them, and I hoped they hadn't recognized me outside of my wedding gown. . . The wedding gown I carried before me.

Once Easton sat by my side, my eyes lifted ever so slightly to the couples. Both the men were playing with their new wedding bands. I lifted my head to Easton and leaned into his ear. "Never going to see them again, huh?" I whispered. His eyes left mine to look at the other passengers. I knew the moment he recognized them when his face flushed crimson. His eyes dropping to the bottom of the panga.

"Are you guys honeymooning on Taiseen, too?" One of the men asked.

"Yeah, man. Congratulations!"

Easton cleared his throat. "Yeah, we'll be there as well. All week. Congratulations to you guys as well," he said. I smiled at the other women.

"Man, I just can't get used to this ring!" One man said aloud. My stomach dropped, and I turned my head away from Easton, looking out to sea.

"I can't either! It's so foreign," the other guy said.

From the corner of my eye, I saw Easton's head drop. I knew he was examining his bare finger. "Hey, you never gave me my ring," he said, quiet enough. I felt the familiar tightness of the dress wrapping around my ribcage, even though it sat draped across my lap.

"You didn't get a ring?" One particularly nosey passenger asked. The two couples stared at us, waiting for an answer.

"Oh, no, we just had a . . . a . . . well, it's a funny story. You see, we basically married before the officiant had time to do his job. So, we were just going to exchange our rings later." Easton shook his head, smiling. I felt his stare sear into me as I pretended not to notice. He patted the side of my arm, drawing me in.

"Huh?" I asked.

"The ring? Do you have it?" Easton asked.

"Oh, yeah! I just . . . it's in my bag," I said, shaking my head. Easton nodded, accepting my answer easily enough. But for how long? How long could he go on believing that his ring was safe in my bag and not . . . I don't know, in the belly of the plane? In a sewage tank? I wasn't sure what happened to the ring after it flushed down the airplane toilet. But I was sure that it was gone, and I had failed my very first task as a new wife. I looked out over the pale blue ocean and wondered how crushed Easton would be when he found out.

When we reached the little island of Taiseen, an islander wrapped a lei around each one of our heads, welcoming us to the resort. I breathed in the aroma of plumeria around my neck. The lei was so beautiful I wondered if I could preserve it and bring it home. I followed Easton mindlessly, looking at the purple and white flowers. "Do you think I could dry these out?" I asked.

"What for?" Easton asked, looking over at me.

"To keep them," I said.

Easton chuckled and wrapped his arm around my shoulders. "Beck, we have lifetimes of leis ahead of us. I promise," he said. My stomach dipped nervously, but I smiled at the thought of endless beaches with the love of my life. Was this really how it was going to be now? Were we to just visit every island on earth, hike every waterfall, and wear all the leis? How did we get so lucky? I squeezed his hand that rested on my shoulder and followed our bags to the check-in desk. Easton handled the check-in while my eyes wandered from the floor to the ceiling and everything in between. Even the ceilings were stunning. Teak wood arches and large wicker chandeliers.

"Room six," Easton said, holding up our card keys. I tucked my hand in the crook of his arm as we strolled through the grounds. Hammocks tied to trees, infinity pools, tiki torches; I'd never been to a place so luxurious in my life. *Lives.* But now that I'd seen it with my very own eyes, I didn't know how Easton would get me back on that plane. I stopped briefly, pulling on Easton's arm, and I kicked off my shoes. I stood for a moment while Easton did the same. The warm sand underneath my feet and in between my toes. I closed my eyes and tilted my head up to the sun. The sun rays kissed my face, and I smiled with open arms.

"Mmm," I hummed.

"I know, right?" Easton said.

"I cannot believe this place," I said.

"You haven't even seen the best part!" He pulled on my arm. I reached down to grab my shoes.

"I don't know what could be better than this? Honestly, I could park it right here in the sand and be the happiest girl all week long."

"Wife," Easton corrected me with a smile. It still sounded weird, and I wondered how long it would take to get used to hearing it. We stepped onto the dock and strolled slowly to our overwater bungalow. I ran my hands down the wood railing as my eyes searched for movement in the water. "I think six is at the end," Easton said. The panga's engine started, and it idled away slowly. When we reached the end of the dock and stood at the doorway of the sixth bungalow, Easton turned to me with a wicked smile. He bent down and scooped me up in his arms. I wailed in laughter as we burst over the threshold.

I squealed, delirious from lack of sleep and the emotional last twenty-four hours. Easton kicked the door closed behind him and took me straight to the bed. He unloaded me, throwing me into the air. I landed on top of a white feather comforter as soft as a cloud. My eyes flickered around the room, taking in my surroundings, but Easton was quick to jump on top of me. I squealed once more before his kiss silenced me, and my focus zeroed in on him and him alone. No more wedding fails, no more plane passengers, no more missing ring; just me, my husband, and this bed.

I arched my hips into his. My hands grew greedy as I grasped and clawed at his back, pulling his shirt off. He planted a kiss from the neck down to my tattoo as I squirmed, kicking off my clothing. I don't know how long we spent showing each other our love, but when I saw it manifest before my very eyes in a warm glowing light between us, I knew that we were making the best of our time on the Taiseen island.

My heart still pounding, I smiled, and the warm tears of joy streamed down my cheeks. I brought my fingertips to the corner of my eyes and blotted my tears. "Are you OK?" Easton asked, his hand tangled in my hair.

I didn't know why I was crying, but the tears that sat on my fingers before my eyes couldn't be mistaken. "Yeah, I think I'm just . . . I don't know? I think I'm just . . . happy?" I said. What else could it have been? I had been so tightly wound with the wedding, and then the airplane incident. I guess being here with Easton was like shedding pounds of fear, worry, and anxiety. And better yet, it was all sinking in. He was my . . . *husband.* I had him for the rest of my life, for the rest of . . . *time?* "I'm sorry, that's really weird isn't it?" I asked.

Easton stroked my hair. "No, it's not weird," he said. I turned to him with loving eyes, and when a smirk escaped him, I grabbed the nearest pillow and thrashed it into his face. "What? What? It's a little weird, but I accept you for you!" Easton cried out through laughter.

I giggled, wiping away the rest of my overly emotional tears, and hopped to my feet. I pulled on my lounge clothes that had been tossed clear across the room and ventured out into the bungalow. The teak wood creaked as I walked to the middle of the living room and looked down through a window on the floor. The aqua blue water lay beneath. "Did you see this?" I looked back to Easton, who was still sprawled on the bed with his eyes closed.

"See what?" He pulled himself up and came to my side. Slowly, I placed one foot on top of the window. When it felt sturdy enough, I put my full weight on the glass. I smiled at Easton, and he grabbed my hand, pulling me to the slider door. "If you think that is cool, check out the deck." Easton slid the door open, and warm, briny air rushed inside the villa. A large deck opened up over the water. Our very own dock. Two lounge chairs and a ladder leading straight into the water.

"Stop it!" I said in amazed disbelief. "I don't know how I'm ever going to leave this place! You spoiled me!" I said, crawling into the lounge chair. "I'm so tired. I could fall asleep right here! But I don't want to miss a thing," I said before I closed my eyes, truly not wanting to miss a single second of this stunning island. When a splash sprayed me, my eyes flew open, and I nearly hopped out of the lounge chair.

"Wow, Beck! It's so warm! You have to come in!" Easton called out.

"I can't just jump in the ocean," I said, wanting nothing more than to be carefree like he was.

"Why not?"

"I don't know?" I looked around nervously. There wasn't a soul in sight. "What about sharks? And stuff?" I asked.

"Beck, if you don't get in this water, I'm coming up there. And you don't want to know what will happen if I do," Easton said before ducking under the water and disappearing from sight. I sighed, not knowing what was holding me back. Other than me, that was. I was always the one holding me back. But I didn't want that anymore. I pulled my shirt off and shimmied out of my joggers, exposing my white lace bra and matching panties. I took one more look around, and when the coast was clear, I ran and jumped off the dock, letting out a small scream before I hit the lukewarm water with a splash. My body submerged for only a few seconds, but it was long enough to bring back the fear of drowning in the river. As quick as I jumped in, I swam back to the ladder and climbed up the dock. Easton splashing me as I did.

"What? I did it!" I said.

"Yup, you sure did," Easton said before he swam to the steps after me. I couldn't tell if he was serious or if it was my own guilt for not being more of a free spirit that sat unsettled in my stomach, but I buried it, either way. This wasn't a place of worry, and I wouldn't let myself get me. I padded into the bungalow with wet feet and fetched us two towels. "Thanks," Easton said after I handed him one.

We dried off before curling up in the lounge chairs and staring out amongst the crystal clear water. Neither of us said much, and I imagined his eyes were closed before mine had finally lost their long battle. Lulled to sleep by the sounds of the lapping water, we slept until nearly noon. And even then, when we woke, I wasn't convinced I had ever stopped dreaming. Life was as beautiful as the island of Taiseen, and I had unlimited time to experience all of it. We did, together.

CHAPTER 10

Day two of our honeymoon and the slow hum of relaxation had fully sunk in. My breathing had deepened, my heartbeat grew to a steady rhythm, and my thoughts quieted. Island life was good for me, and I had already promised myself I would come back. Not just to this island, but all of them. Easton and I would explore every island on this green earth. I didn't care if it took hundreds of lives; it was my first Tethered Soul goal, and it made my heart sing with excitement.

"The sand is so white and fine here," I said, peering out behind my coffee mug to the white beach beyond.

Easton looked down to his bare feet and dug his toes under the sand. "It's beautiful," he said leisurely.

"Do you think they're all like this? All the islands?" I asked.

"No. Some will have brown sand. Some won't have any sand at all. Just shells or small pebbles. You've never been to an island before?" Easton asked.

"Not before this. . . I could live like this forever," a low hum sounded from my throat and my eyes closed for a brief moment, taking in the perfect day.

"It's about to get even better. Want to know what I have planned for today?" Easton asked.

My eyes fluttered with anticipation, and I set my coffee down in my lap. "What's that?" I asked. Easton's excitement brought a smile to my face. If he was this excited, I already knew it would be perfect.

"Skydiving!" he exclaimed.

Coffee spewed from my mouth and misted my legs. Fear froze my mind, and not a single thought had passed as my once calm heartbeat kicked into a gallop. "What?" I asked though I knew I had heard him correctly.

"Skydiving?" Easton replied. His tone, once excited, was now laced in trepidation. He paused, waiting for my reply. A sign of some sort that I was going to be alright. But when it didn't come, he continued. "You may not remember, but in your first life, we had an agreement of sorts. You didn't have long to live, and there were things you had wanted to do . . . to experience. We made a list, and we crossed items off the list as we went. There are still items we haven't crossed off," Easton said.

"I know that! But . . . I don't recall skydiving being one of them!" I said as I wiped the coffee droplets off my legs with a napkin. The truth was, I probably didn't remember half of the things we put on that list.

Easton quieted. "Well . . . technically. . . it wasn't. But it is really close to bungee jumping! And that one *was* on your list."

"Are we really bringing that back up?"

"Well, you didn't get a chance to experience it? So, it's back on the list," Easton shrugged as if I were supposed to have known he would make that ridiculous rule. I sighed, knowing that he was probably right. If there was something on the list that I didn't complete, it made little sense for it to be crossed off. But for the record, I never agreed.

I didn't want to jump out of an airplane. It wasn't my idea of fun. But, there was a small part of me—no matter how small that part may be—that argued it *was* my idea of living. Truly living. Pushing the limits . . . It terrified me. But there was a taste of something else too, something that I could only assume was excitement. What if I jumped and loved it? What if I thought it was exhilarating? Would I want to miss out on that? Of course not. And if I was going to be here as long as Easton had, or longer, shouldn't I know what I like? I guess I would have to jump to understand it. Understand me.

"OK. I'll do it," I said beneath my breath. Easton's face lit up. "But! We are amending that list!" I pointed my finger at him and raised a brow.

"Sure! I'll find a new menu, and we can make a new one!" Easton said. *Menu?* I wasn't sure what he meant about that. Not all of my memory had escaped the shadows, and some details I feared were lost forever. But after a year of asking for clarification, I grew sick of hearing myself question my first life. It only made me sad to think of the memories I had lost. Now, I only asked if I thought it might be important, and this didn't sound very important to me.

My stomach flipped about a hundred times before we even arrived at the headquarters. I'd been quiet during the training session, much like I was for the bungee jumping instruction. My mind a stew of nervous energy, regret, and a touch of nausea. Easton stepped away with his instructor. I watched nervously as he handed the guy cash and patted him on the back. I tried to focus, but my thoughts were scrambled.

"What was that?" I asked Easton upon his return.

"What?"

"That?" I motioned to where he stood with the instructor.

"Oh, just a tip. I figured I better tip him now so that we get the best experience."

"Did you tip my partner too?" I asked, looking between the instructors.

"Of course. It's for both of them," Easton said.

I thought about the tip and what it meant to have poor service from your skydiving instructor. This wasn't the kind of service you would expect from a restaurant. This was my life. And I was about to jump out of a plane thousands of feet in the sky. "You tipped them good, right?" I asked.

Easton chuckled, "I tipped them real good."

The full panic didn't set in until we loaded onto the plane. There was only room for four passengers, Easton and I fit snuggly with our certified instructors.

"This is a Cessna 182, small but mighty. It's the workhorse of skydiving planes," Easton's tandem partner said. A middle-aged man with a fit physique and a weathered face. "It will take us about twenty minutes to climb to 10,000 feet, and then we will jump."

"You have twenty minutes to get it together. Are you ready?" Easton said, leaning into my ear.

I swallowed the lump in my throat. Twenty minutes before I jumped out of a plane? Ready? *Never* . . . I shook my head. Easton grabbed my knee and squeezed it. His instructor went on about the plane's history, but as soon as the engine started, I no longer heard a word of it. My mind in another place completely. I sat still, my breathing shallow. Every now and again, my body would tremble. I knew I was afraid. Terrified even. But what exactly was that? Was it real? Make believe? Could I control it? Conquer it? I had no other choice but to figure it out because, in no time, my instructor stood and signaled for me to stand, too. I was really doing this thing.

I closed my eyes as my tandem partner secured us together. Strapped to my back was a professional. He had done this a thousand times over, and I had nothing to worry about. Nothing to think about. Nothing to do. I was merely along for the ride. Which turned out to be perfect, because my mind had frozen up again. I couldn't be trusted with the smallest of tasks now. Not even breathing.

Easton's instructor waved us ahead. I didn't want to go first, but there was no verbalizing that, or anything else, for that matter. It was far too late for any request. We stepped up to the plane's edge, and I lifted my head high, refusing to look down. The blood drained from my face as I turned to see Easton, his grin wide with excitement. He was handling this much better than when we went bungee jumping in Sin City. If I had only jumped that day, perhaps I would have found the excitement in this, too. I tried to swallow, but the saliva stuck in the back of my throat like tar. I wanted to tell Easton I loved him . . . just in case I didn't make it. But my mouth, along with everything else, was beyond my control, and I could no longer speak. I vaguely heard my instructor talking to me over the Cessna's hum, but I couldn't process what he said. My goggles were tight. Too tight. It was the last complete thought I had before I was pushed from behind.

My shoes scrapped against the platform as I was thrust forward. My stomach dropped, making me want to curl in on myself, and my eyes quickly found the ground that I had refused to look at. Realizing just how far up I was, I wanted to scream, but I had no breath. No voice. I closed my eyes tight. The fear encapsulating me. Suffocating me until I couldn't take it anymore. If there was such a thing as controlling the fear, I hadn't learned it. Far from it. And I'd be damned if I ever gave myself another chance to try.

The wind lashed against my cheeks and flushed through my mouth, hitting the back of my throat and drying it out. I opened my eyes and saw another sky diver flicker in my peripheral vision before quickly closing them again. The ground was so far it made me feel ill, and I couldn't think of anything worse than enduring the fear of falling to my death *and* puking all over my instructor. Though I wasn't convinced that I would live to feel the mortification of it, I still didn't want to die having it be one of the last thoughts in my mind.

My body trembled inside so fiercely my heart felt as if it were vibrating. Some may call it exhilaration, but I was certain I was nothing but petrified. When the landing approached at lightning speeds, I felt the sensation of being pulled backward. It all happened so fast, and I hardly understood it until I bravely opened my eyes and the fall had slowed down, giving my mind a chance to comprehend it all.

I looked around frantically at the world below. More and more detail coming into vision as the earth approached. I looked around me, trying to find Easton, but all I could see was a neon orange and blue parachute flapping in the wind and one other jumper. I looked back to the ground, bracing myself for the land. When we touched down, I was useless. My legs were soft as Jell-O, and my eyes scrunched closed until I was positive I had survived. When I was detached from my instructor, I fell straight to my knees and gripped the grass in my hands.

"Wow! Are you OK?" my tandem asked. I nodded, catching my breath. He put his hand on my shoulder. "Are you going to be sick?" he asked.

"No," I said breathlessly. I willed myself to formulate a question, "Where is Easton?" I asked, looking up at him. My instructor stood, ignoring my question and nodded to the other jumper who had landed beside us.

"Hey, great jump!" the other guy said. I looked over at him, still on my knees like a fool. When he took his goggles off, I did the same, slowly recognizing him as Easton's tandem. My brows pulled tight as I surveyed the grounds. Easton wasn't anywhere in sight. What was going on?

"Where's Easton?" I asked again. This time louder and more demanding. However, it came off as meek and breathless.

My instructor put his hands up, and my eyes shot to Easton's partner. His eyes grew large as he stalled, trying to find the words. "He . . . he's still with the Cessna," he said.

"He's what?" I hissed.

The men chuckled as they helped me to my feet. "Come on; you will see him back at the facility. He's going to meet us there."

"Wait, what?" I asked again, confused. I looked around, not seeing him anywhere. The realization crept into my head that I hadn't seen him in the air either. My jaw dropped open as the pieces fell into place. He hadn't jumped at all. "That . . . little shit," I said beneath my breath.

The men laughed. I heard one of them mutter, "I wouldn't want to be him in fifteen minutes."

My heart still fluttering and my legs still wobbly, I crawled into the van. We had a quick ride back to where we started our training and back to where I would find my cowardly husband. I had no idea what I would do to him when I found him, but I knew one thing. He was about to experience my full wrath. I sat in the van stewing while the men chatted amongst themselves. And when we arrived, I saw the plane parking outside of my window. I watched as Easton climbed out with a smug smile, and my heart rate picked up once more. I wondered where my relaxing vacation had gone.

Easton and I locked eyes from across the tarmac. A smile spread wide across his face, making me even angrier. I strode towards him. All the fears I had previously had turned to rage. How dare he make me jump . . . alone. "You!" I came at him with my finger pointed.

"Me?" Easton looked taken aback. His smile faded with every step closer I got.

"How could you? Just leave me up there, all by myself? You! You! You . . . *asshole!*" I fumed. The instructors were laughing in amusement.

"Wow, wow, wow." Easton held up his hands. "You do recall a certain bungee jumping incident where you begged me to jump with you? Right? And then, on the count of three, I was the only one propelling off the building? You do remember that, right?" Easton asked, eyes defensive.

I couldn't deny it. Not with the instructors present, and not when we had talked about it that very morning. "So!" I fumed.

"So?" Easton laughed. "So . . . you started it!" he said.

Anger boiled under my skin, and I channeled it all towards him. "You're going to pay for that little stunt you pulled, you know that?" I thrust my hand on my hip. My arms still like Jell-O as I tried to look tough. All three of the guys were laughing now, including Easton. It only made me more furious.

"Come on. . ." He said, reaching his hand out for me.

"No!" I jerked back, swatting his hand away. I did the only thing I could think of at the moment. "You're cut off!" I said.

All three of the guys stiffened. "Cut off?" Easton asked. One instructor looked to the other.

"From sex! How's that for a honeymoon?" I said.

The instructors howled with laughter, but Easton didn't find it so funny.

"Wait . . ." He said, reaching for me as I turned to walk away. "Wait! Beck, wait a second!" he called out.

I marched on, crossing my arms and ignoring Easton. It may have been a more dramatic exit if I had somewhere to go or a car to take me away. Instead, I stood by the side of the building, waiting for the guys to catch up with me and tell me where to go. When they caught up, the instructors sat Easton and me down to see the video they had captured, both from a camera on my partner's wrist and one on the guy's helmet that captured the tandem jump. I crossed my arms as they loaded the video and explained the different movie packages they could turn the raw film into. I didn't need a video of me skydiving; I only needed to get out of this place and head back to my sanctuary. Maybe take a long walk on the beach. Alone.

"At least I was brave enough to jump!" I hissed under my breath.

"You were so brave, baby!" Easton tried to rub my shoulder, but I pulled away.

"I experienced it! And that's more than you can say!" I said.

"You're right."

"And it was just like flying. It was amazing, and I'm just mad because you didn't get to experience all the beauty with me," I lied.

"Really?" Easton asked, shocked. "And now you know you love it! Aren't you proud of yourself?" Easton asked.

"Yeah, I am! Are you?" I asked, in a snarky tone. I wasn't proud of myself. Had I not been strapped to someone twice my size, they never would have gotten me out of that plane. I really had done nothing to be proud of at all, but fall ten thousand feet.

"Hey . . . It was just a joke. You can hang it over my head for as long as we live. Just like I'm going to do to you about the Sin City incident. But hey, you can cross it off your list now. Right?" Easton tried and tried to make it better.

"It wasn't even on my list!" I snapped. Crossing my arms tighter as I let it sink in. I had at least been able to say that I had skydived. And I guess that was pretty neat. I'd done it. I didn't like it, but I'd experienced it, nonetheless. And not many people could say as much. At least Easton couldn't. Not today, anyway.

The video started, and I recoiled at the sight of my face. I hadn't recognized myself. It wasn't a face I was used to seeing in the mirror—white as a ghost and fear stricken. My cheeks full of air like a chipmunk as they flapped in the wind. And then… and then something happened. I leaned forward in my seat, closer to the screen of the TV. Easton burst into laughter as my limp, lifeless body hung from my tandem partner's chest. I had passed out. And I hadn't even realized it.

My eyes flickered to the instructors, who stifled their laughter, but it was Easton who let it all out. He stomped the floor with his shoes and wrapped his arms around his waist. Right when I was about to say something malicious, I came to on the video making a moaning sound that reminded me of a cat in heat. I whipped my attention back to the screen and watched as my eyes rolled back into my head as I passed out again, and my face slackened. It happened again.

"Flying?" Easton asked. I gritted my teeth, fuming. I knew I hadn't flown through the sky, but I at least thought I could make it sound like Easton had missed out. Though after watching this video, this living proof, it was clear Easton had missed nothing but a display of my crippling fear. I turned to yell at Easton, but then I came to consciousness on the video, pulling my attention away once more. The terror would return to my face right before I would fall limp again. I'd never seen anything like it.

The embarrassment radiated off my back and heated to a boil. All this big talk about me having skydiving experience, and I hadn't experienced it at all. Unbeknownst to me, I essentially slept through the whole damn thing. I closed my eyes, wishing that I had just thrown up on my partner instead. It seemed like the lesser evil at the time, and by the way he was laughing at me, he deserved it.

There, in a small room with three guys rolling in hysterics, and my embarrassment about to burst into flames, I did the only thing I could. At first, it was a twitch of the lips. I tried to control it. I tried to hide it. I wanted to be furious! But every time I ran through another cycle of consciousness on the TV, I just about died all over again. It was the most ridiculous thing I had ever seen or experienced. And the idea of me not even knowing it was beyond me. A laugh broke loose, and my body jolted forward. I covered my mouth. But as soon as it was out, there was no going back. The guys laughed even louder now that they had full permission, and I covered my watering eyes with my hands, unable to control my rollercoaster of emotions.

My feet were safely planted on the ground, and I had survived a 10,000-foot jump. And I suppose, whether or not I passed out, I could still say that I did it. And the fact that it was so incredibly embarrassing . . . well, that just made for a better story, I guess.

"Yes! We'll take it! We'll take the best video package you offer!" Easton barked between fits of laughter.

"No!" I wailed, jumping to my feet.

CHAPTER 11

Flames twirled between the dancers and over their heads. Their hips knocked side to side with a speed I couldn't possibly comprehend. Their banana leaf sarongs left little to the imagination, but that hadn't stopped me. I couldn't dance like that if I had decades of training. It made me wonder what it felt like to perform a fire dance, but I ultimately concluded that it was just a job for them. An everyday mundane task. Their Monday, and my entertainment. It hardly seemed fair, and I wished they enjoyed it the way I did now. Who knew? Maybe they did?

"Does this ever get old?" I asked Easton across the table. I didn't take my eyes off the dancers, and I wasn't sure that he'd heard me, or even if I had said it aloud. If I truly had lives upon lives to live, would this ever get old? Would something so amazing as raw talent become boring at some point? Had it been boring for Easton now?

"What?" Easton replied, reaching across the table to take my hand.

"This."

"The nearly naked men?"

"No! The show! The talent . . . the extraordinary talent. Does it all become, I don't know, *ordinary* after a while? After seeing it so many times in so many lives, does it lose what makes it special?" I asked, and only then did I pull my eyes from the fire dancers to look at Easton. The glow of the fire waltzed across his face in the dark of the night. I didn't want to hear his answer.

Easton looked from me to the dancers, thinking about my question, and I could only imagine that he was trying to come up with something positive to say. But the truth was probably anything but. It was old news to him. I don't know why I thought it wasn't, but it still hurt a bit. I didn't want to live forever if

I'd be stuck in an endless loop of been there's or done that's. I could see how it would be considered a curse.

"This show doesn't really do much for me. Maybe because I've seen it a time or two before. Maybe because there are men in banana leaves . . ." Easton shrugged. I smiled and briefly scanned the beach for the women in coconuts that were surely going to dance next. "But it hasn't lost its charm. And being here with you makes it almost new again. Being with you is like getting to see it for the first time. I get to see the wonder in your eyes, and honestly, it's probably the most I've ever enjoyed it, which is saying a lot."

"Are you just saying that?" I asked, looking him square in the eyes.

"No, I'm not," he said.

"I used to be afraid of dying. Of not experiencing life. Of not having enough time. And now that I have the opportunity to do it all, I'm just as afraid. But for different reasons." I sighed, and Easton tightened his grip on my hand. "Now I'm afraid of becoming callused. I'm worried that I'll turn numb to all the beautiful things around me. I just feel so at peace here, on the island. And the thought of coming back one day and not feeling this way because I've seen it so many times is just . . . it's just sad," I said. "I don't want it to happen."

"Beck, do you think you could ever, truly, tire of this?"

I looked around. The fire dancers were bowing, and the small dinner crowd applauding. I clapped and watched them walk away. Their tan buns covered by one single leaf. "God, I hope not!" I said. Easton laughed, and before I knew it, a dinner roll hit my chest. I jumped and caught it before it rolled off my chair. "Hey! I'm just saying!"

"I'm just saying… I don't think you have anything to worry about," Easton said, with a twinkle in his eye.

I smiled, placing the dinner roll back on the table. Maybe I was overthinking it. Maybe my predisposition was to worry, no matter what. I would always find something new to fear. I was always going to be my own worst enemy.

A server approached our table, filling our water and giving us a clean plate for the buffet dinner. Easton and I walked to the back of the line that comprised of three honeymoon couples. All young, though we must have had them beat by at least five years. Easton began loading up his plate, and I passed on the smoked pork and macadamia nut crusted sea bass. By the time we walked back to our table, my plate had only gained a single scoop of white rice and a small chicken thigh. And that didn't even appeal to me, but I insisted on getting something on my plate, and it was one of my last options.

"Is that all your eating?" Easton asked, holding a full dinner plate of his own.

I looked down at my pathetic chicken and rice. "I'm just not that hungry," I said with a shrug.

"OK. Well, we can go somewhere else if you want?"

"No, it's not that. I'm honestly just not hungry." I picked up my fork and pushed my rice around on my plate. And when I felt Easton's eyes grow with worry, I forced myself to eat the chicken.

"Are you still mad at me about the skydiving? Is that what this is?" Easton asked.

I looked at him sideways. "Do you honestly think I would starve myself because I was mad at you? What would that accomplish?" I asked.

Easton nodded. "Good point."

"And yes. I am still mad at you," I added.

"Oh? How long is that going to last?" Easton asked. As if it were that simple. We had fought before, sure, but we had never been in a situation where time wasn't fleeting, or the urgency of past memories wasn't creeping out of the shadows and demanding answers. No, we had all the time in the world, and I knew who and what I was. I could simply hold this grudge forever . . . or not, I hadn't decided. "I don't know yet."

"Why don't you show me how mad you are tonight?" Easton's brow rose.

"Nope. You're cut off, remember." I shrugged, looking away just as the women in coconut shells took center stage. Easton looked at them, frowning, and I couldn't help but giggle. "How's that for charm?" I asked. His eyes blazed back to me with a deep burning lust lit from within. I swallowed down a lump in my throat, determined to make him pay for not jumping with me earlier in the day. "No," I said. My mouth suddenly dry.

"No, what?" he asked.

"No. I said no." I looked away, feeling his eyes burrow into me. For the life of me, I couldn't figure out why a smile spread across my lips, but for some reason, I was simply amused. His yearning for me. Me pretending to be strong. Because that's all it was . . . make believe. Just because I was mad at him didn't make me want him any less. He just didn't need to know that part.

Easton finished his dinner, and we ducked out early. The dancers had endless moves, and the show would continue for some time. But there was something romantic about sneaking away while most of the resort guests sat hypnotized by the flames thrown into the sky. Easton pulled my hand, and we ran across the rock paths covered by lush green archways and bountiful flowers. The further we fled from the dinner show, the quieter it became. And when the drums were a distant beat, Easton laid his lips on mine.

He ran his hand up the nape of my neck, deepening the kiss. I all but forgot about what I had said to him back on the tarmac. His hands ran the length of my side before he pulled away, lowering his forehead to mine and taking in a breath. "Let's go back to our room," he suggested huskily. I didn't need convincing. We took off, heading straight for our bungalow. And though the walk was long, the tension built with time. And when we made it back to our room, we had all but collapsed on the bed doing what lovers do best.

My head swam, and the room spun as I worked to catch my breath. My skin was covered in a thin sheen of sweat. "God, you're right!" I grabbed my temples as the spinning slowed, and the room became still once again.

"Always. But what about this time?" Easton asked, panting.

I rolled onto my side and stared up at him as he lay on his back. His hair disheveled like he had been caught in a wind storm. Easton lifted his hand and brushed the hair off my cheek, tucking it behind my ear. "I don't think this life could ever lose its magic," I said.

Easton smiled at me for a sweet but fleeting moment. Before I knew it, I had been swept up in his arms, and he was running straight for our patio. "Easton, no!" I screamed, clenching my arms around his neck. "No!" I wailed as he lept right off our dock, baring less than the fire dancers. The ocean splashed as we plummeted under water, and for a moment, the fear inside me seized up.

I remembered most of my last life, though it had been blurry and the details lacking. But the one memory I relived all the time clearer than the day itself was the accident in which we drowned. I relived it in my sleep, in the shower, and most of all, I relived it when I was near large bodies of water. And plunging into the black ocean was a definite trigger. I fought fiercely, pushing Easton down and climbing up his back like a ladder to my survival. I breached the surface and gasped for air, hungry for the first time that night. I splashed about erratically.

"Hey, hey!" Easton took ahold of me and swam to the ladder. I clung on for dear life. "Are you OK? What was that?" he asked, panting nearly as much as me.

Feeling safer with the ladder in hand, I felt utterly stupid for the way I'd reacted. I nodded, focusing on the moon glistening over the dancing ripples of the water's surface and tried to slow my breath. My instincts told me to get out of the water. Climb the ladder. Get on the dock. But I did no such thing. My legs kicked slowly as my heartbeat slowed. The water was warmer than I imagined it would be, and it felt weird against my skin without a swimsuit on. A tiny part of me almost enjoyed the freedom.

"Come to me," Easton said, floating a couple of feet away. I wanted to, but I wasn't ready to let go of the ladder. "Nobody can see us," he said.

"It's not that." I searched the other bungalows for signs of life, anyway.

"Is it the accident?" Easton asked softly.

I didn't have to answer. My silence confirmed it all. "Trust me," he said, holding out a hand. I did. I trusted him. Not to jump out of a plane with me . . . But I trusted him with my heart and certainly with my safety. I placed my hand in his, and he pulled me to him. The warm water brushed past my bare body. "Turn around and float onto your back," he said.

"I can't. I don't float."

"Just take deep breaths. Fill your lungs and be still. I'll do the rest." Easton pulled on the nape of my neck, holding my face out of the water. My body rose to the surface, and I startled, kicking my legs and arms about. "Shhh. Just relax." I did everything I could to do just that. I took the deep breaths, and I noticed that my body would sink a little when I exhaled. But with every inhale, it would rise again. After some time, I trusted that I wouldn't sink to the ocean floor and history would not repeat itself. Eventually, I closed my eyes, and without my knowledge, Easton had let go. I felt free. Free of the trauma from drowning in the river and free of my worries of the future. The gentle rise and fall of my breath like a life raft in the moonlit ocean. I had been floating all by myself, and all I ever needed was the support of Easton to help me trust myself.

Of course, it all came crashing down the second I opened my eyes to find him several feet away. But until that moment—when he had to help me back to the dock, and I tried to drown him all over again—it was nothing short of magic. It would be a moment I'd look back upon. An example of the many times in my life that I was too afraid to do something I could fully do all on my own.

After my first real dip in the ocean ended, my stomach knotted with what I assumed was hunger for skipping most of my dinner. I placed my hand on my stomach, frowning. "I think I'm going to run to the gift shop and get a snack," I said, toweling off.

"Finally getting hungry?" Easton said as he ran the towel through his hair.

"Yeah."

"Want me to come with you?" he asked.

"No, that's OK. I won't be long," I said, needing time to quiet my mind. Time to feel the water in my lungs and trust that I'm OK now. That *I am OK.* I slipped on my flip-flops and turned to smile at Easton before leaving.

"Hey, Beck?" he said.

"Yeah?"

"We can cross skinny dipping off your list." Easton winked at me, and my smile grew. I hadn't recalled the details of the list he spoke of, but it didn't surprise me that skinny dipping was on it since I made the list pre-drowning. I took in a deep breath as I strolled down the dock. The ocean's sultry brine in the air and the lapping of the water . . . I didn't know if it would be enough three hundred years from now, but I knew Easton would be.

I opened the gift shop door and walked inside. Tiny goosebumps covered my arms as soon as the air conditioning hit my skin, and I rubbed my arms as I walked the isles. Nothing looked appetizing, but I settled on salty crackers and a ginger ale. As I waited in line behind a mother and her daughter, I couldn't help but stare at the chubby curly-haired toddler. "Dis one?" she asked in a high-pitched tone.

"Not that one," the mother said.

"Dis one?" The girl asked for a new candy bar.

"Not that one. . ."

"Dis one?" Each time she asked with the same renewed enthusiasm, and I couldn't help but smile. The excitement in her eyes over each possible candy bar was nearly too much to handle, and I felt a flood of emotion crash into me like a rogue wave. A burn hit the back of my throat, and I wondered what had possibly come over me. The mother and daughter finished checking out, and the little girl never got her candy bar. She screamed as the mom carried her out. I frowned.

"Hello. Is this all for you tonight?" the store clerk asked when I put my crackers and drink on the table.

Had I been emotional over the wreckage? Was it that I had just taken a step in overcoming my fear of drowning? Or was it something even bigger than that? Had I been afraid my life would grow dull without the one thing in this world I knew I couldn't have? I looked back to the clerk and then to the display behind her.

"Um, just one more thing," I said, listening to the girl's cry fade away.

"$22.99, please," the clerk said.

I took out my cash and paid. As I waited for my receipt, I looked back to the glass door and beyond into the night. The little girl was gone, and her cries all but distant. And at that moment, I had to wonder if my emotion came from the fear of never having a little girl of my own. Would my life be enough without it?

CHAPTER 12

The following day was a day of rest. Easton and I lounged on our dock for most of it as I didn't feel well. I should have felt more relaxed as time slipped by, but I felt worse. My stomach hadn't been the same since the buffet, and the crackers I bought at the gift shop did little to settle it. Today was our last full day on the island, and I was determined to make the best of it. My stomach churned, and my mouth watered upon rising in the morning, but I laced my shoes, anyway. I wouldn't miss the waterfall if it were the last thing I did.

When I caught a glance at my reflection in the mirror, I looked peckish. I took a couple of deep breaths through my mouth before dusting on some blush and bronzer. I didn't want Easton to know that I was still ill. It was our honeymoon and the tail end of it, too. I wasn't going to ruin any bit of it for either of us. I didn't want to look back on this memorable trip three hundred years from now and wish I'd just sucked it up for the last day. A little indigestion would not slow me down. *Indigestion* . . . I kept calling it that.

I packed a light backpack alongside Easton as we prepped for our hike to the Wabo Waterfall. It was the most beautiful waterfall on Taiseen Island and well known around the world. We would need to get a ride to the trailhead. Then it would be five miles up and five miles back. It should be easy enough. However, with the humidity and my newfound sensitive stomach, I was expecting a moderate to difficult hike ahead.

"Are you bringing your trunks?" I asked as I shoved leftover crackers in my backpack. Easton motioned to his lower half. He was already wearing them. Black and blue stripes with a white drawstring. He had purchased them here on the island the day we arrived. "Right," I said.

"Are you alright? You seem a little off?" Easton asked.

"I'm good. Just a little tired. Who knew vacationing could be so exhausting, right?" I smiled, and Easton wagged his brows, making me roll my eyes in response. I guess we hadn't exactly taken it easy on the extracurricular activities. My cheeks heated.

"How's your stomach today?" Easton asked, zipping up his bag.

"It's great!" I said, hiding my pale face under makeup. He'd never know.

"Yeah? Do you have your appetite back?"

"Mmm...Yup!" My voice squeaked under the pressure of the lie.

Easton sighed, "Oh good! I was beginning to think your cancer was returning or . . ." Easton stiffened as soon as it slipped from his mouth. Regret washed over his face as his brows pulled in. He avoided meeting my eye.

"No. Never. Just some funky island chicken or something," I said. I had remembered little about my cancer, and it was one topic I liked to stay away from. I had many unanswered questions, but I never dared to ask about them. Was I sad? Was my family heartbroken? Probably. I didn't see how recalling such a difficult time in one of my lives would help me now. Burying the whole thing in the black void of my subconscious was most likely the best place for such memories. And for now, I was content with that. They could sit there for decades . . . centuries . . . Collecting dust for all I cared. As long as they didn't come out from the shadows, I was a strong and capable new me.

"You think you ate that chicken that was walking in circles on the beach the other day?" Easton asked.

I laughed, "That's the one! I know it."

Easton called for a ride to the mouth of the Wabo Waterfall Trail, and we waited in front of the resort for what seemed like a small eternity. Everything moved slowly on the island, and I both appreciated it and was driven mad by the same thing. Today though, I was driven mad. Maybe it was the muggy warm island air, or the sweat cultivating on my back and in between my chest . . . or maybe it was the slow churn of my stomach that made me impatient. Either way, I convinced myself that it would all be better as soon as I could sit in the air conditioning of the cab and rest for just a few minutes before our hike began. I tapped my foot with anticipation.

When the cab pulled up, I had my doubts about feeling better. And when I tossed my backpack inside the old car and crawled in after it, I knew. The cab was like a sauna, and air conditioning was a luxury this little thing could not afford. I swallowed and took a deep breath. Both sweat and cigarette smoke marinated inside the cab and wafted in the air. My mouth watered again. I rolled down my window, crank by crank, and leaned into the muggy air, startling when the cab went over its first twig in the road. Apparently, suspension was also a luxury. Easton took my hand lovingly, and I could tell without looking at him that he was worried. I forced myself to hold his hand, even though it made my whole body feel ten degrees hotter than before.

By the time we got to the trailhead, I all but tumbled out of the car. Opening my door before the car was fully parked, I lurched out of the sweat-infused sauna. I'd been working really hard to keep myself together, but I couldn't do it any longer. I vomited small amounts of stomach acid on the side of the road. And when I was done, to my surprise, the nausea remained. It hadn't eased one bit. I closed my eyes with disappointment in myself. I tried so hard not to ruin the day.

"Are you OK?" Easton asked, rubbing my back.

"Yup. I'm good. That was just the smell. You know. The cab," I said, refusing to look at him. I pointed my finger aimlessly down the road toward the car as it drove away, a cloud of dust in its wake.

"Hey, why don't we just go back to the resort, and you can lie down? Maybe watch a movie or take a nap?"

"No," I whined.

"Beck?" Easton started.

"Please? Easton, I really want to see the waterfall. I don't feel . . . *steller*, but, I believe I can do it . . ."

"You . . . *believe*?" Easton's eyes lasered in on mine, forcing me to look away.

I sighed. "I *can* do it. Come on!" I didn't give him a choice. I wiped my mouth on my arm and took off down the trail, never looking back.

"Beck!" Easton called out. I shook my head in refusal and kept walking. The gravel crunching under my shoes. "Beck!" Easton called out.

"Nope!" I kept walking.

"Beck! It's this way!"

"Damn it!" I hissed, slowing my stubborn pace just long enough to shake off the embarrassment before spinning on my heels and walking back to Easton and the forked trail. Unfortunately, I made the mistake of peeking at him as I passed by. His lips pulled up at the corners as our eyes met. The smirk on his face only made me furious.

My aggravated pace didn't last long, and before I knew it, I needed a break. I kneeled over to retie my shoes, not wanting to look weak. I was able to catch my breath just a little, but it wasn't enough. Shortly thereafter, I officially announced it was break time. We must have only been a mile into the trail, but I was hot and breathless. I cursed the chicken who walked in circles on the beach. And every time a little voice in my head told me it wasn't the chicken, my mouth would run, silencing my mind. I would say anything if it meant I didn't have to hear myself think.

"Think there are geckos out here?" I blurted out.

"Um, yeah. Probably."

"Boas! What about them?" I looked up at the trees, waiting for a long vine to slink through the branches.

"Uh, I don't know. But I don't think you need to worry about that."

I nodded. Opening my backpack to take out my water. I riffled through my bag, and my eye caught on the pregnancy test I had bought at the gift shop two nights ago. "Spider Monkeys! For sure though . . . Right?" I zipped up my backpack without ever taking my water out.

"No. Definitely not. Hey, are you OK?" Easton asked again.

I wasn't OK. I was sick, I was worried, and worse yet, maybe even a little excited. Which, in all honesty, only worried me more. "Yeah. Let's go!" I threw my backpack over my shoulder and jumped to my feet. Easton followed cautiously behind me. What if I actually was excited at the possibility of being pregnant but then found out not only that I wasn't, but that I never would be? What if I was pregnant but wasn't ready? What if Easton wasn't ready?

I didn't take the test yesterday because I was sure I wasn't pregnant. After all, Easton was sterile. He was over three hundred years old for crying out loud. It was impossible. And the only reason I was sick was because of the crazy chicken . . . The one I know was not served that night for dinner. I took a deep breath and admitted to myself that I had seen that very chicken doing donuts in the sand the following day.

"I can't wait to see that waterfall!" I blurted out once more. I was beginning to feel like a crazy person. My physical voice silencing my mental one. They were both fighting for my attention, and neither one of them was winning. At some point, I had to believe that taking the test and finding out that I wasn't pregnant was far better than this slow torture I was putting myself through. I was stressing myself out for no reason at all.

"Do you hear it?" Easton asked.

"Hu?" *Was he talking?*

"Do you hear the waterfall?" I turned back to look at Easton, and his expression was all I needed to help pull me back to the present. And there it was, the deep rumbling calls from a grand waterfall. "We're close!" Easton said. I forced a smile and searched the distant trail for signs of the famous Wabo Waterfall. The sound grew louder with each step, and my gait quickened in anticipation of the beauty that hid just up the trail. My mind snapped back like a rubber band that had stretched too far. *I should just take it. Now. Like right now!* "No!" I said out loud.

"What's that?" Easton asked.

"Talk to me? Tell me something. A story?" I asked, needing the distraction because the lush green scenery was no longer doing it for me. And neither was the fear of an enormous boa constrictor dropping from the trees.

"Um . . . OK, so this one time, during World War I." Easton sighed deeply, taking a moment to gather his thoughts. "It was twenty-four hours before the bullet pierced my chest, and perhaps the craziest twenty-four hours of my lives. It started at twilight during the battle—"

"I have to pee!" I called out, darting off trail and stomping over large spikey bushes till I found one that was large enough to squat behind. I was determined to put my mind to ease. This whole thing was ridiculous. I unzipped my backpack and pulled out the pregnancy test. I clawed the box open and pulled the cap off the stick. Grasping the test tight in my hand, I pulled my pants down and squatted behind the bush. Getting pee all over my ankles and hand, I was sure that I had at least gotten something on the stick itself. My breath quickened as I pulled my pants back on. I returned the clear cap and stared at the window for my future to unveil itself.

CHAPTER 13

My eyes glued to the little window on the pregnancy test. I wasn't sure if I was seeing things or not. I blinked several times to moisten my dry eyes and ensure I was seeing it clearly.

"Are you OK, Beck? Did you see one of those spider monkeys?" Easton called from the trail.

My face heated, but I said nothing in return. The window started to change. A faint blue began to appear in a thin line across the screen. The second I saw it, I stashed the test deep within my backpack and zipped it up, locking my future inside. Unseen. Unknown.

Popping to my feet, I yelled out, "Coming!" I must have been as white as a ghost by the time I got back to the trail, and by the disapproving look Easton gave me, I gathered I might have looked even worse than I originally thought. I didn't know what blue meant on the test, but I did know that blue universally represented boys and pink was for girls. Was I having a baby boy? I cursed myself for clawing open the box without reading the instructions. Here I had convinced myself it couldn't be any worse than the ongoing battle in my head, and yet I had found a way to make it worse. Much worse. Now I had my answer, and I didn't know what it meant.

Did I even want to have a baby? A boy? I was only twenty-two, barely old enough to take care of myself. How was I going to take care of a baby? And what were people going to think? That I got married so young because I was pregnant? Nice. Nice, I thought. I was so wrapped up in my thoughts I didn't realize the five-mile hike to the Wabo Waterfall was complete. The waterfall, bold and beautiful, gushed before me, and in that moment, I couldn't understand what it meant when my hand reached for my belly. I let it linger there for just a little while before I took in the view. The nausea had broken, and I felt at peace.

"Wow, look at that? Have you ever seen anything so beautiful?" I asked. Easton stood by my side, watching me. "Every day," he said. It was so ridiculous to think that I could compete with this world-renowned wonder, but I blushed anyway. Easton leaned over and kissed me softly on the lips. His glacier eyes so accepting. I didn't know why I felt the need to carry this burden all on my own. I knew I didn't have to. "Let's sit over there on that rock. Are you hungry yet? I brought snacks," he said.

I nodded. Not in a way that was a lie, but more of an encouragement. Easton helped me crawl on top of a large boulder, and though it was uncomfortable to sit on, the view was stunning. I pulled my backpack onto my lap while Easton situated himself. Droplets of the waterfall spat at us, and every now and again, it would startle me. "You know I had this dream. A nightmare, really. It haunted me for months when I was looking for you. There were these twin boulders, just like this." Easton slapped the rock. "I was so convinced they would crush me."

"What happened?" I asked.

"They didn't."

"Huh. . ." I watched Easton examine the boulder. It didn't seem much of a dream to me, be he seemed fascinated.

"So, is it everything you hoped it would be?" Easton asked as he laid out a few snacks in front of us.

"It's more. I feel like it's calming all my worries. I just feel at peace here," I said in wonder.

"All your worries? What's wrong?"

"Oh, just, you know. Feeling sick and what not." I opened my backpack slowly and carefully. I pulled out my water and crackers. But not before I took another peek at the pregnancy test results. I was shocked to see it now had two blue lines. I pretended to be looking for something as I grabbed the ripped box and tried to piece the directions together. Maybe it was the pressure of Easton sitting right next to me, or maybe it was the dim lighting within my backpack, but I couldn't tell what I was looking at.

"What did you forget?" Easton peered into my backpack. I snapped the bag shut, causing suspicion to rise in his eyes.

"Nothing!"

"Beck?"

"Nothing!"

"Beck, come on." Easton reached over for my bag, and I pulled it away instinctively. I knew all too well I was only making him more suspicious, but I couldn't help it. It was pure instinct. "What is going on?" he asked when the weird turned to uncomfortable.

"I flushed your wedding band down the toilet!" I blurted out.

"What?" Alarm sounded in Easton's voice as I closed my eyes and tilted my head up toward the mouth of the Wabo Waterfall. I didn't want to know what his face looked like. "You what?" He exclaimed, his voice even higher now. I sucked in a slow, quivering breath. His accusation began, "You told me that—"

"I'm pregnant!" I blurted out.

The humid air grew so thick it was hard to breathe. And the silence grew louder with every passing second. I opened my eyes, but I didn't look at him. I stood up on the boulder and placed my hands on my hips, staring out at countless gallons of water that poured over the steep rocks. Once again, it did something to help ground me. Somehow, calm me. Telling me it would all be OK. How could it not, when something so beautiful as this existed?

After what seemed like a small eternity, Easton stood up and wrapped his arms around me, pulling me into his embrace. I didn't just become unglued, I broke. All the fear of uncertainty poured out of me like the Wabo Waterfall. I cried for a long time—long enough that my legs grew tired of standing, and my eyes had swelled. Easton held me tight through and through. I was thankful for the silence then because after my emotions poured out of me, my mind had finally quieted, and it was nice for a change.

"Are you sure?" Easton asked softly after we sat back down on the boulder. Was I *sure*? The terrible realization came over me that I wasn't *sure*. I was anything but *sure*. In actuality, the only thing I was *sure* of was that I had no clue how to read the instructions.

"Well, I took a test. . ." I said. Then I slowly unzipped my backpack and pulled it out, handing it to him.

Easton's brows furrowed, and he flipped the test over, examining it. "What does that mean?" he asked.

"Um. Boy?" I said, rubbing the back of my neck.

"Boy?" Easton glared at me, and I nodded. "I don't know much about pregnancy tests since I've never taken one, but I know that they don't tell you the gender of the baby." I swallowed the lump in my throat, holding his gaze bravely. "Do you have the instructions?"

"Yes!" I pulled the ripped box out of my backpack and handed it to Easton in pieces. He stared at me until I was uncomfortable enough I had to look away. I knew I had dropped the ball on this one. And while I can honestly say that the wedding band down the toilet was a whole-hearted mistake, this time, I just let my emotions get the better of me. I had to work on that. Staying calm under pressure and all. Gathering all the facts. And perhaps—not telling my husband I was pregnant before I really knew for *sure*—was something I should work on too. Lucky for me, I had all the time in the world to become perfect. I'd put that on my to do list.

"Beck. This is in French." Easton shook his head.

"Cut me some slack! I'm only on my second life here!" I belted out. We stared at each other, his glacier eyes against my emerald ones until he cracked. His smile made me giggle, and my giggle made him laugh. Before we knew it, I was crying all over again. Though for a different reason this time. This time, I felt foolish getting worked up over nothing. But what I hadn't realized before, was that I wasn't alone. I had Easton, and he was a pretty damn good companion to have by my side. That's why I married him after all.

"OK, so I knew French at one time. Bare with me, I'm a little rusty, but I'll do the best I can," he said.

"I thought you were a doctor?" I teased.

"I wasn't an O.B., Beck. And even if I were, we wouldn't have given our patients French urine tests. Blood tests are way more accurate than this hunk of plastic, OK?"

I shrugged. "Whatever you say, doctor," I said, leaving him to it. Easton matched the three pieces of the torn box together and tried to recall his French. He looked at the test several times, perhaps in disbelief. Eventually, he handed everything back to me. "Well, what did it say?" I asked.

"It says you're pregnant."

"It what?" I asked.

"It says your pregnant, but we will have to get a blood test when we get back." Easton shook his head.

"What? Why do you look like that?" I asked. Easton's eyes crinkled with worry.

"I don't think it's accurate, Beck. I don't want you to get your hopes up."

"Wait, why don't you think it's accurate?" Disappointment washed over me. I knew my hopes were already on the rise. I wanted to have a baby. And that was something that I'd never given thought to before now. Knowing it as clear as day wasn't something I could take back.

"I think I may have told you this before, but I can't have kids. I'm tethered. You are tethered. There's no way it can happen."

"But what if being a Tethered Soul is like being your own species? What if you just needed to find another Tethered Soul to make it work?" I asked. My voice whiney, like I was pleading for this to all make sense. It scared me to think how I might react to finding out I wasn't pregnant. And now that I knew I wanted this, what would it do to me to live for an eternity without ever having children? Being a Tethered Soul would surely be a curse then.

"I've never thought of it like that. I mean, I guess it's possible?" Easton questioned.

"Yeah." I nodded, not wanting to give up hope.

"But if that's the case, then the baby would be tethered too. And I don't want to do that to another soul," Easton said.

"Well, you did it to me!" I said.

"I did nothing to you. You followed me back here."

"Is that what I did? I just followed you here?" I waved my hand through the air.

"Look, I don't know what happened, I—"

"That's right! You don't know. So, let's not pretend we know the baby will be tethered because we don't. Fair?" I asked.

It took a moment, but Easton agreed. "Fair." He nodded, and I was a little taken aback by my hostile reaction. The words *mama bear* came to mind. I had to be pregnant. Why else would I be so protective over nothing? "It just hurts me to think that I could bring a baby into this world, and I could only protect it for one lifetime. Then, he would always be on his own. Fighting for himself, fighting to get back to us. I don't want that for him, and I don't want it for you. I would never have chosen this life for you." Easton's eyes glossed over, and I could see the reflection of the waterfall in them. The thought of not being able to protect a child was unbearable.

"I know you want to protect me. I get that, but I'm not so sure this thing is a curse, Easton. I'm just not convinced of that yet," I said.

"That's because you didn't remember for the first twenty-two years, and you had wonderful parents to make you feel loved. That doesn't happen every time. And when you wake up as a young child, and all of your memories come crashing down on you, and you realize it's not a dream any longer . . . that's when it becomes a curse. That's when you realize you're lost, and alone, and you can't find your way back home . . . Because you don't have one." Easton's voice was soft and full of pain.

His words hurt deep in my chest, and I felt for him and our unborn baby. Easton raked his hands through his hair, and it toppled back down in front of his face. "Don't you think we could be that home for him?" I asked. Worry lined my forehead, and I was pleading again. "Every year, we meet at the bridge. May seventh. Rain or shine; we reunite there. And we will be his home." It wasn't a question or a plea now, but a promise.

CHAPTER 14

The following day was a full day of travel. And even though I was nauseous again, I was happy because that meant that I may still be pregnant. I started calling it morning sickness, even though it lasted until well after lunch. The first thing I did when we finally got home was call an OB-GYN and make an appointment. The blood test was scheduled for the following week, and I could hardly wait. I slept like a rock that first night after returning home, and I blamed it on jetlag, but I knew better. I was exhausted from creating a human being. Still, there was a part of me—no matter how small it may be, that was a little superstitious—so I didn't admit it aloud.

The following day, after my sickness had subsided, I ventured to the park by my old house. It was something that I had been doing for the past year. Ever since Easton and I broke into my first parent's house. Sometimes I would sit there and read for a couple of hours. And sometimes, I would see Chloe and my nephew. He was young, maybe four or five, and I imagine she had him unexpectedly. Wes was much younger than my niece, Everly. Rarely, she would show up with Wes in tow. It was easier when she brought him; I never had to worry about being caught. But with Chloe, I did. I wore my spy gear, of course. The large sunglasses and hat. I pulled my hair back too and hid my face behind a good book. Many trips to the park, they would never show, and I would get some valuable reading time in.

Though today, on this sunny afternoon, Chloe and Wes did show. I hid my smiles behind my romance novel and my curious stares behind my mirrored lenses. She never had a second thought about the stranger that often sat on the bench, or if she did, she didn't show it.

Chloe glanced in my direction, giving me a polite wave, and I smiled, raising my book. Keep calm. She's done this a time or two before, she's just being nice. I lowered the book a mere inch at a time and was relieved when she hadn't closed the distance between us. I smiled again when I thought about how mad Easton would be if he found out I was here, playing with fire.

"Ma, who's that?" Wes asked, pointing to me. I was the only other person in the park. My insides twisted, and I squirmed a little in my seat.

"That's a lady."

"What's she doin?"

"She's reading."

"Why?"

"Because she wants to."

"Why?"

"Because it must be a good book."

"Why?"

"Do you want to go on the swings?"

"Yeah!"

I let out the breath I didn't know I had been holding when Wes gave up pursuing me. My heart pounded in my chest. It was closer than they had ever come to talking to me. I raised my book to cover my sunglasses and tried to read the first sentence in chapter seven. I must have read that first line a dozen times, and each time, it made no more sense than the first.

Was I really going to have a baby boy? Would he look like my nephew, Wes? Sandy hair and chubby cheeks. Would he be tethered? And if so, was that really all that bad? I didn't think being a Tethered Soul was a genetic disorder. After all, I only became tethered after falling for Easton. Or so I thought. Perhaps I had been tethered all along? Was that even possible? Had I had lives before that I simply didn't remember? I quickly dismissed the thought. It was far too disturbing. However, if being tethered was not a genetic anomaly, then my theory on being a different species and the whole reason Easton and I could get pregnant in the first place would be blown out of the water. In which case, I didn't know what to think.

The sun beat down on the nape of my neck, but I didn't dare let my hair down. I didn't want to give Chloe another reason to recognize me. I stared at the first line in my book while listening to his soft squeals on the swing. Chloe looked tired today. Maybe even a little sad. She had matured a lot in the last twenty-two years. Not just her clothing or lipstick, but her demeanor. Maybe it was the children that wore her down, but she seemed . . . calm. I worried it might be something else, but always faltered back to age. She must have just settled into her stride. Stopped worrying so much about what other people thought of her. I, for one, never liked her more.

Chloe was a good mom. I had only seen my brother once in my second life, and that was at my dad's funeral, but even then, he looked better than ever. He and Chloe appeared to be strong and happy. As happy as any could be under the circumstances. And I loved her for that. For taking care of my brother the way she has all these years. The fear that she wouldn't was the only reason I had such distastes for her in my first life. I was worried she wasn't good enough for him. Though now, I can see I was wrong. And I couldn't be more grateful. Sometimes while I sat at the park, I wondered if we would have been friends. But as I sat on the bench today, I knew we would be.

A green ball rolled to my feet, startling me from my thoughts. The quick pitter-patter of the little boy running through the grass grew louder as he approached me. Before I knew it, Wes was at my feet, picking up his ball. But he didn't pick it up and run—no—he picked it up and stared at me blankly. My stomach dropped as I slowly lowered my book. Chloe stood on the other side of the playground, watching, waiting.

But when Wes didn't move, and he didn't speak, I did something reckless. I lifted my sunglasses, and I winked at him. He stood stunned for a second, then took off running back to his mom. He pointed at me, repeating himself over and over again. "That's my siser! That's my siser!"

"That's not your sister, baby. That's just a woman at the park. She's reading." Chloe tried to calm him down. She swooped him up in her arms, but he craned his neck, trying to look at me still.

"That's my siser!" he yelled.

"OK. Time to go home, buddy. Come on, let's get your ball." Chloe packed her bag with one hand as she cradled Wes on her hip. She turned around right before leaving the park to look at me one last time. I dipped my head ever so slightly behind my book, regretting my decision to show myself to the boy. I had no idea he would be such a little snitch. Figures, I thought. He's my brother's son.

Chloe started for her car, but I could hear Wes calling louder and louder down the trail. Clearly upset that his mom wasn't listening to him. "That's my siser! That's Everee!"

My stomach sank when I heard my name escape his mouth. What had I done? It was clear that my niece and I looked similar, but how was I supposed to know he would solve the puzzle in a minute flat? Especially when I had been going to the park for an entire year now, and Chloe hadn't figured it out. I shook my head, feeling so stupid. The only reason Wes knew it was me when Chloe hadn't, was not because I lifted my sunglasses. It was because Wes didn't know that it wasn't possible. Chloe may have had a few passing thoughts about us looking alike, but in all her years, she learned that surviving death was not reality. Wes, on the other hand, well heck, he probably still believed in Santa Claus.

I pictured Easton shaking his head in my mind. Disappointed. I was beginning to believe him all those times he told me I couldn't show myself to past loved ones. They don't understand, he'd say. I always believed I could make them, but shortly after I spoke to my dad in the hospital, his heart stopped beating. And now, when I smiled and winked at my little nephew, he immediately went into a tail spin. I frowned, closing the book in my lap and watched her car pull away. Easton was right about this rule. No more, I told myself.

That evening I ordered a couple of pizzas to the house after Tanner had dropped by, and looked like he wasn't leaving anytime soon. Instead, he sprawled out on our sofa, beer in hand.

"Make yourself comfortable," I said.

"I got a place!" Tanner announced. "Rented a home just the next neighborhood over. Only took me six minutes to get here, but that was probably because there was some construction on the main road. I bet when it clears, it will only take three. Or two!" Tanner raised his beer can to me.

"You're staying?" I asked. He had mentioned the possibility before the wedding, but really hadn't said much afterward. At least not to me. But I should have known, since he hadn't quite left our house yet, either.

"Oh yeah! Three amigos. Just like when we were kids," Tanner said, kicking off his shoes and putting his feet up on our coffee table. My eyes dropped to his dirty socks.

"Isn't that great news?" Easton asked.

"Yeah! Congratulations," I nodded.

"And I got all the sign-up info for the academy today, too," Tanner said.

Easton's eyes flickered between his brother and me, and then mine did the same.

"Oh, um, Beck, do you remember when we talked about me becoming a police officer?" Easton said.

I stared unblinkingly at him. Was he serious? Now? When we were going to have a baby? "You mean when we agreed you were too wimpy to become a police officer?" I asked, head cocked.

Tanner laughed, slapping his knee. "Good one, Bec!"

"Well, Tanner and I thought we could join the academy together . . ." Easton said, ignoring my original comment.

I glared at him, willing him to read my mind. Could Tethered Souls read each other's minds? I'd have to try. *Don't put your life on the line when you are going to be a father!*

"Come on, Bec, you can't expect Easton to just sit on the sofa? He's the man of the house now! He has to provide for his family! Am I right?" Tanner said.

Easton pointed to his brother and nodded in agreement. "Can't you provide for your *family* . . . by becoming an accountant? Or a real estate agent? Or literally anything . . . that doesn't put you in front of a bullet?" I asked. The brothers stared at me and then at each other. I could tell that Easton was feeding off Tanner's energy, and I didn't like it.

"Come on, Beck, I'm going to get that six-pack that you always wanted," Easton said.

"Yeah, come on, Bec," Tanner said.

I rolled my eyes. These misfits were impossible. "I mean, I can't tell you what to do, but—"

"Yeah!" Tanner raised his fist in the air and nearly spilled his beer. I rolled my eyes and glared at Easton.

"Everything will be OK," Easton said in a low voice. Our eyes locked for a moment, and by the time our contact had broken, I felt he was sincere. Not that he had any control over what would happen to him in the line of duty, but that possibly he had a plan. Or maybe Brooklyn had shared a dream with him. Either way, his blue eyes from across the living room were soothing, and at some point, I had to realize I couldn't control what happened in my life. Not with Easton, and not with our baby boy.

"All six abs?" I asked.

CHAPTER 15

My nausea grew worse, and vomiting in the morning became routine. It was miserable, and most days, I laid in bed until noon, thankful I had taken a semester off school for the wedding. But when the phone rang with my pregnancy test results, it made it all worthwhile. It was confirmed; I was, in fact, pregnant. The impossible made possible. It seemed to be a theme in my life. The second I got off the call with the nurse, I called Easton. I wanted to surprise him in some fancy way, but the moment was far too precious to hold on to until he got home. The phone rang three times before he picked up.

"Hello?" Easton answered the phone.

"I'm pregnant!" I blurted out.

"You are?"

"Yes!"

"Holy shit! Beck's pregnant!" Easton said, his voice away from the speaker.

"Wait! Don't tell anybody! It's bad luck until I hear the heartbeat!" I said.

". . . Or, nevermind," Easton said.

"Wait, so she is, or she isn't?" Tanner's muffled voice came through the phone.

"No, she really is!" Easton whispered.

I rolled my eyes. "I love you!" I said. It's all that mattered, anyway.

"I love you, too. I'll be home after we finish registering for the academy," Easton said.

"OK. Bye." I hung up the phone, a large grin wrapped around my face. I didn't know I felt this way. Not until my reaction to the nurse's call had I really detected my feelings as excitement. And in fact, it surprised me a little. I was going to be a mother. And I could hardly wait. A mini Easton, following me around all day. My imagination ran wild of a little boy—much like Wes with his shaggy hair—running through the backyard. It was so real. I swore I could see him straight through the glass slider. I had no idea this was where my life had been heading, but now that it was upon me, I couldn't imagine my purpose without it.

I slowly sat down on the sofa, my eyes still fixed on the figment of my imagination playing in the backyard. *I couldn't imagine my purpose without it.* And there it was. The answer. I would live my last life. I watched as the little boy playing in the yard dissipated like a cloud moving past the sky, and I was left with nothing but a sinking feeling of doom. If I had this baby, my life would be fulfilled. And if my life were lived to its full potential, then it would be my last. Easton would be right. Our baby would be left unprotected for centuries to come. I would have to believe deep down in my heart that there were people in this world that would do my job for me when I was gone.

Brooklyn dreamed of the day it would happen. The day we died. She said Easton wasn't the least concerned when she told him. And to be honest, neither was I. Not until now, until it was crucial that I lived forever. Brooklyn devised a plan to evade her premonition. There was only one way to accomplish it, though, and it was as simple as doing nothing at all. Keeping the status quo. What had worked for me in the past was surely going to work for me again. If I could just stay the same—let my fears hold me back from the things I really wanted to achieve and the people I wanted to love—then my life would never be enriched enough to be considered fulfilled. The box simply left unchecked. Simple. I'd been mediocre for as long as I remembered.

Brooklyn was worried when I told her I was getting married until she finally concluded that it wouldn't change much in Easton's and my life. We already lived together anyway and had been doing it for a year. We had loved each other in our past life too, and I still wound back here to live another life. But having a baby was a big change. It was a fork in the road, and we were pivoting. An alternative path altogether, and it sure wasn't the one I had been traveling down for the past two lives. Something told me that being mediocre would no longer work for me and that I'd need to come out of my comfort zone. If I were to shape a person's mind, core, and values ... I couldn't do it half-heartedly. This would be the greatest job I'd ever been given, and I couldn't afford not to give it my best.

Come to think of it, Easton would need to pivot also. While he hadn't lived his life in the shadow of fear quite as I had, he did have a hard time loving. Of course, that would come crashing down the moment he held our baby boy in his arms. Did that mean that his life would be fulfilled too? Was his three hundred years of wandering the same lonely path coming to an end? Was his tether going to fray? And possibly the most pressing matter, was that something that I needed to tell him?

I curled up on the sofa, laying on my side in the fetal position. Tears pricked my eyes, and eventually, they fell at will. I was ready to sacrifice my immortality if that was the cost for opening up my heart to this little baby, and I would do it fearlessly and wholeheartedly. But if I told Easton, would that meddle in his fate? Would he resent me, or the baby, for not living out eternity with him? Or would he simply live his last life too?

I hadn't been set on living forever, though it was something I was told I would do. The thought of traveling the world had become more enticing to me recently. But the possibility of it coming to an end was saddening. And it would be devastating if I weren't there to take care of my child in their next lives. My eyes grew tired from worry, and eventually, before Easton came home, I fell asleep on the sofa and succumbed to the nightmares of the unknown path I was on.

Two very long weeks later, and I hadn't told Easton that I was dying all over again. But weren't we all? I looked around the waiting room at the OB-GYN's office. All of these people were dying; maybe not today—*probably* not today—but they were well on their way. The only difference between them and Easton and I was that he and I wouldn't quite complete the process. Honestly, it was like we failed to launch. We were stuck in some sort of endless time loop. But I knew the way out, and Brooklyn had made me promise not to speak of it. It wasn't my place to change someone's path, she would say, and I believed that.

Easton squeezed my hand when the nurse called us back. My stomach did flips, and my palms were a sweaty mess. Easton did what he could to calm me, but his jokes paled in comparison to the anxiety raging inside me. "Take a seat. I'm going to ask you some questions, and then Dr. Faye will be right with you," the nurse said.

I answered the nurse's questions as she took my blood pressure. We laughed when she stated I was nervous. I thought I had covered it up, but my blood pressure was through the roof. "You're going to put on this gown. Completely undress from the waist down. The opening will be in the back. Easton will have to wait out in the waiting room during the exam," the nurse said.

"Can't he stay?" I asked.

"I'm sorry, it's our policy that during the internal ultrasound, no guests in the room. It's a tight squeeze as it is. But he can come back for the following check-ups." The nurse walked Easton out, but not before he gave me a quick peck on the forehead. I smiled and waved him goodbye. Then, I wrestled with the embarrassing smock. I sat on the exam chair and tried to tuck the paper-thin gown around my backside. I looked around the room while waiting for the doctor, swinging my feet with uncomfortable anticipation. *Should I have taken my socks off?*

A knock on the door sounded before it opened up slowly. "Hello, are you decent?" A man's voice asked from behind a curtain.

"Yes," I replied, checking my gown again.

The doctor pulled the curtain back, and I was immediately taken aback by his tall, broad, and ruggedly handsome stature. "Hello, I'm Dr. John Faye, and you must be . . . Becca Green?" he asked, peeking at his chart.

"That's me. . ." I said, cheeks flushing.

Dr. Faye greeted me, making my hand feel small and cold within his.

"So, is this your first pregnancy?" he asked.

"Yes," I said.

"How are you feeling? Any morning sickness?"

"Oh, yeah . . ." My skin heated. The doctor was twice my age, and his hair was in the first stages of turning grey, but if anything, it only made him more handsome.

"OK, well, that can be a good sign. It means your pregnancy hormones are strong. You've got a little fighter in there, I'm sure. And we're going to take a look today. Are you ready for that?" The doctor asked.

"Yes." I twisted my foot around the back of my leg as I clammed up.

"So this is an internal ultrasound wand; I will be using it to get a better look at the little bean since it's not large enough to see with the doppler just yet." My eyes grew wide at the sight of the large grey stick he held up. The doctor rolled backward on his chair and pushed a button near the door calling the nurse back into the room. "I'm going to have you lay down and scooch your bum to the end of the table," he said.

I took a moment to stare disbelievingly. I didn't know what to expect for today's appointment, but it definitely wasn't this. I laid on my back and closed my eyes tight, wishing my doctor wasn't as hot as he was. It made it so very wrong. "Just relax your knees," he said. The humiliation crowded out every other emotion rolling through my body. "Scooch down, a little more," he said. I scrunched my eyes tightly and moved down another inch. "Good. A little more. . ." I just about *died*.

Mortification ensued until something unexpected happened. "Oh, wow!" the doctor said. My eyes flung open, and I frantically sought out the nurse's face. Had she not been smiling, I might have had a heart attack.

"What? What is it?" I asked.

"Do twins run in your family?" The doctor asked.

"What?!"

"Well, if you look at the screen to your left . . ."

I whipped my head to the left and glared at the screen, but I could only see variations of grey matter. The screen could have been broken for all I could tell. "Do you see the two sacs?" Dr. Faye asked.

"No. I'm sorry, I don't. Did you say twins?" I asked, looking back at him.

"Here, why don't you sit up," he said, finishing the exam and helping me upright. "Sometimes, two eggs can be fertilized—"

"But, you said twins?" I repeated.

The doctor sighed. "Yes. You are having twins. Congratulations." He smiled while the nurse wrote frantically on her chart. I took a deep breath, feeling somewhat lightheaded by the time I breathed out all the hot air.

"I'm sorry, I just... I don't understand," I said. But that's not what I meant. I understood how two eggs could be fertilized. I understood how one egg could divide into two. Twins were no mystery to me; but I never once considered it a possibility for me and my body. I only recently concluded that I wanted a baby at all. But two? I didn't know if I could take care of two kids.

"Do twins run in your family?" Dr. Faye asked again.

"No!" I scrunched my brows and shook my head. Then I remembered I was adopted. My genetics didn't come from my parents now, and not even from this lifetime. I thought back to my first family, and there were no twins that I recalled in their lines either. "No. . ." I repeated, my eyes off in the distance.

I finished talking with the doctor—no longer concerned with his rugged good looks—and finished dressing. I rolled the smock up in a ball and set it on the chair. When I walked out into the waiting room as white as a ghost, Easton popped to his feet. "Are you OK? Is everything OK?" he asked, searching my eyes.

"It's, um. It's . . . two. Twins . . . there's two of them . . ." I mumbled something incoherently.

"Twins?!" Easton's voice echoed in the small waiting room. The few patients there peeked up at us. "We're having twins!" Easton announced. A small applause erupted, and congratulations were expressed. I was barely aware of my surroundings as we walked out to the car. If there was any concern that my life would be fulfilled with the love of one child, there was undoubtedly no questioning that twice the love would bring my life to a complete stop. And this was something that I would need to tell Easton.

CHAPTER 16

The advice on the block was not to tell friends and family of your pregnancy until the second trimester. Got to make sure it "Sticks," they would say. Though, with how nauseous I was, I was pretty sure the stickiness of this pregnancy was like molasses. That's why we were going to tell Brooklyn and Tanner tonight when they came for dinner. Sure, Tanner already knew, but not officially. I was looking forward to seeing his best surprised face. I'd bet that it was terrible.

It was a perfect summer day, hot by morning and just bearable by the evening. It made me yearn for the days of dipping my feet in the pool as a kid. Easton would swim, of course, but I only got as deep as the second step. I smiled as I set the table with fancy napkin rings and peered outside to Easton by the barbecue. It was the first real dinner I'd host as a wife, and I wanted to make it special. Well, that and Brooklyn had been begging me to set her up with Tanner since the wedding. They had been lucky enough to run into each other here or there, but each time it was nothing but awkward. I had the feeling she liked Tanner a lot more than anyone in her recent years and perhaps recent lives. Tanner, on the other hand, played it cool, though he seemed interested enough.

The doorbell rang. I took one last glance at the dining table before answering the door. When I opened it, Brooklyn greeted me with large eyes that glistened with anticipation. She had a crush, alright. I could see her gaze flicker behind me, searching for Tanner. "Come in; he's out back," I said.

Brooklyn stepped in as she tugged on her sundress. It hugged all the right places and was a perfect choice for a summer barbeque. "How do I look? Do I look OK?" she asked.

"Stop, you look amazing. Any guy would be lucky to have you," I said. It was the truth. Brooklyn was a babe, and not only that, she was smart and caring.

"Right, no, I know. I'm not nervous or anything. Just asking," Brooklyn said with shifty eyes and tense shoulders. I smiled.

"Right," I agreed. "Can I get you a drink? I have a seltzer, cold and bubbly."

"Yes, that would be great. So, what have you been up to? I haven't seen you much lately. Is married life all that consuming?" Brooklyn asked though I could tell that her thoughts were elsewhere.

I slid her a seltzer and tied my long hair back in a bun. "I know, I'm sorry. I've been . . . gardening," I said, thinking back to the time I considered buying lilies at the market, but passed on them.

"Oh, I didn't know you had a green thumb. You will have to show me," Brooklyn said, opening her drink. I chewed on the inside of my cheek as her eyes searched the kitchen counter. "You're not having one?"

I swallowed. This conversation was too much work, and I wanted to tell her about the pregnancy at the dinner table; not here, not now. "I'm going to have one a little later," I said.

"Have one now," she pressed.

"Do you want to go outside? See Tanner?" I asked.

"Yeah!" Brooklyn shimmied her shoulders and headed for the back slider. She turned just before I rounded the kitchen counter. "Bring your drink," she said as she disappeared outside. I sighed, then turned around and snatched a seltzer from the refrigerator.

The air was thick with heat and the sky still bright as I joined Easton, Tanner, and Brooklyn near the barbeque. The tension was high, and the conversation had stalled. I cracked open the top to my seltzer, and both boys stared at me with knitted brows. I smiled at them with narrowed eyes until someone dared to break the silence. "So, I hear you two are joining the police academy?" Brooklyn said before taking a sip of her drink. I mimicked her, raising my seltzer to my lips and then pulling it away. I assumed nobody was watching me that closely, and from their peripheral vision, I was most likely pulling this thing off. If anything were to blow my cover, it was going to be Easton's shifty eyes.

"Yeah, you're looking at two of Clover's newest officers right here!" Tanner slapped Easton's back.

"Wait, you already did it?" Brooklyn asked.

"Oh no. But we signed up, so there's that," Tanner said.

"Oh, wow. That's going to be great. I can't wait to see you in a uniform—I mean you guys. I mean . . . not you Easton . . ." Brooklyn sipped her drink and looked around the yard, her cheeks red. Had I really been drinking my seltzer, I would have spit it out right then and there. I'd never seen Brooklyn so awkward and from the look on her face, she hadn't been used to it either. I glanced at

Easton and raised my drink back to my lips and winked at him. "What are you doing?" Brooklyn asked.

I whipped my head over to her. "What?" I asked.

"Are you seriously pretending to drink that seltzer?" she asked.

"Oh, that. . ." I bit my bottom lip, stalling. It wasn't how I wanted to tell her. But after I glanced around our back yard and saw no tell-tale signs of my gardening, I decided it was time to drop the act. "So, I have something to tell you . . ."

"Stop—" Brooklyn started.

"I'm pregnant!" I said in a high-pitched voice, not out of excitement but out of the uncertainty of how it would be received. Brooklyn stared, her face expressionless. I'm not sure why, but I felt like I was in trouble. She took an extra-long drink, finishing her can. I quickly glanced at Easton, and I could tell that he was uncomfortable too.

"Well, I already knew, but officially . . . congratulations," Tanner said before reaching out for a hug.

"He already knew?" Brooklyn said, finally breaking her silence and confirming that, in fact, I was in some sort of trouble with my best friend.

"Well, no. He had his theories and all, but—" I said, pulling out of Tanner's arms.

"No, I knew. Easton told me," Tanner said, making the whole thing worse. I slapped my thigh and gave him a sideways glare. Was it not obvious what was happening here? I caught the slightest glance of Easton's smirk before he turned back to the barbeque. "So, what are you going to name them?" he asked. Tanner asked.

My stomach sank, and I closed my eyes, briefly pinching the bridge of my nose. This couldn't have gone any worse. "Them?" Brooklyn asked, looking between Tanner and me.

"I. I. I'm having twins," I stammered.

Brooklyn smiled a wide toothy grin that didn't come close to touching her eyes. "Congratulations, you guys. I'm so happy for you to have chosen that path," she said. I startled when she grabbed the seltzer out of my hand and started on it. I watched her as she guzzled my untouched drink. "What about you, Tanner? Do you want kids?" she asked. My eyes flickered to his.

"Oh, well yeah—" Brooklyn shook her head no, "—Maybe, no. No." Tanner was quick to change his answer, shaking his head no alongside Brooklyn's.

"Hey, I'm just going to check on the . . . salad. Easton?" I asked, calling his attention away from the barbeque. He followed me into the kitchen, shutting the slider behind him. "What was that?" I asked the second the door closed.

"I know. Why was she mad? Think she's jealous?"

"Jealous? No, why would she be jealous? I mean Tanner. He's practically throwing me under the bus. I thought he knew it was a secret?"

"Well, yeah. But the secret's out," Easton said, confused. I let out a loud audible sigh. Why didn't guys understand that it was never straightforward with us girls? He was supposed to act like he was surprised so that Brooklyn didn't get her feelings hurt for not knowing first. "Am I missing something?" Easton asked.

"No," I said. *Yes.* He was missing something—a very large something—that I couldn't explain right now. I peeked through the slider to see Brooklyn reaching out and touching Tanner's shoulder. "New plan," I said, eyes on the flirting.

"There was an old plan?" Easton asked.

"Stay with me here, Easton! We need them to fall in love." If Brooklyn fell for Tanner, she'd forget all about how I derailed her plan to be best friends *forever.*

"We do?" Easton asked.

"Yeah." Clearly, we weren't on the same page.

"Why?"

"I don't know. . ." *So, she wasn't mad at me?* "Because she likes him?" I said.

Easton shrugged. "Fair enough. What's the plan then?" he asked, steepling his chin and watching the couple by the barbecue.

"Well, we can start by giving them some alone time?" I said. Easton nodded and pulled up a seat at the kitchen counter. "You're just going to sit there like that?"

"Yeah, was I supposed to be doing something else?"

"Well, you can't make it obvious! Here, toss the salad," I said, pulling out the salad that needed our desperate attention.

"So, what do you really think is going on with her? Why wouldn't she be excited?" Easton mixed the salad as I threw in berries and walnuts.

"She's worried things will change between us, and we will drift apart," I said, feeling sad for the inevitable change. I was deflated by how she reacted, but my heart hurt knowing why she did it even more.

"Well, that's ridiculous. I mean, unless she has a thing against babies, there's no reason you two can't still be best friends," Easton said. I wished it were as simple as that. Maybe Brooklyn should give up the act and finish what she started, too. Maybe we all should live our last life . . .

"Shit, here they come. Act natural!" I said, doing anything but. Easton frowned and picked up the salad tongs again.

"Oh, hey . . . We were just tossing the salad," I hated myself the second the words left my mouth.

"OK," Brooklyn said on her way to the refrigerator. She pulled out another seltzer, and I immediately knew it was going to be one of those nights. Although, this was the first time I wouldn't be able to drink away the sorrows alongside her.

When dinner was ready, Brooklyn and Tanner had drunk enough to put them on a different level altogether. They were loud, clumsy, and the flirting was terrible. It wasn't the romantic start I wanted for them, but it was outside of my control. Easton and I observed as the night went sideways on us, but only he found it amusing.

"Did Easton tell you we had a physical assessment today?" Tanner said from across the table.

"How'd that go?" Brooklyn asked.

"He's got some work to do," Tanner laughed, and Brooklyn wailed.

"It's training . . . and you need it too," Easton said.

"Is this where it ends, Easton?" Brooklyn said, and the way she stared at Easton made me believe she wasn't talking about his path to becoming a police officer.

"No, Brooklyn. This is only the beginning," Easton replied, picking up on her shift.

"That's what you think. But your wrong," Brooklyn said.

"It's just training. Haven't you ever worked out before?" Easton asked.

"You can't train your way out of this mess." The room fell silent as Easton and Brooklyn glared at each other. The way they fought, they could have been brother and sister. And now that I thought about it, maybe they had been in another life.

"It's OK, little brother. We will beef up those spaghetti arms. Ain't no chicken legs holding my bro back!" Tanner said.

"OK, first of all, Tanner, I'm older than you—" The moment Easton said it, I could tell he realized he was fighting an uphill battle.

"By sixteen days—" he pointed at Easton with his breadstick.

"And second of all, these aren't chicken legs! I don't know why you keep calling them that. I'm a man of steel. Just ask Beck!"

"Do you mean Becca?" Brooklyn asked. *Oh no. What was she doing?* Easton sighed, clearly not happy with Brooklyn's attempts to derail the night. "Surely you don't mean *Everly?*"

My stomach dropped. Easton slammed his hands down on the table and popped to his feet.

"Who's Everly?" Tanner asked, looking around the table. I bit my lip, my heart pounding.

"Brooklyn! Can I talk to you outside?" I asked sharply. She rolled her eyes but followed me into the backyard. The air was still hot, and it helped to take the edge off the icy conversation inside. "What are you trying to do?" I snapped, harsher than intended.

Brooklyn popped a hand on her hip and laid into me. "You are a liar!" I flinched back. Her tone piercing. "You and I were a team. You told me that you would never leave me. And when you married Easton, you promised me nothing would change between us. But here we are, Becca. You went and changed the plan. And you didn't even talk to me about it. And then you told Tanner before you told me? Do I mean nothing to you?"

"No, that's not—"

"You and I were a team! Did you ever think how you would impact my future if you broke our pact? Did you even think about me at all?" her voice rising with fury.

"Brooklyn, I'm sorry, but—"

"But, what? You made your choice. You dug your grave. I can't help you anymore, Becca."

"I don't need your help!"

"Well, don't think I'm going to stick around to see how it ends for you." Brooklyn's eyes turned sober, making it hurt twice as much.

"That's . . . like sixty years from now, you can't be my friend for the next sixty years?" I asked.

A tear fell off Brooklyn's cheek, and I wasn't sure if it was because she was angry or sad. Maybe a little of both. Easton popped his head out of the slider, and I wondered how much they heard inside. "Dinner is cold," he said.

"This won't end well for you, Becca," she said as she wiped her cheek and breezed past me. Dinner continued just as terrible as the first half, but Brooklyn had turned her attention to Tanner making embarrassing and sometimes crude comments this time. By the end of the long night, Brooklyn had fallen asleep on our sofa, and Easton drove Tanner home. I sat at the dinner table with my hand on my tummy, staring at the untouched food, wondering where the night had gone wrong. It was my first time hosting dinner, and I wanted the night to go perfectly. It was to be a celebration of life but turned into quite literally the opposite. Brooklyn was mad at me for choosing love over immortality. I picked up a cold dinner roll and rolled it around in my hand. Had I really chosen this for myself? Or was the path chosen for me long ago?

I had just started to clean the kitchen when Easton came home. He stood in the entryway staring at Brooklyn for a moment. "Do you want me to take her home?" he asked.

"No. She lives too far. She can just stay here tonight. I'm sure she'll leave in the morning."

"Right." Easton picked up the plates from the dinner table and brought them to the sink. "Barefoot and pregnant," he said.

I smirked at him. "Sorry tonight was such a disaster," I said.

"It's OK. I know I don't have chicken legs." I laughed a little too loud, and Brooklyn stirred on the sofa. "So, she knows about Everly?" he asked, a little surprised.

"Yeah, well, I told her. I had to. I should have said something to you earlier. Sorry."

Easton shrugged it off. "She believed you?" he asked.

"It was the only thing that made sense with her dreams and all. I told her that our death was in the past, and she had nothing to worry about. It actually helped strengthen our relationship." Easton didn't know that I spoke to Brooklyn about being tethered, let alone that she was tethered herself. I wasn't sure why it was so important for her to keep secret, but I would not say anything if it was important to her.

"That's surprising. It's never turned out that way for me. It usually just blows up in my face. I lose my friend. Always." I felt terrible. Especially when I thought back to how my nephew reacted at the park. But I held that information back too. It seemed like I did that a lot lately.

"Well, I'm glad you have such a good friend that she would stand by you, even when you tell her something as impossible as this. But she sure was upset tonight."

"She just feels like I'm leaving her behind. I don't agree with it, but I can understand where she's coming from. She's told me I was like a sister to her, and she hasn't had that since her very first—" I froze. My hands still under the running water.

"First, what?" Easton asked. I'd said too much. It wasn't my place to tell.

"First grade. Since she was in first grade." I started washing the dishes again. Easton and I continued talking till the kitchen was clean, and then I was ready to hit the bed like a ton of bricks. My eyes burned, and I was more tired doing daily tasks now that I was simultaneously building two people from scratch. I waited in the hall for Easton as he walked out into the living room and turned off the lights. Brooklyn stirred once more, and then I heard her . . .

"Goodnight, killer . . ."

CHAPTER 17

Goosebumps prickled my skin as I stood in the dark hallway. There was a bitter moment of stillness before Easton's footsteps padded down the hall. Whatever he felt, whatever he wanted to say back to Brooklyn, it took a lot of strength to hold inside. I felt the ice as Easton passed by me. Closing the door softly behind me, I watched Easton's silhouette disappear into the restroom. The lights from the bathroom lit up a portion of our bedroom, but I stood still in the shadows. Torn between being a good friend and being a good wife.

We got ready for bed in silence, and after lying by his side, unable to close my eyes, I rolled onto my side to see Easton still awake. "Brooklyn means well. I know she came off a little harsh tonight, but she means well," I whispered.

"What are you not telling me?" he asked bluntly.

I sighed, knowing the time had come. "I wasn't supposed to say anything—"

"But I'm your husband. That rule doesn't apply when we're married." He may have been right. I didn't know. Maybe it was a grey area, but I felt that hiding the truth about my friend's life was doing more harm than good. So, I told him.

"Brooklyn is a Tethered Soul, like us," I whispered. It was only the beginning. A long moment passed as Easton's mind bent and folded in on itself. I found it odd he didn't blink. Not once.

"That's impossible," he whispered back.

"No. It's not. I mean, it was impossible for me to be tethered, but here I am."

"Right. But Brooklyn's not tethered, Beck."

"Yes. She is . . ."

"I would know. I would sense it. She's not. She's lying to you. And the real question is, why?" Taken aback by his comment, I was conflicted about defending her while I felt the need to explore the plausible reasons why my friend would deceive me in such a way. There was none. She'd been a great friend to me.

"Well, maybe you don't know as much as you claim," I said.

"I know enough to know she's lying to you. I'll tell you that much. I'm going to talk to her tomorrow, this is ridiculous—"

"No!"

"I should just talk to her now." Easton sat up, and I reached out, grabbing his shoulder.

"No. Please don't," I begged.

Easton ran his hands through his hair, and even through the darkness, I could see the distress he was in. I could feel it in the air. He was trying to protect me. Trying to do right by me. I hated myself for putting him in this position. The tension stretched between us and slinked down my body. I was tired beyond belief, but I acted out of instinct, leaning over and kissing his neck. My intention wasn't to keep him in bed there with me, though it did that too.

In the morning, I woke up stiff and groggy. Easton made coffee, and the clanking of coffee mugs woke Brooklyn on the sofa. She moaned and brought her hands to her head. I poured myself a decaf coffee and smiled at her misery. Somehow it felt better to know that I wasn't the only one suffering from nausea and a headache.

Easton and I sat down in the living room, and I thought it was kind of him to bring her a cup of coffee, even though she accused him of being a killer just the night before. It was something I wouldn't have been able to do so easily. She smiled at him apologetically and then took the mug. Her head hung as she rubbed the sleep from her eyes. And eventually, she began her apology. "Sorry about last night, guys," she said . . . *That's it?* I waited for more to come, but she felt her debt was free.

"So, you know that Becca Reed is Everly Beck, huh?" Easton asked. Brooklyn's brows rose, and she nodded slowly, preparing herself for the long talk ahead of her.

"And now, Becca Green," I mumbled to myself.

"If you knew Becca was Beck, and Beck was Becca, then you would know how important it is to keep that a secret. Why would you bring it up in front of Tanner?" Easton asked.

"Tanner wasn't going to find out. Plus, who really cares if your older brother finds out about Beck?" Brooklyn frowned.

"He's not my older brother—"

"He's *actually* . . . Easton's younger—" I started.

"Whatever. He doesn't know," Brooklyn said, cutting us both off.

Easton shook his head, frustrated with her energy. And I'd have to say he wasn't the only one. "Look, Brooklyn, I know you're upset with me for getting pregnant, but I didn't choose this. I didn't even think it was possible. I swear," I said.

"See, that's the problem, you guys. You're the blind leading the blind. How are you supposed to survive this if you're only listening to him? He doesn't know what he's talking about half the time. You guys don't understand that I'm trying to help you. But you make it so damn hard! Hell, if it weren't for me, you two wouldn't have even found each other again," Brooklyn said.

"What are you talking about?" Easton asked, brows furrowing.

"I knew you were looking for her. I saw it in my dreams. And I saw Becca was lost without you. But do you know how hard it is to make someone fall in love with somebody they can't remember?" Brooklyn rubbed her temple.

"Actually, yeah, I do," Easton said.

"Why? Why did you help us get back to one another?"

"Because she was lost. And she was my friend—" Brooklyn spoke to Easton but stared directly at me with her deep brown eyes. "She's the only friend I've had for so, so long."

"How long?"

Brooklyn pried her eyes off me and looked to Easton, her eyes softening. She sniffed in a broken breath of air and then began a story even I had never heard. "I was born in 1450 in Early Modern Europe. I was a gifted child. Dreaming big dreams that told the future. By the time I was five, it was clear that my future was anything but bright. They called me witch." Brooklyn took a sip of her coffee, and her eyes fell unfocused to her lap.

"Even my own family was afraid of me." Brooklyn cleared her throat, pushing past the memories. "In 1457, at only seven years old, I was burned at the stake in front of my entire village. I watched as my very own sister cheered along with the angry villagers as my skin lit fire and I burned from the outside in. To this day, it was the most horrific, excruciating death."

Goosebumps covered my arms, and shivers split down my back. My chest heavy with sorrow for what she had experienced. I knew she was tethered, but that was about all she had told me. Now I saw why she didn't want others to know. It was a story she rarely wanted to relive.

"Born again the same day, I woke in a wicker basket on a doorstep. As I grew, my dreams were more vivid, and I often spoke of them when I was young. My parents were more loving than my first and shielded me from the villagers until I made one fatal mistake. I ran into my sister. All my rage poured out of me as the memories flooded my mind. She'd betrayed me more than anyone had before. I ran to her, telling her about the terrible man she would marry and all the horrible things he would do to her. I told her how she would die, and I screamed the day it would happen. She took one look at me amongst the villagers and called out at the top of her lungs. 'Witch!' she screamed. I was taken immediately. That's when the cycle started."

"Oh my god, Brooklyn. I'm so, so sorry," I said, my hand heavy over my heart.

"It was over two hundred years later when the infamous Salem Witch Trials began, and by then, they were hanging witches, not burning them. I used my dreams to warn the folk of their impending doom. Time after time, they would rat me out, and we would hang together. That's when I decided I wouldn't use my gift to help others anymore. I became cold-hearted. I had to. It was the only way I could survive. But it was no way to live." Brooklyn said, and Easton nodded with a heavy heart.

Brooklyn took a deep, shaky breath and shrugged. "I'm not that way anymore, though. I only wasted a few lives before I started helping people again. And to be honest, having a friend like Becca has helped me a lot. I wanted to help her find her soulmate. Her love. And when I met you, Easton, I wanted to help you too." Brooklyn's voice was shaky.

"I don't understand. Why do you think that's all going to change? What does having a baby have to do with any of this?" Easton asked. My stomach dipped, and I knew right then and there that I didn't want Easton knowing that fate was calling. Brooklyn's eyes flickered to me, and I gave a quick shake of the head. I didn't have it in my heart to tell him my second chance was fleeting.

"Our friendship isn't doomed, I just felt . . . threatened. Like I would lose her. I mean, having a baby just takes up of all your time. Who is going to go shopping with me and such?" Brooklyn joked. "I'm going to get some more coffee. Do you want any?" She asked.

I mouthed "Thank you" to her, and she responded with a small smile.

"Yes, please." Easton handed her his mug and then turned his focus on me. "But, Brooklyn, one more thing. Why did you call me a killer?" Easton continued to pry.

"Well, you know. I told you that part. That you two died in my dream. Remember? I told you."

"Yeah. But that was our past life. I thought you knew that?" Easton said.

"Yeah. Um, Becca told me that bit. And you know, my dreams change all the time," Brooklyn said from the kitchen.

"So, everything is good? As far as your dreams go?" Easton asked.

"Oh, yeah. I haven't even had one since I talked to you last! That was before you asked Becca to marry you, remember? It's honestly nothing." Brooklyn came back into the room with two mugs of coffee. She wasn't being honest. I knew that much. She had dreams every night. Sometimes about people she hadn't even met yet. And they always came true. Every single time.

"Thanks," he said, taking the coffee. "Brooklyn?" Easton's expression shifted. "If you 're a Tethered Soul, then how come I can't see it?"

"See it?" Brooklyn cocked her head to the side.

Easton nodded. "I can see just how long one's lived. I can see the pain they carry like rings inside a tree trunk. It burns around them like a burning ball of embers."

"Oh, that. That's not what you think it is, Easton," Brooklyn smirked.

"What are you talking about?"

"Hazy? Kind of yellow, orange glow? Sometimes angry looking?"

Easton shrugged. "Yeah. It's how we Tethered Souls know each other. And you don't have it." Easton's tone became accusatory, and I slinked back into my chair.

"Let me ask you this, do you see that on Becca?" They both turned to me, and my eyes dropped to the floor.

"Well, no—but that's only because she's young. There aren't years of pain there, let alone much memory of it," Easton said, and I recoiled. Though it was true, I didn't like being talked about in terms of what I had and hadn't remembered.

"Exactly. She's not *tortured,* Easton. And neither am I. What that warm haze really means is that you are a Tortured Soul. A Tortured Soul can be a Tethered Soul, and more often than not, they are. It takes centuries to build up that kind of pain. The kind that is so deep it invades your energy. But what you fail to see is, a Tethered Soul doesn't have to be a tortured one."

"What—What are you talking about?" Easton's forehead creased with disbelief, and I didn't know what I had thought about it all. I knew one thing, though. I wasn't tortured. The thought of living forever wasn't negative to me at all, and I struggled to see how it ever could be.

"While it's true that I was tortured for many, many lives, I'm not anymore. I've made peace with my past. I no longer want to move on from it. Honestly, it's what makes me who I am, and I think I'm pretty great. I want to live forever! I'm happy, and you can't see that smoldering ember around me, Easton, because it doesn't exist in me." My eyes flickered to Easton.

"And you? You're happy too?" Easton asked me, his eyes holding my own.

"I . . . I mean, you always talk about how it's a curse, and I'm just not sure I feel that way."

"You don't?" Easton was taken aback. "God, Beck. You used to be so tortured. You used to be afraid of the dark because that's when you would be alone with your thoughts. You used to hurt yourself because the physical pain was easier to take than the pain in your heart. Don't you remember any of that? You don't carry that with you?" Easton asked.

"Honestly, I don't remember ever feeling that way. I think it's sad that I ever did. I think it's sad that people feel like that now. But if you asked me if I thought getting to live forever was a curse, I just don't think it is, and I might go as far as to say it could be a gift. I mean, I'm having babies. It has to be a gift, right?" I asked.

Easton nodded his head slowly, then looked back to Brooklyn. "So, all the Tethered Souls I've seen before," Easton began.

"Those are just the ones who don't understand yet. They're lost," Brooklyn said, setting down her empty cup of coffee.

"Lost Souls. . ." Easton said beneath his breath.

"Yeah. Like you. . ."

"Like me?" he asked.

"Yeah. You feel like there's no point; you want to move on but can't. You don't know your purpose here." Brooklyn shrugged like it was simple, and Easton nodded his head, deep in his own thought.

"I do feel that way," he said.

"Yeah." Brooklyn ran her hands through her hair, and I could tell she was getting ready to leave.

"I'm a Lost Soul . . ." Easton said to himself, eyes unfocused in the middle of the room. It was going to be a long day. It was then, when I knew we made the right decision not to tell him about the way out. I wasn't sure he could handle it. Would he race to make his life perfect so he could leave this world behind? Would it be disingenuous? Or would he sabotage himself like I had planned to all along so he could stay behind and care for our children? I had made my decision, but I believed it was best for him to make his on his own and in due time.

"Well, I think that's my cue. I'm going to go. Oh, one more thing. Can I still call you Becca? Or—" Brooklyn weighed both her hands in the air.

"Yeah, oh yeah! Um . . .?" I furrowed my brows, trying to think back to when Brooklyn had become a popular name.

"Don't you dare call me, Beatrix!" Brooklyn said, pointing her finger at me. And had Easton not looked so sad, I might have laughed out loud.

"Promise," I said, opening the front door, my eyes still large with shock. *Beatrix.*

"Love ya," Brooklyn said, passing by and kissing me on the cheek. "Oh, and do me a favor, dear, give Tanner my number!"

CHAPTER 18

All the leaves had turned orange and fell to the ground. Now the trees were nothing more than naked branches in the frigid winter air. Easton had packed on quite a bit of muscle training to become a police officer, and my belly had grown to an astronomical size. I was riddled with back aches, heartburn, and a terrible case of the waddles. But at least the nausea had broken and never returned.

My appointments with Dr. Faye had all been great, and when the time came for him to disclose the twin's sexes, I chickened out at the last minute. I covered my eyes as he laughed. He ended up writing it down on a piece of notepaper and stuffed it in an envelope for me to take home in case it kept me up at night. He said it happened often, and he didn't want a call in the wee hours of the morning unless I was in labor. And you know what? It did keep me up that night. And had I not thrown that envelope in the trash when I walked out of his office, I would have ripped it open the very first night.

Brooklyn and Tanner had started officially dating after a re-do dinner at our house that ended with a goodnight kiss. It worked out kind of perfectly, because they ended up spending a lot of time at our house, and it felt like we were a family. In time, Brooklyn and I asked Easton if we could tell Tanner about our past lives, but he had a firm opinion on that, and since they were brothers, we had to let it go. She ended up telling him about some of her dreams, though, and he thought they were quite interesting. Brooklyn claimed he just didn't understand, and maybe it was better that we never told him about being tethered.

I thought about baby names often and had quite a list going. Brooklyn liked to sneak god-awful names on the list when I wasn't looking. And one time, I wrote Beatrix on there as a joke. She didn't find it as funny as I did. I spent a lot of time at the park, reading. Chloe and Wes hadn't come very often since he called me Everly, and I didn't blame them. But today, when I sat there with Brooklyn, I had a feeling in the pit of my gut that they might show. Brooklyn told me it was just indigestion.

"Do you remember when you told Easton that your dreams changed all the time?" I said, before taking a sip of my hot cocoa.

"Yeah."

"Was there any truth in that?"

"No. They never change. And often, as the event approaches, the dream becomes more frequent."

"Have you had the dream of me dying again? You know, since the first time?"

"No. It was just the one time," Brooklyn said.

"Would you tell me if you did?" I asked. I knew the second she paused that I would never get the full truth from her. I wondered how much she hid from me, even to this day.

"Honey, I'm going to tell you what I think you need to hear. And most likely, not an ounce more," Brooklyn said. At least she was honest.

"Why did you think we could change my fate and live forever if you had already had the dream?" I asked.

Brooklyn shrugged. "I guess I thought it was worth a shot. I mean, I know the formula. The ticket out of here . . . I just figured that if you knew it too, you would make a different choice for yourself. But you are so stubborn, Becca. You were always going to do your own thing." Brooklyn rolled her eyes like I was the most exhausting friend on this planet, and I smiled behind my cocoa.

"You mean like, I would just live the most boring life ever known to man? Or like, I wouldn't bring my pregnancy to term?" I asked, the thought leaving a sour taste in my mouth.

"Yeah. It's a choice, you know. I just didn't expect you to choose them over yourself or Easton."

I frowned. It was honest but cutting. They definitely heard it, too, because I got a sharp kick to the ribs. I moaned and twisted in on the bench. "Well, I do. I choose them. And I'd do it all over again."

Brooklyn chuckled. "You haven't even met them. . ."

"I don't have to!" I rubbed my belly.

"You don't? What if they're assholes?" Brooklyn laughed.

I rolled my eyes. She clearly didn't have the motherly instincts that I had. But before I snapped something rude back to her, I remembered a time before I was pregnant. I probably would have thought the same thing. "They probably will be," I said, causing both Brooklyn and I to laugh. "Oh, stop, stop! I can't laugh anymore. It hurts too much. It all hurts!" I choked out as I looked for a place to set my hot cocoa.

"Ohh, Becca. What am I going to do with you?" Brooklyn asked, wrapping an arm around me. I smiled at her and opened my mouth when a flicker of movement caught my eye.

"I knew it!" I said.

"Is that them?"

"Yeah, only that's Everly, my niece, and the little one is Wes. Chloe must be busy today," I said, watching them get out of the car.

"Awe, he's so cute! And she looks a lot like you. She's got your coloring, that's for sure," Brooklyn said.

"Yeah, I know."

"Well, hey, I've got to run. I told Tanner I would meet him at the police academy for lunch today." Brooklyn gathered her bag and stood up. "Thanks for the cocoa."

"Anytime. I'm going to stay here for a bit and read. Tell Easton I said hi."

"Ha, *read* . . . You know you don't read when you're here."

"I do! Sometimes," I said, smiling.

I waved Brooklyn goodbye and then turned my attention back to my niece. She looked like a young adult. Maybe graduating high school soon? And she did look like me. A lot more so when I was younger. I wondered if it was hard for my mom or brother to watch her grow up. Wes turned his head in my direction right as a sharp pain stabbed into my side. I pushed my hand into the cramp and breathed through it, all too aware that he had seen my face again. As the cramp subsided, I saw Wes tugging on my niece's sweatshirt.

By the look on his face, it was time to go. The last thing I wanted was another disturbance. The poor boy probably had nightmares. I stood up, and a gush of warm water soaked my jeans. I twisted around to see my hot cocoa still full on the bench next to me. I grabbed my tummy. It wasn't long before I gathered my water had broken, and I was going into labor. I still had another month until I was full term, but my doctor told me it wasn't uncommon to deliver early when you were carrying twins. I took nearly two steps towards my truck when a contraction hit, and I called out. Bringing attention to myself was not what I wanted to do. Not when the only people at the park were my niece and nephew. But that's exactly what happened. First, it was Everly. Then, Wes came running across the playground.

"Oh my god. Oh my god. What do I do? Oh, shit—" Everly panicked, placing her hand on my back. I felt a zing of electricity pass through her touch. It was my body recognizing her as my family, and I wondered if she felt it too.

"I'm good. I'm totally OK. I'm just going to drive myself to the hospital," I said, adjusting my oversized sunglasses and tugging at my scarf.

"Can you even drive?" Everly looked back to the fluid that covered the bench. Her expression covered in worry.

"Oh, yeah." My voice became more and more strained as I felt another stir of tightness approaching.

"OK. I'm just going to help you to your truck."

"That would be great," I said, waddling to the parking lot. It was clear to see which vehicle was mine. It was the only other vehicle in sight and right in front of hers. We headed straight for it. "Ahh," I called out, bending over in pain.

"Shit. Shit. Call 9-1-1! Wes, call 9-1-1!" Everly shouted.

"No! No. You. You don't. Need to. Do that," I huffed. "Ahh!" I bent over violently, propelling my sunglasses off my face. Wes hurried to pick them up. I knew the trouble I was in when he saw my face, and I only hoped that my niece hadn't been shown many photos of me. Perhaps she was too stressed out to notice. One could only hope.

"I think I need to drive you. Yeah. I'm going to drive you," she said.

"No, you don't need—"

"You can't drive! You can barely walk!" She had a good point there. I stood as straight as I could, taking baby steps to the parking lot. But when we approached her car and my truck, she was obviously right, and I couldn't drive in my condition. She opened her car door, and I slowly sat in her passenger seat. Wes climbed in the back, where he sat on a booster. "OK. Just hang on."

Everly took off, and I nearly bashed my head into the window. She was a terrible driver. I spread my hands out, one on the dash and one gripping the overhead handle, bracing myself. Between contractions, I thought about how I ended up in my niece's car—and more importantly—how my brother survived teaching this girl to drive. "My name's Everly, and that back there is my little brother Wes," she said.

"Hi," I choked out a breathless reply. I wanted to tell her I knew who she was. I wanted to talk to her for hours.

"What's your name?" she asked.

I had to stop and think about it, which was difficult when my body felt like it was trying to split in two. Beck would be too incriminating, and Everly was surely out the window. "Becca! Ahh!" I cried, gripping the overhead handle. Everly stepped on the gas, and we all but peeled out, rounding the corner into the hospital parking lot. I didn't know what was worse, the fear of inexperienced driving, or the two little people trying to break out of my body. "Thank you," I whispered. My voice disappearing under the pain.

"OK, little man, we've got to help Becca into the hospital. Can you help me?"

"Yeah! I'm gonna help!" Wes said.

I opened my door and swung my legs out of the car, my niece and nephew helping to pull me to my feet. Gravity was not my friend, but Everly did what she could to help support me. Wes stuck by her side, gripping a fist full of her sweater. We were almost to the emergency entrance when the large glass doors opened, and a nurse with a wheelchair rushed to our aid. "Ahhh," I groaned, unable to sit until the contraction passed. Everly rubbed my back, and tears spilled from my eyes. Though they weren't the kind of tears that fell from the searing pain, they had been the kind that fell when you reunite with family you hadn't seen in far too long. The level of love and comfort I had with my niece and nephew—even never having spoken to them before—was far greater than anything I had experienced with a friend. There was something deep and raw between us that ran through my veins, and I wondered if Everly felt the connection, too. I knew the little man did.

"Good luck!" Everly called out as the nurse rolled me away.

"Luck!" Wes echoed.

I craned my neck to look at them one last time before the doors closed, but that involved a full body twist that I was incapable of. I muttered something inaudible that turned into a full sob. I had come so close. I only wished I could convey what they had meant to me; now . . . *then.* I'd say it too if I didn't think I would scare them with my words from beyond the grave.

"Is there somebody I can call dear?" the nurse asked. I'd lost my chance, was all I could think. "Dear, is there somebody I can call for you?"

Easton! I patted my pockets and the side of my wheelchair. I didn't have my phone, my bag . . . nothing. "I don't, I don't know his number," I cried, searching and researching the same pockets. "It's on speed dial. I don't know it . . ." I said. How could I be so *stupid?*

"It's OK. We'll get you checked in, and I'm sure it's on file. We'll find it and call for you. What is the name of the person you are trying to contact?"

"Easton. Easton Green. He's my husband!"

"OK, dear. We'll call Easton then," the nurse reassured me.

Checking in was fast. I was placed in a room and monitored by several people, all who were incredibly nice. I was doing well keeping myself calm until a nurse came in to update me on Easton. "Hello, dear. My name is Judy, and I've been trying to reach your husband for you. He's not answering his phone. Is there someone else we can call?" she asked.

"He's at the police academy. Can you call them? There's only one, and it's in Decord City," I said.

"I'll give it a shot, and I'll let you know what they say," Judy said before disappearing from the room. I closed my eyes, hoping he'd be here shortly, but Decord City was an hour away, and I didn't want to wait that long to see him. I was going to have these babies all alone.

"Becca?" a small voice called from the hall. I opened my eyes to see Everly and Wes standing in the entryway. "You left your bag in my car," she said.

Immediately I began crying again. I waved them to come in, and I could tell that my emotional state made her somewhat uncomfortable, but I couldn't stop myself. Wes jumped on my bed, holding out the sunglasses I'd dropped at the park.

"Wes, no!" Everly snapped.

"It's OK," I said, sniffling. "Thank you, little man. That's so thoughtful of you," I said, careful not to wink at him again.

"You look like Everee," Wes said. I smiled widely and looked up at her. She wore an expression I couldn't quite read.

"Thank you," I said. Everly was a beautiful girl, and if I truly did look anything like her, I was a lucky girl.

"Well, we should go. I just wanted to make sure you had your things," she said.

"Thank you so much." My chest tightened, and I felt like I was losing my chance again. Like they were slipping through my fingers, and there was nothing I could do about it.

"Dear, I called the police Academy, and they said they would pass the message to him," Judy said in the doorway. My heart sank. The quickest Easton would be here would be an hour, and that was if he hit most of the green lights. Everly took Wes's hand and tried to pull him off the bed, but he wouldn't budge.

"Nooo," he whined.

"Wes, don't do this. We have to go."

I swallowed down the uncertainty surrounding what I was about to do and just did it. "Stay?"

"What?" Everly asked.

"Yeah!" Wes cheered.

"Please stay. My husband is a least an hour out. I have nobody here with me. I'm scared. Can you stay? At least until he gets here?" I asked, my voice tapering off as another contraction came. "Ahhh!"

"OK. OK. OK. We'll stay!" Everly took my hand in hers and squeezed it tight. The electric shock ran up my arm.

CHAPTER 19

Everly gripped my hand tight as the contractions wracked through my body. I was practically begging for the epidural by the time it was first offered to me, and I accepted before Judy could even finish talking. Everly held my hand for that too and I stared into her beautiful green eyes—my eyes—as the needle penetrated deep into my spine. Sweat dripped from my hairline and my heart pounded in my chest. My body felt as if it were under attack from the inside out, and my heart felt guarded but full. The last thing I wanted was to scare my niece, and I worried Chloe would walk through the door at any moment. Or worse, my brother.

Having my niece and nephew with me was my chance to tell them everything I had ever wanted. But I couldn't do that with words. I couldn't tell them what I wanted to; the stories of their dad when he was a little boy or what it was like to grow up with their grandma and grandpa. I couldn't tell them that one day—when I was truly gone—I'd watch out over them. Or that I had been doing it now. I'd have to convey the love I had for them in another way. "Tell me about yourself," I said to Everly as the epidural worked its magic and blocked out the pain.

"Well, I'm graduating high school soon, and I'm going to be a graphic artist," Everly said. Her cheeks were red, just like mine had been my whole life. *Lives.*

"Oh, wow. Is that something that runs in the family?" I prodded.

"Actually, yeah. My aunt was going to be a graphic artist too. The talent skipped my dad, but my grandma has it even though she says she doesn't." Everly tucked her ashy blond strands behind her ears and then returned her clasped hands to her lap. She was nervous.

I thought about all the terrible drawings Carter drew as a kid. "Your aunt?" *What was I doing?*

"Oh, yeah. Sorry, she died," Everly waved her hand dismissively.

My gut wrenched, though not from a contraction. Or if it was, I guess I wouldn't have known, as I was numb from the waist down. But there was something to be said about listening to your own bloodline talk about how you died. Especially when they batted their hand as if it were an annoyance. I couldn't blame her, though. The girl had never met me. My brother wasn't much of a talker, so I assumed he hadn't opened up much to anyone about me. She probably heard some stories from my parents now and then growing up, but that still didn't make me real to her. Or important. But if she knew it was me here now, that would change things. . .

"Oh no! I'm so sorry," I said. I was sorry I couldn't stay longer to have met her.

"Oh, it's OK. It was a long time ago," she said.

"Yeah, but . . . I'm sure it's really hard?"

"Um . . . well, like I didn't know her. So. . ." Everly shrugged. *I deserved that.* I had no right trying to dig into her past, *my past* . . .

"Right." I stared at her, searching for hidden feelings deep down inside while she looked around the hospital room nervously.

"Actually, you kind of look like her," she said. A smile tugged at the corners of my mouth. It wasn't much, but at least there was that. And the art; that was special too.

"Look who's talking," I laughed, caught up in the moment. It wasn't until her eyebrows pulled that I realized I had said too much. "Oh, wow. Is it hot in here? It's so hot." I placed the back of my palm against my forehead, and Everly jumped up to feel if I had a fever.

"Should I call the nurse?" she asked.

"No, I think I'm OK. But thank you. So, tell me about Car . . . Your dad . . ." *Shit . . .*

"My dad? He just works. Like all the time. That's it," she shrugged again.

"Hu . . . And your mom?"

"My mom's busy with this little guy—" Everly motioned to Wes sitting on a chair with her cell phone. "He was an oops baby. He's the apple of her eye, though," she said with a smile. I felt bad for her. The poor girl needed her aunt, and I wasn't there for her.

"And you?" I asked.

"I had my time when I was a baby. I had been the only grandkid for many years."

"Huh. . ." I rubbed my belly, never wanting either of the twins to feel like they were second best.

"I have a boyfriend. . ." she said.

"You do?"

"Yeah. We've been dating for a little over a year now. I'm not sure what we're going to do when he moves away to college. I guess we're going to try and make it work. But, it'll be hard. I'm staying local. There's a great university nearby for the arts," Everly said while looking down at her feet, a helpless fog in her eyes.

"Try not to dwell on it. I think everything will work out just the way it's supposed to," I said.

"You think?"

"I know," I said.

It was then that I caught a figure standing in the doorway. Easton. He sprinted into the room and wrapped his arms around me tight. "I'm so sorry. I came as fast as I could. I got a police escort," Easton said, his face buried in my neck.

"It's OK. I've been in good company," I said.

Easton pulled away and stilled for a moment as he looked into my eyes, surveying them. He straightened his back and turned to Everly. "Hello," he said, tight-lipped.

"Hi. Um, I'm Everly, and that's my little brother, Wes. We were just leaving," Everly said, standing.

"Hi buddy," Easton said to Wes.

"Hi."

"Lucky for me, Everly and Wes were at the park when my water broke. They drove me here and have been keeping me company while I've been waiting for you," I said.

"You've been a big help today. Thank you, buddy," Easton said to Wes.

"Yeah. With my sisers. . ." Wes said.

Easton stared at the little boy as he mindlessly played on the phone. Everly shook her head, dismissively rolling her eyes at his comment. Easton's eyes flickered to mine, and the air shifted in the room. Frigid goosebumps prickled my skin.

"OK, well. We better go. I wish you and your baby the best," Everly said.

"Babies. There's two of them," I told her.

"Wow. That's . . . Wow." Everly shook her head. "Come on, little man. Time to say goodbye."

"Bye. Bye. Bye sissser. Bye," Wes waived on his way out the door.

"Bye, buddy. Bye!" I blew a kiss, and the last thing I saw before the door closed was his chubby cheeks pucker into a smile. The moment they were gone, a weight had lifted off my chest that I didn't even know I'd been carrying. I took a deep breath for the first time since my labor had started and turned my gaze to Easton. Who was . . . not happy.

"What?"

"What in the world was that?" he demanded.

"Oh. That. Well, I was at the park—"

"The park?"

I closed my eyes for a moment of regret. The labor had somehow made my lips loose, and I had been divulging too much. "I sometimes . . . go to the park to read, and—"

"You mean the park next to your brother's house?"

"Well . . . that's the only one around. So—"

"Beck, what are you doing?"

"I'm sorry! I'm sorry, I just . . ."

"You're not sorry."

He called my bluff. "I'm not sorry," I admitted, picking at an imaginary fuzz on my hospital blanket. "I sometimes go just to watch Wes play. And Chloe is such a good mom. It's just . . . I don't know . . . It's nice. It's nice to see that the life I left behind was still going, and that I didn't disrupt it too much by leaving. I like seeing them happy. It makes me feel whole," I said, shrugging. I wasn't sorry for making my heart full. It was essential to my well-being.

"That's fair," Easton admitted. His tone heavy with sadness. "Have you ever been caught?"

"No! No . . . But this one time, Wes called me his sister. And then I hid behind a book."

"Sister?"

"Yeah. I think he senses that she and I are alike." I nodded, keeping the part where I voluntarily lifted my disguise, winked at the boy, and probably gave him nightmares.

"So, how did they end up here?" Easton asked, sitting on the bed.

"Well, my water broke—"

"While you were stalking your past life at the park?"

"Yes . . ." A moment of silence stretched between us.

"And your niece happened to?"

"Well, I couldn't drive. Brooklyn had just left, and Everly was the only one there. So, she drove me."

"Brooklyn?"

"Yeah. . ."

"Uh-huh." Easton sighed. I knew I pushed the limits of what he'd been comfortable with. Being a Tethered Soul came with rules, and I didn't follow any of them. But it wasn't an opportunity I could waste.

"Sorry," I said. "I don't want to make you worry."

Easton leaned over me and tucked my hair behind my ear. "You don't need to apologize for wanting to see your family happy." I nodded. Tears pricked my eyes, and my chin wobbled. It's all I really wanted. For them to be happy.

Easton and I chatted until the wee hours of the night when my monitors went haywire. Nurses rushed to my room, checking me and the machines I was hooked up to. I watched them frantically, trying to read their faces.

"Is everything OK?" Easton asked.

Everything happened so fast, it was a whirlwind of nurses and alarms. Panic set deep within the eyes of those who surrounded me. My hand slipped out of Easton's as I was wheeled off to an emergency C-section. I felt my tether pull tight as our distance stretched, and I knew he felt the same.

The room I entered for surgery was eerie and my instincts told me I should run. This was not how I had planned my delivery, and I knew I was in trouble. Panic had set in, my breathing shallow and erratic as a nurse placed an oxygen mask over my head. With large gulps of air, I watched my doctor wash up through a window. Even his eyes were unnerving.

A curtain went up at my chest, separating my line of sight from my stomach. And though I couldn't feel myself being sliced open, my body shook with the tugging of my flesh. I tried to be brave. I tried to keep calm. But I had a sense of fear that came from deep down inside that I couldn't seem to shake. I closed my eyes, steadying my breath, and when I felt brave enough, I opened them and tried to read the expression of the surrounding staff. It was something in the way that Judy looked that told me I'd be able to read her face like a book. I kept my eyes on hers, my heart nearly stopping until the slightest curve of her lips appeared. And then there was a small, distant cry from beyond the sheet.

"It's a girl!" Dr. Faye announced.

I sobbed as the room erupted into claps and cheers of congratulations. My emotions were scattered like a bag of dropped marbles. I felt everything. And when they showed me her pink little wrinkled body, I saw everything I had felt for her, floating in the air. Surrounding us all. Little bits of glowing lights with the warmth of happiness and hope. It was like a meteor shower inside the hospital, and it struck me with wonder, leaving me in awe. I knew I would give anything or be anything for that little girl the moment I laid eyes on her. And giving up eternal life for her was the most honorable thing I could ever do.

I tried to control my sobbing long enough to ask for the nurses to tell Easton, but the tears just kept coming, with no end in sight. They took my little girl away, and I kept busy by watching the stars twinkle softy. Yellow sparkles glowed brightly until something changed.

At first, the brightness had dimmed, leaving the room a darker shade of love and hope. Then it was the warmth that dissipated, turning the room chilly and bitter. My body trembled, twitching and jerking on top of the table. I watched the magic turn blood red before disappearing into thin wisps of smoke, and I was left with the devastation of what I had not yet known but felt in my heart. I swallowed down the rising bile in my throat and lowered my gaze slowly. The staff was silent. Judy would not look at me.

Dr. Faye came to my side and picked up my hand. Before he had the chance to say anything at all, a deep guttural cry ripped through me. "I'm so sorry," he said. The staff stilled, and time stopped. The only thing I could feel was pain. Pain so sharp that I could barely catch my breath. I was being suffocated with the truth of losing a child, and I was going to die right here on this table of a broken, battered heart. I don't know how long I cried for, and I'm not sure how long I lay in the darkness of a room that was once lit with love, but I knew one thing; I'd never come back from this.

CHAPTER 20

When I was lucid enough to understand that this was real life and not some terrible night terror, I was completely gutted. It wasn't just that I no longer shared my body with two babies or that my legs were still numb. It was that my emotions were gone, too. All but one. Devastation. And there was so much of it that I felt hallow inside. I couldn't see the love floating in the air, and I couldn't feel it swell in my chest. I wasn't sure I ever would again. I stared unfocused into the middle of the room as Easton stroked my hair. All I could do was blink because even acknowledging his presence was too difficult for me.

It wasn't until the nurse brought our baby girl into the room that I felt like the worst mother there had ever been. Because even she made me feel nothing. Easton tried to get me to engage, but I just stared at the wall. My mind telling me I was useless. A mother who couldn't protect her child. I never even had the chance. I never got to hold it, and they never felt my love. I failed. My one job, my one purpose in this life, and I failed. How could I live with myself now?

I closed my eyes and rubbed where the crust had formed from countless dried tears. Inevitably I would have to live with myself because now, I'd be living forever. There was no way I could live a fulfilling life now that I had lost a child. Easton was right, after all. This was a tortured life. I could see it now, and I could feel it right about where my heart used to be. I would have to ask him if he saw the burning rings of smoldering ember radiating off me like he had seen with other tortured souls.

The baby cried, and Easton sang a lullaby as he walked her around the room. I was so thankful for his strength to carry on when I couldn't. I didn't know how, but I knew I must find a way to be there for my little girl. Even through the pain and the fog of failure. I was still a mother to one, and I had to be strong enough to be there for her. I opened my eyes. It was the first step. I blinked several times, and I made myself a promise.

You can do this, Beck. You can do this. If you can show up for that little girl, be the mother she needs, I promise . . . you can fall to pieces every other waking second. But for her, you must not give up.

I rolled onto my back, giving it everything I had, and focused my eyes on Easton.

"Hey, there she is. . ." Easton came to me, and I sat up in the hospital bed. "I think she's hungry. You've been . . . out for a while." Easton handed me the wrapped little peanut, and I reached out instinctively to take her. I had hoped that when I took her in my arms, something would change. My heart would light fire again, and I would come back for her. But it didn't, and I was no phoenix. I looked at her little red face, and all I could think was how will I ever love her with a broken heart?

I looked up to Easton, the worry etched deep into my face, and I could see that he understood without having to say it. His eyes watered, and he nodded at me. "It's going to be OK. We're going to get through this," he said in a whisper. I'm not sure why it hurt to hear it. Maybe it was because everything hurt? Maybe because I didn't think it was true. Or maybe I knew one day we would get through it, and that hurt too. I didn't want my child to be something that I one day moved on from. And I didn't think that the doom would ever subside or that my heart would ever be whole again.

"Let's name her Clara," Easton said. I looked up at him. His eyes sad, but there, just on the edges, was a touch of hope.

"Clara. . ."

The time I spent at the hospital went by in a fog. I assume some of that was due to the pain medication, and if I hadn't known any better, I'd say they gave me a little extra to help get me past the first few days after the stillbirth. I slept a lot in the hospital, but even when I was awake, a part of me still lingered somewhere in far-off land. Easton and I had to name our other daughter, but I found it incredibly difficult to give her a name that she'd never use. I wondered if it would hurt more or help with closure. Either way, Easton said she deserved a beautiful name, and I couldn't argue with that.

"What about Molly?" I asked him. He rocked Clara in his arms as we waited to be discharged from the hospital.

"Molly and Clara, I like it," he said. I nodded and then looked away. Molly would forever be the name I associated with the deepest sorrow and the blood-painted smoke in the operation room.

Nurse Judy came in to give us some paperwork. Easton handed me Clara so that he could fill it out. I took her warm little wrapped body in my arms and stroked her forehead with my fingertips.

"Do you have the names yet?" she asked.

"Molly and Clara Green," Easton smiled.

"Those are lovely names. Just keep filling that out. I'm going to get a wheelchair for you, Miss Becca, and a little something someone dropped off for you today," Judy said before disappearing from the room.

"Thank you," I said, not in the least curious what it was or who it came from. When she returned with a small brown teddy bear, I forced a polite smile.

"Here you are. A pretty little girl dropped that off today. Your sister? She looked just like you," the nurse said.

My eyes grew, and I reached for the tag. The instant I saw 'Congratulations,' my stomach churned. It wasn't a good feeling to be told congratulations when a tragedy had just happened. I knew I needed to separate the death from the birth. If I hadn't, poor Clara would forever live in the shadow of Molly's tragedy, and that was no way to raise a child. But I didn't know how to compartmentalize the two. I flipped the tag over to see Everly's name, and it sparked an ember in my broken heart. I'd have to keep this bear safe, and one day, I would explain to Clara just how important it was.

Judy helped me to the wheelchair, and we eventually left the hospital. A part of me didn't want to leave because inside these walls, I was once a mother of two. Somehow, leaving the hospital made it more real, and the reality sank in that I would be going home with only one of my children. When the cold air met my face, I breathed in my new life with the fresh winter air—and reluctantly—I exhaled the old one out. Molly overshadowed all the bits of excitement that I once had to be a mother, and I felt no joy to begin my journey.

Brooklyn and Tanner were waiting for us when we got home. And if that wasn't hard enough to see them, I still had to come home to the house that was prepped for two babies. Brooklyn had expected that, and she and Tanner worked tirelessly removing the second crib, second swing, second . . . everything. There was no evidence whatsoever that I had planned for twins. Not in the closet, not in the drawers, and not on the walls. I was relieved that I didn't have to come home and see it all. But there was also a part of me that hated seeing it gone, and I knew that was the part of me that simply wasn't ready to let go. I wondered if that part would live in me forever.

During this troublesome time, the nights were especially grueling because that's when Clara would stay up crying. And to be honest, it was in the off hours she slept that I would keep my promise to myself. When the house was quiet and all were asleep, I'd slip into the garage, climb inside my truck and shut the door tight behind me. I'd grip the steering wheel and listen to the hum of silence for a few seconds before I'd cry. It happened nightly at first. And when I cried myself to sleep in my truck, Easton just about had a heart attack looking for me. After

I'd confessed to my promise and my nightly belligerent sessions, he would often check on me in the garage if I wasn't in bed. Countless nights he crawled inside the cab with me and held me till my tears ran dry. Sometimes, he'd cry too.

But when Clara was up, that was my time to give her what she deserved. A stable, loving mother. And I loved her right. That was the easy part. The hard part was being stable. I had a good streak going, but I told myself it was OK for all the times I failed and broke down in front of her. She wouldn't remember them, anyway. No, I had a good five years of mistakes before she really remembered what I was like as a mother, and for that, I was thankful.

The shadow that Molly cast on Clara was short-lived. About six weeks after she was born, when I walked into the nursery, Clara smiled at me. It nearly brought me to my knees to see her acknowledge me, and I felt my heart stitch back together. Until then, it had felt like a thankless job, but the moment she smiled at me, I knew it was neither of those things. In the days that followed, I spent my time trying to get her to do it again and then again. Hungry for her little toothless grin because somehow it was the glue that mended my heart back together, and it was Clara who taught me how to love again.

It wasn't long after the smile had renewed my sense of hope that I could hike a trail—albeit slowly—and that is what I was waiting on for Molly's ceremony. I wanted to spread her ashes over the Truly River where Easton and I married in my first life and where we were engaged for my second one. It was a meaningful spot to me, full of memories. And I wanted my Molly to rest in the field where I saw the shape of love for the first time. My parents came, too, and so did Easton's. Brooklyn and Tanner joined as well, completing our family. It was difficult having all the people around, but I was glad they came. And after six weeks, I had finally gathered the strength to face the day I'd say goodbye.

After a slow hike down the trail, we reached the vast opening in the field. It was weird to show up with other people as it had always been a secret spot for Easton and me. Even the day we wed was unconventional. It had just been the two of us. But this felt right, and her memorial was similar in how it too was unconventional. I ran my hands across the tall wet blades of grass and marveled at the beauty beyond the cliffs. My dress soaked up the winter dew much like it had before—and even though we were saying goodbye and my dress was now black—I couldn't help but feel like I had been here before.

The family gathered at the cliff's edge. Easton held my hand and his mother held Clara. A crisp breeze passed by, and I thought it was odd how I hadn't felt the chill, just air that had passed through my hair.

"The most beautiful things on this green earth cannot be seen but must be felt. Molly has touched our hearts, and though she may be gone, she will not be forgotten," Easton spoke softly. I felt a gentle pull in my attention. Like eyes had been watching me from behind. I turned my head, the breeze dancing in my hair. A dragonfly buzzed across the field, lighting it up with love.

Easton let go of my hand to open the urn. I turned around to watch my daughter fly, but all I saw was ash. Black lifeless particles that painted the sky before dispersing into nothing. Molly had not been inside that urn. As everyone cried and embraced, I turned my head back around to the sparkling field and imagined my Molly chasing the dragonflies.

CHAPTER 21

The ceremony marked the beginning of a new chapter for me. The one where I became a mother. Of course, I had been a mother for the six weeks prior, but it wasn't until I saw the ash flutter down in the chilly winter air that I realized it wasn't my Molly. No, Molly was in the fields chasing the twinkling lights. Basking in love that sprinkled between the blades of grass and twirled through the breeze. I didn't say goodbye that day, but I did embrace my present life. And I no longer looked at Clara as a reminder of what I'd lost. It was a hard place in my broken heart to find, but once I found the part that could both love and mourn—side by side—I became a better version of myself. Certainly, a stronger one.

The nights were still difficult, and most days, I felt like a zombie, but Easton was marvelous at picking up the pieces that I either dropped or no longer could carry. When he and Tanner graduated from the police academy, I knew our lives would take yet another turn. I was happy for him, but it didn't make the long hours any less lonely. Easton always said that he wanted to make an honest living, and with a family by his side, he said it was finally time. On the other hand, I was perfectly fine making ends meet in any which way he knew how. I hadn't married him to change him after all. I married him because I couldn't live without him. And some days, it felt like I was.

I'm sure it was hard for anyone to put their life on hold to raise a child. But when you knew that your life would never end, it's a different kind of hard. Don't get me wrong, I wouldn't give it up for the world. *I wouldn't.* But I just wished Clara would talk or *something.* Some days I would get so sick of hearing my voice I'd have to turn on the music to drown myself out. Or worse, call my mother. Sometimes she would come stay with us, and normally that would be too much for me, but now I welcomed the company. I needed to be seen and heard. My mom did that for me, and after some time, we became friends in a way we never had before. She talked about the divorce a lot, and I talked about losing my identity. It seems we both didn't know who we were anymore, and simply knowing that I wasn't alone made me feel better.

A new pastime of mine had become watching the neighbors. I had three particularly sneaky spots around the house that I would spy from; the front window, the mailbox—which had a better view down the street—and the backyard. However, the backyard was better suited for listening. The old lady down the street—I named her Nancy—went missing for a week. When she finally returned, she was in a wheelchair. I think it was a heart issue, but Easton has his money on a stroke. And the neighbors next door fight all the time. He hides the fact that he smokes cigarettes, and he usually sneaks out back after they fight for a nicotine fix.

The neighbors weren't my friends, but they were a nice supplement to keep my mind busy. Of course, Brooklyn was still my best friend several years later, but she and Tanner had become quite serious, and they started spending more time by themselves. They announced they would move in together on Clara's second birthday. I tried to help her move, but Clara made more of a mess than I could help pack and ultimately, we had to leave early so Brooklyn could get proper work done. More often than not, I felt more of a burden than a friend, and I longed for the days when she enjoyed my company again.

I'd be seeing her today though, for a summer wrap-up barbecue I was hosting, and I couldn't be more excited to get the time to talk with her.

Brooklyn came over early to help me set up. It was a small gathering, only Tanner, Brooklyn, and a family down the street with a little boy Clara's age. They were just far enough I couldn't spy on them, which made them appear seemingly normal. They were also the only family around with kids.

"Do you think this is enough silverware?" Brooklyn asked.

"Yeah, for sure. Thanks for helping," I said.

"Anytime! Is Clara's boyfriend coming today?"

"Jackson isn't her boyfriend. They barely even notice each other. It's kind of weird."

"Then why are they coming?" Brooklyn asked. It was a fair question; why would I invite a family with a kid that my kid hadn't even taken notice of. I guess I just felt that she should have a friend come, and since she didn't have friends yet, the little boy would have to do.

"Um, it's for social skills. She's going to start kindergarten next week, and I can't have her unsocialized," I said, shrugging.

"Huh. I just think the parents are super awkward."

"Oh my god, tell me about it! The last time they were over—"

"Wow. Is that for me?" Clara screeched. I spun around to see her standing in her pajamas, clutching her stuffed elephant. "Brooklyn brought that cake for everybody. Doesn't it look good?" I scooped Clara up in my arms, and she smiled a toothy grin.

"It's a party!" she squirmed. I put her down, and she ran to the appetizers.

"You woke up from your nap just in time. The party is about to start. Let's get you changed," I said, taking Clara back to her bedroom. Tanner walked in the front door as I passed, and he gave me a quick kiss on the cheek hello. "Hi, I think Easton is out back setting up the food." I waved to the backyard, but Tanner wasn't looking for his brother. His eyes fell upon Brooklyn.

I was almost finished with Clara's hair when Easton popped into her room. "Wow, you look so pretty. Are you ready for the barbecue? Everybody is here," Easton said. Clara jumped up and down.

"Hold on. Hold still," I said, tying the last bow in her hair before she sprinted out of the room and down the hall. I sighed, looking up at Easton, and he came to my side and rubbed my shoulders. "Oh, that feels so good." I rolled my head from side to side. Easton leaned down to my ear and whispered.

"I have a secret. . ."

I perked up. Secrets were scarce these days. "What? Tell me."

"Can you keep it?" Easton teased.

I looked back to Clara's open door. "Yeah, you know I can. What is it?"

"Tanner is going to ask Brooklyn to marry him," Easton whispered.

"What?" My jaw unhinged, hanging low and open.

"Shhh."

"When?"

"Today, if all goes well," he said, just before walking out of Clara's room. I lingered for a moment, worrying that Tanner would get his heart broken. He didn't know Brooklyn like we did. She was a true free spirit, and I feared she looked at marriage like a ball and chain around her ankle. At least she had before she fell in love with Tanner.

The barbecue went well. Clara and Jackson played together for the first time. And the neighbors kept a good flow of conversation without doing that thing they always did that made Brooklyn and me think they were so awkward to be around. I knew an end of summer barbeque wasn't a romantic setting—not in the least—but the day was next to perfect, and it was amongst the people we cared about most . . . and the neighbors. I knew Tanner would propose soon, and it made me anxious.

When the neighbors had left, and Clara was crazed under the influence of sugar, Tanner took Brooklyn aside. My eyes shot to Easton's, and then we both ran to the master bathroom that had a window opened to the backyard. It was perfect, but only one of us could see at a time, and it wasn't much. Only a sliver of kneecaps could be seen through the slats of the window. But we could both hear crystal clear, and we pressed our ears close to the open window.

"Today was fun," Tanner started.

"It was fun. Clara loved the dessert."

"I really enjoy spending time over here with my brother and his family."

"Yeah. Me too."

"Think that could be us one day?" Tanner asked. I grinned and popped my head up to look through the vented window. He was holding her hands. I panned to his face; he looked pale.

"He's so nervous," I whispered. Easton raised his head to look, and I moved out of his way.

"You want kids?" Brooklyn asked. My breath stilled as I looked at Easton. He had no idea what kept a Tethered Soul bound, and after all these years, I had no intention of telling him.

"I want kids with you. I want a family with you. I want to spend the rest of my life with you. I love you. And if you would let me, I'd—" Tanner lowered down to his knee. Easton and I fought over the small window, our temples competing for headspace.

"Stop!" Brooklyn said.

"Oh, no," I whispered.

"Tanner, I can't have you do this."

"Do what?"

"I can't have you get down on one knee for me."

"I can't see!" I hissed.

"I can't either," Easton replied.

"I can't have you ask for my hand in marriage. . ."

"What's that?" Clara squawked, startling both Easton and me.

"Nothing! There's a bug," I whispered to Clara.

"Can I see?" she asked, her voice much louder than ours. Easton and I ducked below the window, hoping not to get caught.

"Yes. Your dad will show you the bug from the outside. Go show her, honey," I said. Easton glared at me for a split second before turning to Clara with a smile.

"You want to see some bugs? I'll show you some bugs!" He picked her up and took her out of the bathroom. I stood on my tippy toes, pressing my cheek against the window sill. Brooklyn was gone, and Tanner was left staring at the ring in his hands. My stomach dropped. I knew why Brooklyn did it, but I wish she hadn't. I set out to find her. I made it just in time to see her car backing out of the driveway. I ran outside and prompted her to stop.

"Brooklyn, are you OK?" I asked. Tears streamed down her face. It was a stupid question.

"I can't talk right now, Becca."

"I know what happened. I'm so sorry."

Brooklyn threw her car in park and looked up, blinking back the tears. "I can't marry him, Bec," she confessed.

I sighed. If only she knew she had a choice. "I know," I said.

"I gotta get out of here."

"Hey, I think Clara is just going to nap, and Easton can watch her. Do you want some company?" I asked. Brooklyn nodded. I took a moment to run inside and tell Easton and gather my things. When I hopped in her car, her tears had stopped and her face held a vacant expression. We drove around for a little while until Brooklyn stopped at the park. It was the place I found myself often, and the times she had accompanied me were the times we usually had our deeper conversations. Perhaps it was because Clara had entertained herself in the sandbox.

As we walked through the grass to the benches, I watched a dad play with his little girl. She appeared to be Clara's age, and I tried to hide my excitement that she may have a potential new friend.

"The hard part is that I love him. I don't want to break up with him. But it's not like I can stay with him now that he knows I don't want to get married and have kids . . . No offense," Brooklyn said. I frowned for a second, showing my true colors before playing it off.

"None taken."

"I mean, I knew I shouldn't have gotten as close as I allowed myself to get. It's my fault. I deserve this."

"You deserve to be happy, Brooklyn," I said, watching the man push his daughter on the swings. He looked oddly familiar.

"I am happy. Not in this exact moment, but in general. I'm a free spirit. I'm a wanderer. And I wouldn't have it any other way. Love just ties you down . . . No offense." We sat down on the bench, and I placed my bag to my side. I thought about love tying me down, but it wasn't like that for Easton and me. Quite the opposite, really. Easton's love was the one thing that saved me from myself. If I had a tether holding me back, it would have to be *me*. I'm not sure I'd know how to survive without him.

"It's survival of the fittest, Becca. And I need to shake it off if I want to survive. So that's it. I'm done with relationships. Forever."

"Oh my god . . . I think that's my OB-GYN," I said, squinting.

Brooklyn raised her brows, not at all minding the interruption. "Damn, he's hot!" she said. I said nothing, but my head nodded ever so slightly. "And he was the one who gave you all of those exams?" she asked. My cheeks flushed, and my head continued to bob slowly until our eyes met, and we began to laugh.

CHAPTER 22

My hand clung to Clara's as I walked her into kindergarten. Miss Kay's classroom was bright and colorful, and it smelled of crayons and glue. Most of the parents hung around the outskirts of the classroom while one gave their crying son a private pep talk in the corner. I was anxious. I could only imagine what Clara was feeling.

"OK, honey, you need to go sit on the rug. I'm going to stay for a little, but then I'll have to go home so you can learn," I said, kneeling down on one knee.

Clara smiled, her blond hair sticking to her cheeks as I tucked it behind her ears. "OK, mommy." She kissed me before turning to join the other kids. She found her way to the middle of the rug and sat down next to a little girl with long, dark hair. I tried to be happy for her, but I couldn't help but feel like she left just a little too, easy. She never even looked back. Not once. I frowned, looking back to the kid who refused to leave the comfort of his mother.

"How are you holding up?" a dad asked beside me. I looked up at his tall stature, and my stomach dropped. It was my doctor. The same one from the park the week prior and the same one from the exam room. My cheeks heated with embarrassment. Had I felt exposed? This man knew way too much. He'd *seen* way too much. And he'd been there in my darkest hour. . .

"Dr. Faye, so nice to see you again."

"I thought I recognized you. Remind me—"

"Becca Green. You delivered Clara—" I motioned toward the middle of the rug and then wrapped my hand around the nape of my neck and spoke a little softer, "and Molly . . ."

"That's right," he said. I hated how the mood shifted after I said it, but pretending she never existed was far worse. It was something I'd have to get used to, though five years later, and it still hurt. I wasn't sure it would ever change.

"I thought I saw you last week at the park just down the street. Did you just move here or something?" I asked.

"Yes, actually we did. We moved about a month ago. We wanted little Nora to be close to her school so that she could join after-school programs. We thought it might be easier for her to make friends if she wasn't so far away."

I nodded, looking back to Clara. "Is she yours? With the long dark hair?" I asked.

"Yes, and that's . . . ?" he pointed to Clara.

"Yes! That's Clara. Looks like they've already become friends," I said, watching the girls giggle. I'd never seen Clara so chatty, and I assumed it was because the only other friend she had was the boy who lived down the street. I didn't like boys until I had met Easton. I thought back to the day I met him, when I was eight. It was weird to think that Clara could meet her husband in just three years.

"Well, that makes me feel better knowing Nora has a friend," Dr. Faye said.

"Yeah, me too. I can leave knowing she's not alone today," I said with a smile. And while Clara wouldn't be alone on her first day of kindergarten, I would be alone for the first time in years. I did what any mom would do with her day off. I went home and cried. Actually, I didn't quite make it home; I cried in my truck while sitting in the parking lot. And when I arrived home to an empty house, I cried a little more, but mostly I busied myself with cleaning the house. I checked my watch about a million times, worried I'd be late for pick up and Clara would be afraid. I kept imagining her crying on the sidewalk all alone, and it made my stomach churn. If I had learned anything about myself by now, it was that I didn't deal with life transitions all that well. Six weeks, I told myself. Six weeks until this was the new normal.

I checked my watch again and realized it had only been two hours. I threw the sponge in the sink and ran a hand through my hair. There was something about Dr. Faye knowing about Molly that made it impossible not to feel the raw emotions all over again. It seemed like it was yesterday I was lying in that bed, unable to feel my body and watching the room turn. The glowing shimmer of light bleeding away into dark burgundy. I could still feel the chill in the room on my arms and down my back, even now as I stood at the sink some five years later.

I remembered the girl in the field that day we said goodbye to Molly. A little toe head catching the sparks of magic. I wondered what it would be like to look in the backyard now and see two little girls instead of just one. Was it possible it was the reason Clara didn't play with other children? Had she felt it deep down inside that she lost her twin? Was she lonely?

Easton and I had decided to tell Clara about Molly when she was young. Young enough not to understand. And ever since then, we talked about her here and there. 'Your sister Molly would have loved this, something simple as a reminder that she did, in fact, have a twin. I never wanted her to grow up and realize that we kept it from her. I had held on to too many secrets in my time, and I chose for this not to be one of them.

Clara never said much about her sister. Not after that phase passed. But there was a time when Clara would talk to Molly and "play" with her in the backyard. There was always a part of me that wondered if it was really her. Had she come back to play with her sister? She wasn't the typical imaginary friend, after all. A piece of me knew deep down in my heart that I didn't really believe it but that I just didn't want to let her go. It was my way of holding onto hope that Molly was somehow OK. I later realized that if you want something bad enough, your mind will bend in ways it shouldn't. Connecting pieces of the puzzle that really didn't fit in the first place, but if pressed hard enough may appear to work. And I knew that was the case now when I considered if Clara's new friend at school was something more. I knew it was simply my mind playing tricks on me. But as soon as I thought it, I couldn't shake it. What if that little girl had Molly's soul?

I had only seen the little girl's face for a fraction of a second, and what I gathered, she looked just like her father. He was ruggedly handsome, with bright blue eyes. His hair, though grey now, was most likely dark when he was younger. But why had Clara taken to the little girl so effortlessly? Typically, she was a shy girl. She didn't like other kids, and she had only played with Jackson once in all the years they had lived down the street. I knew it was me unable to let go of Molly. I knew it was seeing Dr. Faye and the old feelings resurfacing that made me dig deep for anything I could grasp onto. And I knew the silence in the house wasn't helping either. But what had stopped Molly from being a Tethered Soul? And if it were genetic, wouldn't both girls be tethered? Molly could be out there somewhere.

It wasn't . . . *impossible.*

By the time I got to school, I was an hour early. I simply couldn't take the waiting any longer. And my mind had been playing mean, mean tricks on me. A rush of adrenaline coursing through my veins told me this was a very dangerous mindset for me to be in. This wasn't as simple as spying on the neighbors. This was a family. A good family. And this was my daughter, the one I'd never met. The one who died. *God, Beck, get it together!*

I gripped my steering wheel, barely holding on to my sanity when Miss Kay's class walked single file before my truck. I sat up tall in my seat and lowered my sunglasses to the bridge of my nose. I peered down the line of kids until I found Clara. Her hand behind her as she held on to Nora's little fingers. My stomach dropped. *See?* They had the same figure. Same stature. They looked . . . similar. Fair skin, chubby cheeks. Nora had dark hair, and Clara was a toe-head . . . But that meant nothing. The fact that they were holding hands *did,* though. They had a bond. But was it a sisterly bond? That was the question. I watched until the class disappeared into the room, and then I had the idea of a lifetime. I lept out of my truck and marched to the front office.

"Hi. I'm a parent of one of the kids in Miss Kay's class, and I wanted to sign up to volunteer," I smiled at the lady behind the front desk.

"I'm sorry, but we don't allow volunteers the first quarter," she said.

"I'm sorry—what?"

"We don't allow volunteers," she repeated.

"You don't *allow* . . . free help?"

"Not for the first quarter, no. It's harder on the little ones when the parents are hanging around. After the teachers establish a routine, and all the kids are used to being dropped off, then we open volunteer enrollment."

I stared at her for a long awkward moment. It was the stupidest rule I'd ever heard. "So I can't sign up?"

"No, ma'am. Not until quarter two. And that's if you make the list."

"The list? I might not make it now?" I asked.

"Many of the parents want to volunteer, and there are only so many spots we can offer before it's a distraction for the kids."

"Can I sign up now?"

"I'm sorry. You'll have to wait until the sign-up e-mail gets sent out," she said. I sighed and checked my watch. I still had ten minutes before Clara got out.

"OK. Thanks," I said, deflated. So much for my brilliant plan. I'd have to find another way to spy on the little girl. *Oh god.* Could I hear myself? Was I going crazy? Was this how my life turns out? I wind up with a restraining order from a five-year-old? And did she really call me ma'am?

Dr. Faye walked up to me as I stood on the curb contemplating my bright future. "You couldn't wait either?" he asked.

I smiled, my eyes wide with alarm. If only he knew what I had been plotting. "I was anxious, I guess," I said. That much was true.

"Yeah, me too."

"Where is Nora's mom?" I asked absentmindedly. "Oh my god. That was really rude of me to assume. . ." I said, searching his face and wishing I could take it back.

"No, it's alright. My wife and I work at the hospital, so our hours are atypical."

"Oh, yeah. Right. Well, I know you just moved here, and our daughters seemed to hit it off, so if you want to get them together at the park, that would be fun. . ." I shrugged. The class let out, and the kids were released one at a time. I watched, waiting for Clara, hoping that she would wear a giant smile on her face. And I may or may not have been looking for Nora, too.

"That would be wonderful. Do you still have my number?" Dr. Faye asked.

"Huh?"

"My emergency number, it's my cell phone."

"Oh, no. I don't have it anymore." I said. Because that would be weird if I hung on to it.

"Let me give it to you then," he said.

I pulled out my phone and typed his name in. When his contact came up with both office and personal cell phone numbers, I pretended to enter it all over again. Clara ran up to me during the last two digits and slammed into my legs.

"Mommy!" she screeched. I kneeled, giving her a tight hug. It was only my first day alone in the house, but I missed her much more than I expected. As I grasped my daughter tight, Nora came up behind her back, and our eyes met for the first time. If I hadn't known any better, I'd think my heart stopped beating for one breathless moment. She was stunning. Her blue eyes, her dark hair, the way her nose turned up ever so slightly. She stole my breath away because, deep down inside, I knew her. Was she really my Molly? Did she recognize me too?

"How was school, Nora?" Dr. Faye asked his daughter.

"Fun. I met a friend," Nora said, pointing at Clara. I stood up slowly, with caution. I was beginning to feel unwell.

"Are you alright, Becca? You look like you've seen a ghost."

I stared at the doctor as he held his blue-eyed daughter. She looked so much like him. There really was no explanation for what I had conjured in my head.

"I'm fine, doctor. Just a little light-headed is all," I said.

"I'm not your doctor anymore. Call me John."

"OK, John," I said, even more uncomfortable now that we were on a first-name basis.

"And do call me. We'll get these girls together," he said.

I blushed, "I will." I watched them walk away before I gathered myself. When Clara and I fastened our seatbelts, she began telling me about her day. A lot of it had to do with her friendship with Nora, and I may have pried just a little.

"So you two are friends?" I asked.

"Yeah!"

"That's so great! How did you know you were friends?"

"What?"

"Like how did you know you wanted to be her friend?" I adjusted my rear-view mirror so that I could see her face.

"Um, because, Mommy. I just know," she said, and like me, it was the only explanation that I could come up with too.

CHAPTER 23

Easton didn't get home from work until nearly midnight. He walked into our bedroom stealthily, trying hard not to wake me, but I hadn't been able to sleep. I watched his silhouette weave in and out of the bathroom, each time wearing one less layer. When he slipped in bed, I reached my hand on top of his chest and placed my head on his shoulder. I opened my mouth several times to tell him about Nora, but every time it ended in silence and shame. I knew that the hole in my heart had never healed from losing Molly. And I knew that this was my way of coping with that loss. I would have believed anything if it made her whole again. And there was the problem.

"What's wrong?" Easton asked when my tears dribbled to his shoulder. "Hey, what's wrong?" he sat up and wrapped his arms around me.

"It's Molly," I cried.

"Oh, honey. It's OK. Shhh. It's going to be OK," he said, rubbing my shoulder like he'd done a million times before.

"No. It's not that. Easton, I think she's alive," I said, sitting up.

"You what?" Easton shook his head.

"Clara met a friend today at school. She said she just *knew* that they were meant to be friends. She just knew!" I searched Easton's face lit by the moon for any inclination he might believe me. I saw no signs.

"Clara made a friend today?"

"Yeah, but she's not just a friend . . . She's her twin!"

"What? She looks just like Clara?" Easton's voice rose, and his back stiffened like a board.

"Well, no. Not just like her. I mean, actually, they don't look alike at all. But —" I stammered.

"I'm sorry, Beck. Help me understand right now, because I can't wrap my mind around this. You think Molly is alive because Clara made a friend?" Easton's tone was now sharp, and I could tell his patience was wearing thin.

"I know. I know I sound crazy. I'm not, though. There's something there. Something in the way she looked at me. Easton, you've got to believe me!" I cried. The desperation in my voice scared me. I didn't recognize myself. Easton sucked in a deep breath and hugged me tightly. I knew this wasn't what he wanted to come home to after a long shift, and it only made me feel more guilty for losing my wits. "I just miss her so much. I have this hole in my heart, Easton, and it won't heal. It never heals!" I sobbed, unsure of when it would ever end. If it ever could end. I cried until I was too exhausted to lift my head, and the tears had run dry. It reminded me of the nights I'd spent balling in my truck when Clara was a newborn. I hadn't cried like this for months, maybe a year.

"I'll tell you what. I'll do a little research when I have some time at work. Just get me some names, and I'll see what I can find," Easton said. I don't know if he said it because he was curious about Molly being tethered or if he said it to make me feel better, but either way, I'd sleep a little better knowing that this wasn't over yet. If my little girl was out there, I had to know about it.

"It's Dr. John Faye . . ." I whispered.

". . . Wait, wasn't that your doctor?" he asked. I looked up to him with all the strength I had left and watched him lose faith in me all over again. "You're not telling me you think he stole our baby . . . Are you?" Easton pulled away.

"I mean, I hadn't thought about it like that but . . . now that you say it . . ." My head spun with the possibilities.

"No. Beck No. I'm sorry. That's just not—"

"I know. I know. I just thought that maybe she became tethered, but now that you say it, he *was* there. Maybe he just stole her." I had been on drugs after all.

"Do you really think he would steal our baby and then move to our neighborhood?" Easton asked.

I thought about it. It would be pretty reckless, and he was a smart guy. "Yeah, you're right. He wouldn't do that."

"Beck, do you think you need to talk to someone?" Easton asked gently.

"Look, there's nothing a therapist is going to tell me I don't already know. So, no. I don't need to talk to anyone. I'll let you go to sleep, but just promise me you will look into Dr. Faye," I said.

"You really want me to look into your doctor?"

"Yes."

"Then promise me something in return. You won't do anything stupid."

"What? What would I possibly—" I started.

"Breaking into somebody's house. Does that sound familiar?" Easton crossed his arms over his chest.

I lifted my hands into the air and glared at the ceiling, remembering that

Easton had been my partner in crime once upon a time. Now, he was a cop. "Yeah, I promise. I will not do anything stupid!"

My alarm didn't have to wake me in the morning. My eyes had still been strapped to the ceiling by the time it went off. I startled, turning it off quickly so that it wouldn't wake Easton. I'd been so ashamed of my late-night conspiracy theory that I hadn't been able to fall asleep. I tried to tell myself it was ridiculous, but when I dropped Clara off at school, and Nora looked at me, my hair stood on end. It took everything in me not to take her in my arms and squeeze her tight. Thank god I didn't. I'd probably have been taken away. As my luck would have it, Easton would be the one to cuff me. I pinched the bridge of my nose and inhaled slow and methodically.

I'd felt hopeless before when Molly passed, but this was a whole new kind of hopelessness. I hoped Nora was Molly. I hoped she was OK. I hoped I wasn't . . . insane. It felt that way sometimes, and now more than ever. I wished that Easton and Clara wouldn't see it. Though that crazy part of me was stronger than I wanted it to be, I'd do what I could to keep it hidden. I didn't believe it was the best side of me.

I sat in my empty house, growing more and more leery of Dr. Faye as the silence ticked by. I cleaned the house from top to bottom and had ventured into an old linen closet just to keep my body moving. It didn't help my mind from wandering, though, and most of my thoughts revolved around what I could do to ensure that both of my daughters grew up in a happy and healthy home. I thought of the future and wondered how I could finagle my way into the girl's life and not be cast aside if she were to move again.

A lawsuit was the only thing I could think of . . . Apart from kidnapping, but that went against my simple rule of not letting my family see just how crazy I'd become. Whatever I did, I couldn't jeopardize my life with Clara and Easton to chase after a life with Molly that may or may not exist. I'd already done that in the first six weeks of Clara's birth. It wasn't fair to any of them, Molly included. And though it was hard to look at Clara and not be reminded of what I'd lost in Molly, I learned to do it over time. I felt terrible that it was an instinct of mine, but there was no right or wrong with mourning the loss of your child. It all had to unfold in its own unique way. I was just grateful that my way ended with Molly coming back to me.

Concealing the battle within me was more difficult than I expected it to be. The best way I knew how was distance. I put as much distance between the Faye family and me as I could. It had been nearly four months since I laid eyes on Nora, and since then, my mental state had declined considerably. Easton and I would argue every time I brought it up, and eventually, I stopped talking about it. But every day at school pick up, I watched from the parking lot. John picked up most days, but on the days he didn't, a nanny would. They were on their second nanny, and I wondered what happened to the first. I hated seeing my daughter go home with a stranger. It had been isolating to watch from afar, and I wasn't sure I could do it any longer. Before today, I had barely been able to hold myself back. I knew my patience was wearing thin.

I bit my lip when Clara and Nora surfaced from their classroom, holding hands. It took a lot of willpower to hold myself back from asking Dr. John Faye for a play date. That's why I stood just outside my truck door when the doctor was under the overhang of the school. Originally, I was trying to wait for Easton to get back to me with his police research, but he never did. I waved when John glanced in my direction, then continued to bite a hole into my lip until the copper taste of blood had surfaced. I shook my head, trying to dispel the crazy, but I knew now it wasn't possible. All I ever wanted after having children was to protect them, and that was instinct. Instinct wasn't a habit that could be changed. I knew from experience. As much as I hated this obsessive, burning side of me, I had to learn to live with it.

Maybe it was the taste of blood in my mouth, or simply that my willpower had finally worn out, but before I knew it, something in me snapped. My legs were moving across the parking lot towards the overhang. My mind a battlefield, my legs taking long forward strides.

"Hi John, how are you?" I asked, coming up by his side.

He turned to me and smiled. "I'm well. How are you doing?"

"Great, hey, I was going to take Clara to the park after school today. Did you two want to join us?" *Don't Beck...*

"Um . . . Sure, I think we have time for the park," John said, reluctantly.

"Great! Oh, but it's kind of cold outside today. Should we just go to my house instead?" *Stop this Beck. . .*

"Umm . . . OK. That would work too."

"Yeah, because I have hot chocolate for the kids, so. . ." I nodded.

"Right," John shrugged, peering at me oddly. Did he think I was coming on to him? Was he into it? My eyes darted about and landed on my daughter.

"Hi, honey. Nora is going to come over for a play date today. Won't that be fun?" I asked, kneeling beside her and taking her backpack.

"Really?" She squealed. They both did. I stood, tossing her bag over my shoulder and smiling at the doctor.

"Follow me?" I asked. He nodded, looking somewhat unsure. I checked my watch. Easton would be home in the next hour, and I wondered if this fell under the 'doing something stupid' category or not. The thought dissipated when I realized I did not have hot chocolate at the house. How was I supposed to be luring this man and his daughter to our house when I didn't even have hot chocolate for the kids?

John pulled into our driveway after me, and when I opened the door, the girls ran down the hall towards Clara's room leaving John and me alone. My face flushed at the awkwardness of it all, and as a result, my mouth ran a mile a minute, trying to fill the silence.

"Come on in. Can I get you some tea? Soda? Water? Um, I don't think I have hot chocolate, now that I think about it, but I'm sure I have some of the fun-sized chocolate bars leftover from Halloween if—"

"No, thank you."

"Oh. OK," I stopped rambling off the contents within our pantry to the man I thought may have stolen my child and closed the cabinet doors. I swallowed the lump in my throat and walked over to the sofa. Sitting across from him, I had to ask myself why he appeared so comfortable. Had he known that I knew? Was he going to steal Clara too? "So tell me about . . . Um. . ." The words caught in my throat as the girls came barreling down the hall, giggling.

"Man, I don't think I've ever seen Nora this happy," John said. I smiled, my eyes lingering on his before looking to the girls. Maybe this wasn't a reckless idea after all. The girls were having fun. Nora squealed and clapped her hands right in front of Clara's face, causing Clara to jump back. Both girls peeked into Nora's hands as she opened them ever so slowly. When her palms were open wide, they both giggled . . . identically. It was music to my ears. Did every little girl have a similar laugh? I didn't think so.

"What are you girls doing?" John asked.

"We're catching lights!" Nora said. My smile melted, leaving me with a low-hanging jaw. Then *smack!* Another clap. This one caught with a skip and a jump. I watched the girls peek inside Nora's hands with renewed hope and scream with delight when nothing had been there. I closed my mouth, but I couldn't stop my eyes from watering. Had this simply been how little girls played? Or had Nora been catching the love she saw surrounding her sister?

The front door opened, and Easton walked in. He stalled taking in the doctor on our sofa, and I used the distraction to blot my eyes. I stood up with trembling hands and motioned to Easton. "You remember Easton, my husband," I said.

Easton placed his hand on his gun, giving John a subtle warning that did not go unnoticed by either of us.

CHAPTER 24

"Easton, so good to see you again." John held his hand out, and I turned away from both of them to pull myself together. Easton had been such a loving and supportive man that I feared the reason he felt the need to warn the doctor with his subtle gesture. Easton was no longer the tall thin guy I had fallen in love with, he had packed on the muscle for his training, and his frame was quite impressive. When he was in uniform, his bullet-proof vest added to his bulk, making him quite intimidating. Why he needed to grip his gun in his own home was beyond me. Had it been because John was so good-looking? Easton had never been jealous before. Or was it something deeper than that? Had he discovered something about him? Something incriminating?

"Doctor," Easton said, taking his hand. The tension was so thick it could be cut with a knife. I sat back down, rubbing the back of my neck and looking anywhere but either of them. I could feel Easton's eyes burrowing into mine, and I knew he was cursing me for taking it a step too far. I didn't blame him. "So, I hear the girls have become fast friends," Easton said, breaking the ice. I took a deep breath, thankful for his presence.

"Yes, I was just telling Becca that I'd never seen Nora take to anyone quite like she has your daughter. It's refreshing to see."

"Is that so?"

"Yeah, it's been such a blessing, really. . ." John said.

"That's great. And you just moved here?" Easton asked as the girls ran down the hall, a trail of fireflies following them.

"This is Nora," I said. Easton looked toward the little girl, and I thought I saw it behind his eyes . . . The recognition. But it was my own emotions that hindered me from reading his face clearly. He watched her carefully, his eyes more than curious.

"Yes, we were closer to the hospital for work, but the schools out there—" John's voice echoed in the background as I watched Easton's eyes on Nora. It was then that I realized something . . . My eyes traveled from him to her. Nora didn't have dark hair and blue eyes like her father. Instead, she had them like Easton. She was nearly his spitting image, whereas Clara had looked just like me.

John continued to talk as Easton turned his attention to me. His eyes were filled with emotion, and I knew he'd seen what I had. I popped to my feet, breaking our gaze, and padded to the restroom before I lost it in front of John. I closed the door, locking it tight before pushing my back up against it. I sucked in several shattered breaths, none of which filled my lungs. I turned to the sink, gripping the cool porcelain top, and closed my eyes. *I was not crazy.* I was *not* crazy. When I opened my eyes and I saw my reflection staring back at me in the mirror, I was no longer a mother with a gaping hole in her heart. I was a mother with hope. I nearly didn't recognize myself.

I knew I couldn't hide in the bathroom forever, and it was a cowardly move in the first place to leave Easton out there alone. He'd probably been going through the same thing that I had been, but he was out there on the sofa having to act his way through it. I felt bad for him and all the acting that he had done in his lifetimes. I went to rescue him, but not before splashing cold water on my face.

"Hey, are you OK? It looks like you've got something up with your eyes?" John asked the second I sat back down.

"Oh, yeah. I'm allergic," I said.

"To what?"

"Cats," I said.

"Dogs—" Easton said.

"Oh?" John looked between us.

"Well, it's fur, really. I'm allergic to fur."

"That's too bad. It's probably me. We have a big cat at home. He's got the long fur and everything."

I snapped my fingers. "That's got to be it," I nodded.

"Well, I should get going. I don't want to make you sick," John said.

"Oh no, you just got here. . ." I checked my watch again. "Hey, I don't know if you guys are busy next Sunday, but it's Clara's sixth birthday, and we were going to throw her a little party. If you guys could make it?"

"Next Sunday?" John asked.

"Yes, just a small party. A couple of friends and the neighbors," I shrugged.

"That's so weird. That's Nora's birthday too."

There it was, the proof I didn't need. I tried to speak but couldn't. "A. Um—" I stammered.

"All the more reason to celebrate," Easton said, opening the front door with a stoic face.

"Yeah, you're right! Let me just talk to my wife and make sure she doesn't have any plans, and I'll get back to you," John smiled before calling for his daughter. *Our* daughter. Easton, Clara and I stared as the two of them walked down our driveway with sad eyes and heavy hearts. Watching her go was hard on all of us. Easton closed the door but didn't say anything. He only stood motionless with his head hung.

"Mommy, Nora says that we all have glowy lights," Clara said, raising her hands in the air.

"She does? *All* of us?" I asked.

"Yes. All of us," she said. My heart skipped a beat, causing me to cough. "What's the matter, Mommy?"

"Nothing, baby. I'm just so happy you made such a good friend." I kneeled in front of her and tucked her blond hair behind her ear. "Um, so do you see these glowy lights, too?" I asked.

"No. I can't see them. But she says they're there. She says she's going to catch one and give it to me." My chest tightened. I didn't know what it meant, but judging by the feeling it left behind; it wasn't a good thing. I turned and looked up at Easton to see the same grave look on his face that I felt in my heart. "Why are you sad, Mommy?"

I turned my attention back to Clara. "Well, baby, she's a good friend for trying. Those little glowy buggers can be hard to catch sometimes," I said, thinking back to the time that I tried to catch one myself. They were as real as the breath in my lungs, but when I grasped at them, my hand only passed through a pocket of warm air.

"I'm hungry," Clara said, snapping me back to the present. I stood up and passed by Easton to get Clara a snack, but not before I snuck a quick glance at him. His face was pale and somber. Eyes transfixed, distant. I didn't know what it all meant, but there was something in his demeanor that told me he did.

Dinner passed incredibly slowly as the conversations we needed to have hung just out of reach. I was bursting inside with every emotion. So much so that I couldn't pick the most prevalent one. My mind was running a marathon while my heart was sputtering. Clara talked about her new best friend—her only friend—while Easton and I stole glances at each other over the roasted chicken. Neither one of us had much of an appetite, and most of dinner had to be packed up as leftovers. By the time Clara went to sleep, and we finally had our chance to talk, neither one of us could find the words.

I sat on the sofa with a lap blanket pulled up to my chin while Easton made a wood-burning fire in the fireplace. Once the fire ignited, he sat next to me, and I draped his lap with half the blanket. A minute of heaviness passed between us before my head found his shoulder. The flames grew taller and wider, crackling and popping. My eyes glued to the white-hot flames. I still didn't know how to feel about the recent news, but at least I wasn't alone. I knew I could get through anything with Easton by my side. I had before. Surely, we would get through this, too.

"You know, I thought I was losing it? I thought I was actually going crazy. I felt myself slipping away . . . and this . . . monster . . . taking over me. It was a monster," I trailed off.

"You could never be a monster, Beck," Easton reassured me.

"I wanted to steal that little girl and run away with her," I said.

"Oh." Easton looked down at me, and I lifted my head off his shoulder to meet his gaze. "Really?" he asked.

"Well, I wasn't going to do it!" I said defensively. "For better or worse. You married me, for better or worse, just in incase you needed a reminder . . ." I said. I raked my hands through my hair. "I don't know. . .I just felt so helpless. And all I wanted to do was protect her as a mother should. It's my only job, and I failed."

"You didn't fail. You're an amazing mother. You've done everything you could—"

"But I lost her. I lost Molly." It was the absolute truth.

"Beck, I didn't want to tell you, but I did some background searches some time ago. Some of it was illegal, and some of it was—most of it was—on social media . . ." I straightened my back attentively. In all my crazy moments, I'd thought of kidnapping, breaking an entry, stalking . . . But I'd never thought of looking up the doctor's social media profiles. It should have been alarming to me, but I moved past it effortlessly. I never claimed to be a saint.

"And?" I asked.

"And, it looks like they adopted Nora when she was around six weeks old."

"They adopted her?"

"Yes."

"So, it *is* . . . Molly. . ."

"I can't say for sure. But—"

"But you know, don't you? You know deep down inside, that little girl is our Molly, don't you?" My voice was broken with the pain. It was in six weeks that I finally turned the corner on my depression. It wasn't because we had a memorial and I said goodbye to Molly; it had been because Molly was no longer alone. Someone adopted her and showed her the love she had deserved all along. That someone should have been me. Easton's eyes locked onto mine as he held in what he really wanted to say. He wasn't fooling anybody. I saw the way he looked at her.

"You know, she has your eyes. . ." I said.

And that's when Easton broke. He held his head in the palms of his hands. Elbows digging into his knees, his back began to quake. I didn't intend to hurt him, and the sight of him crumbling before me wasn't easy to witness. But I knew it was the sight of his confession. He didn't have to say he knew it was Molly because his body was screaming it from the inside out. We both knew it.

I rubbed Easton's back as mindless tears ran down my cheeks. I watched the fire dance till it no longer raged. Then, when Easton had no more left to give, he laid on the sofa and pulled me close to him. My back pushed to his chest and his arm wrapped around me tightly. I traced my finger over his skin mindlessly as I wondered if my life was back on track to becoming untethered. Surely having Molly back would put me on the path of living a happy and fulfilled life. That was if I could find a way to stay in it. Because it was a tremendous threat that the doctor would move, or even something so simple as stop returning my calls. It was all so fragile, like a house of glass. I needed to watch my every move, become strategic. Calculated. Because this was one game I couldn't afford to lose.

After Easton fell asleep, my fingers trailed from the skin of his arm to the metal of my cell phone. I was afraid of what I might find on the internet. All the secrets that were hidden right there in plain sight this whole time. Finding the doctor was easy. Too easy. Within seconds I was browsing through private moments. A baby wrapped tight in a blanket, a close up of Nora that looked identical to Clara. It stole my breath away, yet somehow my thumb found the strength to continue scrolling.

Several pictures with groups of people, family reunions, medical awards—I skipped it all. I scrolled and scrolled until I chanced upon the close ups of my precious daughter. Nora laughing with the tongue of a dog licking the side of her face. Nora at a dance recital when she was so tiny, her pink tutu could have swallowed her whole. Nora blowing out the candles on her third birthday. That's where I stopped because I could no longer take the sight of everything I had missed and shouldn't have.

CHAPTER 25

The week passed by slowly in anticipation of the girls' birthday. Every day a challenge new in itself, but one day closer to spending our first milestone with Nora. It was the driving force that kept me moving through the week. I would need to make this memory the best one yet. The birthday party had to be perfect, and I had to make a good impression on Nora's mother. We had exchanged a few texts about the party throughout the week, and she seemed nice enough, but if she didn't absolutely love me, it would destroy my chances of watching Nora grow up.

The doorbell rang, causing me to sweat through my second blouse even though it was the dead of winter. I opened the door, relieved to see it was only the neighbors. "Hi, Jackson! So nice to see you!" I said, waving the family inside.

I was changing my top for the third time when the doorbell chimed again. I took off running down the hall and ripped the door open—Brooklyn. "Oh, thank god you're here. I'm freaking out. I can't do this," I said, fanning myself in the doorway.

"Hey, hey, it's OK. You're going to be great. They're going to love you."

"You don't understand. They invited their parents too. I have many people I need to impress. And what happens if they recognize the similarities between Nora and Clara?" I asked.

"Come on," Brooklyn said, taking my hand and leading me back down the hall.

"Where are we going?"

"You can't meet them with sweaty armpits, and we can't have this conversation here in the doorway, either," Brooklyn said. I lifted my arm again and huffed at the sight of my underarms. I really had to pull myself together.

Brooklyn closed the bedroom door behind me, and I ran my hands through my hair. "Look, remember what I told you? It's all going to be alright. You have to calm down," she said.

"But how do you know Brooklyn? How do you know?" I searched her eyes, looking for a sign that she knew something I hadn't. She sighed, then turned away from me to dig through my closet. "Brooklyn? Did you have a dream that you're not telling me about?"

"This one. Put this one on," she said, holding up a sun-kissed yellow top.

"Not that one, because yellow is cheery, and I don't want to appear too bouncy or energetic because what if she's an introvert and I just—"

"Put it on!" Brooklyn barked, causing me to jump. I did as she said. I would self-detonate if I didn't have her in times of weakness.

Brooklyn tweaked the buttons, and I asked again. "Did you have a dream?"

"I—" The doorbell rang, and I sucked in a breath. "Forget it. Let Easton handle it," she said. My eyes flickered from my closed bedroom door back to Brooklyn. "I . . . I haven't had a dream, but I know everything will be fine. Who wouldn't love you? Just go out there and be yourself." It was the worst advice. If only she had known just how unstable I had grown to be over the last several months.

I could hear the guests arriving, and I instantly regretted inviting the entire kindergarten class. I did so hastily when I thought the doctor was hesitant about my eagerness to have them over. I figured he couldn't say no if the entire class was coming. It turns out, I was right. He accepted the invitation for the shared birthday party when I announced to the class that invitations would be passed out after school. I had to run home and print off twenty invites that day. High-pitched squeals sounded through the walls, and I assumed Nora and her family had arrived.

"But what if they see through me? What if they can tell that something is off? We're not exactly the family next door," I said, rubbing out the worry across my forehead.

"And I'm not the girl next door, but I do a pretty damn good job of covering that up, don't I?" Brooklyn asked, placing her hands on my shoulders.

"That's because you 're a witch," I joked.

"I'm no such thing." Brooklyn smiled.

"Easton's an actor. He's been doing it forever. It's normal to you guys."

"Becca, Clara is six. You have been doing this for the past eight years now. You have got this. Nobody is going to think a thing about you or the girls. Honestly."

I took a minute to relax. Fill my lungs with one last breath before stepping into the interview of a lifetime. "I'm scared, Brooklyn. I don't want to lose my chance," I said.

"Honey, what's waiting for you out there is not a loss by any means," Brooklyn said, and for the first time, I believed it. I believed that life happened this way for a reason. I couldn't possibly know what that reason was, but I had to believe that I could make the best of it. I smiled and nodded. I started to walk out of the bedroom and into the rest of my life when, "Wait! That yellow is all wrong!" Brooklyn said.

When Brooklyn and I finally emerged from my bedroom, I wore a sky blue sweater and jeans. The house was filled with kids and parents alike. I waded through the crowd, handing out pleasantries and getting caught up in warm hugs. The small talk was encapsulating, and I excused myself several times as I looked for John and his family. I spotted Easton and made my way to him. His eyes looked me up and down, and a grin set in. "You, look—"

"Are they here? Have you seen them?" I asked, my eyes searching the crowd.

"Um, no. But your mother is," Easton's brows rose.

"My mom?" I asked. Last I heard, she would not make the party and living so far away it was completely understandable. Easton tipped his head in her direction, and I followed his line of sight to where my mom stood talking to Clara. I passed by Easton. "Mom?"

She turned to me and smiled pleasantly enough. "Becca! You look marvelous."

"What are you doing here?"

"Well, that's not a warm welcome," she stated dryly.

"I'm sorry. Hi. Hello." I hugged my mom, and Clara took off running when she saw new friends show up. So far, none of them had been Nora. "I just didn't think you were coming," I said.

"I know, but then I got thinking. This weekend was probably better than next month anyhow. Plus, I couldn't miss my only grandchild's sixth birthday party! What kind of grandmother would I be if I did that!" *Only grandchild.* The words rang through my mind, swirling till I felt dizzy. "I see your father didn't come. . ." My mom said. I didn't know what she had against the man. As far as I knew, she was the one who sabotaged their relationship. I shook my head, dispelling the unnecessary stress, and spotted Tanner making his way to the backyard dressed in uniform.

"Excuse me, Mom. I've got to say hello to my brother-in-law," I said, squeezing her shoulder as I left her side. As I approached Tanner, I saw Brooklyn intercept. I hadn't seen them together since the day they ended their relationship. I knew they had spoken, I just hadn't seen it myself, and it was nice to see them together. Tanner was smiling, and it actually looked genuine. I looked down at my watch, which revealed that John and his family were now nearly an hour late. My heart sank, thinking they might not show. I checked my phone to see if they had left any messages when Clara stopped me and asked if we could do the piñata. I sighed, looking around at all the kids. They were growing restless. Regardless of whether the Faye's showed up, I had an obligation to throw one heck of a birthday party.

"If everyone would like to grab a bag over here, and write their name on it, then we can line up and take turns at the piñata!" I called out. The kids ran to the bags, and I fought against the crowd to get to my cell phone. When I did, I had several messages unseen, but only one that I cared about. John had a delivery and would show up late if they could make it at all. Disappointment washed over me, but I still had a sliver of hope that they would come before the party was over. Either way, the show must go on. I owed it to Clara. And for the moment, she hadn't noticed that her sister wasn't here. *Sister.* I hadn't allowed myself to say that word until now, and it made my stomach flip.

I turned on the outside speakers and pushed through some party music. The kids jumped and danced in anticipation for their turn at the piñata. Easton yanked the rope, sending the candy stuffed unicorn soaring through the air. Clara spun, missing her strike, and we all cheered her on. She smacked it when Easton let her, and the crowd of parents clapped. The grin on my face, once wide, shrank when I scanned the yard again. It's an odd thing that happens when you're surrounded by people, yet still feel alone.

The party continued, and I threw myself into hostess mode. There was only an hour left before everyone would head out. Even so, my Molly had not yet arrived. Presents and cake had yet to pass, but I couldn't wait any longer. I sat Clara down in front of her gifts, and she shredded them. I set aside the gifts labeled Nora and the ones that were addressed to both girls. The pile of untouchable gifts grew with the times I checked my watch. Clara screamed over the dolls and stuffed animals while tossing the clothing behind her back. My cheeks burned as I reminded her repeatedly to be kind and thankful. When I looked out into the sea of parents, it was clear that none of them had expectations of graciousness at this age, and many of them laughed it off and nodded, saying their children were the same way.

When Clara's chubby cheeks dimpled, I lost my stomach. The air had turned brisk, and a chill settled down my back. Her sister had arrived; I was sure of it. The loud chatter quieted until I heard nothing at all. Time slowed frame by frame as beautiful Nora swept through the crowd leaving a trail of glowing lights behind her. My heart soared seeing her wide smile as her eyes fell upon Clara and the gifts. Soft tresses of dark hair curled around her face and sprawled over her shoulders.

I watched her in slow motion pull from her mom's hand and dash towards Clara. The sea of kids and parents parted, letting the second birthday girl through. And as the parents took a step back, my eyes stretched from the hand that was left behind. It was when I saw the doctor's wife—the woman dressed in scrubs with blue eyes and dark blond hair—that time had frozen completely. Just for a moment. My heart fluttered . . . faltering. Because I had never foreseen that the mother of my child would be Lindsay.

My best friend, Lindsay, from my first life. The one I hid my cancer from. The one I loved so deeply that I was afraid to let her down with my diagnosis. The one I hadn't seen in twenty-nine years. The mother of my child.

Time resumed, and the noise became deafening. I whipped my head away and ducked through the crowd. I ran from Lindsay. I raced into the house, heading for the confines of my bedroom, when John intercepted me along the way.

"Becca! I'm so sorry we're late. I had a delivery mid-morning," John said, giving me a quick handshake. I looked down at our hands, barely able to discern what he was saying. "Oh, and this is my mother, Mary, and my wife's parents are coming, they're just a little slow," John said, motioning down our driveway. I shook Mary's hand as my eyes stretched to see Lindsay's parents pushing their walkers towards us.

"Nice to meet you. Um, make yourself at home. Everyone is out back. . ." I said as I backed up slowly before turning on my heels and running down the hall. When I reached my bedroom, I slammed the door closed and pushed my back up against it, breathing heavily. The door pushed open, and I lurched forward. Easton and I collided in a spell of panic.

"Where's my hat?" he said, breathless. His eyes scanning the bedroom before landing on mine. I didn't know where his disguise was, and in the moment, I couldn't comprehend much more than the sound of my heart gushing in my ears. But one thing was resoundingly clear—this was the path that would set me free.

WHEN I WAS BECCA GREEN

When I was Becca Green

CHAPTER 1

Had I known that this would be my last life . . . I wouldn't have changed a single thing. That doesn't mean it was perfect. Not by a long shot. My time here wasn't without heartache, pain, or blood-curdling fear, but that doesn't mean it wasn't filled with pride, growth, and unconditional love. Because this life had purpose, and that's all I could ever ask for. And at the end of my days, I knew I'd earned my happily ever after . . .

It was the dead of winter, and the storm had yet to reach its peak. I was warm inside the house and comfortable enough. The medication helped to ease the pain, and though I still felt a great deal of it, the sensation paled in comparison to the emotional pain I'd felt over the years. The knowledge of that perspective was strong enough to knock a few notches off the pain chart. I did my best to hide it from Easton. He had a fire going in the fireplace, as he often did during storms like these. And he played music in the early mornings. The sweet piano notes floated through the air. They drifted down the hall until they reached my heart, placing a smile in my eyes that couldn't quite meet my lips. I wasn't sad, though—only tired. My body ached, and my sleep had been restless. I had a long day ahead of me.

I sat down at my vanity to get ready for the day. I dusted my face with powder and swiped on a bold red lip. It was a little much for the early morning, but I didn't know if I would get the chance to wear it again, and I wanted to feel pretty. It didn't look the way it used to. It settled in the cracks and crevices of my dried lips, and I knew it wouldn't be long before it bled out from under my lip line. It never stopped me from trying, though. I sighed, reaching forward and drawing in a small crystal box I kept my wedding bands in, along with a few other sentimental pieces. I pulled out the tiger's eye drop earrings and slipped them into my lobes. I wasn't as fierce as the tiger, but I liked to think I had some fight left in me. These earrings always reminded me of that.

The room flashed, and thunder cracked, sending Tiny Tommy running to cower under my seat. A small grey mop of hair found solace between the legs of my chair. "It's OK, TomTom. You're OK," I said. I reached down and picked him up. His four pounds felt like a dozen in my weak arms. His tiny frame trembled, and he licked my hand as he cuddled close. "I thought you were supposed to be *my* emotional support pet?" I sighed, looking in the mirror.

I didn't like looking into the mirror. Not because I detested my reflection, but because I didn't recognize it. I had been aging my whole life, but at some point in time, I must have rejected it. My appearance—though Easton would tell me I was beautiful—simply wasn't me. I had always been the same girl in my core. My looks had stretched over two lifetimes. But this? This reflection was new. And I wasn't. It was a hard concept to cope with, even now, after trying for so long.

My hair was stark white and brittle. What was left of it anyway. My eyes seemed to droop, even when I was happy. Everything did. Gravity wasn't a friend of mine. My body had been losing its battle with it for seventy years. It wasn't all bad, though. If I looked closely enough—and sometimes I did—I would see the seventy years of laughter running deep in the lines around my eyes. I would see the decades of love in my cloudy, cataractous eyes. And I would be reminded of the best of times from my overworked smile in the way my cheeks hung like marionettes. It was the face of a well-lived woman, and I had earned it. I was proud of that fact, but it didn't resonate with me.

Until recently, I had felt like my youthful self trapped inside a withering body. But in the past several weeks, that had changed as well. My body hadn't been the only thing to grow weak. My thoughts were slowing down. And sometimes I felt less than capable.

I put Tiny Tommy on the floor and pulled a scarf out from within a drawer. Standing in front of the mirror, my eyes dropped from my bold red lip to my neck. I swallowed, the lump rising and falling before I covered it with my teal scarf. I tied a bow, fluffing it as much as I could to hide what lay beneath. It wasn't a secret by any means—not this time—but it didn't have to be a constant reminder.

I walked down the halls, enveloped in the piano's melody, and found Easton sipping his coffee on the porch. His grey hair swished slowly back and forth in the rocking chair as he watched the storm. Wrapping a blanket around my shoulders, I joined him, sitting in the rocker beside him. He placed a cup of coffee by my chair every single morning. It's where we had started our day for the last thirty years. This porch, that view, a cup of black coffee. I looked out to the grey sky and could barely make out the horizon. The rain pelted down between the cliffs, and it looked like we were caught in a cloud. I wondered if this was what it would be like after I passed and lived in the clouds. Though sunsets were my favorite, this storm was a sight to behold. I sipped my hot coffee and peeked over at Easton when I set my mug down between us.

His eyes were on my scarf. And though I wore it proudly, my heart sank when his gaze met mine and he nodded curtly. His lips pursed as he tried to be strong, but it was mere seconds before the tears broke from deep within. He had tried so hard to stay strong for me. Though he didn't need to. Easton's grey hair shook with his sobs, and my stomach dropped with guilt. He wrapped his arms around his chest in an attempt to stabilize himself. I lowered my gaze, and the teal scarf caught the corner of my eye, reminding me of a time in the past. A time when I desperately needed to hide behind it . . . but for different reasons than now. I pulled the blanket tight around my shoulders. It was hard to witness your best friend bend until they broke. Especially knowing that you were the reason.

CHAPTER 2

As Easton broke, I was taken back to a time when youth was upon me. When my eyes still shined and life was set at a quick and vibrant pace. It was Clara's sixth birthday party, and I was hiding in my bedroom. My heart was pounding, and my eyes wide as I stood in front of the mirror. I picked up my teal scarf, tying it every which way. Nothing I did changed the fact that I had died almost thirty years ago but was still an active member of the Clover community. I couldn't hide who I had been or who I was today. If our friendship meant what I thought it did, Lindsay would know the second she laid eyes on me. And this sheer scarf couldn't hide me from my best friend.

Easton rummaged through the bedroom, doing what he could to disguise his appearance. Hats flew over his shoulder one by one. "How's this?" Easton asked. His trusty old baseball cap was pulled down to his brow, and a pair of sunglasses blacked out his eyes completely.

"You? She's not going to recognize you!" I said scornfully.

"Perfect!" Easton spun on his heels and reached for the doorknob.

"Easton, wait!" I shouted.

"You should . . ." He hung in the balance, eyes traveling the length of my body. "You should stay here . . ."

"Stay here? How am I supposed to stay in our bedroom while I'm hosting our daughter's sixth birthday? Her entire class is out there waiting for me!" I said, running my hand through my hair.

"How are you supposed to go out there? Lindsay will recognize you. It'll be a disaster! A very *public* disaster! Could you even imagine? Just stay here. I'll tell everyone you aren't feeling well," Easton said with a quick but lasting glance of empathy before disappearing down the hallway.

I couldn't stay in our bedroom. Clara and Nora hadn't blown out their candles yet. I'd miss the whole thing. I tied the scarf around my hair, but it did nothing to shield my face. I panicked. Picking up my phone, I dialed the only person I could in a moment like this. Brooklyn. She picked up on the second try.

"Becca? Where are you?" she asked.

"Shhh. Just come to my bedroom. I need you," I hissed.

"Is everything OK?"

"No! Hurry up," I said.

I was standing in front of my mirror, trying to contour my face into a version my best friend wouldn't recognize when Brooklyn walked in. "Brooklyn, I need your help," I said, pulling her into my bedroom and closing the door behind her.

"What's going on? You're missing the party. I doubt you're going to make a good impression while you're hiding in here." Her brows furrowed as she took in my less than stellar makeup.

"It's Lindsay," I said, staring at Brooklyn's unregistering eyes.

"Who is?"

"Molly's mother is *Lindsay*!" I said through grated teeth.

"You mean Nora's mother?"

"Yes!" I hissed.

"OK. Maybe we should just call her Nora from here on out, because it's getting a little confusing . . . and . . . am I supposed to know who Lindsay is?" Brooklyn asked calmly.

I took in a deep breath. I didn't have time for back stories. "Lindsay is my best friend!" I raked my hands through my hair as I paced back and forth.

"I thought *I* was your best friend?" Brooklyn asked, one eyebrow arched.

"You are *now*! But she was *then*," I said.

"Wait, are you saying that your daughter's adopted mother"—Brooklyn placed a finger in the air, trying to connect the dots—"is your best friend . . . from your past life? *That* Lindsay?"

I felt the blood drain from my face. Seeing it with my eyes was one thing, but to hear someone repeat it back to me was a whole new revelation. Recognizing what I was up against, I took a seat on the bed, my head swimming. "Yes. That's exactly what I'm saying. Brooklyn, I don't know what to do. You've got to help me."

"Yeah. Anything. But what can I do?" Brooklyn asked. I raised my head to meet her gaze. Neither of us knew how to remedy the situation. And even though Brooklyn had lived through some tricky times, she'd never been faced with a former loved one playing such a substantial role in a different life. I needed Lindsay to know and love me as the parent of her daughter's friend. But I couldn't have Lindsay recognize me as the girl she had grown up with—the one who had tragically died. It was more than impractical. It was impossible.

The "Happy Birthday" melody erupted in the backyard, and my eyes flicked from Brooklyn's to the window and back again. My face fell. I was missing it. I needed this to be the best birthday ever, so I would make a good impression on Nora's mother. So I could stick around for years to come. So I wouldn't miss moments like this. Like now.

"How am I ever going to be in Nora's life if I can't show my face to her mother?" I asked Brooklyn, my lip quivering.

"It's OK, Becca. We're going to find a way. I promise," Brooklyn said, pulling me in for an embrace. I fought the hug. My arms hung by my side as my head grew heavy on her shoulder. Clapping sounded from the backyard, and I wondered what each of my girls had wished for. I knew my wish.

"You should get a nose job."

I pulled away. "What?"

Brooklyn nodded in all seriousness. "Yeah. You should get a nose job. It's perfect. Lindsay will be *reminded* of her best friend, and she'll love you. But you'll be different—just enough."

"You want me to get plastic surgery?" I asked.

"Everyone's doing it." Brooklyn shrugged.

I scowled, looking into the mirror briefly. Should I? Was that the only way? My trembling hand reached up toward my nose before I dispelled the thought with a shake of my head. Brooklyn turned to the mirror, examining her own profile.

"What if . . . what if *you* pretend to be *me*?" I said.

"What? Now, that's crazy." Brooklyn scowled.

"It's better than surgery! I mean, you just go out there and pretend to be me. How hard can it be?" It was the perfect idea. And I wouldn't have to go under the knife.

"Doesn't John know what you look like; inside and out?" A smirk spread across Brooklyn's face, and I shoved her arm—aggressively.

"Stop that!" I said. She was right though. There was a slight problem. John had been my OB-GYN. He delivered both the girls, and we had been talking for months now at school. There would be no fooling him with a stand-in.

"I don't know what to do, Brooklyn. Can you at least go get some pictures of the girls for me before it's too late?" I asked. I didn't want to be left alone in the confines of my bedroom, but a picture of my girls was something I could cherish for years to come. I hoped someone had snapped a picture of them blowing out their candles. Perhaps Lindsay had.

I sat in bed for the next hour while the party wrapped up. Texts from Brooklyn came in one at a time. Photos of Clara with her arm around her sister. A close-up of Nora with blue cake frosting on her cheeks. And a couple of candid pictures of Lindsay. I zoomed in. The years had been kind to her. She was the same beautiful girl I had known and loved in my last life. My heart ached, knowing my best friend was so close yet so far away. I wondered what it would be like to pick up where we had left off. And it pained me knowing that we could never do such a thing.

Few families lingered behind, but it wasn't until Easton came into the bedroom to retrieve me that I knew it was safe to show myself. Nora's family had gone home, and the threat of being exposed as a Tethered Soul was finally behind us—for the time being. Though I knew more obstacles would be waiting for me in the days and weeks to come.

I helped clean up as the last of the guests parted ways. Clara didn't notice my disappearance, and I was both thankful and crushed at the same time. I threw out dozens of juice boxes and several half-eaten pieces of cake before I cut my own slice. Tanner and Brooklyn flirted in a way they hadn't in a long time, and I stole tiny glances in their direction. I watched him brush his hand against hers as they reached for the same empty soda can. Her face lit up even though she was the one who had ended their relationship. I knew she wanted what she wasn't willing to give. She feared the commitment more than the broken heart. Familiarity has a way of doing that to a person.

Easton took a seat beside me. Removing his disguise, he ruffled a hand through his hair, disheveling it. He offered a small smile, and I fed him a bite of my cake. Neither of us had to speak to know how the other was feeling. In fact, words wouldn't accurately describe it anyhow. We were caught somewhere between a curse and a gift. And it was up to us to decide which one it was going to be.

"Never thought it would be Lindsay," Easton said, ripping a napkin into minuscule pieces.

"Nope," I replied. Clara walked up to Brooklyn and asked for help to remove a doll from its packaging. I watched her struggle before taking the doll to the kitchen in pursuit of a knife. Easton followed.

"Maybe it's a good thing? At least we know Nora will be taken care of properly. Lindsay is probably a good mom, right?" he asked.

"Oh yeah. The best," I said. But that wasn't the part I was worried about. I freed the doll from its packaging and handed it to Clara. She ran away with a smile on her face. I shoveled the last bite of cake into my mouth and resolved to clean up the backyard. Easton and I talked little about it after that. And a part of me felt like my dream was over. There was only one way that I could be in Nora's life now—two if you counted the nose job. But it was risky business. And when losing the chance to have the girls grow up together was on the line, I wasn't sure I could do anything other than fold.

How would I react if my best friend came back from the dead? I played out several scenarios in which Lindsay or Brooklyn had dug out of their grave, but all of them turned into short zombie features in my head. That was the last thing I wanted Lindsay to think of me as. Forget having Nora over for playdates if her mom thought I was of the undead race. I kicked myself for not having made some kind of pact with her. A safe word of sorts.

Later that night, when the lights were out and Easton and I lay in bed and his breathing was far too fast for slumber, I rolled onto my side, staring at him until he asked, "Can't sleep either?"

"No." A long stretch of silence passed, and had I not been watching his eyes blink, I might have thought he'd fallen asleep. "Think we're jinxed?" I asked.

"I do. I think we're plagued with having everything we wanted . . . just out of reach. I mean, you . . . our love— it just ended. Us, when we couldn't find each other. And when we did, you didn't remember." Easton winced, the pain of our reunion still fresh in his mind. "Nora, lost . . . then found. And now this. We've had everything we always wanted dangled right in front of us. What else would it be if it weren't a curse?" His forehead creased, the lines drawn from years of stress.

"I don't know . . . *luck*?" I wasn't sure why I said it. Perhaps I was just playing the devil's advocate. Maybe it was hope. But if luck had anything to do with Lindsay being the guardian of my lost daughter, I'd be forever indebted to somebody or something.

CHAPTER 3

It was a particularly chilly morning the following week when Nora's nanny didn't show at drop-off. I had forgotten Clara's lunch box and was retrieving it from my truck when I spotted Lindsay walking Nora in from the parking lot. *Shit!* My heart beat thunderously as I scampered to my truck, ducking. I hid my face behind my bag, probably drawing more attention to myself than I originally would have. It was silly, really. Lindsay wasn't even looking in my direction, and I nearly had a heart attack. It was easy to see what I had been doing wasn't working. I started my ignition with shaky hands, and the second they disappeared into the school, I sped off much too fast for a twenty-five-mile school zone.

I couldn't live this way indefinitely, and actually, I was surprised I had gotten by as long as I did. That nose job was looking better by the day. With my mind a wreck, the school disappeared in my rear-view mirror. I looked beside me at a stoplight to see Clara's pink lunchbox still waiting to be delivered to the school.

"Dammit!" I hit my steering wheel, and the horn whimpered. Why couldn't it just be easy? Why couldn't Nora's mom have been anybody else? It was at times like this I felt the universe was testing me. And I was pretty sure I was failing. Miserably.

I scoured the parking lot as I came in. There were no more parents dropping children off, and I was pretty sure the coast was clear. My adrenaline was still coursing through my veins as I grabbed Clara's lunch and headed for the front office. I swung the door open, and as soon as I did, I knew I had made a terrible mistake. I stared directly at the back of Lindsay's head as she spoke with Sarra, one of the administrative staff members. The door slammed closed behind me, and I jumped. My jaw hung while I waited for Lindsay to turn around as she inevitably would. But their conversation continued seamlessly. I should have run. I told myself to. But my legs were frozen in fear. Or perhaps . . . just maybe . . . I wanted to be discovered.

"What about Tuesdays?" Sarra asked.

"I don't have a set schedule that I can come in on. I'm a nurse, and my hours rotate week by week. Can't I just pop in the morning of and ask if you need help?" Lindsay asked. Her dirty blond hair had darkened over the years, and her figure had filled out with age. I was frozen still. Afraid to stay and afraid to leave. I didn't know which would make less of a scene.

"I'm sorry, ma'am. You need to sign up on the schedule."

"But I can't commit! How can I help when I can't commit to every single Tuesday?" Lindsay's voice was elevating. She turned to glance at me, where I stood waiting behind her. "Sorry, I just . . ." She whipped her head back around when Sarra continued. I sucked in a deep breath.

"Ma'am. We need consistency for the kids. If you can't volunteer on a set schedule, then we can't have you volunteer in the classroom." A thin sheen of sweat covered my skin, and I kept my eyes trained on the floor.

"But what about parties? I saw you needed help for the class party. I think I will be available." Lindsay flipped through what I imagined was a pocket calendar.

"You need to sign up on the e-mail." Sarra's monotone never changed. If she had good days or bad days, nobody would know the difference. She was neither patient nor impatient. The only thing she ever was . . . was repetitive.

"So, I can't sign up here?" Lindsay asked, her patience wearing thin.

"Ma'am, you need to sign up—" Lindsay shook her head and threw a hand up in the air. Having heard enough, she sighed and spun around for the exit. I dipped my chin and ran a slow hand through my hair, covering most of my face the moment she looked at me.

"Can't even work for free these days without jumping through hoops," she hissed under her breath as she strode by. I sucked in a deep breath when I heard the door close behind her and I knew I was safe. I dared to look behind me, and I watched through the glass door as she walked away.

"Ma'am?" Sarra asked in the tone she wore so well.

I held up the pink lunch box. "Just dropping this off," I said.

"Drop-offs go in the bin to the left," she said, motioning behind her desk. I looked up but didn't see what she had been referring to. I smiled and began to wander. "In the bin. To the left," Sarra said once more. I startled, further embarrassing myself. Once the drop-off bin was located with no help from the staff, I left Clara's lunch and headed for the door.

Relief washed over me as the fresh air reached my lungs. I started my truck and then paused. The engine running, and my hand on the gear. I knew I should let it be, but I couldn't bring myself to drive away. I picked up my phone. My thumb hovered over Lindsay's last text message. I knew she was frustrated, and I desperately wanted to reach out. I wanted my friend back. But sending a text now would be like opening Pandora's box. I typed out a carefully thought-out message, and before I could hit send, I deleted the entire thing. I tossed my phone into my lap and pulled my gear into drive. I had no business texting Lindsay like we were friends.

The torment in my head raged on, and by the time I was halfway home, my cell phone had found its way into my hands once again. I typed out my message, eyes ticking up to the street between each word.

Hey there. I was thinking about volunteering for the class party, but I can't find the e-mail. Can you forward it to me? I don't know why they make these things so difficult!

A horn blared, and the phone fell to my feet. I whipped my head around to see a car nearly side-swiping me and a red traffic light passing overhead. My heart hammered against my chest, and my hands trembled as I gripped the steering wheel. Reaching down toward the floorboards—careful to keep my eyes on the road—I retrieved my phone. And as safely as I could, I opened the text message I had started and hit send.

Then, to keep my mind off the line of communication I had just opened, I called Brooklyn. She was at Stanford's Coffee, and I was on my way. What I needed now was a friend. A friend that knew me and what I was going through. And probably coffee, too.

I entered the coffee shop, and Brooklyn waved me over to a table for two in the corner. A coffee was waiting for me on the table, and I smiled when I saw the foam latte heart. Inevitably, it reminded me of Lindsay and how she used to teach me latte art.

"Hey. I got you a cappuccino. How are you?" Brooklyn asked.

I lifted my bag off my shoulder and draped it across the back of my seat. "You didn't have to do that!"

"My treat." Brooklyn smiled.

"Thank you. I think I needed this. I nearly crashed my car after running a stop sign. I just can't focus lately," I said, taking a sip.

"Sounds like you need to be more careful. What's got you rattled? Is it your friend?"

I shrugged. Of course, it was, but I didn't want to bother her with all of my problems. It seemed to be one-sided lately, and I felt like an awful friend for it. "It's nothing. How are you? How are things going with Tanner?"

Brooklyn's eyes lit up. "We've been texting again. I know it doesn't mean much, but I missed it." The bridge of her nose turned pink, and the blush spread to her cheeks.

My cell phone pinged, notifying me I had an incoming text. I bit my lip. "Do you want to get back together with him?" I asked, glancing down at my bag.

"I don't know Bec. I do, but I know it's no good for either of us. He wants a family. I can't give him that." A sadness crossed her eyes as she looked around the room.

"Why not? I don't get it, Brooklyn. Why don't you give up this free spirit act and just let yourself be happy? I mean, you want him, don't you?" I asked.

"I . . . It's not that easy."

"Actually, it is. Take it from me. I did it."

"But we're not the same, you and I," she said.

"Well, I don't see why not. Have you had any dreams about it?" I asked.

"I don't have dreams about myself. It's the only thing I don't dream about."

I frowned, and my phone pinged again. This time, I reached for it, unable to resist my curiosity any longer. "Well, that has to be frustrating," I said. After reading Lindsay's text message complaining about Sarra and the school's protocol on volunteering, I cracked a smile and let out a stifled giggle.

"What's that?" Brooklyn asked.

I typed back a snarky text to Lindsay with a goofy smile on my face. "What?" I asked, my eyes glued to my phone.

"Who are you texting?"

"Oh, it's nothing." I quickly stashed my phone in my bag.

"Oh my god!" Brooklyn's jaw dropped.

The tables quickly reversed, and now I was the curious one. "What?"

"Are you having an affair with the hot doctor!?" Brooklyn cupped her mouth.

"What? No! I'm . . . I'm texting Lindsay!"

Brooklyn's face fell. "Oh," she said, with a hint of disappointment.

I rolled my eyes. "I ran into her today at school. She didn't notice me, but we've been texting," I said. My phone pinged again.

"You know that's never going to work, right?"

I sighed, knowing she was right. When I read the incoming message, it was so classically Lindsay that it made me sad. Like a little taste of a memory that I could never get back. And it reminded me of what Easton had said about everything we ever wanted being just out of reach. "I know," I said, shrugging. "Um, she's asking if Clara could go home with Nora on Friday after school. Would you be able to stand in for me and pick her up?" I asked. An unsure grin on my face.

"You want me to pretend to be you?"

"Yeah, I mean, you don't have to do much. Just be polite and pick up Clara. It's not like you have to stay and chat or anything."

"And what if John is there? He'll know I'm not you." Brooklyn's eyes searched mine.

"Well, just say you're my friend then, and that I was unavailable. Think you can do that for me?" I asked. I knew it was a big ask, but only another Tethered Soul could truly understand.

Brooklyn sighed, looking down at her coffee. "Yeah. I can do that. Better me than you," she said.

"Thank you! I'm going to text her right now," I said, typing out a reply as fast as I could. I knew it wasn't a fix for the future, but it was a decent patch for the time being. And I was excited that the girls could hang out again.

That Friday, Clara was thrilled to be going home with Nora after school. I hadn't been to the Faye's house before and I was curious to hear every last detail from Brooklyn. When Lindsay texted me their home address, I immediately made plans for a drive-by in the near future. I exchanged a few texts between Lindsay and Brooklyn during the day regarding pick-up. And when the evening came, I had pizza ready for dinner as I waited impatiently for Brooklyn to arrive with Clara. I ate breadsticks while staring at the front door. And when a car pulled into my driveway and headlights brightened my windows, I rushed to the front door.

"Mommy!" Clara ran into my arms.

"Hi, baby! How are you?"

"Good. I had so much fun!" she said.

"You did?"

"Yeah! I want to go again!"

"Hey," Brooklyn said, with wide, telling eyes, and I immediately knew that my plan hadn't played out as seamlessly as I hoped.

"Oh no. What happened?" I asked. Brooklyn stepped inside, and we both peered down the hall to make sure the little ears were out of earshot.

"So, I went to pick up—"

"Was their house nice?" I asked.

"Yes. Focus," Brooklyn said.

"Right. Sorry."

"And Lindsay opened the door. She shook my hand and said, 'You must be Becca, it's so nice to meet you,' or something like that. And I just smiled and shook her hand. She didn't think twice, and she invited me in while Clara gathered her things." Brooklyn spoke fast and quietly.

"OK. Good. There's pizza here, by the way," I said. Brooklyn glanced at the pizza and ultimately grabbed a slice. "Go on." I encouraged her.

"So then, she said, 'I ended up volunteering at the class party. I was surprised I didn't see you there,' and then I said, 'Volunteering isn't my thing,' and she gave me this weird look, and things went sideways from there."

"Oh no! You didn't!" I said.

"What?"

"I told her I wanted to volunteer for that party," I said, placing my forehead in my hand. "She thinks I'm a total flake now."

"Well, if she didn't then, she definitely did when John rounded the corner and she found out I was an imposter!" Brooklyn said nonchalantly.

"What!?" I grabbed hold of my head, making sure it wouldn't spin around completely.

"Yeah. He said, 'Who's this?' And Lindsay was like, 'What do you mean? It's

Clara's mom,' and he was all, 'Um, no. It's not actually—'" Brooklyn made her best male doctor's impression.

"Holy shit. Please stop! This is unbearable!" I said, standing up from the dining table and pacing the length of the small kitchen. Before today, my chances of watching Nora grow up were slim, but now that they thought I was lying about who I was, it was nearly impossible. I might as well say goodbye to Nora all over again.

"It's fine. I mean, I don't think it was *that* bad."

"What do you mean?" I asked.

"Well, I just explained to them that you were busy, so I was helping out." Brooklyn shrugged it off.

"But you said that you were me?" I asked.

"No! No. Technically, I didn't say that. It's not our fault that Lindsay interpreted it that way," she said with arched brows.

I came to sit down beside her at the table. "Brooklyn, I'm so screwed," I said, my forehead resting on the table.

"Hey, I did the best I could under the circumstances," she said.

"I know. Thank you. I'm not saying any of this is your fault. It's not. It's my fault." I looked up at Brooklyn and forced a smile. ". . . I should have just gotten a nose job."

Brooklyn giggled just as Clara reached the table. The three of us picked at pizza for dinner while Easton worked late. And it wasn't long before two of my favorite people in the entire world made me forget all my problems. However, it was long after Brooklyn had gone home and Clara was down for the night that I lay in bed thinking about all the worst possible scenarios that may come from baring my face to my former best friend, and now, the mother of my child.

Any way I sliced it, the risk was exponential. What if she thought I had faked my own death? What kind of person would do that? If Lindsay didn't believe me or, worse, thought I was driven by dark forces, I'd lose Nora all over again. But, if Lindsay accepted me, I'd lose my tether, and this would be my last life with Easton. It was no surprise that my only two options made me sad. The stakes were high in each likely outcome. But there was only one thing driving me now, and that was to protect my girls. And I was willing to give up my immortality if it meant I could do so. My mind was set. I'd confront Lindsay, and I would tell her everything, whether or not she was open to hearing it.

CHAPTER 4

It took nearly two weeks before I could get Clara a playdate with Nora. Lindsay had been slow responding to my text messages, and I was convinced that John had a cold shoulder at pickup. I knew the stunt I pulled with Brooklyn was bad news, but it was clear after the following weeks that it was worse than I imagined. I tried to explain, but it didn't translate well. On this particular evening, both Easton and John were working late. I used it as an excuse to have a glass of wine with Lindsay after our kids played. I must have practiced what I'd say to her a dozen times. None of it was right. I'd have to wing it, and I had never been good at that.

The bottle of wine had nearly slipped out of my sweaty palm just before I rang the doorbell. Her house was beautiful. Massive compared to mine. Rose bushes lined the walkway leading up to decorative double steel front doors. A blurred figure approached as I watched through the glass behind the steel. The small security camera in the corner hadn't gone unnoticed, and I knew there was no turning back now that I'd been on camera. The ominous dusk sent chills down my spine as the figure approached and I heard the footsteps. Was it Lindsay? Her nanny? I kept my sunglasses on so I wouldn't startle her before my entry. If there was one small goal that I had for today, it was to make it past the threshold. The knob turned as a lump stuck in my throat. This was either the stupidest thing I had ever done in my life or the bravest and most courageous act of love I could think of. Either way, I was about to pass out.

The door opened, and Lindsay smiled before me. She had a casual air about her. Jeans and a T-shirt, twisted leather sandals. She waved me in, and I could see her brows pull together as she assessed me for the first time. Her house was beautiful from what I could see, but dark through the lenses of my sunglasses.

"Hi, it's so nice to finally meet you. I brought some wine; I hope you like red," I said, my head spinning.

"Oh, yeah, I do. Thank you," Lindsay said, taking the wine from my sweaty grasp. "Come on in." I wiped my palms on the legs of my jeans as I followed her through the house. I passed by photos on the foyer table and pulled my glasses down to the bridge of my nose, glancing as I passed by. A grand vase of fresh tulips dressed her dining table. It looked like something out of a magazine. I folded my glasses in my shaky hands and sucked in a broken breath of air before we reached the kitchen. A large granite island with a farmer's sink graced the center of the room. French doors opened up to a patio fountain, and the trickling sounds of water helped ease some of my anxiety. Lindsay busied herself fetching wine glasses from the cabinet as I set my things down on the countertop slowly. I stood meekly in the corner, arms crossed over my chest as I waited for the shrill that was about to come.

"We're still settling in, so sorry for the clutter. It's just been so hectic around here with work and school . . ." Lindsay said, opening the wine. The house was meticulous. Not a box in sight. I came to her side, timid and slow as a cat on the prowl. Lindsay smiled, her eyes finally lifting to mine as she held out my glass of wine. The stem slipped from her hand, and her smile shifted from poised to panic. And right before it came crashing down, and red wine surged everywhere, I thought I saw a hint of grief. That look . . . that horrified look, like all the pain of the day I passed had flooded back for just one second.

Wine spattered everywhere, and the glass scattered across the floor. "Oh, god! I'm so sorry!" Lindsay said, immediately bending down to pick up the broken pieces of glass. I looked down at her; my jeans stained with wine. She murmured something inaudible, shaking her head in distress. I lowered, slowly. My eyes focused on her.

"I don't know what's gotten into me," she said.

I took a deep breath and reached for a broken piece of glass by my feet. "I do," I said. Lindsay deliberately raised her gaze to meet mine. Our eyes connected, hers in inquiry. A moment passed as wonder traveled through her eyes. Then she was on her feet. Quickly, she spooked. Taking a few steps back. Her mouth gaped, and her hand, full of broken glass, began to tremble.

"Mommy!" Clara shouted.

Both Lindsay and I shouted back. "Glass! Careful, there's glass!" It was all it took before the girls giggled and took off running in the opposite direction. My eyes flickered between Clara's back as she disappeared down the hall, to Lindsay's face of utter disbelief. Both of our arms outstretched to keep the girls away. Silence stretched between us, but I had no words to make this any easier.

"I . . . I'm sorry. I . . . It's just, you look like someone I used to know," Lindsay said. She laid the glass down on the table behind her and dusted off her hands. Her eyes filled with hurt. I could only imagine what it was like for her to lose me. If I had lost her, nearly thirty years ago, I would be beside myself. Would it be easier for her if I were back? Would it be better that she could talk to me again? Was this a gift of friendship?

I cleared my throat yet spoke softly. "Everly," I said, in a knowing tone.

What passed through Lindsay's face was unrecognizable to me, but the single tear that rolled down her cheek was no mystery to either of us. "How did you know that? Who are you?" The sorrow melted away with the hint of conspiracy.

I took a step forward, the glass crunching under my shoes. Lindsay took a step back. She was afraid of me. I dropped my gaze to the puddle of wine beneath my feet. I often wondered how I had ended up in this mess. And this very moment was no different.

"It was nearly thirty years ago. I had cancer. I was terminal," I started. Lindsay grabbed her stomach and started heaving. I started for her but then stopped myself the moment she cowered. I stood at a distance as she worked through it. I wasn't sure she was listening, but I continued anyway.

"I didn't want to tell you. I was afraid our friendship would change. I was afraid you would pity me. And that was the last thing I needed. Not just from you, but from anyone," I said. Lindsay spun around. She staggered out of the kitchen, her hand grasping at the wall for support. I followed her, keeping my distance. I needed her to hear me. And I needed to say it now before I was no longer allowed in her house.

"I was afraid of dying, but I was even more afraid of change!" Lindsay grabbed the back side of her sofa, her knees faltering just before she went down. "Lindsay!" I lunged to her side. I patted her cheeks, and her head wobbled ever so slightly. She was out cold. I surveyed the room for help. John was working late tonight. The girls must have been playing outside. "Lindsay?" I asked, patting her cheek some more.

She moaned, twisting her head and wincing. She reached up to grab the back of her head as her eyes parted. Just as I came in to focus, she screamed. Eyes wide with horror, she scooched back on the floor, gaining as much distance from me as she could. I glanced around, worried the girls might be alarmed.

"You! You!" she stammered.

"Lindsay! It's me! I'm not going to hurt you!" I said. She rose to her feet, but her legs were wobbly as she shifted her weight from side to side. "You should really sit down. Can I help you sit down?" I motioned to the sofa.

Though Lindsay looked at me with fear in her eyes, she did what I said. Slowly, she made her way to the sofa. I reached out to support her elbow, and she yanked it away, glowering at me. I held both hands up in the air like a white flag if I ever had one. "There, do you need anything? Can I get you some water?" I asked, glancing back at the kitchen.

"Wine. You can get the wine," she said. I nodded and rose to my feet. "Bourbon! Get the bourbon . . ." Lindsay pointed to a cabinet across the room. I rummaged through the countless bottles of hard alcohol before I found the bourbon. Shot glasses were on the side of the cabinet, and I placed two on top of a cutting board that was adorned with limes. I slowly walked back to Lindsay, careful not to spill on my already stained jeans. She took hers, knocking it back before grasping for my shot, too. It looks like I'd have to do this sober.

"You're not Beck. It can't be. It doesn't make any sense." She took another sip of her amber shot. Her eyes unfocused before her.

"Easton was easy to love," I continued. "He was the only one who understood me in a time I didn't know myself. He knew things, too. He knew about the path I was on. How unfortunate I was. How it felt to have a death sentence. He knew what I was going through . . . and he knew what I was up against. Because he had done it all before."

"Done what before?"

"Died," I said.

Lindsay's gaze lifted to meet mine. "He'd died before. Many times."

"No. No, this doesn't happen," she protested, her mind clamping down on what she had known to be real for all these years.

"His soul . . . it was immortal. No matter how many times his body died, he would come back to do it all over again. I don't know how. I don't know why. He said it was a curse." I hunched over my crossed arms as I sat opposite from Lindsay. I felt the need to reach out to her, but she was too far away.

"So what happened to you then? They said you died. I went to your funeral." Lindsay knocked back the rest of her shot, and the girls ran by the window outside. I watched them with fear in my heart. I truly hoped this wouldn't be the last time Clara could play with her sister. I had to choose my words carefully.

"Easton became my only support. I pushed him away. But I needed him. The day I gave into him was . . . well, I don't remember much, but it was the best choice I had ever made for myself. I wanted to marry him. Even if it was for a short while. I wanted him to know that he was the love of my life. And I had little to give in my final months. So, I gave him my hand in marriage. It was beautiful. It was private. And I knew that my parents were throwing a reception for us when we got back. It was supposed to be a surprise, but I had overheard them planning it one morning. I knew you were there when the cops showed up."

"How? How did you know? They said you died!"

"I did. It was my fault. I . . . I distracted Easton from the road. It was raining, and he swerved into oncoming traffic. The car went over the bridge." My voice trailed off into the distance. It was the one memory I kept clear as day. The one I wished I could forget. "We drowned," I said in no more than a whisper.

Lindsay cupped her mouth. Any conspiracy she had thought of me had temporarily been dwarfed by compassion and empathy for her former friend. "You drowned . . ." she repeated.

"We survived the crash. It took me a little while before I came to, but when I did, my seatbelt was jammed. The doors wouldn't open. And Easton wouldn't leave my side. We didn't die from the crash, we drowned in the river. After it happened, I saw everything. I saw the past and present. I saw the future. And then . . . and then, I did it all over again. Same soul, same body. Different family, different life."

Lindsay sniffled and swiped a tear from her cheek. She fetched another two shots of bourbon, but this time, she offered one of them to me. "And you . . . you just . . . what? Started over?" Lindsay evaluated me, head to toe, as she counted out the years on her fingers. Her face flushed when she realized this was no tall tale.

"Yeah, I did. I just started over. I didn't think a thing of it. I had no memory. Just an unfounded and irrational fear of the water. And if I'm being honest, when I look back, there were some nightmares, too."

"How are you here? Now?" Lindsay asked, confused in her own right. I didn't expect this to be easy for her to understand. It was impossible, after all. I didn't know what kind of world I was living in, but it wasn't the one I had always known to be true.

"It's a long story. But I guess the short answer is . . . fate?"

CHAPTER 5

Lindsay sat coiled on the sofa, hugging a shot glass filled to the brim with warm, silky bourbon. She stared at me sideways, waiting to call my bluff, when the doorbell rang.

"Pizza!" Nora screamed. Clara rounded the corner after her sister as they barreled toward the front door. Lindsay pulled her gaze from mine, looking over her shoulder at me before disappearing into the foyer. I closed my eyes and took in a deep breath as I slouched against her deep-seated sofa, expanding my lungs until they hurt. I ran my hands through my hair and looked around. Dusk had given way to nightfall, and it was dark outside. I made my way to the kitchen and began to clean the spilled wine with paper towels. I could hear the girls make their way to the dining room. Shortly thereafter, Lindsay came into the kitchen to fetch plates.

"Oh, you don't have to clean that," she said.

"It's OK. I don't mind." Lindsay grabbed the broom and swept. Neither of us spoke, though I imagined her mind was anything but quiet. With the two of us working together, the mess was cleaned up in no time. We joined the girls at the dining table for dinner. Lindsay stole sideways glances at me in between the fragmented conversation and bites of piping hot pizza. Every time I caught her questioning eyes peeking in my direction, my stomach would drop with frightening speed.

"So, John is working late tonight?" I asked, even though I already heard he was. It was the very reason I had picked tonight to have wine. I couldn't have had him here while Lindsay melted down.

"Yes. And he was your doctor, correct?" she asked, trying to put the pieces together.

"Yes! He was. Small world, huh?" But Lindsay only stared at me with a deep crease in her forehead. "Um. Girls?" I pried my eyes from Lindsay's suspicious eyes. "Did you know that?" I asked.

"What?"

"That Nora's dad was the doctor that delivered . . . Clara?" I said, nearly faltering in the end.

"What?" The girls giggled.

"It's true!" I laughed with them, though my laughter was rooted in nervousness, not humor. Lindsay's eyes softened, but she was far from laughter. "Nora's dad was the first one to hold Clara as a baby. I remember the day like it was yesterday. He handed her to me and announced that she was a baby girl—"

"You thought I was a boy?" Clara asked, and Nora laughed.

"I didn't know what you were. I didn't find out beforehand."

"Why?" she asked.

"Well, that's a good question. And one I don't have an answer for. I guess I thought it would be fun to have a surprise. Like being surprised on your birthday. You know what I mean?" I asked.

Clara nodded, deep in thought. "Mom, did Dad deliver me, too?" Nora asked. My heart lurched and I let out a forceful cough. It pained me to hear her ask. A girl should know where she came from, and Nora did not. And neither did her mom.

"No, honey. I had a different doctor," Lindsay said.

"Why?" Nora asked.

"Um, because, it's standard practice to not have personal relationships with your doctor."

"Why?"

"Because it can cloud judgment, honey. Now eat your pizza," Lindsay said, her eyes shifty. Only I had known the real answer. And I could now tell that Lindsay was uncomfortable for more reasons than one. She had never told Nora that she was adopted.

When the girls finished their pizza, Clara asked if we could stay a little longer. I glanced at Lindsay, assessing her capacity for my presence. But when I couldn't get a gauge on it, I told Clara we could stay for just a bit longer while I helped clean up. The girls squealed as they scampered off, leaving dirty plates and half-eaten crust in their wake. I smiled apologetically at Lindsay as I picked up after the girls.

"If you really are Beck, then where did we work together?" Lindsay asked, narrowing her eyes.

"Easy! Fresh Grounds! You always had the best latte art. Mine was a muddled mess," I said, remembering the days when Easton would walk into the coffee shop and my heart would be set ablaze.

"When did we meet?" she asked. Brows raised.

"Come on. The sixth grade." I shrugged. If she was testing me, she would have to try harder than that.

"What teacher?"

"Mr. Richio," I said with confidence.

Lindsay stared at me, unblinking. "Anyone could have known that." She shrugged.

"Try me again?" I dared her.

"OK. Who was my first kiss?" Lindsay asked, squaring off with me as she popped a hand on her hip. A smile spread across my lips because this was a game I knew I would win. And this was something she had never told another soul. Something she had barely confided in me in the first place. And something I couldn't forget.

"Grant Stevenson!" I pointed my finger at her chest. Her eyes rounded and the thin, straight line of her lips softened. "He was your first kiss. It was in second grade, and you kissed behind the slide. He told everyone, and you denied it for years. He turned into a giant nerd, and you were his only claim to fame. You were so afraid that if anyone found out he'd been your first kiss, your reputation would go down in flames!" I pointed.

The best part was seeing her finally crack, giving in to everything we both wanted but were so afraid to reach out and take. Our friendship.

"And you know what the funny part is? He's totally hot now!" I said. Lindsay laughed, and I chuckled. "It's true! I saw a picture of him online!" The internet was a mysterious world, both wonderful and overly invasive at the same time.

"How do you know that? I never told anyone that!" Lindsay said, wiping her eyes.

"You told me. And I remember it because that's the kind of thing a best friend keeps locked up tight." I shrugged. Our eyes locked onto one another's, and she smiled at me, not completely understanding but accepting nonetheless. "I remember. It's me. I'm here," I said, wrapping my arms around her and burying my head into her shoulder. I cried when I felt her slowly reciprocate, embracing me.

"I've missed you so much!" Lindsay cried.

"I've never stopped thinking about you!" I confessed.

"Never!" she agreed.

"You've always meant so much to me! I love you so much! I should have told you more often! I'm sorry. I'm so sorry!" I bawled. All the stress that had built from the moment I laid eyes on Lindsay at the girls' birthday party had peaked and now was spilling out as I sobbed on her shoulder.

"No, I'm sorry! I love you, too!" We stood there in the kitchen. Two friends reuniting. Thirty years after one's early departure. And it was like no time had lapsed at all. We weren't kindred spirits like Clara and Nora but similar in an unexplainable way.

The hours flew by. Both Clara and Nora fell asleep during a movie while

Lindsay and I rehashed old times. Her memory was far better than mine. She told me how she and John had met. And how she swore she had recognized Easton at the coffee shop, and then again at the house. She told me about my Pop—which I had known—and then she told me about my mom.

"I work at Sunny Hill Assisted Living. Your mom is a patient there. She has dementia. I've been taking good care of her."

"My mom has dementia?"

"Yeah. It's bad. She no longer remembers who I am." Lindsay scratched her head, deep in thought. "Maybe you should visit her?" she asked after some time.

"Really? You think?" I asked.

"Well, I mean, if she doesn't remember you . . . maybe it's kind of . . . perfect? In a way..." Lindsay said with empathy-filled eyes.

"Yeah. I guess you're right. Would you be able to get me in?" I asked.

"Absolutely! Just say you're a volunteer, and I'll sneak you onto the schedule. Let me know whenever you want to come in, and I'll have you directed to her room, even if I'm not there. But, if you are going to come, I would probably plan it soon. I'm not sure how much longer she has," she said. I nodded, remembering the time I said goodbye to my pop. It didn't end well.

My phone buzzed. A text message from Easton. "It's late. I should probably get going."

"Yeah. I'll walk you out."

I scooped up Clara's limp body and walked her out to the car. I buckled her in and shut the door before turning to Lindsay. "I'm going to see you again, right?" I asked, worried that she would wake in the morning with regret.

"I mean. I would like that. Would you like that?" she asked.

"I just want us to go back to how we were, before . . ." I shrugged. Lindsay chuckled.

"We're not kids anymore. Have you seen my hair?" she joked.

"I mean, like the way things *should* have been."

"Yeah, only you've still got your youth," she teased.

"But you can overlook that, right?" I asked.

"Look, I can overlook your youth if you can overlook my grays. Deal?"

It was a deal I couldn't pass up.

"Deal," I said. I gave her a hug and told her I loved her. And we planned to meet up the following day at Sunny Hill. Overall, it went better than I could have hoped for. I had my friend back, and things were looking up. There was only one small piece of information I hadn't disclosed. And that was because I was sure it would send Lindsay scaling the walls. Surely, she would put as much distance between me and my family as possible if I told her I had not only come back from the dead but claimed my stake on her daughter, too.

Secrets were terrible to keep. The weight heavy upon my back. I had carried so many of them throughout the years, I'd learned they often weren't worth it. But that didn't keep me from withholding the truth. There was an art to timing, and I knew that the timing wasn't right with this particular secret. Lindsay had a lot to unpack after our talk, and I needed her to trust that my heart was pure. I didn't want to take Nora from her, even though I wanted nothing more than to have her under my roof. I'd still be honored if I could watch her grow up under Lindsay's wing. She was doing a fine job. And I was content with that.

Easton helped me unload Clara from the car. She slept peacefully in his arms and slipped into bed without ever waking. As soon as her door was closed, he turned to me in question. "How did it go?"

"Well, at first, not great. I think I ruined my favorite jeans," I said.

Easton looked down at my thighs. "Then?"

"Well, then she fainted and started knocking back shots of bourbon."

Easton looked at me sharply. "I'm afraid to ask what happened next," he said, brows furrowed.

"Then she believed me! And we're friends again!" I said, a gigantic smile plastered on my face. Easton cracked a grin and pulled me into his chest.

"Oh, I'm so happy. I really needed that win," he groaned.

"Long day at work?" I asked.

"Long, long day."

"Well, I might be able to help with that?" I pulled away from his grasp and unbuttoned his top button. The desire to celebrate the turn of events flickered inside me.

His eyes gleamed down on me, and his hands responded by running the length of my body. I unbuttoned three more buttons before spreading his shirt opened and planting kisses on his chest. His hand wrapped around the nape of my neck as he pulled me in, kissing me deeply. I closed my eyes and let the stress roll off me in waves, crashing at my feet.

I pulled away for a breath, biting his lower lip gently, and our eyes caught just before he grabbed me and threw me over his shoulder in one swift motion. I screamed in delight and clapped a hand over my mouth, afraid to wake Clara. Easton ran down the hall as I muffled my wails of laughter in my hands. He nearly decapitated me with the door frame when he spun around to close the door behind us. I screamed again. Then, I was falling onto the bed. I braced myself as Easton jumped on top of me, silencing my squeals with his kisses and unwinding my anxious body until I longed for the night's sleep.

CHAPTER 6

I checked the directions on my phone one last time, making sure I was headed in the right direction. It didn't seem like a road that an assisted living home would be down, but I drove slowly, checking the signs anyhow. When I came upon one that said Sunny Hill Assisted Living, I pulled in and found a parking spot. It was sad to think that my mom had ended up here after losing her daughter and husband. And I wondered how often my brother visited her with the kids.

The live-in facility smelled like a mixture of hospital antiseptic and crocheted blankets. A small gathering of seniors sat quietly in an open game room to the left. None of them spoke, and none of them were watching the TV. I bit my lip as I approached the front desk, worried about what state I would find my mother in, and worse yet, if she would recognize me.

"Hello. Um, is Lindsay Faye working today?" I asked, playing with the collar of my shirt. Even though it hadn't been tight, it felt somewhat restricting.

"One moment." The lady picked up the phone and spoke softly into the receiver. "She will be out shortly. You're welcome to take a seat," she said, with an open palm. I saw the few chairs lined against a wall and smiled before sitting. I clutched my bag in my lap, wringing out the straps. I didn't know why I felt so nervous. If my mom couldn't recognize Lindsay, and she was in the late stages of dementia, surely she wouldn't recognize me. Especially after not seeing me for thirty years.

Lindsay and I had been on good terms when I left her house the night before, and I doubted that she'd reconsidered in such a short time. I rubbed my arms, though I was anything but cold. It was an uncomfortable feeling knowing I, too, could end up in a place like this. Or more like a *state* like this. I knew a little bit about what it was like to have memories escape you. And I knew enough that I didn't want to experience slowly forgetting my loved ones. To watch them hurting, having no control over it.

"Beck!" Lindsay rounded the corner with open arms.

"Hi!" I stood, giving her an anxious hug.

"I still can't believe it!" she whispered in my ear.

"I know. I'm sorry," I said. I never wanted to be a burden on anyone, and I could tell by the way she was looking at me that I'd rocked her world. Everything she knew to be true had been obliterated when I walked through her door just the night before.

"I was up all night! Just thinking about it." She shook her head, staring at me like it was the first time. Like we hadn't just had a full night of disbelief.

"I know it can be a lot to take in. I didn't sleep well either," I said, thinking back to how torn up my bed had been in the morning's light. I tried to hide the coy smile that wanted nothing more than to spread its wings.

"Well, we can talk more about it later. I'm sure this isn't the place. Why don't I show you to your mom's room, and then we can chat before you need to take off," Lindsay said.

"That sounds great." I nodded, and my memory of being tangled up in Easton faded away. I followed Lindsay, taking multiple twists and turns until we reached one room in particular that made my stomach flutter.

"Are you ready?" she asked.

"I think so?"

"Just be patient with her," she said, opening the door. "Good morning, Mrs. Beck. I brought a friend with me today. I hope you don't mind. This is . . ." Lindsay looked at me, stumbling over her words and prompting me to answer. But all I could see was a woman who resembled my mom.

She was smaller than I remembered, but that may have been the way her back hunched. A dark green duster covered her shoulders, and her hair was fluffed in a way she'd never worn it before. She looked at me, her face etched with the years of heartache, and she . . . she looked right through me. Not an ounce of recognition. No eternal bond that was strong enough to pull her mind from the depths of deterioration. Nothing but an empty gaze. And I loved her all the same.

"Uh, uh, Becca," I said. Staring.

"This is Becca." Lindsay turned to me, and whispered, "Just text if you need anything. I'll be available all day." She clapped my shoulder as she passed by. I nodded. Quiet blanketed the tiny room, and I startled when the door clicked shut behind me. My heart floundered in my chest, and I didn't know what to say or do. I wrung my clammy hands and cracked several knuckles, buying myself time. Then, I took a step toward the woman I used to call Mom. My mouth felt dry. The words I had practiced earlier had vanished entirely and were replaced with an unfortunate melody in my head.

I couldn't for the life of me understand why this would happen to somebody. She had already lost me. And no parent should have to experience that. But then she had lost my dad too. She'd lived alone for years thereafter. And as if she hadn't lost enough, now she had lost her memory? It didn't make any sense at all. *Why* would this happen? *How* could this happen?

I pulled up a chair and took a seat next to my mother. Her hair was thin. Her skin so lean, it was translucent. Her eyes, yellow. She looked . . . sad. She looked caged within her body. A body that no longer served her. She looked . . . *Tethered.* Had this been what Easton had felt like all these years? Like his soul had outgrown its body? Like he'd been ready to move on but couldn't? Trapped?

There was a muffled knock. Must have been the room next door. I listened to the muted conversation and then the laughter. Joy spread through the walls and out of the vents when I was sure nothing could penetrate them. I looked up to the vent in the wall and smiled at the vitality next door. Mom did, too.

She only smiled, but it was enough to get me through the fear of seeing her current state of mind. At least now, I knew she was capable of joy, and that not all had been robbed of her. It wasn't long before there was a knock on our door, and I met Tommy. He was a therapy dog, a beautiful black lab. He smiled just as much as my mom did. His jowls hung as he panted big heavy breaths. He was polite in the way he held back his wet slobbery kisses. Mom clapped her hands ever so softly—a habit she had picked up from Chloe. I used to hate when she did it. Now, it touched my heart.

Tommy's wet nose bumped her face, and she lit up. Her body shook with laughter as she stroked his back, giving him as much love as she could within her brief window of Tommy time. "This is amazing," I said. "Do all the residents respond like this?" I asked Tommy's caretaker, a middle-aged man with dark skin, soft eyes, and scrubs adorned with hotdogs.

"Most do. It's really something to see how they come alive with a furry friend," he said.

"How often do you come?" I asked.

"We come once a week," he smiled.

It seemed scant. Why didn't the facility have its own live-in therapy pet? "Wow. Can't you come more often? Like every day?" I asked.

"That would be wonderful. But we just aren't capable of that right now. Hopefully, one day we will grow, but it's a small mom-and-pop shop. And there is only one Tommy," he said. I looked over to my mom, completely connected with this dog, when moments before I hadn't realized that she could engage at all. His tail slapped the backs of my knees with excited energy. And I wondered if I, too, could get a Tommy. What was stopping me from having a service dog? I could bring joy to all the residents here, and I could do it daily. Why should they have to wait a whole week? My mind raced with the possibilities.

"OK, Mrs. Faye, we need to go, but we'll see you next week," he said. Mom gave Tommy one last hug before he jumped off her bed and down to the ground.

"Um, do you have a business card? I'd like more information," I said.

"I don't carry business cards, but I can give you Lisa's phone number. She's the owner, and she would be happy to answer any of your questions."

"That would be great," I said, taking out my phone and entering Lisa's number.

When Tommy left, the letdown was immediate. Mom was quiet, her eyes plunging through gloom before landing on vacancy once again. I had seen others walking through a garden when I came in and texted Lindsay to see if that was something we could do. I imagined getting some fresh air and sunlight would be good for my mom and her mood. When I got the green light, I helped Mom put her shoes on. They were more like house slippers than anything else. She leaned heavily on me as I slipped them on. She was more than willing to go with me on the adventure, but her gate was no faster than a crawl. At this rate, it would be nightfall by the time we made it to the garden and back again.

Things moved a lot faster once I secured a wheelchair. It had been abandoned in the hallway, and I assumed it was for situations like this. I sat her down and took her for a spin outside. Her face lit up, but nothing compared to when she saw Tommy, which hadn't been anything like when she saw me. I lowered a red rose to her nose, and she smelled it with a slight curvature in the corner of her smile. I knew I wasn't supposed to, but I picked it. The gardens must have taken so long to maintain, and the flowers were meant for everyone to enjoy, not take. But roses were my mom's favorite, and I wanted nothing more than to get her smile back. I was breaking the last couple of thorns off the stem when I heard footsteps come up behind me.

"You know you're not supposed to pick the flowers, right?"

I turned to see Lindsay. My heart kicked some extra beets. "Oops. No, I didn't know that. I'm sorry," I said, shrugging. I gave the thornless rose to Mom, and she took it with a slow, trembling hand.

"So how's it going?" Lindsay asked.

I took a deep breath. I didn't know how to answer honestly. And I was still in the presence of my mother, whether she was following our conversation or not. "Good," I said, my pitch high and sharp.

"Oh, no. What's wrong?"

I sighed. Even after three decades of absence, she still knew when I was lying. "Nothing, it's just . . . she doesn't recognize me." It came out before I knew that it'd been what bothered me the most.

"But that's a good thing, right?" Lindsay asked.

I shrugged. "I guess so. I just didn't expect it to hurt like this." I tightened my grip on the wheelchair's handles, forcing it over a lump in the grass as we strolled through the garden.

"I know. It's hard for me too, and I see it every day. I see the family members come in with trepidation and leave with disappointment. Eventually, many of them stop coming. And that's the worst. That's when the patients usually start to decline, and they do so pretty rapidly. So, it seems like they don't notice, but they do . . . in their own way," she said, sitting on a stone bench by the fountain. I parked Mom beside us and took a seat next to Lindsay. "You know, that's going to be us one day," she said.

"I know. I think about it all the time. You'll have to tell me what it's like," I said, smirking.

"Oh, come on!" Lindsay shook her head. "I'm old enough to be your mother," she said, exasperated. And it was true. She was.

"Yeah. In this lifetime," I agreed, looking at my mom's paper-thin hands. Lindsay bumped my shoulder with hers, and I forced a small smile. I didn't want to feel like this. Like I was helpless. Like I was a victim of whatever life threw my way. "Hey, are you going to the rain forest play at school next Friday?" I asked.

"I'm going to try to make it. I'm scheduled to work the night shift, but I think I can get off an hour early. My co-worker said she could cover for me. John's hoping to be there, too. Nora has been fretting over her lines all week."

"What part does she play?" I asked.

"She's the snake."

"Clara is the humming bird. I'm happy to help them learn their lines. They could practice together this week?" I asked, checking my watch. Time had been creeping up on me, and I would have to leave soon to get Clara from school.

"That would be great."

"OK. Good. Well, I should get going," I said.

"Yeah, it's about pickup time, huh? I'll bring your mom back in and get her settled. It's movie night tonight," Lindsay said, standing.

"OK. Thanks." I bent over, giving my mom a hug and a kiss on the cheek. Her hands never leaving the rose in her lap. "I love you," I whispered in her ear.

I pulled away to see the same distant gaze in her yellowing eyes that I had seen most of the day. I was hoping she would give me the same warm glow she gave to the service dog, but it wasn't even close. My love had simply gone unregistered. The lifetime of memories, gone with the wind. Never to resurface again.

I sighed and forced a smile for Lindsay. I didn't want her to see just how naïve I had been about my mother's condition. As I drove to the school, I tried to focus on the positive—though there had been little of it. Even so, my mom's dementia was the only reason I could visit her, and a small part of me wondered if it was fate twisting in its mysterious ways.

CHAPTER 7

Easton had the day off. He didn't get them often, so picking Clara up from school was something new and exciting for him. But nobody could be more thrilled than Clara herself. She wanted to show her dad off to her new friends at school. I was excited too because I was going to a therapy animal center with Brooklyn. The drive was two hours with no traffic, but I intended to hit some traffic on the way home. I wasn't going to buy a dog, even though I'd come to want one since meeting Tommy. But today, I planned to start my research by asking questions in person. And a few friendly pats on the head were always welcome if the opportunity presented itself.

The facility was a little difficult to find. Tucked behind an industrial park sat the small run-down animal center. "Is this it?" Brooklyn asked.

"I think so."

"Do they train the dogs here?"

I browsed the lot, looking for life. "I don't know. It looks a little small. Let's go find out," I said. We entered the center and found not a single soul. The front desk was bare, and the chair sat empty. "Hello?" I called out.

"Hit the bell," Brooklyn whispered. I looked down on the counter, and tucked behind several flyers was a small silver bell. I tapped it twice. When it was clear that nobody was coming, Brooklyn and I began to roam the property. She slipped her hand into the crook of my arm, and we explored the premises at will. The hall gave way to multiple kennels. Only a couple of them had dogs. One was a lively boy, sure to alert the owners that they had company. The other was an older dog. His black fur hid his sad face, and he lay motionless on the floor.

"Awe. What's wrong with him?" I asked.

"I don't know. Is he sleeping? I think he's sleeping."

"He wouldn't be sleeping through all this commotion. I think he's sick," I said.

"Maybe he just needs a home . . ." Brooklyn gave me puppy dog eyes of her own, and I slapped her shoulder. She wanted me to get a dog, too. And together, we were a terrible combination.

"Stop that. I'm not getting a dog. I haven't even talked to Easton about it."

"He knows you're here though, right?" she asked.

"Yeah, but he thinks I'm looking into working with the therapy dogs. Not bringing one home. I can't just come home with a dog," I said, mostly for my own ears to hear.

"What's that one's deal? Aren't they supposed to be calming?" Brooklyn pointed to the golden retriever, who hadn't stopped barking since we walked into the kennel.

"Can I help you?"

Brooklyn and I jumped. I spun around to see a middle-aged woman with short curly hair and a stained smock.

"Hi. Um, I rang the bell up front, but nobody answered. I'm sorry . . . I just wanted to speak with someone about the therapy dogs?" I asked, twisting my fingers into knots.

"Are you here to pick up?" the woman asked.

Brooklyn elbowed me in the side. "Oh, no. I was just going to ask some questions. You see, my mom is in a nursing home, and I'd really like to get more service dogs to visit the residents. And since that won't happen on its own, I was thinking maybe I could get involved. Maybe I could bring a service dog to visit? I wasn't really sure how it all worked," I rambled.

"I see. Well, my name is Sandy, and we have a new litter on the ground now. They're out back. This yellow guy is completing his training next month, and he's already been purchased," she said, pointing to the kennel.

"What about him?" Brooklyn motioned to the other dog.

"Him? Oh, he's not for sale. He's deaf."

"Oh, got it." Brooklyn nodded.

"But why isn't he for sale?" I asked, not wanting to give up on him just yet.

The lady shrugged. "Well, nobody has ever wanted him. He's been with us for years. It would take a really special person to take care of him. And he can't get fully certified because of his hearing. Do you girls want to see the puppies, though? They're a real hoot!" she kicked her thumb over her shoulder.

"Puppies!" Brooklyn said as she blew past me. Sandy led the way, and my eyes fixed on the deaf dog as we passed his kennel. The closer we got, the louder the puppies became. And as soon as Sandy opened the door, five little ankle biters rushed to our feet, licking, nipping, and tripping over themselves. "Can I pick one up?" Brooklyn asked.

"Sure. I've been wrestling with these guys all morning. I'm sure they could use some fresh blood. Have at it," Sandy said.

Brooklyn chose a curly-haired black and brown one to hold first. But before we left, I knew she would hold them all. Brooklyn was an animal lover; she always had been. But she had a rule about that too. "Love them and leave them," she'd always say. Something about getting the best of both worlds. Snuggles and kisses without picking up after them.

I never thought about it until that moment, but it was more of a life mantra than a rule that applied to pets. As I watched her—eyes squinted and mouth puckered as she tried to escape the direct contact of a tiny tongue—I realized she was the very same way with Tanner. She clearly loved him, but she wouldn't allow herself the commitment. She was always one foot out the door. At the least, I felt blessed she had never been that way with our friendship.

I kneeled down, and paws pranced upon my thighs, climbing me like an obstacle course. I did my best to pet them all, but their appetite for attention was voracious. Brooklyn and I giggled when one pup turned feisty. Its growl wasn't yet fierce, and its size was anything but powerful. Still, the little bundle of curly hair continued to call out one of its brothers or sisters to a duel. They remained unaffected.

"Do you see it?" Brooklyn whispered. I looked around the small fenced-off yard. Several training stations. Food and water. Sandy.

"See what?" I asked. But she simply motioned to the surrounding air with a soft smile. I looked up, and though I couldn't see the love like she had, I smiled, knowing it was there. Sometimes I would see it, but I guessed that most of the time, I did not. My sight wasn't as strong as Brooklyn's or Easton's, and I couldn't see all the emotion and energy that they had described to me. I took another look, letting my eyes lose their focus just above the playing puppies, but nothing came into sight. It never did when I tried.

Sandy let us play with the puppies for quite some time, and when she got tired of watching us, she went inside for coffee. I glanced over at Brooklyn, who wasn't slowing down in the least. I knew she could play with these critters for hours. I on the other hand . . . I couldn't stop thinking about the deaf dog that slept through our arrival. "I'm going to go talk to Sandy. Did you want to stay here?" I asked Brooklyn.

"Do you have to ask?" she replied.

I chuckled. It was the exact response I had expected. I headed inside and found Sandy at her desk with a mug of piping hot coffee. The steam rose under her nose, and she blew on it before taking the tiniest of sips, careful not to burn herself.

"Hey, Sandy? I was wondering if I could spend a little time with the black dog." I motioned back towards his kennel.

"Bodie. Yeah, we can go see him." Sandy put her coffee down and took me to see the dog with the buried eyes. "Deaf dogs get startled easily. Here's a little trick I use to wake him up," Sandy said, getting down on her hands and knees. Bodie lay sound asleep, just like he had been when we arrived. Then, Sandy took a deep breath and blew on his face. The air ruffled his bangs, and his paws twitched in response. A smile spread across my face as she tried again. This time more air. Bodie's nose flared and his brows lifted. His eyes were partially visible for the first time. Finally, he wagged his tail, slapping it on the ground. Sandy got to her feet and opened the kennel door.

Bodie sat up, taking me in. "Hi! Hi! What a good boy you are!" I cooed.

"Now, remember, he can't hear you," Sandy said.

"Oh!" I stopped to give Sandy a look of regret. I wasn't sure how to talk to a dog who couldn't hear me, and I was embarrassed for not thinking it through.

"It doesn't mean you can't talk to him. Go ahead if that's what you want to do. But you can't give him verbal commands. They have to be visual." I nodded, brows furrowed.

But when I turned back to Bodie, and his hidden black eyes, I did it again. "That's a good boy!" I said, under my breath. His mouth parted, and he panted, opening his enormous mouth and displaying his sharp teeth. "Is he trained to be a therapy dog?" I asked.

"Well, yes and no. He is, but he has restrictions. Most of the therapy relies on sight and smell. But he is at a disadvantage without his hearing. If someone were to fall or call for help, Bodie wouldn't know unless he was within proximity to see it happen," Sandy said, leaning up against the wall.

"Could he visit a nursing home?" I asked.

Sandy sighed. It was clear she thought Bodie was a lost cause, but I wasn't giving up on him just yet. "Yes. He's fit for an ESA."

"An ESA?" I asked.

"An emotional support animal," she said. I turned to Bodie, petting his fluffy head, and I swore he smiled at me.

Brooklyn wandered down the hall, her face pink from the mid-morning heat. "I thought I would find you here," she said.

"This is Bodie," I said. His tail slapped the ground as he looked up at her with his big black eyes.

"He's perfect. How much?" she asked. Surprise sparked in Sandy's eyes.

"Look, he's not for everyone—"

"I'm not everyone!" I said, hopeful.

"Well, he seems to like you. Let me talk to my husband. If you want to leave your information with me, I can get back to you. But are you sure you don't want a pup? They will be fully trained in under two years—"

"Two years?" I interrupted.

"Yes, but—"

"How much will a fully trained pup cost?" Brooklyn asked.

". . . $8,500.00 with full training, but—"

"Wow," I said. I had no idea they would cost so much. I only wanted a dog to make my mom happy. Put a smile on her face more often than once a week. I scratched behind Bodie's ear. "Sorry, guy," I whispered, knowing he couldn't hear me but that maybe he could sense my expression.

Saying goodbye to Bodie was difficult. I hated to think of him sitting in that kennel alone because of his deficit. But I left with Sandy's card, and she promised to speak with her husband regarding Bodie's fit for someone like me.

"Can you believe how much they cost?" Brooklyn asked when we reached the truck.

"I had no idea. Why can't I just bring any old dog into the home? As long as they're nice, I don't see why they need to have special training."

"Maybe you can?" Brooklyn shrugged.

"I'll have to ask Lindsay," I said. Then, I started the truck and pulled out onto the main road.

"About that . . ."

"What?" I glanced over to Brooklyn. Her face marked with guilt. "What did you do?" I asked, reluctantly.

"I may or may not have led you to believe that revealing yourself to Lindsay was a bad idea. It wasn't. It never was. And I knew all along. I'm sorry," she said.

"What!?" My jaw dropped, and I scowled at Brooklyn beside me for as long as I could keep my eyes off the main road. "Why would you do that to me? I spent weeks hiding from her! It tore me apart, and you knew that!" I barked. Weeks had passed since the birthday party where I hid in my truck at pickup, fearful I'd lose Nora all over again. Every time I confided in Brooklyn, she would urge me not to show myself to Lindsay. She never said it outright, but she hinted at it being a mistake. One that I wouldn't be able to take back.

"I know! I know! I had a dream—"

"You said you *didn't* have a dream about it!" I said.

"I lied. I'm sorry. I'm telling you now. What else can I do, Bec?" she said, her face wrapped in defense, but her words apologetic.

I sighed. I was infuriated by her choice, but she was right. What else could she do but come clean now? I had already told Lindsay everything. "Well, are you going to tell me about the dream, or?"

"Well, don't be mad at me!"

"I *am* mad, Brooklyn. That's my right. OK? You don't know how much I worried about that. Should I tell her? Should I not? Will I lose Nora? And it all could have been prevented if you had just told me what you dreamed about. So, will you just tell me what you know?" I pulled onto the highway.

"I had a dream. There wasn't much to it. But you and Lindsay were best friends again. You were happy. The kids were happy. Everyone lived happily ever after! Is that what you wanted to hear?" she said, annoyed.

I should have been relieved. My life was complete. Job well done. I'd been successful at raising a happy family. But I couldn't understand why that had been a bad thing. And why Brooklyn's disturbance had overshadowed the bit about living happily ever after. "So, what's the problem, Brooklyn? What am I missing here?"

Even more frustrated now, she said, "Me! You're missing me! Where do I fit into this perfect life? If I'm not your best friend anymore, and you don't need me? If I'm not Tanner's girlfriend? Then I'm just a wanderer. Again. Then, this life has been another waste!" her voice wavered in a moment of weakness.

"Brooklyn! What are you talking about? You're always going to be my best friend!"

"But what about Lindsay?" she asked.

What about Lindsay? She had been a pillar in my life since I was young. "Why don't I get both? Why can't I have a best friend from each lifetime?" I asked.

It made little sense until I considered her insecurities. "Look, you can't compare our relationship with one that I have with someone else. That's not fair to you or me. You did that when I got married to Easton, too. And you're doing it now. I'm starting to think that your problem isn't insecurity within our own relationship but within yourself. Maybe you see me getting close to other people, and it makes you realize you're not doing that for yourself! And maybe you should be!" I said, stealing a quick glance at her while I drove. I couldn't see much, but I could tell that her jaw had been clenched tight by the hallows in her cheeks. "Does that sound right?" I asked.

Brooklyn stared out the window, her frustration keeping her from speaking.

"Brooklyn? Could you be mad at yourself for not committing to Tanner? Maybe that's why you're putting so much pressure on our friendship to carry you through? Maybe that's why you don't want me to be friends with Lindsay?"

She took a long while to mull it over in her head, chewing her cheek and fighting back tears. And when she finally opened back up, all she could say was, "Tanner's seeing someone else."

CHAPTER 8

It was the following day when Easton texted me from work saying that we'd have company for dinner. Tanner was coming over with his new girlfriend. She was someone he'd met at the Decord Police Station. Of course, I wanted to meet the girl that could be my sister-in-law, but a part of me felt disloyal to Brooklyn for doing so.

I promised myself I wouldn't make the same mistake twice, though. When my brother brought home his girlfriend and announced that he was engaged, I'd hated his fiancée. Chloe was completely wrong for my brother. And of course, I had already picked out the perfect girl for him. It took me quite some time to realize I had been wrong, but it wasn't until a lifetime later that I realized just how wrong I had been.

Not until I saw Chloe at the park did it resonate with me that love wasn't a choice. If it had been, Carter would probably have made the obvious choice. A sweet girl that everyone liked, and one that he got along with well. But his heart chose Chloe instead, and it was hard for me to see why. Eventually, I made peace with the fact that their relationship was meant for them to feel, not for me to see. And I didn't want to make assumptions about Tanner's relationship in the same way, just because I had picked Brooklyn for him instead of whomever he was to bring over.

I spent the day preparing lasagna, breadsticks, and salad. I cleaned the house and still managed to take Clara to the park for a half-hour. I had just placed fresh flowers on the dining table when I heard a knock on the door.

"Your uncle's here!" I announced to Clara.

"Uncle Tanner!" Clara wailed, running down the hall.

Normally, Tanner would let himself in, but he must have been trying to be polite in front of his new girlfriend. I opened the door, Clara by my side. Tanner was dressed a little nicer than normal, and his hair was done for the first time in a long while. His girlfriend was a cute girl. My guess was that she was a redhead by nature, with the dusting of freckles over her nose and cheeks. But as she stood on my doorstep, her hair was a dark chocolate brown. Eyes blue, and skin fair. "Hello!" I said.

Tanner introduced us. "Becca, this is Charlie. Charlie, Becca."

I shook Charlie's hand and welcomed them inside. Tanner picked up Clara and threw her into the air. She squealed, free-falling until he caught her again. A pink hue crossed Charlie's cheeks as she beamed up at Tanner and my daughter, and I could see the appeal he had on women. He was handsome, fun-loving, and a terrific uncle. "Can I get you something to drink?" I asked.

"Oh, I brought wine," Charlie said.

"Perfect!" I took the bottle, uncorked it, and poured two glasses. I knew Tanner would want a beer, so I pulled one from the refrigerator as well.

"Thanks. Where's Easton?" Tanner asked, taking a sip of beer.

"He should be here any minute," I said, checking my watch.

"Come see my doll house!" Clara said, pulling on Charlie's jacket. Her eyes flickered between me and Tanner before agreeing.

"Oh! Here, take this!" I said, holding out the glass of wine. She smiled and took it with her to Clara's room. "You're going to need it," I mumbled under my breath. If I knew my daughter, I knew she would keep her busy for hours, and at some point, I would have to rescue her. But for now, Clara could show Charlie her room, and Tanner and I could chat, privately.

"So?" I asked Tanner, wagging my brows.

"So, what?" he played dumb.

"So . . . tell me everything! How's it going? How long have you been seeing her? Oh . . . is this your first date? Tell me this isn't your first date?" I asked, leaning across the kitchen counter.

Tanner pulled out a barstool and took a seat on the other side. He rolled his eyes at first, but then dove in more than willingly. "It is. I mean, we've had lunch together at the station, but we've never gone out before. Can you tell? Is it obvious?"

". . . And you brought her *here*?" My neck craned at the absurd thought of a romantic first date being spent in my daughter's bedroom. *Alone.*

"Well, I thought it would make her more comfortable since she knows Easton and all." Tanner nodded his head, proud of his considerate ways. Still, he was missing the mark.

I didn't want to crush him, so I didn't remind him that his new girlfriend was playing dolls in a bedroom with a six-year-old instead of being swept off her feet. "I see . . . You're so thoughtful," I said.

"I don't want this to be weird between us because Brooklyn is your friend and all," Tanner said, one cheek lifting into a forced, empathetic smile.

"Oh, no. Please don't worry about that. I've already committed to having an open mind. And all I really want is for you to be happy. I mean, I want Brooklyn to be happy too, of course—"

"Of course—"

"But, it's separate. They're two different relationships, and honestly, they're not mine. So have at it," I rambled.

"So, you're OK with this?" he asked.

"Yeah! Of course," I said, my face warming under the lie of it all. I *was* OK with it. I was happy for him. But that didn't mean I couldn't also feel guilty—like I was doing something wrong by having her over for dinner. Like I had helped Tanner fall for another girl, despite my friend being in love with him. But he didn't need to know all that. I raised my wine glass to my lips and let it linger before drawing in a long, tart sip. "Do you love her?" I asked.

"Charlie?" Tanner flinched.

"No, Brooklyn . . ." I whispered, craning my neck to peer down the hall.

Tanner looked over his shoulder, then lowered his voice. "Bec, you know I can't."

"I know."

"She doesn't want me. I was ready to give up having a family for her, but if she doesn't want to marry me, regardless of having a family, then what's the point?" Tanner said, resting his chin in the palm of his hand, hopeless.

I only wished Brooklyn could see she had choices. That her life wasn't black and white the way she always made it to be. "I love Brooklyn. You know that, but if she can't get out of her own way, she can't expect you to wait around," I said, shrugging. It wasn't the way I wanted it to be. But I was ready to accept it. Tanner already had. "Charlie seems nice though," I said.

"She is. She's got a real sweet temperament too. Everyone really enjoys being around her at the station."

"Good. That's good. You need a nice girl. Speaking of, I guess I should go rescue her from Clara, now."

Tanner smiled. "Yeah, and put in a good word for me while you're at it."

I raised my eyebrows as I passed by, but I never made it down the hall. The doorbell rang just as I left the kitchen. I was shocked to see Lindsay standing on the other side of the door; a bottle of wine in her hand and an apologetic look on her face.

"Lindsay! Is everything OK?" I asked. Her hands twisted nervously over the neck of the bottle.

"Yeah! I'm so sorry for coming by unexpectedly, but I wanted to talk to you about something. Do you have time?" she asked, peeking inside. I didn't. But I couldn't turn her down. She needed me, and it had been a long time since that happened.

"Yes, come in! Come in!" I said, waving her inside. "This is Easton's brother, Tanner."

Tanner shot from his seat and shook Lindsay's hand. "Hello," he said.

"And his girlfriend, Charlie, is playing with Clara in the bedroom," I said, worry warming my cheeks. It had surpassed the time I was going to allow Clara to steal our guest of honor away.

"I'll go keep her company," Tanner said with a smile, taking out another beer from the fridge. "You two can talk."

I laughed because playing dolls was hard work, and sometimes a glass of wine or a can of beer helped bring out the creativity. Tanner was quick to learn, as he had played dolls a time or two before. I mouthed "Thank you" to him and patted his shoulder as he passed by.

"I actually have a bottle open if you want some of this one?" I held the bottle of red wine up, trying to read the label, but it was in French, so I didn't try to pronounce it aloud.

"Perfect," Lindsay said. She sat down where Tanner had been, and I poured her a glass of wine. "I know you have guests. I'm so sorry. I just . . . I'm having a hard time believing you're back. So, forgive me for popping by. I just wanted to see you in person. I should have called. And—"

"No, no, no. Don't apologize. You can stop by anytime! OK?" I gave Lindsay her glass of wine.

"And . . . I have a proposition for you," Lindsay said, dipping her chin into her chest.

"Huh. Why does this sound like a bad thing?" I asked.

"No! It's not! Unless . . ."

"Unless, what?"

"Unless you don't want to do it, and then you feel like you need to because I asked." Concern spread across her face and settled in the lines of her forehead.

"OK. Just ask. You're making me nervous."

"OK, I'm sorry. Well . . . you know Penny? My nanny?"

"Yeah. I mean, I know *of* her."

"Well, we caught her stealing, and I had to let her go today."

"No way! What? How?" I stammered. The thought of a thief watching Nora made my stomach twist.

"We have nanny cams around the house. They're these little cameras you can hide in plants or stuffed animals. Wherever really. We caught her on one of those. I had been suspecting it for a little while now, so I set up the camera in my bedroom where I keep my jewelry." Lindsay sighed.

"She stole your jewelry?"

"No, that's the funny part. She bypassed the jewelry and stole some of my perfume. Go figure." Lindsay shrugged.

"Yeah. Huh. Maybe she thought the jewelry would be too obvious?"

"Yeah, maybe?"

"Well, I'm glad you caught her. I know you have gone through a couple of nannies, though, so that's hard," I said.

"Well . . . that's the thing . . ." Lindsay took a long swig of wine and looked anywhere but at me.

"What's the thing?"

"I was wondering if maybe, *you,* wanted to do it?" Lindsay asked, her face scrunched with worry.

"Me?"

"We would pay you! But it's not because I think you need the money or anything! I mean, I know you don't have a job right now . . . Not like that means you're looking, or that staying at home is bad, or—"

"Lindsay, stop! Stop! I'll do it," I said.

"You will?"

"Yes. I love Nora. I love you. I'm happy to help in any way I can," I said. And she didn't know how true that statement was. I hadn't yet told Lindsay that Nora was of my flesh and blood. But even if she hadn't been, I would have loved her for being my best friend's child.

Lindsay nearly knocked the barstool over as she jumped from her chair and gave me a tight hug. The back of my throat burned, and I told myself not to cry. This was the best news I could have received. I had the privilege of being in Nora's everyday life? Everything was falling into place.

"I love you, too, Everly." My stomach dropped. It was the first I'd heard my name in a long time. It sounded foreign but still pulled at my heart strings. I blotted the corners of my eyes.

When Lindsay pulled away, she too was misty-eyed. We both chuckled at each other. She took a seat and pulled out a folded-up piece of paper from her bag. A schedule. As it turned out, Nora was a busy girl. She had school, dance, and piano. I took the piece of paper from Lindsay and studied it.

"Is it too much?" she asked.

"Oh, no. That's not it. I was just thinking, I should probably enroll Clara into the dance class too if I'm going to be there anyway," I said. "I think she'll like that."

"Um, so . . . sometimes we work the night shifts. And by that, I mean a lot of times we work the night shifts."

"OK," I said, nodding.

"Usually, Penny would stay the night at our house. She was a partial live-in."

"Oh?" I hadn't known that.

"Yeah, but since you have a family, maybe Nora could stay here some nights? I'm trying to change my schedule to the day shifts. I'll take a pay cut, but I think it will work out nicely because one of my co-workers is saving for a house, and I think she wants to switch schedules . . ." Lindsay shrugged. "Anyway, I think the sleepovers will only be for the first two or three weeks, and then the schedule will be normalized. Are you sure you're OK with this?" she asked.

"Of course. Anything you need." And I meant that. I'd do anything she needed me to do.

"I owe you. I can't thank you enough!" Lindsay placed her hand across her chest and took a sigh of relief. I smiled, knowing that I was of help to her. But nothing was better than knowing we would spend more time with Nora.

I could hear that Tanner was growing bored when his voice boomed through the walls. "Oh, how rude of me. I forgot you have guests. I'll be on my way." I checked my watch. Easton was more than an hour late to dinner. Worry spread in the pit of my stomach as I reached for my phone to text him. I had a missed call from a number I didn't recognize. Lindsay stood and gathered her things. I held up a finger while I checked my voice mail.

I felt the blood drain from my face the moment the recording began referencing a local hospital.

"Is everything OK?" Lindsay whispered.

I sucked in a deep breath. "It's Easton," I said, my voice shaky and small.

"Easton?"

"Tanner!" I yelled. He came barreling down the hall wearing a pink princess crown and gobs of makeup.

"It's Easton. He's in the hospital!" Goosebumps prickled my skin. Lindsay gasped. I turned to her. "Watch Clara?" I asked, squeezing her forearm.

"Yes. Absolutely."

"I'll text you as soon as I know anything," I said, grabbing my keys and purse as I ran toward the door.

"I'll drive," Tanner said. I gave him a quick nod and headed for his police car parked in our driveway.

CHAPTER 9

Tanner drove like a bat out of hell. His driving put Everly's to shame, but the flashing lights and piercing siren made it not only acceptable but normal. We were weaving in and out of traffic so fast that other drivers couldn't lay eyes on us, which was a good thing because if they had, we would have struck them as crazy people. I had been so worried about Easton that I hardly noticed the clown faces on both Tanner and Charlie. Or the pink tutu tucked just under Charlie's armpits. But for those out there that weren't petrified to lose the love of their lives, I'd imagine that two pretty pink princesses driving a cop car screaming down the highway was quite a sight.

I couldn't think of Tanner and Charlie, though. And honestly, I couldn't think of Easton either. What if he didn't make it? What if he died, never having seen his girls grow up? What if he left me behind? What then? My mind raced to places it had never been before and places it never wanted to see. Thankfully, it wasn't long before I was on my feet again. Charlie and I on the flank of Tanner. He ran with one hand on top of his head, securing the plastic tiara in place. The emergency doors slid open as the three of us ran to the front desk.

"Decord P.D. My partner's just been admitted. Easton Green," Tanner said, flashing his badge. The receptionist's eyes grew to the size of saucers before falling back to her computer screen. She must have seen a lot come through those hospital doors, but I imagined this was a first. My heart raged in my chest, and I thought for a moment that I might pass out. My hands trembled and knees wobbled. I was going to be sick to my stomach. Tanner shot Charlie a weary glance. One that I wasn't supposed to see but did.

The receptionist told us to have a seat. She said that someone would be out shortly with an update. At least, that's the gist of what I understood. The fear that coursed through my veins did little for my cognitive function. When Charlie headed for the waiting room, Tanner nudged my arm, beckoning me to follow. Without his cue, I may have stood there alone, frozen in worry, still waiting for instructions.

Even though I followed Charlie to the waiting room, I didn't sit with her. I paced back and forth, biting my nails mindlessly until shards of pain would light up a nerve. Only then would I shove my hands into the back pockets of my jeans before taking them out and chewing on a new nail. I jolted every time I saw a person walk into the waiting room, hoping it would be Easton's update.

But they were families like us, coming to wait for news that may change their lives. Maybe it would just be for the night. A missed date or no time to study for a test the following morning. They'd be the lucky ones. Because as I looked around the waiting room, I knew that the inconvenience for some would pale in comparison to others. Some might spend their time teaching their loved ones to walk again. Some might lose their chance to have their father walk them down the aisle. Or a chance to tuck their child into bed at night.

A young boy, maybe six or seven, was curled up on his mother's lap, asleep. They'd probably been here for hours. Across from them was an older couple, presumably husband and wife. They held hands and shared the same worried look on their faces. And in the corner sat a woman all by her lonesome. Her foot bobbed as she scrolled through her phone much too fast to know what she was looking at. They were all similar. Loved ones, sick with worry. Waiting.

A middle-aged man dressed in blue scrubs walked into the waiting room, and everyone craned their necks hopefully. My heart stopped until the doctor spoke. "Carmichael?" he called. The mother and son perked up, and the rest of them fell back in their seats. My shoulders fell, and I turned away from the doctor, giving them an ounce of privacy. I glanced over my shoulder as the mother and son followed the doctor into the nearby hall. I wondered when I would get an update on Easton. It shouldn't be taking this long. Why was it taking this long? I took out my cell phone to text Lindsay that we were at the hospital waiting for an update when I heard a blood-curdling scream.

My back went rigid, my thumbs froze on top of my cell phone, the text message coming to a halt. Just beyond the corner where the waiting room met the hall, the mother had sunk to her knees. The little boy patted her head as she sobbed—uncontrollable and erratic cries of grief. My stomach dropped. I had heard the cries of loss before when they escaped my own mouth. They were unlike anything else I had ever heard. It's a guttural cry and sounds nothing like the pain of a broken bone or a cut knee. Saved for a time when your heart leaves your body and searches for a loved one that is no longer there.

I watched as the doctor kneeled down, cupping her shoulder. It did nothing to console her. Nothing would now, except time itself. My heart ached for the little boy who hadn't yet understood how his life would be forever changed. All he knew now lay in front of him, and that was his mother, broken in pieces. The heartbreak spread like a virus, and I could see it in the faces of the elderly couple and the lone woman. My eyes met Tanner's, and it was evident that he, too, had been startled by the woman's cries. I switched hands, biting into a fresh nail.

"Green?" a doctor called out.

"Yes!" I waved frantically. Tanner and Charlie sprung to their feet. And as the doctor flipped through his chart and began the update, all I could think was how happy I was that he hadn't called us into the hallway.

"Easton is currently in surgery. He's been shot in the abdomen. We couldn't save his kidney and had to remove it. You've got a couple of hours before he is out of surgery, moved to another room, and can have visitors. You're welcome to stay here and wait . . ." The doctor's eyes traveled from Tanner's tiara to Charlie's tutu. "Or, you can go home and return when he is ready for visitors if that meets your needs," he said.

"No. No. I'll be right here. Waiting," I said, taking a moment to catch my breath. "He'll be alright, won't he?" I asked, reaching out and grabbing the doctor's arm.

"Oh yes. You can live a good long life on one kidney," he said, smiling.

I turned to Tanner and buried my head in his chest. I don't know why I cried. Relief, I suppose. I didn't know what I'd do without Easton by my side. I wasn't the mother I knew I could be, and he helped fill in the gaps where I could be stronger. He put a light inside me that made me whole. Without him, I'd be my worst self. And he . . . he'd be starting over again. Cast out into this world like a fish released back to sea. I'd spent my whole life looking for him, and I wasn't convinced I'd be as lucky as I was my second time around. Or even my first, for that matter.

By the time I gathered myself enough to pull away from Tanner's arms, the doctor was long gone. Charlie stood awkwardly, stroking my back. I gave her an apologetic smile as I wiped away my tears. "Why don't you two get going? You must be hungry. We never ate dinner," I said.

"Oh, no . . . we're OK," Charlie glanced up to Tanner, unsure.

"Um, maybe I should take Charlie home. Then I'll come back?" Tanner asked.

"Honestly, I don't mind," she said. The three of us stood there for a moment, undecided. Until Charlie chased away the silence. "Here, I should give this back to you before Tanner takes me home," she said, tugging on the tutu. She pulled it down, but it was far too tight to get over her chest.

"Here, let me help you," Tanner said, taking the pink gauzy ruffles and trying to pull it down. It didn't budge.

"Maybe go up?" she asked.

"Let's go up," he said. He tried to lift it over her head. One quick tug and it breached her shoulders. The crack of the band ripping as it caught under her nose. "Oops!" Tanner froze. Charlie was stuck with her arms high in the air, and she glared with embarrassment through the holes in the gauze.

"Don't stop! Help me!" she hissed.

Tanner looked at me, "Sorry Becca, I'll have to get Clara a new one," he said.

"It's OK. Help her!" I waved him on, quickly glancing around to see how much of a spectacle we'd made. He ripped the tutu in half, freeing Charlie from the confines of the skirt—and the embarrassment. Her pink lipstick had smeared under her nose where the skirt had caught. Tanner handed me the shreds, and I balled them up in my hands.

"I'll be back as soon as I can," he said.

"It was nice meeting you. I'm sorry this wasn't the night you had in mind," I said to Charlie.

She took me in her arms and squeezed me tightly. "Please let me know if you need anything. I can help. I want to help," she said. I smiled warmly at her. It was then that she won my heart. I knew she'd be good for Tanner, and I was happy for him. I patted him on the back as the two of them left the waiting room with pink lipstick spread halfway to their ears. Matching purple eyeshadow and fake eyelashes glued right beneath their eyebrows.

"Wait!" I called out, just before they disappeared beyond the automatic doors. They turned around with concern. I ran to them, pulling out my cell phone. "I want a picture," I said.

Tanner's head fell back, and his eyes rolled up. The tiara fell off his head, and he bent over to pick it up off the ground. But when I held my cellphone up to take a picture, they both plastered on a forced grin. I smiled, accepting the picture for what it was—a brother who was worried sick and his awkward first date. "Thanks. It was just too good to pass up, and I know Easton will have wanted to see this, so . . ." I held up my phone and gave it a shake.

Tanner left to take Charlie home, and I imagined he'd take a little extra time to eat and wash the makeup off his face before returning. I sat quietly in the waiting room. The mother and son were nowhere to be found. The lone woman was grasping her phone under her chin. And the older woman was starting to doze off on the shoulder of her husband. It wasn't long before newcomers came. And slowly, one by one, someone would get called back. I was especially happy to see the woman riddled with anxiety receive good news.

I spent my time thinking about how I needed to tell Easton about the laws of a Tethered Soul. How we weren't sentenced to roam this earth forever. I needed to tell him how my time had come and how a mortal life had found me—or at least that I believed it had. I never wanted to tell him for fear it would change the course of his destiny, but as I sat in the waiting room and he lay in surgery with the idea that he was some sort of immortal hero, I knew this information was no longer a best-kept secret. He needed to be more careful.

I looked around the stagnant waiting room and racked my brain. I needed something to do. I made my way to the receptionist and asked where I could find a cup of coffee. She pointed me in the direction of the hospital cafeteria. I was walking through the halls when I ran into Dr. Faye. "John!" I said, somewhat in shock.

He gave me the same perplexed look that I had given him. "Becca? What are you doing here?" he asked, looking over my shoulder.

"Looking for coffee," I said, pointing down the hall. He nodded, confirming I was headed in the right direction.

"Yeah, down there. But what are you doing here? Is everyone OK?"

"Oh, that! Yes, um, Easton was shot. He had a kidney removed. The doctor said that he could live normally off one kidney, but that didn't sound right?" I asked, unsure if it was true.

"Oh, shit! I'm sorry to hear that! I'm heading into a c-section right now, but when I get out, I'll check up on him. Are you going to be around?" he asked.

"Yeah, I'll be here. Lindsay has Clara, so I'll be here all night. Come and find us."

"OK. Take care, I'll see you soon."

"John?" I asked.

"Yes?"

"Just one kidney?"

"Oh, yeah. He'll be fine!" John said, before disappearing behind the elevator doors. I took in a deep breath, thankful that Easton would be OK. Thankful that Clara was in good hands. That there was a doctor here I knew and trusted. And soon . . . soon, I'd be thankful for a warm cup of coffee while I waited for Easton to wake up.

CHAPTER 10

It was late when the nurse called me back. Much later than I was expecting. Even so, Tanner hadn't come back yet. I followed the nurse through a maze of hospital twists and turns—none of which I'd remember. When we came upon a single row of rooms, she gave me his room number and left me to it. Slowly, I opened his door, unsure of what I might find.

Easton lay motionless in the hospital bed, tubes under his nose and running into the crook of his arm. He looked good—better than I was expecting—like he was sleeping. His chest rose and fell under the gown, which was split slightly open. He was tucked underneath a thin sheet of the hospital bed. Not long after, a doctor came in. He checked on a few things while he updated me. The surgery went as well as expected, and he would be home soon, but he'd need to take it easy during his recovery. I took a seat next to his bed, and put Easton's warm hand in mine.

My thumb ran back and forth over his rough knuckles as I surveyed the minor scrapes and scuffs on his forearm. I tried to imagine what had happened—the shooter, the words exchanged, the trigger pulled. How he landed and how the scrapes came to be. At first, it was simple curiosity, but quickly became a disturbing intrusion of imagery that I could no longer shut off. The fear behind his eyes would plague my dreams for years to come—even being purely speculative.

It took a while for Easton to wake. I sat patiently by his side, imagining the best way to tell him I had no more lives left—and that maybe, just maybe, he didn't either. I didn't want him to put his life in danger, but how was I to know? That could have been the thing that made his life full. It could be his key to untying his tether. And as far as I knew, it was what he wanted. He wanted the freedom to move on from this life. Could putting his life on the line to help other people be his life's fulfillment? Either way, I was afraid to tell him. So much had changed since we last talked about it. We had a family now. And who knows, maybe he'd had a change of heart?

A knock on the door startled me from my deep, troubled thoughts. I pulled my eyes off Easton and found John standing at the door. "John! Hey, how was your c-section?" I asked.

"Great! Eight pounds, six ounces. Healthy baby boy. The mom wants to name him Wilber, but the dad won't have it. How's Easton doing?" he asked, taking several steps closer to read the monitors.

I shrugged. "They said he would be awake any time, but I don't know. He's been sleeping for a while, and it doesn't look like that's going to change soon," I said, resting my gaze back on his face.

"Everyone reacts differently to the anesthesia and the procedure. He's been through a lot and just needs time to rest. It's not indicative that something is wrong. Who's his doctor?" John asked.

"Um, Dr. Sonders? Or Sanders?" I said.

"Oh, Dr. Sanders. He's a great doctor. I'll talk to him—let him know you're a friend. And if you have any questions, don't hesitate to ask. He's really personable," John said, tapping the door. It was late, and he was probably ready to go home and get some sleep between deliveries.

"I won't. Thank you," I said.

Brooklyn walked by just as John was leaving. Her eyes were puffy and face bare. "Brooklyn?" I called out as she passed by the window.

"Bec?" She popped her head in, and her face lit up as soon as she saw me. For the first time, I let go of Easton's hand, and I ran straight into Brooklyn's arms. "He's going to be OK. It's all going to be OK," she repeated.

"How did you know?" I asked. "Did Tanner call you?"

"Did I what?" Tanner asked, walking in behind her.

Brooklyn stiffened, drawing her hair behind her ear. She gave me a quick shake of the head, her eyes wide with alarm. I'd known by now what that look had meant. She must have had a dream.

"Tanner! You're back!" I said.

"Sorry it took me so long," he said, an apologetic look on his face and the remnants of pink lipstick etched into his cheeks. His eyes flickered to Brooklyn's for a quick and awkward moment, and though it was short-lived, I saw the conflict that lived in his heart. I knew he still loved Brooklyn.

"That's alright. He hasn't woken up yet," I said.

"Um, I'm not supposed to be here. They said no visitors, so I just snuck in. I've been wandering the halls for the past ten minutes hoping to find you. I'm glad I did. You haven't been answering your phone—"

"Yeah," Tanner agreed.

"Oh? It must be dead?" I picked up my phone and tried to turn it on. The screen remained black.

"But now that I've got a hold of you, and I can see you're in good company, I should go," Brooklyn said.

"No. Stay!" I replied.

Brooklyn opened her mouth, but as soon as she did, Tanner said it too. "You should stay." A soft-spoken statement that meant way more than the words themselves. Brooklyn smiled, looking down to the floor, and I brought my gaze back to Easton.

His lids twitched. Then, his brows knotted. "Hey, he's waking up!" Brooklyn said.

I squeezed his hand. "Easton? Can you hear me?" I asked. His eyes fluttered open, and his limbs woke, bending and twisting. A moan growled deep from within his throat. "Easton?" I squeezed his hand. His eyes landed on me, though they remained unfocused. He cleared his throat and tried to talk, but nothing came out except for breathy noises. "Can we get some water?" I asked, looking around the room.

"Here! There's some on this side!" Brooklyn handed me the water. Tanner stood at the foot, arms crossed and emotion clouding his face. I held the straw up to Easton's lips and he drew in a small sip. I watched as his eyes took in his brother and Brooklyn. "How are you feeling?" she asked.

"Hey, brother. You scared us," Tanner said.

A small smile spread across Easton's dry lips. "No. You don't need to be scared," he said in a raspy, hushed tone. I wiped away the single tear that dropped from my eye and smiled as relief washed over me. I kissed his knuckles repeatedly. "Where's Clara?" he asked, searching behind me.

"Lindsay has her. She's fine," I said.

"So, what happened? And why the hell didn't you have your vest on?" Tanner scolded.

Easton tried to sit up but only made it a couple of inches. I tried to help by bunching the pillows underneath his head, and Brooklyn pushed buttons on the side of the bed's arm rails. Once situated, Easton told us what happened in so many words. "I was off duty. I was coming home for dinner when I remembered I was supposed to get those drinks Charlie likes." Tanner and Brooklyn's eyes met like magnets before quickly polarizing. Her face was washed in heartbreak, his in guilt.

"I was in the back of the gas station pulling out the drinks from the refrigerator when a guy pulled out his gun. He tried robbing the clerk, but he was a stubborn son of a bitch. He wouldn't give him the money."

"Oh shit," Tanner mumbled into his cupped hand.

"Yeah. He turned his gun on a mom and her son. As soon as he did, the clerk pulled out his own gun. I made my way to the boy and his mom. I took the perp down, but not before he got a shot off." Easton rubbed his hand over the bandage.

"Oh, man. You should have just stayed in uniform until you got home!" Tanner said.

"I was off duty!"

"Still!"

"But I had dinner," Easton said. "Honestly, it was a freak accident. I was lucky to be there when I was."

"Lucky?" I hissed.

"Yeah. I was able to save that boy and his mom. Who knows what would have happened if I wasn't there," Easton said, his voice full once again.

"But who knows what would have happened if you were shot a little higher?" I scowled.

"I do," Easton said, challenging me. But the truth was, he didn't know. None of us did. Except for maybe Brooklyn. But if she did, she wasn't talking about it. I shook my head, barely able to control myself in front of Tanner. I looked away, mauling the inside of my cheek.

"I saved not one life but two! I did it!" Easton said, looking up at his brother.

"You did it . . ." Tanner said, a proud smile across his face.

"I can't wait to do it again!" Easton coughed and grabbed at his side, wincing. Tanner came to his side, and their hands met before he enveloped him in a hug.

"You did it," Tanner repeated. I don't know what goals they had set when becoming police officers, but I was teetering on the edge of concern and alarm.

"I'm glad you're OK, but don't do that again!" Brooklyn said.

"Thank you!" I said in response to her statement.

"What? No! That's my job!" Easton frowned. Both boys turned against Brooklyn and me.

"Your job is to get shot, off duty?" she asked.

"Hey, that's not fair." Tanner came to Easton's defense.

"Well, maybe if he had worn his vest until he got home . . ." she said.

"Well, maybe if he vowed to protect the innocent, then he should do that at all costs and not just when he's on the clock," Tanner dug in. At this point, it was clear they weren't arguing about Easton's safety anymore.

"OK. OK. Can we just celebrate that the boy and his mom are OK? That I'm OK?" Easton asked. And as worried as I was that he may have laid down his life under false impressions, I could agree to celebrate his safety—along with that of the mother and child.

"Yes," I said. "We're so happy you're OK."

"Wait, what about the clerk?" Brooklyn asked. And when Easton gave a slow shake of his head, the room fell silent. ". . . And the shooter?" she asked a moment later.

"I don't think he's going to make it either. They weren't loading him into the ambulance when I was taken away." The room grew quiet once more.

"Hey, looks like you're awake . . ." A nurse walked in, surveying the room. "And there's a party in here. Visiting hours are over. Didn't anyone tell you that?" she asked, one hand on her hip.

"Oh, yeah. I was just leaving," Brooklyn said.

"Me too." Tanner placed his hand on the small of Brooklyn's back and ushered her out. She turned, blowing us a kiss goodbye. And I watched them walk away together. His hand was still resting on her back as they disappeared down the hallway.

"And you, Miss?" the nurse asked me.

"Me? I'm his wife," I said.

"I'm sorry. But no visitors overnight. You can come back in the morning," she said.

"But— "

"It's OK, Beck. Nurse . . ." Easton squinted at the nurse's name tag. "Nurse Shannon is going to take good care of me. Isn't that right?" he asked.

"That's right, Mr. Green. Now say your goodbyes. I'll give you a minute, but then I'm coming back for your checkup," she said. I watched the nurse until her back disappeared from view before turning to Easton.

"I don't want to leave you," I said.

"It's OK. I'll be alright. It's just one night."

I frowned. He didn't know that any more than I did. I stood, bending over the bed, and kissed his forehead. "I love you," I said.

"I love you, too. Honestly, I'm OK. And remember, even if I wasn't, we have a backup plan. May 7 we meet at the bridge. Never forget," Easton said. And for the first time since he woke, I could see the seriousness of the situation touch down upon him. Our plan had always been that if we were to separate, we'd meet again on the bridge. On our anniversary.

"Honey," I said, half-joking, half-serious. "Don't make me change your diapers."

"What?" Easton said. Shocked, he grabbed at his side.

"If you didn't make it . . . I wasn't going to wait until you were old enough to meet me at the bridge. I was going to find you. Now. I was going to call every hospital in the world to find you. And when I did, I would have adopted you." Easton smiled at me with admiration. "But, you know what?" I asked.

"What?"

"You wouldn't be my husband anymore . . . You'd be my son. And that shit's weird. So don't do it!" I jabbed my pointer into his chest. I was serious, but he was laughing, even through the pain. "I'm serious, Easton!" I said as the nurse came in, tapping her watch.

"OK. I won't. I won't do that to you. I promise," Easton said, holding up his hands.

I gave him my most serious glare before turning my back on him. The nurse chuckled when she saw Easton's face wrapped in both pain and pleasure. And as I walked out of the room I heard her say, "Oh, you're in trouble, aren't you?" I nodded silently because he was.

CHAPTER 11

The next couple of days, Easton spent recovering in the hospital, and I juggled my new position as Nora's nanny. It was in Easton's absence that Nora's company was even more than a joy, it was a welcomed distraction. Having her in my car, at my dinner table, and under my roof was more than welcomed. It filled a hole in my heart that I once thought would never heal. And I caught myself frequently with my hand over my heart and tears in my eyes.

Nora was a Tethered Soul. She had already proved that to be true. But occasionally, I thought that Clara wasn't. And that idea had come more often since I had been acting as Nora's nanny. I watched her carefully, and she'd become distracted frequently. The "lights," she'd call them. She tried to hide it as much as possible in my presence, and it made me sad to think she was uncomfortable around me.

However, when she didn't think that I was watching or listening, she spoke of them freely, like an imaginary friend. Clara loved it and asked questions every time it came up. I wondered what Lindsay thought of it all, but that only reminded me I had to have a very serious conversation with her one day about Nora, and I didn't want to think about that.

It was only a couple of days that Easton spent recovering in the hospital, but I quickly became used to my new routine. I took the girls to school in the morning, visited Easton in the hospital, picked up the girls, took Nora to dance, went back to the hospital, and then home for dinner. Nora was picked up each night at varying times, and it was the night that Easton was discharged from the hospital that Nora was staying over for the first time. Lindsay had the night shift, and John was on call for delivery. It was the first night that my family would sleep under one roof, and I couldn't be more grateful for Lindsay's schedule. Nora seemed happy, too.

Easton tried to eat dinner at the dining table, but he was too uncomfortable. The girls had no problem joining Easton on the sofa with their dinner plates. And I could barely eat I was so excited. I had my husband home, safe. And I had both of my girls giggling before me. But as I had learned before, it was in happy moments that sometimes I'd feel the sorrow creep in. I knew it wouldn't always be like this, and that one day, Nora would sit in the living room with a different family, feeling lost and lonely. We'd all be nothing but memories for her to fall back on. When I couldn't shake the thought of it, I cleared plates and cleaned up in the kitchen.

"It's time to turn the lights off. You have school tomorrow, and we need to wake up ready to learn. Did you girls brush your teeth?" I asked. Both girls tucked under the same blanket. One towheaded, one with dark wild hair, and both with pale dimpled cheeks.

"Yes," they said, giggling.

I turned out the lights and stumbled over the bedside. I hugged Clara and whispered, "I love you."

"I love you," she said.

Then I reached over Clara and wrapped my arms around Nora. "I love you," I said.

Nora jolted back, and I worried that I'd upset her. "What's that?" she asked.

"What's what?" I looked around in the dark, and my eyes were adjusted enough to see Nora holding her arms out wide and looking between the two.

"Oh. It's nothing." She reached for me again, and I wrapped my arms around her for a second try. This time, she jumped back. "What is that?!" she gasped.

"I felt it too," I said.

"It tingles?" she asked.

"It's like electricity," I laughed. Nora nodded in agreement and laughed, too.

"I want to feel!" Clara grabbed me and knew I had to act quickly. I dug my fingers into her ribs and tickled her.

"Buzzz!" I said, tickling both girls. They squealed and jumped, giggled and squirmed. I laughed until the room glowed with twinkling stars as bright as the northern sky. And though Nora said nothing, she too had fallen quiet with searching eyes. It wasn't fair that Clara couldn't see the love, but what was most important was that she could feel it. And that she had. I kissed her forehead, and she smiled up at me, unaware of the twinkling night sky within her four bedroom walls, and we said goodnight.

I lay down on Easton's lap in the living room, and he ran his hands through my hair. I didn't say anything for a long while. Not that I didn't know what to say . . . but that I didn't know how to start.

"Hey, Easton?" I asked.

"Huh?"

"I think Nora is Tethered." It pained me to say it.

"Oh, yeah. For sure," he said.

A moment passed before I continued. "But I don't think Clara is . . ."

Easton sighed, and it took him some time before his eyes met mine. "I think you may be right. We're just going to have to give her the best life we can. Encourage her to live it right the first time," he said.

"Well, I mean . . . we need to teach them both that, right?"

"Yeah. But you know what I mean. Nora will have more time to learn it all."

"But what if we're not here to teach her?" I asked.

Easton frowned. "What do you mean? We'll always be here for her." Easton had been thinking it was Clara that he had limited time with, while I was worried about Nora living eternity, alone.

It was then that I found myself with the opportunity to tell him what I had been holding back for so long. "I think this is my last chance, Easton. I don't think I'll be moving on to a third life," I said.

"What are you talking about? Of course, you will. That's how it works," he said, concern still at bay.

"But what if you don't know how it works?" Easton's fingers froze in my hair, and his palm rested heavily on my head. "Brooklyn has been around for much longer than you, and she says there's a way out."

"A way out?" he said, craning to look at me clearly. I sat up when his leg shifted under my head.

"Yeah. Do you want that?" I asked. Easton's jaw dropped open and hung as his eyes searched mine for answers. "I mean, I know you *did*. But do you *still?*"

"Well, a lot has changed, Beck. Why are you just telling me this now? How long have you known there might be another option for us?" he asked.

"Um, for a while," I admitted.

"How long, Beck?"

I looked away. "Since before we married," I said, softly.

"What?!" his voice raised.

"Shhh, the girls are trying to sleep," I said.

Easton twisted and groaned, grabbing at his side as he tried to stand. I reached my hand out to help, but he didn't accept it.

"Let me explain . . ." I pled.

"I just . . . can you just give me a moment? I need to wrap my head around this before we go any further," he said, heading for the door.

"Wait!" I called out, but the door closed behind him. I stood in the middle of the living room, my thoughts on Easton alone. I didn't want him to be mad at me, and I probably should have told him sooner. I *definitely* should have told him sooner. It took everything I had to sit back down and give him the space he needed, but I did so staring at the door knob, willing him to come back. When I heard his car door shut and the window lit from his headlights, I promised myself that I'd never keep a secret from him again. No matter how big, how small, or how hurtful. I'd never do it again.

Easton came home that night before I fell asleep. When he walked in and saw me sitting right where he left me, his face softened. He strode toward me and took a seat by my side, grimacing as he leaned back. Once comfortable, he nodded. "OK. I'm ready. Explain," he said.

I took a deep breath and began. "Brooklyn says that we're tethered because we had an unfair disadvantage. We were taken before our time for one reason or another. Most likely for the greater good. That being a Tethered Soul is like getting alternative compensation—only, some of us don't want it. She says that it was never meant to be forever. And that more often than not, a Tethered Soul will only take one extra life." I spoke clearly and slowly, allowing him the time he needed to take it all in. But he didn't need more time than he had already taken on his drive. He urged me to continue.

"She said that our tether would last as long as needed to get one *full* life in. Once we achieved our best life, then we would be rightfully compensated, and we would move on. Just like everyone else."

"A full life? What does that even mean?" he asked.

I pulled my leg up on the sofa, gripping my shin. I couldn't tell how he was taking the news, and I worried more with every bit of new information I gave him. "Brooklyn said that sometimes, being tethered can backfire. And that's when a Tethered Soul becomes stranded and ultimately turns to a Tortured Soul." I watched him carefully. "She says that's what you are . . ."

"What about her? She's been here longer than I have. Why hasn't she lived her one life then?" Easton asked, skeptical.

"Because she doesn't want to die. She likes it here." I shrugged.

"Then how is she continuing to live? How does she make sure she doesn't have a full—" Easton paused, his eyes trailing off into the distance. "She won't marry Tanner," he said softly. I nodded. "She doesn't want kids . . ." he said, cupping his mouth. His eyes met mine in question. "You knew this *before* we married? *Before* we had our girls?"

"I did," I admitted.

Easton ran his hands through his hair. I knew what he was thinking. He was thinking that I chose a life with him that would end, when I could have chosen one that lasted forever.

But that's not what I saw. I saw the quality of our lives meaning more than the minutes, the days, and the years we'd spend here. "I didn't want to tell you. I thought I'd be messing with fate. I wanted you to live your best life, but I only wanted it for you when you were ready to take it. I didn't want to be the reason you forced it. I didn't want you to go . . . *uncompensated*," I said with a shrug. I didn't know how else to say it.

"Do you think that I've lived tortured all these lives because I wouldn't allow myself to love?" he asked. It hurt to hear. To think that he had been walking this earth for centuries trying to protect his heart, but all he was doing was hurting himself in the long run.

"It's not for me to say. Maybe?"

"And now, that we have each other . . . now that we have our daughters, you think we're living our last lives? That our time is limited?" he asked.

"I believe mine is." I couldn't explain it. It was just a feeling I had.

"And mine?"

"I don't know, Easton. I don't know what a full life looks like for you. All I know is that I feel it in my heart. I feel it when I look at you, and I feel it when the girls giggle. I feel it when I laugh with Brooklyn, and when Lindsay hugs me. I just know that I was lucky to have another chance at life. And I know that I took it."

Easton's eyes locked onto mine as he absorbed what I had said. "I never took it. I was too broken to even try." Easton hung his head and mindlessly rubbed his side where his kidney had once been.

"You have to be careful at work, Easton. You might not be coming back again," I said. He looked at me, his eyes wide with the realization that things weren't what they seemed. "You might not be as invincible as you once thought."

The corners of his lips curved ever so slightly. "I can graduate," he said.

"What do you mean?"

"All my lives, it was like never graduating. Never moving on to the next level. No progression, no advancement. But now, I can earn it. And I want to. I've wanted to earn it since the day I met you. My lives were stagnant before I met you. But they've been in motion ever since. You opened up my heart and not just to you but to everyone. My brother, my adopted parents . . . You gave me Clara and Nora . . . You gave me my full life. If Brooklyn was right, and that's all it took to graduate, then I was already on my way."

Easton took my hand in his and kissed my knuckles. "I don't want you to ever think that you need to hide something from me. We're in this together. Right?" he asked.

"Right. You're so right! I'm so sorry, I don't know what I was thinking. I'll never hide anything from you again. I'm done with secrets!"

"Promise?" he asked.

"Promise."

"Then you need to tell Lindsay about Nora," he said.

It hit like a ton of bricks dropping into my lap. "I know I do. Soon." I nodded.

"Soon." Easton pulled me into his arms and called out when I leaned against his wound.

"Oh! I'm so sorry!" I said. He shook his head and pulled me into him again. I hugged him more carefully this time. I lay on him, feeling light as air. Feeling closer to him than I ever had before. The heat from his chest warmed my cheek, and I took in one long, cleansing breath. A breath that was pure and hopeful. Until . . .

"Poor Nora . . ." he said.

CHAPTER 12

I found myself in the parking lot of Sunny Hill Assisted Living, unable to bring myself in. I knew I'd face my mother, and she'd face a stranger. I'd be no different to her than any other person she would see today. Another face in a sea of people she could no longer recognize. The relentless fear in her eyes was heartbreaking, and I knew that today would be no different. I felt the guilt flow through my veins as I sat in my truck. How dare I not be eager to see her . . . to try and improve her day. But I *wasn't* eager. I didn't want to look into the eyes of my flesh and blood—the eyes of the woman who raised me . . . and know she saw nothing in return. I didn't want to do it.

It would be different if I had Tommy. Or even Bodie. Because if I walked through those doors with a leash in my hand, I'd know that I could bring a smile to my mom's face. She wouldn't recognize me, of course, but she would be smiling. Her fear would be pushed to the outskirts of her mind, and for a moment . . . just a moment . . . she'd be happy. As happy as she could be these days. I wanted that for her. I wanted to be the one to bring that to her. And selfishly, I wanted to walk through those doors and know that my heart wouldn't be ripped from my chest.

I sighed. Taking my bag in my hand, I locked my truck and started for the doors. Lindsay wasn't working today, so I'd be on my own. I could do it. At least that's what I told myself.

"Good morning. Are you visiting today?"

"Yes. Beck in room 306."

"Oh, lovely. She could use a smile today. Just sign in here." I looked at the woman behind the desk, trying to decipher what she meant when she said that my mother could use a smile today. It didn't sound like a good thing, and I was sure I needed to prepare for an uphill battle. My stomach twisted, tying in knots.

"Thank you," I said, setting the pen down. I stalled before the door, my eyes fixed on the 306 tacked to the wall. I knew some days were better than others; Lindsay had warned me of that. And I had only seen my mother a couple of times since she had been in the home. Each time had been like the time before. She was quiet. Timid. Distant. I didn't have it in me to see her on a bad day, but I couldn't give up on her. What kind of daughter would I be then? I twisted the knob and slowly opened the door, peeking my head in.

"Hello?" I said. Mom sat in bed, gazing out the window. "Good morning, Mrs. Beck. How are you today?" I asked, knowing I wouldn't get an answer. She didn't acknowledge me.

I placed my bag down on the table and sat at the edge of her bed. When I took her hand in mine, she slowly turned to look at me. I smiled warmly at her, and for a second, I thought she felt something. But then, like every other time, she turned away, indifferent. I wanted to shake her—tell her she had to remember me. Tell her I missed her and that I was sorry for leaving her the way that I did. That I was sorry for ruining her life.

"Look," she said, pointing out the window.

Look? She's talking?

I looked out the window, arching my back to see what she had been pointing at. I craned my neck, looking all around, but saw nothing. "What is it?" I asked.

"Look . . . an angel . . ."

Cold chills ran down my spine. I saw no angel beyond the window pane, and I had seen no such thing when I died, but that didn't mean she didn't see it now. I looked out the window again, but still, there was nothing but the lush green garden of unpickable roses. I turned back to her, the morning sun lighting up her eyes. "It's beautiful," I said.

I wiped my clammy hands off on my jeans and pulled my hair back into a ponytail. Her gaze remained on the angel. "Breakfast time, Mrs. Beck." A young nurse backed into the room, holding a tray of food. "Oh! I didn't realize she had company!"

"Hello," I said, helping her guide the tray to a nearby table. "I'm B . . . Becca."

"I'm Christine. Nice to meet you. She hasn't been eating very well lately. Would you mind trying to get her to take a few bites while you're here?" Christine asked.

"Oh, sure. I don't mind."

"Thank you. I'll be by later to get the tray," she said.

"Thanks, Christine." She gave me a polite smile and moved on to deliver more breakfast that would go uneaten and unacknowledged. *It must feel like a thankless job*, I thought. The eggs looked wet and the toast brittle. "Are you hungry, Mom?" I asked. My heart-stopping as it slipped from my mouth. But her gaze was still set on the angel outside her window, and I realized that she didn't know any better. I could call her Mom if I wanted. And I could tell her all the things that I wished I had before I died. I had a golden ticket here to say whatever I wanted . . . Whatever, I *needed.* And why shouldn't I?

"Mom?" I whispered, looking for subtle hints of recollection in her eyes. "Mom, do you remember me?"

Not so much as a blink of her eyes. I was relieved at first, but on the edge of that relief was regret for not getting to her sooner. *I should have* . . . I squeezed her hand and took down the facade, piece by piece.

"I should have . . . come back for Easton's shoe." I dropped my gaze to our hands. Both similar—one kissed by the wrinkles of time and the other gifted with renewal. Our fingers were the same shape . . . or had been before her knuckles grew with arthritis. It was likely the reason that she didn't wear her wedding band.

"I should have knocked on your door. Journals in hand. We could have gone through them together. I know you would have been sad. Maybe even a little angry, and that would have been OK, too. But I should have come back for you. And I didn't. I should have done it the very second I remembered my life with you and Dad. I should have . . . I *could* have . . . haunted Carter." I chuckled.

My cheeks were tight as I pondered the many ways I could have gotten him back for all the pranks he played on me as a kid. But they slackened when my fun-loving imagination showed me the more realistic fallout. Carter wouldn't find it funny and neither would I. I sighed, dispelling the thought that any of this could ever be fun.

"I'm sorry I left you. It wasn't by choice. I never would have gotten in that car had I known I would've done that to you and Pop. I know my time was limited as it was, but I had months longer to say the things I needed to, and it was all taken away too fast. Maybe I would have come to grips with the idea of dying, and I would have opened up more. I could have accepted it, and then I could have told my friends, my aunt, my teachers, and co-workers. I could have told everyone, and I could have felt the love and support that I know everyone was robbed of giving me. I could have leaned on them. On you. And it would have given you time to prepare, too. I'm sure there are a lot of things you wanted to say to me that you never had the chance to get out. Or simply hugged me a little longer . . . but we can do that now, can't we?" I asked.

Afraid to look at her, I refused to raise my eyes. My body felt heavy like someone had draped a weighted blanket over my shoulders, and I succumbed to the pressure. Folding in on myself, I let go of my mom's hand and laid my head down on her lap. Her tiny lap. I curled myself onto the edge of her bed as she lay still. It didn't feel like it had when I was a kid seeking the comfort of my mother. She was no longer the stronger of us, and I was no longer afraid. I didn't lay across her lap because I was scared, but more because I needed her love, and she wouldn't give it to me. She *couldn't* give it to me. So, I rest my head on her thin, brittle legs, and I pretended that she pulled me into her embrace like the last hug I never got.

When I felt her hand drop to the edge of the bed, my eyes dampened, wishing that it had fallen to my shoulder or that she had played with my hair the way she once had. "You're going to be OK, Mom. I know you've had a hard life. No parent should ever have to bury their child. Even I can't understand what you went through, and once upon a time, I lost my Molly. I know you questioned life for a long time after I died. And I know you never found an answer. But the world kept spinning, and you kept living. It's hard to live with a broken heart. I know that. I've felt that. But Pop is waiting for you. Somewhere, he's waiting for you. And you're going to be alright." The door cracked open, and I startled, jolting the bed.

"Oh, I'm sorry to interrupt. I'm collecting trays." A nurse backed into the room, wheeling a cart. I sat up and wiped the tears from my eyes.

"It's OK," I said.

The nurse looked at me for just a moment and nodded. She had seen it all before. "Family?" she asked, softly.

I had never seen this nurse before, and Mom wouldn't say any differently. "Yes," I admitted. She smiled with empathy.

"She likes the pudding the most, but even that she hasn't been eating. I see today is no different. I'll leave it behind for her, in case you can get her to take a few bits, and I'll take everything else with me."

"Thank you," I said, as the nurse excused herself.

I peeled back the lid and sank a plastic spoon into the vanilla pudding. I held out a small spoonful, but she was disinterested. "Still looking at your angel?" I asked. Her face lit up with a rosy glow, and the corners of her lips pulled upward. I chuckled to myself, and she found it to be contagious. When she started to laugh, I did too, and it snowballed from there. Before I knew it, Mom and I were laughing together, just like old times. Only this time, I didn't know what we were laughing at, and neither did she. As soon as the laughter came, it passed by like a rogue wave—there one minute, gone the next. And the wake was just a silent reminder of all the things we didn't have to share because of her dementia.

I stood by the side table, setting her pudding pack down. My attention kept finding its way back to my bag and the contents that hid within. I glanced at my mom, who was watching the garden like a feature film. "Hey, I brought something I wanted to show you," I said, making my way to the bag. I slipped my hand inside and pulled out my journals, tied once again with the burlap bow. Just like my mom had them displayed. "Do you remember these?" I asked, bringing them to her side. She looked down at them, her expression unchanged.

"I told you not to read them because there were some things in here I didn't want you to see. I always figured you'd read them, anyway. But you didn't." I untied the bow, and she watched, more intrigued than I had seen her since coming to Sunny Hill Assisted Living. I flipped to the last few pages in the journal where I had kept my goodbye letters. I took out the envelope marked "Mom" and opened it for the first time, running my finger underneath the seal. I unfolded the letter and held it in my shaky hands. Nine pages of goodbyes and regrets.

"Mom," I began. "I'm sorry I never told you about my illness. I don't want you to worry. And I can't bear to look into your eyes for my final months and see a broken woman. I just want everything to remain as normal as could be. I need it too. I need my parents to be strong and supportive because if you were anything less, then I might crumble. And I don't have the strength for that, nor the time." I paused in reflection, remembering a life where time was fleeting.

"I'm so tired, Mom, and I can feel my body deceiving me. Forgive me for keeping that burden to myself, but it's not one that I want to share. You don't have to worry about me. I'm not alone in this. I've met someone. He's kind of cute in his own way. Not really my type, but I think he found his way into my life for a reason. It's weird because I feel like I can talk to him. And I need someone I can open up to right now. Someone who can support me but who isn't already a pillar in my life. I hope you understand."

I flipped the page, appreciating the bittersweetness to the memories of a time when Easton was just an ember in my heart. A mysterious stranger. I'd hoped he would be a light for me in a time of darkness, but little did I know that he would be so much more. I read page after page of memories that I held dear to my heart—and a few apologies for things I never moved on from. My eyes burned by the time I reached the ending.

"Mom, I know you will be sad when you read this one day, and that's the last thing I want for you. So for me, if you don't mind, could you look back and remember me for all the good times? The laughs, the messes made, and lessons learned? Because the suffering pales in comparison to all the fun we had and the love we shared. And I'll be fine. I don't know what will happen to me after I'm gone, but I'll be OK. Because I'm the strong and capable woman you raised me to be. So, thank you for giving me the best parts of yourself. It was the best part of my life. I love you, always. Till we meet again, Everly . . ."

Till we meet again. I never thought it would be like this. Slowly, I folded the nine-page letter and tucked it back into its envelope. Mom's frail hand grabbed hold of my wrist, and I was taken aback to see her looking into my eyes. Not past them or through them but directly into them. Not just who I was now but the girl I'd always been. She saw me. *Me.* Tears welled in her eyes. She said nothing, but she didn't need words to express all that she had in that moment. I could *feel* it. "Mom?" I whispered, heart thumping in my chest.

"How did she do?" the nurse asked, barging in on the most fragile and, unfortunately, fleeting moment. As soon as I looked away, the bond had broken. Mom's grip was still tight around my wrist, but she was no longer looking at me or anything in particular. Not even the angel in the garden.

"Um . . ." I began. Not wanting to move on.

"You said this was Mom? I think your brother just got here!"

"What?!"

"Yeah, Mr. Beck just signed in. You have to see these flowers he brought . . ."

I pried my mom's fingers from my wrist. My heart pounding in my chest as I jumped to my feet and fled the room. The nurse whirled around as I burst through the door. I nearly ran straight into Carter, a pair of legs walking a grand bouquet of white lilies. "Oh!" I gasped, spinning on my heels as he lifted the bouquet to see who he'd nearly run into.

"Sorry! Didn't see you there!" he said. But I was already down the hall in a half-jog. And I knew that while I'd managed to grab my bag, I left behind the journals and all of my goodbye letters . . . including Carter's.

CHAPTER 13

It was a perfect Sunday morning—lazy, slow. I was tangled up in bedsheets and Easton when the doorbell rang. Only, I hadn't been expecting anyone. "Who's that?" I asked Easton. He shrugged, just as confused as I was. I slipped on pajama pants and a robe and hobbled down the hall. I saw Brooklyn through the peephole, holding a tray of coffees. But when I opened the door, she was no longer the center of my attention, and neither were her caffeinated gifts.

Black shaggy hair covered the lonely eyes of Bodie as he sat on my doorstep; leash wrapped around Brooklyn's hand. "What?!" I shrieked. The dog lurched forward to smell me.

Brooklyn shrugged, a big smile on her face as she held out the leash for me to take. "He's all yours," she said. My throat swelled and my eyes burned as I kneeled down slowly. Bodie's tail wagged slowly as he sniffed my face.

"Hi, Bodie! Hi!" I said, scratching behind his ears.

"What's going on?" Easton came to the door in a pair of sweatpants and nothing else. His incision was purple and still somewhat inflamed. My eyes dropped, lingering on the shadow of his obliques. "Morning, Brooklyn. Who's this? Did you get a dog?" Easton leaned down to pet Bodie.

"He's deaf," I said.

"He's *yours*," Brooklyn laughed.

Easton stiffened, pointing in question to his bare chest. Brooklyn nodded as we waited to see how he would take the news. "Mine? Like here? In *this* house?" He pointed to the hardwood floor, frozen like a statue, but I imagined his mind was racing.

"Please!" I said, hugging Bodie around the neck.

"How old is he?" he asked. I looked to Bodie and the tips of white hair on his chin.

Brooklyn's shoulders dropped as she thrust the tray of coffee toward Easton's chest. "Seven or eight," she said, letting herself in.

"Come on. Come on, Bodie," I encouraged. But he didn't need to be babied; he was all smiles and tail wags.

"Well, is a deaf dog going to be safe with Clara?" Easton asked. I stilled, looking to Brooklyn for answers. He hung in the doorway, unconvinced.

"He's perfect for her. I had a dream about it. They're already best buds!" she said.

"Yeah!" I agreed, fully trusting Brooklyn's gifts. Easton sighed, knowing he had lost the battle before it even started. He set the coffees down on the kitchen counter, and I took the leash off Bodie.

"Thanks for the coffee," Easton said, taking a sip and making himself comfortable on the sofa.

"Yeah, thanks for the coffee . . . and the *dog!* How did you even get him? They never returned any of my calls. Oh, my god . . . Did you steal him?" My mind spun a web of lies—all of the things I would say if we ever got caught.

"What? No!" she said.

"Of course not," I shook my head, thankful.

"I've been working with Sandy behind the scenes. I asked her to keep it a secret from you, and she was more than willing." I looked up at Brooklyn, remembering the conversation we had in the car. She was worried that I didn't need her now that I had my first best friend back in the picture. I jumped to my feet to give her a hug. Bodie flinched, and I froze midway to her. Then, ever so slowly, I wrapped my arms around her. "You don't need to do that," she said.

"Thank you, Brooklyn. He's the best gift anyone's ever given me . . ."

"Hey!" Easton grumbled from the living room.

"Did you hear that, Easton?" Brooklyn laughed. "Well, you're welcome. You deserve him. And I think he'll make you happy."

"Yeah, and my mom, too!" I said. I'd been so excited, scratching the back of Bodie's ear that I barely caught the troubled look in Brooklyn's eyes as she turned away.

"So, you said you had a dream that Bodie would be good for Clara?" Easton asked.

"Uh-huh," Brooklyn sipped her coffee.

"Do you remember, back at campus, when you told me you had a dream of Beck and me dying?" Easton asked, and the air shifted in the room, turning the buzzing energy into a frigid chill. Where was he going with this?

"Yeah, I remember."

"Well, I always thought that you dreamed about the car accident. I thought it was weird that you had a dream like that, but we had already died, so I just thought nothing of it—"

"Shhh, keep your voice down," I said, my neck craning towards Clara's room. Her door was still closed.

"—but now, I'm worried that what you saw wasn't a vision of the past."

Brooklyn sat across from Easton, and I remained on the floor with the dog, watching, waiting.

"No. It wasn't of the car accident, though I saw that, too," Brooklyn said, pausing for a long moment.

"Can you tell us what you saw then? Because you show up with this dog and these dreams, and I know there's always more to the story than you willingly tell."

Brooklyn's eyes flickered to mine, and my stomach dropped. Did I want to know? She'd never shared this with me before, and I assumed it was for good reason. But then again, I'd never asked. It could have been as simple as that.

Before I knew it, both of them were looking at me in question, and I knew it was up to me to decide if I wanted to hear about how I would die. Just because I had done it once before, didn't make it any easier. It was still just scary and unnerving. "OK. It's OK," I said, seeking comfort in the eyes of Bodie.

"Are you sure you want to know?" Brooklyn asked.

"I mean . . . I don't know? You tell me," I said, dumping the decision on her.

She nodded, then began. "It's a terrible storm. Worst one in a decade—"

"Wait!" I said. "Are you sure?"

Brooklyn stared at me, considering my doubt, but ultimately began again. "You're older—seventy maybe. Your hair is white." Brooklyn motioned to her head as her eyes lost their focus. Chills crawled down my spine, and I pulled Bodie close.

"You're wearing a teal scarf and these tiger's eye drop earrings that you cherish. I don't know why. Your lips are red like you know it's your last day and you want to dress up one last time," she said, brows knitted. I could see the hurt in her eyes as she walked through her vision.

A moment passed—long enough for Easton and me to worry. Our eyes met the moment she began again. "It's peaceful. You're in bed, nearly sleeping when it happens. There are flowers. They're beautiful . . ." Brooklyn trails off, her eyes squinting as she tries to pull herself back to the present moment. I rubbed the goosebumps from my arms and failed to meet the eyes of my husband.

"And she doesn't come back?" Easton asked, softly. "Her tether . . . It's broken?"

I looked up to Brooklyn and found that her face was twisted in grief and something else—maybe regret or uncertainty. I couldn't tell. "I . . . I'm not certain she ever *was* tethered," she said.

"What?" Easton asked.

I opened my mouth, but the words never came. The room was silent for what felt like an eternity. "I'm not sure! I don't know! I mean, yes, she was tethered . . ." She stumbled over her words. I let out a breath of air and glanced at

Easton, worried. ". . . but, maybe not in the way that you always thought her to be."

"What are you talking about, Brooklyn? If there's anything you know, you need to say it now. Just say it," Easton demanded.

"You see, Easton and I are tethered to this earth, right? But, I *think*—I don't *know*—that Becca is tethered to *you* . . ."

"To me?" Easton asked.

"Yes, you." Easton and I looked at one another, and I felt gravity itself shift beneath me. "Easton, you couldn't get your life to make sense. All your chances and you never seemed to get it right. But there was an answer to all your questions. It was as simple as love. But not just any love. It had to be a love so strong and so deep that it would flip your world upside down. Becca was the only one that could do that for you. And in the process, I think her soul got wrapped around yours. The circumstances weren't quite right with her cancer and all. Your heart needed more time—more experience. The only remedy was a second chance at first love."

"So, I never had more lives?" I asked Brooklyn.

"No. At least, I don't think so . . . While your life wasn't perfect by any means, it was still enough. A Tethered Soul is usually seen when a child is taken too soon. You were far from being a child when you received your diagnosis. And that's why I can't help but wonder if you were ever tethered at all."

"Then, why all the talk about living forever? About mediocracy being the key to eternity? Why would you lie about that?" I demanded, anger boiling under my skin, making the nape of my neck heat.

"Well, like I said, I don't know for certain. And it's confusing. I'm only human. I make mistakes, too!" she said defensively.

"How do you know any of this? Any of it at all?" Easton pried.

Brooklyn sighed, throwing her head back onto the sofa. "OK. I'm . . . a caseworker, if you will. It doesn't really have an official name, but that's beside the point. The point is that my gift, coupled with my Tethered Soul, makes me a unique piece in this game."

"Game?" I asked.

"Well, no. It's not a game, but for the sake of analogy . . . if it were a game of chess, and everyone was pawns taking one step forward at a time, your Tethered Souls would be the horses. You move in unique ways compared to all the other players. Different rules apply to you. But then there's me, and I'd be the queen because I can move almost any way I want to."

"Who's the king?" Easton asked.

"What?"

"The king. If we're playing chess, who's the king?" he said.

"No. We're not playing chess. All I'm saying is that it's my job to protect you. It's my job to help you get to the other side of the board. And I do that with my gift. My knowledge of the past and future. It's like the queen's ability to move in many directions around the board."

"So, no king," Easton confirmed.

"I was there the day you two met. On the bridge. Did you know that?" Brooklyn stood and paced the length of the room.

"I had been following Easton's case after having a dream about him. I found him nearly a month later after having a dream every single night about his empty heart. His need for a soul unlike any other. The perfect companion suited for his special situation."

"You were there?" I asked in awe.

"Situation?" Easton asked.

"Yeah. You had lived so long, everyone bored you. Everyone was predictable," she said, and Easton nodded in agreement. "You had to fall for a heart that needed you as desperately as you needed it. And that was none other than the dying heart of Everly Beck," she said.

My insides twisted with a weird sensation; like butterflies in the stomach, but much higher, swirling in my chest and escaping into my throat where the cancer had once been.

"I started having dreams of the both of you at dinner with a note—a contract of sorts. A stolen kiss in the parking lot. And dancing in a field, till the rain fell. I knew it was my job to help secure the path for you. And when Easton was having trouble with his car on the day you two met and he walked to the bridge in that awful storm, I knew the entire plan would be thrown out the window."

I glanced at Easton as his eyes fixed on recollection. I never knew he had car troubles that day, but I had always wondered how he got to the bridge without a car in sight. It gave merit to Brooklyn's story, though I didn't need it. I already believed her.

"I went to Beck's doctor's appointment, pretending to be the patient before her. I ate up twice as much time as the doctor allowed. When your appointment was pushed back an hour, you hadn't even noticed," she said.

"You saw me?" I asked, and Bodie nudged my hand gently.

"Yeah, I saw you in the waiting room. You were so lost. You needed Easton just as badly as he needed you after roaming this earth for three hundred years . . . I watched you two at the coffee shop, and I was there at that wedding you crashed. I crashed it too," she said with a laugh. The memories came back to me like shattered pieces of glass—there but distorted. Had I seen Brooklyn at the wedding?

"When you two died, I had another case I needed to work on. I wrapped it up as quickly as possible. It was a year's time before I could follow you."

"You followed us?"

"I had to. I'd never loved a case as much as I did yours. I knew Easton would spend his life trying to find you, so I set out looking for you first, Becca. I got parents near your home, and I made sure we became friends. I was always there for you, even when you didn't know it," she said.

"But how? How did you pick your parents?" I asked.

"Remember, I move differently. I have more options because I've dedicated myself to helping people just like you. People who are lost . . . the tethered and tortured," Brooklyn said, the pacing finally slowing to a point where she could sit back down. It helped put me at ease, but nothing worked quite like Bodie when he rested his head on my lap.

"The case of Easton's heart captured mine in a way no other case had. But nothing was better than being your friend, Becca. At first, it was just part of the job, but quickly, I opened my heart to you in the same way Easton had. And I hadn't done that in a very, very long time. It was so nice having a friend—a genuine friend—that sometimes . . . I lost my way. Sometimes, I didn't want the job anymore. And sometimes, I'd have given it up to keep you as a friend. I didn't want to lose you any more than Easton did. And I knew that once your hearts connected and you fulfilled each other's deepest desires, you would be gone. And I would remain. And then, I would be the one with an empty heart."

I wrapped my hand around the nape of my neck—a worry set deep within. I hurt for her. She'd been a soul dedicated to helping others, and her own basic needs had gone unmet as a result. It was the ultimate sacrifice, and she'd been doing it ever since they called her a witch and burned her at the stake.

"I'm *so* sorry, Becca . . . I should have done better—"

"No, don't be! I love you so much—" I began.

"No. Not for that—" she said, as the phone rang.

A chill set in, sending a shiver down my spine. The phone rang a second time, and the three of us looked at one another. Only Easton and I were uncertain of the doom that hung in the balance. The phone rang a third time, and nobody moved to pick it up.

It was then when Brooklyn said, "It's your mother . . ."

CHAPTER 14

The day was long and the night restless. Not just for me, but Easton, too. Clara had spent the day introducing Bodie to every square inch of the house. While I followed them supervising, my mind was off in a distant land. Had I really not been a Tethered Soul? All this time? My tether was born not of the cancer that stole my life but from the man who stole my heart? Had it been a symbol of our undying love? If so, it hadn't been a curse at all.

My life was cut short but nothing like the horrific events that both Easton and Brooklyn had to endure. I had time to experience friendships and a loving family. I was lucky enough to have fallen in love. And if I really thought about it . . . I had a damn good life. The funny thing was, I never knew it. Until now, that was.

It was so easy to think of all the experiences I would never have. And it was so easy to see the ill-fated existence, that I never opened my eyes to the remarkable life around me. I may never have seen it without the privilege of knowing Easton or Brooklyn. Their struggles were so real, so heartbreaking, that they thoroughly put my first life into perspective.

I'd had . . . a wonderful life until my diagnosis. And even then, the worst part was feeling alone, and I think I did that to myself.

I really had been my own worst enemy. Because life was what you made of it, and I'd been skipping out on all the things that made it worthwhile. I always thought life had to be long to be fulfilling. Or that you had to change the world in some grand way to matter. But that wasn't true at all.

I watched as Clara showed Bodie her favorite stuffed animal and I wondered if she would grow up with the perspective that I had in my first life, or if it was something I could teach her now. And as Bodie sniffed around her room, I began to wonder about Nora and how much more difficult it would be to teach her what so few knew.

That night, when Clara was fast asleep—with Bodie at the foot of her bed—I lay on Easton's chest, my eyes refusing to close for slumber. Easton's fingers trailed up and down my back as he, too, was filled with thoughts so loud he couldn't sleep. I had known for some time that I was living my last life, but this was a first for him, and I could feel the tension radiating from his skin. Maybe it was because my heart had been so tangled up with his, or maybe this was how everyone loved, but I could feel his troubles just like they were mine.

"What is it?" I asked, even though I was pretty sure I already knew.

"I'm just having a hard time with all of this. I thought we had forever. I don't know if I believe Brooklyn or not, but I can't shake the thought that maybe, one day, you'll be leaving me."

"You don't know if you believe her?" I asked.

"She said she didn't even know if she was right. She said it was only a theory. How can I believe her when she doesn't even believe herself?" He had a valid point. But I knew how I felt inside, and that was all I needed.

"I think she's right," I said. "I've only known a few Tethered Souls before, Nora being one of them, and they were all much younger than I when they were taken. I was so conditioned to think that my life was unfair. I mean . . . it was, but, what I never realized was it had its moments, too. I met you. I fell in love. I wasn't robbed in the way that I always believed. And if I really think back, I was a lucky girl," I said, planting a kiss on his bare chest.

"You really think that?"

"I do."

"You're a better person than I."

"That's not true. Don't say that," I said.

"Beck, I don't know what's going to happen, but I don't want to lose you," he said.

"You're not going to," I said as I rolled on top of him, straddling him.

"And how can you be so sure," he asked, placing his hands on my hips.

I planted a kiss on his cheek. "Because, my heart is anchored in yours," I whispered. Then, I moved to kiss his other cheek. "And where you go, I go . . ."

He wrapped his hand around the nape of my neck, pulling me in for a deep and long kiss. "Promise?" he asked in a breathy, heady voice.

"I promise," I said. And I meant it. I would try my hardest to stay with him wherever he may roam.

He rolled me over, moaning into my mouth. "Are you OK?" I asked, trying to see his wounds through the darkness of the late night. I felt his bandage scratch the inner part of my thigh and I lowered my knee down against the bedsheets. He nodded just before taking my breath away.

His hold a little tighter, his urgency more intense. My hands gripped tightly as my heart pounded in a way that felt fleeting. Time was slipping through our fingers, and it was more important than ever to show just how deep our love had grown.

Time had passed swiftly, the weeks coming and going with the blink of an eye. My mom's funeral was nice. It was a quiet service. Lindsay attended with the small crowd. Every now and then, she would look over her shoulder at Easton and me in the distance. She was too far away for me to read her expression, but even so, I knew she was wishing I could be there with her and my family.

It was after the service I could tell that her wheels had spun. She looked at me in a way that she never had before. At first, it worried me, but soon it became a look of comfort. And sometime after the service, she had our family over for dinner for the first time. It had been a little odd knowing that John didn't know our secrets, but it was just like when we used to have dinner with Brooklyn and Tanner. Tanner being on the outside of a very secret life we all shared. Lucky for us, John had been such a busy guy that he hardly had the time to consider all of it.

"If you don't mind, John and I would like to talk to you guys about something important," Lindsay said. Dinner was done, and the girls had run off to play in Nora's room.

"Of course!" I said, glancing at Easton.

Lindsay looked at John and took his hand in hers. She gave him a quick nod, and he replied with a wide-eyed look that I couldn't quite read. "I wanted to talk to you guys about Nora. It might come as a surprise, but she's adopted. We took Nora in when she was a baby," Lindsay said. My stomach dropped, and my eyes ticked toward Easton's. He played it much cooler than I.

"I had no idea," he said, simply.

"Yeah. I had a hysterectomy some time back because of cancerous cells."

"Oh, no!" I said.

Easton nodded, "Uh, huh."

"It's OK. We caught it super early. But the devastating part was that I couldn't get pregnant. We had always wanted to have a baby, and I was especially looking forward to taking advantage of John's 3D ultrasound pictures," Lindsay said with a nervous laugh. I chuckled along with her, equally nervous about where the conversation was going.

"Anyway, we applied for adoption. It took some time, but we were approved. One day, when I was visiting him in the hospital, this beautiful baby caught my eye. I remember she stole my heart right away. It wasn't long after that we received a call from the adoption company assigning a baby girl to us." Lindsay's eyes started to water and her voice rose several octaves. "It was her. It was Nora. I just knew it was meant to be . . ."

I felt a tug at my heart, knowing that she was meant to be ours above anyone else. That fate had twisted unconventionally to give Lindsay what she'd always wanted. And that it was I who suffered the consequences. It left a bitter taste in my mouth, and I was rendered speechless.

"And just as Nora was meant to be in our lives, we believe that your family is a part of that plan. You have become so important to us in such a short time," Lindsay said, her eyes flicking to her husband's. "Would you take Nora in, should anything happen to us?"

I stared into Lindsay's eyes, my emotions scattered like a dandelion pappus riding in the wind. It had been everything I ever wanted—both my girls under my wing. But not at the expense of my oldest friend.

"We would be honored. The girls are already best friends, and Becca nannies Nora; it would be seamless for our family to take her in. You have nothing to worry about in the off event that something happens to you prematurely," Easton said, reaching for my hand.

I looked towards John, who had somewhat of a suspicious look in his eyes. Easton had been confident and strong, and Lindsay a weeping mess. I gazed at each of them through what felt like a lens of slow motion. It was when Easton squeezed my hand that I jolted back into the present moment, remembering that I, too, needed to speak.

"Nothing would make us happier . . . I mean . . . No, not like that!" I fumbled over my words. Lindsay chuckled through her tears, and John's scowl deepened. "I mean, you have our word. We would do everything in our power to raise her" —I swallowed, my throat dry as could be—"as our own . . ." I choked out.

Lindsay covered her mouth, crying into the palm of her hand. She stood, the chair screeching along the tile behind her as she made her way to me.

"I've written your family up in our will," said John. "The papers will be recorded later this week. Let us know if you change your minds. It's no problem at all for us to amend the will at any time. Any time at all," he added, being crystal clear.

Lindsay squeezed me tight, and I patted her back, still wounded from her earlier comment. Through Lindsay's hair, I caught John shrugging as he shook Easton's hand. "They've just become so close, so fast," he said, meaning for only Easton to hear. It was clear he didn't understand what was going on between Lindsay and me, or even the girls, for that matter. And from what I gathered, he was skeptical but not necessarily opposed.

"Yeah, they're like kindred spirits—or old friends," Easton said in return.

Lindsay pulled away and wiped the tears from her cheeks. "Thank you. You don't know how much this means to me. When I saw you at the funeral, I just realized how much you're like family to me. And I want you to know that," Lindsay said, quiet enough for only us to hear. She looked back at John, beaming at him from across the dining room.

"Is he OK with this?" I asked.

"Oh, yeah. Of course," she said.

"Um, you're like family to me, too. And Nora . . . she's . . . she's . . ." I couldn't say it. I couldn't say anything that wasn't true any longer. Nora wasn't *like* family, she *was* family. "Hey, can we talk?"

Lindsay's brows came together in concern. "Yeah, is everything OK?" she asked.

"Everything's OK. But there is something I need to tell you. And it's . . . private," I said, looking back at the boys. Lindsay's gaze followed mine. She took a deep breath before nodding her head.

"Um, John?" she said.

"Yeah?"

"I forgot dessert. Becca and I are going to run out really quick to pick up some ice cream."

"Are you sure? The girls won't even notice," he said.

"Of course they will! Plus, we're celebrating!" Lindsay said. I offered a smile of encouragement.

"Well, why don't I go? You can stay here?"

"Oh no. That's OK. We'll be right back," Lindsay said, pulling me in tow. I passed Easton with lifted brows and I saw him bring his hand to his stomach nervously.

"Be back soon!" I said before turning away.

CHAPTER 15

It was s'mores ice cream, a pink plastic spoon, and my last secret. Lindsay and I sat in the parking lot of the ice cream shop with the headlights turned off and the music playing softly in the background. I dug through my ice cream, looking for a place to start. I preferred it to be a thick ribbon of marshmallow, but I had more pressing concerns at the moment.

"Are you sure you're OK with my request? I know it's a lot. And I know I'm older than you now, but I—" Lindsay said, waving her spoon around in the driver's seat.

"No! That's not it. That's not it at all." I said. A long pause stretched between us when I didn't follow up.

"Then what is?" she asked.

"I . . . I don't know how to say it," I stammered.

"Beck, just spit it out. I literally asked you to take my daughter if I die. The least you can do is talk to me about whatever's bothering you," she said, spooning her mint chip ice cream.

"OK. I'll just say it. But you have to promise me you won't get mad at me. And that things will not change between us. Because I couldn't handle that."

"What are you talking about? Nothing is changing!" Lindsay brought her hand up in question.

"Just promise me, Lindsay."

"OK. I promise. Now say it."

I took a moment. Her promise was short and sharp, not at all what I wanted to hear before saying that her adopted daughter never should have been up for adoption in the first place—that it was all an accident. "Nora . . ." I started, but fear swelled my throat shut. What if she turned on me? What if she thought I was trying to take her away? What if they moved and I never saw Nora again?

"Beck, you're starting to scare me . . ." Lindsay lowered her ice cream into her lap and laid her eyes on mine. The pressure was peaking at an all-time high.

"No, I'm sorry. That's not my intention. I'm just scared," I said.

"What about Nora?" Lindsay asked.

"Nora . . . Nora is mine," I said. It came out all wrong. It was true, but it sounded off. The words hung in the air and I watched as Lindsay tried to grasp at them.

"I don't . . . What does that mean? I don't—" She ran a hand through her hair.

I set my ice cream on the dashboard and turned to my oldest friend, remembering the worst day of my lives. "Clara was a twin. Do you remember?"

"Yeah, I remember John said it was terrible. I'm sorry, but what does that have to do with—" Lindsay's voice cut out abruptly, and her eyes wandered down to the console between us. My stomach dropped as I could see the puzzle pieces finding their counterparts behind her misty eyes. "No. No, your baby *died!*" she said. The word stung like a hot iron branding my skin.

"My baby *passed*, and on the very same day—as Tethered Souls do—she came back, for a second chance at life," I said, my voice quiet but clear.

"And you think, that your baby is Nora? That's oddly convenient, don't you think? Do you even hear yourself right now?" Lindsay scolded. It was everything I was afraid of, and it was coming at me like a tidal wave. Reckless and unrelenting.

"Didn't you think it was weird how quickly the girls took to one another?" I asked. Tears streamed down Lindsay's cheeks. "Didn't you think it's weird how you had an automatic connection to her? Above any other baby in that nursery, it was her that you felt something for. Don't you think that's odd? Or how they share the same birthday? I mean, look at me! I'm living proof that not all things end in death! And Nora is the same way!"

"Stop it! Stop it! Just stop!" she yelled, cradling her head between her hands. It was then that I realized she was just as afraid as I was.

"Lindsay . . . I know you're scared. I am too. My biggest fear right now is that you will leave me and you'll take Nora with you. I'm so afraid that I won't be able to have her in my life," I said.

"You're afraid? I wake up every day scared that some court order will take her away from me! And now you're telling me that she's yours? And you never wanted to put her up for adoption?"

"No, Lindsay, that's not what I'm saying. I mean it is true—" Lindsay cried harder.

"It's true! I never wanted any of this! But it happened, and I'm so happy that it happened with you! Could you imagine if she was adopted by another family? Or if she never had a second chance life at all? I got my baby back . . ." Tears stung the back of my eyes.

". . . And I got a daughter," Lindsay added.

I reached over the console and grabbed her hand. "We can do this, right? We can raise that beautiful girl. And she will have four loving parents. And a sister!" I said.

"I don't know, Beck . . ." Lindsay pulled her hand away.

"What do you mean?"

"I don't want her to know that you're her biological mother, if that's even what you are. That will jeopardize *my* relationship with her. I'm her *real* mother!" she said. It stung once more, and I closed my eyes briefly to get through the pain.

Then, with everything I had, I said, "Thank you for raising her when I couldn't."

It sent not only Lindsay over the top, but me too. We cried together, both mothers afraid of parenting. I wiped my nose on the back of my hand and caught a glimpse of Lindsay doing the same. When I saw how much pain we had put ourselves through, I began to laugh. We were best friends who both loved Nora deeply. What was there to cry about? At some point, Lindsay and I found ourselves laughing together.

"You spilled your ice cream!" I shrieked. Lindsay picked up her bowl and tried to wipe her pant leg with a napkin, and the ice cream spread down her jeans. We both laughed harder.

"I know. I'm a train wreck," she said.

"No, you're not. I'm the wreck."

"I'm the one that's afraid you're trying to take my daughter away from me ..."

"What? No, I'd never do that. I'm scared you're going to take her from *me!*" I said.

Lindsay looked at me, the lines in her forehead prominent. "I wouldn't do that, either," she said in all seriousness. "I mean, I just called you guys over to ask if you would take her if we died in some terrible w—oh, sorry, I didn't mean—"

"No, no. It's OK," I said.

"All I'm saying is that I'd never take her away from you. Whether she's Clara's sister or not, I'm not going to lose you again. You're like family to me," she said.

"Then it's settled. We'll just keep everything the same. I'll be Nora's 'nanny,' " I air quoted, "and she will just think we're close family friends."

"I'm OK with that," Lindsay said.

"And you know, if you ever want to tell her, we can do it together," I said.

"Deal," Lindsay said, offering me a small smile.

"Deal." I picked my ice cream off the dashboard and sighed. "It's melted."

"At least it's not all down your leg," she said, trying one more time to clean up the mess. Ultimately, she crumpled up the napkin and threw it in the backseat. "Hey, Beck?" I looked up from my melted s'mores, and something in her eyes worried me.

"What is it?" I asked.

"Can we get a DNA test? Not because I don't believe you or anything . . . Although, I think we can agree that would be perfectly just, if I didn't. But more or less, just for me to see it. I think it would really help wrap my mind around the idea," she said.

"Of course. Do you think we can do it secretively?" I asked.

"Yeah, nobody needs to know. I think Nora will cooperate."

"OK, then let's do it," I said, suddenly afraid that maybe I'd been wrong the whole time. But I couldn't be. *Could I?*

"Well, we should get back before the guys start to wonder what happened to us," Lindsay said, pulling down her mirror. "God, I look like death!" she said. I pulled down my mirror and moaned before trying to wipe away the black mascara that had settled in the crevices under my eyes.

We rode back to Lindsay's house, mostly in silence. I worried that I had made the whole thing up in my head and that the only piece of concrete information that I had been counting on was that the girls shared a birthdate. It was odd but not impossible for two friends to share a birthday. But then I remembered her glacier eyes. The icy blue that reminded me so much of Easton, and I knew in my heart that the DNA test would show she was our own flesh and blood.

"Hey, Lindsay . . . There's one more thing we should discuss while we're alone," I said.

"Oh, shit, Beck. Honestly, I can't take anymore!" Lindsay glanced at me sideways before returning her gaze to the traffic lights just down the road. The neon green light lit the side of her face.

"It's nothing like that. But have you ever heard Nora talking about the lights?" I asked.

Lindsay raised her arm, and her hair was standing on end. "You're really freaking me out, Everly! I'm covered in chills! She talks about them all the time. Are you trying to tell me that's some weird Tethered Soul thing and not a normal little kid thing? I knew it wasn't normal!"

I smiled, pushing her arm down to her side. "Well, it's no normal little kid thing . . ."

"Dammit! Why do you have to do this to me?" Lindsay whined. She never liked scary stories or anything she couldn't see in the daylight.

I laughed at her. "I'm not doing anything! It's just that she can see things."

"No!" Lindsay protested.

"—Weird things that normal people can't. Things like emotion. She can see the pain that people carry. It looks like a weird glow of hot embers. And she can see love, too. And that's the lights she always chases when she's with Clara," I said.

Lindsay placed one hand over her heart, and her chin wobbled back and forth. "That's the most beautiful thing, I've ever heard," her voice cutting out. Lindsay nodded, deep in thought. "She sees most of her lights when she's around Clara," she agreed.

I smiled, happy that Lindsay and I ended what could have been a disastrous discussion in the same positive place. "It's because they're sisters," I said.

"Sisters," she whispered, deep in thought.

When we walked back into the house joking with one another, we were taken aback by the guys' expressions.

"What?" I asked.

"Good lord, where did you go to buy ice cream? I thought you'd never come back," John said.

Easton laughed nervously. "You got ice cream, right?" he said, looking down at our empty hands. My jaw gaped open. We had forgotten to get the girls' ice cream.

"Oh, um, they were all out," Lindsay said, unconvincingly.

"Is that ice cream on your pants?" John pointed to Lindsay's leg. Her face flushed, caught in the lie, and all I could do was laugh at her. I grabbed her elbow and hid my face behind her back. And I laughed even harder when she stuck to her guns and continued on with her story, even though nobody was buying it.

Finally, she ended the fabrication with some extravagant story about how we bought ice cream but ended up dropping it in the parking lot and we were too embarrassed to go back inside and buy more. At which point, John gave up on his suspicious endeavor and threw his hands in the air, all but giving up. Lindsay never had to say what really happened, but I imagined it wasn't difficult to piece together.

The night was late, and Lindsay and I were beyond tired. When I scooped Clara up in my arms, she fought me tooth and nail, not wanting to go home.

"No! Can't she stay? Please!" Nora asked Lindsay.

"Not tonight, but soon, OK?" Lindsay said.

"It's not fair! She always takes the sparkling lights with her when she goes!" Nora stomped her foot, and Lindsay shot me a look, her face pale as a ghost.

John sighed, batting his hand dismissively. "She's got this thing. It's like an imaginary friend, but she says they're lights. We've been trying to ignore it, hoping it will go away when she sees we don't pay it any attention," he said, leaning into Easton. Lindsay bit her lip, looking between John, Easton, and me.

"Hey, Nora . . . we all have to get a good night's sleep tonight, but I promise you we will have so many sparkles next time you come over that you won't know what to do with them all!" I said. The corners of Nora's pout curved ever so slightly as she nodded.

"But I never get to see them! Why should she be the only one to play with them?" Clara yelled out. I brushed the hair from my face and looked at Lindsay with exhaustion. If it wasn't one, it was the other, and nothing was ever fair.

"Come on, Clara." I picked her up, ignoring her rant. I'd heard it before, and I had spent countless nights worrying over it, but when I said goodnight to Lindsay, it was clear it was her first time understanding the depth of my family affairs. Her eyes trailed from mine to Clara as she pulled Nora in close. She rested her hands firmly on her shoulders.

"We'll be in touch," John said, waving us goodbye. I blew the girls a kiss, and Easton wrapped his hand around my shoulder as I hugged Clara to my hip.

The door closed behind us on our way out, and I took a long, deep sigh of relief. "You know Clara, some people can *see* sparkles, but you know what? You have the ability to *feel* them . . . right, here," I said, patting her heart as we walked down the Faye's driveway.

CHAPTER 16

A crack of thunder rattled deep inside my old, timeworn bones, scaring me and Tiny Tommy alike. The storm hadn't let up the entire morning. And I was worried about Easton when he slipped out after our time on the porch. I knew he needed space. Time to gather himself, find his strength. Because I knew he wouldn't want me to see him crumble any more than he already had. He didn't want me to worry in that way. But I worried now because he had gone out in the storm.

I picked up the leather-bound journal I had been working on for the last several months since receiving my diagnosis. Whenever I had a memory—something worth sharing—I jotted it down. The book was nearly full, and by the end of the day, it would be complete. And although I had written nearly two hundred pages in the journal, it was the last four that would be by far the most difficult. I had written goodbye letters before, but that didn't make writing them today any easier.

I wrote to Clara, telling her what a gift she had been in my life and how honored I had been to raise her. I pleaded with her to remember me with a smile. It always crushed me to see the guilt that plagued survivors long after the passing of a loved one. Being a loved one myself and having the fortune to come back to see it firsthand was not a pleasurable experience. I may venture to say that their sadness was worse than the death itself. Although I never went to my own funeral, I had seen the damage that unfolds after the departure. A broken heart takes time, and I let her know that was OK, too. I wrote that sometimes we lose someone special. It's inevitable, really. I knew how deeply it hurt but that one day, she'd be able to laugh again, love again, and live again. She may not get a second chance like I did, and possibly the best thing she could ever do was not count on it. Make this the one life in which she shined her brightest. And to remember, all things lost can be found. She just needed to know where to look.

And as for me, I told her she could find me in the gentle ocean breeze, the warm summer sky, and the wind beneath a dragonfly's wings. I told her I would look out for her children and grandchildren, and that I'd do everything in my power to warm her heart when she needed her mother's love.

I licked my finger and turned the page. I took a moment to reflect, as my mind moved slower these days. I found myself gazing out the window at the rolling sheets of rain and cloudy condensation covering the windows. I pulled a cardigan over my shoulders and began my letter to Nora. I could never be sure, but it was my gut that told me Nora would take after her father and that her life fulfillment wouldn't be earned on the second try. I knew she had a long road ahead of her, but I promised that I would help in any way I could. I encouraged her to take chances and open her heart. I wrote that pain is growth and that it would always be better to love with loss than to never love at all. She needed to believe that deep down in her heart of hearts if she wanted to earn her rite of passage. I knew she would one day.

I leaned back in my chair and remembered a particular moment in time that led me to believe Nora was in it for the long haul. She was a teenager in high school. The girls looked so beautiful in their winter formal dresses. I remembered taking pictures of them with their dates outside in the rose garden.

The air was crisp, and the girls were anxious. Nora was dating a perfect gentleman—a favorite of all the parents. Landon treated her with such respect, and I believed he loved her. She was easy to fall for. Many of the boys she hung around had puppy love deep in their eyes. Nora, on the other hand . . . she never opened herself up to Landon's compassion. And sometimes I wondered if she even noticed it at all.

"Just one more. Trent's eyes were closed," I said. Trent huffed before wrapping his arm around Clara's waist again. Trent was a good guy, but I couldn't help but compare him to Landon. And I always hoped Clara would find a boy that treated her like Landon did Nora. I snapped another picture. It wasn't perfect, but I knew the kids' patience was wearing thin. I waved them on.

"Can we go now?" Clara asked. She always took on Trent's impatience and wore it like a cloak of anxiety. I never liked him for her, but she swore she saw something in him that no one else had. I took her word for it. I had no other choice.

"Yeah, you can go. Have so much fun! Take lots of pictures! And call me if—" The car door slammed. Nobody was listening to me. My head fell to the side, and Easton wrapped his arm around my shoulder. At least I had him.

"Goodbye!" yelled Landon out the window. I smiled, finally settled. We watched the car pull out of the driveway, and I hoped they would have a memorable night. I never imagined they'd be coming home so upset.

Several hours had passed when the girls came home—alone. Easton and I were in the middle of a heated poker game, and I had just uncorked a bottle of wine. I jumped when the front door slammed and the girls came barreling in, arguing.

"Wow, what's going on?" I looked at my watch, trying to focus on the tiny numbers. "You're early," I said.

"Well, that's what happens when Clara gets dumped," Nora said. I couldn't understand why Nora was angry about that.

"You got dumped, honey?" I asked Clara. Her eyes were red and puffy, telling me everything I needed to know. She said nothing, only came bounding into my arms, crying. "Oh, Clara, I'm so sorry!" I said, stroking her hair. "I'm so sorry, honey!"

Nora stood by the doorway, arms crossed over her chest. When Clara pulled away, she excused herself to take a hot bath. She didn't say one word to Nora as she disappeared. Easton cleaned up the cards, and I took my wine to the kitchen. "Um, Mrs. Green? My car is at home. Do you think you could give me a ride?" Nora asked.

"Oh, sure honey!" I said. I turned my attention to Easton, who had adopted my freshly poured glass of wine. "I'll be back soon," I said, gathering my bag. He nodded. I looked down the hall toward Clara's room as we walked out of the house. I knew she was upset, and I figured she would be even more upset now that Nora wasn't staying over.

"Is everything alright? Sounds like you guys had a rough night," I said, starting the ignition.

"It was a disaster! I feel terrible for Clara, but she kind of did it to herself. She never listens to me!" Nora said.

"So, what happened?" I asked.

"Well, Trent is a dirtbag—that's what happened. He used her. I'd been telling her all along that he wasn't *the one*. And she didn't listen."

"The one?" I asked with trepidation.

Nora fell quiet, which was a rarity for her. "You know . . . *the one* . . ." She said.

My stomach dropped as I recalled the tears in Clara's eyes when she ran into my arms. "Oh no . . ."

"Yeah, and then he dumped her! What an asshole!" Nora said, tongue sharp. "I saw it all over him. His vibe was weird and jagged. I didn't like the way it sat on his skin, and it always seemed like he changed her vibe, too. But not in a good way. She had the lights for him, but he never did for her. Or anyone, for that matter. That boy is incapable of love! I can't believe she fell for it!"

"Huh . . ." I nodded, knowing that I had never liked Trent, either. Not that I ever saw jagged edges on his frame, but a mother knows unexplainable things in her own right. Nora was talented when it came to seeing the lights, but for whatever reason, I rarely saw them. And I wished I had known before so that I could warn my daughter of the love that she gave but didn't receive. "And you told her all of that?" I asked.

"I told her countless times," she said.

I thought about what she said about the lights, and I wondered if she could see her own, or if her emotions clouded her own manifestation, making it incapable for her to see. "And do you have lights for Landon?" I asked.

"Me? No. Landon is just a boy . . . He's cute though, right?" she joked.

"He's very handsome, but you don't have that connection with him?"

"Um, no. He could vanish tomorrow and I couldn't care less."

"Well, honey, you have to be careful. I think he might have more significant feelings for you. You don't want to hurt him," I said, worried about the impressionable heart of his youth.

"He's great! I like having him around. But, I just . . . He doesn't know anything about me. Like, I'd never tell him I could see emotions and whatever. We don't really talk in that way. We just go to parties together . . . I've actually been thinking that I don't really want a boyfriend anymore. And now that Clara is single, maybe I'll break it off with Landon, too. He felt really bad about what happened to Clara. God, if I didn't know any better, I'd say he has feelings for Clara!" There Nora was. The one I'd come to know and love. The one who spoke everything on her mind no matter how fast those thoughts were moving.

"Oh! Well, that would be a mess, huh? Why do you think you haven't given Landon a chance to get to know you?"

"Oh, I don't know. Nobody knows me like your family does. I just feel like people don't get me. So why even bother, you know?" She shrugged and looked out the window. She looked so pretty in her dress, and I wished she had the confidence to show the world just how special she really was. But Nora was good at putting up walls. Her exterior was hard as nails, and sometimes icy, too. Only I knew it was an act. A way of protecting herself from a broken heart like Clara had experienced after the winter formal.

". . . Honey, if you don't have a connection with the boy, the sooner the better, so you don't lead him on. He's such a great guy. I'd hate to see him get hurt beyond what's necessary," I said.

"You're right. There . . . Done."

"What's done?" I asked, looking over at Nora. Her eyes focused on her phone.

"I just told Landon that we aren't right for each other." Nora's face glowed from the light of her cell, and not an ounce of remorse reflected in her eyes.

"Just now?" I asked, shocked.

"You know what? It's for the better. I never loved him like Clara loved that dirtbag, Trent. And maybe now Clara and I can look for new boys together." Nora shrugged, unbuckling. "Thanks for the ride, Mrs. Green!" she said, hopping out of the car.

I watched in disbelief. That poor boy. Nora was a heartbreaker, and I feared it stemmed from feeling like an outcast her whole life. She didn't know that she was a Tethered Soul, but she knew she was unlike others. And I could only believe she knew that she didn't quite fit in with her family either. Sometimes, it looked a little like resentment toward Clara for having the family she felt most accepted with. Other times, it looked like she was cruel and selfish. But I knew her heart, and it was made of gold. I did what I could to make her feel loved. And I knew that Lindsay and John did, too. So, there was no shortage of love in Nora's life, but being an outsider in her own home and amongst her peers must have been a deep ocean of turmoil for her. And I didn't think she was handling it all that well.

When I got home, I gave Easton a quick peck on the cheek. I told him not to wait up and that I'd be having a girls' night in Clara's room.

"Clara?" I asked softly as I opened her door. She lay on her side, hair wet and eyes still red. "Are you OK?" I asked.

When she didn't respond, I curled up behind her and hugged her tightly. Her body quaked with silent cries, and I held her through the regret of giving herself to the wrong person.

"I loved him, Mom! I don't understand . . ." she cried. "I know you didn't understand him, but he was special. He cared so much about his little sister. You never saw that. And he tried really hard to get passing grades, even though it didn't come naturally to him. He worked really hard. You didn't see it like I did," she said, defending him still.

I wanted to tell her that she was so young that she didn't yet know what love was, but I knew what she felt for Trent was real to her. She had such a kind heart that she would see the best in anyone that she looked at for long enough. "He just wasn't the right one. Shh, I know it hurts," I said, soothing her as much as I could. "Heartbreak hurts."

"Why? Why does it feel like this? I'm so stupid. How could I not have seen it?" she murmured.

"It's hard. Our emotions cloud a lot of our better judgment—"

"But Nora has the best boyfriend in the world! He's so caring and thoughtful, and she treats him like shit! I don't get it!"

There wasn't much I could say, but I could hold her. She went on and on about how Nora had everything she didn't and how she ended up with the short end of the stick. I wanted to tell her that Nora saw it just the same way, but I only listened.

It was after Clara fell asleep that I knew Nora would need more than one lifetime to get her heart straight. And I couldn't help but wonder if she had known the truth about being a Tethered Soul—and our past lives—if she would have grown up with such a bulletproof exterior? And would she have needed it, had she known just who she was?

Little did I know that the time when she would find out exactly who she was and how she came to be was just around the corner.

CHAPTER 17

The following year, when the girls were seventeen and fighting for their independence, they took it too far one evening when they failed to come home. I was used to the unanswered calls and the stretching of curfew, but this was different. It was an hour later than I expected to see Clara at home, and she hadn't been answering her phone. By the second hour, I called Nora to no avail. It was unusual that neither of the girls would answer. When I spoke to Lindsay, she had said that she thought the girls were staying at our house, but that was never the case. Not that I knew of anyhow.

Three hours into the silence and I was on the phone with Easton. He had been at work all evening, which most likely gave him better access to finding the girls. He was surprised when I said I hadn't heard from either of them, but he wasn't as worried as I'd become. He did what he could to reassure me that everything would be OK. And he promised to look into it. He had special equipment at the station for tracking cell phones and credit cards, all of which he'd used to check up on the girls before. By the time I'd gotten off the call, I felt better about the expected outcome of the evening.

But when Easton had called to say he found nothing, worry stirred in my chest. He said he checked the location of the girls' cell phones, but the last known location pinged from their high school a little after lunch hour. "The phone must have died. Do you know if it was charged?" Easton asked.

"She's really good at keeping it charged. Do you really think that both of their cell phones would die at the same time?" I asked.

"Well—"

"And why haven't they come home?"

"Right. It doesn't add up. Did Clara say anything? Any after-school plans? New friends? Anything you can think of?" Easton asked.

"No. Nothing!"

"Did you talk to Lindsay yet?"

"Yes, and she said that Nora told her she was staying at our house tonight," I said.

"But she wasn't?"

"No, Clara never mentioned that."

"OK, well, it sounds like maybe they turned their phones off and went to a party or something. Just stay by your phone, and I'll keep my eye out," Easton said, calmer than I would have liked. I didn't need him to worry like I had been, but I didn't want the anxious storm in my chest to be invalidated, either.

I couldn't understand what would have happened, and at school no less. Why would they turn their phones off at the same time after lunch hour? It's not like a party would start in the middle of the school day. Unless it had? Unless they ditched? But it was a Tuesday. My mind ran wild, trying to fit the puzzle pieces together. But there were too many missing pieces to make out any semblance of a picture.

Easton drove the streets, looking for the girls after his shift had ended. I sat on the sofa, my cell phone in hand. I had worried myself sick watching the minutes tick by. I made a list of hospitals and called them all. Every time I was placed on hold, I would feel my heart kick out. And every time the operator came back on the line with no known patient, I was relieved. No news was good news, I told myself. But it was the no news that left a gaping hole that I desperately needed to be filled.

It was about two in the morning when my knee began bouncing relentlessly. My cell phone was clutched in my hand. Volume on high. I knew Clara was a happy girl, and that she would never choose to run away or worry me unnecessarily. That's why the pit of my stomach had filled with doom, and my knee wouldn't stop from vaulting. Because maybe it wasn't her choice at all.

When I couldn't take it any longer, I did what I swore I'd never do. And hadn't done so, until now. I called Brooklyn. I called, looking for answers from her unconscious premonitions. It was a cheat in my book. I didn't think it was right for me to ask, but in my moment of weakness—my back against the wall—I had no other choice. At first, Brooklyn didn't answer. But by the third try, I'd finally woken her up.

"Becca? Do you know what time it is?" she answered the phone.

"I need your help Brooklyn," I pled.

"What? What is it?" she asked.

"It's the girls. They haven't come home, and neither one of them is answering their phones!" I said.

A moment passed where all I could hear was the deep breaths of Brooklyn over the phone. And then she asked, "Is it October?"

"Yes?"

"And the girls are seventeen, right?"

"Yes!"

"OK. Yeah, they ran away," Brooklyn said sleepily.

"What!" I shrieked.

"Uh, huh."

I sat on the other end of the line, rattled with disbelief. How could my sweet Clara run away? More importantly, *why* would she run away?

"Hey, Becca?" Brooklyn asked.

"Yeah?"

"I'm going to go back to bed now. They're going to be alright. Just try not to lose it, OK?" she said.

"What? Are you serious? That's it?" I asked.

"What did I say? Hold it together. Oh, and Becca?"

"Yeah?"

"Show them some sympathy . . ." It was the last thing Brooklyn said and the furthest thing from my mind.

When Lindsay was finished with her night shift at Sunny Hill Assisted Living, she came directly to my house. It was still too early for the sun to rise, but I made a pot of coffee anyhow. She was worried sick, as I had been, but I told her what Brooklyn had said. She was fascinated by Brooklyn's story. One I vowed not to speak of to anyone, but since I had been breaking all the rules tonight, I let it slide. Plus, it gave us something to talk about. A much-needed distraction.

Easton called with updates, though they weren't much to go by. "A girl seen in the parking lot of a shopping mall" or "teenagers pulled over for speeding down the highway." None of them turned out to be our girls, until he had a lead he was going to check on that was an hour away. He thought it was worth the drive, and I encouraged him to look into it. The surveillance feed was pixilated, but he'd been going off a feeling, and I always encouraged those.

Lindsay and I spat speculations until the sun rose, casting a warm hue in the sky. And when Easton called to say he had found them and they were on their way home, my relief was strong but short-lived. Soon after the call, my relief turned straight to white-hot anger, and I wasn't the only one. Lindsay had been just as angry as me. I didn't know their story, but I knew how afraid I had felt for the past twelve hours, and I was going to punish them until they knew my pain.

When Easton walked through the door with the girls in tow, Lindsay and I ran to them, hugging them tightly out of pure instinct. Only, neither of the girls reciprocated that love. Clara could have been a block of ice pulled close to my chest and I'd never have known the difference. Her body was stiff and cold.

I pulled back, trying to look into her eyes, but she refused to acknowledge me. My anger melted into worry as Easton sighed with a heavy look of empathy.

How could he empathize with the girls after all they'd put us through? I couldn't understand.

"Where have you been?" Lindsay demanded.

"Do you have any idea how worried we were?" I added. But our words had fallen on deaf ears.

"We need to have a talk. All of us," Easton said, locking up his gun. "I'll be right back." Then, he headed to the bedroom to change out of his uniform. The girls didn't speak. Their eyes were glued to the floor. Maybe it was the lack of sleep or maybe it was the sting of secrets, but the air was frigid and their hearts cold.

"What is going on?" Lindsay asked. Nobody answered. The girls made their way to the sofa, and I shook my head in frustration. When Easton returned, we sat down, three to two. Three parents directly across from the two misfits who had stayed out all night. Running from nothing but the unconditional love that we had all given them. And it was clear they were prepared for a fight.

"I picked them up in Winchester—" Easton began.

"Winchester!" I barked.

"They were using cash on the local bus transportation, so we couldn't track them. They were running away," Easton confirmed. The girls looked guilty and maybe even a little regretful. Lindsay had been surprised that Brooklyn's forecast was correct.

"I had a buddy pick them up on surveillance. We're lucky, as their next stop would have been the city." I gasped, thinking of my girls in the city, alone, and in the middle of the night. It was a dangerous place—one of the worst in terms of crime.

"What do you have to say for yourselves?" I asked them. It was no surprise that Nora was the one to speak up first.

"Us? What do *we* have to say for ourselves? Why don't *you* tell *us* what you've been hiding all these years?" Nora said, with one eyebrow raised and a smoldering stare.

I opened my mouth to protest, but remembered what Brooklyn had said about showing sympathy. I didn't know how much the girls had discovered about our secret past, but I knew it was time for our surrender.

CHAPTER 18

I looked to my right at Lindsay, worried, but she was far more worried than I. Her eyes glassed over, and her forehead was perspiring. Easton, to my left, encouraged me to continue with a curt nod. "Clara?" I asked, hoping she hadn't shut me out just yet.

"Do you know what we did in school today?" Clara asked. I looked at Lindsay, but she didn't know any more than I did. "We reviewed the DNA tests we took at the beginning of the semester." My stomach dropped, and Lindsay let out a shudder. Her head went down into the palms of her hands.

"We will never forgive you for this," Nora said, not just to Lindsay but to Easton and me as well. "We only have one question for you guys," she said.

I took a deep breath, knowing that the conversation should have come a long time ago but that it was Lindsay's deepest desire to keep it secret. I knew how I felt about secrets. They were destructive, deceptive, and sometimes cruel. But if Lindsay allowed me to be part of Nora's life, I would have taken that secret to my grave.

"We will answer any and all of your questions. Together," I said.

"We're sisters?" Clara asked.

I nodded, ever so slightly. But when the girls continued to glare at me, I answered in a full-bodied voice. "Yes. You are."

"*Why* did you do this to us?" Clara asked.

"*Why* did you give me away?" asked Nora, tone cutting.

I had trouble swallowing the lump in my throat. I looked at Lindsay, giving her an opportunity to speak, but she was melting down. "Why don't you take this one, honey?" I asked Easton. I knew it was unfair, but he was the best suited. His face was void of stress, and only slight tiredness hung in the corners of his eyes. If Easton excelled at any one thing in all of his lives, it would be finding strength in the most vulnerable of times.

"We never gave you away, Nora. It was an accident—" Easton began.

Lindsay spoke for the first time since the girls sat down across from us. "No! You don't have to do that. You don't need to protect me or John. We need to tell Nora the truth."

I looked to Easton, who was in the middle of a fabrication that would last a lifetime.

"Tell me what truth?" Nora demanded.

"All of it? Do you think it's best?" Easton said, huddled behind my back.

"For Nora, it is," Lindsay said, behind me.

"But for Clara, do you think it's best she knows, too?" he asked.

"What the hell Mom? I can hear you!" Nora spat.

I saw the problem that lay before us clear as day. Nora most likely grew up feeling like an outsider with her gifts of sight. She was different than her family but comfortable with ours. And now, as the truth unfolded, Nora would feel accepted for once in her life. And she deserved that. But it was Clara who would pay the price. She would swap places with her sister and become the girl who didn't fit in. She would know that both her parents and sister were tethered while she was not. I didn't want to do that to her. But it was the truth, and they deserved to know the facts.

"No more lies. She's going to find out, anyway. These girls can't keep a secret," I said.

"Mom? What? Just tell us," Clara called out. Easton and Lindsay straightened, facing the girls once more, prepared for whatever might come our way.

"It's true. Nora is your sister. But we never knew that until you two became best friends in kindergarten," I said.

"So, you gave one up for adoption, and kept the other?" Clara asked.

"No," I said.

"She basically gave me away because my mom couldn't have kids. How much did you sell me for?" Nora scowled.

"I didn't sell you!" I rose to my feet. My chest burned like a blade had pierced into it. Easton grabbed my arm and pulled me back down. I sat begrudgingly. "When you died, it was the worst thing that had ever happened to me!" I said, breathless.

"Wow. OK, what your mother is trying to say is—"

"I died?!"

"Stop! Everybody stop!" Easton's deep voice silenced the room. "This will be easier if I tell the story from start to finish. You can ask questions when I'm done. Deal?" Everyone looked around the room, and not a single word was issued.

"There is a special gene inside our DNA, right? You've been learning about DNA . . . That gene can be flipped if something terribly unjust happens to you at a very young age. It has to be when fate bends and twists in ways it was never supposed to. And sometimes, for the greater good, a life is stolen. And when this happens, the gene of the person whose life was taken gets flipped. And that's when the person is born again. This happened to Nora when she was stillborn." Easton steepled his chin, and the girls gawked at us parents in disbelief.

"So, to answer the first question, we never gave you away. And your second question . . . yes, you died, when you were little. But you were reborn, and we never knew. Then the Fayes adopted you since they couldn't bear their own child. We have been so lucky to have since found you. And we have been working with the Faye family as much as possible to incorporate you into both families," Easton said. Lindsay and I nodded in agreement and I patted Easton's leg.

"How did you know I was Clara's sister if I was adopted?" Nora asked, still skeptical.

"Well, for starters, the lights—"

Nora clapped her hands and jumped to her feet. "I knew it! I knew I wasn't crazy!" she said. Clara slouched back into the sofa.

"And you shared a bond unlike anything I had seen before the instant you met your sister," I added.

"We do look a lot alike," Clara said beneath her breath. The girls looked similar when they were children, but now it was obvious they were twins. People commented all the time about it. It was surprising they hadn't figured it out until now. Besides Nora's dark hair and blue eyes, Clara and she looked almost identical. Nora was somewhat taller but not by much.

"You're twins," I said. And it was the first positive breakthrough we had. Both girls smirked, looking at one another. Lindsay wilted beside me as she tried to stifle her sobs. The girls held hands, and I noticed Nora's eyes lift just above Clara's head.

"So why didn't you take me back?" Nora asked of me.

"I . . . I couldn't. I couldn't do that to you or to your parents. They're such good people, and you had already spent six years under their roof. I thought it would be too disruptive. And to be honest with you girls, the whole genetic thing is really, really rare. So rare, that most people in the world have never heard of it," I said.

"Then how did you hear about it?" Nora asked.

"It happened to—"

"Wait . . . you said you saw the lights, too," Nora said.

"Yes," I admitted.

"So how exclusive are we talking here? Have you all had the gene switched?" she asked.

"No, not all of us. Easton and I have, and Brooklyn, too. It's so secret that John doesn't even know about it. Most people wouldn't understand. It's probably best if you keep it quiet," I said.

"Yeah—" Clara started.

"What if we don't?" Nora questioned.

"Well, take it from me," Easton said. "You won't have many friends if you tell them you've had multiple lives."

The girls frowned, and Clara looked at Nora with concern. "Maybe you shouldn't say anything?" she said.

"You guys can't be serious," Nora's voice rose again. She must have felt like we were pulling the wool over her eyes, and I understood where she was coming from. It was difficult to grasp the impossible as sincerity. Lindsay would have never known had she not recognized me.

"Would you rather we told you there was a mix-up at the hospital?" I asked. It was the very lie I had planned on spinning, and how Easton had begun. I figured I wasn't the only one.

Nora shook her head, clearly frustrated with the entire event. I knew she didn't believe us, but it felt better knowing that there was a foundation of truth laid down before us. I planned to show her the plaque on the bridge one day where Easton's and my name rest. I would show the girls our graves and tell them stories of not only their grandpa but their pop, too. We would be as open as possible, no matter how difficult it would be to face.

"So, what happens now?" Clara asked.

I looked between Easton and Lindsay, whose eyes were swollen and filled with worry. "We keep going . . ." I said.

"Let me be the one to tell your father," Lindsay asked Nora.

"That I'm Clara's sister? Or that I'm some rare genetic mutation?" she asked.

"Well, for now, the sister part. I have a feeling he's going to be quite upset with me, as you are. But let's keep the mutation thing to ourselves until I find a way for him to understand. Your father doesn't do well with belief. He needs proof, and I'm afraid I don't have that right now," she said.

"Well, they have the DNA test. This is going to get messy since he delivered Clara and knows what happened to Molly," I said to Lindsay.

"Who's Molly?" Nora asked.

"That's um . . . that's what your name would have been if you stuck around a little longer," I said. Nora's lip pulled up on the left side. From the looks of it, she was glad she hadn't stuck around.

"Can we go home? It's eight in the morning, and I haven't slept," she said.

"Yeah, go home. I think that's enough for one night. Or morning," I shrugged.

The girls hugged one another but didn't want to separate. They whispered amongst themselves. "Can I go to Nora's?" Clara asked. And as much as I wanted them both to stay, I nodded. I knew if the girls stayed at our house, Lindsay would go home devastated.

"Sure honey. I'm glad you two are home safe. I love you girls," I said. And my heart broke when neither of them said it back. Betrayal was a nasty road to travel, and I hoped it would be a quick path for our family.

CHAPTER 19

The girls healed as time unraveled, and eventually, things went back to normal. The only change that I could see was that the girls had a stronger relationship. They weren't just best friends anymore but sisters—*twins.* They felt the shift that came with knowing the truth. Nora had been a little leery of Easton and me, and I gathered that was because she didn't fully believe the story we'd spun. I feared she still worried I had given her up for adoption. And I didn't blame her for having trouble accepting she'd lived another life before this one.

But there was a switch in Nora's eyes after I showed the girls our memorial plaque on the bridge. The change was so pronounced, it echoed in Clara's face as well. We spent a long time their answering questions, and all three of us came back sunburnt. Still, I never felt fully accepted by Nora in the way a mother should. I told myself it would take her years or maybe even lives to open up to the idea of me being her mother. Especially if she took after Easton in so many ways. I was patient.

But on one special morning—not any morning, but the first Mother's Day since the girls found out the truth—I lay awake, eyes closed as the smell of bacon wafted through the air. Indistinct sounds of clacking and clanking came from the kitchen, and tiny voices could be heard through the walls. I rolled onto my back and stretched contently, the bedsheets like silk across my skin. My eyes fluttered open and adjusted to the morning light. It was then, when not only Clara walked through the bedroom door holding a plate of bacon, eggs, and toast but Nora too, holding a mug of coffee.

It was my first mother's day with both of my girls, and in that moment, I had never felt more honored. I sat up in bed, and a smile stretched across my face that lifted well into my eyes. "Good morning, girls," I said, my voice groggy.

"Happy Mother's Day!" Clara said.

"Good morning," Nora said.

Clara placed the hot breakfast on my lap, and Nora set the mug down on my nightstand. My stomach grumbled at the sight and smell of the bacon below. The girls sat down on the edge of the bed as I bit into the salty bacon. "It's so good. Thank you, girls. You have no idea how much this means to me. But Nora, won't your mom be upset that you're not with her this morning?" I asked.

"Oh, she's working, so Clara and I were going to surprise her at work later today," she said.

"Oh, that's right."

"Can I have some?" Clara asked.

"Yes, help yourself!" I offered, lifting my plate towards both the girls. In one quick swoop, the bacon had vanished. Next was the toast. And before I knew it, the plate was clean, and the girls were giggling just like they had when they were kids. I held my coffee close, the warmth rising under my nose.

"Um, well . . . we got you something," Clara said.

"You did?" I said, smiling.

"Yeah, both of us," Nora said, tucking her hair behind her ear. She pulled a little silver box topped with a bow from the pocket of her hooded sweatshirt and handed it to me.

"Oh, I love things that come in tiny boxes!" I said. I took the gift from Nora, whose eyes were a deeper blue than I had been used to. I untied the bow and lifted the lid off the box. Inside, nestled in white velvet, was a pair of earrings. Small studs that dropped down into a beautifully polished tiger's eye. They were both unique and absolutely perfect for the occasion. "I love them!" I exclaimed, reaching over to hug each of the girls. "Thank you, so much!"

"Happy Mother's Day, Mom," Clara said, wrapping her arms around me.

"Yeah, Happy Mother's Day," Nora said. Her embrace was anything but present. It had meant the world to me that she wanted to celebrate Mother's Day with me, but I couldn't help but want more. I wanted her to engage. I wanted her to look at me. And I wanted her to hug me so tight that I could feel her love. But she had done none of those things since she found out she was my daughter, and I could argue that we once had a better relationship when I had only been her best friend's mom.

"We saw those, and we knew they were just as special and unique as you were. It was between those and these other ones, but we picked the tiger's eye because we'd never seen anything like them before." Clara took the box from me and removed the earrings one by one, placing them in the palm of my hand. I didn't need a mirror to slip them into my lobes, but I stood to look at them dangle once they were secured.

"They're beautiful," I said. The girls smiled, and Clara picked up the empty plate from the unmade bed.

"Well, we're going to meet Kayla and Kyndal at the coffee shop this morning if you don't mind."

"No, not at all. Go have some fun," I said, still admiring the earrings in the mirror.

"OK. I'm just going to shower really quick, and then we can take off," Clara said. I smiled at her when she walked out of my bedroom and wondered if it had been some sort of setup to leave Nora behind. Her eyes were still down—always down. The pink of her cheeks came out, and I could tell that she was growing nervous. It was the last thing I wanted for her.

"Oh, honey . . . what's wrong?" I asked. Her back quaked several times before she couldn't hold it in any longer. She crumbled before me, falling into my lap. "It's OK . . . what is it, Nora? You can talk to me . . ." I rubbed her back in the same manner I had when she was young and couldn't sleep because our house had different sounds than her own.

She cried for some time. And when Clara peeked her head into the bedroom with wet hair and saw Nora huddled on my lap, she backed out quietly, giving us the time we needed.

"Nora? Talk to me," I pled when her tears died down.

"I've always felt like an outcast. I've always been misunderstood. Nobody has gotten me like your family does—not even my own. Clara was always my safe harbor, and I was jealous of her for having a home that I felt so comfortable in. At times, I never wanted to leave. But I love my mom. I do!" she said, conflicted.

"Shh, it's OK. You don't have to choose, Nora. You have us both."

"I just feel like I'm betraying her when I'm over here. And I feel like I can't love you without taking from her. And I know she's not my mom, but she raised me. I mean, you kind of did too . . ."

"She *is* your mom. She is!" I said.

"But, then what are you?"

"I'm . . . I'm your mom too. But you don't have to see it like that if it makes you feel torn. You can picture me as an aunt or just your sister's mother. Whatever you feel comfortable with. But I'm here for you, either way."

"I can't have two moms!" Nora huffed.

"Why not?" I asked.

"Well . . . because, nobody else does," she said, wiping her cheeks free of tears.

"Honey, I think we already know we're unlike any other family. Being unique is just a part of who you are. How many kids can say they survived death?" I asked, and Nora chuckled. "Seriously, you're so special. And you have a long road ahead of you. I don't mean to worry you, but you could use all the support you have. Let me be there for you."

"You are there for me. You always have been," Nora said, craning her neck and looking into my eyes for the first time in a long while.

"I have been and always will, but you've got to let me in."

"OK," she said, sitting up. As if it were that simple. "Do you remember my old boyfriend Landon?" she asked.

"Yes."

"There was a time when I felt like I was starting to care for him . . ."

"Yeah . . ."

"And I shut it off. Like a light switch, I just shut it off. I got scared, and I pulled back. And I told myself I'd never be as stupid as Clara. I saw what it did to her, and I saw the lackluster way Trent looked at her. I knew she would get hurt, and I knew she was allowing herself to do so. It just seemed so . . . so avoidable. I don't know why anyone would do it. I just wished that she was smarter, you know?"

I thought about what she said. She was right, in a way. Clara did get hurt, and it could have been avoided had she read the warning signs and made different decisions. But she gave herself to that boy, and her heart broke. "While Clara got hurt, I'm so proud of her for allowing herself to fall—and for trusting herself."

"You're proud of that?"

"I am. Her judgment was off"—I shrugged—"but if we can't trust ourselves, then who can we trust?"

"True . . . I hate to admit it, but I never wanted Clara to be loved back by Trent. She already had this place, she had you and Easton, and she always knew who she was. I still don't know who I am. I feel like she and I are so similar but so, so different. If that makes any sense at all. I know I'm rambling."

"I understand," I said. "But please don't be jealous of your sister. She never chose this life—none of us did. And Nora, nothing good ever comes from being closed off. Just ask Easton about that."

Nora frowned. "Ask Easton? Why?"

"Well, he could tell you better than I, but he spent many lives loveless. He too saw all the pain, and he closed himself off to the world. And if you can't grasp what really matters in life, honey, then you're going to wind up back here repeatedly, until you get it right."

"I know," she said, saddened. "What will happen to all of you?"

"Good question," I said with a small smile.

She pulled her knees up to her chin and wrapped her arms around her shins, content on the edge of my bed. "I like this. I think I want more talks like this."

"I like this too. And we can talk all the time! Day or night, you know I'll be here. Even if you just want someone to listen."

"OK. Thank you."

"You don't have to thank me," I laughed.

"Um, Mrs. Green? Do you think I could call you Mom?" Nora's eyes glassed over, and I could see that she was nervous to put her heart on the line. It was a big step for her. Without thinking, I grabbed her and squeezed her close.

"I would love that!" I said. The tension slowly but surely drained from Nora's rigid body, and she came to embrace me the same as I did her. It was the first time I felt her love since she thought I sold her on the black market. And I couldn't have thought of a better Mother's Day gift.

"Well, I should get going. I know Clara has been waiting for me," she said.

"Patiently! Very patiently!" called Clara from the other side of the door. We all laughed, breaking the tension.

Nora rose from the bed, and just before she walked out, she turned and said, "Happy Mother's Day . . . *Mom.*"

I smiled as she disappeared into the hall. My throat stung as my heart swelled, and I was left alone in the quiet house, reflecting on how far I'd come. I rubbed the tiger's eye stone hanging from my ear as I heard Brooklyn's voice ring through my head. *"You're wearing a teal scarf and these tiger's eye drop earrings that you cherish. I don't know why . . ."*

CHAPTER 20

When Clara was called on stage to receive her high school diploma, I jumped to my feet, screaming. The pamphlet was beaten and battered by the wild clapping. And when she moved her tassel from one side to the next, my heart jumped. Time stood still, and I beamed with pride. It was deep within that pride that I forgot to take a picture. "Shit! I didn't get a picture!" I said, jaw dropping. How could I be so irresponsible?

"I got it," said Brooklyn to my right. She cupped her hand over her camera, checking the picture.

"Oh, thank god!" I said, fanning myself with the battered pamphlet. The day was hot, and the lotion I had put on my legs was melting into a slick, sweaty mess. Tanner leaned forward, craning his neck to see Brooklyn as she spoke. He had recently announced his divorce, and since then, was spending extra time at our house. And if I didn't know any better, he'd been spending extra time looking at Brooklyn, too. She felt it. We all did, and it made for a very awkward graduation.

I loved Charlie; we all did. But over the years, she and Tanner grew apart instead of growing together. It had been a long time since I saw Tanner look at Charlie with love and admiration in his eyes. It was common—more common than I'd like to admit. But many of our friends had separated over the years. It seemed that "till death do us part" was rare these days. I still spoke to Charlie and would continue to do so, but it would never be the same between us. I knew she would eventually need to put distance between herself and our family to heal.

Brooklyn leaned back in her chair, out of Tanner's line of sight. She leaned into me and whispered, "Is he still looking at me?"

I didn't have to look at Tanner to know. He was still perched on his elbows, his stare blistering like the sun. "Uh-huh," I said, lips pursed.

"I think Nora is coming up," Lindsay said from the row behind us.

"Oh, OK! I gotta get a picture!" I said, fumbling with my phone.

Brooklyn placed her hand over mine. "I've got this. You just enjoy the moment." I smiled, grateful for such a thoughtful friend. I'd probably butcher the picture anyhow, and Brooklyn was a talented photographer.

"Nora Faye!" I jumped to my feet once more and hollered as loud as I could. Easton laughed, patting me on the shoulder. I reached my hand up high in the air and waved my pamphlet, hoping she would get a glimpse of us. I couldn't be so sure, but I thought I saw her spot us in the crowd. She moved her tassel to the side of her cap and my heart fluttered once more. My cheeks hurt from smiling, and there was a possibility that I would have no voice by the next morning. I may have been more excited than the girls themselves, but that was just a part of being a mother.

Nora walked off stage, and we all took our seats once more. "Seriously? Every picture is of Becca's arm!" Lindsay said. I slumped down in my seat, afraid to turn around. Lindsay thrust her phone over my shoulder to show me the pictures of Nora receiving her diploma. Only my blurry arm was visible.

"I'm so sorry!" I said, turning around to see Lindsay. Her brows were knotted, and her jaw clenched tight.

"How's this?" Brooklyn showed her the pictures she had taken. I watched relief wash over Lindsay, and I knew that I owed Brooklyn for saving me not once but twice that graduation.

"Thank you," I said, leaning into Brooklyn.

"Any time. Is he still looking?" she asked.

This time, I needed to check, and when I did, Tanner's eyes flicked to mine. I looked away as quickly as I could and then stared straight ahead. "Yup," I said, watching the girls' friends walk across the stage.

"Is it seriously this hot outside? Or is Tanner boiling my blood right now?" she asked in a low tone.

"No, it's really this hot. I'm drenched," I said, fanning myself with the weakened pamphlet. I looked down the row at Easton and Tanner and then behind me at Lindsay and John. Everyone looked like they had just emerged from a sauna, and pamphlets were waving everywhere throughout the sea of parents.

When the ceremony was over and we found the girls in the sea of graduates, I slipped leis over their heads and tried not to cry. Brooklyn snapped several pictures of the girls together. Clara's pale blond hair against Nora's dark. They were the perfect yin and yang; complementing each other in the best possible ways. Later, I would frame one of the several pictures from that day of both the girls, and it would be one of my favorites of all time.

Since Tanner's divorce, he had been spending all of his free time at our house. The girls had moved out for college, and Tanner had practically moved in. It was fitting for all of us because neither he nor Easton and I wanted to feel alone. And in the absence of Clara, that is exactly how we felt.

Having an empty nest was an odd mix of emotions. I was beyond proud to have raised Clara so that she was mature and resilient enough to take care of herself, leaving the safety of our home to venture out into this world alone. But at the same time, I didn't want her to leave. I didn't want her to grow up. I knew I didn't have a choice, though, and I tried my hardest not to let the girls see that I was barely holding it together. When they left for college, I promised I would visit them and they made me promise . . . not too much.

So, the days settled with Easton, Tanner, and me. Much like it had been before we ever had children. I'd cook dinner for three and have extra beers in the fridge. I'd leave clean sheets in the guest bedroom and a spare toothbrush in the bathroom. And even though Tanner had been my brother-in-law, I sometimes looked after him like a child.

But when Easton and Tanner would leave for work—they'd been putting in extra hours because of a staff shortage—I stayed home and felt the effects of the empty house. There were no more little footsteps running through the home. Bodie had passed long ago, and everything remained untouched in silent stillness. I spent my time at the park, coffee shop, or on long drives that ended in the same place they started. I did anything to get out of the house—that quiet vortex that left me anxious.

One particular day, when I missed the girls deeply—and no amount of cleaning or errands seemed to help—and Easton had his first day off in a long while, he came to me with a flower picked from the side yard. The small daisy twirling between his fingers and a wicked smile reaching across his face.

"It's been really quiet in this house lately, and I know I've been spending so much time at work. Let me make it up to you. Let's go out today? We can hike and have a picnic at our spot by the Truley River? It's been years since we've been there . . ." Easton said, handing me the daisy.

I took the flower. "I'd love that," I said, bringing the flower in for a sniff. We packed a brunch—ham and cheese, croissants, and a thermos of hot coffee—and then we were on our way. Easton was in a pleasant mood, and if I didn't know any better, I'd say he was hiding something. A surprise of sorts. I tried not to let my mind wander for fear of disappointment, but it ran the gauntlet, anyway. He could have already set up a romantic picnic there early this morning. His face had seemed a little flushed when he approached me with the flower. I thought back to the daisy; had it been from our side yard like I originally thought? Or had it been a species that grew wild in the fields of the bluff?

The bluff . . . I thought little about the last time we had been there, but now that my mind was searching for answers, I let it wander. It was the first time I had been cleared since my c-section to exercise. Clara had started smiling at me for the first time. It was something I'll never forget—the moment she recognized me as the person who loved her most. And though it was a monumental event in my life, it hurt knowing that Molly should have been right alongside her . . . smiling at me for the first time, too. Every good thing that happened was laced with the bitter taste of mournfulness, and I found it hard to be happy. It seemed like ages ago.

But something happened when we went to the bluff that day to release Molly's ashes. I watched her playing in the fields behind me. A little girl chasing dragonflies. It wasn't her, of course. It had only been a figment of my imagination; but when I saw the ashes flutter through the sky, I knew it hadn't been her. I couldn't explain it then, and I still struggle to find the words now. Not that I knew she was still alive—I didn't. I only knew that she wasn't in that urn, and that was enough to carry me for many years to come.

I hadn't been back to the bluff where Easton and I married when I was sick—the place where he proposed to me a lifetime later. I hadn't been back since we said goodbye to Molly. And I worried it would bring back the emotions of losing her, and that I'd be lost in the darkest memories of crying myself to sleep in the garage nearly every night. I was afraid to go back to a time when I thought I may actually die of a broken heart.

"You're awfully quiet," Easton said.

"I just . . . haven't had my coffee yet," I said. I took in a deep breath and looked out the window as we pulled off the side road where the head of the trial began.

"Ready?" Easton cupped my shoulder with a wide smile.

"Ready," I said.

I followed Easton when the trail grew narrow, and we walked hand in hand when it widened. We talked about the day we were there last and speculated on how it may have been different had we known then what we did now. When we were close and the trail grew narrow again, Easton stopped me, rifling through his backpack. "Wait one second."

"What are you looking for?" I asked.

"Just hold on," he said. He pulled out a red paisley bandana from his pack and rolled it.

"What are you doing?" I said in a coy tone.

"It's a surprise. The bluff is just around the bend—"

"I know that—"

"I want you to put this on. And I'll lead you," he said, holding out the bandana.

I smiled. "OK." He tied the cloth around my head and secured it tightly in the back. I reached up, adjusting it around my eyes. "OK, I can't see a thing. Don't let me trip."

"I won't. Follow me," he said, taking my hand and leading me forward.

The trail comprised of packed dirt, and as long as I kept my feet one in front of the other, I'd stay on the trail easily enough. The grass grew taller as we rounded the bend and nipped at my shins with every step. Easton's hand was warm and clammy, and I could tell he was nervous about the sunrise. It only made me nervous about my reaction. I hoped it would be everything he wanted.

"OK, stop right there." I reached up towards the bandana. "No! Wait!" he said. I dropped my hands, listening for clues. And when there had been no sound other than the wind rustling in the trees, I pictured our picnic blanket near the cliff, a bottle of champagne and orange juice.

Easton said nothing, but I felt his proximity close in. And even though I couldn't see, I knew I had been eclipsed by his shadow. I felt his hands press against my bandana and the pressure on my eyes eased as he lifted it off my head. Easton gazed into my eyes with loving trepidation. I couldn't read what had been behind them, but when he leaned in and kissed me deeply, I imagined it was desire that I had misread as apprehension. With my eyes closed and his mouth on mine, I was taken back to the bliss we once shared in this very field. A small moan left my lips.

Easton pulled back, his hands still cupping my cheeks. And his blue eyes twinkled before he stepped out of my line of sight. I sucked in a piercing breath when I saw the surprise. It wasn't the picnic planned for two, a bottle of champagne on a rose-covered blanket, but a deserted construction site and the makings of a custom home overlooking the Truley River. My jaw dropped and hung open as I took several steps forward, unable to believe my eyes. A large tractor sat vacant off to the side. The field was dug up, exposing the rich soil. Exposed beams framed the home, as work had begun some time ago.

"I know you've been struggling with the girls moving out. And it had always been my dream to build you a home here. I was going to wait until it was complete to show you, but you've been so down lately. I just thought that maybe if you knew why I had been 'working late,' then maybe you would have a reason to shift your focus from an empty nest to the next chapter in our lives. There's a lot that needs to be done, and I was hoping you could help. I know you've been driving around aimlessly." Easton shrugged, looking back toward the home. "Now you can drive here, instead," he said.

"This . . . is ours?" I asked. Easton laughed, but it was no joke; he was serious. "This is ours?" I repeated.

"Yes! This is our new home! We're going to have coffee every morning on the porch. It's going to wrap around the entire house. We're going to open our windows at night and listen to the river run . . ."

"Can I throw flower seeds all over the field? And have a white picket fence?" I asked.

Easton laughed, "You can have whatever you want!" he said.

My chest fluttered, and I blinked several times, trying to regain composure. I turned to Easton, the man who never ceased to amaze me. "I want you," I said with deep desire. The next bits were a blur, but before I knew it, we were making *new* memories in a place I'd one day call my kitchen.

CHAPTER 21

I couldn't take the chill any longer. I didn't know if it was the cancer, the raging storm outside, or the simple fact that I was frail and my body had lost its efficiency in my older age. I cranked up the thermostat several degrees and made a pot of tea. Once my bones warmed some, I sat down at my desk to finish my farewell letters. I was halfway through Nora's when I was caught in a memory and the chill set in, rendering me useless.

I tapped the pen on my lips, remembering when John had passed. We were all beside ourselves. But we found strength in each other. At least that's what I had thought. Although, Lindsay never fully recovered and she didn't wait too long before following John. I wrote to Nora about how wonderful her parents were, and how much her mother meant to me.

As I sat there—pen in hand—I reflected on my relationship with my own mother, and how we never spoke of my adoption. She passed unexpectedly, and I never took the chance when she was alive to tell her that I knew her deepest secret. That I loved her even more for raising me when she didn't have to. I knew holding that in was a great detriment to her wellbeing, but even so, I never took the opportunity to talk to her about it. Because, well, it was awkward. I shouldn't have allowed something so meaningful to get swept under the rug like that. Had my mom known that I accepted her, blood or not, it very well could have lifted a burden so heavy that it changed her life. Perhaps she would have lived longer. It was something I thought about all the time. Something I regretted. And I was so thankful that the day had come when we had the opportunity to tell Nora the truth, as difficult as it had been.

I focused my eyes back on the page and realized I was running out of room. I pressed the pen to the paper, and I wrote for Nora to love fiercely. Love like she couldn't be broken and when she fell apart, broke and shattered—and that she would—to do it all over again.

I told her to live fully. Live like fear didn't exist. Live like there's no time like the present . . . because perhaps there's not, and living with regret is no way to do it. I had learned that lesson once upon a time. And I was still learning it today.

And lastly, I told her to laugh. Life is a whole lot better with deep, gut-wrenching laughter. And if it makes her cry or even makes her wet her pants . . . that's the good stuff. I told her not to take life so seriously, and when she finds the person who makes her laugh harder than she ever had, to hold on to them tightly. They don't come around all that often.

I sipped my tea and stared out the bedroom window. The rain pelted down, turning into hail momentarily. I stopped to watch. Clicks and clacks spackled my window, and I listened to the melody of Mother Nature. I was going to miss the rain, among many other things. I swallowed, but the lump in my throat remained. I knew I had two more letters to write and that I was running out of time. I worried about where Easton had run off to and quickly dispelled the thought of him trying to leave this world first so that he could be the one to greet me with open arms. That wouldn't be very gentlemanly of him. I sighed and gripped my pen to write my dearest friend, Brooklyn, a few words to take with her after I passed.

I told her that she had been a guiding light for me all these years. That I would have been so lost without her. I thanked her for all the sacrifices she made in her own life to help the lost souls that wandered this earth long after they should have. And I asked her to take a chance on herself sometime. It didn't have to be now, or even in this lifetime, but that she should strive to find a balance between giving and receiving. While she had always been happy to give, she refused to receive anything entirely for herself. And she needed so much more than she had allowed herself to have.

Brooklyn always reminded me of the speech given on airplanes before takeoff, when they say to put your own mask on before helping others. She never abided by that rule, and sometimes I would see her struggle with little oxygen. If she only realized that she could help the other passengers more effectively if she could get a full breath; then, I think her life would find balance. And I wanted that for her.

I asked her to look after Nora. I knew Nora would walk this earth for some time. Stuck in a vortex that she didn't yet have the strength to find her way out of. I asked that Brooklyn guide her and, when necessary, push her. I knew she would take care of my daughter long after I had gone, and I couldn't thank her enough. But it didn't stop me from trying. And by the time I finished, I had tears in my eyes.

One letter left. And it was the one I couldn't find the words for. How would I say goodbye to the love of my life? My soulmate, and yet, so much more. Easton wasn't just a husband or a lover. He had been an anchor in my life. He'd been my home.

I tried not to let the tears fall as I wrote the one thing I could. The one thing I knew how. A simple sentence. Written in cursive diagonally across the middle of the blank page. I stared at the paper and the blinding white of the empty lines. The ink blurring in and out of focus. Should I have said more? No. I didn't think so. He already knew. But this . . . this one line . . . this was a promise.

I closed my journal and wrapped it with a large burlap bow, much like the one my first mother used to wrap my childhood journals in. I left it on my desk —one last goodbye gift. Easton already knew that he needed to share the journal with all the girls. Brooklyn included. And that I'd like everyone to read it at one point or another. It was my voice that would carry on long after I passed, and that made me happy.

I stood, in pursuit of one last gift I wanted to leave with the journals, when I heard the front door close and Easton shudder down the hallway. I walked slowly, my hand trailing the walls for support. Easton stood sopping wet in the living room, holding the most beautiful bouquet of white lilies and pink roses that I had ever seen. He closed the distance between us, leaving a trail of wet footprints on the floor. I smiled, taking the bouquet from him. I smelled the invigorating aroma of fresh flowers and I closed my eyes as the baby's breath tickled my nose.

"I just couldn't let you go without giving you flowers one last time," Easton said. My smile faded as his words sank in. His hair was plastered to his forehead, and rainwater dripped down the sides of his temples. Droplets clung to his lashes. And his eyes were red. Though he was much older now, it reminded me of the first time I looked into his eyes on that fatefully stormy night. He had been rain-soaked then, and his eyes were filled with the same heartbreak I saw in them now.

"Thank you. They're so beautiful," I said, looking out the window. I couldn't face him knowing that I had been the one that hurt him.

"What is it?" he asked.

"You know, I was just thinking of the first time we met. You were on the bridge and I had just received my diagnosis. The first time." I shrugged. "We were so young and hopeless. You just reminded me of that evening," I said.

"I did?"

I reached out, cupping his wet cheek. "You did." I dared to look into his eyes.

He turned ever so slightly, kissing the palm of my hand. And though my final curtain was drawing near, I still got butterflies in my stomach when his lips pressed against me.

"I think . . . I think I want to feel the rain. I want to feel it one last time. And I want to remember that day that we met and our lives changed forever."

"You want to go outside? But it's cold—"

"I'm doing it!" I said, leaving. "Well, are you coming or not?" I asked, halfway to the door.

"I'm right behind you," he said. And together we stepped out of the house and stood on the edge of the covered porch. The rain was lighter than it had been that morning, and I was glad there was an opening for me to step out into the rain and not be swept away. I slipped my hand into Easton's as we stepped out into the storm. At first, it was jarring. The rain pelted down, smacking my head and slapping my cheeks. I squinted as the assault took place. I fought to open my eyes enough to see Easton. But when he stood in front of me, hands out to my side and a concerned look on his face, I felt the need to be my strongest self. I wanted to show him that I could do it and that I was still the same soul I'd always been even though my body had been failing me. "Are you OK? Let's get you inside!"

"No! I want this!" I shouted over the rumbling thunder. I held onto Easton's arm for support and slowly tilted my face up to the sky. My eyes closed as the raindrops fell onto my cheeks and dripped down my lips. I parted my mouth and caught the rain on my tongue—drinking the angel's tears. It was a marvelous feeling—the freshwater that fell from the clouds on top of my skin.

On a day that I thought I wouldn't feel anything other than the pain, I smelled the fresh roses and I drank the rain. It washed away any fears that I had lingering in the depths of my mind. And I knew that whatever force of nature was out there, that I'd soon be part of it. Maybe I'd been the one to draw in the thunderclouds? Or paint the fields with wildflowers? Maybe I'd be the girl who sent stars shooting through the sky when someone needed a wish? A smile parted my lips. I could be anything I wanted when I died. I wanted to try it all. Easton's laugh echoed and rose above the storm.

I turned to see him, and his head was tilted back, a hand crossed his chest. He was laughing harder than I'd seen in years. It reminded me of the time he saw the tattoo etched across my ribs in Sin City. And though it had faded quite a bit, I still smiled when I saw it in the mirror to this day. Easton bent forward, his laughter building still. And I watched one of the most beautiful sights I had ever seen. His unruly wet hair and flushed cheeks brought me back to a time when I was young and the days were endless. I felt that way now—that my time was infinite. And I knew that while my body was anything but, that something inside of me would go on forever.

Easton took me in his arms, wrapping one hand around my back, and holding my hand in his, and we danced. Right there in our field overlooking the Truley River—fogged in and mysterious, wet and spontaneous—we danced. Slowly, we swayed from side to side. A melody that only we could hear. Our feet never leaving the ground. I pressed my head against his chest and whispered, "I'm going to miss this." And I was glad when the storm overshadowed my voice.

I closed my eyes, my heart spilling over until the storm grew cold once more. Lightning lit the sky, and I opened my eyes just in time to see the electricity snap above the canyon and scatter into finger-like voltage. We turned slightly to watch as the blue glow lashed downward, and when the crack of thunder hit, rumbling the very ground we stood on, we knew our last dance had come to an end.

Easton ushered me inside. My teeth were chattering and my hair dripping. He ran a warm bath straight away and helped me peel the wet clothing off my frail body. "I'm so cold," I said. My voice had strained from calling out in the storm and was now no more than a hiss.

"I know, I know. This bath should help warm you up," Easton said, his hand under the faucet. I turned to see myself in the mirror and didn't recognize the woman staring back at me. Her eyes were sunken and her lips blue. Her clavicle prominent on her bony frame. Ribs covered in gooseflesh. My eyes trailed slowly down her body as I refused to believe it was mine.

Easton helped me step into the tub, and I sat down, shivering uncontrollably. He enveloped my hand in his own and blew hot air to warm my frigid fingers. I leaned forward, grasping my knees as the water rose just above my ankles.

"Don't worry, I'm going to get you war—"

"Easton?" I interrupt him. "Do you remember when Nora graduated from law school?" I asked.

He looked at me, confused. "Yeah?"

I struggled to control my breathing, which was growing ever more labored. My body was having a hard time regulating basic needs like breath and temperature. But I no longer felt the cold. "It's our granddaughter's birthday in three days . . ." I whispered.

Easton stilled, his clothes dripping on the bathroom floor. "I know . . ." he whispered back as his gaze left mine for the running bathwater.

CHAPTER 22

Smile!" Lindsay called out. I squeezed Nora's waist, and she stopped whispering to Brooklyn for a moment to smile for the camera.

"OK, now you get in here!" I said to Lindsay.

"I'll take the picture," Brooklyn said, nodding at Nora. The two of them had been talking quietly all day, and it only made me more curious. Lindsay put her arm around Nora, and the three of us beamed with pride. "Wow, that's a great one!" Brooklyn cried, examining her camera.

"Hey, what have you two been talking about all day?" I asked casually.

"Nothing," Nora said, never making eye contact. I sighed. I hated when the girls hid something from me. I spotted Clara in a blue summer dress wading through the sea of law school graduates.

"Did you find the restroom alright?" I asked.

"Yeah, it's a hike, but it's on the far side of the building if you need it," she said.

"You missed all the pictures!" Brooklyn griped. "OK, one more, guys!"

Nora threw her head back in protest as Clara joined in. The twins in the middle and the moms on the outside. "Seriously though, I can't take one more picture!" Nora said.

"You sound like your father!" Lindsay said.

I kissed Nora on the forehead. "Wow, my sweet Nora—a lawyer!" I said.

Nora rolled her eyes. She was embarrassed, but somewhere behind the annoyance, I could see a hint of a smile. "I still have to take the bar exam, Mom."

"But I thought you were a lawyer now?" Clara asked.

"I am."

"Then why do you have to take another test? You just graduated," Clara said, frowning.

"Because I'm not an attorney until I pass the bar."

"What? That doesn't make any sense." Clara's voice was sharp as she became aggravated. The sun was warm, and the crowd of graduates was a lot to take in.

"She's a lawyer now that she graduated, but she still needs to pass the bar exam. When she passes, she can then work as an attorney in that state. She's not an attorney until she can work. Did I get that right, honey?" I asked. Nora nodded, barely listening.

"So you just went through seven years of school, and you're not qualified to work?" Clara said.

"No—"

"Why isn't the bar exam just the finals then? Like why are we even celebrating if you're not done yet?" Clara asked. She had a good point, but I knew she was trying to get under Nora's skin. Nora shot her a look that could kill.

"Clara, stop. We're celebrating because it's deserved," I said.

"Ready to get out of here?" Lindsay asked. The look in her eyes told me she had been ready to part from the crowd long ago, and she wasn't the only one.

"Yes!" Nora said.

"OK, we just have to find the men," I said, scanning through the crowd.

"They're right where we left them," Lindsay said, pointing to the graduation seating. They never came with when we moved around campus in search of backdrops for our photoshoot. If I stretched my eyes as far as they would go, I could make out a couple of tiny black suits occupying two seats in a field of white fold-up chairs. We made our way back to Easton and John as I positioned myself behind Nora and Brooklyn, trying to eavesdrop on their secret conversation.

"How much?" Nora asked.

"A lot," Brooklyn said.

"But how much? Do you know?"

"Millzsss." *Millzsss?* Millions? Were they talking about money? I hurried, stretching my neck as close to the secret as I could.

"Wow . . ."

"And that's only the first one," Brooklyn said. Nora turned enough for me to see that whatever they had been talking about had made her ecstatic. The sunlight danced atop the apple of her cheek as I caught her profile. Clara hung back to walk with Lindsay and me. And it was clear that she, too, wasn't part of the secret conversation.

"Are you OK?" I asked Clara.

"Yeah, it's just hot."

"That it is," I said, watching Nora and Brooklyn laugh. "What do you think those two are up to?" I asked.

"Nothing. Brooklyn's just handing out fortunes like she's a gypsy is all," Clara said, her tone deflated.

My stomach dropped. Brooklyn didn't speak of her dreams all that often, and when she did, it was because it was important. Monumental. Life-altering, even. I worried what she would possibly say to Nora that she hadn't said to me first. And I wondered why Nora had found so much joy in it.

"Did she tell you yours?" I asked. We were coming up on Easton and John, and it looked as though they had finally found common ground to stand upon. They, too, were deep in conversation.

"Yeah, but it wasn't anything like what she's telling Nora. She basically told me I was going to be a loser."

"What?" I highly doubted that. Although it was unlike Brooklyn to be talking about her dreams with the girls in the first place.

"Yeah, nothing even happens in my life. I just get married and have kids. It's totally predictable. Totally safe. Totally boring!" Clara crossed her arms, and the blue summer dress pinched beneath her arms.

"What!? No! Having a family isn't boring! You girls are the best thing that ever happened to me!" I said, reaching out for her arm.

"Whatever," Clara said, accepting a life of complacency.

"What did she tell Nora?" I asked, my concern growing, as Brooklyn and Nora had been inseparable throughout the graduation ceremony.

"Oh, nothing much. Just that she's a multimillionaire, super-successful attorney who dates all these famous actors and models—"

"What?"

"While I'm here marrying Nora's high school sloppy seconds, Landon."

"But I thought you loved Landon?" I asked, watching Clara's chin begin to quiver.

"That's not the point, Mom. The point is that my life is boring. I might as well die now," Clara said, her voice barely hanging on.

"Hey! Don't say that!" I hissed. I was going to have a talk with Brooklyn as soon as we got home. Easton joined my side, taking my hand in his as we walked to the parking lot. Clara and I fell quiet, the tension thick.

"Everything OK? I'm sensing—" Easton began.

"It's fine, Dad!" Clara cut him off just before she walked ahead of us. Easton raised his brows and then turned to me for answers.

I sighed. "It seems that someone has been handing out premonitions as graduation gifts . . ." I motioned to Nora as she walked, interlocking arms with Brooklyn.

"Ahh. And Clara is jealous?" he asked.

"Well, yes. But it's only a matter of perspective."

It was late when Lindsay and John took off. Both Nora and Clara had parted immediately after dinner to spend time with their friends while the rest of us enjoyed each other's company and drinks at our house. Easton pulled out a deck of cards, intending to play poker, but the conversation never stopped long enough for him to deal. Every now and then, he would re-shuffle the deck, arch them into a bridge and tap them on the dinner table.

"Well, I should head out, too. It's late, and it's been a long day," Brooklyn said, as the door closed behind Lindsay and John and the room fell quiet.

"Actually, I wanted to talk to you about something," I said.

"Oh, boy," Easton said, leaning back into his seat. Brooklyn crossed her arms, already expecting a lecture.

"Did you tell the girls what their futures hold?" I asked, already knowing she had.

"Yes. It was a gift to Nora. But then Clara felt left out, so, I told her, too," Brooklyn said unapologetically.

"I thought we agreed that would not benefit them. That it would interfere with how their life progressed, and their efforts in doing so, that it would—"

"—Yeah! We did! But Nora has a really bright future ahead of her, and I wanted to share it! You saw how happy she was today!" Brooklyn said. It reminded me of the way some grandparents spoiled their grandchildren with cookies, candies, and cakes, only to send them home to the parents, a sugar-high terror.

"I did. But did you notice how *unhappy* Clara was?" I asked.

"I mean, she has a great future, too. It's just not as flashy as Nora's. But flashy isn't really Clara's speed, anyhow."

"Well, I know that, but she doesn't," I said.

"What do you mean by flashy?" Easton asked.

"Oh, you know, dating supermodels and rolling in cash," I barked. Brows raised and lips pursed.

"I didn't say that!" Brooklyn defended.

"That's what Clara gathered from the conversation."

"Look, I may have mentioned some men she would meet as being big names in the industry, and I may have mentioned something about the mega cases she would win . . . but what's the big deal? She's happy!" Brooklyn's mouth hung in the balance.

"I don't want her dating all these male models," Easton said, his eyes unfocused as he undoubtedly imagined something scandalous that he couldn't unsee. I frowned, just thinking about it.

The room quieted as both Brooklyn and I questioned Easton's point of view. I took a deep breath, feeling defeated. What was said was said, and there wasn't much point in arguing about it now.

"Can you promise me you will stop telling the girls about your dreams? It just doesn't feel right," I said. There wasn't much else I could say, but I knew I wanted the girls to walk their own paths, not the one Brooklyn dreamed up.

"OK. I can promise you that. For now. But when you're gone, and it's just Nora and I . . . I don't know if I can keep that promise," she said.

"Brooklyn, just try. Just try to imagine you have her best interest at heart, OK?" I asked, taking a dig.

"I do have their best interest at heart. I just don't believe it makes a difference if they know what will happen before it does. And you want to know why? Because it doesn't! I've seen it! And the picture never changes, whether or not I tell it. So, why not have a little fun where fun is needed?" she asked.

"I don't know. Obviously, I don't see what you do. It's just a protective feeling I have. It's like cheating or something," I said.

"And you don't cheat?" she asked.

"No! I don't cheat!" I snapped. Easton shuffled the cards with a smile on his face. He knew a different story. It only made me angry.

"So, you don't want to know the thing I was going to tell you about your future?" she asked.

Heat rose to the surface of my cheeks, and I knew instantaneously that I had shoved my foot in my mouth. I swallowed the lump in my throat and dared to look at Brooklyn. A slow smile spread across her face as she took in what I knew were beet red cheeks of remorse. Triumph touched the corners of her eyes. "Uh-huh," she said, a smug look on her face as she leaned back in her chair and crossed her arms.

Brooklyn had been like a sister to me. She was there through thick and thin, and when we fought, she never took it for more than what it was.

"What thing about my future?" I asked.

Brooklyn threw her head back, laughing. Easton chuckled as his cards fell out of order and spilled onto the table, the joker face up. "Oh, but I thought you didn't think it was morally acceptable. Wasn't it you who said it was *just like cheating*?" Brooklyn teased.

"Just tell me!" I said.

"Say you're sorry—"

I sighed, looking at Easton. His brows were raised in anticipation. Clearly, I was on the opposite side of the fence. "I'm sorry that I'm weak and can't resist temptation. I want to know what my future holds," I said.

"While that wasn't a genuine apology, I'll still allow it," Brooklyn said, eager to move on to the juicy bits. She uncrossed her arms and leaned forward, the front legs of her chair hitting the hardwood floor. I leaned forward in preparation for a glimpse into my future.

"You heard that Clara marries Landon, right?" she asked, voice low and mysterious.

"She does?" Easton asked with a broad smile. We all liked Landon, even when he had dated Nora for a few short months back in high school.

"Yeah. Try to keep up," Brooklyn said to Easton, her eyes soon flicking back to mine. "So Clara and Landon have two children. Kinsley and—"

"No! Don't tell me their names!" I snapped, wanting to preserve some element of surprise.

"OK. Weird. But, on her eighteenth birthday, she gets into a terrible accident."

"Who does!?" I asked, alarm rippling through me with a shudder.

"Kinsley."

"Oh, no!" I said, cupping my mouth.

"It's OK. She'll be OK. That's what I wanted to tell you. The odds are stacked against her, and it's a very difficult time in Clara's life. I just wanted you to know that she will pull through."

"Oh my god, thank you!" I said, grateful for the knowledge. I probably would have been sick with worry, but now, at least, I'd have hope.

"I mean, you won't be there to see it, but you'll still play an instrumental part in her recovery," Brooklyn said.

Easton's gaze snapped up from his deck of cards, and the room dropped several degrees in an instant. Tiny goosebumps prickled my arms as I nodded slowly, taking in the information. I wouldn't be alive to see my granddaughter's eighteenth birthday. Clara wasn't married yet, but she and Landon were in love. I probably had twenty years left. Every passing second was one I'd never get back.

"How do you mean I'll play a part in her recovery?" I asked in haste, cutting through the grief and focusing on the information at hand. Easton sat motionless, the deck of cards still for the first time that night.

"You see, Kinsley will be in a coma for some time. Her spirit will be just beyond the veil. Not dead but not quite alive in body or mind. You'll be able to reach her there. And she'll need your guidance and encouragement to keep fighting. You two will have a special bond, and she'll look toward you for the support she needs to survive," Brooklyn said, withdrawing her hands from the table.

I should have felt devastation. Fear of the unknown. Heartache for knowing that I only had twenty years, give or take, to live out the rest of my life. But I felt none of those things as I focused on the one piece of information that would keep me going strong in the final chapters of my life. And that was purpose. The purpose I had beyond my death.

CHAPTER 23

When Brooklyn's premonition came true, Clara married Landon at our new home on the bluffs above the Truley River. It was the push we needed to finish the last ten percent of odd jobs. I watched my firstborn marry in the same field I had. And it felt like I'd come full circle. Easton squeezed my hand tightly as they read their vows, and I knew he had the same tugging in his heart that I had.

Clara dated several characters over the years. Some were OK, and some were not. Some were right, but the timing was wrong. Landon had remained friends with both of the girls after Nora dumped him in high school and he grew fond of Clara's kind heart. She never let the potential of hurt stop her from finding the one. And one day, she realized that he had been right in front of her all along.

Landon was easy to accept into our family. He'd been hanging around long before he and Nora ever started dating. And he would be around long after. Somewhere along the way, he had become Clara's best guy friend. He felt at home when he was over, and I often caught him making lunch in our kitchen when I hadn't realized any of Clara's friends were over. She always said that he was just a friend, but I had a hunch that she was saving him for the right time.

I watched his heartbreak when she would date other guys, and I saw the same in her when he would become close to other girls. It was clear that they cared the most for each other, so we all rejoiced when they finally gave up the act and declared they were dating. I'd never forget the look Clara gave me when I said, "Wow, your *last* first kiss . . ." but deep down, she knew it, too.

I looked to Nora, who stood confidently behind her sister as her maid of honor. Both the girls looked stunning, but only Clara was a bleeding heart. Nora had passed the bar exam three months after graduating and immediately got to work at a large firm in the city. She was on the cusp of her first big case and I could only imagine it was the one that Brooklyn had told her about. Nora had been withdrawn as she stood behind her sister. And while her heart was also made of gold, it had been misled somewhat along the way, and dollar signs reflected in her vacant stare.

When Clara kissed her groom, Easton leaned over and planted a kiss on my lips that surely rivaled that of the newlyweds. And when we took family photos welcoming our new son-in-law, he would secretly drop his hand from the small of my back and pinch my butt. There was something liberating watching your daughter marry, and I didn't know if it was the high of the celebration or the shift in responsibility from us as parents to Landon as the husband, but it made me feel like a kid again. And judging by the playful manner in which Easton and I flirted like we were teenagers, I imagined that he felt the same way.

Clara's marriage felt like our success. It felt like we were celebrating not only her beginning but our validation. Because in that moment, we had a successful launch. And though Clara's marriage was the glaringly obvious reason to celebrate that night, Nora had become successful in her own right, too. She had learned that hard work pays off, and she never backed down from hard work like she did the opportunity to let someone in. I had to remind myself that everyone has different strengths and that one day, she too would master love in the same way she had her career.

The last reason for Easton and I to celebrate was the freedom from construction that we had been living with for what seemed like an eternity. The constant table saw screaming in the background, the drywall dust that never ended, and the lack of privacy in our own home were finally things of the past. And anywhere we looked that evening, be it at Clara or Nora, or even past them and into the rose bushes, the three-tiered fountain, or the baseboards that had stolen a month of my life. . . I was so tenderly proud of it all. And I beamed all evening long.

I celebrated that night in a way I never had before. In a way, I had always wanted to but was too embarrassed. I danced. I danced with Easton, I danced alone, I danced barefoot. And when the night was still young, I earned the name. . .

"Dancing Queen," Easton said, his hands on my hips. I threw my head back into his chest and laughed. We fit together snugly—like two pieces of a puzzle. I had always been too insecure to dance, and sometimes I even tricked myself into thinking I didn't want to in the first place. But I always wanted to. I just didn't know how. But tonight, none of that mattered. I had a reason to celebrate, and my lack of musicality wasn't reason enough for me to stop now.

"Eww, get a room!" Nora said, passing us on the dance floor as she led a tall and handsome man behind her.

I laughed, batting my hand at her when I caught the spark in Easton's eye. "What is it?" I asked.

"We do have a room . . . We have *three*," he said, his eyes pointing toward our bedroom. My lips pursed the way they sometimes did when I felt I was doing something sneaky. Easton pulled my hand, and we passed through the crowd and vanished unnoticed. We walked through the foyer, smiling at the lingering guests inside the house. Fewer guests yet, were meandering through the kitchen, and I suspected that they knew what we were up to when we passed them in a hurry, my heels clacking down the hall. I burst out laughing, but just like the dancing that took place that night, the embarrassment didn't touch me.

Easton slammed the bedroom door and backed me up against it, kissing me eagerly. I felt the smile on his lips in the bedroom shadows. "My dancing queen," he said.

"Oh, you like that?" I asked, shoving him away from me and locking the bedroom door behind me. I reached back and unzipped my dress, swaying my hips as it slid down my body and pooled at the floor. I stepped out of the dress, my heels clacking slowly with each step I took toward Easton. And for every step I took, he took one back. A simple game of cat and mouse.

"Show me what you got," he said.

I spun, feeling the heat creep up into my cheeks as I laughed at myself. I wasn't this girl. The girl who was sexy. The one who could dance fluidly. But I was the only one that found it funny. I was the only one that thought I wasn't her.

Easton's eyes were ablaze, and as soon as I saw them, my smile faded. I rocked my hips slowly, side to side, lowering down and then back up again. I watched his eyes trail the length of my body, encouraging me to keep dancing. I strode towards him, running my hands through my perfectly pinned hair. I knew I would regret it later, but that wasn't my concern at the moment. When I reached Easton, I pushed him down on the side of the bed. I spun to face the door, and his hands reached out to greet my curves.

Sometimes I still wonder who I was that night or what had come over me. And then I simply wish I could summon it with a snap of a finger. Live as the dancing queen when the party had all but gone. Dance while I was making dinner all alone. Maybe I would even do it in my heels.

I smiled, thinking of all the opportunities I had on a regular day to be carefree and maybe even a little sexy. We made love then, in a way that was new and exciting to us. Easton collapsed against me, and the sound of the band became loud once again. "How long have we been in here?" I asked, suddenly losing track of time.

"Not long? I don't think," Easton said, reaching for his slacks and pulling them on.

I hurried to the restroom and was thankful I had glimpsed the wild beast that lived inside before hitting the dance floor. My perfect hair was distorted, slanting to one side and nearly concave on the other. "What . . . the . . ."

"Oh, wow," Easton said, looking at my hair. "You should see the back." I frowned at him before trying to finger comb the nest into order. Easton finished buttoning his shirt, tucked it in, and buckled his belt while I directed all of my efforts to fix my hair. It wasn't ever going to look the same, but when I got it to a point that looked like maybe I had just danced the curl right out, I left it. The sun had dipped behind the horizon some time ago, and I was confident that nobody would look at my hair. And if they did, they'd see a healthy marriage, and I was proud of that. Easton zipped up my dress and kissed my shoulder. His lips lingered for a moment before he pulled away and whispered, "I love you," in my ear.

"I love you, too," I said. The fire was gone in his eyes, but in its place was the warm and consistent glow of embers that he kept for only me.

Easton peeked his head out of our bedroom door. "It's clear," he said, opening the door wide. I threw my shoulders back and strode down the hallway. As luck would have it, nobody was lingering inside the house, and nobody had witnessed our bedroom exit. At first, I was grateful, but then I wondered, *why*? I squeezed Easton's hand as soon as it hit me.

"The cake!" we said. We took off running across the kitchen and down the foyer.

When we snuck into the crowd, almost unnoticed, I could see Clara with a dot of frosting on her nose. Landon had cake up the side of his face and pressed into his ear. I smiled, placing my hand over my heart, and mumbled, "Good boy," to no one other than myself.

The guests dispersed, some to the dance floor and some to their chairs. But Easton and I stood still as we watched Clara and her new husband make a memory that would last a lifetime. I rested my head on Easton's shoulder as I spotted Brooklyn across the room. She had been watching Clara with the same pride in her eyes that we had. I thought about how she would remember this moment for far longer than the one lifetime. And how the memory would live as long as she graced this earth.

Brooklyn's head whipped around as Tanner slipped his hand in hers. She looked pleasantly surprised. I watched as a quick exchange ensued, and then he pulled her onto the dance floor. Brooklyn put her head on his chest, and he slid his hands down the small of her back. They rocked slowly from side to side, and I marveled at just how perfect they were. How perfect they had always been when they were together. I loved Charlie. She'd found a special place in my heart, but at some point in time, she and Tanner found they were better people when they were apart. It wasn't like that with Brooklyn, though. They always brought out the best in each other.

"Do you want to dance? Or are you all tuckered out?" Easton asked.

I smiled and wrapped my arms around his neck. "Never," I said.

He held me close as we slow danced. My head pressed against Easton, I searched the crowd for the bride. She was wiping down Landon's cheek with a napkin. He turned to her talking before leaning forward and licking the frosting off her nose. I giggled. They were well on their way to a happy marriage. I searched for Nora. I found her wrapped in the arms of the handsome stranger that I'd seen her with earlier. She danced with her eyes closed and a small smile on her lips. And just for that single moment under the stars that evening, everything had been perfect.

CHAPTER 24

The phone rang in the dead of the night. Alarmed and disoriented, I reached for my cell phone. Easton rolled over as I fumbled to answer it. "H—Hello?"

"Are you ready to be a grandma?" Landon asked on the other line.

"It's time? It's time! Easton, it's time!" I slapped the bed.

"We just got admitted to the hospital. Clara has hours ahead of her, but you're welcome anytime. We're on the third floor," he said.

"We're coming! We're on our way!" I shouted.

"Christ, Beck, he's having a baby, not going deaf! He can hear you!"

"Shut up and put your pants on! We've got a baby to catch!" I ran in circles frantically.

Landon laughed on the other end, and I could hear him faintly say, "Your parents crack me up . . ." Clara moaned.

"OK, we're coming! See you soon!" I said, bumping into Easton in the dark.

When the lights switched on, I was wearing a sheer lace cami and a pair of sexy boy shorts. It was a habit I started when Clara moved out of the house because why not? I didn't expect it to last longer than a week, but there I was, completely unacceptable outside of our bedroom. I looked at Easton, who was fully dressed in an impossible amount of time. I couldn't wrap my mind around it. It was mere seconds since the phone had rung.

"What just happened?" I asked.

"Do you remember when I said you would cave under the pressure? And you had the audacity to take that bet?" he said with a smug smirk.

I said nothing but rolled my eyes, in search of clothing.

"Remember when you upped the ante by saying that I would never get ready as fast as you when the call came in?"

"No! That's not what I said!"

Easton laughed.

"That's not what I said . . ."

"Then, what did you say?"

"I said . . . that I would make it to the door first," I said. And as soon as it came out of my mouth, we were racing to the front door. All in the name of diaper duty. I reached my hand for Easton, who was ahead of me by several feet as we ran through the dark house. I dug my nails into the back of his shirt, trying to grasp a handful. Anything I could use to pull him backward and propel myself forward. But it didn't happen like that.

"Door!" Easton called out as he hit the door. I slapped his shoulder and then thrust my hand on my hip. "What? Were you ready to go to the hospital, in that?" Easton's eyes trailed down my silk and lace silhouette.

"No . . ."

He laughed again. "Then why did you even race me? Just admit that I won the bet!" he said.

"I—I raced you out of pure instinct, first of all," I admitted. Easton threw his head back, laughing, and a small smile tugged the corners of my lips out of embarrassment. "And second of all," my eyes trailed down Easton's shirt, jeans, and shoes. "Did you sleep in that?" I asked.

Easton leaned in, and though the house was empty, he whispered. "I had secret intel."

I growled ferociously. Easton was impossible to beat at a bet. I had made it my lifelong goal to win just once. But every time I lost, I only wanted it more. I spun on my heels and stomped down the hall, defeated, when Easton reached forward and slapped my butt. The thin fabric of the shorts, like a second skin, did little to protect against the sting. I paused and took a deep breath as he chuckled in triumph. Then, I continued on my way.

"Come on, Beck. We've got a baby to catch!" Easton called out down the hall.

On the way to the hospital, I couldn't help but be reminded of the time that my first niece, Everly, nearly took my life when she rounded the corner into the parking lot. I couldn't believe that we were here again. And I couldn't be more grateful that it wasn't *me* who was having another baby . . . in another lifetime.

I felt the nerves and the thrill wind up in my chest as we waited outside of Clara's delivery room, but most of all, I was excited. I'd never been a grandparent before, and neither had Easton. I imagined it was all the best things about having kids, with none of the work. I vowed to myself that I would help Clara as much as I could . . . As much as she would let me. And even though I lost the bet to Easton, I didn't mind changing dirty diapers.

"Push!" the doctor said. I looked up at Easton, his shoulder leaning against the wall.

"OK, now breathe. Breathe. Good."

We listened through the partially opened door. I chewed on my lip, and my heart pounded in my chest as the seconds ticked by in slow motion.

"OK, now push! Push!"

Easton and I locked eyes again, waiting. We held our breath, listening.

"Good, you're doing great. Breathe." I breathed laboriously. I wasn't in labor, but I was right there alongside Clara, going through the motions. I wished I could hold her hand, so I held Easton's instead.

We breathed together. Long deep breaths in and out. And though she couldn't see us on the other side of the wall, we were there, cheering her on. I reached my clammy hands out to Easton's, and he pulled me close for support. "It's going to be OK," he whispered. I nodded against his chest.

"Now push! Push!" the doctor instructed. I pulled from Easton's embrace and sought comfort in his light blue eyes. Goosebumps pricked my forearms as I heard the first tiny, tiny cry of my grandchild.

The emotion swept over me, and tears spilled down my cheeks. I bowed my head into Easton's chest, and he rubbed my back as I wept happy tears. I knew on the other side of that wall that Clara had her eyes on her firstborn for the first time. For the first time, she had a face for all the love she'd carried for nine months. She was a mother now, and I knew just how remarkable that felt. And then . . . and then, I was taken back to a time when the miraculous feeling had slipped right through my hands, and everything had become darkly devastating. My world upside down.

I knew it would be alright because Brooklyn had told us so. But I still couldn't help but remember losing Molly, and a small part of me worried it could happen to Clara, too. But it was just fear. Fear of my own tragedy projecting onto her. And I cried it all away. Clara's baby was healthy, and it wouldn't be a Tethered Soul, either.

The doctor walked out of the room and saw us embracing outside of the door. "Ah! You must be Mom and Dad?" he asked.

"Yes," Easton said. I wiped my tears and attempted to gather myself.

"Congratulations, Mom and baby are healthy. You can go in now," he said with a pat on Easton's back.

I leaned toward the open door and called out, "Honey?" in a broken voice.

Landon popped his head out, startling me. "You want to meet your granddaughter?" he asked.

"Granddaughter?" I said, placing a hand over my heart. Pigtails and pink frilly dresses danced before my eyes. I had an entire box filled with Clara's favorites from when she was a child that I had been holding onto just in case.

"Yeah, come on in," Landon said while opening the door. Easton cupped him on the back, congratulating him as a father while I headed straight for the baby. She was a beauty. Puckered, blush, wet lips, short blond strands, and a wrinkled little face. My tears dropped on Clara's bed as I leaned over to admire my granddaughter. Clara chuckled and wiped away her own tears.

"She's beautiful, Clara," I said. Easton came up behind me, gasping in awe, as we marveled at the tiny human that captured our hearts.

"Do you want to hold her?" Clara asked.

"Me?" I smiled. I couldn't think of anything better. Clara lifted the bundle, and I took her in my arms carefully. Her face flexed in and out of a wrinkled frown, and her lips bowed and parted. I patted her back as I swayed slowly back and forth.

Holding my grandchild differed from holding my own. I wasn't sure if it was the confidence I found in the experience of raising Clara or that this was a completely different delivery than I had, but when I held my granddaughter it was like all the worry had been stripped clean, and only a fresh start remained. It was peaceful.

"Do you have a name picked out?" Easton asked.

Clara looked to Landon and smiled. "Kinsley," she said.

"She looks like a Kinsley," Easton said, and I could hear the smile in his voice. I smiled too, remembering that one day, not too long ago, it was Brooklyn who dreamed this very moment. Her voice rang in my ears *"Kinsley and—"* But I didn't know it would feel this magical to hold her, and I was beyond myself that, one day, there would be another.

But then something else surfaced in my memory. True to form, the yin and yang of contrary forces were coming together. Always together. It was something that crowded out the light, chasing it to the outskirts of my mind and leaving darkness in its place.

My smile faded when I remembered what else Brooklyn had seen in the realm of her dreams that night. It was an accident—the severity of which I couldn't yet know. However, I knew two things. The first was that Kinsley would overcome her accident and make a full recovery one day with the help of her friends and family, and maybe even me. That piece of information did a lot in terms of reassurance, and I was thankful Brooklyn had told me, even though I gave her a hard time for spilling the future.

The second thing that rang true and that I couldn't shake—I was just shy of eighteen years away from my death date. Eighteen years seemed like a long time until you realize there was no more time after it.

"Mom?" Clara asked.

"Huh?" I looked down at Clara, and then across from her at the nurse. They were waiting for something. I hadn't even seen her come in.

"I need to feed Kinsley," she said, her hands outreached.

"Oh! Right!" I leaned over the bed, passing sweet Kinsley back to Clara.

"She's so in love, I don't think she even heard you," Easton said, his hand wrapped around my shoulder.

I smiled. "We're going to get some coffee. Just let us know if we can get you anything," I said. Landon walked us to the door and we parted ways. We hung around the hospital for a couple more hours before giving the new family time to be alone. It was hard for us to do, but we knew it was what Clara and her family needed to bond.

When we left the hospital, I had Easton take me to the local bookstore. I browsed for nearly two hours. The smell of the books was oddly calming, and I ran my hand across the spines until one called to me. By the time Easton had pulled me from my escape, not only one book had spoken to me but many. I walked out of the bookstore, balancing a stack of books.

One for Clara on what she could expect as a new mother. A few for me to fill the nights when Easton worked late and I couldn't sleep. A psychological thriller, a mystery, and a romance. And several fairytales for Kinsley. Little Red Riding Hood, Beauty and the Beast, Rapunzel, and a couple of other classics sure to capture her heart and fill her head with imagination.

The next several months were some of my favorites. I would spend my time rocking baby Kinsley. And even though Easton handed Kinsley to me every time she soiled herself, I always took her proudly. And then I wouldn't give her back. In the evenings when Landon came home from work and Easton was heading out for a night shift, I would busy myself with babyproofing the house. Every now and then, I would get a glass of wine and talk to Nora on the phone.

Nora ended up winning her first big case like Brooklyn had said she would. But because she had known about it since law school graduation, she had a lot of time to think about how she wanted to spend the money. By the time it hit her account, most of it had either been spent or was already spoken for in various investments. And after the first big case was won, another followed. Then another. Eventually, Nora had made quite a name for herself and opened her own law firm.

She and Easton had long talks late at night about the things she could do to squander away a stash of money for her next life. And one time, he took her on a special father-daughter trip to meet some special people that would help hide her assets for her next life.

It didn't take long before Nora started dating men I had seen on the cover of a magazine or playing small roles on the big screen. They all dazzled her. Entertained her for sure. But none of them captured her heart. And during the family dinners that she brought them to, I'd always watch Easton's eyes to see if they rose above her head. I knew I had never seen her love glow for anyone other than family, but my vision wasn't as strong as hers or Easton's, and there were never wandering eyes as far as I could tell.

Some nights, I would try to pick the reason why her boyfriends weren't the ones for her, and some nights, I'd give up and throw my hands in the air. I'd blame it on Nora for not opening her heart up. But ultimately, I knew she was waiting on someone special in the way that Easton had. The very specific soul that would capture her heart, whether or not she was ready for it. And the truth was, that soul could be lifetimes away.

CHAPTER 25

The heater kicked on, and the low sound of its hum shed little hope of warming my bones. Even though I had soaked in a hot bath and Easton had dried my hair, it didn't change the fact that I was dying today. My body was frail, fatigued, and beyond the point of repair. Chills racked my body, ripping through my knobby spine. And when Easton gave me hot tea to sip, I spilled it down the front of my bathrobe in one swift convulsion.

Outside, the storm was relentless, and inside it was no different. It reminded me of the doom that once painted the sky and made its way into my heart—the day of my first diagnosis, and the day I'd met Easton. I remembered how powerful the storm was that night. And the moment I stepped out of my truck—my shoes soaked through, immediately drenched, afraid, and all but ready to give up. Just like Easton was that night.

But if I had only known what I do now, maybe I would have spread my arms and drunk the rain. Maybe I would have looked into Easton's eyes and smiled instead of judging him for where he was in his life at that very moment. Maybe I could have made him laugh. Or maybe I would have asked him to dance in the middle of the wild storm like he and I did today.

Tiny Tommy curled up next to me on the bed, and I pet him mindlessly. He was a gift from the girls when they found out my cancer had returned. They recalled a time when I told them of my first mother and how much joy a therapy dog brought her. They remembered sweet Bodie and how loved he had been by everyone who met him. And they wanted to gift me the same support my mother once had. But Tiny Tommy wasn't a therapy dog, and I wasn't a patient who received weekly visits. The little grey dog quickly became Easton's out of necessity, because I was too tired to take care of him. But at rare times like this, when he was calm and cuddly, I found it soothing to run my hand around his ears and down his back, twisting and tangling my fingers in his long, silky hair.

"I have them," Easton said, entering the room with my two engagement rings—one old, one new. One Beck's, one Becca's.

"Can you bring the journal that's on my vanity?" I asked, pointing a knobby, quivering finger.

Easton brought me the journal and set it on my lap. I unraveled the bow and then plucked one ring from the palm of his hand and slipped it over the burlap tie. Then, I did the same with the other ring. Simple, yet challenging with dwindling motor skills. "I want Clara to have the new ring. She's made such a wonderful life for herself," I said, re-tying the bow to secure the journal. The two diamond rings dangled below the burlap.

"I want Nora to get the old ring. The one we stole from my parent's house. She will need the reminder one day that her path, while less traveled, is one that we've taken before. And that there is love on that path if she's patient."

I lifted the journal, and Easton took it gently from my hands. "There's a note for you in there. You can read that when you're good and ready," I said. Easton paused momentarily before placing the journal down on our dresser next to the bouquet he'd given me that morning. I noticed his head drop ever so slightly, and I wanted nothing more than to make him feel OK. "Easton?" I asked, my voice raw from yelling in the rain and the tumor that pressed against my vocal cords.

"Yes?" He turned around and joined me on the side of the bed.

"I don't want you to be sad," I said.

"I know you don't." He reached out for my hand, and the heat of his body felt nice against my skin.

"I'm not scared. You asked me one time if I was scared to die. Do you remember that?" Easton nodded, slowly. "I was then. But I'm not now. I feel ready. I don't want to leave you, but my body no longer works in the way I'd like it to, and it's holding me back. It hurts, and it's heavy to carry. I'm looking forward to being set free. I'm ready. I'm *ready*." I nodded.

Easton's back hunched, and he could no longer keep himself together.

"Did you hear me? I'm ready!" I said, stressing that my life wasn't being taken from me—that I wasn't a victim, but that I had earned my way out.

"You have given me such a beautiful life, Easton," I said, even though I feared he could no longer hear my whispers. I lay down on the bed and curled up on my side.

"No." He shuddered and curled up behind me, wrapping his brawny arms around my bony waist. And even though I weighed next to nothing, my body felt incredibly heavy, like it might sink into the bed and fall straight through to the other side.

The sky had been dark and stormy for days, and I had no way of knowing what time it was. But that didn't matter any longer because it was *my time*. "Tell me a story?" I asked. Though I didn't want a story and I didn't need the distraction, he did. And I wanted to hear the sweet sound of his voice, the melody of language, his unique intonation.

"A story? Um, I can do that." Easton cleared his throat and took a moment to collect himself. "Once upon a time, there was a boy—"

"Was he handsome?" I asked.

"He was *so* handsome. He was the most handsome of all the boys!" Easton said. I wanted to laugh. It felt like I had. Only, there was no sound and there was no movement.

"This boy. Despite being ruggedly good-looking, was down and out. His life was an endless loop of unfulfillment. And one day, he sought to end it. But just as he was about to take what he had thought was his only option out, he saw another path. That path was a difficult one too, as he knew it would inevitably hurt his heart more than ever before. But she was the fairest in all the land, and she had a light within her that he couldn't resist. A light so profound that he could never look back."

I imagined that night and the first time I looked into his eyes as I listened to the honeyed rhythm of his voice. His subtle inflections lulling me to sleep.

"Her light was so special that she kept it guarded—safe from the others. And sometimes, she did that so well that she forgot it was there at all. But he saw it, even when she did not." Easton tightened his grip around me and I grew even heavier.

"The boy opened his heart to the girl, and eventually, she did the same. They didn't know it then, but they had been each other's missing puzzle pieces, and once found, their masterpiece was complete. The girl couldn't understand why the boy was sad. She had been happy that their work was done. But the boy explained to her in only the way that he could. He said he enjoyed putting the puzzle together so much that he didn't want it to end."

My breathing slowed as my body continued to sink into the bed. And ever so slightly, I felt a release. A part of me was lifting, while the part that no longer served me sank. My memories, thoughts, and all of the love rose above the brittle body that was once Becca Green. And my breath fell to trivial, undetectable levels.

"But she looked at that boy . . . that ruggedly handsome boy, and she said, 'Dear, I know you enjoyed making this masterpiece with me. I enjoyed it more than you will ever know. But the best part of making art is stepping away from a finished piece and marveling at your creation.' "

I listened to the story as it rang true in my heart of hearts. My life with Easton was a masterpiece, and I wouldn't have it any other way. I looked down at Easton's arm wrapped tightly around my waist, but I no longer felt it.

"She said, 'Dear, won't you let me step away, so that I may marvel over our masterpiece?' And though he didn't want her to go, he couldn't keep her any longer. He released her, and she took several steps back. Far too many in his opinion, but the further away she got, the bigger her smile beamed. Until one day, she got so far and her pride shined so brightly that she became the sun."

I tried to lift my hand to his arm, but I could no longer move. I tried to speak, but nothing translated. I pulled back and was suddenly standing beside the bed, looking down on myself wrapped in Easton's arms. I wasn't sure if or when I had passed, as it felt like the smooth transition of falling asleep after a long day of work. I felt incredibly light, though, like I was everywhere and nowhere at the same time. But all I wanted was to be here, now. I wanted to hear the end of the story.

"And it was her sunlight that shone down on the boy every day that warmed his heart. And he, too, began to step back and see the puzzle as a masterpiece in its completion," he said. Easton paused for a moment before his head jerked upward. Swiftly, his arm that held onto my waist was on the fleeting pulse of my neck. "Beck? Beck? Just stay. Stay a little longer. Don't go. Don't go, honey," he cried.

Easton's frantic tone slowed into a vibration I could feel stirring within me. His woodsy scent came alive, dancing around me like a phantom in the night. I looked down at my hands, which were no longer trembling. The chill I couldn't shake shifted into something new—something tantalizing . . . like pleasure prickling down the nape of my neck to the small of my back. I let out my last shallow breath of air and watched and waited for the inhalation that would never come.

And then it happened. The faint beat of my heart ceased to exist, and Easton collapsed over my body, weeping in a blur of slow motion. There was a shift in my axis. The buoyancy I felt before paled in comparison. I was larger than life itself as I became a part of all the things—seen and unseen. I was limitless. Lawless. I was no longer bound by the laws of physics, suppressed by the human mind, or confined to the body that had jailed me for all the years and lives. I was untethered.

I watched Easton's back rise and fall over my body. His cried like a sad piano symphony that I could feel in my heart and hear all around me. I reached out to touch it as it whirled by, and my hand slipped inside. I pulled it back, examining my fingers. It wasn't like the first time I died, when I saw the events of loved ones before the blackness swallowed me whole, but perhaps that was because my heart was here with Easton. And I wouldn't be returning to another life on Earth.

It was nice to pass with no major regrets. I felt I had done a good job this time. I had balance. Love and happiness. I raised two of the best people I knew. It was an odd thing to look back at your lives and see them in their completed form. I had been so used to seeing it in motion. Seeing life as it unraveled before me. But now it was fixed, only a memory. A memory that Easton was still stuck in. I didn't know why I departed earlier than he or why he couldn't have come with me, but I knew one thing . . . I would wait for him.

CHAPTER 26

Take me with you," Easton cried as he hunched over me. What used to be me. I watched from the corner of the room, unable to interfere. It wasn't what I wanted to see, and it hurt me to be there witnessing his cutting pain. I felt it in ways I'd never felt anything before. Bold colors painted the room. A bitter taste filled my mouth and drumming coursed through my veins—energy where blood had once been. But I couldn't leave him. My heart belonged to Easton, and his to me. And when I said forever, I meant it. I would be Easton's personal angel for as many lives as he needed to live before he came home to me.

Easton cried until he nearly turned grey. I once would have worried that he would die right then and there, but now I knew. I knew he had a long life ahead of him. His work wasn't done yet; his body wasn't weak. And it was hard for him now, but he would one day look back at me with a smile. I'd do everything within my power to urge that day to come sooner than later, but for now, I'd have to ride out the storm with him. And it was the worst storm we'd seen in a long time.

"Beck . . ." Easton called out. I wanted to comfort him—show him that I was there and he need not worry. I tried. I reached out, but my efforts went unnoticed. I was invisible. Inaudible. Untouchable. I was only a memory. But I wasn't just a memory to me; I was here! I was alive! I was thriving like never before! I begged him to notice me. I grabbed his arm, firmer yet, but my grasp turned empty every time. I tried to knock over a lamp on the bedside table, but I passed straight through it. I tried to take my love and wrap it into a ball and push it toward him with all the energy I had conjured. Nothing worked. He cried all night long.

It was difficult to watch Easton cling to me. I wanted to tell him it wasn't me. I wasn't me! But he couldn't hear all the things I had to say. I watched as Easton's eyes grew heavy and my remains turned cold. The hours passed by, slow and painful. And though time didn't have the same meaning to me any longer, I knew this had to be the longest night in history. Easton's eyes fixed to nothing in particular as his heart rate slowed and the fight inside of him simmered down. It had been a good fight, but not a battle he could have won.

His eyes began to blink for longer, more restful moments. And when sleep finally took him, I came in close and whispered, "I'm here," in his ear. I watched for a sign that he heard me, but there was nothing except his twitching eyelids to tell me if my voice had reached him. I stayed there for some time, making sure he drifted off to sleep. And when I was sure that he had, I moved to the window to watch the storm lighten.

It was all but a mist when the sky lightened. The windowpane was fogging before me, even though I had no breath to share. I tried to draw a heart in the fog, but my finger passed through it. Part of me was inside the bedroom with Easton, and part of me was outside in the crisp morning air. I felt neither of them. Because I wasn't just in these two places at the same time, but I was everywhere all the time. I felt the beating heart of Clara, slow and steady. I saw my passing replayed in Brooklyn's nightmare. I felt Easton's emotions quiver like a fish on the line. I knew the rain had a distinct smell, but I no longer smelled it. I knew the early morning air was cold, but I didn't feel it.

I passed through the window with great ease. I felt no physical touch. But emotion—that was a different story. I felt everything near and far. I felt every living soul all at once, and I knew which of them were my loved ones. I dimmed the emotional potency of all others. I don't know how I did it. Instinct, I guess.

My soul buzzed with the vitals of the select handful of souls I wanted to watch over. Easton, of course. Clara and Nora. Clara's husband, Landon, and my granddaughter, Kinsley. I'd watch over Brooklyn and Tanner, too.

The moment I thought of Lindsay and my parents—the moment I thought of all the loved ones that had passed before me—a warm energy glowed in the distance. I stared at the burning light, entranced by its beauty. I knew, without a shadow of a doubt that if I wanted to, I could leave this place. This grey sky. This grief-stricken heart.

I knew I had that choice, but inside that home that Easton and I built and inside that bedroom, lay a heart that beat for me—a heart that I belonged to. And though I knew it was my time to pass on, I chose to wait instead. After all, I had been a Tethered Soul. Because I wouldn't leave Easton if it meant living an eternity unseen and unheard.

As soon as I looked away from the gleaming light, the sky grew dark in its absence. I knew I'd be here and it would be waiting. I watched the sunrise, and I felt the living rise with it. Easton's sleep lightened when Tiny Tommy jumped off the bed, and I came back inside to be there for him when he woke, not from a nightmare but to his new reality. It was harder than I imagined. I stayed close, trying to plant memories in Easton's mind. Good memories of times we had shared. He cried despite them.

By mid-morning, my body had been collected by the coroner. Brooklyn had shown up before Easton called the girls, and she did what she could to support him. It was more than I could do.

"I know it hurts, but she's in a better place," Brooklyn said.

"How do you know? How?" he asked, eyes swollen. "Did you have a dream?"

A dream? I wondered if I could penetrate Brooklyn's dreams and patch a message through to Easton. It was worth a try. I had the time anyhow.

"I did," Brooklyn said. And I knew this was the side of Brooklyn that used her insight for good—because she didn't have a dream about me—but she had the power to help ease Easton's pain. And she knew that.

"I don't know, Brooklyn. I don't know that I can live without her," Easton said.

"You've done it for so long. You can do it again."

"But that was before I knew her. Everything has changed now. Everything," he said.

"I know." Brooklyn peered out the window. "Hey, there's a rainbow!" she said, standing. Easton and Brooklyn hurried outside and stood under the most brilliant rainbow, which stretched across the sky and sank into the field. Our field. I marveled as the rainbow's end lit the long blades of grass and wildflowers. Easton's trembling hand cupped his mouth, and Brooklyn wiped away the silent tears that spilled onto her cheeks. And I stood with them, resting my head on Easton's shoulder as I took in the colors of light that spilled onto the damp field.

"The storm is finally over," Brooklyn said.

But nothing was over. Just different. I opened my senses for all things living. I sifted through the quivering lines until I found one so delicate and so hopeful that I reached out for it, sending a long breath of wind for it to ride all the way to us. When it showed, its teal wings flickered under the light of the rainbow.

Easton hadn't felt me when I grabbed for his arm, and he didn't hear me when I spoke soft words of encouragement to him as he drifted off to sleep. But he recognized my presence when I sent him the dragonfly. His jaw clenched tightly as he ran a hand through his hair. He nodded. Said nothing but he didn't have to.

We watched the rainbow until it faded away and the time had come for Easton to make two very difficult phone calls. Brooklyn asked Easton if he wanted her to stay, but he asked her to tell Tanner instead. One less phone call for Easton to make. She agreed and left shortly thereafter. Easton sat by the phone for a long time before picking it up. I wasn't privy to his thoughts, but I didn't need to be to know he was planning on what to say. I tried to give him the words. I whispered them in his ear. And I held him while he broke the news.

When it was time for Clara to break, I left Easton to be by her side. She had the support of her loving husband and her two kids, and I was thankful she took it better than Easton had. I tried to comfort the family, but I knew they'd be going through a rough patch. If they broke today, I knew they would shatter in two days' time. Kinsley was about to turn eighteen, and she'd be fighting for her life as she transitioned into adulthood. It would be the darkest time in Clara's life, but it would make her so much stronger.

Kinsley took the news harder than I expected. She and I had a special bond, and I was the first real loss that she experienced. She couldn't understand how I was there one day and gone the next. She questioned life's purpose. And I did, too. But I encouraged her to stay strong and support her mom. I watched as Clara and Kinsley talked on the sofa for hours about love and life. I listened to her theories and basked in the sporadic laughter. And though it was my passing that gave them the opportunity to bond, I was so grateful that Clara would have this moment to fall back on when she had no hope left.

Nora turned inward. She sat alone in her loft high above the city and drank wine while she watched the world below pass by. She took one day off work—which was more than I had known her to do before—and she eased her pain with alcohol. She didn't shed a tear that day, though I knew they would come in time. I thought about how difficult it was to watch Easton mourn, and then how much more difficult it was to see Nora resist it. I watched as she placed brick over brick, securing her walls. Making them stronger and even less penetrable—obscuring the signs of pain. But Nora didn't need thicker walls; she needed to remove them. Bust through them and completely crumble. Like a phoenix, she needed to burn so she could resurrect.

I reached out for her, but like Easton, I couldn't get through. However, there was a difference when I tried to comfort Nora. There wasn't a need. She didn't want my comfort. She only wanted to skirt around any authentic emotion. She wanted to bury her heart and busy her mind. And when she could no longer focus on distractions, she would numb herself in other ways. If I was invisible to Easton, it was like I had never existed to Nora. Her hurt ran deep and twisted. Branching out in unconventional paths. If there was one thing that hurt more than grief, it was knowing that you couldn't feel it at all. I knew that I couldn't help her. Time and only time would be her antidote.

I closed my eyes to Nora in her loft above the city and found myself home with Easton. He sat on the sofa, his feet up on the coffee table, warmed by the wood-burning fire and Tiny Tommy by his side. The flames flickered in his eyes, and his face wilted with defeat. On the coffee table lay my journal. The burlap bow untied, and the page open to Easton's letter.

Find me.

It wasn't a goodbye letter like the others had been. It was a challenge. If there was anything that Easton excelled at, it was a challenge. Like he had the first time our lives parted, I knew Easton would find me one day. And until then, I'd be here before his very eyes. I curled up in his lap the way I used to, and I settled in for another long night.

CHAPTER 27

I hadn't been dead for more than three days when Kinsley had her accident. I didn't need a phone call to know, and I certainly didn't need a ride to the hospital. I had been preparing for this moment for the last twenty years of my life. It was the very reason I hadn't feared dying. I knew that there was something left I had to do, and I was the only soul for the job. It brought me wells of comfort to know that I was still needed. I didn't know how I could help Kinsley during this difficult time, but I knew I could figure it out along the way. After all, everything else had come so naturally for me on the other side.

The moment it happened, I felt Kinsley's senses shift like a sharp edge. And when she fell unconscious, her emotions slipped into a void that I could no longer reach. I rode with her in the ambulance. I held her hand as the paramedics attended to her. I checked in with Clara and Landon, but the news hadn't reached them yet.

Brooklyn had only told Easton and me about the accident. And even though she spoke of it only once, and so long ago, Easton and I talked about it often—and thought about it even more. It was a marker in time that signified the end of my life. At least, the end of the predictable part.

When Kinsley reached the hospital, the pain came back tenfold, and she stirred, though her eyes remained close. The doctors rushed all about, passing through me while I stood still. I didn't know what I was looking for, but I knew I was close to finding out.

"Help me! Help!" Kinsley screamed. For a moment I stared at her face as she writhed in pain. Her body thrashed against the pillow as the doctors pushed medications. "Help me!" she screamed. I looked around me and then rose above to look down. Kinsley's calls weren't emanating from her body. In fact, they weren't from this dimension at all.

I closed my eyes and instinctively—like I'd done it a million times before—I pushed backward into the next dimension. There were many of these layers, like an onion, they'd say. And I had time to explore them all, but I wanted to do so with Easton. And until now, I'd never had a reason to leave Easton's world.

The realm was still except for Kinsley as she frantically ran about calling for help. I approached her with caution. "Kinsley? Can you see me, dear?"

Kinsley's eyes stilled, and I thought she had been looking at me, but I wasn't sure. She gasped for air, looking me up and down. I turned my attention inward. I looked almost real. Like I had when I was alive. "Kinsley?" I asked.

"Gran? Is that you?" she asked, panting. Her cheeks were flushed and pupils dilated.

"Oh, Kins—"

"—You're dead! But you're dead!" She looked down at her own body, and the fear that settled when she laid her eyes back on me now tripled.

"No! No!" I shook my head.

"Yes! You died! Three days ago! You died!"

"I . . . I—"

"Am I?" she asked.

"No!"

"Gran, am I dead?!" Kinsley cried out hysterically.

"Baby, no! You're not dead! Listen to me!" I grabbed ahold of her and was shocked when I made contact with her skin. I pulled her in close, wrapping my arms around her and stroking her hair. It felt incredible to hold her again. "That's why I'm here. I need to tell you that you're going to be OK. It's all going to be OK," I said.

Kinsley cried against my shoulder, and I could swear that the tears were real. "Gran, I'm scared!" she said, her voice splintered with fear.

"I know you are. But I'm here. I'm right here with you." A loud sound crashed down like thunder, and Kinsley jumped. "What was that!?" she shrieked.

I looked around, but there was nothing. The whole place was like a void. A waiting room for those who were split between two realms. And if I hadn't known any better, I would have guessed that we were in a cloud. Not a puffy white cloud that resembled a cotton ball but a dark grey one, misty and thunderous. I didn't feel it, but the dimension appeared cold and damp. Kinsley's arms were prickled with goosebumps, and while I worried that she could still feel the discomfort, I was relieved because it meant that she was still alive. "I don't know," I said.

"Gran, I don't want to die," Kinsley said in a hurried voice. She pawed at me frantically.

"No, it's not your time, dear. You *will* get through this. I promise."

"What's that?!" She raised her arms, searching the length of her sides for answers. I saw nothing.

"What's what, dear?" I asked.

"What's happening?" Kinsley became even more panicked, spinning in circles like a dog after its tail. I reached out for her arm to steady her, but this time . . . this time, my hand went through her and tiny shards of her arm splintered and drifted away. Kinsley's eyes were struck with fear, and there was nothing I could do about it. She reached for her missing arm and the sudden movement left a trail of particles in its wake.

"Gran!" Kinsley lunged for the safety of my embrace and all but dissolved into the cloud. "Gran!" she called out, and her voice echoed all around me. I searched and searched, but I couldn't find her. Boldly, I pressed through dimension after dimension, searching for my granddaughter, but she had slipped into a space that even I couldn't penetrate.

I let myself fall back into the void of a brewing storm. Kinsley was no longer there, and her cries were replaced with the low whining that reminded me of the bowels of a ballast howling under the weight of the ship. The place was eerie, and I hated that Kinsley had to see it. That she had to feel the frigid air. I pondered how I could help her. And wondered if I could change the things she saw or felt so that it wasn't such a scary place the next time she visited. Because I knew she'd be back.

Kinsley was very much alive but under the sedation of Propofol—a drug-induced coma. She was in a dimension that few could reach. Though I didn't think it was impossible, I only knew that I hadn't found it yet.

I pushed forward into Easton's world. He and Brooklyn were in the waiting room of the hospital, and Clara and Landon were on their way. I gave them as many green lights as I could. It was the small things, and a traffic light was the least I could do for Clara now. I felt for her as she had already been broken down from losing me. It wasn't fair that she had to deal with this, too.

But I knew that no matter how difficult the struggle may be that she could—and would—push through. And when she did, she would be a stronger version of herself. Her perspective would shift, and she would become her best self. I just had to get her to the other side. And already failing my first mission, doubt swirled through the air as I wondered if I could do much for Clara.

When she and Landon arrived, I sat beside her in the waiting room, and I watched Brooklyn's calculating eyes. Many failed attempts later, Brooklyn finally had her chance to talk to Clara when Landon left to find a restroom.

"Clara, you have to listen to me. I don't have much time," Brooklyn said, looking over her shoulder toward the men's restroom.

"Huh?" Clara groaned.

"It's important, Clara. Focus. Kinsley is going to be alright. It's thirteen days. It's thirteen days of pure hell, but it's thirteen days. You can and you will get through this. And Kinsley will too."

"She will? You know?" Clara focused on Brooklyn. Easton listened in.

"She will. You will hear many terrible things while she is in that coma. Setbacks that will threaten to end you. Don't listen. Please!"

"But she's going to be alright, right?"

"Yes. More than alright. She'll make a full recovery." Brooklyn looked over her shoulder. "And one more thing—your mom is with her. She's not alone," she said.

Easton shifted in his seat.

"She is?" Clara asked, wiping her tears with newfound strength and hope.

Brooklyn looked over her shoulder again as Landon emerged from the restroom. "She is . . ." Brooklyn said, nodding.

Clara took a deep breath, and I felt the relief that washed over her. Brooklyn turned to Easton and grabbed his hand. He forced a smile for her, but I knew he was having a hard time knowing I was with Kinsley but that he couldn't reach me. But what Easton didn't know was that he *could* reach me. It was *I* that couldn't get through to him. Not right away, anyhow.

After a long night in the hospital, I sat on the edge of Kinsley's bed during Easton's first visit with her. She was finally stabilized, and guests were allowed back inside, one at a time. I knew that while he held her hand, he wondered if I was near. He spoke to me, at first, in his mind, and eventually, he did so out loud. I heard it all.

"I know you're there, Beck. I know you're with Kinsley, watching over her. But if you could just give me a sign. Something to let me know. Please," he said, under his breath.

Lights sometimes worked for me, but not here. Not in the hospital, where so many lives depended on the machines that they were hooked up to. I didn't want to tamper with the electricity. I had been experimenting with air but hadn't yet been successful with it. Still, I tried. I sucked in a long, bottomless breath and I pushed it with all the might I had. All the love I could spill, I exhaled. And with all the energy I could move through the veil, I tried with everything I had. Easton's back stiffened, and his eyes fixed. I came in close to see the tiny hairs on the back of his neck standing on end. And I smiled.

"Beck?" Easton whispered. I was so happy I could cry. I wanted to yell at the top of my lungs, *I'm here! I'm here!* But I didn't have a voice. Not one that he could hear. "I can feel you," he said when I didn't answer. It was like music to my ears, and I smiled, knowing that I was able to let him know that I was alright.

Over the next thirteen days, I lived in the hospital. I searched for Kinsley in the other dimensions, near and far, and I frequented the last place I had made contact with her. I spent time there, in the void, reciting the stories I had read to her as a child. Folklore and fairytales. And I told her stories I thought she might enjoy now as an adult. And occasionally, she resurfaced.

I'd come to realize that our connection was based on the depth of her drugs. When the doctors lightened her dosage to run various tests . . . that's when I could reach her. I did what I could to cloak the void in which we had our brief meetings, and I believed it worked. I couldn't control the sounds or the temperature that she experienced—it was always far too cold—but I managed to turn the dark thunderous void into a comfortable place.

And on the few occasions that we met, I'd tell her to fight. I'd encourage her to be strong, and I'd let her know we were all rooting for her. I tried to show her the way out, but it was beyond our control. I counted down the days. Our time was always short, but I treasured the brief moments I had with my granddaughter. And it made me a little sad that when she'd wake up, I'd no longer get to visit her.

After thirteen days, when she was brought out of her coma, we celebrated. Kinsley still had a long time to get back to her full self, but we cheered her on every step of the way. And one day, months down the road, Kinsley told Easton of her visits with me while in the hospital.

CHAPTER 28

Three years had passed. Some days were harder than others, but I was there for all of them, nonetheless. Easton had aged more rapidly in my absence, and the girls were worried about him. They took turns visiting and then had long talks on the phone about the funny and sometimes absurd things he would say. But I knew Easton was living out his seniority in a way he never let himself do before. And I think there was a part of him that liked it. Not the brittle bones or the lonely home, but the lack of responsibility that came with being in his old age.

Easton would eat cereal for dinner if he wanted to. He wouldn't get dressed some weeks until Wednesday rolled around—because that's the day one of the girls would come to check on him. And he would spend countless hours putting together the most difficult puzzles or playing solitaire across the dining table. Some nights, he would watch old cop movies and laugh out loud while he remembered his time as a police officer. I'd laugh, too.

But today was a big day for Easton. He had pants on for starters, and he was on his way to Clover's historical chapel. I pulled at his bow tie in the back of the cab. I couldn't straighten it, but I never let myself stop trying. It made me feel involved. I could have skipped time. I could have appeared at the wedding for all the good parts. I didn't. I took the cab. Because I didn't want to be there for just the good parts. I wanted to be there for every stride, big or small.

We got to the chapel with plenty of time to spare. Nora was there early with a handsome man on her arm. She looked stunning, as always, in a fitted navy dress. Happy too. "Hey Dad, how are you feeling today?" Nora asked as she hugged Easton.

"I'm good. How are you? Is this Beau?" Easton asked.

"Hello sir," Beau reached for Easton's hand. I could tell that Easton liked him. Nora did, too. But he wasn't the one. Beau was, however, the first one to stay for a while, and the first one to teach Nora balance. But ultimately, he'd just be the first one who got away. And there would be many after him.

"Let's go get a seat." Nora led the way into the small chapel. Stained glass windows lined each side of the walls, and white ribbon bows dressed the pews. It was simple. Classic.

"So, I hear you play golf? Is that right?" Easton asked Beau as they took their seats in the front row.

"Dad . . ." Nora sighed.

"That's right. Do you play, sir?"

"No. I never spent my time chasing balls."

"Dad!" Nora glared at Easton. Beau chuckled. And I did too.

"What? I didn't," Easton grumbled.

"That's alright. What do you do for fun, then?" Beau asked Easton.

"Well, now, not much. But in my day, I chased the bad guys."

Nora leaned over to Beau. "He means, he was a police officer," she said.

"Oh, wow. I bet you have some crazy stories then?" Beau asked.

"I do!"

"Did you ever get shot?"

"I did!" Easton started to pull at his bow tie.

"Dad! Keep your clothes on! Beau doesn't want to see your bullet hole!" Nora said, her hand over Easton's.

Clara and Landon walked in like a breath of fresh air. Clara wore a yellow sundress and brown leather sandals. She smiled warmly and hugged everyone, including Beau, who she'd just met for the first time. When Beau took his seat, Easton leaned in and said, "You know, I've never been this old before?"

Beau stared at him with empty eyes, and I threw my head back, laughing. Sure, it sounded odd, but it was true. He hadn't let himself get that old before. This was new to him.

"Is that so?" Beau asked, head cocked.

Soon after, Clara's kids came in. Though they were anything but kids. Kinsley's arm interlocked with her boyfriend's, and her little brother, Conrad—who was now tallest in the family—was with his girlfriend. A bubbly, bright personality that reminded me of Chloe. They were all nice kids and genuinely happy to be at the chapel. They sat on the same side of the church, huddled together, chatting amongst themselves when Tanner came out from behind a curtain with the minister.

They spoke briefly before Tanner took his place on stage, giving Easton a brief, nervous smile. The music started—not the traditional wedding march, but a soft romantic symphony. And our small group stood and turned their attention to the back door, but I couldn't wait.

Brooklyn, dressed in white, stood on the other side of the church doors, her hand frozen on the doorknob. It was a sight I'd wanted to see my whole life. However, I was thrilled I could see it now in the afterlife. I had a better view from here anyhow. More beautiful than Brooklyn's hair or her dress was her heart, which she opened up just enough for Tanner to find his way back into. Still, she stood frozen with trepidation.

Tanner and Brooklyn had been together since I passed away. Tanner would drive to Brooklyn's place every single morning to have coffee and do crossword puzzles with her. Then, they would take a leisurely walk around the neighborhood. It had been that way for so long that the driving to and from no longer made any sense. The only thing that would change after they married in their seventies was that Tanner would spend evenings with Brooklyn, too. And when they went to bed as early as they did, it really meant just sharing dinner.

Still, Brooklyn was afraid. She'd always worried that marriage would steal her immortality. I placed my hand on top of hers. I whispered in her ear that I loved her and I told her congratulations. She didn't feel my hand on top of hers, and she didn't hear my voice in her ear. But she did find the courage to open the door. She walked into the church with her head held high. And since her parents were long gone, I walked beside her. And it was I who gave her away to Tanner.

Easton cried throughout the ceremony, and when Clara placed her hand on his shoulder, he told her he had something in his eye. But I knew he was thinking of me, because I was thinking of him and the time we wed in the barn. There was a time when Easton only felt sorrow, and while he was on the brink of looking back at our lives together with nothing but fondness, he wasn't there yet. This was a bitter-sweet moment for him.

After dinner, Beau extended his hand to Nora for a dance. I pushed her out of her seat, chanting, "Do it! Do it!" She blushed while taking his hand. Beau pulled her close, gripping Nora's waist and down the small of her back. They danced slowly as she looked into his eyes. If I hadn't known any better, I'd say she was falling for him. But I did know better, and it would stop there. But tonight was the height of the relationship. She was happy and so was he.

"Well, Brooklyn, you did it. You finally did it," Easton said, alone at a table with the bride.

"I finally did. It took some time to get here, but I'm glad I did. I've always had a soft spot for your brother." Brooklyn took a sip of champagne. The golden liquid shook with the tremors of her hand.

"Yeah. He's never given up on you, that's for sure . . . except—"

"—Except for that one time?" Brooklyn chuckled.

"Yeah, that one time he married someone else. That was just a moment of weakness, though," Easton said with a laugh.

"Look at him, dancing with Clara." Brooklyn pointed a finger at Tanner on the dance floor. It was surely a sight to behold, but the best part was the sound Clara made when she laughed at her uncle Tanner.

"Let me get some of that?" Easton reached for Brooklyn's champagne.

"I thought you weren't supposed to drink with the medication you're on?" she asked.

"Oh, it's just a little bit. It won't kill me. And if it does?" he shrugged with a sly smile on his face. I shook my head. "So what's next for you?" Easton asked Brooklyn.

"Bed! It's way past my bedtime!" Brooklyn said.

"No, I mean, what comes after this life now that you've married?"

"Oh, that. I don't think this will change my path. My fulfillment has always been helping people get where they need to go, and I have more of that to do in the next life. Maybe the next several. I may be here for a while . . ." Brooklyn said as she gazed at Nora, who danced with Beau across the room in a dark corner. He had her hair wrapped around his finger, and she wore a flirty smile.

"You're going to watch out for my girl?" Easton finished the flute of champagne.

"You know I am," she said.

"Good. Good." Easton watched Nora with worry in his eyes.

Tanner came up to Brooklyn, sweaty and excited. "I love this woman!" he said to Easton before he kissed her on the cheek.

"I love you, too, hubby," she said.

"I'm going to run to the restroom. Do you need anything from the bar when I come back?"

Brooklyn looked at her empty champagne glass and then at Easton. "No, thank you," she said.

Tanner danced off, and with him left the fun-loving energy that he had always brought to the table. "I miss her," Easton said. And it was so fast that it was almost automatic. Like he had no control over the confession he spilled.

"It's not your time," I said.

"I know you do. We all do," Brooklyn said.

"Have you had any dreams?"

"Not since the last time you asked," she said with a teasing smile. He'd asked two hours ago.

"I've felt her near. I know she's there. Sometimes I get a cool breeze on my arm or hand—" Brooklyn looked down to the hand I had touched outside of the chapel, and she smiled. "And sometimes I hear her voice. 'I'm here,' she'll say," he said in a whisper.

I watched his eyes turn from dry to moist as I thought of all the times that I'd wanted to scream it. *I'm here!* I said it to him all the time. I had no way of knowing which of them he had heard, but all that mattered was that he knew. He knew that I hadn't left him. "But it's never enough. I think, perhaps, I'm going crazy. She doesn't visit like all my loved ones before, and I worry that something's wrong. Like maybe I've made it all up, and she's out there again."

"You think she came back?" Brooklyn asked.

"I don't know. She could have."

"No. No. No. She didn't come back. I would have known. Trust me, her case is closed. She made it to the other side . . . unless—"

"Unless what?"

"Well, unless, she's here. With you," she said.

"Could that happen?" he asked.

"Yeah, if she's stubborn enough," she said.

Easton smiled. "Then she's here," he said, as a matter of fact.

"I have a feeling she may be keeping an eye out for you. Making sure you don't mix your medications and whatnot."

"Yeah. You're probably right. She's probably here now," he said.

"Probably." Brooklyn looked around for me. But I was right by Easton, and her eyes moved swiftly through my path. "What do you think she'd be doing if she were here now?" she asked.

Easton chuckled. "Dancing. She'd be dancing." I smiled.

"Well then. Shall we?" Brooklyn asked. A wicked smile split across Easton's face and the two of them slowly made their way to the dance floor. I trailed behind them with ease. Easton, though stiff in his old age, still had moves, and he didn't hold any of them back. He danced as if I were there. But this time, I think he believed I was. Tanner came to dance with his bride and soon everyone was on their feet. I drifted back and forth like a deep-ocean current.

When the night was over and Easton lay on our bed alone, he fell asleep with peace in his heart. It was the first time since my passing that the light had crept in. The chapter had finally come to an end where his despair ruled all else. And I looked forward to the next eight years Easton had left. Even though I'd be invisible to him, I was patient. More than I'd ever been capable of before. Death did that to you.

When time was no measure of currency, impatience ceased to exist. And it only made me happy to know that he was living again. Even in my absence, the next eight years would be some of his happiest times. And I wouldn't miss it for the world. I'd be the sunlight that shined down on him on a warm summer day, and I'd be the crackle in the fire that hypnotized him on a cool fall evening. I'd be there by his side until the day that he was there by mine.

CHAPTER 29

Auburn and mustard leaves masked the bluffs eight times over. Easton's time was running out like the sand in an hourglass. He had made several new friends over the years. And getting dressed only one day a week became a thing of the past. He kept a busy schedule, and on most nights, he was in bed by seven, resting for his next full day. Time flew by, not only for him but for me, too.

While Easton filled his days the best he knew how, I tinkered with electricity, tampered with dreams, moved small objects, and sent dragonflies, butterflies, and songbirds on paths to a smile. I danced by myself in the shadows of our dark home. And when it rained, I would scale high above the clouds and wait for the first sign of a rainbow to paint the sky. I'd watch until the world below was covered in the ethereal glow, and I'd imagine it was art.

Easton joined the police department's volunteer group and would sometimes drive around in a police car. His favorite was talking to the new cops that were just starting out, both eager and afraid. He'd tell them all the things he'd learned over the years. In the weeks that Easton didn't volunteer, he would meet up with other retired cops in the program and often hosted a poker night at the house.

Poker nights were the best. The men would complain about many things. The pills their doctor put them on. Their aches and pains. How they couldn't do this or that any longer. But when they complained about their wives—their old ladies—Easton would fall quiet. I knew he'd give anything for the chance to complain alongside his buddies, but I was no longer around to annoy him, and he'd all but forgotten the ways I used to drive him crazy.

They were a funny group of men, though, and I enjoyed listening to their stories about past jobs they'd been on and the crazy things they'd seen. I'd play with the cigar smoke that rose underneath the dining room light and I'd try to manipulate it in ways that could get someone's attention. Practice for later, when Easton was alone. But he never smoked cigars alone. Not until the day he became a great-grandpa.

When Kinsley had her first baby, Easton smoked a celebratory cigar with her husband. I tried to manipulate the smoke, but only once did I think that maybe Easton had seen it. Something in the way his eyes focused and his brows knitted made me think he saw me etched in the smooth lines of his cigar smoke like a charcoal drawing. I felt his heart pick up speed, but if it were true and he had seen me, he said nothing to allude to it.

On the days that Easton spent holding his great-grandson, he was the happiest. The baby boy would sleep in his arms, and Easton would just watch. I watched too, and I couldn't have been prouder of Kinsley and the family she made for herself. Sometimes, when she rocked her baby to sleep, she'd read the old books I bought for her when she was born. They were torn and tattered now, but that only meant they were well-loved. It didn't take long before she became pregnant again, and I had a feeling that one day she would have a large, boisterous family.

When all the poker games and police volunteer work had become far and few in between, I could feel that Easton's heart had weakened, and I could see that a marked tiredness had taken over his body. He still wanted to do all the things he had done before, but getting up to do anything made him short of breath. And one day, I caught him writing in a journal that I'd never seen before.

I peered over his shoulder, surprised to see my name at the top of the page. He wasn't writing goodbye letters to the girls like I had—but a love letter to me. He wrote slowly, concentrating on his penmanship. He talked to me like I was still alive. He told me how much he missed me. How much he had seen me in everything he did. He told me how much I had missed. About our great-grandson, about Nora's firm, and Clara's emerging passion for pottery. He told me how he missed my tattoo and how sometimes he'd still laugh at the funny things I did. Or at how mad I got when I lost a bet.

But what he wrote next I couldn't pry my eyes from. And my focus lingered there for some time.

I'll be seeing you soon.

Easton stared at his love letter—my love letter. And I studied the last line. When he was satisfied, he folded it up and left it on his desk. Then, he slipped on an olive button-down sweater and his brown leather loafers and left the house. A cab showed up at the door, and when I saw he had directed the cab driver to the grocery store, I deemed it safe to leave him to grocery shop while I answered the call I had from Nora.

Nora sat on a blanket by my grave at the cemetery. A single tear rolled down her cheek as she picked petals one by one out of a pink rosebud. She missed me. And she was having a hard time. I ran my hands through the grass and listened to her talk about her struggles. I tried to pull the stress out of her, but it was something that she would have to do on her own. I only had the power to be there for her, but even that had gone unnoticed.

Nora didn't come to the cemetery often. None of them did anymore. But today there weren't only roses from Nora, but sunflowers from Brooklyn, too. On days like today—a special occasion—there would be more visits to the gravesite. But they never needed to come here to see me or show me their love. I always felt it. Every time a memory would spark warmth in their hearts or they'd wake from a dream of me. Any time my name left their mouths—it was just like them bringing flowers to my grave. I felt their affection all the same.

When Nora's eyes dried and she fell silent, I told her about Easton. I told her how he wrote me the sweetest letter. How he said he'd see me soon. And how I felt excited for the first time in a while—like I had a date coming up. I hadn't been on a date in years. When she said goodbye, I said goodbye to the grave too. Because I was coming with her, not staying. Nora climbed into her luxury sports coupe, and while I loved riding in it with the top down, I knew she was headed to the house to see Easton, and I wanted to beat her there.

But when I came to the house, something was off. Something was different. I didn't sense Easton at first, like I usually would have. My tether seemed to have slackened, and I found myself unsure of where I belonged. I went to the desk where he had left my love letter, and beside it was a grand bouquet of red roses adorned with wooden twine and baby's breath. A note stuck out from roses with a simple note saying.

Happy Anniversary, my love.

I glanced around the empty room, listening for the drum of Easton's heart. And it was in the silence that I remembered our plan. The only plan we had ever made in case of an emergency. I looked at the calendar pinned to the wall above Easton's desk. May 7 circled with a red heart. It was all I needed to be on my way. I fled the house, catching a glimpse of brown leather loafers sprawled across the kitchen floor and Nora's sports car pulling into the driveway on my way out. It all happened in a blur as I hurried to our spot. It was there that time stopped completely.

A silhouette stood in the middle of the road on the New River Bridge. Even though I didn't recognize the figure in the distance, I didn't need my eyes to trust that my heart had found its counterpart. He turned, taking in his surroundings, and I lost my stomach as I imagined he was looking for me. But I wasn't sure that he could see me. I'd been invisible for so long.

I caught the sunlight that lit the side of Easton's face, and when it lit his glacier eyes to a shade of blue that I'd never seen before, I knew that there was nothing standing in our way. Not time, not dimension, not even fate could touch us now. His eyes drew upon mine with the pull of two magnets, and the corners of his lips pulled into a flirty smile. I made my way to him slowly. His face youthful as I approached him. Easton looked just like the day I'd met him, only this time, he was strong, proud, and happy.

I stopped just before him. His hair lifting in the gentle breeze. "You found me," I said.

He smiled. "I knew just where to look." He looked over me, his smile never fading. "I'm sorry I kept you waiting."

"It wasn't long at all," I said.

"You look young. Like when I met you, but healthy, strong."

"It feels that way, doesn't it?" I asked.

"Yeah. It does," Easton said as he looked at the back of his smooth hands, not a wrinkle or age spot to be found. I took his hands and slowly, ever so slowly, lifted onto my toes and planted a feather-light kiss upon his lips.

When I pulled away, he stared in wonder. "I can't believe I found you . . ."

"I knew you would," I said, taking his hand and leading him down the middle of the bridge.

"So, what do we do now?" he asked, looking around as if seeing the world for the very first time.

I threw my head back, laughing. "Just wait, it's only the beginning . . ."

The end

THE END

WITH LOVE,

Laura C. Reden

www.ingramcontent.com/pod-product-compliance
Lightning Source LLC
Chambersburg PA
CBHW020721310726
48979CB00004B/1012

* 9 7 8 1 9 5 4 5 8 7 1 9 9 *